A TRANSLATION OF THE CHINESE NOVEL
CHUNG-YANG (RIVAL SUNS)
BY CHIANG KUEI (1908-1980)

Rival Suns graphic by
Janet Ross.

A TRANSLATION OF THE CHINESE NOVEL
CHUNG-YANG (RIVAL SUNS)
BY CHIANG KUEI (1908-1980)

Translated from the Chinese by
Timothy A. Ross

Chinese Studies
Volume 8

The Edwin Mellen Press
Lewiston•Queenston•Lampeter

Library of Congress Cataloging-in-Publication Data

Chiang, Kuei.
  [Ch' ung yang. English]
  A tranlsation of the Chinese novel Chung-yang (Rival suns) by
Chiang Kuei (1908-1980) / translated from the Chinese by Timothy A.
Ross.
     p. cm.-- (Chinese studies ; v. 8)
  ISBN 0-7734-8188-5
  I. Ross, Timothy A. II. Title. III. Title: Rival suns.
IV. Series.
PL2844.K8C4513   1999
895.1' 352--dc21   98-31939
                                          CIP

This is volume 8 in the continuing series
Chinese Studies
Volume 8 ISBN 0-7734-8188-5
ChS Series ISBN 0-88946-076-0

A CIP catalog record for this book is available from the British Library.

The Edwin Mellen Press
Box 450
Lewiston, New York
USA 14092-0450

The Edwin Mellen Press
Box 67
Queenston, Ontario
CANADA L0S 1L0

The Edwin Mellen Press, Ltd.
Lampeter, Ceredigion, Wales
UNITED KINGDOM SA48 8LT

Printed in the United States of America

Rival Suns

Chiang Kuei

CONTENTS

Acknowledgments	i
Preface	iii
Author's Note	xi
Foreword	xiii
Chapter I	1
Chapter II	23
Chapter III	49
Chapter IV	75
Chapter V	101
Chapter VI	131
Chapter VII	159
Chapter VIII	187
Chapter IX	221
Chapter X	253
Chapter XI	279
Chapter XII	311
Chapter XIII	341
Chapter XIV	371
Chapter XV	399
Chapter XVI	427
Chapter XVII	455
Chapter XVIII	483
Chapter XIX	509

Chapter XX   537

Chapter XXI   563

Chapter XXII   593

Chapter XXIII   621

Chapter XXIV   649

Acknowledgments

The translator gratefully acknowledges the encouragement and patience of his wife Janet, the invaluable editorial assistance of his daughter Sarah, and the willing and unselfish help rendered by his readers, Drs. Jeffrey Kinkley and Constantine Tung. Special thanks are due Dr. David D. Buck who contributed the Preface.

The translator also wishes to thank Dr. C. T. Hsia of Columbia University, in whose book *A History of Modern Chinese Fiction* the translator first became acquainted with the writing of Chiang Kuei.

Preface

Wang I-chien, writing under the pen name Chiang Kuei, wrote three impressive novels while living in poverty in Taiwan. Wang had been a radical student activist in the May Fourth period, a political worker in the Chinese Nationalist Party in the 1920s, a railway official in the 1930s, an Army officer in the war against Japan, and finally, a commission agent in Shanghai after 1945. In the 1930s, he wrote and published some minor novels associated with modernist, romantic, and patriotic themes in Chinese literary circles.

Shortly after coming to Taiwan with his family in 1948, Wang failed in business and managed only to eke out a living for his wife and three children by working as a custodian in a Catholic church in the southern city of Tainan. Many Chinese, displaced from their lives on the mainland, found the strongly regional Fujianese culture of Taiwan unfamiliar and inhospitable. Taiwan was a poor place in the 1950s and outside the top echelon in political and military circles, most Taiwanese and mainlanders had little in the way of resources or prospects. For Wang I-chien Taiwan meant poverty for himself and his family; there seemed little prospect that he could recoup his fortunes. Even his menial livelihood depended on a demanding, arrogant foreign priest. In 1952 his wife, Yen Hsueh-mei's heath failed and she remained bedridden for the rest of her life. After she died in 1961, Wang was charged and convicted of her early death. Proclaiming his innocence, Wang struggled for more than three years in the courts to reverse the verdict, but failed. However, he never served time in jail for this conviction.

During these years, when Wang I-chien was in his forties and early fifties, he produced, under the pseudonym Chiang Kuei, three long novels set clearly and accurately in the history of twentieth century China. The first, entitled *Hsuan-feng* [*The Whirlwind*] (published 1957), concerns the decline of a landed gentry family and the younger generation's involvement with radical politics; the second, *Ch'ung Yang* (published 1961), translated here as *Rival Suns*, depicts the pull of the Nationalist and Communist parties through the men and women caught up in the Northern Expedition of 1927 when leftist elements in the Nationalist Party, together with Soviet advisors and Chinese Communists, established a short-lived radical regime in the city of Wuhan; the third and still untranslated, *Yen-tzu lou* [*Swallow Tower*] (published in book form in 1964) deals with a railway official who becomes caught-up in the anti-Japanese war that began in 1937. Each of these novels draws clearly on the author's own life and circumstances. *The Whirlwind* uses Wang's own family and personal involvement in radical politics as background in the novel; *Rival Suns* centers around young men in their late teens and twenties who fomented and directed mass activities in the city of Wuhan for the Chinese Communist and Nationalist parties just as Wang I'chien had done; and finally, *Swallow Tower* clearly reflects Wang I'chien's experience as a railway administrator, separated from his wife and with a long-standing attachment to a former singing girl.

The narrative direction in the three novels derives from the events of recent Chinese history, but Chiang Kuei does not attempt to make his characters into heroic nationalists or admirable revolutionaries. Indeed, in *Rival Suns*, none of the revolutionaries is depicted in a favorable light and little is said about how the protagonists, Hung T'ung-yeh and Liu Shao-ch'iao, youthful heads of the mass organizations in Wuhan at the height of the revolutionary tide, carried out their responsibilities. In spite of Wang I-chien's own background in such activities, Chiang Kuei tells us almost nothing about the actual business of making revolution, either from a Communist or a Nationalist perspective.

At the time these books were first published in Taiwan, conservatives criticized Chiang Kuei as departing, as he clearly does, from the Nationalist Party's then ideological orthodox position of representing the Communists as devils incarnate. Liberal critics' praise suggests that Chiang Kuei had managed to recapture the indeterminacy of the 1920s and 1930s when the long-term struggle between the Communists and the Nationalists—still not settled today, some sixty years later—was unclear to all the participants. At the same time, Chiang Kuei's own particular strong anti-Communism comes through clearly in all of his books.

Indeed, the Communist characters in *Rival Suns* are presented in an exceptionally negative light. Liu Shao-ch'iao, the son of a Hunanese merchant family who leads the Wuhan city Trade Union movement, is depicted as a vicious bisexual predator who preys on men and women while dressing up his lust as an attack on prevailing Confucian morality. Written years before the Cultural Revolution in China, *Rival Suns* contains chilling accounts of students denouncing their parents in mass school rallies, trumped up accounts of sexual and physical abuse against political opponents that led to arrest, torture, and murder in which the Communist accusers redouble the supposed offenses of their captives. The main protagonist of the novel, Hung T'ung-yeh, is presented as basically a well-intentioned young Nationalist who becomes enmeshed in the clutches of the Communist immoral bully, Liu Shao-ch'iao, and dragged into complicity with Liu's crimes though his own character weaknesses and a lack of leadership by elder Nationalist leaders in Wuhan who should have served as his mentors. At the end of the novel, Liu Shao-ch'iao, the embodiment of immorality masquerading as revolutionary idealism, survives; others, representing traditional or misguided modern values, perish.

It is hard to see Chiang Kuei as soft on the Chinese Communists. Probably more disturbing to Nationalist authorities was the author's depiction of them as ineffective and cautious men who, far from risking all for anti-imperialistic and nationalistic revolution, chose their own personal comfort above everything else and trimmed their sails to sail with the prevailing political winds. In the 1950s, the Nationalist Party on Taiwan began to reshape itself into a force for economic and social progress after its defeat on the Chinese mainland; no one wanted to be reminded of the Nationalists' own shortcomings, so sharply depicted in Chiang Kuei's novels.

In Chiang Kuei's novels the apparent struggle is between the Nationalists and the Communists, but the real struggle is between the old ways of cultured Chinese life and the mixture of refined high culture and vulgar mean culture coming to China from outside. Chiang Kuei's own stance is clearly cosmopolitan, finding good among both particular Chinese and foreign individuals, just as he finds weaknesses and evil in others. The most sympathetic foreigner in *Rival Suns* is a Japanese physician, Itakura Minoru, who runs a charity hospital with his daughter. In general, Chiang Kuei shows his younger characters as drawn to the new, modern, and foreign ways, but also finds much to praise, in softer tones, about traditional Chinese values. In the account of the Communist Liu Shao-ch'iao's arranged marriage to Yeh P'in-hsia, Chiang Kuei portrays the young P'in-hsia as devotedly attempting to live up to the traditional role of a wife in the face of her husband's violent iconoclasm. Chiang Kuei presents other examples of how new practices can bring rewards, as well as examples of how older Chinese practices impede the lives of other characters. Still, Chiang Kuei lovingly describes traditional Chinese values and practices, while not always upholding older values. It is this very split judgment about the traditional and modern that has given Chiang Kuei's novels their lasting appeal.

What I find most appealing in *Rival Suns*, is Chiang Kuei's attachment to the topics and narrative approach of late traditional Chinese fiction inside the guise of the modern vernacular novel. It is here that his real genius lies; let me give four brief examples.

First, in the long accepted narrative style of Chinese fiction, Chiang Kuei freely introduces new characters in long episodes only marginally connected to the main story line. The account of the student Chu Ling-fen's denunciation of her father, Chu Kuang-chi, an old Nationalist Party stalwart serves to further darken the portrait of the Communists, while the account of the French arms merchant Raymond's sojourn in Manchuria serves to make manifest the evils of imperialism, but neither is essential to the main narrative.

Second, Chiang Kuei's male characters are well-drawn but also clearly flawed while several women are depicted as wise, caring, morally strong, and compassionate. In this novel several women with good character, sound values, and often some education, are depicted as being without the limiting character flaws of his male characters. Hung T'ung-yeh's younger sister, Chin-ling, is portrayed as being a person with much stronger character and better values than her brother. Her goodness is encouraged by another young woman, Ch'ien Shou-yu. In this Chiang Kuei continues a Chinese tradition of depicting women as more conscious of the sufferings of life and thus more capable of virtuous lives than men.

Third, Chiang Kuei eroticizes the life of the wealthy, upholding a literary value most fully realized in *The Dream of the Red Chamber* written by Ts'ao Hsüeh-ch'in (1715?-63), an author like Wang who wrote in reduced circumstances of the extravagances of a former life. The most highly eroticized parts of *Rival Suns* concern Hung T'ung-yeh's service as a pedicurist to the wife of a French arms merchant, Madame Lefebvre. The theme is resumed when Hung T'ung-yeh is sent to Hankow and meets Anna Raymond, who runs a lingerie shop. As in so much Chinese fiction, we find here the linking of wealth, leisure, privilege, and eroticism. The theme disappears abruptly as the pace of Hung T'ung-yeh's revolutionary activity picks up; the representations of sex in connection with the revolution emphasize violence and force in place of the leisurely eroticism of the privileged. For Chiang Kuei revolution kills the erotic.

Fourth and probably most important, in *Rival Suns* Chiang Kuei remains focused primarily on the web of family and human relationships in which people find themselves. This web, in which an individual is bound by ties deriving from the parents and family, is carefully depicted as being extended through marriage, school, work, and acquaintance. Chiang Kuei shows how this web of relationships pulls and shapes the characters' lives in ways that usually are not emphasized in Western fiction, where fathers, sisters, and friendships seldom override a character's individual fate.

It is the playing out of these and other conventions of traditional Chinese fiction in the context of war, revolution, and other phenomena of twentieth century China that makes Chiang Kuei's work so rich. It is this special blend of the modern and traditional in his fiction that will make later generations of readers turn to these novels for their plot, character, and action.

Timothy Ross is Chiang Kuei's main interpreter to the English reading world. He wrote an excellent short biography of him in the Twayne World Authors series, *Chiang Kuei* (1974), that discusses Wang I-chien's life and work through 1972. Wang lived until 1980, after Ross published a translation of *The Whirlwind*. Now Ross presents a clear and flowing translation of *Rival Suns*. Ross captures the mood and tone of these novels, and his text maintains the fast flowing narrative style of the original. Without Ross' dedication and effort, Chiang Kuei's wonderful novels would remain unknown to the vast majority of those who do not read Chinese. I hope that through Timothy Ross' translations, many readers will come to treasure the novels of Chiang Kuei, one of the most readable and able practitioners of the art of the novel in twentieth century Chinese literature.

David D. Buck

Professor of History (Modern China)
University of Wisconsin, Milwaukee
July 25, 1998

Author's Note

The author of this book offers it on the fiftieth anniversary of the founding of the Republic of China and the three hundredth anniversary of Cheng Ch'eng-kung's opening of Taiwan.

Foreword

On October 1, 1961, in the foreword to *Chin t'ao-wu chuan* (*Tale of the New Leviathan*), later put out under the original title of *Hsüan-feng* (*The Whirlwind*), I wrote the following few words:

In 1927, I was an eyewitness to that episode of the Communist Party's in Hankow; the next year I returned to Nanking, with the memory of that year of destiny still fresh. In 1931, I wrote my third novel, *Hei-chih-mien* (*The Face of Blackness*). I felt that the Communist Party belonged to the category of things "the reverse of bright", and could have no future of which one could speak. But, as for technique, I was still not satisfied with this novel. After some time had passed, I burned it.

Later on, I again thought of writing something, only I had no opportunity. Naturally, having no opportunity, neither did I have any resolution. And as to what *The Face of Blackness* had really been about, already I no longer completely remembered. Two years ago, walking in the street, I happened to see the sign of a building called *Hua-ti* Technological Society, and just then I was reminded of the principal character in *The Face of Blackness*, called "Hua-ti". "Hua-ti" is a kind of facial makeup for women; we have sometimes seen plumes stuck into the hats of Western women, and now women also use plumes, of a color suitable to their hair, to bind their hair; probably "hua-ti" is some such thing. In the past, when men went out to hunt, and caught rare birds and unusual beasts, they would offer plumes and pelts to those they liked, using them to show their love. The use of plumes by women to adorn themselves probably originated thus, and this is the so-called "hua-ti". As for what *The Face of Blackness* was written about, one can perhaps imagine from seeing the name of this principal female character.

The Communist Party regards class interest as important. This class is a "new aristocratic class" from which is formed the violent strength of the Communist Party itself, and it is absolutely not the so-called "proletariat". This new aristocratic class does not regard the interest of the nation's people, and neither does it regard the free rights and privileges of the individual. By now, every man who is instinctively free and upright needless to say already understands this truth.

But it has already given us a look at the "pattern" in the Wuhan of 1927. If we are concerned with the national fortunes, we should all carefully regard this "pattern", and should all carefully regard the many "excesses" which they carried out which are manifested within that "pattern"; this should serve as a forewarning. If, cautious and fearful, we could have positively eradicated those factors which produced the Communist Party, then today the mainland, as of old, could necessarily be included in the free world; this is certain.

President Chiang is an anti-Communist of foresight and vision. But during the past thirty years he has constantly suffered numerous domestic and foreign hindrances, both concrete and intangible, and he could not carry out his will. This was China's misfortune, and it was also the world's misfortune. Reading his book, *Soviet Russia in China* really makes one feel regret over all kinds of matters.

The "Central Government" established at Wuhan during the period of the Northern Expedition influenced the most remote "split". In Chapter Four, Section Two of *China's Destiny*, President Chiang said:

At this time, in 1926, Wang Chao-ming and the Chinese Communist Party within the Chinese Kuomintang and within the National Revolutionary Army positively advanced the work of splitting, to ruin the base of the Kuomintang and to destroy the life of the National Revolution.

This "splitting work" of stirring up clashes between the Left and the Right factions within the Kuomintang, to incite the class struggle of social revolution among the citizens and the society, caused the people's inherent virtue to be cast aside. President Chiang said:

> Severe floods overflowing, are almost beyond remedy. Now, thinking back to the years between 1931 and 1936,....everywhere soldiers caused calamities, village gates were as wasteland. Thus today, recalling past pains, and tracing the trouble back to its origins, it came from nowhere else but this tragedy of the "Ning-Han Split" created by the hand of the traitor Wang Chao-ming.

Later on, President Chiang gave the following analysis of this "tragedy" in Section Twenty-five of Chapter Two, Book One, of *Soviet Russia in China*:

> The "Resolutions of the China Question" of the seventh session of the Executive Committee of the Communist International, were originally the product of Stalin. Stalin's plot concerning the Wuhan political regime was to organize it as the "democratic dictatorship of the proletariat, peasantry, and other exploited classes", or, in simple terms, it was to be the "democratic dictatorship of the workers, peasants and petty bourgeoisie." In March, 1927, the situation of the Moscow Communist International in this party's national revolution was that the Northern Expedition had developed to some distance, and reality made its initial calculations unattainable. It was barely able to use the organization of the Wuhan Left Faction, and the title of the Joint Conference, but it absolutely could clash with the Nanking Central, and still less could it destroy this party, or hinder the goal of the Northern Expedition. At that time it only had the power to make Wang Chao-ming return to his country from France via Russia. Once Wang Chao-ming arrived in Shanghai, he, together

with Ch'en Tu-hsiu, proclaimed their Common Manifesto, advocating the organization of the "democratic dictatorship of all oppressed classes, in order to suppress counter-revolution." This declaration was obviously the first of Stalin's resolutions. The conference of the Central Party Branch of the "Left Faction" at Wuhan, of which Wang Chao-ming was the head, and its government, was completely under the plundering of the Communist Party's elements, and their popular movements' units were all led by the Communist Party and its fellow travellers. . . The Communist Party elements had seized control of the majority of the political sections at various levels of the National Revolutionary Army stationed in Hunan and Hupeh. Among the various armies, still more did they suffer from the dissension sown amongst them by the Communist Party, and there were no means of harmonizing the opinions of one with the other. In fact, the people of Hunan and Hupeh could not endure the Communist Party's terrorist government and social struggle. The Wuhan Left Faction, at this point, began to awaken and realize the plot and ambition of Moscow to utilize our Kuomintang to arrive at the goal of turning China red, and they determined to split with the Communists, and to break with the Chinese Communists.

The subtitle of this section is "The Tragedy of the Wuhan Left Faction".

Now, it is just this tragedy that I sought to write about in *Rival Suns*.

But, in my view, this man "Ch'ien Pen-san" does not represent the "Left Faction". A number who were of the Left Faction at that time changed their plans suddenly later on, and never again lost their orthodoxy as members of the Kuomintang, and no doubt are worthy of praise. Whereas Ch'ien Pen-san is merely an opportunist. In whatever newly arisen force, it is unavoidable that there will be such opportunists; the question is only whether or not it can shake them loose when it pleases, protect its original character, and avoid being increasingly corrupted. It is not something shameful for a healthy man to accidentally get ringworm. The Kuomintang's reorganization of 1924, its general registration in 1928, down to the Reconstruction after coming to Taiwan, all had such a function of leaving corruption and putting on muscle; that is something which everyone knows.

Ch'ien Pen-san had three cases of capital, he could have engaged in any sort of business. Perhaps he had his own opinion, but he only indulged in accepting reality, he followed the current, and was completely ignorant of "choosing the good and sticking to it". He was one of those "self-sacrificed" of that time, who voluntarily fell. He and Hung T'ung-yeh were really men who followed the same path, only separated by the fact that one had good fortune and the other did not.

Within this novel there are also several "gentlemen of a friendly state"; since there was no better method of showing the complications and confusions of that period. I used M. and Mme. Lefebvre and M. and Mme. Raymond as examples, in the hope that they will "neither be oppressed or indulged". The concessions of that period, called the "adventurers' paradise" were asylums of evil. I would not wrong nor provoke these gentlemen of a friendly state, nor have I any intention of being discourteous to them. President Chiang, in Section One of Chapter Three of *China's Destiny*, said:

> The secret activities of the imperialists in various places were the greatest cause of the turbulent battles of the warlords after the founding of the Republic. Extraterritoriality was quite sufficient to protect their spies and special agents. The leases and concessions, the railroad zones and such kinds of specially privileged territory, and the special rights of the Powers in levying on railroads and shipping lines, also were quite sufficient to serve as storehouses and emporiums for munitions of war, for the supply of local bandits, and helping along internal disorders for profit.

President Chiang has analyzed the political, legal, economic, social, ethical and psychological influences of the unequal treaties, and this also involved religion. In Section Five of Chapter Three of the same book, concerning the Protestants' readiness to be held in high esteem, he also wrote as follows:

In the past one hundred years, because the Protestant churches had the unequal treaties to rely upon, enjoyed special rights, and did not regard the popular spirit of the Chinese people, therefore some men saw the foreigners' preaching as cultural aggression, they became suspicious of it, even to the point of regarding it as an enemy and opposing it.

These were all the actual conditions of that time. It is fortunate that after the abolition of the unequal treaties, these improper phenomena can never be restored. Now, in *Rival Suns* only the smallest part of this scene is written about, and my intention was to paint around it using the art of the novel.

"A viewpoint of racial superiority" rendered the missionaries' propagation of righteousness as though dark, and without light, and without justification. The time having come to the seventieth year of the 20th century, in many places they are still arguing and racking their brains over this question, to the point of spilling blood, and even the free, democratic America has been unable to avoid it. Hence, thirty-odd years ago, in the context of the influence of colonialism, the evil of the situation may be imagined.

Historical fiction is indeed not history, and the story of the *Rival Suns* is completely imaginary. Because of this, if people and things in the book are proved to bear the shadow of real people and things of that period, it is completely accidental.

My aim is only in recreating the singular atmosphere of that period, to give people a renewed impression, and a renewed understanding, as a "reminder of warning". Perhaps there are those who consider that this viewpoint is near to that of an old schoolteacher, or that the time is already late, but I am not so pessimistic. Mr. Hu Shih-chih time and again has pointed out that "A job worth doing is worth doing well," and I agree with this saying.

At the same time, I have never believed that the Communist Party dropped down from heaven. We must dare to analyze those factors which produced it, and late we can hope to extinguish it. Cursing and insulting perhaps can express our rage for a fleeting moment, but in fact will not be of much use. It goes without saying that "concealing the disease and forgetting the doctor" is dangerous indeed.

To oppose Communism, one must be objective, and one must be prudent.

My origin is that of a petty-bourgeois medicine-shop household, and I'm used to recognizing that one seeks reasonable profits through reasonable management, and I seek a private life, for the individual and the household, of enjoying benefits and avoiding annoyances.

My anti-Communist thought has this level view as its foundation. I am not a fearless fighter.

But in putting *Rival Suns* thirty years after *Black Face*, I still felt deeply bashful. Facing such a disordered time, what I could not bear was a boundless solitude.

I began to write *Rival Suns* in September 1959, and it took me nineteen months in succession to have it ready for the printer. Indeed it was not that I was making extra work, or producing some relatively good writing, or getting "ten chills from one storm", or writing by fits and starts. The longest delay in the process was seven months.

This is really too inauspicious.

This book had already had an original draft, and I had had no intention of sending it out into the world. Towards the end of 1960, I returned to the south after living for a short time in Taipei, and suddenly I developed a sort of "to understand an ugly wife one must look at her husband's father and mother" viewpoint, causing me to change my earlier feelings, and decide to print the book, as it stood, and lay it humbly before the readers. And when it came time to set it up and print it, I hurriedly revised it in this manner. Although it was not entirely different, still in my own feelings I considered in general that the new did not match the old.

I have already explained in detail that so far as writing fiction is concerned, I am completely an amateur. If you can constantly remember that you are reading an amateur novel by an amateur writer, then you will not be disappointed; this writer will have attained his aim and can then gain still greater forgiveness and generosity, and will not be anxious that all is lost.

That truly is merit without measure.

Chiang Kuei

Tainan, cottage by the East Gate
March 28, 1961

Chapter I

Hung T'ung-yeh graduated from middle school.

During the four years of his education, he happened to encounter the May Fourth Movement which developed from Peking. This movement extended to Shanghai at once, and spread to the whole country, causing many young students to lay down their school books and leave their classrooms to take part in the movement against the government of the Peiyang warlords. Hung T'ung-yeh was one of these.

The political movement could not but directly influence education, and when the Principal delivered his speech during the graduation ceremonies, he frankly criticized Hung T'ung-yeh's class as the most lacking in scholarship and grades to graduate in many years. With feeling, he said:

"I am responsible for education. I take my stand upon pure education, and I demand that political movements get out of the schools, and that students take no part in political movements."

Immediately after the Principal had delivered his speech, a teacher of Chinese literature automatically mounted the stage to deliver his speech, and rather indirectly explained his own opinions.

"The value of the May Fourth Movement is in its educative effect upon thought. To accept science and democracy, to allow the spirit of science and democracy to penetrate politics, the economy, society, and the life of the people—

that is the principle of life for the Chinese people. We cannot preserve the thought of more than two thousand years ago, and never change!"

The Chinese literature teacher's point of view was obviously different from that of the Principal. After the graduation ceremonies, a great disagreement developed between the two men, and the Chinese literature teacher was not willing to yield a step; he held his ground and argued, making the Principal so angry that his whole body trembled. Naturally such a quarrel could not be resolved, and during the summer vacation the Chinese literature teacher did not receive an invitation to continue his duties, and finally he could only roll up his mat and depart.

Hung T'ung-yeh's school work was not good, as he himself candidly admitted. In ranking within his class, he had just barely attained the score necessary to receive a diploma of graduation. According to the Principal's way of looking at things, he should be considered the worst among the bad.

Although it was thus, his mother, who had been a widow for many years, still hoped that he could enter college, because an adolescent middle school graduate, neither literary nor martial, really had no very good prospects. And when she thought of his father, she felt even more the necessity of giving him a good opportunity. Otherwise it would cause no end of regrets for both the living and the dead, and she would be disturbed forever. How could she forget the reputation of the Hung family? She was always thinking that she must not bring disgrace upon this illustrious family, and it would be better still if the family's reputation could be enlarged and glorified by the hand of Hung T'ung-yeh—then she would feel that she could face her late husband.

Originally Hung T'ung-yeh's father had been an assistant secretary of the Ministry of War in the Nanking provisional government; he died of illness while in office. He left his wife and a son and daughter, and the son and daughter were Hung T'ung-yeh and his little sister Chin-ling. Although Assistant Secretary

Hung attained recognition as one who had sacrificed himself for the revolution, after his death and burial no estate remained. This meant the greatest difficulties in the lives of his survivors.

Hung T'ung-yeh had a paternal uncle, who had studied the fine arts in France. But when his studies were completed and he returned to his own country, he had taken up his duties at once in the field of transportation, and had served for years as bureau chief of various railway lines north and south; he was reckoned a person who had gotten where he was in a roundabout way. Yet no one knew the real reason why he treated the family of Hung T'ung-yeh, his flesh and blood relatives, as though they were strangers, and did not look after them at all.

Later on Hung T'ung-yeh's family drifted into living quarters in the Chapei district of Shanghai. The mother and the little sister worked as temporary workers binding books in the Commercial Press factory, and with the money they earned with blood and sweat, by eating less and using less, they were able to send Hung T'ung-yeh to school.

It was his mother who urged him to go to college, and Hung T'ung-yeh himself was willing. But figure it as they might, they could not afford it. The mother was anxious for several days. At last, in a spirit of "trying it once under pressure" she took Hung T'ung-yeh and broke precedent to go to the uncle who was the Bureau Chief. The uncle had been married for many years, but he had no sons or daughters, and Hung T'ung-yeh was the last generation of the Hung family. By rights, he should have accepted the responsibility of supporting him to maturity, because this was what a man with money should have spent it on. But the uncle had no interest whatever in this request, and positively refused.

The mother then could only retreat, and make a second request. Hesitantly, she said:

"I hear that there is work on the railroad, and that it can be quite profitable. Can't you give him an introduction?"

"If T'ung-yeh didn't bear my own surname, I could consider giving him an introduction. As he does bear my surname, it won't do, because I can't bring in my own people."

The Bureau Chief crooked his neck, thought a bit, and then said:

"Look here. I have a French friend, who operates a foreign shop on Shuang-fei Road, and sells sporting guns. A little while ago he asked me to find him an apprentice. As I see it, you tell T'ung-yeh to go there. He'll learn a little French, and if he does his job well, by and by he'll become a compradore, and be even better off than I am as a Bureau Chief."

So the matter was settled.

Every day Hung T'ung-yeh would go to work at the foreign shop, and wash the windows, polish the floors, wash the car, clean the toilets, and also polish the shoes of the Manager and the Manager's wife, and wash their underwear. The job of washing the underwear was particularly strange: early every morning there would generally be one or two pairs of underwear sent down to wash, sometimes a man's underwear, sometimes a woman's, and sometimes both, but only let the Manager remain at home and without fail there would be some. Hung T'ung-yeh happened to ask the cook, Old White-hand Wang, why it was that he had to wash only underwear. Old Wang laughed.

"Little Hung, I ask you, how old are you?"

"Eighteen."

"Eighteen, and you still don't understand? Stupid!"

As he spoke, he laughed, and although Hung T'ung-yeh laughed, his face flushed.

Very few people were employed in the foreign shop; besides this Old White-hand Wang, there was the man who sat at the desk writing, and sometimes people called him "Compradore". It seemed that the French Manager used this compradore of his for all sorts of tasks, and he always called him by the single name "Chang". High or low, inside or out, everything fell upon him alone. The Manager would often send him outside to take care of something, and also blame him for mishandling some work in the house.

Besides these, there was also an odd-job man called Little Wang; after Hung T'ung-yeh came to work, his livelihood was cut off.

Hung T'ung-yeh had no particular interest in the bright prospect of becoming a compradore, which his uncle the Bureau Chief had prepared for him, and in any case it remained to be seen what would happen after "Chang" the Compradore left. But sometimes the job is not selected by the person; when one runs into a line of work and there are no other opportunities, one can only attend to it.

Every day after work, he would buy something or other to eat in order to fill his belly, and then go to a night school to study French. Sometimes, when he had no money, he would skip the evening meal and simply tighten his belt. Every month the French Manager gave him four foreign silver dollars, for food money, and added two dollars for other expenses; in all, six dollars. However, he needed eight dollars a month for his school expenses, studying French, alone. Because of this he had to rely, as before, on the wages of his mother and little sister to get along.

A year passed. Hung T'ung-yeh had learned some French phrases, and he had also come to understand a little of the situation at the foreign shop. The sale of sporting rifles was only a blind; he didn't know if they sold even one or two in the course of a year. The Manager, whose name was M. Lefebvre, in fact dealt in military guns. He was always travelling to various provinces, and making connections with the local warlords; he imported military guns from Europe for them, and he also had means of taking the opium from their provinces and selling it abroad.

Once, while fighting for a relatively large piece of business, M. Lefebvre clashed with a Japanese arms dealer. Late at night, when he was returning to the foreign shop and had just gotten out of the car, someone hidden in the dark fired three shots at him. He may be counted lucky, for all three shots hit him but none inflicted fatal damage. Upon coming out of the hospital, after a few weeks' rest, he was as active as ever in the arena of his old business. But he kept a memento of that incident; he was a bit lame.

Thinking of his mother who was entering old age and of his sister who was growing up, neither of whom was very fit to go working outside the home, Hung T'ung-yeh worked even harder, carefully obeyed the Manager, the Manager's wife, and their son and daughter, and studied French even more diligently. His hope was very simple: to fulfill the term of his apprenticeship a little earlier, to sit at the writing-desk and to earn a little salary, that was all. He saw clearly that this was not a place where one could make a rapid advance in his career; in this place, high hopes were doubtless in vain.

Every Saturday afternoon the Manager's wife would call a pedicurist from the public baths to the house to trim her toenails. The Manager's wife used the simplest of methods to keep her hands and feet white and tender. She washed them with perfumed soap, wiped them dry, then used perfumed soap again and scented oil and rubbed them together, producing a great deal of bubbles, and finally she did not rinse with water, but rubbed the foam away with soft new towels. Once, on a very cold winter day, Hung T'ung-yeh's hands grew chapped, and several cracks opened; the pain was intolerable. He tried the Manager's wife's method, washing them by stealth a few times, and not only were the cracks healed, but his hands were softened. Because of this he greatly admired the Manager's wife for her cleverness.

The man who usually gave the Manager's wife her pedicure was Little Huang the Ninth of the Cleansing Virtue bathhouse, and every Saturday afternoon at three o'clock he would punctually report. By that time, the Manager's wife would just have emerged from the bathtub, and she would seat herself in a soft chair, and extend her foot to rest upon the knee of Little Huang the Ninth; sometimes the foot still had drops of water on it, not yet wiped off. For the Manager's wife, Little Huang the Ninth used a set of instruments and a whetstone; when he was finished, these were kept by the Manager's wife.

As a rule the Manager's wife would read a picture magazine during her pedicure, and at the same time she would smoke. She liked receiving the benefit of Little Huang the Ninth's "art", or perhaps it was even a "fine art"; he really trimmed very well, but she did not care for Little Huang the Ninth's yellow face. Taking up a big pictorial magazine, and holding it open with both hands so as to separate herself from that yellow face, she would temporarily give him her feet, and the Manager's wife knew a complete and beautiful happiness.

Little Huang the Ninth also had a kind of disquieting enjoyment, which he should not have had, but had nonetheless. Sometimes the Manager's wife's bathrobe slipped down off her leg. Whenever this happened, Little Huang the Ninth would put down his knife, and pull her bathrobe back up for her. The Manager's wife seemed to be absorbed in her pictorial magazine, and took no notice of these things. Little Huang the Ninth caught her foot, and directed his knife carefully, just like a sculptor creating a work of art.

It happened by chance. Three o'clock passed, the Manager's wife had bathed long enough, and Little Huang the Ninth still had not come. Hung T'ung-yeh telephoned to inquire and the reply was that the person had already gone out.

The Manager's wife sat on the soft chair, waiting impatiently. She saw that it was already past four, and still he hadn't come. Then the Manager's wife said to Hung T'ung-yeh:

"You really ought to study pedicure. When you've learned, you can cut mine, and then what's happened today can't happen again. I'll speak to the Manager, you'll learn pedicure."

For a moment, Hung T'ung-yeh did not know how to respond to this order, which came so suddenly. Embarrassed, he said:

"Pedicure and operating a foreign shop selling sporting rifles aren't the same line of work."

"How not? I'm the wife of the Manager of the foreign shop. If you do my pedicure, it's exactly the business of the foreign shop."

At four-thirty, Little Huang the Ninth arrived. He had gotten into a quarrel with someone on the streetcar, and had gone to the police station, and so he had just arrived. The Manager's wife told Little Huang the Ninth that she wanted him to accept Hung T'ung-yeh as an apprentice.

"As for his tuition, I'll pay whatever you like."

Hung T'ung-yeh translated her remarks for Little Huang the Ninth. Little Huang the Ninth understood at once, and said to Hung T'ung-yeh:

"When you learn how, then she won't want me to come."

Hung T'ung-yeh was afraid she would be displeased, so he lied and said:

"Not at all. She's taking precautions so that if she should have to go back to her own country, you couldn't go, and she'd take me."

"I'm willing to go to France too."

"To tell the truth, I don't want to study it either, it's her idea. I'll tell her now that you're not willing to teach me, that you refuse her, all right?"

"No need to do that. Let's see how much tuition she can pay."

Beginning the next day, after Hung T'ung-yeh had finished his French lesson in the evening, he went to the Cleansing Virtue baths to study pedicure. It was after midnight when he was able to return to the foreign shop and sleep, and before dawn he had to rise again, busier than ever.

This was the first time since Little Huang the Ninth became a teacher that he had accepted an apprentice, so it was a serious matter. He knew that Hung T'ung-yeh had no money—he ran back and forth, not even riding the streetcar—so he set up a single banquet table himself, and in front of many of his colleagues he burned incense to the patron deity, and told Hung T'ung-yeh to kowtow to his teacher, and to his teacher's teacher, and his teacher's friends.

One morning, when Hung T'ung-yeh was bent over, waxing the floor, the Manager's daughter, holding a toy hunting rifle, ran over and climbed onto his back, as though he were a horse, and told him to gallop. The girl was eleven years old, and plump, and must have weighed seventy or eighty pounds. She pressed down on Hung T'ung-yeh so that he could scarcely draw breath. Hung T'ung-yeh knew that she was the Manager's wife's darling, so he went through the motions for her, and galloped forward a few steps.

"All right, I've galloped, get down."

She wasn't willing to, and wanted him to gallop some more. The nine-year-old boy also climbed on. Big Sister sat on his back and Little Brother sat behind. The girl hit him on the head with the toy rifle to make him gallop. Those blows weren't struck lightly in fun, but were in earnest, and after a few of them, Hung T'ung-yeh saw golden stars. He couldn't help getting angry, and stood up roughly, and the two children slid off onto their backs. Little Brother got up and started to bawl. Big Sister began to beat Hung T'ung-yeh wildly with the toy rifle, hitting him on the head and the face until blood ran from several places.

The Manager's wife heard and came running out. She drew the girl away, asked how it had started, and scolded Hung T'ung-yeh.

"They are your Little Masters, and you're their horse. If they tell you to gallop, you should gallop. You shouldn't drop them on their backs!"

After soothing the children, the Manager's wife brought out a thick book and said to Hung T'ung-yeh:

"I've wanted to say a few words to you for a long time. It's very dangerous for a person like you to have no religion to believe in. You see that our whole family goes to church every week, and prays early and late. God is with our whole family. Loyally serving your master and little mistress is like serving God, and God will like you. If God likes you, then you'll be able to get along. If your master beats you, and curses you, and treats you like a horse or a dog, you must bear it, and you can't have any spirit of resistance or dissatisfaction. Because God says, if someone hits you on the left cheek, you must offer him the right cheek too. Let him beat you, and never strike back, even die without getting angry; this is God's will. Man cannot disobey God's will. Then after you die God will invite you to come up to Heaven and enjoy blessings. Your uncle helps my husband to do business, they are friends, so I want to help you by telling you about this advantage. Ah, this is the Bible, you take it and read at least a chapter every day; don't skip anything. This is in French; I don't know if you can read it or not?"

The Manager's wife, then, with her intimate expression, and her gentle tone, so sweet and honeyed, really seemed to be a different person than her usual self. Hung T'ung-yeh saw that this foreign Manager's wife was treating him with respect, and all at once he was alarmed by this favor, and despite himself his body seemed to grow as light as that of a bird. He rubbed the blood off his face with his hand, and blushing, he accepted the Bible; he was really so moved that he could not speak.

The Manager's wife went back inside, and seeing that the girl was still angry, she said:

"You simply should not get close to that yellow man! Naturally God will punish him, will send down calamities on him, just as He sent down calamities on the Egyptian Pharaoh."

Thus the sister and brother immediately knelt down before the bed, and muttered their prayers.

"God, God, send down calamities on that yellow man! Send him maggots, send him plague, send him blood! . . ."

God lived with them; they were soon happy again. From then on, they no longer paid any attention to Hung T'ung-yeh, nor looked at him straight on; however, at times they would call out in loud voices to him: "Yellow dog!"

As for the "yellow dog", the addition of the "Bible-reading" class further reduced the time he had for resting and sleeping. His command of French was still incomplete, and moreover this was a "heavenly book", so although the dictionary never left his hand, it was still a terribly difficult thing to read. Since the Manager's wife had personally given it to him, perhaps he looked on it as part of his work, and feared that it wouldn't do not to read it.

Sometimes he thought it might be more convenient to find a Chinese edition. But the Master had not told him to do so, that was certainly not what the Master meant, and he didn't dare.

Three years passed in the blink of an eye.

During those three years, Hung T'ung-yeh had achieved certain results. He had learned to speak French, and he had learned to read ordinary French newspapers and books, including that difficult Bible. Even more unexpectedly, he had learned pedicure. Moreover, he had been disciplined to the greatest patience, which could suppress a rage as ardent as fire. Although when others praised his good temperament, he usually felt a little uncomfortable.

What worried him was that there was no definite news of his hope of ascending to the writing desk. He didn't know how long he'd have to go on being a six-dollar-a-month apprentice. He stole the time to go and talk it over with his mother, and his mother went to see his uncle the Bureau Chief, meaning to ask him to speak to the French Manager. The Bureau Chief said:

"That's quite unnecessary. I know M. and Mme. Lefebvre are excellent people, who treat others very well; absolutely no mistake. Wait until the time comes, he'll naturally have a way for T'ung-yeh. It wouldn't do for me to bring it up. Wouldn't that make him feel 'What, you don't trust me?'?"

So Hung T'ung-yeh could only go on being patient.

But Mother's health got worse and worse. She would start to cough after midnight and be unable to get back to sleep, and although she had taken various medicines, and seen doctors, she didn't get better. She was already so emaciated that she seemed to be only bones, and still she had to go to work every day. If she didn't get to work, then the problem was even greater: how were the three of them to eat?

One afternoon when she was at the factory, her stomach suddenly began to hurt severely. Her daughter Chin-ling helped her into the factory infirmary, and the doctor was certain that it was appendicitis; she must be sent to the hospital at once. Chin-ling hastily asked the doctor:

"About how much will it cost to send her to the hospital?"

The doctor figured it for her: counting the operation and the sickroom, it would be at least sixty dollars. Chin-ling went to telephone her brother T'ung-yeh, told him about the illness, and asked if he could borrow some money from the French Manager. Hung T'ung-yeh himself was uncertain; he put down the phone, and went to look for the Manager. Fortunately, the Manager and his wife were just having tea, and Hung T'ung-yeh went up and spoke to them. The Manager lifted his teacup and said:

"How much money did you say you wanted to borrow?"

"Sixty dollars."

"Sixty dollars? That's your wages for ten months. Are you joking?" As the Manager spoke, he shrugged at his wife, and drew down the corners of his mouth.

"I hope you'll help me, to save my mother."

"You go on now, and don't worry!" The Manager's wife said with a smile. "Wait until I pray for you, and ask God; God will arrange things for you. If God wants your mother to go to Heaven, man can't keep her back."

Hung T'ung-yeh, greatly disappointed, retreated. Sweating in desperation, he hurried to borrow Old White-hand Wang's bicycle. Old Wang knew why he wanted it, and said:

"Little Hung, you don't have any experience. Who can lend you sixty dollars just like that? Such a big sum, you've got to get it together bit by bit. Just now you should have borrowed six dollars from him. When you got six dollars, then it would be a bit easier to think of a way to get fifty-four dollars."

As he spoke, he reached to his waist, brought out five dollars, and gave them to Hung T'ung-yeh.

"Who escapes illnesses and calamities? Anyway, just figure I'm helping you with this money. You don't have to pay me back."

This moved Hung T'ung-yeh so that he couldn't speak. He was about to go and seek the Manager again, but Old Wang said:

"Just now you tried and failed. If you go back again, he won't even be willing to loan you six dollars. Don't delay any longer. Get on that bicycle and go think of some other way. Remember what I said: nobody is going to loan you sixty dollars just like that. You've got to get it together little by little."

Hung T'ung-yeh mounted the bicycle, wishing only that he could make it go faster than a car. His first stop was the home of his uncle the Bureau Chief. The Bureau Chief wasn't at home, but his wife said:

"Your uncle is so poorly paid as a Bureau Chief, how could he give you any money?" As she spoke, she opened her handbag. "Take this, this is my miscellaneous money."

The hand she extended to him with the money wore a silver bracelet over an inch wide.

Hung T'ung-yeh took the money, saw that it was three dollars, and felt the greatest resentment. He thought of refusing it. But he remembered what Old White-hand Wang had said, restrained himself, thanked her, and left.

When he got to the factory in Chapei and saw his mother, her agonized face was white as a sheet of paper. Chin-ling, hearing that neither the French Manager nor the Bureau Chief uncle had been willing to loan money, was so anxious that she started to cry. Some women workers, who were looking on, said all together:

"Saving her life is what counts. We can't let Mother Hung die! We'll get some money together."

So a good many people took out their purses. A little here and a little there, and all at once there was over ten dollars.

The doctor saw that there were beads of sweat standing out on Mother Hung's temples, and said:

"We can't delay any longer, we've got to send her to the hospital right away! I'll call ahead, we can make up the money later."

That evening, in the hospital, Mother Hung was operated on, and her condition was greatly improved. Only her incessant after-midnight coughing threatened to burst open the new stitches on the incision, and added greatly to the worries of the duty physician. Finally he injected her with a suitable amount of morphine, and then she ceased coughing and slept peacefully.

Hung T'ung-yeh telephoned the French Manager and asked for three days' leave. While Chin-ling looked after their mother, he devoted himself single-mindedly to devising a way of raising the money. Wherever he had the slightest acquaintance, or there was half a thread of hope, he went, hesitantly and fearfully, to try his luck. But after two days of fruitless running about, he had gotten nothing.

Early on the third day, Hung T'ung-yeh called his sister Chin-ling out into the corridor outside the sickroom, and quietly asked her if there was anything in the house that could be sold. His sister thought for a while, and couldn't think of anything. Everything in the house was broken and shabby; what was there that was worth any money?

Just as brother and sister were facing this difficulty, a middle-aged man in a long gown of coffee-colored beige, wearing glasses for near-sightedness, appeared and asked the nurse for Mother Hung's room.

Hung Chin-ling said softly to her brother:

"That's the foreman of the temporary workers in the binding department. He's called P'eng Wen-hsüeh."

The next moment the man came over. Because his near-sightedness was severe, he had to draw near before he recognized Hung Chin-ling. Hung Chin-ling introduced him to her brother. He inquired about Mother Hung's condition, went inside to have a look at her, and then came out into the corridor. Turning to face Hung Chin-ling, he handed her a hundred dollars, and said:

"I hear you're having a problem with your medical expenses. This money is to help you out. This is a gift, not a loan, so you don't have to repay it."

This "public assistance" struck them both dumb. Hung T'ung-yeh said:

"How can we? The medical expenses won't come to this much."

"After she leaves the hospital, Mother Hung won't be able to come to work for a while. With old folks, it's most important for them to recuperate after an illness."

Brother and sister thanked him and thanked him again. Hung T'ung-yeh saw him to the door, and they stood talking for a time.

After P'eng Wen-hsüeh had gone, Hung T'ung-yeh returned to the sickroom and asked Chin-ling:

"Do you know him pretty well?"

"No. When we temporary workers go to work every day, we give him our time cards to register, and when we leave, we give the time cards back to him. Although we all know him by name, I've never spoken to him. Besides, he's nearly blind. Unless he comes very near, he can't recognize anyone. We often make jokes about him."

As Chin-ling said this, she laughed, and their mother, on her sickbed, also laughed softly.

"How much money does he earn in a month?" Hung T'ung-yeh asked.

"I don't know, but I don't think it can be more than thirty or forty dollars."

This person had miraculously saved Hung T'ung-yeh and his old mother and young sister from their great anxiety. Although Hung T'ung-yeh thought it strange, and did not understand the reason behind it, he was naturally pleased and joined his mother and sister in their laughter.

Brother and sister had been so worried for the past two days that they had had no interest in food and drink. Now that the money question was resolved, they felt hungry. Leaving their mother resting peacefully, they went to a small Cantonese restaurant near the hospital and ate dinner. For Hung T'ung-yeh and his sister, this was a most bountiful dinner. Hung T'ung-yeh even drank a cup of Tientsin Wu-chia-pi wine. They were so hungry that they cleaned up all the dishes, leaving nothing.

After dinner, they sat savoring their tea. Once more, they pondered the real meaning of that hundred dollars. Obviously, it was not simply to help the sick, he had to have another motive, only they could not guess what it might be.

Hung T'ung-yeh suddenly had a strange thought. Looking at his sister's white, delicate face and her youthful, captivating bosom, and then thinking of that middle-aged and nearly blind P'eng Wen-hsüeh, he felt that they were as much of a contrast as a lovely flower and cow-dung, and certainly not a pair. He couldn't help laughing.

When Chin-ling asked what he was laughing at, he made some excuse, and then stood up. He deliberately let his sister go first, and inspected her from behind. What a slender waist, what a figure. He kept shaking his head, and muttered:

"Oh, not a match, not a match!"

"What did you say?"

"I didn't say anything."

"I think you're a little drunk. Come on, Mama's waiting for us."

Because the next day was Saturday, the day on which the French Manager's wife had her pedicure, Hung T'ung-yeh returned that evening to the foreign shop, terminating his leave and getting back to work. When the Manager and the Manager's wife saw him, they acted as though they had nothing on their minds, and did not ask at all about his mother's illness. Hung T'ung-yeh returned the five dollars and the bicycle to Old White-hand Wang, and told him what had happened. When Old Wang heard, he was also completely amazed. He said:

"Little Hung, I've watched you for over three years now, and you're really a good fellow. You're still young, and if you stick with the Manager, and don't hang back, sooner or later there'll be a vacancy and you'll get to be the compradore. This business of P'eng Wen-hsüeh giving you a hundred dollars just like that means your Star of Fortune has moved. It won't be long before you make it. You're already changing. Little Hung, I'll be watching you."

The next evening, when Hung T'ung-yeh was going out to eat, Old Wang stealthily handed him a paper-wrapped packet. As he walked down the street, Hung T'ung-yeh found that the packet was slightly warm. When he opened it up to see, it was a big piece of fried beefsteak.

Mother Hung, after she had recovered from her illness, several times discussed inviting P'eng Wen-hsüeh to dinner, to express their gratitude. Had it not been for P'eng, the medical bills would have ensnared them. But they lived in half a room at the front of a building, and their quarters were as crowded as a pigsty; there was really no way to invite a guest inside. Hung T'ung-yeh thought it over, and said:

"Before long the French Manager and his whole family are going to Pei-tai-ho to avoid the summer heat. Wait until I've talked to Old White-hand Wang, to see whether we can borrow the foreign shop's kitchen to invite Old P'eng. We could also ask Old White-hand Wang and Chang the Compradore. It's a good chance to invite guests. Ma, you haven't seen the Manager's kitchen, it's got screen shutters and screen doors. It's a big, bright, airy place, and they cook with gas, and it's so clean—it's really great!"

The mother laughed politely and said nothing. Chin-ling put in:

"Every year when we go to call on our Bureau Chief uncle at New Year's, I see that their toilet is better looking than this half of a room of ours. As for their kitchen, that goes without saying!"

When Hung T'ung-yeh heard this, he said impatiently:

"Don't mention that Bureau Chief uncle. I hate him!"

"I don't understand either," Chin-ling said, pursing her lips. "He and Papa were brothers, so why does he hate us so? You see that Uncle Chang in the back room facing the landing treats his nephews and nieces better than his own children."

"It's not because of anything," said Hung T'ung-yeh, shaking his fist, "It's only because he has some stinking money! People with money look down on poor people, even their own fathers and mothers. What a thing! Selling military guns, selling opium, collaborating with foreigners to cheat his own kind, and he thinks that I don't know!"

From this simple conversation, Mother Hung discovered that T'ung-yeh and Chin-ling were already gradually changing and losing their patience. Patience is like a sheet of paper, and paper cannot contain fire. She saw that family relationships according to the ancestral laws and the ritual doctrines could no longer have any suppressive effect; the young people were considering, and picking and choosing. In general, when children grow up, they are no longer willing to hide their feelings, and one can no longer compel them to hide their feelings.

Mother Hung felt that the time had come to tell them the true story. The events of ten years ago were reflected before her eyes again, as clearly as though it were the present.

She was in Nanking then. It was not long since her husband had died, and the children were still small. Mother Hung had gone out to get some money for the next day's expenditures. When she returned, it was late, and it began to rain heavily. There were no streetlamps. Mother Hung was careless and slipped and fell into the ditch beside the road. The water came up to her waist, it was slippery, and for a long time she couldn't climb out. Mother Hung struggled, and called out, and finally a passerby helped her up, and moreover saw her home.

This man was a merchant, but he sympathized with the revolution. He had long heard the name of Assistant Secretary Hung. After they became acquainted, he would often help them out, in order to express his respect for the family of a revolutionary hero. Sometimes alone and sometimes bringing his wife and his son and daughter, he would come and inquire after them, as though they were old family friends.

Mother Hung softly told her son and daughter:

"Unfortunately, at that time there was a former subordinate of Papa's who had been a minor official in the Ministry of War. He caused trouble, after me from dawn until dark to marry him, and bothered me nearly to death. I had no idea of getting married again. I only know about preserving my chastity. I only know that when one loses one's husband, one obeys one's son. But because you were still small, I could only use pleasant words to make him understand, and beg him to forgive me. How did I know he was a mean person, and as soon as he saw that I wouldn't marry him, he spread rumors, saying bad things about that merchant and me. He also intimidated that merchant, scaring him so that he didn't dare to come see me any more. And he deliberately put those baseless rumors into the ears of your uncle, the Bureau Chief, so that from that time on, your uncle hasn't liked us. At first, it wasn't too good, still outwardly he put on a show."

When Hung Chin-ling heard this she felt hurt, and although her mother didn't cry, she began to cry.

Hung T'ung-yeh was obviously angry, and asked his mother:

"That rotten egg, who said bad things about you—where is he now?"

"Later on we moved to Shanghai, and I haven't had any news of him."

Hung T'ung-yeh suddenly stood up. He could no longer hold back his anger.

"Uncle's all mixed up! How could he not know what kind of person Mother was? An outsider casually says a few words and without distinguishing blue from red, or black from white, he believes it! From now on I don't recognize him as my uncle, I'll just call him 'mixed up uncle', the mixed up thing! Next New Year's I'm not going to pay respects to him."

"That won't do; an uncle is an uncle after all." His mother, seeing that he was angry, spoke very quietly.

Unexpectedly, Hung T'ung-yeh clapped his hands together and started to laugh. He patted Chin-ling on the shoulder, and said:

"Sister, don't cry. I'll tell you a bit of news. The Bureau Chief's wife has taken rooms at Ts'ang-chou Villa, where she's supporting a few boyfriends, and spending rolls of money on them. I've also heard from the French Manager's wife that when the Bureau Chief was in France, he caught a venereal disease, gonorrhea, so he can't have children, his line is cut off . . ."

Hung T'ung-yeh spoke joyfully, and would have gone on joking. But his mother picked up her chicken-feather fan and hit him on the head with it. Hung T'ung-yeh dodged away, and Chin-ling took the chicken-feather fan from her mother's hand. Their mother was so angry her face had gone white.

"If you dare go on with this wild talk, I want your life! I never thought you'd act like this. You're worse than your uncle by far!"

Mother Hung suddenly felt hurt. She hugged her daughter and wept. Snuffling, she said:

"If your father were here, things would never have come to such a pass."

When Hung T'ung-yeh saw his mother crying, he was no longer angry. He helped Chin-ling to calm their mother, and promised that he would never again curse his uncle, and so it was settled.

Finally, their mother resolved the matter, and decided that they would invite P'eng Wen-hsüeh to dine at the Cheng-hsing-kuan Restaurant near the North Station. She told Hung T'ung-yeh to go and fix a time with him. Borrowing the foreign shop's kitchen to invite guests was not respectful, and she didn't approve of it.

Chapter II

Having learned P'eng Wen-hsüeh's address, Hung T'ung-yeh found the time to call upon him. Because of the sudden appearance of the hundred dollars, Hung T'ung-yeh had had a peculiar feeling about this "blind brother". From thinking of P'eng Wen-hsüeh he was led, without knowing how, to thoughts of his sister Chin-ling, as though the idea had just appeared in his mind.

Shaking his head slightly, Hung T'ung-yeh smiled to himself.

P'eng Wen-hsüeh lived on an old alley in the French Concession. The mouth of the alley was occupied by a street stall, where money was changed and cigarettes were sold. There was also a cobbler, and on the opposite side a shop selling hot water, so that the passage was almost entirely blocked, and traffic was most inconvenient. Opposite this alley, across the street, was the North Station. The human tides swept back and forth countless times every day, and seldom was there a moment of quiet amid the din.

Hung T'ung-yeh squeezed into the alley, and found the doorplate. He became aware of a strange smell assaulting his nostrils. He had never smelled anything like it before, and he didn't know what produced it.

The landlord lived downstairs, and used the room where water was boiled. He rented the back rooms to P'eng Wen-hsüeh. When Hung T'ung-yeh came to call, P'eng Wen-hsüeh welcomed him eagerly, and invited him into the front room to sit down. He said:

"I live here with a friend. Come and sit down in the front room."

The front room was divided into two rooms. One, against the stairs, was quite dark and contained beds and bedding. The other, which had the window, contained a writing desk and several broken-down sofas. The friend who lived with P'eng Wen-hsüeh was just then bent over the writing desk writing something. When he heard P'eng Wen-hsüeh's voice, he shoved whatever he was writing into the drawer and hastily stood up. Hung T'ung-yeh looked him over. He was several years older than Hung T'ung-yeh, tall and thin, with a wildly dishevelled head of hair. He was bearded, and it must have been several weeks since he had shaved.

P'eng Wen-hsüeh introduced him. He was called Liu Shao-ch'iao, he was Hunanese, and he knew how to speak a few words of the Shanghai dialect. After the commonplace pleasantries were disposed of and they were seated, Hung T'ung-yeh thanked P'eng Wen-hsüeh, and explained the purpose of his visit. P'eng Wen-hsüeh was delighted, and exclaimed:

"Since Mother Hung has invited me to dinner, how could I dare to refuse? Only, Brother T'ung-yeh, I hope you'll also invite Shao-ch'iao. He's no stranger, we've gotten along together on cakes and fritters, we're brothers in adversity."

"That's just what I was thinking. I hope Mr. Liu will come too."

"If there's something to eat and drink, I never refuse." Liu Shao-ch'iao ran a hand through his hair, leaned on the couch, and laughed. "Only, you can't call me Mr. Liu. I've got a name, so call me by my name. I don't like it when people call me 'Mister'."

"That's the kind of straightforward person Shao-ch'iao is. Brother T'ung-yeh, I feel like I've known you a long time, and we're all friends here, so don't stand on ceremony."

"Well, then, you've been calling me Elder Brother, but you're older than me, so I can't accept it. You should change that too, all right?"

"Very well, I'll certainly do as you say."

Liu Shao-ch'iao offered Hung T'ung-yeh a cigarette. He didn't smoke, but he couldn't refuse in front of these two happy friends, so he accepted it and tried to smoke it. Liu Shao-ch'iao said:

"A person's name is only a label. This is called a cigarette, this is called a match, this is called a table, you're called Hung T'ung-yeh, I'm called Liu Shao-ch'iao, but there's no difference. A few years ago, someone advocated doing away with surnames, and I heartily approve. Ch'ien Hsuan-t'ung was the first to suggest it; he changed his name to Doubt the Past Hsuan-t'ung—an example we young people could well have imitated. But these two characters 'Doubt the Past' don't go far enough. The past—that is to say, what's old, or ancient. What's old or ancient certainly can't be anything good, so destroy it—what is there worth doubting?"

P'eng Wen-hsüeh extended his hand with a thumbs-up gesture to Hung T'ung-yeh, saying:

"You've got to listen to this theory of Shao-ch'iao's. He often writes articles for the newspapers and magazines; he's got a bit of a knack for it."

"So you're a writer?"

"No, I'm not a writer," Liu Shao-ch'iao said, shaking his head. "I only like to study."

Hung T'ung-yeh, looking around the room and seeing no books, felt puzzled: could someone who often wrote essays not read books? But then he saw a thin magazine on the table. He casually picked it up and glanced at it. The cover bore the title *The Guide*. In his several years of apprenticeship at the foreign shop, Hung T'ung-yeh had single-handedly studied French, and had paid no attention to Chinese books and magazines for a long time. It was the first time he had seen *The Guide*, and as he riffled through it, the titles and the authors' names were all unfamiliar. He read a few lines, but didn't understand what the author was saying. He couldn't help saying to himself: "What magazine is this?"

"This is the organizational journal of the Chinese Communist Party," Liu Shao-ch'iao said casually.

The phrase "Chinese Communist Party" shocked Hung T'ung-yeh. He stared, and said in a croaking voice:

"The Communist Party? I've heard that the Communist Party shares property and also shares wives."

"Who told you that?"

"Lots of people say so."

"Have you seen it?"

"No."

"How can you believe something you haven't seen?"

Hung T'ung-yeh had no answer, and Liu Shao-ch'iao went on:

"Communism is an ideal for the benefit of mankind, but at present few people understand it. If you're interested, you can study it and gradually you'll come to understand. It's not something that can be explained in a few words."

"Where did you get this magazine?"

"I bought it at a bookstore."

"Do bookstores openly sell Communist Party books?"

"Why not? Many of them do. If you take the time to go and see for yourself, then you'll know. Even Chang Ching-sheng's *History of Sex* is openly displayed in the windows for sale."

Hung T'ung-yeh felt ashamed of himself before this new friend, because he didn't even know what kind of book this so-called "Chang Ching-sheng's *History of Sex*" was. He wanted to ask, but he was embarrassed, and without realizing it he blushed a little. Liu Shao-ch'iao saw, let out a loud laugh, and said to P'eng Wen-hsüeh:

"Who'd have thought our new friend was such a kid, so innocent?

"He's not all muddled, like you!"

At this Hung T'ung-yeh blushed even more. He said hesitantly:

"I've been working in a French company for several years. I've been busy, and I don't know anything about what goes on outside. I've really turned into a dummy."

As he said this, he felt slightly ashamed, and hated himself a little.

"I think, I'm backward. Please don't laugh at me."

P'eng Wen-hsüeh took pity on him, and hastily said:

"Shao-ch'iao, we won't talk of this. It's late, let's take T'ung-yeh out to eat."

"How so?" Hung T'ung-yeh jumped up. "I came to invite you to dinner."

"Mother Hung's invitation isn't for today; today it's on me. We're only going to eat something to fill our bellies, it isn't like inviting a guest."

As Liu Shao-ch'iao spoke, he went into the back room and brought out several books wrapped up in newspaper. He handed them to Hung T'ung-yeh and said, with a laugh:

"It's our first meeting and I haven't anything to give you. You take these few books to read. If you're thin-skinned and afraid of being embarrassed, it's best if you lock the inner door and read them before going to sleep. You can discover for yourself the Great Way of human life. It's marvelous."

"What are these books?"

"You needn't ask that now. In general, 'reading enriches the mind'—I wouldn't fool you."

P'eng Wen-hsüeh said with a chuckle:

"I see you're spoiling Mother Hung's good boy."

"What do you understand? Stop talking nonsense!"

As they were about to leave, Hung T'ung-yeh again caught a whiff of that strange smell which he had encountered before outside the back door. He felt a little nauseated. It was really hard to bear. The smell seemed to be blown in through the front window. He asked:

"What kind of smell is that?"

"There's a little factory across the street where they render lard. That's the scent of lard," Liu Shao-ch'iao said.

"You call it scent, but I say stink. I really can't stand it."

"After a while you'll get used to it, and then you'll be all right. Don't you know the saying, 'After a time those who work in the pickled fish shop don't smell the stink'?"

"I'd rather get away from it, I don't want to get used to it."

"If circumstances force you to stay here, I'm afraid you won't be able to get away from it."

In a burst of laughter, the three of them went out.

Hung T'ung-yeh felt somewhat uneasy accepting the books Liu Shao-ch'iao had given him. What books were they anyway? How could they be good books, since he told me to shut the door before I read them? Thinking along these lines, he grew a little anxious, and the hand with which he carried the package clutched it more tightly. He was afraid that passersby on the street could see his books.

After they had dined, Hung T'ung-yeh went home and told his mother that the guests had accepted. His sister asked:

"What's that you've got in your hand?"

"Books."

"What books? Let me see."

"No, I haven't read them myself yet."

When his sister came over to grab them, Hung T'ung-yeh ran away.

He returned to the foreign shop and arranged things, preparing to go to bed.

Then the French Manager's wife came to tell him:

"I've already discussed it with the Manager. We're going to Pei-tai-ho this summer to avoid the heat, and we're taking you along, because I can't do without you to do my pedicure."

Hung T'ung-yeh heard this, and felt a bit put-upon, but he didn't know how to respond. The Manager's wife pressed him:

"What? Did you hear what I said?"

"I heard."

"Well, will you come with me?"

"I think, I am studying the business. I ought to stay and help the compradore to do business."

"The Manager's real business is in Pei-tai-ho. Every year, in the summer, he deals with many generals there. The Manager also wants you to come and help him."

Since Hung T'ung-yeh didn't answer, the Manager's wife went on:

"Pei-tai-ho is really fine, and you'll have plenty of chances to enjoy yourself. What's the use of sitting around Shanghai? We'll teach you to swim; the beaches there are the best for swimming. Besides, I can introduce you to other women who'll want pedicures. There are many foreign women there. You can fix a price, and give them pedicures. You can make a lot of money in a single summer. And you can keep the money you earn, only don't ask the Manager to pay your travel expenses. You pay for your own travel, and come with us to Pei-tai-ho."

"What if I don't make any money when I get there?"

"I guarantee you'll make money. I'll introduce you to many, many foreign women, and they'll all be willing to spend money to have their feet done."

Hung T'ung-yeh thought it over and agreed to come.

The Manager's wife ran over and kissed him on the forehead, saying:

"Now that's my good boy!"

As she spoke, she was gone. Hung T'ung-yeh felt sleepy, and shut the door of his room. For the past several years he had slept in this dark room under the stairs, which contained nothing besides a fan, a lamp, and a pile of cleaning supplies. This triangular bed-chamber, with its slanting ceiling, had no room for anything else. He had suspended a dim lamp over his bed; lowering it a bit, he opened one of the books Liu Shao-ch'iao had given him. He was anxious to have a glimpse into this mystery.

At the first glance Hung T'ung-yeh's "sleep-demon" fled away. He felt wide awake all at once. With his mind unprecedentedly tense, and his breath coming faster, he flew off into a new world.

That book, after all, was that world-shaking "famous work" compiled by Chang Ching-sheng, and there were several other books of the same kind.

Hung T'ung-yeh didn't sleep all night, and early the next morning he dragged his exhausted body to start his sweeping, beginning a whole day of troublesome and strenuous labor. Because he was not well-nourished, his face was yellow; he had become a "yellow man" whose name matched the reality. Today, there was some white amid the yellow, especially around the lips. Dark rings surrounded his heavy-lidded eyes.

As he worked he berated himself: in his hankering to become a compradore, he was wasting his precious youth. Life is precious insofar as it accords with one's wishes, and Hung T'ung-yeh was already beginning to feel that he ought to pursue some other goal.

From then on, without really being aware of it, of his own will he began to draw closer to Liu Shao-ch'iao. Almost every day he would find the time to go and see him, to pass the time of day. Liu Shao-ch'iao, ever since he had been "struck by the beauty" of Hung Chin-ling at Mother Hung's dinner, had also grown more intimate with Hung T'ung-yeh. He was always calling him Younger Brother, and referred to himself as Elder Brother. Hung T'ung-yeh also dropped the formality, and in front of others or alone addressed him as Brother Ch'iao. By this time, that blind brother P'eng Wen-hsüeh had been pushed to the rear. Because of this he felt uncomfortable, and a little jealous. He had not expected that Hung T'ung-yeh, whom he had introduced, would get the better of him. Once, when Liu Shao-ch'iao was going out with Hung T'ung-yeh, he pushed P'eng Wen-hsüeh back upstairs. When he called out and they paid no attention, P'eng Wen-hsüeh got angry. Standing at the top of the stairs, he shouted:

"Rabbit-boy! Rabbit-boy!"[1]

His glasses slipped down on the bridge of his nose, and spittle flew from his lips.

Liu Shao-ch'iao turned his head and glanced at him, then pulled Hung T'ung-yeh along, telling him quietly "Never mind him", and they went off together.

Two months passed, and Hung T'ung-yeh returned from Pei-tai-ho. Not counting the travel expenses paid back to the French Manager, he had cleared over two hundred dollars. This represented his accumulated wages for the work of pedicure, "hard-earned money" gotten snip by snip, and it was also the largest amount of money Hung T'ung-yeh had ever earned in his life. For many years, Hung T'ung-yeh had had an ambition. It was the hope that by his own efforts, he could take care of his old mother and look after his little sister. But now his ideas and his feelings had undergone an obvious change, and he no longer considered that he had such a responsibility and a duty. Since each person ought to nourish himself by his own efforts, how should his mother or his sister be exceptions?

---

[1] Rabbit-boy: colloquial term for the passive partner in a male homosexual relationship.

There were many people in the world, and according to Liu Shao-ch'iao, to be constantly thinking of one's mother and sister was really a cheap and selfish false humanitarianism.

"When your father and mother went to bed together, did they have a blueprint to create such a precious boy as you, and spend their last drop of sweat? You just came along unexpectedly, the dregs of a necessary function, that's all! People who eat food have to wash that filthy and greasy bowl, and you're just that bowl. You must understand! They've just got to force themselves to wash that bowl, but they don't have to really love that bowl."

Listening to Liu Shao-ch'iao's strange theory broadened Hung T'ung-yeh's experience, but there were still some things he didn't understand, so he said:

"But why would they spend as long as ten or twenty years raising a son and a daughter?"

"You're young, you don't see the truth even when it's right before you. If they didn't look after you, how could you look after them?"

Hung T'ung-yeh thought about it, and it did seem reasonable.

So he divided the money he had brought back from Pei-tai-ho, giving half to Liu Shao-ch'iao and keeping half himself. He quietly told Liu Shao-ch'iao:

"Don't let P'eng Wen-hsüeh know, I'm afraid he'd want that hundred dollars medical expenses back."

Liu Shao-ch'iao laughed when he heard this.

"Stupid, do you still think that hundred dollars came from P'eng Wen-hsüeh? That was mine!"

Hung T'ung-yeh was amazed.

"You didn't know us, how did you come to do that?"

"P'eng Wen-hsüeh brought it up to me. Otherwise, how would I have known? I heard about your situation, and felt that a person like you might be useful, so I told P'eng Wen-hsüeh to give you the money. When I throw rice, it's in order to steal a chicken. I don't do things out of compassion. When I repair the bridge, and mend the road, it's so people can come to me."

"So I've fallen for your plot!"

As they spoke happily, Liu Shao-ch'iao seized Hung T'ung-yeh and kissed him on the mouth. Hung T'ung-yeh fought free and wiped his lips with a handkerchief.

"I can't stand your tobacco stink!"

Liu Shao-ch'iao pursued him, still trying to embrace him. Hung T'ung-yeh ran down the stairs.

From upstairs, P'eng Wen-hsüeh jerked open the door and yelled:

"Rabbit-boy! Rabbit-boy!"

Hung T'ung-yeh's trip to Pei-tai-ho resulted in an even greater benefit. When he was on the beach, quite unexpectedly he became acquainted with the renowned Professor Kuo Hsin-ju and his wife.

On the swimming beach the French Manager's dressing cabin was next to that used by a Chinese couple. The Chinese gentleman, who seemed to be a member of the gentry, wore his hair long, and had a little mustache in the style of Charlie Chaplin. His face was pale, and he was of middling height. His wife was also short and plump, with coarse hands and big feet, and a round face. But her husband was attentive and considerate of her, and looked after her with affection and care.

The couple seemed to bathe and rest at about the same time as the Lefebvres. When they conversed they often used French, and they often used German, and when they spoke Chinese it was with a heavy Peking accent. This aroused Hung T'ung-yeh's interest; he felt they were a refined couple, and at times he couldn't help watching them. Professor Kuo and his wife noticed Hung T'ung-yeh because of his pedicure activity. Such a delicate-looking youth, who spoke such fluent French, must be the son of a great house. But his occupation did not match his appearance at all, for after all he was a foot specialist. There were always a great many foreign women after him to give them pedicures, and afterwards they would give him money, and he would accept it and thank them.

One day the Lefebvres had all gone down to the ocean, and Hung T'ung-yeh was resting in the canvas chair under the canvas awning. Professor Kuo and his wife came over. Hung T'ung-yeh then addressed him for the first time.

"Sir, you've come a little late today."

"Yes, we're a little late today. Did you come early?"

As Mrs. Kuo spoke, she sat down. Looking at Hung T'ung-yeh, she asked:

"You came with the French from Shanghai?"

"Yes."

"Do you work in a bathhouse, and they hired you to come?"

"No, I don't work in a bathhouse."

"Well, then, how is that you can do pedicures?"

"I learned it, originally, just so I could serve the Manager's wife." Hung T'ung-yeh's face grew red, and he felt a little embarrassed. "Now, in order to earn a little extra income and to make up travel expenses for the summer vacation, I—"

"Do you only do pedicure for foreign women?"

Hung T'ung-yeh hesitated, and then nodded.

"Yes."

Mrs. Kuo looked at Professor Kuo and laughed. Professor Kuo asked:

"Do you go to school?"

"I've graduated from Middle School."

"You speak French pretty well."

"Because of the hard work I've put in on it, my French is better than my Chinese."

"Do you like your present occupation?" Professor Kuo had taken a liking to Hung T'ung-yeh, and so he asked him this question.

"No, I don't like it."

"Well, then, why don't you change your job?"

"I haven't any opportunity, my uncle won't let me change my job."

"What does your uncle do?"

"My uncle," Hung T'ung-yeh paused, and finally said, "My uncle is Hung Pai-chuang, who's chief of the Railway Bureau."

"Hung Pai-chuang?" Professor Kuo seemed to breathe more easily, and sat up in his chair. He said: "I knew him when he was studying in France. Well then, your father was?"

"My father, Pai-li, died long ago."

"Hung Pai-li? In the Provisional Government at Nanking in 1912—?"

"Yes, he was the Vice-minister in the Ministry of War."

"So, no wonder I felt from the start that there was something different about you."

Kuo Hsin-ju sighed, and said feelingly:

"It's all because politics has gotten off the right track that the son of a revolutionary hero has fallen so low. And Pai-chuang shouldn't be so careless; he ought to take responsibility for you and send you to school."

Now that the matter had been brought up, Hung T'ung-yeh could not explain it all at once, so he said:

"I haven't asked you, sir, but I guess you must be someone of importance."

"I am Kuo Hsin-ju."

"Professor Kuo, the leader of the May Fourth Movement?" Hung T'ung-yeh unconsciously grew more respectful, and said delightedly: "Even when I was in primary school I looked up to you, sir, but I didn't know that my uncle knew you."

"We parted company after we came back to this country. He had his own affairs, and we haven't been close for many years."

Professor Kuo saw, in the distance, that the Lefebvres were bringing their children back from the water, as though they were coming back to rest. He asked:

"What business is your French Manager in?"

"Outwardly he sells hunting rifles, but in fact he deals in military weapons and drugs."

"Well, don't let him know what we've talked about. Such people disgust me."

As Kuo Hsin-ju spoke, he and his wife went into their dressing cabin.

After this, they had many opportunities for conversation. The situation of Hung T'ung-yeh's family, and his own experiences, elicited the greatest sympathy from Professor Kuo and his wife.

Professor Kuo had always cherished the youth and placed all his hopes in the younger generation. He and his wife had been married for over a decade, and his wife had never borne a child. The popular view was that to have sons and daughters represented good fortune, and they had no heirs to continue the family line. Still, the truth was that, on this account, they loved young people all the more.

Kuo Hsin-ju considered that Hung T'ung-yeh ought to leave M. Lefebvre, and quickly find another job.

"Your father Pai-li was an elder member of the T'ung-meng-hui, and you ought to continue his work, and follow the same path."

Hung T'ung-yeh agreed.

"In my opinion, you not only cannot work for M. Lefebvre for six dollars a month, but even if it were sixty, or six hundred dollars, you still couldn't work for him. The imperialists use the compradore class to carry out the economic plundering of the colonial peoples—surely you're not willing to do such a thing?"

"Of course not; it was my uncle's idea!" Hung T'ung-yeh said in a voice to divide steel and cut iron. "As soon as I return, I'm going to quit, I'm ready to go to work in a factory."

"You don't have to go to work in a factory." Professor Kuo Hsin-ju thought a bit and said: "If you have the will to travel your father's road, I can arrange something for you in Shanghai. You can study while you do this work."

Hung T'ung-yeh, having failed to get what he wanted, hastened to thank him.

"I have a few more words to say. Please don't be offended," Professor Kuo said with a laugh. "From now on, please don't give any more pedicures. It's not a very refined occupation, and it doesn't become your family or yourself. Does Pai-chuang know that you've been giving pedicures?"

"He knows that I give the French Manager's wife her pedicure, and he doesn't oppose it."

Professor Kuo smiled coldly, and said to his wife:

"I wouldn't have thought Hung Pai-chuang would have fallen so low."

Mrs. Kuo also sighed sorrowfully.

When he returned from Pei-tai-ho, Hung T'ung-yeh carried a letter from Professor Kuo. The Professor had instructed him:

"See this man, he can give you something to do."

Hung T'ung-yeh first told his mother about it. Mother Hung knew clearly that it was pointless to go on as they had been doing for the past few years, and that if there was an opportunity, it would be well for him to change his place. She said:

"Anyhow, you must first tell your uncle, the Bureau Chief; he recommended you for the job in the first place. But you'd better go and see that man first of all, and see what he has to say. If it doesn't work out, you don't want to make two mistakes."

"Even if it doesn't work out, I won't go on working at the foreign shop," Hung T'ung-yeh said with decision. "I'm ready to be a temporary worker."

So he went to see his uncle. Hung Pai-chuang was taken by surprise, and sought his reason. Hung T'ung-yeh said:

"Does Uncle know a Professor Kuo Hsin-ju?"

"We were quite close in France, but I haven't seen him for many years."

"He's going to find me another job."

"What?" Hung Pai-chuang, startled, stared at him and asked: "Kuo Hsin-ju is the revolutionary party's representative in Peking; what kind of a job can he give you? How did you get to know him? Have you joined the revolutionary party too?"

Hung T'ung-yeh stared back at him, and did not answer. Hung Pai-chuang grew anxious and slapped his hand down on the table.

"Answer me, answer me!" he said.

The aunt had been sitting with them, listening, and at this she left, saying:

"You young people can't act like this! Your uncle got you your chance at the foreign shop, laying out a bright path for you. You've been at it for several years now, what a shame it would be to throw it away."

"Professor Kuo says," Hung T'ung-yeh suppressed his anger and spoke softly, "that it's a shame I've been working all this time as a six-dollar-a-month apprentice, and giving the Manager's wife her pedicure as well."

"So you've let him stir you up against them, isn't that so?" Hung Pai-chuang said with a sarcastic laugh.

"I think that what he had to say was right. He treated me like a human being." Hung T'ung-yeh spoke very calmly, and his face showed no expression.

"What work did he really find for you?"

"He told me to go to Ch'ien Pen-san at No. 4 Ch'ing-lung Road, and said that I could work at No. 4, or if I wanted I could work in the newspaper office."

"I say you've been taken advantage of, and no mistake," Hung Pai-chuang said, in a rude, contemptuous tone. "No. 4 Ch'ing-lung Road is the headquarters of the revolutionary party. Ch'ien Pen-san is a member of the National Assembly, a famous troublemaker, and the representative of the revolutionary party. If you go there, can anything good come of it? Those revolutionaries specialize in using young people, sending them charging into the enemy's lines to spill their blood and sacrifice themselves, while they sit by and enjoy the benefits. If you take this wrong step, you're ruined!"

Hung Pai-chuang glared at Hung T'ung-yeh, but Hung T'ung-yeh said nothing. After a moment of silence had passed, Hung Pai-chuang could no longer stand it, and he cried:

"What about it? Say something!"

"I'm willing to go with them."

"Well, then, get out of here!"

Hung Pai-chuang gestured for Hung T'ung-yeh to leave, and Hung T'ung-yeh turned and left.

Skirting a small fountain, Hung T'ung-yeh left Hung Pai-chuang's peaked gray building. The withered yellow fallen leaves of the French plane trees were swept back and forth by the wind on the cement path. Over there a new cassia, which was probably blooming for the first time, emitted a fresh fragrance which gave one the feeling of having just awakened. Some of the chrysanthemums in the plot were already half-opened, and the gardener was busy potting them, so that they might be conveyed to the refined mansions of the wealthy and the grand, for the enjoyment of the virtuous daughters of the gentry. At festive wine banquets, amid the clear singing and the delicate dances, a few branches of nameless yellow flowers would be their ideal companions. Their brief lives served to brighten the youth of certain people.

As he was waiting within the iron fence to be let out at the gate, Hung T'ung-yeh stood for a moment and looked around. The master of this flowery garden, this fountain, this little building, acted for many years as my Bureau Chief uncle. This Bureau Chief uncle, Hung T'ung-yeh thought, was my invisible cangue; he diminished my hopes for the last ten years, and what I have gotten is a wound, a piece of dirtied nothingness.

"Finished, that's finished!"

Hung T'ung-yeh heaved a long sigh, as though he were expelling a chestful of accumulated depression. He felt a little regret. If this act were a ritual of leave-taking, it was obviously unnecessary. When a bird flies off to another branch, why should it keep thinking about the old branch?

The old fellow who kept the gate came out of the gatehouse, and without a word opened the iron gate no more than a foot. Clearly he was opening the gate for Hung T'ung-yeh, but his eyes were fixed on the dark gray sky, and his attitude was as though there were simply no one there in front of him. Hung T'ung-yeh likewise paid no attention to him, and slipped sidewise out the gate.

Hung T'ung-yeh got to see Ch'ien Pen-san in the reception room at No. 4 Ch'ing-lung Road. Ch'ien Pen-san took Kuo Hsin-ju's letter of introduction very seriously, and expressed his great respect, both in a public and a private capacity, for Kuo Hsin-ju.

"We always need people," Ch'ien Pen-san said, inviting Hung T'ung-yeh to sit down. "And expenses are always especially difficult. We welcome your taking part, only we can't treat you very well. Are you single?"

"Yes."

"That's much easier to manage, then. I can give you a place to live."

Ch'ien Pen-san then explained in greater detail about the organizational headquarters and the newspaper office, and asked Hung T'ung-yeh to choose. Hung T'ung-yeh said quietly:

"My aim is to be your 'apprentice'. I want to follow you, sir, and get some experience with a senior revolutionary."

"Speak a little louder, I'm hard of hearing."

Hung T'ung-yeh blushed, and repeated what he had said. He was not used to flattering people to their faces, and although what he had said were no more than the ordinary polite phrases, mere social talk, he already felt very embarrassed.

Ch'ien Pen-san heard, and shook his head, but murmured his thanks. This at once confused Hung T'ung-yeh, who couldn't tell if the other's response were genuine or not. Ch'ien Pen-san struck the bell on the table, and a middle-aged man in a jacket and trousers came in. Following Ch'ien Pen-san's explanation, he understood that this was the custodian. Ch'ien Pen-san said:

"You move in first. I come here every day to meet guests, so you'll be seeing me."

When the matter was settled, Hung T'ung-yeh went straight to the foreign shop. The Bureau Chief's car was parked in front. He knew that this had to be got through, so he braced himself and went on in. As soon as Chang the Compradore caught sight of him, he said:

"They're waiting for you; hurry on upstairs!"

Hung T'ung-yeh nodded and went upstairs.

M. and Mme. Lefebvre were sitting with Hung Pai-chuang. When Mme. Lefebvre saw Hung T'ung-yeh, she jumped up, led him to a seat, and served him coffee; never before had she been so polite. The Bureau Chief led off, speaking in Chinese:

"We've been discussing your affairs for some time. You certainly cannot leave! With five years of effort, and ever so much care on the part of Manager Lefebvre and his wife, we've just made a man of you. You've just grown your wings, and you want to fly away. How can you face them? For the sake of my face, you were given this once-in-a-lifetime opportunity. Don't you have any regard for my friendship with M. Lefebvre?"

Hung T'ung-yeh did not answer, but only said to himself: for five years I suffered for him and put up with his temper, and what did he make of me? A few words of French, not worth half a cash, and didn't I learn that myself by hard study? Besides, I learned to do pedicures . . .

At the thought of pedicures, he glanced at the Manager's wife's feet. She was wearing a pair of soft-soled Chinese women's slippers, of yellow satin embroidered with a dragon pattern. Perhaps the slippers were a little small, so that her instep protruded, and her silk hose wrinkled above the slipper.

The Manager's wife immediately became aware of Hung T'ung-yeh's gaze. She raised her feet, looked, and pulled up her hose. Although she didn't understand Hung Pai-chuang's words, she knew what he must be talking about, and interjected:

"In any case we can't allow you to go. It's hard to find someone like you, who can do everything, and is willing to do it, and we've been quite moved. Do you remember where it says in the Bible—"

"I'm promoting you to Assistant Compradore," M. Lefebvre broke in on his wife. "Starting today, I'll give you sixty dollars a month. Your work won't change; if you're willing to do a few things, go on doing them, because you're already familiar with them. There are many jobs which, if you don't do them, there's no one else to do them."

Hung T'ung-yeh was inwardly slightly shaken, but he quickly calmed himself, and as before said nothing.

"See," exclaimed Hung Pai-chuang joyfully, "how good the Manager is to you! I knew he could never wrong anyone. Well, this is fine. You've learned for several years, and you've learned pretty well. Even I can take some pride in that."

"Remember, it says in the Bible—"

"No."

Hung T'ung-yeh spat the word out harshly. His uncle's joy had aroused the opposite feelings in him, and he had really heard enough of the Bible's good words. He no longer placed any hopes in those words divorced from acts, that false benevolence of honeyed words which concealed a bad heart.

Hung Pai-chuang and the Lefebvres were startled by this "no". That he should refuse such a sweet morsel was completely unexpected.

"I've already explained to you the matter of No. 4 Ch'ing-lung Road. Now I'm going to move over there."

Hung T'ung-yeh stood up and made a bow.

"Thank you for your sincerity, Master and Mistress, and goodbye."

Having said this, he went directly downstairs. He heard only his uncle spit out the words:

"Muddled thing! Don't ever come see me again!"

And the Manager's wife started to cry.

Hung T'ung-yeh hardened his heart and ignored the tender sound of that crying. That sound was even more affecting than those sweet words of hers. Hung T'ung-yeh had never before heard the Manager's wife cry, and unexpectedly he heard it as soon as he resolved to leave.

His baggage was simple, and made ready at once.

Hung T'ung-yeh picked up a little knife which he had used in giving the Manager's wife her pedicure. He had meant to throw it away and not to take it with him, but for some reason he couldn't discard it. It had been given to him by his teacher when he became an apprentice. His teacher had said:

"I welcome you into our trade. May you single-mindedly study the art, hand it down, and spread it far and wide. It is said that this trade of ours has never produced any amateurs. You can be an amateur opera singer, but you can't be an amateur pedicurist. If pedicure has any amateur practitioners, you're the first."

So said Little Huang the Ninth, making the teacher's teacher, the teacher's maternal and paternal uncles, and the senior students at the banquet all laugh, and they had another cup of wine. With these words still in his ears, he felt that he must abandon his amateur's status. A kind of mysterious, insubstantial feeling of longing suddenly rose in his heart, and Hung T'ung-yeh picked up the little knife, which he had tossed under the bed, and began to examine it. He rubbed the dust from its leather case and polished it bright with his sleeve. Lovingly he placed it into his kit, and put it to sleep together with his safety razor.

The safety razor, in its gilded case, had been given him by the Manager's wife. She felt that he ought to shave his face every morning, just as she must have her pedicure very week, so she had given him the thing. The pedicure knife given him by his teacher had originally come with a coarse wrapper of blue cloth. But the Manager's wife hadn't liked it; she had given Hung T'ung-yeh some money and told him to have a case made to order. The case was of deerhide, with two German-made gilt knobs on top.

Five years had passed, and Hung T'ung-yeh had had his fill of it. The Manager's wife often smiled, and the name of God was often on her lips, but unfortunately her heart was wolfish and cruel. Liu Shao-ch'iao asked him:

"How many hours a day do you work?"

"Twenty-four hours."

"You're joking."

"I'm not joking, it's true. Although I get four hours a day to sleep, sleeping is also part of my work. First, I have to sleep under the stairs. Second, although I do sleep, they can call me to get up at any time. Third, when they tell me to sleep, it's not because everyone has to sleep just as everyone has to eat, for that would be to say that man has a 'right to sleep'. They let me sleep, so that I can restore my strength and my spirits, so that after I wake up I can work for them some more . . ."

Hung T'ung-yeh wanted to go on, but Liu Shao-ch'iao waved his hand and said:

"All right, enough, don't go on. That's because you yourself are willing, you can't blame others only."

"So it's my fault?"

"Yes, because you're naturally a slave."

"What do you think I should do?"

"Resist!"

Under Liu Shao-ch'iao's 'incitement' Hung T'ung-yeh's consciousness was gradually awakened, and he began to have the courage to face the French Manager, the Manager's wife, and even his uncle the Bureau Chief, and to act the man. Ordinarily he had to do mostly with the Manager's wife, and it was she whom he despised the most. Now that they were going to part, and each go their own way, it was this little thing the Manager's wife had given him that he most prized. Hung T'ung-yeh himself felt that this was a contradiction. He drew down his lips, and smiled contemptuously.

Chang the Compradore and Old White-hand Wang appeared. They stood outside the little four-foot high door, and bent over to beckon Hung T'ung-yeh to come out. Hung T'ung-yeh came out and told them goodbye.

"Don't say goodbye, we want to keep you. We're asking you not to leave."

"There's really no way, because I've already accepted another job."

"You've already got a job here, why do you need another one?"

"You know what my situation here is."

It was at M. Lefebvre's suggestion that these two had come forward to detain Hung T'ung-yeh. M. Lefebvre understood, and his wife understood even more clearly, that it was simply a dream to think they could ever find another like Hung T'ung-yeh. He could do both rough and delicate tasks; he was willing, and he was patient. For the past five years he had done the work of two, or even of three men, and had gotten along on what little money his mother and sister could spare him. M. and Mme. Lefebvre had intended to discipline him and to make a man of him. Now they saw that he had made up his mind to leave, and they felt that they had disciplined him a bit too well. In M. Lefebvre's dispassionate reckoning, there were plenty of men, but to start afresh and discipline another like him was really too difficult. At the least, it was hard to find another as amenable to training.

The couple knew that since matters had come to this point, oppression was no longer of any use. On the contrary, they remonstrated with Hung Pai-chuang and asked him to calm his rage and go home. M. Lefebvre discussed it with Compradore Chang, and gave him complete authority: the greatest weight of social relations must be brought to bear to force him to stay. Compradore Chang knew that Hung T'ung-yeh was friendly with Old White-hand Wang, so he suggested adding Old Wang to this cooperative venture. Compradore Chang said:

"This isn't something that can be settled with a few words. I'll invite him out to have dinner and a good time, and gradually talk him around. From what I've seen of him, he's not a completely obstinate person."

M. Lefebvre looked at his watch. It was just four o'clock in the afternoon. He thought a moment, nodded, and said:

"You and the cook both go, then. This evening we can fix something to eat for ourselves. I don't care how late you come home, I'll be waiting for news of your success. Give me an accounting of whatever you spend."

When he was finished speaking, he limped off up the stairs.

Compradore Chang had worked for M. Lefebvre for over ten years, and had never known him to be so generous and so liberal. He did not respect M. Lefebvre, but he respected Hung T'ung-yeh who had been able to get the best of M. Lefebvre. He told Old White-hand Wang, and they went to get Hung T'ung-yeh. Compradore Chang said:

"I'm inviting you out to dinner, so we can talk this over at length."

"How can I impose on you?"

"What does a dinner matter? If you refuse, it means you look down on me."

Old White-hand Wang added:

"The compradore and I are playing host—does that give you enough face?"

"How can you leave?" Hung T'ung-yeh thought that he must be joking.

"I asked the Manager for time off. You just wait a moment, while I go and change my clothes."

Hung T'ung-yeh could no longer refuse. Old Wang changed his clothes and reappeared. He asked Compradore Chang:

"Where shall we go?"

"I'd like to drink some wine."

"Well, what does Little Hung have to say?"

"I'm the guest; I'll abide by the host's decision."

With all this polite talk, the three men reached the street, and in the end, according to Compradore Chang's wishes, they got on a streetcar and went to Pa-hsien Bridge.

Chapter III

"It's still too early to eat and drink," Compradore Chang said. "Let's find a place to sit down first."

So the two men followed him. Turning a corner, they gradually left the clamor of Pa-hsien Bridge, and entered a relatively quiet alley. Stopping before a rather old-fashioned stone gate, Compradore Chang knocked with the brass ring. Old White-hand Wang made a "six" sign with his right hand toward his lips, and asked Compradore Chang:

"Is this it?"

Compradore Chang nodded.

"Little Hung hasn't been here."

"I know, I have something else nice for him."

As he spoke, the door opened with a creak, and a maidservant let them in. A great many miscellaneous things were piled so thickly in the small yard that one could hardly find a place to set one's foot. But the sitting room was nicely arranged, with a six-lamp chandelier, and redwood furniture. The maidservant, following them, said:

"Please go upstairs, Compradore Chang."

At the head of the stairs they were welcomed by a middle-aged woman with oiled hair and a powdered face. The three men were invited into a side chamber, where an opium tray rested upon a redwood mandarin's bed. A girl of eighteen or nineteen lit the lamp, and then served tea. Now and then Compradore Chang would smoke a couple of pipes of opium. Although he didn't have the habit, he enjoyed it. Now, he introduced Hung T'ung-yeh to the middle-aged woman.

"This is Mr. Hung, the Assistant Compradore of our foreign shop." He gestured with his opium pipe. "He doesn't smoke this, but he likes something else, so you be a matchmaker for him. You see he's young and good-looking, and besides he's a virgin, so find somebody suitable for him."

These remarks made Hung T'ung-yeh blush all over his face, and he became very uneasy. He didn't say anything, but he felt willing enough to go along with it, and was hoping for just such a meeting. He had studied the theories of Chang Ching-sheng, and had experimented several times with Liu Shao-ch'iao, but none of this had satisfied him. Since he had given pedicures to the French Manager's wife and to the many foreign women at Pei-tai-ho, his taste in women had become Westernized. His spirit leaned toward white skin and tall, full-bodied figures, and these were the attributes which Heaven had not bestowed upon most Chinese girls. He hoped to meet his ideal partner, and he was always prepared to repay such a partner with his body and spirit. But he grieved that because of his own shortcomings, such a thought was in vain, for he would never have such an opportunity.

"How about it, Little Brother?" Compradore Chang asked deliberately, amused to see him in such an awkward state.

"How can I? I don't do that kind of thing!"

"Food and sex are natural, and not bad things. It's much healthier than reading Chang Ching-sheng's little books on the sly."

Hung T'ung-yeh felt even more uncomfortable at hearing the mention of Chang Ching-sheng, and he said defensively:

"I don't understand."

"Little Brother, stop this nonsense!" Compradore Chang said, laughing. "What were those books under your pillow? I say, Little Brother, from now on we'll be frank with each other. Let's open the windows and speak plainly, and not fool each other any more. It's just Old Wang here with us, we all muddle together to eat from the foreigner's rice-bowl; what do 'benevolence, righteousness, and virtue' have to do with you and me?"

"Right, the Compradore has said it very well! That's exactly what I mean," Old White-hand Wang said, gesturing the middle-aged woman toward Hung T'ung-yeh. "You take him along now. Play first, then we'll talk more. We won't cause you any trouble."

"I'm the host tonight; whatever it is I'll settle for it," Compradore Chang winked at the middle-aged woman, and the woman took Hung T'ung-yeh away.

Watching him go, Compradore Chang asked Old Wang:

"Well, what do you think? Do you want to join me in a couple of pipes, or call a girl?"

"Me? Neither," Old Wang drank some tea, and said, "You smoke, I'll keep you company. I'm waiting to drink some wine."

Compradore Chang lay down, and the girl leaned down to heat the opium for him.

Just as he was finishing the first pipe, the woman came back and sat down on the edge of the chair in front of the bed. Shaking her head, she said:

"That friend of yours is really hard to please! He doesn't want any kind of girl. He's only thinking of a foreign girl—French, Russian, no matter if they're fragrant or smelly—he only wants white girls. Compradore, you know, where am I going to find a white girl? Isn't that just making fun of me?"

When Compradore Chang heard this he laughed. He said:

"So all along he wanted to try a foreign girl. . .That's easy, leave it to me."

"No wonder you said he liked something else. He usually keeps things to himself, but inside he's pretty complicated," Old White-hand Wang said, chuckling.

"All right, ask him to come on back," Compradore Chang told the woman.

In a little while Hung T'ung-yeh came back, blushing.

"The kind you want," Compradore Chang told him, "can't be found here. I know where you can find foreign women, and I'll take you there. I'm only afraid, Little Brother, that when you're face to face with the enemy you'll find you've bitten off more than you can chew."

"I'm just curious," Hung T'ung-yeh bashfully explained.

When Compradore Chang was finished, the three of them began the rest of the program.

At the restaurant they drank five bottles of Flower-pattern wine. Compradore Chang and Hung T'ung-yeh together couldn't finish one bottle, but Old White-hand Wang forced it down. Strangely enough, he wasn't yet completely drunk, but his speech was slurred, and he didn't know what he was saying.

Compradore Chang called a car, and the three of them left Hongkew. As they passed a Japanese dance-hall, Compradore Chang asked Hung T'ung-yeh:

"Do you want to try a Japanese girl?"

Hung T'ung-yeh shook his head.

Compradore Chang ordered the driver to stop, and paid. He led them into a Japanese hotel, saying:

"There's an old Japanese woman behind there; she has a few Russian girls, who specialize in receiving Japanese and Chinese customers."

"She really understands international equality," Hung T'ung-yeh said happily.

"Not so, she doubles the price for Chinese."

"Well, why play the fool?" Old White-hand Wang said loudly, rubbing his nose.

"She uses the curiosity of the Chinese, who are willing to be taken advantage of."

While Compradore Chang was still talking, two drunken Japanese blocked the way. One of them came up face to face with Old White-hand Wang and chattered at him. None of the three understood Japanese, nor did the Japanese understand French or English. They were momentarily stalemated, until a Chinese wearing a cap and a jacket and trousers came over, and explained what the Japanese meant.

"The Japanese blames that big fellow for talking too loud and disturbing others."

"Oh, and what kind of place is this?" Old White-hand Wang snorted angrily. "They charge you double and you're not allowed to talk—isn't this just cheating people?"

"They only want you to talk a little softer."

"It's my nature to carry on like this, and it's nobody's business," Old White-hand Wang said, pointing at the Japanese. "Look at him! He's gabbling even louder."

"Here, he can, but you can't."

"You're a Chinese too!"

"I eat the rice of the Japanese, so I interpret for them."

The Japanese "dwarf" saw that the big fellow was sticking out his fingers and waggling them to and fro, and felt that he was rude. Catching him off guard, he seized his hand and bit it cruelly, causing Old Wang to squeal like a hog being slaughtered.

The old Japanese woman who had the Russian girls came out from the back. She recognized Compradore Chang, and she could speak a few words of English, so she resolved the matter, sent the two Japanese and their Chinese interpreter who ate the Japanese rice away, and took Compradore Chang and his companions upstairs in back.

The two small wounds on the back of Old White-hand Wang's hand were bleeding, and the old woman bound it up for him with some mercurochrome and bandages, and repeatedly bowed in apology. Old Wang got over his anger and said, laughing:

"There are good Japanese too."

"Her business is looking after you."

"Little Hung, I've been wounded in action so that you could enjoy yourself with a foreign woman, how can you face me?"

"I'm sorry. If I'd known before, we wouldn't have come."

"When you come to such a disreputable place to have fun," Compradore Chang said with a laugh, "it's not strange if you stir up some trouble. Old Wang, I think you'd better have a Russian girl, too, so as to make up for it."

"All right, shall I try a foreign dish too?" Old White-hand Wang grinned widely. "I've been a master chef for many years, but I've never eaten Russian food. I'm only scared that if that short old lady of mine finds out, she'll bite my tongue off."

"We'll keep your secret," Hung T'ung-yeh added hastily, feeling that he must have someone to go with him.

"All right, but it's your responsibility. If my old lady finds out , I'll just say you dragged me in here," Old White-hand Wang said, pointing at Hung T'ung-yeh.

"Doesn't that go without saying?" Compradore Chang said. "It's a question of Little Hung's face."

There was a peal of laughter, like brass gongs, on the stairs, followed by the mixed up sounds of heavy footsteps, and a wind swept up the steps. Three mother yakshas appeared, and one of them, who was at least six feet tall, and happened to be standing closer, reached out, seized Hung T'ung-yeh, and kissed him on the mouth.

An hour later, the three men rented a room in a big hotel near Hongkew to rest for a while. Compradore Chang again brought up the matter of Hung T'ung-yeh leaving the business. Old White-hand Wang added:

"Little Hung, just forget about that. Since you've been promoted to Assistant Compradore, just carry on anyhow. If you went to Ch'ing-lung Road, wouldn't it still be to wait on someone? The taste of waiting on someone is pretty much the same all over, and moving isn't as good as staying on."

"No mistake, that's just how it is. I've got the title of Compradore, and you know how it is with me. If I really got angry with them, wouldn't I have died of anger early on? Just so I have a bowl of rice to eat, that's all. I wear this Compradore's skin, and it looks good on the outside; I get enough to eat, and people respect me; these are all advantages. Once you work with Chinese, your position in society at once drops ten thousand feet, and who will look up to you?"

Compradore Chang yearned to dig out his own heart and show it to Hung T'ung-yeh, the better to make Hung T'ung-yeh understand his sincerity; very seldom was he genuinely concerned about anyone. Naturally, his loyalty to the French Manager was one reason. But a still more important factor was his own selfishness: he wanted an assistant like Hung T'ung-yeh.

But none of this talk agreed with Hung T'ung-yeh's intention. This new Hung T'ung-yeh was an awakened person, and he naturally reacted against the taste of Compradore Chang's complete slavishness to the foreigner. But they had entertained him all evening, and the novel and provocative taste of the Russian woman was still fresh, so from the standpoint of human relations there was really no way he could argue.

Hanging his head and hiding his anger, Hung T'ung-yeh had nothing to say.

"Very well, then you'll forget about leaving," Compradore Chang settled the matter with a word. "So Old Wang and I have some face after all! Tomorrow, I'll talk to the Manager, and look for another apprentice to handle the odd jobs; you're the Assistant Compradore."

Old White-hand Wang also said:

"Little Hung, I've always been good to you, and you've acknowledged it yourself. If you ever talk of leaving again, I'll be angry with you."

"No mistake, that's how I think too," Compradore Chang said with a loud laugh. He leaned on the sofa, and said slowly: "A man can't cut himself off completely and leave no way back. It's not that there's no such thing as changing your job, it's just that you can't go too far in doing so. That's like burning your old house down before you know if your new house is suitable or not. Rushing ahead without looking back can get you in trouble."

"Never mind that now. If you want to go, just wait a bit and look for an opportunity, and go in a proper manner. Who can guarantee that this bowl of rice is good for a lifetime?" Old White-hand Wang said with a laugh. "It's late, and I'm really tired. If I don't go back now, that old lady of mine will make me 'kneel and await my punishment'."

Someone knocked at the door, and Compradore Chang called an answer.

A middle-aged White Russian man, carrying a great Russian fur rug folded over his shoulder, came in smiling and chuckling. In crude Mandarin, he asked them to buy his fur rug. The three men refused him.

But he didn't leave, and kept on at them. Over and over he told them that his goods were of high quality, his price was low, and that if you didn't buy it at once, you were making a mistake, and would regret it for the rest of your days. That was the general meaning. He didn't speak Chinese clearly, and would mix in words of English and French, but his English and French were equally incapable of conveying his meaning.

"Little Hung," Compradore Chang said, "you like Russian women, do you like Russian men too?"

Old White-hand Wang heard this and said with a loud laugh:

"That, I'm afraid he couldn't handle! How about it? Little Hung, are you interested?"

Unexpectedly, the White Russian had also understood the words "Russian women" and at that he stopped trying to sell his fur rug. At once he asked:

"Do you want a Russian girl? I've got one, you come with me. Really pretty."

Compradore Chang turned to Hung T'ung-yeh.

"He wants, he wants."

The White Russian then turned on Hung T'ung-yeh, wanting him to come along. Hung T'ung-yeh paid no attention to him. The man kept circling him, wishing that he could drag Hung T'ung-yeh away by force. He brought out of his pocket a couple of Imperial Russian decorations, gesticulating wildly, and gabbled on without pause. They thought they understood him to say that he was one of the Tsar's military officers, and had been awarded these decorations for merit, and furthermore that he knew the wives of high-ranking Tsarist army officers, and could introduce Hung T'ung-yeh to them. Finally, he seemed to be saying that a woman was cheaper than the fur rug, and was worth a try.

"A rare opportunity," Compradore Chang said to Hung T'ung-yeh. "Do you want to go again?"

Hung T'ung-yeh, smiling, shook his head.

Compradore Chang rang the bell, and told the waiter to call a taxi. He said:

"We'll take Little Hung back to the foreign shop first. Just now as we passed the Odeon Theater, I saw that Fan P'eng-k'o's 'Moon Palace Casket' is playing. Let's come and see it another day. Little Hung, do you like to watch movies?"

"I very seldom go."

"You must have seen Fan P'eng-k'o. Do you like him? I hear that in 'Moon Palace Casket" he treats a Chinese wearing a queue like a bear. He's sure to be a lot of fun. You've just got to see good shows."

"I rather like Chaplin."

"No mistake, he can really make you laugh, and he's got a routine. Unfortunately, he's always suffering, and getting taken advantage of in his movies, and it makes one feel uncomfortable. Whereas Fan P'eng-k'o has women, money, fame, and position, and takes advantage of the whole world."

Compradore Chang, in high spirits, put out his thumb and waggled it under Hung T'ung-yeh's nose. He said:

"Shouldn't a gentleman be like Fan P'eng-k'o, eh?"

The taxi arrived, and the three men went downstairs.

The White Russian, seeing that he had talked for a long time without doing any business, blushed down to his neck, shouldered his rug, and went away angry. He was muttering, probably in Russian, and probably curse words.

"People who have lost their country are really pitiful," Compradore Chang said. "The men sell rugs, or pimp, and the women sell themselves."

"It's their own fault, because they had it too good before," Hung T'ung-yeh said.

On the sidewalk in front of the hotel, an English army officer in a red jacket was anxiously following a Cantonese prostitute. That 'salt-water sister' was tall and slender, with a dark complexion, finely drawn eyebrows, and wore high-heeled shoes on her bare feet. There was a strong feeling of the south about her. Hung T'ung-yeh was captivated; he felt that she really represented a strong contrast with the plump, pale, Russian girl, and that each of them had their good points.

Compradore Chang deliberately slowed down, and made way for the English officer. Hung T'ung-yeh looked around, and looked again after that salt-water sister's back.

A night had passed, and Hung T'ung-yeh was an Assistant Compradore. A writing desk was designated as his. But he still had to rise early, sweep the floor, clean the toilets, wash the car, and wash underwear. Whatever he had done before, he now still had to do. The Manager said:

"Wait until we find a new apprentice, and he'll do these things."

"Except for giving me my pedicure," the Manager's wife added.

The Manager shrugged, and smiled sourly.

The Manager's wife kissed Hung T'ung-yeh on the forehead and said sweetly:

"You're really a good child. God will be with you forever and ever!"

Hung T'ung-yeh's face grew hot, and he thought of the previous night and that Russian yaksha.

Hung T'ung-yeh told Ch'ien Pen-san that for the time being he couldn't leave the foreign shop, and so he could not come to Ch'ing-lung Road. Ch'ien Pen-san made nothing of it, and only said:

"You write a letter and tell Professor Kuo Hsin-ju that I welcomed you. Actually, according to what you told me of the situation at Lefebvre's foreign shop, it's just as well not to leave. He's quite active politically, and maybe it will prove useful to have you on the inside. A revolutionary, wherever he is placed, can serve; he doesn't necessarily have to run off to the headquarters. I think there's no reason you can't join the party now."

Ch'ien Pen-san took a couple of forms for entering the party from a drawer.

"You fill this out, and stamp your seal on it. Kuo Hsin-ju and I will be your sponsors. There's a table."

Hung T'ung-yeh sat down and read it through, asked about the parts he didn't understand, and then filled it out neatly. Ch'ien Pen-san looked it over, and said:

"Stamp it with your seal."

"I didn't bring my seal."

"Well, you go back and get it; I'll wait for you here. It has to be stamped with the seal."

"Is there a bicycle here? I'll borrow one and ride it to get my seal."

Ch'ien Pen-san rang the bell, and told the man to loan him a bicycle. In a little while he was back with the seal, and he stamped it, and Ch'ien Pen-san inspected it. He then signed Kuo Hsin-ju's name as a sponsor, noting that it was Ch'ien Pen-san who was signing it for him, and stamped a seal on it. After this he signed his own name and stamped it. Then he said:

"Now you're a party member, and you must work for the party. Working at the foreign shop is your occupation, and the revolution is your profession."

"I don't know what I should be doing."

"That's not certain. I'll be in direct contact with you, and I'll be giving you your orders from time to time. At present the party's most important items of business are, internally, to knock down the warlords, and externally, to knock down imperialism. These obstacles to the revolution must be cleared away first."

"I've seen a magazine in my uncle's home, called something like *Awakened Lion,* and on the back cover it had paired couplets: 'Destroy the traitors within, Resist the tyrants without.' Does that mean the same thing?"

Hung T'ung-yeh asked in all candor. Ch'ien Pen-san smiled, looked at him, and said:

"You're speaking too loudly."

"You're hard of hearing, sir, and I was afraid you wouldn't hear me," Hung T'ung-yeh said doubtfully.

"I'm not that hard of hearing." Ch'ien Pen-san smiled at the corners of his mouth, and said: "Does Hung Pai-chuang read *Awakened Lion*?"

"He reads every issue, and he saves them."

"He's just amusing himself. If we really destroyed the traitors within and resisted the tyrants without, where would he go to look for business? I tell you, this *Awakened Lion* belongs to the Nationalist Party. The Kuomintang is different from them."

"I've got another friend who reads *The Guide*."

Hung T'ung-yeh was attempting to understand the direction of Ch'ien Pen-san's thinking, so that he could serve him the better, and so, pretending to speak offhandedly, he had made this remark.

"*The Guide* belongs to the Communist Party. Is your friend just reading it for fun, or is he a Communist Party member?" Ch'ien Pen-san asked casually.

"I think perhaps he was just reading it for fun."

"The Communist Party is even more vague," Ch'ien Pen-san said with great certainty. "Talk about 'suiting the remedy to the disease'—China is a backward agricultural society, it certainly doesn't need communism. Besides, China's national character is only willing to accept gradual change. Shang Yang, Wang Mang, Wang An-shih, Hung Hsiu-ch'üan—in history, these great and violent changes all failed very quickly. To practice communism in China—that's a dream."

"Russia is also a backward agricultural society."

"After the October Revolution, I went to Russia to investigate. The result of the October Revolution was to create a famine in the whole of Russia." Ch'ien Pen-san laughed, dismissing the subject. "Surely no one needs to create a famine for China?"

"But famine wasn't the aim."

"I know, famine was a means, or perhaps a stage. But in any case, communism cannot be practiced in China."

Ch'ien Pen-san paused a moment, thought, and then continued:

"The content of the May Fourth Movement was science and democracy, but the result of the May Fourth Movement has not been the establishment of science and democracy. The old anti-scientific and anti-democratic tradition and spirit may have been destroyed. At least they've been shaken, and will gradually fall; even supposing that they briefly revive, it won't be for long. This has created an era of emptiness, in which man doesn't know where to turn. In this empty period, everyone, without any standards, is pursuing new things; this is an indicator of historical progress. This attitude of marvelling at and valuing the new is a good thing, but naturally it also has its bad aspects. It's no wonder that such things as discarding one's surname, unfilial conduct, Chang Ching-sheng, and the Communist Party all flourish. After a time, the dust will settle, and they'll disappear. But in this grand time of change, it's hard to avoid having some people who will take the wrong path. When one analyzes their motives, they're not all necessarily bad. I think your friend may be such a person. What do you think?"

"He's got his own theory."

"That doesn't matter. But the Communist Party cannot succeed," Ch'ien Pen-san said seriously. "We must make them our friends, because we need strength. You can bring him to see me."

"But suppose he's not sincere?"

Hung T'ung-yeh spoke softly, and Ch'ien Pen-san did not hear. Hung T'ung-yeh then raised his voice a little, and repeated himself.

"An all-embracing, noble spirit can certainly convert anything," Ch'ien Pen-san said, laughing.

When Hung T'ung-yeh came out of No. 4 Ch'ing-lung Road, he had thoroughly discussed everything. He had discovered two things: Number One, Ch'ien Pen-san's self-confidence was strong, and Number Two, when speaking with him, one had to pitch his voice just right—too low, and he couldn't hear; too high, and he became irritated.

Hung T'ung-yeh turned onto the road which led into the French Concession. The little lard-rendering factory was in operation, and the odor of hog-lard permeated the alley. Hung T'ung-yeh could force himself to endure the odor, unlike the first time he had encountered it, when he hadn't been able to stand it.

"'Those who work in the fish-pickling shop soon get used to the smell'—that old saying is quite right."

Hung T'ung-yeh was pleased with this thought, and a smile drifted across his face. But then he shook his head, and assumed a sober demeanor. He thought, better be careful with that remark, and not tell Liu Shao-ch'iao. Liu Shao-ch'iao is opposed to old things, so I mustn't tell him 'that old saying is quite right'; since old sayings certainly can't make any sense, how could they be 'quite right'? By the same token, he'll be greatly pleased to hear you say: "That saying about 'those who work in fish-pickling shops', Shao-ch'iao, you were just right about that."

Hung T'ung-yeh was assuredly clever. He had known Liu Shao-ch'iao for not quite half a year, and Ch'ien Pen-san for no more than half a month, and he had come to understand each man's temperament, and the similarities and differences between them.

Even so, there were times when he couldn't help clashing with Liu Shao-ch'iao.

Liu Shao-ch'iao came from an old family of west Hunan. His family had managed a cotton factory for several generations; they had a thousand looms, and their piece-goods were used in nearly all the counties of western Hunan and eastern Szechuan. Although the Liu family were both manufacturers and merchants, they did not abandon farming and studying. There were those who farmed, and planted cotton for their own use, and there was a Licentiate, who had won a degree in the examinations so as to reflect glory upon the family.

As for foreign trade, Japanese cotton from Shanghai and Hankow slowly penetrated the rural villages. This cotton was broad, and of good quality, and moreover the price was cheap. Gradually people came to prefer it, and there was no longer a demand for the Liu family's cotton, which was produced on wooden looms by old-fashioned methods. Liu Shao-ch'iao's father was an enlightened person, and knew that one had to welcome the progress of the times. He went in person to Hankow and Shanghai to investigate, and then sold his original industrial and mercantile property, and established a completely modernized cotton factory in Hankow. He also sent Liu Shao-ch'iao, who had graduated from Middle School, to Nan-t'ung, to study at the Textile Institute operated by Chang Chien. He single-mindedly struggled to build an up-to-date enterprise, and hesitated not at all.

But when his cotton factory, after two years of preparatory construction, opened, it went under in less than a year. The Japanese factories combined to undersell him, and he was simply unable to break into the market. His goods were really in no way inferior to the Japanese goods, it was only that they were native goods, and a new brand, and he could not gain the trust of the consumers. He thought of cutting his prices, or pegging his prices below that of the Japanese goods, which meant that he had to cry his wares like a medicine-plaster hawker, and employ some social stratagems so that the wholesale merchants would be willing to do business with him. He invited them to drink, he provided prostitutes, and gambled with them, and all of these things were also a great expense.

At first, Old Mr. Liu put forth both goods and capital, and exerted himself to compete with the Japanese merchants. He knew clearly that the financial strength of the Japanese merchants was great, and that he could not contend with them, yet he struggled on. But he saw that he could not go on spending like this.

Besides the petty levies and miscellaneous taxes on the local scene, there were also "special collections". Most of the "special collection" came from the military. An invitation would arrive, and one would have to go to a banquet. If someone wasn't acquainted with the host and thought to avoid the occasion, he would be forcibly invited; armed officers of the guard would stop their car in front of his door. They weren't polite about it; one could not but attend.

The general, facing these wealthy merchants and great businessmen, who had all gone pale, spat heavily, wiped the grease from his lips, and began to speak. Old Mr. Liu experienced such a scene in person. He heard the general say:

"My army is stationed here to defend this place, and we thank you for the concern you've shown for us. Now, our division can't get any money from the Ministry of Finance in Peking, they just won't give us any, it's completely muddled. Sooner or later this business is going to cause disorder—maybe our division will fight its way into Peking and change the cabinet minister!"

The general, by this point, was obviously extremely bitter and angry. Drops of spittle flew from his lips, and fell in a cloud over the table before him. The merchants and businessmen held their breath, and leaned backwards.

"Now my soldiers haven't received their pay for six months, and they've been very upset the last couple of days. I've heard they're going to make trouble. If they really start to loot, Wuhan will suffer—how awful that would be! So, in order to protect the gentry and merchants of Wuhan, I'm asking you today to make up the soldiers' pay."

He cried in a loud voice:

"Quartermaster!"

An officer, seated behind the general, stood up at once and responded.

"Here!"

Next, he read off clearly the sums required for the "special collection" from a roster of names he had prepared beforehand.

"All right," the general said, standing up. "You drink and enjoy yourselves here, and send out for the money. When the money comes, you can go home."

Having finished, he strode off with his head held high.

There were those among the merchants and businessmen who couldn't get enough money together, and after amusing themselves in the general's reception hall for three or five days or even ten days, were allowed to go home to their families—that was a blessing amid misfortunes.

Foreign businessmen, and even Chinese businessmen operating under foreign commissions, never had such "military disasters". Not only that, but petty levies and miscellaneous taxes were much less for them.

Old Mr. Liu knew that under such conditions it would be difficult to maintain his factory. So he discussed matters with the Japanese cotton manufacturers, thinking that he could sell them his factory. When the Japanese heard this, they laughed, and asked:

"Who wants those broken-down machines of yours?"

"Everything in my whole factory came from Japan, and it's all new."

"Don't fool yourself, those are old machines made new."

"Do you mean I've been swindled?"

"Take him to court, make him give you new ones."

In pursuit of this affair, Old Mr. Liu took a lawyer to Japan on two or three occasions, but he got nothing, and spent a good deal of money on travel expenses besides. Because he was feeling bad, and was an old man, he amused himself with a young Japanese woman in Tokyo, and spent another batch of money on her. Then, with sunken heart, he came home.

Finally, he sold his machines as scrap iron, and so he disposed of his new factory. Fortunately, the factory stood on a good location, and he was able to clear up his debts with the proceeds from the sale of the land. He took the few thousand dollars left over and opened a dry-goods shop on the corner of Chiao-t'ung Road where it turns by the Chiang-Han-kuan, and did a retail business. The old man, a widower for years, had his second son and several clerks, who had been with him for years, to help him look after the business. The household affairs were taken care of by Liu Shao-ch'iao's wife and by a housekeeper. Despite the old man's defeat, he was still able to enjoy good fortune.

He had, altogether, six sons. Liu Shao-ch'iao was the third, and he was studying at Nan-t'ung. The others were back at the family homestead in west Hunan, where the eldest son directed them in farming, and they could not leave. The eldest son, who was a man of firm character, had all along opposed his father's setting up a factory in Hankow. Perhaps because his wife's parents were famous big landlords, he had come under their influence, and he felt that business enterprise was risky, and not as secure as farming. The old man felt that his son's view had some reason to it, so they agreed that each would go his own way, and they would press ahead separately. Fortunately, their goals were the same; for the prosperity of the Liu family each did the best he could.

Liu the Second was deformed. When he was small he had climbed a tree, and fallen, breaking his back. He was a hunchback. He was over twenty, and not four feet tall. Because of his shortcomings, he had developed a feeling of inferiority, and he always felt that people had no good intentions toward him, and were all out to cheat him. He had a violent and easily aroused temper. The old man knew that he especially didn't get along with his aunt—First Brother's wife—and so he told First Brother:

"Let Second Brother come and learn the business with me, and Third Brother can go to school. There are still three, they're small, and I have no way to look after them. I'll leave them here at home, and you look after them. Wait 'til they're grown and then we'll see."

First Brother agreed to take them. The old man also told First Brother's wife:

"As the saying has it, 'the elder brother's wife is like a mother', so you just treat them as your own children, and I'll trouble you to look after them."

First Brother's wife also agreed to take them.

Thus the old man left their homestead of several hundred years, and taking the two boys and some followers, he went to Hankow.

Liu Shao-ch'iao's wife, Yeh P'in-hsia, was originally a distant cousin on his mother's side. Although her family was not as well off as the Lius, they were well-respected in Ch'ang-sha; she was the daughter of a family whose scholarly reputation went back for several generations. Not only was she meek and chaste, with a headful of the Three Obediences and the Four Virtues, but in addition she was a beauty. There was a photography studio in Ch'ang-sha which had already hung a large color photograph of her in the window, to attract business. The people of that time considered this an insult, and Yeh P'in-hsia's father had lodged a complaint about it with the local Court of Justice: it was necessary to punish that photography studio. Afterwards, although the manager arranged to resolve the matter, Yeh P'in-hsia's reputation as a beauty had already spread far and wide.

Old Mr. Liu was often in Ch'ang-sha on business, and he often called at the home of his relative. As it happened, he also took part in the mediation of the photograph case, and he took the opportunity to arrange Liu Shao-ch'iao's engagement. Although he had six sons, he had always favored the third, and he had the greatest hopes for his future. He felt that Yeh P'in-hsia and Liu Shao-ch'iao, a beauty and a talented youth, were a match made in heaven. When he first suggested the marriage, Yeh P'in-hsia's father was unwilling, because the Lius raised cotton and managed a cotton factory; they smelled too much of cash, and not enough of books. Someone then suggested to Old Mr. Liu that he buy, for five thousand dollars, Ch'iu Shih-chou's *Authentic Portraits of Fox-spirits Quarreling* in twelve scrolls, and present them to the renowned literatus of Ch'ang-sha, Yeh Te-kuang. Nowhere else could help be sought; only by seeking his help could the marriage be arranged. Yeh Te-kuang belonged to the generation of Yeh P'in-hsia's grandfather. He was the most famous scholar of the Yeh family, and his achievements in the study of old editions were particularly great. Yeh P'in-hsia's father respected him as an elder. Yeh Te-kuang had all along looked down on the Lius as cotton merchants, but this time it was hard to refuse. He advocated it with all his might, and Old Mr. Liu got Yeh P'in-hsia as a bride for his son.

When Yeh P'in-hsia's father heard that Yeh Te-kuang had obtained an advantage, he too raised a secret demand. Old Mr. Liu could only send Yeh P'in-hsia's father the sum of ten thousand dollars for the cost of the bride's trousseau. What does the money matter? he thought. Just let my son be properly married, and it will be well worth it.

Before going to Hankow to set up the factory, the old man went to Ch'ang-sha to complete the arrangements for Liu Shao-ch'iao's marriage.

Liu Shao-ch'iao opposed this marriage from the beginning, because the arranging of marriages by parents' orders and the words of matchmakers was an unreasonable system which ought to be abolished. Young people had the right to determine their own marriages, and parents should not interfere. Besides, he said:

"You spent fifteen thousand dollars to buy a wife for me. Surely you don't think I haven't the ability to get a wife for myself?"

"Finding a wife is easy, but finding a good wife is hard. You can meet a good wife, but you can't ask for her. Since I met one, how could I let the opportunity pass? Never mind fifteen thousand, even for fifty-five thousand I wouldn't have given up that opportunity."

The old man spoke as though he were still glad, and chuckled.

"You spent the money to get her, so figure she's yours. I don't want her," Liu Shao-ch'iao said, obstinately and rudely.

The old man couldn't help feeling a little angry, but he restrained himself. His eldest son was also dissatisfied with this marriage. His eldest son believed in seeking local talent, and since there were many young women before his eyes at home, one could choose to suit oneself. There was no need to go so far as Ch'ang-sha, and moreover to spend so much money—wasn't it clearly an injustice?

His eldest son's wife also had much to say:

"When I came into the Liu household, not to say how much, but I brought a dowry which won't be used up in a whole lifetime. Now, what is it about the Yeh family of Ch'ang-sha? I've seen people like us spend money to buy a concubine, but I've never seen anyone buy a wife!"

The old man listened to this, and knew that he could never explain himself. He said to himself, it's worth it having them grumble about me, if only Shao-ch'iao has a good wife. Now, unexpectedly, Liu Shao-ch'iao himself did not approve, nor did he shrink from offending his old father over the matter. It was no wonder the old man got angry. But he still did not regret it, and said:

"I won't say any more now. Wait until you're married, you'll naturally be satisfied. She's famous for her beauty, and she's kind and good. What more do you want?"

"I don't want beauty, and I don't want kindness and goodness, I only want to decide for myself! I want to decide my own business, I don't need you to look after me!"

The old man thought, you're a little child, what do you understand? Isn't it a good thing that you have an old father to be concerned about you? If you chose someone else, would you have such good luck? But he didn't say this, for he knew well enough that the boy wouldn't accept it. He kept on thinking, wait until after the marriage, the boy will be satisfied, and the matter will be over with.

On the wedding night, Liu Shao-ch'iao looked over his bride. She really was pretty enough; his father had not deceived him. As for whether she was kind and good or not, that couldn't be determined at once, but by just looking at her docile expression and actions, one could tell she wasn't far below standard. Liu Shao-ch'iao had been tired all day, but now he suddenly grew excited, and blew out the candles and the lamp with one breath.

"What?" The bride, surprised, cried out loudly in the darkness. "You can't blow out the light tonight."

"Never mind that!" Liu Shao-ch'iao pushed at his bride. "Quickly, take off your clothes!"

"How can I? Three nights have to pass, then I can take off my clothes." The bride was thrown into confusion by her bridegroom's lack of understanding, and did not know how to respond.

In the darkness, Liu Shao-ch'iao no longer answered, but only went about tearing off her clothes. The bride cried, sobbing:

"Good man, good man, I beg you!"

"Don't talk nonsense. I paid fifteen thousand dollars for you, how can you disobey me?"

When she heard this, the bride's resistance weakened, and she could only weep tears of hurt.

Afterwards, Liu Shao-ch'iao lighted the lamp, straightened his clothes, and said, with a nod of approval:

"Fifteen thousand dollars, and the taste's not bad, after all."

He pulled up a rug, put it on a long couch which stood opposite the bed, and covered his head and went to sleep.

Beginning the next day, Liu Shao-ch'iao would only address his bride as "Fifteen Thousand"; this became a new name for her. Yeh P'in-hsia couldn't hold up her head before people.

Old Mr. Liu spoke ever so many good words to Liu Shao-ch'iao, and almost went to far as to bow apologetically. The old man said:

"You haven't even the patience to live with her a while and see, so how can you decide that she's no good? When you hurt her, you're hurting me. Don't you have any filial feeling for me at all? Don't you know that of all my six sons I love you the most? Did I spend so much money to get a wife for any one of them? Let's drop the matter here, you understand, and don't be so headstrong about it!"

Liu Shao-ch'iao laughed coldly and said:

"But I didn't hurt you, and I'm not hurting her; I only want to hurt that commercialized marriage system. I'll never be convinced why, when a man wants a wife, he can't decide for himself, and has to have someone else arrange it for him."

When the bride paid her return visit to her mother's family, on the third day after the marriage, she wouldn't say a word, and would only weep incessantly.

The Yeh family had intended to invite the bridegroom to a banquet, but since he refused to attend, they could only call it off.

The Yehs were numerous and influential, and it was not good to cross them. They raised serious questions with Old Mr. Liu. The old man had to accept their rebukes, and agreed that the bride might remain with her family temporarily, while he undertook to instruct his son.

After more than a month, Liu Shao-ch'iao's anger seemed to have considerably dissipated. The old man suggested to the Yehs that the bride might return and accompany them to Hankow. The Yehs immediately refused.

"Here in her own place, she doesn't have to accept such ill-treatment. If she goes off to Hankow—a distant place, where even a long whip won't reach—who can guarantee her security?"

The old man beat his breast helplessly, and said, smiling:

"Let it all be on my head. If by any chance the wife suffers any wrong, you can settle accounts with me."

"You can't even control your own son. Nobody can believe you."

"I'm still asking for the wife to go with us. A young person's temperament can change for the better after a time. If you keep her here, the two of them will be separated, and will never have a chance to get along."

So, after ever so much talk, the Yehs decided to consent. Yeh P'in-hsia's father said to his daughter:

"Since things have come to such a pass, advance and retreat are both difficult; it's no good to go, but neither is it good not to go. The wood has already been made into a boat, and it's no good for me to regret it now. I only blame Te-kuang for this; if it hadn't been for him, I wouldn't have agreed to this marriage. Now, there's no use in saying these things. You'd better go with them. If the son-in-law is headstrong, you can gradually reform him. You're a young couple and the days are long. If you truly can't stand it, write a letter, and I'll come to Hankow to see you, and bring you home."

There was nothing for Yeh P'in-hsia to do but take a maid from her mother's household, and go with the Lius to Hankow. Fortunately, Liu Shao-ch'iao no longer addressed her as "Fifteen Thousand" and except for using her at night, he paid no attention to her. When they met it was as though he did not recognize her, as though she were a stranger on the street.

So, Yeh P'in-hsia felt that she could bear to muddle through.

And Liu Shao-ch'iao began to develop an interest in her maid.

Chapter IV

This servant had originally been the personal maid of Yeh P'in-hsia's mother. When she grew up, she was given in marriage to a man who made firecrackers. Because the couple did not get along well, in less than half a year she came running back to the Yeh family to be a maid again, and was utterly unwilling to return to her husband's house. After several rounds of negotiations and quarreling, matters stood as they were, and the couple remained permanently separated, husband and wife in name only.

Originally she had been called Pai-ch'a. When she returned, after her marriage, everyone called her Aunt Liu. Although Aunt Liu's fate had not been too fortunate, still she had grown up fair and plump, with delicate eyes and a round face, which gave her an aristocratic air. Moreover, she had learned characters from Yeh P'in-hsia, and had taken the time to apply herself, so that after all she could both read and write. Her only shortcoming was that her two legs were of unequal length, and she walked with a swaying gait.

After she got to Hankow, Yeh P'in-hsia knew that she could not obtain her husband's approval. She assigned all of the tasks which involved contact with Liu Shao-ch'iao to Aunt Liu. Aunt Liu's bearing was by no means smart, but she could talk, and she loved best to pass the time of day; when she got to talking, she could forget a meal and talk without rest or pause. Liu Shao-ch'iao was helping his father get the factory ready for operation, and he was busy every day. Later, the old man said to him:

"Shao-ch'iao, you'd better review your lessons. This summer, you take the examinations for Nan-t'ung. If one doesn't know the ropes, it just won't do. I had some trouble myself at first; this is completely different from our old methods. If you don't know your engineering, it's not easy to manage."

From then on, Liu Shao-ch'iao shut his door and stayed inside. He bought new copies of several of the textbooks he had read in Middle School, and began to review. His father and Second Brother ate and slept at the factory construction site, where there were several rooms. Only Liu Shao-ch'iao, and Yeh P'in-hsia and her maid, lived at the newly bought house on Chiao-t'ung Road, a three-story building with a storehouse in the rear. Yeh P'in-hsia lived by herself on the second floor. Liu Shao-ch'iao had a place to sleep on the first floor, but now, because he was studying, he had moved into the storehouse in the rear. This storehouse was as large as a basketball court, and nearly as high as the three-story building in front. Inside, it was swept clean, but it was quite empty; there was nothing there. Liu Shao-ch'iao was perfectly satisfied with a bed, a table facing the bed, and a few simple pieces of furniture.

Liu Shao-ch'iao and Yeh P'in-hsia always took their meals separately, and each time Aunt Liu had to bring them their food. One day at noon, it began to rain heavily, and Aunt Liu raised an umbrella, and put on an old-fashioned pair of oiled boots. She brushed off the table, arranged the dishes, and said:

"It's raining hard today, so I couldn't buy vegetables. I killed one of the laying hens for you. Half of it is red-cooked, and half is boiled."

"Why go to such a bother? I only want a dish of hot peppers, and a bowl of rice," Liu Shao-ch'iao said as he came over.

"This was my mistress' idea. She said since you were studying so hard, you ought to eat a little better. She's always so good to you—really, why do you hate her so?"

Aunt Liu saw Liu Shao-ch'iao sit down, so she served the rice, and stood beside the table.

"You wouldn't understand that."

"*Ai-ya*, I'm just stupid, so stupid I don't understand anything!" Aunt Liu, unwilling to submit, said with a laugh. "You pretend to pay no attention to her, but late at night you go to her room—how can I understand?"

"How do you know that?"

"I live behind her room, with just a single partition separating us, and I'm not deaf, so how could I not hear?"

"Well, then, do you wait up every night to listen?" Liu Shao-ch'iao asked with a grin.

"Shameless!" Aunt Liu deliberately covered her face with her hands.

"You must not sleep all night."

Aunt Liu picked up her umbrella and turned to go, but Liu Shao-ch'iao grabbed her around the waist.

"If you'll come here in the evenings, I'll never go upstairs."

"You're making fun of me," Aunt Liu said, pushing at him. "I know I can't compare with my mistress in any way."

"I disagree, I feel that she can't compare with you. You're much stronger than she is." Afraid that she would get away, Liu Shao-ch'iao held her more tightly.

"You cheating devil!"

"I'm not cheating you. At least, with you, I'm choosing for myself."

Aunt Liu didn't understand, but she didn't inquire further. She snuggled up to him, burying her head in his chest, and wiping a greasy stain on the front of Liu Shao-ch'iao's shirt.

"Come on, eat with me."

"No, there's not enough rice, and there's no bowl or chopsticks. You hurry up and eat."

"Next time you bring rice, bring two portions."

Aunt Liu agreed.

As Liu Shao-ch'iao ate, he kept smiling in an infatuated manner as he gazed at Aunt Liu. He felt a kind of happiness that was almost supernatural, and difficult to explain; it was something he had never experienced before. After he finished eating, Aunt Liu gave him a towel, and he wiped his lips, and stood up. He watched her clear up. He felt as though his heart itched and he couldn't scratch it. Impulsively, he said:

"Aunt Liu!"

Aunt Liu responded, turned her head to look at him, and smiled. Then she said:

"I don't like people to call me Aunt Liu."

"Why?"

"I'm already finished with that fellow named Liu, I'll never see his face again, so why should I still be 'Aunt Liu'?" Aunt Liu said, shaking her head.

"Well, suppose I call you Aunt Liu of our Liu family?"

"I don't have such good luck! They used to call me Pai-ch'a; I like to be called Pai-ch'a."

Aunt Liu had finished clearing up, but she didn't leave.

"What does this name Pai-ch'a mean?"

"Originally I was called Ch'a-hua." Aunt Liu slitted her eyes and said in a self-satisfied tone. "Because my skin was white, everyone called me Pai Ch'a-hua, and later they dropped the 'hua' and called me Pai-Ch'a. In fact, I feel that Pai Ch'a-hua is better."

"Well, from now on I'll change and call you Pai Ch'a-hua."

"Will you urge the mistress to call me that too?"

"You know I don't talk to her. You tell her yourself."

"I've spoken to her about it many times. She says, 'marry a chicken, follow a chicken; marry a dog, follow a dog' and since I've already married that fellow Liu, I'm a member of his Liu family forever, and how can I just change it?"

"Her way of thinking disgusts me. Stubborn!"

Liu Shao-ch'iao shook his head, spoke, thought for a moment, and then pencilled a note, which he gave to Pai Ch'a-hua.

"You show her this."

Pai Ch'a-hua took it, read it for herself, and then, smiling delightedly, she went off with it. Not stopping to eat, she went right upstairs, and gave it to her mistress. When Yeh P'in-hsia heard that it was a note from her husband, she felt that it was odd. She saw these words, written in a careless scrawl:

> Aunt Liu doesn't like Brother Liu, so she's no longer to be considered a member of his family. To stubbornly insist on calling her Aunt Liu is to damage her freedom of choosing her own name. She is a person too. She married a chicken and he didn't want her; she married a dog and the dog rejected her. You'd better agree to her restoring the use of her original name of Pai Ch'a-hua, and not raise any objections. Otherwise the consequences don't bear thinking about. Don't say you weren't warned.

Although there was neither salutation nor signature, Yeh P'in-hsia understood. Hurt, she held back her tears, looked at Aunt Liu, and asked:

"What did you say to him?"

"I only said that I didn't like—"

"Never mind," Yeh P'in-hsia cut her off. "I understand already. From now on I'll call you Pai Ch'a-hua."

As she spoke, she began to cry, and hastily wiped at her tears with a handkerchief.

"Why does it hurt you that I change my name?" Pai Ch'a-hua was a little puzzled.

"According to what he's written here, he just won't recognize me as a member of his Liu family."

"Mistress, you ought to take a broader view. If they don't want you here, there are other places. You're young and beautiful; what are you afraid of?"

Pai Ch'a-hua said only half of what she had in mind. The other half was: see, even I, Pai Ch'a-hua, have an unexpected opportunity—the master can love me after all. But she felt she had her place to keep, so she didn't say this.

"You can go on downstairs," Yeh P'in-hsia said slowly. Then she pulled up a blanket, and fell asleep on the bed in her clothes.

Pai Ch'a-hua grinned, hurried down to the kitchen, and hastily ate. She did not wash the bowl, nor wipe the wok, but dashed out to the store-room despite the rain. As soon as Liu Shao-ch'iao saw her, he embraced her, and put her on the bed. Pai Ch'a-hua said anxiously:

"Wait 'til you shut the door."

"What are you afraid of? There's no one."

"Mistress is upstairs, if she—"

"I just wish she could see."

At a certain moment, Liu Shao-ch'iao pushed Pai Ch'a-hua roughly away, and jumped off the bed. This gave Pai Ch'a-hua a great fright. When she saw that he wasn't fooling, she asked him:

"What was that about?"

"That's what I always do."

"Why?"

"I don't want children."

"You don't want me?"

"It's not that. Didn't I say I always do that?"

"I don't understand."

As Liu Shao-ch'iao was going back to sleep, he said:

"It's on account of my father."

"I really don't understand."

"Let me explain, then you'll understand. Papa bought me a wife, but just so that I could get some grandchildren for him, and not for my sake at all. So he arranged the marriage, and he wouldn't let me decide. 'Of the three ways of being unfilial, not to have offspring is the worst'. I'm attacking that saying; I'd rather not have children, and disappoint his hopes. Sooner or later they'll realize that if only one party is willing, the sum will never add up—between heaven and earth there just isn't any such thing!"

"So that's how you feel—just like me, after all. I'm that way too; I wouldn't go with that Liu fellow, and it made them so mad!"

Pai Ch'a-hua embraced Liu Shao-ch'iao and kept kissing him, congratulating herself that she had finally found someone who understood her.

"Why didn't you like him?"

"Because they weren't finding me a husband—they were really making a fool of me, looking down on me, not even treating me like a human being." As Pai Ch'a-hua spoke, it was clear that she was still a little angry.

"Really, why?"

"You didn't know that fellow Liu was a cripple. When he made the engagement for me, Old Master told me: 'He's lame in the right leg, and you're lame in the left leg, so when you walk you can lean in the same direction; the two of you are a match made in heaven and established by earth.' When I heard this I didn't dare say anything, but I was so angry inside. After I got married, I wouldn't live with him, I wouldn't sleep, and I wouldn't work, I smashed the platters and broke the bowls, and fought with him all the time. I wasn't afraid of anything. They could beat me, curse me, I didn't even want to live. At last, when I'd given him enough trouble, he himself was willing to let me go."

As Pai Ch'a-hua spoke of this page from her glorious battle history, she felt happy, and she narrowed her eyes, and chuckled. Pleased with herself, she asked:

"See—aren't I resourceful?"

"It's marvelous, your dealing with them like that."

Originally Liu Shao-ch'iao had had only a passing interest in Pai Ch'a-hua. Unexpectedly, in all her actions she matched his own temper. She had plenty of the spirit of resistance, and the courage to destroy tradition. A burning feeling of 'self-recognition' stirred Liu Shao-ch'iao to shed a few tears.

"What is it?" Pai Ch'a-hua hurried to ask.

"You move me. It's the first time I've met a like-minded person."

In her heart Pai Ch'a-hua was pleased, but she only said lightly:

"That's not worth crying about."

She smiled, and said:

"There's a story: there were a father and mother who brought up the matter of marriage to their son. But the boy didn't want this bride, and he didn't want that one; he rejected all of them as not pretty enough. At last, he himself found a one-eyed bride. He told his father and mother, and said he'd decided on that one. His father and mother scolded him for not knowing beautiful from ugly. But he said: 'Other people have two eyes, and when I look at them, I always feel they've got one too many, and they aren't good-looking.'"

Liu Shao-ch'iao was amused, and said:

"This is called 'beauty is in the eye of the beholder'."

"In fact, Master—"

"Stop calling me Master; I can't stand it."

"Then what shall I call you?"

"Call me Shao-ch'iao."

"If Mistress hears, she'll blame me."

"If she does any blaming, I'll blame her. Besides, you don't need to call her Mistress. Isn't her name Yeh P'in-hsia? You should call her Yeh P'in-hsia. The reason people have names is so that they can be addressed by them."

"I'm afraid I can't change all at once."

"Even if you can't change, you've got to change. If I hear you call me Master again, I'll be angry."

"All right, let me try. I think I can, if no one's around, but I don't dare in front of people. They'd laugh at me."

Pai Ch'a-hua threw on her clothes and got up. She looked outside. It was still raining.

"What was it I was just going to say?" She thought a moment, and said: "Right, I was going to say: Shao-ch'iao, do you think I walk prettily?"

"Everything you do is fine."

"When a woman's one leg is shorter than the other, then she sways when she walks, and that's good-looking. Don't you think I walk like a butterfly in flight? A butterfly in flight—how pretty it is!"

"You're exactly right, my butterfly."

As Liu Shao-ch'iao spoke, he pulled her down on the bed again. Pai Ch'a-hua said:

"I can't go back to sleep. I must get up and prepare the meal."

"Prepare what meal? Wait a bit and I'll take you out to eat."

"That won't do, there's Mistress."

"Can't she fix food for herself? Starting tomorrow, I'll tell her to fix the food, and you can just stay here with me. The two of you ought to trade places—from now on, you're the mistress and she's the servant."

"What are you thinking of? That couldn't happen in ten thousand times ten thousand years!"

"Since it's in my power, it can certainly be done."

The couple dressed. Pai Ch'a-hua couldn't get over her distress at Liu Shao-ch'iao's insistence on taking her out to eat.

"What can I say to Mistress?"

"You don't need to say anything to her."

The two of them went out, sharing an umbrella. Pai Ch'a-hua said:

"The gates have to be locked; we'll have to call Mistress to come down."

"Just pull it shut, that way neither spirits nor ghosts will know."

After drinking wine and eating dinner in the restaurant, Liu Shao-ch'iao took Pai Ch'a-hua to a photography studio. Their pictures were taken together and Pai Ch'a-hua's was taken alone. After that, they went to see a film. This was the first time Pai Ch'a-hua had ever been inside a movie theater. She was aware only of flashing movements and bewildering changes on the screen, and she didn't understand at all what was going on. The patrons were few, the theater was pitch-dark, she was snuggled close to her intimate friend, and she delighted in the feeling, she enjoyed it to the utmost.

Love was a new thing for both of them, and this was really their "first love".

When they came out of the theater, they hadn't gone but a few paces when the street lights went out, and in an instant all was darkness. The oiled-paper umbrella had been torn or something. Liu Shao-ch'iao, his hand resting on Pai Ch'a-hua's shoulder, braved the rain and led her home. Liu Shao-ch'iao was tall and slender, while Pai Ch'a-hua was round. When placed together, they made the letter "d" of the English alphabet.

Pai Ch'a-hua was like a butterfly in flight.

Upstairs, on the second floor, Yeh P'in-hsia tried for a long time to fall asleep, but the harder she tried, the more awake she felt, and she felt sad as well. Getting up, she put on a spring robe of light serge, and stood before the front window for a while, gazing down at the street. It was still raining, and the street, usually so busy, was deserted.

She was a little hungry, but reluctant to go downstairs. She took a cracker from the cracker-box, nibbled half of it, and then threw it down. She looked out into the street again, and then turned and rested herself on the high-backed leather sofa. She stretched out her elegant legs, and rubbed her silk-stockinged foot over the thick, yielding nap of the carpet. She felt that it tickled a little. The design of a lovely and captivating phoenix facing the sun was embroidered on the fine yellow Peking carpet. Yeh P'in-hsia placed her foot on the phoenix's delicate eye, covering it.

"You're not allowed to look at me," she said softly.

Getting up suddenly, she stood before the full-length mirror. This head of luxuriant hair, this face, this slender waist, these long legs—who could say that this was not a beauty? Yeh P'in-hsia bore no resentment toward her father, nor towards Uncle Te-kuang, nor did she even resent her strange husband; she only felt sorry for her sad fate. But she was grateful to her father-in-law, who was starting a business enterprise in his old age; in the midst of his own busy affairs he had fixed up this building for her, and had done everything to furnish it comfortably. It was to serve as a lure, in hopes that Liu Shao-ch'iao would be "lured" upstairs. Shamefacedly, the old man had said:

"If he doesn't come up, you can live here. You can read, and write, and pass the time quietly for awhile, then we'll see. I'm the one who's hurt you, and I'm sorry."

As he said that, his tears flowed freely.

Yeh P'in-hsia, for her part, wanted to comfort him, but she did not know what to say, so she could only cry with him. Her heart was filled with gratitude. What she meant was: "I don't blame anyone, I only blame the bitterness of my fate!"

Yeh P'in-hsia thought of Li I-an's "Autumn Emotions" and softly intoned:

Searching, searching,
Looking, looking
Lonely, lonely
Grieved, grieved
Mournful, mournful
When warmth turns suddenly to cold
It is most difficult to bear.

But Li I-an, she thought, at least had a talented and affectionate husband, and although they couldn't grow old together, they did have some good days, so that at the end of her life she may be reckoned to have left some record of her spirit. But I, what do I amount to? I'm really not up to her at all! And she thought, perhaps Li I-an was a person of passionate emotions, a bold person, even a bit unconventional? She certainly wasn't reserved and weak like me! Unconsciously she nodded, and said softly:

"Can it be that my reserve and my weakness have caused my misfortune?"

Thinking thus, she felt herself much more determined, and she seemed to have the strength to support herself. She stood up tall, and taller.

Behind the glass, she caught a glimpse of the book <u>Nora</u> in the bookcase. The title seemed to radiate light, provocatively tempting her. She thought:

"If I left, where would I go? And after I left, then what?"

If this were only a pool of mud, then with a single step she could begin a new life. But she was afraid that the sea of sin was boundless, and she would be lost forever. She lacked that spirit of seeking the new, which prompts the explorer to press forward, so she shook her head. Softly she intoned the lines:

> If I've become slender of late,
> It's not on account of being ill from wine,
> Nor from lamenting autumn.

The sky had darkened, and Yeh P'in-hsia switched on the electric light. It was, she thought, time to be preparing the rice. How was it that she hadn't seen Aunt Liu all afternoon? No, it was Pai Ch'a-hua; she hadn't seen Pai Ch'a-hua all afternoon. Every afternoon she would sit in the front room and pass the time of day until Yeh P'in-hsia got after her, and then she would stop talking and go downstairs. What had happened today?

In the midst of her surprise, she heard someone downstairs say:

"Who's upstairs?"

It was her father-in-law's voice. Yeh P'in-hsia hastily put on her shoes and went downstairs.

"So Papa and Second Brother have come back. I really didn't expect it, it's raining so hard."

"Isn't it?" the old man said. "When it rains, we can't work. We came back to see you, and eat dinner with you. How is it that the gate is partly ajar, and there's no one about downstairs? Where's Shao-ch'iao?"

"I don't know, I haven't been downstairs all day," Yeh P'in-hsia said doubtfully. "Isn't Aunt Liu here either? There's only me upstairs."

"Strange—the two of them?" The old man's voice expressed his surprise.

"Papa, Second Brother, come and sit down. I'll bring tea."

When Yeh P'in-hsia entered the kitchen, the cookstove was cold, and not only was the rice not boiled, but even the bowls and the chopsticks were still soaking and hadn't been washed. Coming out, she saw that the storehouse was dark as a cave within, as though no one were inside. She made a circuit around the verandahs which ran under the eaves of the wings of the house, and peered inside, and she saw only an unmade bed, with pillows and blankets in careless heaps.

"Surely he and Aunt Liu can't have . . ."

Yeh P'in-hsia thought of the business of changing her name to Pai Ch'a-hua, and her face grew hot. She went back to the front room, and said:

"Neither of them are here. Just wait while I go and make tea and fix rice."

"That's not necessary, wait a bit and we'll go to the restaurant across the street to eat." Thinking that she might not be willing to go to the restaurant, the old man added: "Or we'll ask them to send something over here, that would be better."

So Yeh P'in-hsia sat down. The old man said:

"You see, I was right to buy this building. When the factory starts producing, this will be the retail section. This place is close to the customs wharf, you couldn't find a better place, right in the commercial center. You and Shao-ch'iao will live upstairs, and the clerks and I will stay in the two wings, and this room will become the sales room. It's really most ideal. Besides—"

Looking at Second Brother, the old man said:

"We'll reserve the third floor, and when Second Brother gets married, it can be his nuptial chamber."

The old man was completely sincere in these words. He spoke in this way to cheer up Second Brother, thinking to increase the happy atmosphere of the scene. Never had he imagined that the other would be instantly provoked. His face flushed red, he glared at his father, and said furiously:

"Anyhow, I am your son, you shouldn't make a fool out of me!"

"I didn't mean any such thing," the old man protested hastily. "I meant what I said!"

"I'll never get married," Second Brother looked at Yeh P'in-hsia and said, blushing, "You haven't thought—who would be willing to marry me?"

"As long as my business goes well," the old man said loudly, with a smile, "there wouldn't be any difficulty even if you wanted three wives and four concubines."

"What Papa says is right," Yeh P'in-hsia said, encouraging him. "Second Brother, you needn't despair. See, even Aunt Liu had a man who wanted her."

As soon as she mentioned Aunt Liu, Second Brother calmed down a little. He had always thought that, since he was a cripple, this marriage business would be hard to arrange properly. It would be best to find a crippled girl for his mate, and then the situation could be saved.

Aunt Liu's image, her gait like that of a butterfly in flight, appeared before Second Brother's eyes. He exhaled a long breath, and responded mysteriously:

"Yes, Aunt Liu."

"Papa," Yeh P'in-hsia took the opportunity to tell Old Mr. Liu, "Aunt Liu used to be called Pai Ch'a-hua, and she doesn't like to be called Aunt Liu. Shao-ch'iao wants us all to start calling her Pai Ch'a-hua."

Mr. Liu had no opinion on this, and nodded.

"Pai Ch'a-hua," Second Brother said approvingly, "What a pretty name!"

The hour was late, and Liu Shao-ch'iao and Pai Ch'a-hua had not returned. Old Mr. Liu was at a loss, and could only say:

"We won't wait any longer; let's send out for dinner."

After dinner they sat and talked. When it was almost ten o'clock, they saw Liu Shao-ch'iao and Pai Ch'a-hua coming back in the rain, both of them wet through. Old Mr. Liu couldn't help asking:

"What, the two of you went out together?"

"Yes," Liu Shao-ch'iao said happily. "I invited her to eat dinner and see a film, and we had a fine time all evening."

Pai Ch'a-hua, obviously very embarrassed, looked at Yeh P'in-hsia, and timidly asked:

"Mistress, have you eaten?"

"We've all eaten," Yeh P'in-hsia, outwardly calm, said. "Hurry and go with Master to change clothes. You've gotten so chilly all over, you don't want to catch cold."

"She doesn't call me Master; from now on she calls me Shao-ch'iao."

As he spoke, the two of them went off to the rear of the house. Yeh P'in-hsia, Mr. Liu, and Second Brother sat dumbly, looking at one another, and not knowing what to say. Finally, the old man heaved a long sigh.

After a while, Liu Shao-ch'iao came back, and told his father:

"We've already talked about it. I want to marry Pai Ch'a-hua."

"That's nonsense, you already have P'in-hsia!"

"Her? She's the daughter-in-law you bought, but she's not my wife. She belongs to you, and Pai Ch'a-hua belongs to me; she is really my wife."

When Second Brother heard this, he flew into a rage. He cried out in a loud voice:

"You've already got one, and now you want a second, while I haven't even got one! That won't do, Pai Ch'a-hua is mine!"

Liu Shao-ch'iao had never imagined that Second Brother would contend with him for Pai Ch'a-hua. He gave his brother a slap. Second Brother, who wasn't willing to stand for that, rushed at him, and the two of them fell to the floor, struggling. Old Mr. Liu, after shouting at them to no avail, went forward to pull them apart.

Yeh P'in-hsia could not bear to go on watching. Taking advantage of the fact that no one was paying any attention to her, she opened the gate, and despite the rain dashed blindly out into the street. After a desperate run, she found herself in utter darkness, without a trace of light. In front of her the great river rushed by. Yeh P'in-hsia thought, so this is my home after all! Without a moment's hesitation, she leaped, and the turbid stream swallowed her at once.

When Old Mr. Liu, with Pai Ch'a-hua's help, finally got the two brothers separated, Second Brother had already taken a beating. Pai Ch'a-hua saw that his forehead was bleeding, and went to wipe it for him with a dry cloth. Liu Shao-ch'iao saw and cried:

"Don't touch him, you're mine!"

"No, she's mine!" Second Brother was not ready to yield either.

Mr. Liu hastily told Pai Ch'a-hua to go to the rear of the house.

After sitting in melancholy silence for a while, Mr. Liu felt that he was already without the strength to control his children; no words, no means could make them return to the right path. He simply did not understand them, their way of thought, and it seemed that they could not understand his way of thought. He thought, can it be that times are changing? Thirty years before, during his own youth, he thought that he certainly had never had any differences of opinion with his father, or even with his grandfather. Their ways of thought, and their viewpoints, were often the same.

What was the reason, after all, that now there were great divisions between father and son, elder and younger brother, and husband and wife, and simply no means of bringing them together?

So Mr. Liu thought, but could not understand. Suddenly, he felt that his efforts were in vain, and without meaning, and a feeling of complete discouragement arose in him. He looked at Liu Shao-ch'iao, sorrowfully shook his head, and said to Second Brother:

"Let's go back to the factory. This is my fault; if I hadn't suggested coming to visit them, none of this would have happened."

Second Brother's whole body ached, he was unbearably fatigued, and really had neither strength nor will for another fight, so he nodded in agreement. They called a foreign concession cab, and father and son, with hanging heads and gloomy demeanor, departed.

Liu Shao-ch'iao ordered the gate shut and the lamps extinguished. He wanted to sleep. Pai Ch'a-hua said:

"I haven't seen Mistress; where is she?"

They looked upstairs and downstairs, in every room, without finding her. Liu Shao-ch'iao said:

"Never mind her! She's a grown-up, how can she get lost? It's late, let's go to bed."

"Let me wait for her here in front, so I can open the gate for her," Pai Ch'a-hua said.

"Can't you wait until she rings, and then get up and open it? I fought Second Brother for you, aren't you going to thank me? Come on, to bed!"

So the two of them went back to the store-room.

Yeh P'in-hsia did not return that night.

In the next morning's paper they discovered the following news:

Beautiful Young Woman Throws Self in River, Rescued
Unwilling to reveal name, origin, or motive for suicide. By the richness of her clothes and jewelry and her refined manners, she obviously belongs to a wealthy family. Tearfully, she refuses to be photographed and begs to be allowed to die. She is now at the Mutual Benevolence Society Hospital waiting for some family member to identify her.

When she did not see Yeh P'in-hsia in the morning, Pai Ch'a-hua grew a little afraid, because she knew for certain that the other had no place to go. When she saw this article, she hastily said to Liu Shao-ch'iao:

"Could this woman be our Mistress?"

"If it's really her, I'm sorry."

"Sorry for what?"

"Sorry that she didn't drown."

"You hate her so much—it's too cruel! She's really a good person."

"I didn't say she was a bad person. I only hate that tradition and society which she represents. To allow oneself to be executed, to willingly sacrifice oneself without the slightest resistance. Not to resist, and to sacrifice oneself—what kind of a way is that? If she could be like you, that would be well."

"Her background and mine aren't the same, so we can never be alike."

"So, I don't sympathize with her."

"All right, all right, never mind. Let me go to the hospital and see if it's really her or not, and bring her back."

"You absolutely cannot go, I won't allow you."

The next morning, the police station sent two policemen, bearing summonses, to order Liu Shao-ch'iao and Pai Ch'a-hua to come to the police station for questioning. Liu Shao-ch'iao took it casually, but Pai Ch'a-hua, as soon as she heard of a police station summons, naturally grew frightened. In an unsteady voice, she asked:

"Why?"

"We don't know," the policeman said. "We hear it's a case of someone throwing herself into the river to commit suicide, and it has something to do with you."

"If someone throws herself into the river, what does it have to do with us?" Liu Shao-ch'iao asked, glaring.

"As for that, it's no use you talking about it with us; let's go to the station."

"I beg you—I had nothing to do with it, don't make me go." Pai Ch'a-hua was nearly in tears as she spoke.

The two policemen were no longer patient, and took handcuffs from their belts.

"Come on now, no more delaying. It doesn't look too good to wear these."

"What are you afraid of?" Liu Shao-ch'iao wasn't used to seeing Pai Ch'a-hua looking so pitiful, and he too helped to hasten her along. "Come on, come on!"

They locked the gate and went off to the police station. Liu Shao-ch'iao caught sight of Engineer Sung from the factory, and Lawyer Chang, and asked them:

"How is it that you're here too?"

"The police station sent for Mr. Liu for questioning, and we came to represent him."

"What is it, anyway?"

"You still don't know?" Lawyer Chang pulled him aside, and said gravely: "Your Young Mistress threw herself into the river, and the result of the police investigation is that they consider the three of you—your father, you, and Aunt Liu—under suspicion of abetting a suicide. The police chief was a student of Mr. Yeh Te-kuang's, and he's very unhappy about this business. I'm afraid the case may be sent to the Court of Justice, and it could turn out to be a lot of trouble."

"This is really malicious talk! Who helped her commit suicide?"

"Grumbling and casting blame are no use right now. We've got to have a way to settle this case." Lawyer Chang was obviously anxious.

"Look here, Lawyer Chang," Engineer Sung interjected. "You're familiar with the police station, suppose you go in first and see what they're thinking. Then wait and see what their reply is."

Lawyer Chang agreed, and hurried in. After a long time he came out again. Wiping the sweat from his head, he sighed and said:

"Bother! I couldn't get anywhere! The police feel that, because the Yehs of Ch'ang-sha aren't willing to let it go, they've got to pursue the matter."

"According to them, how could it be settled?" Liu Shao-ch'iao asked.

"According to them?" Lawyer Chang, obviously very embarrassed, said: "They feel that if you and Aunt Liu leave Wuhan, and if nothing else happens afterwards, this will be considered a commitment to the Yehs."

"Where do they want me to go?"

"They only want you to leave; there are many places in the world."

"What's hard about that?" Liu Shao-ch'iao grew joyful. "I'll take Pai Ch'a-hua and go."

"Can they count on that?" Lawyer Chang wanted to nail him down.

"Of course."

So Lawyer Chang went inside again, and after a while came out, saying:

"Very well, I've got it all arranged for Mr. Liu. It's undertaken that within three days you and Aunt Liu will leave, and the case will more or less be considered closed, and they won't inquire into the reasons behind it. Come on, we'll go to the factory, and discuss your departure with Old Mr. Liu."

Pai Ch'a-hua, who had been anxious and uneasy all along, released her breath and calmed down when she heard, and went with them to the factory.

When Mr. Liu had seen the article in the morning paper the day before, he had grown a little afraid, thinking that, from the time the boys had fought the evening before, until he and Second Brother had left, he hadn't seen Yeh P'in-hsia. But at the same time he had paid no attention, and had not inquired.

"Could she have been the young woman who threw herself into the river?"

Thinking along these lines, Mr. Liu did not delay, but immediately hired a taxi cab and went to the Mutual Benevolence Society Hospital. He had not been wrong in his expectation: it really was the daughter-in-law of his own family.

Yeh P'in-hsia was sleeping in a hospital bed. When she saw her father-in-law she wept, but said not a word.

Mr. Liu was also pained. He thought a moment, and then said:

"Since things have gone this far, to say it all in a word, I've wronged you. Now that I think back on it, I made all the wrong moves, and there's no one to blame but me! Well, the person who tied the bell on the tiger's neck has got to take it off again. Now, I'm going to take the responsibility of resolving this matter."

He looked at Yeh P'in-hsia and saw that she was still listening attentively, and continued:

""Now I'm going to ask you a few questions, and you must answer me honestly. First, do you want to go back and stay with your parents in Ch'ang-sha for a while, or not?"

Yeh P'in-hsia shook her head.

"Second, do you want to live apart from Shao-ch'iao for a while?"

Yeh P'in-hsia nodded.

"Shao-ch'iao has often made loose talk about divorce. How do you feel?"

Yeh P'in-hsia shook her head.

"You'll certainly approve of sending Aunt Liu back to Ch'ang-sha?"

Yeh P'in-hsia nodded.

"Very well, since this is how it is, you just relax, and rest here in the hospital. When I have things all arranged, I'll take you back to Chiao-t'ung Road. I'll hire another maid for you, and you can stay there by yourself. Will that be all right?"

Yeh P'in-hsia nodded.

Mr. Liu said a few more soothing words, and left. He paid the bill in the cashier's office, and returned to the factory. Until then, he had always taken care of his own household affairs, and had never before sought the help of outsiders in

his own family matters. But that would no longer do; he already knew that he
didn't have that kind of strength. He was no longer afraid of washing his dirty
linen in public, because the problem was growing ever more serious, and plans to
resolve it absolutely had to be made.

He said to Lawyer Chang and Engineer Sung:

"You two help me manage the factory, and we're friends. I have a family
problem, and I'm not afraid that you'll laugh. I know I can't solve it myself, and I
want to ask the two of you to help."

Naturally there was no question about it, and the two men made some
polite talk. Mr. Liu told them everything about the matter of his daughter-in-law
throwing herself into the river, and explained his plan to remedy the situation.

"This third son of mine is an unfilial child, and that Aunt Liu is no good
either. If they won't listen to me, and they won't go, what is to be done?"

Lawyer Chang thought a bit, and then presented his plan. They discussed
it, and Mr. Liu considered it feasible. Lawyer Chang set to work with Engineer
Sung to put the plan into operation. That evening they entertained a table of
guests, all of whom were friends from the police station.

After having been to the police station, Liu Shao-ch'iao and Pai Ch'a-hua,
who had not gotten into any trouble, were willing to leave.

Liu Shao-ch'iao's destination was settled; he had wanted to go to Nan-
t'ung, and now he would go a little earlier. But he meant to take Pai Ch'a-hua
with him, and Mr. Liu could not agree to that.

"Pai Ch'a-hua belongs to the Yehs of Ch'ang-sha, and she has to be sent
back to Ch'ang-sha. 'The thing returns to its owner'. What right do you have to
take her?"

"She belongs to me now, and doesn't belong to the Yeh family."

"Since you're going to go to school, you must act like a student," Engineer Sung urged him. "I've never seen a student who brought a maidservant to school with him."

Nonetheless Liu Shao-ch'iao insisted that unless he took her with him, he couldn't go.

Again, Mr. Liu absolutely could not consent.

Lawyer Chang, seeing that matters had reached an impasse, made a sign with his eye to Mr. Liu and Engineer Sung. He drew Liu Shao-ch'iao aside, and said softly:

"Sending Pai Ch'a-hua to Ch'ang-sha is only to make a show for the benefit of the Yehs, and it's no use you fighting it. Now I'll tell you a way: give her a few dollars, and tell her to hurry and come back to you. When you get to Nan-t'ung and get well settled in, rest for a while, and then write her a letter and tell her to steal away to Nan-t'ung. That way it won't be the old man's responsibility, and you'll be satisfied too. What do you say?"

Liu Shao-ch'iao listened to this with interest, and then said:

"That's a little better. I can consider it."

"Then you'd better go now and talk it over with Pai Ch'a-hua, and explain the route clearly to her," Lawyer Chang prompted him.

After Liu Shao-ch'iao and Pai Ch'a-hua had discussed this in secret, they both expressed their very pleased acceptance of the plan. But there was a condition: Pai Ch'a-hua must take a thousand dollars, to provide for travel expenses on her future elopement.

"Right, you don't have to say a word, I'll take care of it for you."

Lawyer Chang, having gotten Liu Shao-ch'iao quieted down, went to tell Mr. Liu.

"The two of them have agreed to break off their relations from now on, and to have nothing to do with one another. But there's one little condition: Aunt Liu wants a thousand dollars; when she gets it she'll go back to Ch'ang-sha."

Mr. Liu was delighted, and said:

"Give it to her, give it to her. What does a thousand dollars matter, just so this business is settled?"

With the agreement made, Liu Shao-ch'iao took Pai Ch'a-hua back to the photographer's studio on Chiao-t'ung Road to pick up their printed photographs and to part company. Pai Ch'a-hua liked best the photograph which showed the upper half of her body. Her hands were clasped behind her head, she was squinting her eyes, and her lips were split in a big smile.

"See, in this one I'm sticking my elbows out to the sides, like two wings, just like a dappled butterfly."

"Well, you write a few words on this one for me."

"What shall I write?"

"Whatever you please."

"I can't write—you tell me what to write."

"If I tell you what to write, it won't be the same."

Pai Ch'a-hua thought a bit, and then, blushing, wrote:

"Shao-ch'iao, see your dappled butterfly Pai Ch'a-hua!"

Liu Shao-ch'iao was delighted, and said teasingly:

"If you work at it a bit, you can surely become a lady poet."

A few days later, Mr. Liu sent someone to take Pai Ch'a-hua back to Ch'ang-sha. That person carried a long letter for Yeh P'in-hsia's father, asking him by all means to intercept any letters which Liu Shao-ch'iao might send to Pai Ch'a-hua, and to pay attention to any letters which Pai Ch'a-hua might send. After Yeh P'in-hsia's father had read the letter, he released his bellyful of accumulated rage upon the body of Pai Ch'a-hua. He ordered his men to tie her up, and beat her half dead with split rattans and leather whips. The thousand dollars was taken from her luggage. From then on, Pai Ch'a-hua was kept under surveillance; she was forbidden to go out, and she lost her freedom.

Engineer Sung, who had once been an instructor at the Nan-t'ung Textile Institute, was ordered to accompany Liu Shao-ch'iao to Nan-t'ung. At first he was enrolled as a special student, and when the school term began, he was formally enrolled. Liu Shao-ch'iao resumed his student life, and, for the time being, settled down. He thought constantly of Pai Ch'a-hua, and wrote her many letters, but they all vanished like stones thrown into the sea.

Chapter V

After the failure of Mr. Liu's new factory, Liu Shao-ch'iao left Nan-t'ung, and transferred to another school in Shanghai. At that time, there were two newly established colleges in Shanghai, both of which had strong political colorations. They propagated the new thought and advocated rapid advance.

Liu Shao-ch'iao changed his major to economics, and before long he had a batch of new friends. He threw himself into a new environment, and every day he was busy about nothing; studying had become a mere excuse. And before long he simply abandoned his studies. There were those who called upon the youth and loudly urged: reading dead books in school was meaningless, and not worth the effort. "If the skin is gone, what is the hair to cling to?" If the country is truly lost, will there still be schools to study in? Naturally, first there is the country, and then there are schools. Thus, to leave school and to take part in the revolution, to take part in the political struggle, was the brave choice of noble youth.

Although the factory had failed, even the broken boat had a bottom, and the shop was still doing a good business. Liu Shao-ch'iao often received financial aid from his father. His father, after all, did not know just what he was doing in Shanghai. His father, who no longer had too many illusions about him, did not really inquire into it, because his son was beyond his reach and nothing could be done about it.

Liu Shao-ch'iao led an erratic existence, but he found that it satisfied him. His greatest problem was still women. When he received no letters from Pai Ch'a-hua, his feelings cooled after a time, and he no longer thought of her. Momentary relief was not at all difficult, but a proper match was extremely hard to find. This was because, in the circles in which Liu Shao-ch'iao moved, there were no proper women.

As soon as Liu Shao-ch'iao set eyes on Hung Chin-ling, at Mrs. Hung's appreciation banquet, he felt as though he had known her for a long time. At once, and without the slightest reserve, he poured out for her a chestful of warm feelings, and toasted her with glass after glass of wine. Later on, he had had two or three opportunities to see her. He said to Hung T'ung-yeh:

"Your little sister is really good; Chin-ling is really good!"

Hung T'ung-yeh just smiled, and did not respond.

That little face, still innocent, and that slender figure completely overthrew Liu Shao-ch'iao. Once he happened to observe that, as far as appearance went, Hung Chin-ling really looked as Yeh P'in-hsia must have looked when she was a girl. That abusive madness which he had displayed toward Yeh P'in-hsia became, in his subconscious, the desire to pursue Hung Chin-ling; he knew what it was that had been lacking in his life.

He needed such a woman; Pai Ch'a-hua could not serve in her place.

At a photographic exhibition he ungrudgingly paid double the price for a famous photograph, which he hung at the head of his bed. A beautiful model, tall and lovely, who wore not a stitch of clothing except for a pair of high-heeled shoes, was bound in iron chains. A leather whip was thrust menacingly toward her, and her face expressed helpless terror.

He could no longer be patient, no longer wait. He went right out to find Hung Chin-ling.

The apartment house was unexpectedly quiet. Liu Shao-ch'iao, wearing shoes with soft rubber soles, quietly felt his way up the dark, narrow and steep stairs. He paused on the landing to calm himself. Why was it so quiet? Perhaps they weren't home? Thinking in this way, he did not call out, but stood beside the cloth screen, peeping in.

"Ma!"

Hearing this call from inside, he stood stock still, held his breath, and listened.

"What is it?"

A light, chirruping laugh.

"What are you laughing at?"

"Ma, how old do you think that Liu Shao-ch'iao is?" It was Hung Chin-ling's voice.

"Your brother said he was over twenty, he's older than your brother."

"I'm afraid he may be over thirty."

"Don't be silly, he's still young."

"He's got such a beard, as though he doesn't even cut it. How filthy!"

Mrs. Hung laughed, and said:

"Your brother says he's very interested in you, though."

"Brother also says he's low-class."

"It's no wonder, because he's young; in the future he may straighten out."

"Let him dream his dreams—I'll never let him get the best of me."

Mother and daughter both laughed.

Liu Shao-ch'iao was so angry that he wanted to rush right in, but he restrained himself, and withdrew back down the stairs. Clenching his fists, he hurried straight back to his apartment. Without taking off his shoes, he got into bed and tried to go to sleep. But he couldn't sleep, and after turning over several times, he jumped up. He pulled a camphor-wood box out from under his bed, turned it over, and shook out a photograph, which he nailed to the wall. But, feeling that this wasn't good enough, he took it down, wrapped it up in newspaper, and hurried downstairs. At the mouth of the lane he got into a rickshaw, and said loudly:

"Hui-lo Company."

Ordinarily Liu Shao-ch'iao most despised those big companies, and he especially disliked the Hui-lo Company, calling it "The Kitchen Window of Imperialist Aggression" and "The Scab on the Englishman's Head" and "The Colonial People's Chancre". But, for some reason, this time he chose that firm, and for eighty dollars bought a made-in-England, gilded, flower-bordered mirror-frame.

Liu Shao-ch'iao felt a kind of satisfaction.

A pair of slender and fashionable women passed by, talking. Liu Shao-ch'iao felt that their faces were most familiar, only he couldn't remember where he had seen them. So he followed them, inspecting their faces, figures, and gaits, as he went. He heard them speaking Cantonese. Liu Shao-ch'iao suddenly remembered, and grabbed one of them, crying happily:

"You're Yang Nai-mei!"

Unexpectedly, the girl glanced at him, startled, and said in Shanghai dialect:

"Swine! Bum!"

Then, tugging at her friend, she made swiftly off.

The onlookers who had seen this little performance laughed, and some of them repeated:

"Swine! Bum!"

Liu Shao-ch'iao's face turned white with rage, and he said bitterly:

"These chancres - you wait and see!"

Grasping the mirror-frame, he returned, and hung it up beside that picture of the naked woman in chains being beaten with the leather whip. Liu Shao-ch'iao looked at it, kissed it, and slowly his anger dissipated. Softly he read the words written on the photograph:

"Shao-ch'iao, see your dappled butterfly Pai Ch'a-hua."

Taking off his shoes, he went to bed in his clothes. He felt unbearably tired.

After discussing his decision to keep working, for the time being, at M. Lefebvre's foreign shop with Ch'ien Pen-san at Number 4 Ch'ing-lung Road, Hung T'ung-yeh went to the French Concession. Liu Shao-ch'iao, lying on the bed, talked with him, and when he learned of the change in plan, he lazily got dressed, and even put on his shoes. He coldly pointed to the front room, and said:

"You go and wait for me."

He went into the back room and talked with P'eng Wen-hsüeh. After a while they came out, Liu Shao-ch'iao in front and P'eng Wen-hsüeh behind, carrying a glittering knife of the kind used to slaughter hogs. Their faces were set like iron as they quietly came into the front room. Hung T'ung-yeh, seeing this behavior, was somewhat at a loss. P'eng Wen-hsüeh first lowered the black curtain at the front window, and then, standing beside Hung T'ung-yeh, poked the point of the knife into the small of his back.

Liu Shao-ch'iao sat down, lighted a cigarette, and smoked. He seemed very cool, and said slowly:

"Quitting your job at the foreign shop and going to Ch'ing-lung Road was your idea to start with, and you yourself asked me to seek the consent of our superiors. At that time, they were still suspicious of you, and feared you couldn't be relied upon. You definitely said you would go to Ch'ing-lung Road to sleep, but maybe you're working for Ch'ing-lung Road and you've turned and come back to sleep here—then what's to be done? No one can trust you! At that time I, Liu Shao-ch'iao, guaranteed you, and because they trusted Liu Shao-ch'iao they agreed to your proposal. Didn't I already tell you these things?"

"Yes, you already told me," Hung T'ung-yeh quickly responded, and a chill ran up his spine as P'eng Wen-hsüeh's knife stuck in a little closer, nearly puncturing his clothing.

"Good, you still have a memory. Don't go back on it! But you ought to know that when our superiors agree to something, it's an 'iron-clad decision' and besides, I guaranteed it. You have no right to change it on your own. Let me speak a little more clearly: I run Chapei; the French Concession is someone else's responsibility. Our superiors detached you, alone, from that area and gave you over to my guidance, because they weren't quite sure about you, and they told me to be responsible for you."

Liu Shao-ch'iao spoke gently and coolly, his voice pitched very low.

"Your having dared to spoil the decision of our superiors really comes from your innately defective consciousness, for the 'human feelings' of a compradore slave of the foreigners for a counter-revolutionary White Russian woman. Little Hung, say it yourself—shouldn't you be disciplined?"

"I should," Hung T'ung-yeh said weakly, from trembling, pale lips.

"Little Hung, always remember, I love you very much. If it wasn't for you, I couldn't even go on living."

Liu Shao-ch'iao threw away his cigarette and stood up. He seized Hung T'ung-yeh and kissed him again and again. Then he pushed him away and said:

"We often discipline those we love. Whoever we discipline, it goes without saying, are certainly those we like. Anyone we don't love, we look on as rubbish, not worth a glance—they are not fit to receive our discipline. Do you understand?"

"I understand."

"Are you willing?"

"I'm willing."

Liu Shao-ch'iao turned to P'eng Wen-hsüeh and said:

"Today I'm going to beat him, not kill him."

P'eng Wen-hsüeh smiled and nodded.

"Little Hung, I'm going to beat you now. First, you're not allowed to dodge, and second, you're not allowed to make a sound. When I'm finished beating you, that's all there is to it! I know the art of beating people: I can beat you so that every part of your body will be hurt, but I won't damage your muscles or hurt your bones, and I won't break the skin or draw blood. On that, you can relax."

Liu Shao-ch'iao smiled from the corners of his mouth, and asked:

"Do you see that knife at your waist?'

Hung T'ung-yeh nodded.

"Speak, do you see it?"

"I see it."

"Is it sharp, or not?"

"Sharp."

"It wouldn't take much effort to stick that knife into your middle, would it?"

"Not much effort."

"If he dodges or wiggles to protect himself, or cries out, or lets any sound slip out, then stab him."

"Yes."

"I'm afraid he's a punk, and doesn't really understand. Spread out that oilcloth, you don't want to wait until you really have to use the knife and then have blood running down the stairs—it wouldn't please the landlord."

P'eng Wen-hsüeh gave the knife to Liu Shao-ch'iao, spread out the oilcloth, and told Hung T'ung-yeh to stand in the center of the oilcloth. Then he took back the knife from Liu Shao-ch'iao, and stood behind Hung T'ung-yeh, holding the knife against Hung T'ung-yeh's back so that it pointed toward his heart. He said:

"Rabbit-boy, you're going to get it today!"

Liu Shao-ch'iao glanced at him, and suddenly stood up. Without a word he began.

After a time, it was over. P'eng Wen-hsüeh put down the slaughtering knife, pushed his spectacles, which had slipped down his nose, back up again, wiped the sweat from his lips, and helped Hung T'ung-yeh to Liu Shao-ch'iao's bed to rest. Then he took the slaughtering knife back into the back room, and took the thermos bottle down to the hot-water seller at the mouth of the lane to buy some boiled water. When he came back, he mixed a big glass of condensed milk and gave it to Hung T'ung-yeh, telling him to drink it for the warmth.

Liu Shao-ch'iao was resting on the couch with his eyes closed. Then he stood up and stretched, lighted two cigarettes, and walked languidly into the bedroom to give one to Hung T'ung-yeh. Hung T'ung-yeh's face was yellow as wax. He looked up weakly, accepted the cigarette, and took a couple of puffs.

"Turn over and let me have a look at you."

Hung T'ung-yeh, gritting his teeth, turned over. It was obviously costing him much effort, and he did it clumsily. Liu Shao-ch'iao said to P'eng Wen-hsüeh:

"Go and tell Old Wen to come and give him a shot."

P'eng Wen-hsüeh nodded and went off.

Liu Shao-ch'iao sat on the edge of the bed, bent over, and kissed Hung T'ung-yeh on the face. He ground his short, tough beard against the other's face, causing Hung T'ung-yeh to hurt and itch; he shoved him, and then he leaned over even closer, and laid down beside him.

"Little Hung, remember, I love you. Everything, everything comes from my loving you."

Liu Shao-ch'iao said intimately:

"I'll never stand to see you leave me. The day I see you're leaving me, I'll have your life, and even if we die together, I'll have no regrets. You've had your first lesson today; do you understand it?"

"I understand it."

"Explain for me, so I can see the degree of your understanding."

Hung T'ung-yeh thought it over for a moment, and then said:

"Suppose there's a treasure, no, not necessarily a treasure, just anything, even a person. If you can't get it, if it won't come under your control, then you'll destroy it without the slightest hesitation."

"Why?"

"If it doesn't come to you, then its existence loses all value. If you didn't destroy it, then wouldn't you have to obey others' decisions? And then you wouldn't be able to make decisions for others."

These words went right to Liu Shao-ch'iao's heart, and pleased him so that he couldn't be still. He couldn't restrain himself from embracing Hung T'ung-yeh tightly, and paying no attention to the other's aching body, he began to roll about with him on the bed.

"Since you've comprehended my philosophy of man and of action, you can never leave me. I've already taken you, you're mine."

He kissed Hung T'ung-yeh, and asked:

"Are you happy?"

Hung T'ung-yeh bore the pain, and said softly:

"Of course I'm happy."

As he spoke, P'eng Wen-hsüeh came in with Old Wen. Old Wen took his stethoscope and gave Hung T'ung-yeh a cursory examination. He stared at Liu Shao-ch'iao with wide eyes and said, in a tone of warning:

"After this be careful, don't hit so hard, or something might happen."

"He didn't suffer any harm, not even a single bruise on him." Liu Shao-ch'iao glared back at him, not giving in.

"Sometimes internal injuries are even harder to treat."

Old Wen, who seemed unwilling to waste any more words, hastily ended the discussion, saying:

"I wasn't talking about this one, I was talking about from now on."

Hung T'ung-yeh, worried, asked:

"Do I have internal injuries?"

"No." Old Wen pressed his hand gently on Hung T'ung-yeh's lips, and shook his head. "If you had internal injuries, could you be this comfortable? Now, I'm going to give you a shot to make you sleep. This evening, you do whatever you have to do, and don't worry about anything."

After giving the injection, Old Wen left. Liu Shao-ch'iao told Hung T'ung-yeh:

"After this, no matter where you run into that piece of goods, it's important that you pretend not to recognize him."

Hung T'ung-yeh nodded.

"All right, you rest quietly."

Liu Shao-ch'iao closed the door and went into the front room to read. He seemed to feel as though there were something he wanted to write, but when he had spread out his writing paper and taken up his brush, he did not write a word. Cigarette followed cigarette as he smoked without pause. The fumes of hog lard from next door, as deeply intoxicating as wine, invaded the room. Liu Shao-ch'iao's eyes were blinded by exhaustion, and finally he laid his head down on the desk and slept.

"Shao-ch'iao, see your dappled butterfly Pai Ch'a-hua!" This sound wove around his ears.

Liu Shao-ch'iao suddenly woke up. He experienced a flash of light, and his spirits were increased a hundredfold. His inspiration came pouring like a tide; he smoothed the paper and began to write.

> Liu Shao-ch'iao is a lonely and solitary man.
> This lonely and solitary man
> With respectful hands and fragrance offers
> > these ten thousand tender sentiments to
> My dappled butterfly Pai Ch'a-hua who understands my heart—
> You are my precious
> You are my empress
> You are the tapeworm in my stomach
> You are the moisture between my toes
> You are my midwife
> *Ai!* Clearly, I am your toad.

When he was finished writing, he tossed his brush onto the table, read the poem through again, and thought approvingly: what a grand ten-line poem! He meant to add a title, but after thinking it over he could not find a suitable one. Finally, he wrote the phrase: "A Grand Ten-line Poem" to serve as the title. Putting it in an envelope, he sent it off to a poetry journal.

One evening, three days later, Liu Shao-ch'iao told Hung T'ung-yeh that the Revolutionary Army of Kwangtung, having already pacified the interior of that province, was preparing to launch the Northern Expedition. The main force of the Northern Expedition army would come down from Shao-kuan upon Hunan and Hupei.

"I've received orders to hand over affairs here to P'eng Wen-hsüeh; I'm going to Hankow. That's because that's my old home, and I'm familiar with conditions there, so it's more convenient for the work."

Liu Shao-ch'iao patted Hung T'ung-yeh on the back, and said:

"From now on, you'll come under Old P'eng's jurisdiction."

P'eng Wen-hsüeh, who had been standing to one side, immediately came over and seized Hung T'ung-yeh's hand tightly. With great sincerity and courtesy, he said:

"Please help me, brother. Once the Northern Expedition gets under way, the work in Shanghai will naturally become more urgent, and our responsibilities will be even heavier."

"Brother needn't be polite; whatever it is, you need only order me. Just as I obeyed Old Liu, so I'll obey you, brother; there can't be the slightest problem."

Hung T'ung-yeh also squeezed P'eng Wen-hsüeh's hand. Behind the thick-lensed spectacles, he saw tears in P'eng Wen-hsüeh's eyes. He asked:

"What, are you troubled?"

"I feel the weight of responsibility deeply, and I'm really a little afraid."

"What are you afraid of?" Liu Shao-ch'iao added. "I'm giving you back your rabbit-boy."

"That's a joke, later on it won't do," P'eng Wen-hsüeh said, blushing. "Little Hung, please don't hold it against me."

"I've heard enough of this polite talk of yours."

Liu Shao-ch'iao pulled Hung T'ung-yeh away, and they all sat down.

"Little Brother, I know you have a wish," Liu Shao-ch'iao smiled, sniffed the hog lard fumes from next door, and said to Hung T'ung-yeh: "Now that we're parting, I'm going to realize this wish of yours. Then you'll know that you can't go wrong by knowing someone like Liu Shao-ch'iao—and P'eng Wen-hsüeh is the same."

"What wish? I don't understand," Hung T'ung-yeh said, surprised.

"Aren't you always thinking about a Frenchwoman?"

"No, I'm not."

"Every day you rub the back and trim the toenails of Lefebvre's wife, and cause her to get you all stirred up, so you're always thinking about a Frenchwoman. At first you thought a Russian woman would fill in for her—how could you know it wouldn't work? And since you tasted a Russian woman, you've been thinking all the more about a Frenchwoman. Isn't that so? Am I right?"

"You really understand psychology," Hung T'ung-yeh said in embarrassment.

"I can see through even that little bit of stinginess in you, so it's no use to think of rebelling," Liu Shao-ch'iao shook his head, obviously very pleased with himself. "Come, I'll tell you. First, you go to Number 4 Ch'ing-lung Road, and see what's going on there. When you leave Number 4, someone you won't recognize will call you by name. You just relax and answer, and go with him."

"To go and do what?"

"There's a reward."

"What reward?"

"That, you don't need to be told beforehand. That person has prepared a Frenchwoman for you, and when you see her, and speak to her, you'll know. She's a prostitute, but she's especially pretty, and has no disease. When you're finished, go; that person has already settled the bill for you."

"Who is he?"

"Naturally he's someone who takes orders from me; do you need to ask?"

"Why go to all that trouble?"

"It's absolutely necessary."

As Liu Shao-ch'iao spoke, he offered them cigarettes. Amid the swirling smoke, he delivered a new lesson for Hung T'ung-yeh and P'eng Wen-hsüeh, to serve as his parting words of advice. Calmly, he said:

"This is one sort of 'technique of leadership'. You've seen a certain high-ranking deity? In one hand he holds a sword, and in the other he grasps the sutras. Who serves me lives; who defies me dies. And you've seen the little Tibetan bear in the circus? After each performance, they give him a piece of beef. His trainer holds a dog-beating club in one hand, and a meat dumpling in the other. This is the most artful technique of leadership. Little Hung, you've already tried my dog-beating club, and you understand what it is. Today, I'm giving you a meat dumpling."

These words left Hung T'ung-yeh looking embarrassed, but Liu Shao-ch'iao was utterly pleased, and he laughed with satisfaction. He inhaled deeply twice, and tossed the remaining half of his cigarette into the ashtray, and seemed even more excited. He looked at Hung T'ung-yeh and continued.

"Little Hung, you ought to be glad, and rightly so, because my superiors treat me in the same way. In the future, when you lead others, this will be a 'treasure of the Law handed down from the ancestors'; you mustn't forget it. Use violent force, use sweet words, or use a beautiful dream of the future—use anything. But never expect that anyone will make one-sided sacrifices for you over a long period of time, without some hopes of his own. On the one hand, satisfy his desires, whether they are subconscious or animal desires, and on the other hand, whip him. Then he'll naturally accept your leadership, and 'throughout the empire, everyone's heart will turn to you'."

"Surely there are exceptions?"

"Of course there are. If you happen to meet an exception, root him out, pull him up by the roots and destroy him! In that case, you need tact, speed, and decisiveness; you cannot have the slightest hesitation."

"Let me compare it to playing mahjongg," Hung T'ung-yeh said lightly, smiling. "That's like playing a full house against a full house and losing. Right?"

"Exactly right, my Little Brother." Liu Shao-ch'iao patted Hung T'ung-yeh on the cheek, and kissed him.

"Rabbit-boy, rabbit-boy!" P'eng Wen-hsüeh called softly, smacked Hung T'ung-yeh hard on the buttocks, and ran off.

After he had been to Ch'ing-lung Road, Hung T'ung-yeh returned to tell Liu Shao-ch'iao:

"Ch'ien Pen-san has gone by boat to Canton; they say he'll be back soon."

"It's definitely because of the Northern Expedition. They're getting busy too. I've got to prepare to leave soon for Hankow," Liu Shao-ch'iao said, and then asked:

"How was that French prostitute? You ate a treat, aren't you going to thank me?"

"If you want to go, I'll give you the money."

Hung T'ung-yeh made a triumphant gesture, expressing his satisfaction.

After about a month, Hung T'ung-yeh received a short note from Ch'ien Pen-san, inviting him to come over for a talk. He had returned from Canton. The authorities at Canton, because of his many complicated connections with the Peiyang warlords, had ordered him to take up residence at Hankow, and to do preparatory work for the Northern Expedition which was about to be launched. He received a great sum for operating expenses, and was to direct espionage work to disrupt the enemy army. He said to Hung T'ung-yeh:

"Now the time has come for youth to dedicate themselves to the nation. I thought of Mr. Kuo Hsin-ju's hopes for you, and decided to ask you to go to Hankow, to help me. You really cannot go on working at the foreign shop now."

Hung T'ung-yeh could not have anticipated that this would be brought up at their meeting, and for a moment he really didn't know how to respond. He hastily said:

"I understand Mr. Ch'ien's good intentions. Wait until I go and discuss it with them, and then I'll come back and give you my answer."

"You must make up your own mind about this," Ch'ien Pen-san smiled, and said affably. "Once you start to discuss it, then there are ever so many nameless obstacles, like last time."

"At least I've got to tell my mother, because she's not in good health." Hung T'ung-yeh also smiled, bowed, and retreated a pace.

Ch'ien Pen-san pulled a long face, stared at the floor from under the rims of his spectacles, yawned, and said:

"Very well—go!"

Hung T'ung-yeh bowed, withdrew, and went straight off to find P'eng Wen-hsüeh. Since Liu Shao-ch'iao had gone, P'eng Wen-hsüeh had moved to the front room, and a new face had moved into the back room. Hung T'ung-yeh had always considered P'eng Wen-hsüeh an agreeable and honest person, but since he had taken Liu Shao-ch'iao's place, it seemed there had been a sudden change. His face, originally ruddy and sleek, had become dark as iron, and from being a person who was always talking and laughing, he had become gloomy and short of speech, as though he still bore a numbness from the cold wastes. Hung T'ung-yeh felt that this man was even harder to get along with than the brilliant Liu Shao-ch'iao, and in his heart he dreaded him a little. He had suffered many pains at the hands of Liu Shao-ch'iao, but he had always had a feeling of intimate friendship for Liu Shao-ch'iao, a kind of spontaneous love. As for P'eng Wen-hsüeh, although they were together every day, he always felt as though a great gap separated them.

Having told P'eng Wen-hsüeh in simple terms of Ch'ien Pen-san's words, Hung T'ung-yeh stood at the corner of the desk waiting for his directions.

P'eng Wen-hsüeh took off his spectacles, rubbed his eyes with a handkerchief, and then said a single word:

"You."

Hung T'ung-yeh understood as soon as he heard, and hastily said:

"I haven't any opinion; whatever you say, goes."

"Liu Shao-ch'iao is in Hankow."

"You're my contact now, and I obey you."

"Come back early tomorrow morning."

Hung T'ung-yeh knew that the other had to go and ask someone else. He assented, and went downstairs. The new face from the back room was just leaning against the wall at the stairwell, and gave him a cold glance. Hung T'ung-yeh nodded to him, but did not recognize him; he had never seen him before. Hung T'ung-yeh glided down the stairs like smoke, threaded his way through the room with the stoves, and drew a deep breath, smelling that lovable scent of hog lard which made him think of Liu Shao-ch'iao.

He returned to Chapei. He saw his mother, whose wasting disease seemed to be getting worse and worse. But his sister was even taller; she was growing up like a bulrush, and her small bosom was filling out. Hung T'ung-yeh, with his back to his mother, beckoned to her, and went quietly out, with Hung Chin-ling following behind. The two of them walked through the noisy, dirty, and stinking lane, and out onto the street with its flying dust and soot. Hung Chin-ling kept a small handkerchief to her nose. Hung T'ung-yeh looked at her and said:

"Let's go to the Self-restraint Society for a Western meal."

"If you'd said so earlier, I could have changed clothes."

"It doesn't matter, there are no strangers here."

"I don't eat Western dishes, I can't chew those pieces of half-raw beef, and besides it's not time to eat."

"I just want to find a place to sit and talk. You don't have to eat beef, who said you had to eat beef?"

As soon as Hung Chin-ling heard this, she halted, looked all around, and pointed to a nearby local restaurant. She said:

"Well, right here, then. Why do we have to go running off to some far-off Self-restraint Society?"

The two of them went upstairs. All of the seats were empty, and they picked a spot in the corner near the window and sat down. They had tea, and a tray of fried noodles to go with it. Hung T'ung-yeh took a hot towel to wipe his face, and said:

"I may have an opportunity to go to Hankow; it'll be decided early tomorrow."

"Is Liu Shao-ch'iao sending you?"

"No, Ch'ien Pen-san."

Hung T'ung-yeh explained it to her, and added:

"If I do go to Hankow, I'd like very much to take you with me."

"What about Mother?"

"Mother is old, but young people are even more important than old people. It's not right to hold back young people for the sake of old people."

"What could I do?"

"Help Liu Shao-ch'iao—he's a man with a limitless future."

"He has a wife, and he also has that Pai Ch'a-hua. What would I be to him?"

"Be his friend, that is of even greater value than those other titles."

"I don't know why, I just don't like him."

"What kind do you like?"

"I don't have any definite model, but Liu Shao-ch'iao doesn't suit me."

"Very well, we won't speak of that. Tomorrow, if it's really decided that I'm going, you go with me, and then we'll see."

Hung T'ung-yeh loved his little sister, and had to be concerned for her. He measured her with a glance, and said with a smile:

"Sister, you've grown up, and you can't just sit at home. The house is like Mother in its age and physical condition; it doesn't have many days left. What's the good of you sticking to it?"

"I haven't decided to stick to it forever. Let's talk again tomorrow."

So Hung T'ung-yeh allowed his sister to return.

Early the next morning, he went to the French Concession to hear the word. P'eng Wen-hsüeh gripped his hand in parting. His earlier warmth of feeling was restored, he talked and laughed, and Hung T'ung-yeh saw again his ruddy, sleek countenance. He was allowed to follow Ch'ien Pen-san to Hankow, and already the relationship of obedience between them no longer existed. P'eng Wen-hsüeh said:

"After you get to Hankow, you'll be under Liu Shao-ch'iao again. Give him my regards. Tell him our situation here is very good."

P'eng Wen-hsüeh, aping Liu Shao-ch'iao's style, tried to playfully punch and kiss Hung T'ung-yeh on the face, but he was pushed away by Hung T'ung-yeh's hand. P'eng Wen-hsüeh said spitefully:

"You rabbit-boy!"

Hung T'ung-yeh paid no attention to him, and left. Outside the room with the stoves, he deliberately paused for a moment, and sniffed the odor of hog lard from next door.

He told Ch'ien Pen-san that his mother had agreed that he should go to Hankow, and moreover that he might take his little sister Chin-ling.

"Let her go out to see the world too. She has friends in Hankow."

"Do you have means to get away this time?"

"I certainly do." Hung T'ung-yeh had already hit upon a good idea. "You buy the boat tickets, and when the day comes, my sister and I will go directly on board."

Ch'ien Pen-san gave him money, and directed him to buy one single cabin ticket and one double cabin ticket. He explained that he was to be sure and buy tickets on an English boat, and if there were no English boats, then on a Japanese boat. This was because there were inspections by military and the police at the customs station on the river bank, but they were rather careless about foreign vessels, and it would save much nameless bother. Moreover, order and sanitation were relatively good. If it were a Chinese boat, then the situation was completely reversed: not only were the inspections en route a hindrance, but disbanded soldiers and irregular troops, like so many thievish rats and dogs, were liable to pillage them. Besides, the stench from the toilets spread to the four directions, and mucus and phlegm were everywhere; the disorder and filth were insupportable. Still more to be feared was seizure of the boat by the army. If that misfortune occurred, the passengers would be driven from the boat, which would temporarily be put to military use, and its destination would be obscure. Many travellers, obstructed in mid-journey, could neither go back to the villages, nor return to the inn, and if their funds were cut off, their lot was even sadder.

Hung T'ung-yeh bought the tickets and reported to Ch'ien Pen-san. He also informed his sister Chin-ling, asking her to bring some things with her, and, when the time came, to deceive their mother and steal away to board the boat. This was because he knew that Mother would not consent to Chin-ling leaving, and it had to be done by stealth. At first Chin-ling was a little troubled, and unwilling, but later she agreed in spite of herself. Although she was a girl, she too hoped to see the great world, and she did not want to go on living in poverty with her mother. Mother's endurance had meaning: to remain faithful to her husband by not remarrying, to raise her son and daughter, and a still more important reason was her own poor health and old age—if she did not endure, then what? But what sort of thing was it for the newly risen generation, the youth, who ought to be making their own new lives, to keep her company in her endurance? Wasn't it an unavoidable wanton misuse of Heaven's gifts? Too pitiful, too pitiful.

Hung T'ung-yeh returned to the foreign shop, did not alter his obedient manner, and performed his duties as usual. He sat at the assistant compradore's desk, where there was much accumulated work to be done, but he felt that there was nothing he could do. He looked out through the big glass window upon swarming Avenue Joffre. A fat, middle-aged man, who looked like a member of the gentry, and who pressed close to a refined-looking girl, stopped before the window. He peered intently at the hunting guns displayed in the window, pointing at them as he said something, and then turned and was gone. A skinny, shabby fellow wearing a visored cap, a short jacket, and trousers, who had also been standing looking at the guns, kept looking to the right and to the left as he puffed on a cigarette butt he had already lighted in his hand.

Hung T'ung-yeh felt that everything was boring.

The new apprentice brought a cup of hot tea. Hung T'ung-yeh looked at him and nodded.

A cigarette flew through the air and dropped on his glass desk-plate. Hung T'ung-yeh looked up and saw Compradore Chang, leaning against his own desk and watching him with a grin. Hung T'ung-yeh thanked him and lighted the cigarette.

Compradore Chang beckoned to him, and he went over.

"The Manager's wife doesn't understand why you're going out so much these days, and you're not around much."

Hung T'ung-yeh inhaled smoke, looked toward the ceiling as he exhaled it, and didn't answer.

The Manager's wife appeared at the head of the stairs and beckoned him to come up. He crushed out the cigarette in Compradore Chang's ashtray, and went upstairs.

The Manager's wife allowed him to sit down facing her, and asked him if he wanted coffee. He shook his head.

The Manager's wife's mood was dispirited. Fixing her eyes on him, she said:

"Lately you've changed."

Hung T'ung-yeh flushed, and did not answer.

"You're not around much since the Manager went to Peking."

Hung T'ung-yeh didn't say anything.

The Manager's wife raised her right foot in front of Hung T'ung-yeh's face, and said:

"Look!"

She hadn't worn her shoes, and had come out onto the stairs in her bare feet.

Hung T'ung-yeh played dumb, and sat still. The Manager's wife, seeing his indifferent attitude, flew into a rage. Furiously, she pressed her face close to his, and cried in a loud voice:

"You haven't given me a pedicure in two weeks!"

Then Hung T'ung-yeh suddenly came back to himself. The images of the Russian yaksha and the French prostitute flashed before his eyes like electric sparks, and he felt it was rather funny, so he laughed.

When the Manager's wife saw him laugh, she could not contain her rage, and shouted even louder:

"You've made me so mad, and you can still laugh—you conscienceless thing!"

Hung T'ung-yeh restrained his own anger, and took a cigarette from the low table. Inhaling, he said quietly:

"Is there bath-water now?"

"You're stupid—when is there bath-water in the morning?"

"You calm down a bit. I'll go and heat water for you."

So saying, he went upstairs.

After a while, Hung T'ung-yeh took off his long gown, rolled his sleeves up high, and prepared the Manager's wife a basin of steaming hot bath-water. He told her:

"Don't be angry, please wash. Do you want me to rub your back?"

The Manager's wife made a spitting sound, went into the bathroom, and loudly locked the door from the inside. She felt that Hung T'ung-yeh's manner today was slightly disrespectful, and that she had lost some of her dignity. But she did not feel insulted; on the contrary, she took a kind of mild comfort in it.

After the bath, she put on her clothes and came out, and leaned against an easy chair. She was delighted to see that Hung T'ung-yeh was already waiting there. At once she thrust out one damp, salty foot onto his knee. Hung T'ung-yeh, with his pedicure knife in one hand, nonchalantly planted a kiss upon the arch of her foot. The Manager's wife cried angrily:

"You bad egg! Wait 'til I tell the Manager, he'll kick you to death!"

Hung T'ung-yeh glanced at her, and began to trim her toenails with his little knife. This time the Manager's wife did not read her illustrated magazine, but kept both eyes on Hung T'ung-yeh, so that he wouldn't try anything worse.

Late at night, when everyone else was sleeping and the street was quiet as well, Hung T'ung-yeh packed his simple bags. He placed a letter, which he had written before, upon the empty bed. Since M. Lefebvre was not in Shanghai, the letter was to be given to the Manager's wife. Hung T'ung-yeh, in the letter, first thanked the Manager's wife for the care she had given him these several years, and then said that he had already gone into partnership with a friend in a commercial organization in Hankow. It was so that he could be independent, and he could not but go. Since his last attempt to resign had not worked out, this time he had had to change his method and leave without saying goodbye. But all of the matters which he had handled had been honestly done, and his conscience was clear. Finally, Hung T'ung-yeh expressed his deep regrets, and added: "I hope that we will have an opportunity to meet again in the future, and when that time comes, I hope that you will still care for me, as you have done for so long."

He also had letters of farewell for Compradore Chang and Old White-hand Wang.

He slipped out the back door, and locked it. Picking up his luggage, he had gone no more than a few steps before a strong light shone in his face, so bright that he couldn't open his eyes. A French constabulary officer with a flashlight looked him over, and then recognized him. He asked:

"Where are you going, this late at night?"

"The Manager wrote a letter from Peking," Hung T'ung-yeh said quickly. "Something's come up and I have to go there."

"What train can you get at this time of night?"

"I'm going to Chapei first, to see my family, and catch the early train."

The constable, without waiting for him to finish, had already gone.

Hung T'ung-yeh went a little way, and hailed a rickshaw. After crossing the Avenue France, he found a small hotel in which to rest. On the other side of the wall, a couple kept chattering to each other. When they weren't talking, they were shaking the iron bedstead as though they were going to break it, with a *ding-ding* sound. Hung T'ung-yeh couldn't get to sleep the whole night. Just as dawn was breaking, the couple in the next room got up and left, and then he slept.

When he woke up, he looked at his watch: it was ten o'clock. He thought, the boat leaves at noon, so I'll go now and have a bite to eat, and then it will just be time to meet Ch'ien Pen-san on the boat. He left his baggage in the hotel, greeted the clerk, and went out.

After he had eaten, he took a rickshaw to Ch'ing-lung Road. As soon as he entered the reception room, he saw his little sister Chin-ling with Ch'ien Pen-san, and also last night's French constable. The French constable, seeing Hung T'ung-yeh come in, said:

"Good, you've come. Fortunately you didn't take the early train to Peking."

Compradore Chang came to work at eight o'clock, and it was Compradore Chang who had told Mme. Lefebvre, so she knew that Hung T'ung-yeh had already gone without saying goodbye. Having hastily read the letter, she was furious, and anxious, and she stamped her feet all the way down the stairs. She ordered Compradore Chang:

"You go to the police station and report that he has stolen important things."

"What things? You must explain clearly; the police will want to register it."

"A lot of cash, and my jewelry besides," the Manager's wife said thoughtlessly.

Compradore Chang felt uneasy. He hesitated a moment, and then said:

"I'll call up, and you can talk to them, all right?"

"Fine!" the Manager's wife cried impatiently.

After the telephone call, some policemen arrived, and the constable who had been on patrol the previous night was among them. This constable had been very close to M. and Mme. Lefebvre for many years, and he often came to their shop to sit, drink tea, and joke with them. Mme. Lefebvre and her two children all liked him. He was called Dumas.

Mme. Lefebvre gave them Hung T'ung-yeh's letter to read, and she herself wrote out a list of missing articles for them. Dumas looked over the list, figured a moment, and then shrugged and said:

"This amounts to twenty or thirty thousand dollars. It's no small case."

He told of the circumstances under which he had seen Hung T'ung-yeh leaving, the previous night, and everyone made up their minds that, as a first step, they must go to Mother Hung's home in Chapei, and investigate. But the French constable could not operate in the "Chinese city" and they would have to hand over the case to the local police authorities in the "Chinese city". They feared that "leisurely action would not help in a desperate crisis".

It was the Manager's wife herself who had an idea. She asked Compradore Chang to go.

"If he's at home, ask him to come back with you, so that we can talk everything over face to face. If he's not at home, you ask his mother to think of a way to get him to come back."

And she repeatedly instructed him:

"Whatever you do, don't bring up the matter of theft, and frighten him so that he'll be afraid to come back."

Compradore Chang thought that this was a troublesome business, from which, either way, he stood to lose. If Hung T'ung-yeh had really gone, she will suspect that I leaked word of it to him; if I bring him back, he'll suffer for it and won't he say that I helped the foreigners to do him harm? So he refused, saying only that the implications of this business were too great, and he didn't dare to get involved. He would rather the Manager's wife called him a "bad egg" and he wouldn't agree to go. He added:

"It's better to send somebody from the police station."

Old White-hand Wang suddenly decided to take part in this affair. He was very upset. Had Little Hung stolen and run away? It wasn't clear, and the Manager's wife's tricks were too secretive and cruel. He couldn't help saying:

"Since Compradore Chang isn't willing to go, suppose I go?"

When someone proclaims himself rashly courageous, naturally there are none who do not approve. Old Wang rode a bicycle to Chapei. When Mrs. Hung heard his news, she was so frightened that her legs went weak; at once she started to weep and snuffle, and she did not know what to do. Hung Chin-ling had an idea, and said:

"Please, Uncle Wang, you go back, and tell them not to worry. I'll go and try, and see whether or not I can find Brother. Once he shows up, won't the matter be easily handled?"

After she had seen Old Wang off, Hung Chin-ling urged her mother to go to bed and rest. The rays of the sun were just coming in the window. Hung Chin-ling took especial care to plump up the pillow, and shaded her mother's eyes.

"Ma, you relax, and sleep; I'll go and get him."

So saying, she changed her clothes and shoes, and took the little bit of luggage which she had stealthily made ready beforehand. At the thought that the rice-jar was empty, the oil-pot and the salt jar were empty too, and Mama's old-fashioned purse was also empty, she really felt a little inexpressible grief and sadness. Holding back two eyefuls of tears, she went downstairs and out.

At the mouth of the lane, she took a rickshaw to the North Station, where she changed to a rickshaw of the English Society and rode to No. 4 Ch'ing-lung Road. Having asked and learned that her brother wasn't there, she asked to see Ch'ien Pen-san. When Ch'ien Pen-san heard that the little sister of the Hung family, who was to travel with them, had arrived, he told her to sit down in the reception room.

No sooner had they begun to speak than Dumas arrived with two Annamite policemen. When Old Wang returned to say that Hung T'ung-yeh had not yet returned home, the Manager's wife had thought of No. 4 Ch'ing-lung Road, and she remembered why he had wanted to leave the last time.

"Maybe he's gone there again."

Ch'ing-lung Road was in the French Concession, so it was easily managed. Dumas immediately got into his car and went there. As it happened, none of those in Dumas' party could speak Chinese, and none of the several people at Ch'ing-lung Road who could speak English or French were there, so the two sides could not understand each other. Ch'ien Pen-san knew, from what Hung Chin-ling had said, that the Manager's wife of the foreign shop was behind this affair, but since he couldn't communicate, there was nothing he could say.

Just at that moment, an exhausted Hung T'ung-yeh dragged himself in.

Dumas also understood what Mme. Lefebvre had in mind, and at first, with a pleasant manner, he urged Hung T'ung-yeh not to go, but to return to his job at the foreign shop. After Hung T'ung-yeh had refused, he brought out Mme. Lefebvre's list of missing articles, and asked with a frown:

"Well, where are these stolen goods? Where did you put them? Lead me to these stolen goods!"

Hung T'ung-yeh read the list, and knew that a case had been trumped up against him, and the matter was serious. He composed himself, and said calmly:

"You saw what I carried out of there last night. Those things are in a little hotel across the sand-bank; I can take you there to examine them."

Dumas clapped his hands, and the two Vietnamese policemen, one to each side, marched Hung T'ung-yeh out. Hung T'ung-yeh understood that, with matters having gone this far, it was really a case in which, though right was on his side, he couldn't explain himself, and the circumstances were such that he couldn't just give up. In a loud voice, he said:

"Mr. Ch'ien, if I miss the boat, please take my little sister to Hankow, and I'll come along later."

Ch'ien Pen-san heard, and looked at Hung Chin-ling. Hung Chin-ling hid her face, weeping. Ch'ien Pen-san found himself thinking that the Party's present slogan of beating down the warlords and beating down the imperialists was certainly most correct. In order to realize this political demand, we shouldn't hesitate to unite with any source of strength.

Seeing that the time had come, he took Hung Chin-ling aboard the boat. The boat left the wharf, passing the mouth of the Wu-sung, passing Chen-chiang, and passing Nanking, and in the end they never saw Hung T'ung-yeh board the boat

Chapter VI

After they had gone to look for the stolen property, and since none of the articles on Mme. Lefebvre's list had been found in Hung T'ung-yeh's luggage, Hung T'ung-yeh was locked up. Two weeks later, he was released for lack of evidence. During these two weeks, although Hung T'ung-yeh did not personally taste the police station's famous electric torture or water torture, he was strung up and flogged, and he suffered no few hardships. Mme. Lefebvre deigned to visit the police station and came to see him on two occasions. She kept urging him:

"If only you'll agree not to go, and come back to work as before, this theft case will quickly disappear. It's all for your own good, don't you understand?"

But on this occasion Hung T'ung-yeh was unreasonable, and except for shaking his head, he ignored her. Mme. Lefebvre, seeing that words would not move him, held back her tears, and took a New Testament, in French, from her handbag. The leather was stamped with gold, and it was beautifully bound. She held it out to Hung T'ung-yeh, and said sweetly:

"When one is in difficulties, one cannot leave God. While you're here, you ought to pray more, and read the Bible more, then God will be with you."

Hung T'ung-yeh closed his eyes, shut his hands, and would not take it from her.

"You cannot refuse God, child!"

Hung T'ung-yeh was upset, but he paid no attention to her, and she got angry and left.

After he left the police station, Hung T'ung-yeh went to the French Concession to see P'eng Wen-hsüeh. He rested for a few days, and then bought a boat ticket for Hankow. Before leaving, he thought of going to see his mother. But then he felt that it would be pointless; it would do no good, on the contrary it would be a lot of bother, so he discarded the idea. He thought:

"If I saw that she was sick, or saw that she was hungry, what could I do about it? Do I have the means to make her well, or provide her with food?"

Naturally the answer was in the negative.

"Old people are close to death; they belong to the world that is past. We of the younger generation have the responsibility of creating the future. Each side must turn its back on the other and go its own way."

With this explanation, his conscience was at peace.

The Yangtze River was considered China's important waterway, yet as one passed upstream, one often went for a long time without encountering a single ship. When one chanced to be seen, nine times out of ten it flew a foreign flag. The naval warships were ever so big and grand, and they, too, all flew foreign flags. The Chinese naval craft flew the five-color national flag of red, yellow, blue, white, and black, and the naval ensign of the white sun in the blue sky on a red ground: a pitifully matched pair, which looked like something just bought from a curio shop.

Hung T'ung-yeh looked upon the vastness of the river and the sky, and felt that this land, with its lovely rivers and mountains, was indeed a land of great possibilities. And the first step, the step that had to be taken, was to expel the power of the foreigners, to knock down imperialism. If imperialism was to be knocked down, then the domestic warlords, who depended upon imperialism, had first to be destroyed. He thought, those two slogans, put forward by Mr. Sun

Chung-shan's Kuomintang, meet completely the demands of the nation and the people. The tide was running, and it was bound to achieve its goal; there was no doubt of that.

He thought of the Communist Party, and felt that if the Communist Party decided to depend upon the Kuomintang, to be the Kuomintang's helping hand, that would really be an intelligent policy, because the Kuomintang had already grasped the essentials of the problem. Outside of this, there could not be any other road.

Marx? Capitalism had not formed in China.

Lenin? China had no serfs under the rule of the Tsar.

The Paris Commune, the February Revolution, the October Revolution— none of this series of events were of the sort that could have happened in China.

When Hung T'ung-yeh had thought to this point, a dark shadow seemed to fall over his emotions. A white water-bird darted swiftly across the boat's course, flying from the south back to the north, and standing out sharply against the gray sky.

Full of misgivings and hesitancy, Hung T'ung-yeh arrived in Hankow.

On the opposite bank was Wuchang, the starting point of China's October Revolution. The bloodstains of a decade past had not yet dried, yet the world had already changed and changed again. The passengers were all in a hurry to disembark, while Hung T'ung-yeh, who had been ready well before time, stood on deck, gazing about in all directions. In the distance were several great chimneys, from which no smoke issued. Hung T'ung-yeh guessed that they might belong to the once-famous Hanyang Steel Works.

The boat drew up to the wharf, and the passengers began to disembark. Hung T'ung-yeh picked up his two pieces of luggage—his bedding and his leather suitcase, which altogether weighed perhaps thirty pounds, and followed the others down the gangplank. Alighting, he beckoned and called to a porter.

"Carry these off the wharf for me."

The porter folded his hands, and lazily surveyed his little bit of luggage. He said:

"Thirty dollars."

When Hung T'ung-yeh heard this, it gave him a start. But he considered that he had just arrived, and was not familiar with the local accent; perhaps he had heard wrong. He bent his neck and asked:

"How much?"

"Thirty dollars!" The porter, so that he would thoroughly understand, first thrust out three fingers, and then, with both hands, made the sign for "ten", thus giving him both a visual and an oral demonstration. Hung T'ung-yeh was taken aback, but he held his temper and pursued the matter.

"You're joking—just a few steps and you want so much money?"

"How should I be joking with you?" The porter looked at him with indifference, and said carelessly: "Thirty dollars, a copper less and it's no go."

Because his opponent was a wharf-coolie, Hung T'ung-yeh could not look upon him as a stranger. Although he wasn't very reasonable, and was lacking in good manners, that was just the proper spirit of resistance and struggle which his class exhibited toward another class. It was worthy of approval, and even deserved to be publicized. Hung T'ung-yeh used his intelligence to control his emotions, and thus avoided losing his temper in the face of sacred labor. Laughing, he said:

"Seriously, how much do you really want?"

"Aren't I being serious with you? Thirty dollars!" The porter raised his voice, fiercely expressing his resolution.

Hung T'ung-yeh, seeing that he couldn't make himself clear, said no more. There were only two small pieces of luggage, and he didn't absolutely have to have the porter carry them, so he picked them up himself. Unexpectedly, the porter got in front of him and blocked his way, and gave him a shove on the chest. It was a hard shove, and Hung T'ung-yeh stepped back two paces, and nearly fell down. Several idlers, sitting on the rails of a receiving lighter, saw this little episode and laughed all together.

The porter, seeing that someone appreciated his provocation, was even more pleased with himself. Arms akimbo, he grinned nastily at Hung T'ung-yeh. Hung T'ung-yeh again tried to go around, and the porter shoved him again. This time, he used his strength, and Hung T'ung-yeh could not keep his feet. He slid to a sitting position on the oily, filthy deck of the lighter. His hands waved and he lost his luggage.

The audience of idlers again laughed loudly.

Hung T'ung-yeh, still more mortified and irritated, blushed. He abandoned the luggage, got off the lighter straightaway, and mounted the bank, where he stood for a moment. He saw a big tall policeman passing by, and Hung T'ung-yeh, according to the conditions in Shanghai, took him to be a wheatcake-eating northerner, and went up to him to say "Pardon me" and tell him what had happened. But unexpectedly, without waiting to hear it all, he shook his head, and strode off with his head in the air.

With that, Hung T'ung-yeh was truly solitary and friendless. He saw how it was, he would have to break out his money, because his luggage certainly could not be abandoned. He took the wallet out of his shirt-front and had a look. He still had enough money. But in his heart he felt truly wronged, and not at all willing.

Standing at the side of the riverbank, Hung T'ung-yeh hesitated, undecided. An old woman beggar happened to come lurching along, and Hung T'ung-yeh immediately departed. He despised that so-called "shallow humanitarianism", considering that the dispensation of charity destroyed the beneficiary's will to struggle, and the will to struggle was the motive force of human progress; without struggle there could be no advance, and mankind would be forever sunk in delay.

So thinking, Hung T'ung-yeh's spirits immediately rose a hundredfold, and he was even happy. That thirty dollars would just serve to encourage that porter's will to struggle, and would serve, for him, as still another proof of that indestructible truth: only struggle could obtain for one the benefits one ought to have.

Thus, he no longer hesitated, but hurried straight back to the lighter, gave the thirty dollars he had counted out to that porter, and said:

"Pardon me, I've troubled you, thank you, thank you."

And he accompanied this with a smile.

All this politeness mystified the porter. He took the money, said not a word, carried the two pieces of luggage ashore, and watched the other ride off in a rickshaw. Then he said to himself:

"Mother's—these days unless you act a bit rough, unless you're unreasonable, you needn't figure on getting any money."

The old woman beggar was just pursuing a haughty woman who was crossing the street. She stuck out a dry, withered hand to beg, and the other woman, in order to avoid the bother, escaped by hurrying off. The porter, who had seen this, took a big bar-copper worth a hundred cash and thrust it into her hand. Snorting, he said:

"Rich people won't give you anything, it's no use asking."

When he found the Liu family's dry goods store, on Chiao-t'ung Road, Hung T'ung-yeh got out of the rickshaw. Just after having confused that dishonest porter on the wharf, he had seen a rickshaw, and had gotten into it and left, without having explained the destination nor agreed upon a price. Now, Hung

T'ung-yeh got his wallet out as he asked the rickshaw coolie how much money he wanted. The rickshaw coolie replied carelessly:

"Two dollars."

This time Hung T'ung-yeh understood what he heard, and he couldn't help gasping, as he realized that he had run into more trouble. Although he might say that it was to nurture their will to fight, and a few dollars didn't matter, still it was really hard to put up with being cheated once and then a second time. He said:

"From the wharf to here was only two turns, and as for time it didn't take more than five minutes. How is it you want so much?"

"It's two dollars, no mistake," the rickshaw coolie said, restraining his irritation and smiling.

"In Shanghai, this little ride wouldn't be more than ten little coppers at the most."

"That's Shanghai, this is Hankow."

"There can't be that much difference."

The rickshaw coolie saw that he was not being forthcoming, and gradually grew impatient. In a loud voice he said:

"Hurry up and give me the money, so I can go. You can't ride without paying!"

"You crook, I won't give it to you!"

"Who are you calling a crook? You can't ride without paying."

The rickshaw coolie seized Hung T'ung-yeh by the front of his shirt, and bawled out:

"You rode without paying, and now you want to beat me!"

Hung T'ung-yeh spread his hands and asked desperately:

"You're talking nonsense, when did I beat you?"

The rickshaw coolie held his shirt even tighter, and kept bawling:

"Fine, you beat me, and now you're cursing me!"

And he cried out:

"*Ai-ya*, you're killing me, you're killing me!"

At once they were surrounded by a crowd of onlookers. Hung T'ung-yeh was intimidated to the point of helplessness, and he could only give up and say:

"All right, all right, I'll pay you."

He gave two dollars to the rickshaw coolie, who, as soon as he saw the money, remembered his manners, released his grip, and went off with his rickshaw. As he went, he snorted:

"You didn't want to give it but I got it anyway!"

Hung T'ung-yeh was so angry that his four limbs grew weak. He settled himself down, picked up his luggage, and examined the nameplate. He mounted the stoop and went into the dry goods shop. Mr. Liu and Second Brother had been out in front of their door watching the quarrel, and they hadn't expected the stranger who had been involved in the quarrel to come into their shop. Mr. Liu felt a bit dubious, and his ruddy, much-wrinkled face took on a cold expression. In a stern voice he called to Second Brother:

"Come in."

Second Brother came behind the counter and climbed onto the tall stool behind the cashier's desk. He kept staring coldly at this unfamiliar guest who was coming through the door. Hung T'ung-yeh put down his luggage, and asked:

"Please, is there a Liu Shao-ch'iao here?"

No one answered him. A young clerk, with his eyes on his employers, said nervously:

"Not here."

Hung T'ung-yeh, completely baffled, again inspected the doorplate and the nameplate.

"This is the right place, how can he not be here?"

Hunchbacked Second Brother, in a pleasant voice but with a mean tone, said to the young clerk:

"Explain to him!"

The clerk heard, and as though no longer apprehensive, said crisply:

"There is such a person, but he's already moved out."

"Moved to where?" Hung T'ung-yeh asked anxiously.

"Number 108 Ssu-fen-li."

"Where is Ssu-fen-li?" Now that he had an address, Hung T'ung-yeh relaxed.

"Not far from here. Ask the passersby and you'll find out."

Hung T'ung-yeh hesitated a moment, and then said with a smile:

"May I trouble you to call a rickshaw for me? And settle the fare? I just got here and I'm not familiar, you saw what just happened. It's very embarrassing to squabble on the street, and I hate to spend two dollars besides."

The clerk looked at Mr. Liu, but Mr. Liu's face expressed nothing. He looked at Second Brother, and the hunchback nodded, so the clerk said: "All right."

In a moment a rickshaw had been summoned, and the fare was settled on at two-tenths of a hundred-cash bar-copper. Hung T'ung-yeh calculated. It was about six-tenths of a silver dollar. When they arrived, he looked at the time. The ride had taken twenty minutes.

It was a newly-built alley, wide and spacious. Hung T'ung-yeh at first felt that the place was a little mixed up, because in front of at least half of the houses hung big shaded glass lamps, bearing the professional names of courtesans, as in a Shanghai red-light district. He went to the last house, and it was No. 108. There was a tailor shop downstairs, and Liu Shao-ch'iao lived in the front apartment above.

When Liu Shao-ch'iao returned to Hankow, he had at first stayed in the store-room behind the dry goods shop. But now the store-room was no longer completely empty as it had been before; it was heaped with many things. Besides the dry goods, there was tung oil. Since they had opened the dry goods shop, Mr. Liu had told Second Brother to take on more responsibility, intending to give him some business experience. "Can I look after him all his life?" he would often ask himself, and so he did not concern himself too much with the business.

Unexpectedly this ugly Second Brother proved to have a natural talent for business. He was frugal, he calculated clearly, and his eyes were sharp. The shop was a dry goods shop in name, but profits in the business were extremely limited, and he relied on cautious speculation for most of his profits. Most recently he had been accumulating tung oil. Without knowing from whence the inspiration had come, he felt that the production of tung oil was going to decrease, and the price would rise; the export price, especially, was bound to rise. This view of his was his "military secret"; he kept it to himself, and didn't even let it slip out in front of his father. He was afraid that if the slightest hint got out, everyone would start to hoard it, and the price would be driven up so that he wouldn't be able to buy it cheaply.

Because the goods were piled up inside, naturally the building had to be locked, and Second Brother kept the key. But Liu Shao-ch'iao didn't want to stay anywhere else, he preferred the store-room, and so the two brothers began to quarrel. This happened before Liu Shao-ch'iao had been home for even an hour. In the end the elder, feeling that he was wronged, yielded to the younger brother, and let him move in. Liu Shao-ch'iao pushed in to see Yeh P'in-hsia, but she would neither recognize him nor listen to him. In the middle of the night he went up to her room. Unexpectedly, Yeh P'in-hsia was no longer as she had been before; the door had already been locked from the inside and she pretended not to hear him. Liu Shao-ch'iao got angry, and began to shout, shove at the door, and run up and down stairs, so that everyone was awakened by the noise. After quarreling for half the night, he departed in a rage, saying:

"The next time this happens I'll bring kerosene and burn down this cowshed of yours. Maybe you've got a lover in there?"

Early the next morning, as soon as he got up, he wanted money. It was now Second Brother who managed the money. This Second Brother, when it came to anything else, could be reasonable, but when it came to money, he was like someone with a grudge eight generations long; he was a hundred times unwilling, unwilling to the end. And he also knew that this Third Brother was no good, and not lightly to be provoked. He asked:

"What do you want the money for?"

Liu Shao-ch'iao considered this question unnecessary, and was slightly annoyed. He replied smoothly:

"Money has lots of uses! Eating, drinking, whoring, gambling, and carrying with you to smoke opium—how should one not want money?"

"You've got food and a place to live, you don't need money. Papa and I have never taken a cent from the till; we're businessmen."

As they talked back and forth the brothers began to quarrel again.

Mr. Liu suppressed his anger, and said to Liu Shao-ch'iao:

"Since you left, we've all gotten along very agreeably. Everybody concentrates on doing business, and there's been a flourishing atmosphere. Ever since you came back, there hasn't been half a moment's peace, but it's been so noisy that even chickens and dogs can't rest! It's not that I've been partial among my children, it's that you're really too wicked! I don't want you! I understand completely now, as long as you're here, this family can't exist!"

"You don't want me! Fine!"

"Well, get out!"

Liu Shao-ch'iao stuck out his hand, smiled coldly, and said:

"Give me some money, and I'll go."

"I'm willing to give you a hundred dollars a month, just as when you were in Shanghai, and you can get along. If you're going to stay in Hankow, leave your address, and I'll have the cashier send your money there at regular intervals."

Mr. Liu, in extreme disgust, shouted:

"Don't you ever come back!"

"All right, all right, certainly," Liu Shao-ch'iao said. "But I have one condition."

"What condition?"

"I want to divorce Yeh P'in-hsia."

"That won't do!"

"Then I'll come back every day and quarrel with you, and you won't be able to stand it!"

"Papa," Second Brother interrupted, "you ought to ask Third Brother's wife about this divorce business. If she's willing to agree, why should you hinder it?"

"Because I know she would certainly not agree!" Mr. Liu said, furiously stamping his foot.

"You can ask her, at least."

"All right, it might work, we'll ask her. If she's willing, I won't oppose it."

As Mr. Liu spoke, he went to the foot of the stairs, intending to call Yeh P'in-hsia. But as it happened, she was just standing halfway down the stairs. He beckoned to her to come downstairs.

Yeh P'in-hsia had changed. Her hair was drawn back into a round bun, her face was yellowish and pale, and she wore no cosmetics. Her clothes—dress, shoes, stockings—were all blue, and all of cotton. Although she was still clean, her charm and beauty had completely disappeared. Liu Shao-ch'iao felt that she greatly resembled a widow. He spat, turned away, and left.

Mr. Liu was just going to open his mouth when Yeh P'in-hsia spoke first:

"I heard everything you said. From childhood I learned the Three Obediences and the Four Virtues, and getting a divorce is something I shall never do. I won't ask what he does outside; even if he gets married again I won't care. I only want to keep the name of a wife of the Liu family, so that I can face the father and mother who bore me—that's enough for me."

As she spoke, tears ran down her face, and she dashed up the stairs.

"Very well. It's my retribution." Mr. Liu's heart was troubled. "We won't speak of the divorce again. It can't be done, and there's nothing for it."

Liu Shao-ch'iao shook his head, and sighed. He felt that the woman was already deeply poisoned, and there was no use in seeking, neither through ferocity or liberality, a remedy. One could see it was of no use. So he no longer insisted, but took a hundred dollars, and went out onto the street to look for a room.

Originally he had had no intention of living on Ssu-fen-li. It was just the first rental notice that he had seen on the street. He saw that the area was heterogeneous, with all kinds of people coming and going. The apartment was spacious, and seemed suitable, so he rented it.

Hung T'ung-yeh went upstairs, and found the door closed. He knocked, and someone opened the door a crack and peered out. Seeing it was Hung T'ung-yeh, this person slipped out, and then closed the door as before. It was Liu Shao-ch'iao. He happily seized Hung T'ung-yeh's hand, and said:

"You've come! Good, good!"

Lowering his voice, he added:

"There are several friends inside, and it's not convenient for you to come in just now. Leave your bags here, and you go to that little Yang-chow restaurant at the head of the lane. I'll come shortly and get you."

Hung T'ung-yeh, seeing his half-serious, half-joking manner, suspected that he was being deliberately mysterious and asked him in a lowered voice:

"Men friends or women friends?"

"Men and women both."

"Let me look in at the crack of the door, all right?"

As Hung T'ung-yeh said this, he moved to open the door, but Liu Shao-ch'iao suddenly put out his right hand and chopped down hard on his palm, and then pinched him on the thigh. In both instances he used considerable force, and Hung T'ung-yeh felt such pain that he nearly cried out. Liu Shao-ch'iao shoved him away, and said viciously:

"No fooling around here! Go on!"

Hung T'ung-yeh, aware that he had been rebuffed, hurried downstairs, and then slowly traversed the alley. Sure enough, there was a small restaurant selling Yang-chow snacks, and it was called the Little Half-fast. Across from it there was a Cantonese restaurant, whose sign read The Two Rivers. Hung T'ung-yeh felt hungry. He looked at his watch, and it was twelve o'clock, just time for the noon meal. He liked Cantonese dishes, and he wasn't interested in the Little Half-fast. But Liu Shao-ch'iao had directed him to the Yang-chow restaurant, and he was afraid that if he changed the place, the other wouldn't be able to find him. He thought, I'd better stand by the side of the street and wait until he comes out, and we'll eat together at the The Two Rivers.

The street was spacious, prosperous and bustling, and fairly festive. Unfortunately the paved street was also very dusty. Now and then several young women would pass in and out of Ssu-fen-li. Their accents were northern, their dress was nondescript, and doubtless they were shop assistants. Hung T'ung-yeh, who worshipped Western women, had no particular interest, so he merely glanced at them.

In a little while, Liu Shao-ch'iao came out of the alley with four or five people, old and young, men and women, and as they came face to face with Hung T'ung-yeh, Liu Shao-ch'iao made a devilish grimace and winked at him, telling him to keep silent. So Hung T'ung-yeh did not hail him. He saw Liu Shao-ch'iao accompany them into The Two Rivers. He thought, this must be the reason he directed me to go to the Little Half-fast. Fortunately he hadn't gone rushing into The Two Rivers.

Hung T'ung-yeh was upset. He felt that since his arrival in Hankow, everything had gone wrong. The waterfront porter and the rickshaw man had cheated him, the people in the Liu family shop had been cold to him, and Liu Shao-ch'iao's cruelty had made him feel that he didn't even know who he was.

"Don't I have a single friend, a single partner?"

Resignedly, he entered the Little Half-fast, and chose a secluded seat. He had some salted dried pork-shreds, and he drank four ounces of kao-liang liquor as he sat there alone. He thought, I've often heard people speak of 'drinking to banish melancholy'; probably that's what I'm doing.

What was he melancholy about? Hung T'ung-yeh hadn't thought of that. Although he had thought about it, he had never imagined that the greatest sadness must be when a man couldn't choose his own path, and couldn't even choose his own preference.

When he had finished the kao-liang liquor, Hung T'ung-yeh felt quite silly. He smoked, and sipped tea. He watched the other diners, and seemed to himself to be an idler. Then Liu Shao-ch'iao arrived.

He stood in the door, looked at Hung T'ung-yeh, and beckoned to him. Hung T'ung-yeh settled the bill, and went out with him.

Liu Shao-ch'iao did not return to his apartment, but led Hung T'ung-yeh down the road. Gradually they got away from the busy area, and came to a quiet spot. As they strolled slowly along, they talked. Liu Shao-ch'iao said:

"Little Brother, what's on your mind? You seem a little different today."

"How can you tell?"

"I've got a natural gift for it."

"Guess."

"Probably you're a bit upset."

"Why just probably?"

"After all, I'm not an immortal spirit; I can only make out probabilities."

"All right. Since I'm face to face with a sage, I'll speak the truth," Hung T'ung-yeh said with complete candor. "First, I feel that the Kuomintang has correctly raised the slogans of 'Down with the warlords' and 'Down with imperialism', and they correspond exactly with the present political demands of the nation and the people. No one can shout slogans that are better, or have greater drawing power."

"You say that no one can shout better slogans." Now that he was truly studying the problem, Liu Shao-ch'iao seemed to have grown calm, and even cool. "What do you mean?"

Hung T'ung-yeh did not dare to answer.

"You can say it, it doesn't matter," Liu Shao-ch'iao smiled. "If you don't say it, it's the same thing if I say it for you. You mean the Communist Party."

"That's right." Since Liu Shao-ch'iao had caught his meaning at once, Hung T'ung-yeh no longer dissembled. "That's exactly what I meant."

"Just because a slogan is loud doesn't necessarily mean it's of any use. If you just shout "Down with imperialism!' in general, you will certainly stand alone, because the world's great powers are all imperialists. The Communist Party is an international organization, and the Soviet Union is a reliable friend forever. Your opinion is partly right. The Peiyang warlords, even if they were more vigorous than they are, are like a candle in the wind; they're in their last years, and even if nobody knocked them down, they'd destroy themselves. The

Kuomintang's situation is very different; they're moving with the tide of the demand for new thought since the May Fourth Movement, and if they use it properly, they can certainly stand."

Hung T'ung-yeh, seeing that Liu Shao-ch'iao had accepted his point of view, advanced a step, and asked:

"Then what position is the Communist Party going to take?"

Liu Shao-ch'iao thought deeply for a moment, looked all around, and then put a question in turn to Hung T'ung-yeh.

"What's the second thing on your mind?"

"You still haven't answered me."

"When you finish telling me, I'll give you a general answer."

"It's really nothing. I only feel that too much stirring up of the spirit of struggle, as far as the evil tendencies of mankind are concerned, may deepen the capitalist spirit of monopoly and selfishness."

"Struggle can strengthen one, and can suppress, and even destroy, one's enemy; it's indispensable."

As Liu Shao-ch'iao spoke, he suddenly grew a little impatient. He stood up, and stuck out his right hand. He asked:

"Look, what's this?"

"Are you talking about your hand?"

"Yes. But you'd better understand, this is the Buddha's hand."

"What do you mean?"

"Suppose that you're Sun Wu-k'ung in the *Journey to the West*, and you can never escape from this Buddha's hand of mine. You do too much careless thinking; it's most dangerous. Do you understand?"

"I understand."

"If you want to save yourself, the best way is to obey orders, and don't use your brain so much."

As they spoke, they started to walk back. Liu Shao-ch'iao, in a serious, quiet voice, said:

"At present the Party's method is to hinder the progress of the Northern Expedition, and to spoil the relations between the Kuomintang and the masses, and at the right moment to provoke a direct clash between them and the imperialists. On the positive side, the Party faces the task of establishing the armed strength of the worker and peasant masses, in the belief that sooner or later there will come a day when we can forge ahead of the Kuomintang."

Hung T'ung-yeh felt at once that there was some confusion here, but it was extraordinarily dim, and he couldn't grasp it clearly. He turned pale in the face, and felt short of breath.

Liu Shao-ch'iao glanced carelessly at him, and continued:

"I believe that I can control you; you cannot waver. Once you waver, you're done for. I talked about this with you in Shanghai."

Hung T'ung-yeh hastily said:

"Don't worry, I won't."

"That's fine."

As Liu Shao-ch'iao spoke, he turned, embraced Hung T'ung-yeh, and kissed him on the cheek. Hung T'ung-yeh struggled free, blushing, and said:

"What's this, on the street?"

Liu Shao-ch'iao laughed gleefully.

They had attracted several passersby, who stood around watching, not understanding what the two of them were up to. Hung T'ung-yeh, half-running, hurried ahead. Liu Shao-ch'iao called after him:

"Little Hung, slow down, why are you running so fast?"

Hung T'ung-yeh spent the night in Liu Shao-ch'iao's apartment. The two photographs of the naked, chained girl being whipped, and of the "dappled butterfly" Pai Ch'a-hua, hung on the wall. Beside them there was pasted a strip of paper, on which was written:

One origin, two poles
The world has its adjoining boundaries
History is connected
The mind of the proletariat is linked
Ice and charcoal are irreconcilable
North and south are two poles

"Is this a poem, or a notice?"

Smiling at Hung T'ung-yeh's question, Liu Shao-ch'iao answered:

"It's both; this is a notice-poem."

"How do you read it?"

"This contains my complete revolutionary philosophy. The first line explains that China and the Soviet Union are neighbors; China's proletarian revolution does not stand alone. The second line means that the European war influenced Russia's October Revolution, that the European war and the October Revolution influenced China's May Fourth Movement, and that the October Revolution and China's May Fourth Movement influenced the founding and growth of the Chinese Communist Party, and also influenced the reorganization of the Kuomintang in 1924 and the Northern Expedition that is about to begin. These all move to the same beat; they have reciprocal influence upon one another."

Liu Shao-ch'iao picked out an English "Pirate" brand cigarette with two sallow, stained fingers, and inhaled fiercely. His eyes flashed. In a tone of deep satisfaction, he said:

"But history is made by man; man creates history, and it is not history which determines man. The third line ought to be taken from this point of view. Look, isn't this a good poem?"

In the morning, they went out for a little breakfast. Hung T'ung-yeh wanted to try a few dishes at The Two Rivers, but Liu Shao-ch'iao took him to the Little Half-Fast again, and so he could only go along.

Ch'ien Pen-san was reckoned to come from the same district as Wu P'ei-fu. He had no few old friends among the Peiyang warlords, but he had never been acquainted with Wu P'ei-fu himself. Originally he had been a member of the Parliament. During the episode of Protecting the Constitution, when Dr. Sun Yat-sen convoked the Extraordinary Parliament at Canton, he went to Canton, and it was then that he became a member of the Kuomintang. He managed a daily newspaper in the north, and both overtly and covertly propagated the political position of Dr. Sun. Under the indiscriminate and reckless power of the Peiyang warlords, this was assuredly no easy matter.

He was not yet thirty years old when he was elected to the Parliament; he had attained his goal while still a youth. In Peking's official circles, it was difficult to avoid becoming more or less corrupted. His advantage lay in his ability to decide: in the space of a single thought, one can repent and find salvation. He recognized that the Peiyang warlords, with the way they went about things, certainly could not have a long life, while the Kuomintang was the only newly risen force which had a hope. He had read Yen Fu's translation of *Evolution* over and over, and by diligent study had learned the greater part of it by heart. He knew that the new was better than the old, and that the younger generation had a greater future than the old. He had gone on a tour of investigation through the Soviet Union during the famine period of the October Revolution, and while he recognized that the Soviet Union's experiment was "new" he did not believe that popular feeling in China would find that stage of famine acceptable. He was an advocate of mild revolution. Although one may come to power on horseback, one can never govern from horseback.

Now that he had been ordered to Hankow, his principal duty was to influence the northern army to respond to the Northern Expedition. His younger brother Ch'ien Pen-ssu was a graduate of the School of Law and Politics, and was a qualified lawyer, but he had always been a teacher, and had taught in both primary and middle schools. Ch'ien Pen-san, through his secret connections, had gotten him introduced into Wu P'ei-fu's Thief-punishing General Headquarters as a military judge with the rank of lieutenant-colonel. Then, using Ch'ien Pen-ssu's office, he had rented a building in the British Concession. Ostensibly it was Ch'ien Pen-ssu's office; covertly it was the site of Ch'ien Pen-san's secret organization. Ch'ien Pen-san's daughter Ch'ien Shou-yü was a student at Peking Women's College; she had already studied for three years and would soon graduate. Ch'ien Pen-san had urged her by letter and telegram to come to Hankow, to help him in carrying out the work of the temporary organization in the British Concession. On the gate of the organization's building there was pasted up a long white paper, on which was written in characters as big as fists: "Thief-punishing Headquarters, Office of Military Justice. Mr. Lo's Office." In the midst of them was a stamp of a large red seal.

Ch'ien Pen-san himself lived in the Hotel France in the French Concession. This was a hotel which a Frenchman had opened in order to attract Westerners; its furnishings were simple and its prices were high. Chinese could stay there too, but in that case the price of a room was doubled. The small room in which Ch'ien Pen-san lived cost sixty silver dollars, or about twenty American dollars, a day.

Ever since Ch'ien Pen-san had dedicated himself to the revolution, his life had been fairly difficult, and now to make such a large expenditure was painful, but for reasons of security it could not be avoided. Wu P'ei-fu used the term Thief-punishing, but to whom did the word "thief" refer? There was really no telling. Loosely interpreted, all those whom the emperor disliked were thieves, and thieves could be lawfully executed. Truly it was a case of the Licentiate meeting the soldier—although he has reason on his side, he cannot make himself understood. Ch'ien Pen-san, moreover, was a personage of some small reputation, and his caution was not without reason.

When Wu P'ei-fu, like East Mountain,[2] rose again, he assembled a good many miscellaneous units, numbering between three hundred and five hundred thousand men. Outwardly they were quite impressive, but in fact there weren't so many of them who were truly reliable. On this account, General Wu was extremely anxious as he disposed his troops. Since the front line had to resist the enemy, there must be reliable picked troops, and reliable picked troops were also needed to guard the rear. From where were so many reliable picked troops to come? General Wu had a Japanese military adviser who usually offered suggestions, and made various kinds of necessary calculations. But the General, only half paying attention, would sometimes laugh with a snort, and say:

"Japanese—what do they understand?"

Actually, he valued adviser Yen P'ing, but only as an ornament, and in fact the Japanese did not get to do any advising. However, every day he got together with those secretaries and counsellors who specialized in physiognomy and fortune-telling, and when they had time left after drinking wine and composing verse, they would use the *I Ching* to determine the disposition of troops and the battle plan.

When his eye fell upon the name of Liu Yu-ch'un, he was delighted, and he shook his head, saying:

---

[2] "East Mountain Rises Again" is a reference to the Chin Dynasty General Hsieh An, who, having withdrawn to a Buddhist monastery, later returned to active secular life. Wu P'ei-fu, in 1926, was re-emerging after a period of inactivity.

"This 'Liu Yu-ch'un' means that there is some 'spring' left over, and that the 'spring' won't be all used up. What an auspicious name!"[3]

Recalling that the man was a division commander, he summoned him at once and gave him the responsibility for holding Wu-ch'ang. Among Liu Yu-ch'un's subordinates there were two regimental commanders who had secret connections with Ch'ien Pen-san.

Such were the ways of General Wu.

Hung T'ung-yeh saw his little sister Chin-ling in Ch'ien's office, and through Chin-ling he was introduced to Ch'ien Shou-yü. Ch'ien Shou-yü had a slender figure, but her legs were plump, and she swayed from side to side when she walked. She treated Hung Chin-ling like a little sister, and was always praising her to Hung T'ung-yeh, and saying that she had so many good points.

"She's so clever, you ought to let her go to school."

Hung T'ung-yeh looked at his little sister, and smiled, but said nothing. Hung Chin-ling said:

"Sister Ch'ien has been teaching me to read *Collected Foreign Stories* these days."

"What stories?" Hung T'ung-yeh asked.

"Foreign stories, translated into the literary language. It's not easy to understand," Hung Chin-ling said.

"Since you don't understand it, why not read it in the colloquial?"

"That's the reason I want to teach her to read them. There are many things in the literary language; if one can't read the literary language then there aren't many books one can read."

"Aren't we advocating the colloquial language?"

---

[3] General Wu is analyzing the name of a subordinate officer, Liu Yu-ch'un. By changing Liu and Yu for two other characters which sound the same, the meaning is changed to "remaining" or "left over" "spring". Spring is considered auspicious.

"That applies to the present and future. All the books of the past are in the literary language."

"Things of the past are old, we needn't read them."

When she heard Hung T'ung-yeh say this, there was a great deal that Ch'ien Shou-yü wanted to say to him in argument, but she reflected that it wouldn't look well to squabble with him on their first meeting. So she said:

"This is a big question, and can't be cleared up in a moment. You two sit down. I still have some work in the back, I'm going."

With a nod, she went swaying off.

Hung Chin-ling lowered her voice, and asked her brother:

"When you left Shanghai, did you go to see Mama?"

"I didn't."

"Why?"

"I felt there was no need."

"I keep thinking that when I left," Hung Chin-ling said sadly, "she wasn't in very good health, and there wasn't anything to eat or to use in the house. I don't know how she's getting along these days. Acting as though we hadn't the slightest responsibility towards her—we've really wronged her!"

"That's your old-fashioned thinking."

"New thinking doesn't have any use for Mama?"

"You can't say it doesn't have any use for her. But a person always has to labor. She can be a temporary worker, and earn her living."

"She's old, she can't work."

"Then there's no way she can live," Hung T'ung-yeh shook his head, and smiled bitterly. "In the future, when the revolution has been achieved, the nation will have old folks' homes. The present is a period of change, when last year's harvest doesn't last until this year's, and naturally it can't be avoided that there are many small tragedies."

"Do you call this a small tragedy?"

"Yes, just now we have even more proletarians who are suffering hardships."

"When we can't even look after our own mother, how are we up to finding ways for the affairs of so many other people?"

As Hung Chin-ling spoke, her tears came rushing down. She hid her face with both hands, hiccoughing uncontrollably.

After a time, she felt someone patting her shoulder, and someone said:

"What's this? Sister Hung, don't feel bad."

She opened her eyes, and saw that it was Ch'ien Shou-yü. She asked:

"My brother?"

"I came out and didn't see him; probably he left."

Hung Chin-ling wiped her tears with a handkerchief, and heaved a long sigh. She felt infinitely wronged. Ch'ien Shou-yü would have gone to fetch her a hot towel, but Chin-ling held her back. So Ch'ien Shou-yü stood beside her, twisting her two glistening braids of black hair, and asked in a familiar manner:

"Why were you crying?"

Hung Chin-ling stood up and clasped Ch'ien Shou-yü with both hands. She raised her face and gazed at the other for a moment, as though she wanted to speak but could not. Ch'ien Shou-yü said:

"If there's something, just tell me. Perhaps I can share your sorrow."

"Sister," Hung Chin-ling said, blushing, "when I left Shanghai, I didn't tell my mother goodbye. I was deceived by my brother, and once I was stirred up, I acted recklessly, and ever since I've regretted it."

"That's not so bad."

Ch'ien Shou-yü made her sit down, poured a cup of hot red tea from the thermos bottle, added a little sugar, and gave it to her. Hung Chin-ling thanked her, took it, and drank.

"Now you must hurry and write your mother, explain what happened, and beg her to forgive you. There's still time."

"You don't know. Mother was sick in bed, alone, with no relatives and no friends, and there wasn't a copper in the house, nor a grain of rice! I'm really afraid that she may be dead by now."

As Hung Chin-ling spoke, she again wiped painfully at her tears.

When Ch'ien Shou-yü heard this, she stood up. She said:

"Well, we mustn't delay. We'll go and send some money by telegram. When we come back, you can carefully write a letter."

She went inside to get her purse, and came out.

"I've money here. Come on, come on!"

She pulled Hung Chin-ling out onto the street.

In a little while, they came back. Hung Chin-ling thanked her again and again.

"Sister, I've learned something—there really are good people like you in the world. I've lived almost twenty years, and all the people around us were bad people, starting with our uncle, the Bureau Chief. Because of that I thought that all people were bad, but today I know that isn't so."

As she spoke, two shiny tears appeared again. Ch'ien Shou-yü smiled, and asked:

"Do you like to cry?"

"I never used to," Hung Chin-ling said, very embarrassed. "But since I carelessly wronged Mama, I don't know where all these fresh tears are coming from."

As she said this she burst out laughing.

"Every family has its painful memories," Ch'ien Shou-yü sighed. "Your mother makes me think of my mother. My mother had a different kind of pain."

"Where is she now?"

"At the old home in the country. Father gave her twenty *mou*, and let her support herself. He severed relations with her, and they're husband and wife in name only. Father forbade me to have anything to do with her. Already it's been more than ten years."

As Ch'ien Shou-yü said this, she shook her head. Hung Chin-ling couldn't help asking:

"Why is he so serious about it?"

"He blames Mother. Country folk don't recognize a single character, and besides they're reckless by nature. Such people are more dangerous, they'll do anything!"

"What did she do?"

"It wasn't anything." Ch'ien Shou-yü spoke quietly and tonelessly, as though she were speaking to herself. "Father killed a cook, and almost got taken to court."

"Oh." Hung Chin-ling didn't really understand, and said nothing.

"At that time, Father used a little servant, someone pretty much like your brother. Father liked him, and paid no attention to Mama," Ch'ien Shou-yü muttered, as though dreaming. "So you can't blame Mama alone."

Hung Chin-ling, mystified, stared at her. Ch'ien Shou-yü suddenly seemed to awaken from a dream, and at once seized Hung Chin-ling's hand, and said in a sorrowful voice:

"Always love your Mama, never forget her!"

As she spoke, her tears flowed down.

Chapter VII

At the Hotel France, Hung T'ung-yeh saw Ch'ien Pen-san.

The ochre curtains were drawn, and although the sun was bright outside, within the room it was so dim as to call for the light of the electric lamp. Ch'ien Pen-san wore an iron-gray satin-collared robe, and sat in a deep, low easy chair covered in white cotton, sucking at a large cigar. He constantly and habitually removed, replaced, and then removed again a pair of large, thick, dark glasses with tortoise-shell frames, which he wore during all seasons of the year, early and late; this was done with his left hand. His right hand was busy with the cigar. His two hands were incessantly busy, causing those seated beside him unavoidable vexations and difficulties, while he himself was quite at ease. He was usually optimistic, but at any moment he might snort like a captive general in a Peking opera grieving for his parents; it was said that he imitated T'an Hsin-p'ei.[4] He could get angry easily; at times he would fly into a thundering rage, and abuse people with the most unpleasant colloquialisms: your mother's this, your mother's that. Then he would turn about, and again be quite calm, forgetting that he had just been in a rage.

His most recent trip to Canton had been one of the most gratifying occasions in his life. But his happiness had not been complete, and had left him with a little regret. When he was taking part in an important meeting, there had been a talkative old woman who had something to say on every question—she spoke in Cantonese-accented Mandarin, and Ch'ien Pen-san couldn't understand even half a sentence of it. Seeing that she chattered incessantly, he became annoyed. He turned to his neighbor, a party elder, and softly asked:

"Who is that old lady?"

"Madame Chung."

"Chung the martyr's widow?"

"Yes."

Ch'ien Pen-san inadvertently started to rise out of respect. He greatly revered the martyr Chung, and he knew that the man's widow was a heroine among women. He thought, no wonder everyone respects her, and is always praising her.

After the meeting broke up, Ch'ien Pen-san thought to pay his respects to Madame Chung. He approached her, all smiles, reverently murmured "Madame" and extended his hand. Madame Chung glanced coldly at him, but did not speak. She turned her head, and went off to another corner of the room to speak to the big-nose adviser Borodin.

Ch'ien Pen-san was embarrassed and annoyed, and he thought bitterly:

"So this old lady doesn't recognize her supporters."

Because he hated the widow Chung, he transferred a nameless anger to Borodin, and from hating Borodin, he hated the Communist Party. He subjectively, or what was worse, intuitively, felt that the Communist Party in China was certainly laboring in vain, and that their ideals were no more than illusory. Originally he had felt that the Communist Party could be utilized, and this had slowly become the belief that the Communist Party could be played with. But there was a great difference between utilizing them and playing with them.

---

[4] T'an Hsin-p'ei: a Peking opera actor, much admired by the Dowager Empress.

His younger brother Ch'ien Pen-ssu was of a different opinion, and they had often wrangled about it, sometimes arguing until they were flushed and hoarse. Ch'ien Pen-ssu placed special emphasis upon the international character of the Communist Party: when they shouted "World Revolution!" they weren't just shouting for the fun of it, nor were they trying to intimidate people. Rather, it was an honest sign; that was their ultimate goal. In the process their strategies might change, but the goal was fixed. The saying, "The workers have no fatherland" had its own internationalist meaning, and it was not necessarily to say that the workers' fatherland was the Soviet Union.

Ch'ien Pen-ssu would often say:

"The Communist Party's method is to destroy all that is old, while they fire up the crucible for a new beginning. They've got a new blueprint, but it's not certain that it's a reasonable model which can actually be realized. They have the advantage of class and organization, and they don't have freedom of the individual."

Because of this, his conclusion was:

"If we want to defend the tradition of the nation and the people, if we want to protect the freedom of the individual, then we certainly cannot allow the Communist Party to exist. Exterminate them, and never mind being polite!"

Shaking his head, he said to his third brother:

"Do you think you can play with them? Be careful, don't let them play with you."

"The Communist Party doesn't suit human nature, and doesn't agree with our national spirit," Ch'ien Pen-san laughed, and said in a tone of utter unconcern. "If they could succeed, then Huang Ch'ao, Li Ch'uang, and Chang Hsien-chung[5]

---

[5] Huang Ch'ao, Li Ch'uang, and Chang Hsien-chung: notoriously destructive rebels in Chinese history.

and those historical figures would have gained power long ago, so how could they succeed today?"

"If you take them too lightly, and don't guard against them, then you're giving them an opportunity."

"Old Fourth, I'll make a bet with you!" Ch'ien Pen-san pulled off his dark glasses and put them on the tea table. He waved his cigar and said: "If the Communist Party can rise after all, you can cut off this head of mine!"

So saying, he laughed loudly. He thought, how is it this Old Fourth is so mixed up?

"According to this attitude of yours, the Communist Party can certainly rise."

Ch'ien Pen-ssu glared impatiently at his brother; he was ready to leave in his anger. Then someone knocked at the door. Hung T'ung-yeh had arrived. Most recently he had been paying especial attention to Third Brother's visitors, and this one was a stranger, whom he had never seen before. So he sat down again. Ch'ien Pen-san asked Hung T'ung-yeh about his situation, and introduced him to Ch'ien Pen-ssu.

"Kuo Hsin-ju has also gone to Canton. Have you written him?"

"When I left Shanghai, I'd already written to him in Peking, telling him that I was going to Hankow with Mr. Ch'ien. But I don't know if he got my letter."

"We talked about you in Canton. He had a very good impression of you," Ch'ien Pen-san went on, asking: "Where are you living?"

"I haven't any place. Last night I stayed temporarily at Liu Shao-ch'iao's for the night."

"I've a place for you to stay," Ch'ien Pen-san indicated Ch'ien Pen-ssu, saying, "In his office. Your sister is staying there too."

"Just now I was by Fourth Master's, and I saw my sister and Young Miss."

"I'll call someone to fix the place up for you," Ch'ien Pen-ssu said, welcoming Hung T'ung-yeh. "You come right over."

Ch'ien Pen-san put on his dark glasses and scratched a match to relight his cigar. He smiled, and said:

"A few days ago Liu Shao-ch'iao came by here, and we got along fine. After all, he's like you in temperament: straightforward! He agreed to help in everything from now on, and wanted me to look out for him.—What news from his place?"

As Ch'ien Pen-san spoke, he realized that Hung T'ung-yeh had been standing since he had come in, and he told him to sit down on the round, cushioned stool beside the table. Ch'ien Pen-san offered him a cigarette. Hung T'ung-yeh shifted on his seat, thanked him, and refused. He meant to act older than his years in front of them.

"Last night, he said that the Communist Party didn't approve of a Northern Expedition at this time," Hung T'ung-yeh said cautiously.

"I learned that in Canton." Ch'ien Pen-san looked at Ch'ien Pen-ssu, and took off his dark glasses. "Do you know why?"

"I don't know. There must certainly be a plot."

"Not necessarily a plot. The Communist Party feels that their own strength is still insufficient, and if the Kuomintang carries out the Northern Expedition at this time, they'll be building a foundation for themselves, and the Communists won't have any part in it. So they advocate delaying the Northern Expedition for as long as possible, until they've had time to grow their own feathers. Then they may be able to divide the honors equally with the Kuomintang."

As Ch'ien Pen-san said this, he smiled.

"What a joke! Look, what a naive way of thinking. Could the Kuomintang be so foolish?"

"Kwangtung probably cannot become a problem." Hung T'ung-yeh kept his face impassive, and spoke in a serious tone. "Liu Shao-ch'iao said the Communist Party had seven hundred thousand peasants in the East River region—a good foundation!"

When Ch'ien Pen-san heard this, he laughed loudly.

"Seven hundred thousand peasants! Who gave them to them?"

"Naturally they organized them themselves."

"You believe his fantasy! Peasants are deeply localistic and conservative, would they be willing to sell their lives so that the Communist Party could conquer the empire? That's too strange!"

"Since that's what he said," Ch'ien Pen-ssu was provoked by the obstinate way in which his brother took it so lightly, "perhaps there's something to it. If it turns out to be right, then what?"

"The Communist Party is expert at boasting. The Kuomintang has existed for quite a few years, and I dare say they don't have any seven hundred thousand organized peasants."

Ch'ien Pen-ssu stood up, took his woolen cap from behind the door, and said:

"I've something to do, I'm going. The two of us could talk forever and never agree."

This military judge with the rank of a lieutenant colonel in the Thief-punishing Headquarters always wore a blue cotton gown, and his bald head was shaven and shiny. Ch'ien Pen-san removed his dark glasses, watched him leave, and glanced wolfishly after him. Then he said to Hung T'ung-yeh:

"This Fourth Brother of mine isn't a modern-minded person. When you're staying with him, you'd better take care. He hates the Communist Party."

"That doesn't matter," Hung T'ung-yeh smiled, "since I'm not a Communist."

Ch'ien Pen-san hummed to himself a moment, and said lightly:

"A pity the rent here is too expensive. Otherwise, you could get a room and stay here with me. It would be most convenient."

Hung T'ung-yeh did not know how to respond politely to this, so he said nothing. Ch'ien Pen-san added:

"There's no reason you can't go to Liu Shao-ch'iao's often, and see what they're up to."

Hung T'ung-yeh agreed, and stood up.

Ch'ien Pen-ssu wrung his hands as he left the Hotel France, for he was unusually frustrated. He was developing deep doubts of Third Brother's attitude of taking the Communist Party lightly. In some mysterious manner he intuitively felt that while neither the Peiyang warlords, nor even the imperialists, were truly unconquerable, the Communist Party was most to be feared. The stupid warlords saw every newly-risen thing as Communist, and recklessly killed, suppressed, and blocked off such things. They sternly spoke of protecting the traditional culture, but in fact they were merely destroying what differed from themselves. The result was that they drove away in terror many people of good will, and thus helped the Communist Party to expand. He thought:

"But the kind of viewpoint represented by Third Brother is no different from opening the door and bowing the robber inside. It's giving him the opportunity to grow freely. That's even more frightening."

Ch'ien Pen-ssu could not think of the best way to suppress the Communist Party. He only felt that matters were not right, and this aroused his disquiet. He crossed the road, and sat for a while on a stone bench on the river bank, gazing at the river scene. Loftily in the distance rose the celebrated Yellow Crane Tower. He had once ascended it. Ten years and more ago, Wuchang had fired the first shots of the Chinese people's new life, and had raised the flag of righteousness. Unfortunately, it had been a disturbed and disorderly scene ever since. Foreign ships and foreign flags were to be seen on the river. The Communist Party's sprouts and seedlings were springing up in dark places, in corners people neglected. There was still a leftover chill in the late spring weather, and Ch'ien Pen-ssu shivered. He felt that he could sit there no longer, and he got up and left.

He went on foot to the Office of Military Justice of the Thief-punishing Headquarters. Although he wore civilian clothes, the sentries all recognized him. When they came to attention, he was startled, and aroused from his deep thought. His right hand touched his cap-brim as he returned the salute. He went straight into the office, and sat down in his place. There were several official papers on his desk; he looked at them without interest and shoved them into a drawer. Then he spread out a sheet of paper, dipped his brush in the ink, and wrote a report to his superior officer, the chief of the Office of Military Justice. The gist of it was:

"It is rumored that a secret organization of Red bandits has been established at No. 108 Ssu-fen-li, and that the ringleader is one Liu Shao-ch'iao. It is requested that someone be sent to search and seize."

After he had signed it and stamped it with his seal, he folded it and went to find the chief of the office. When he arrived outside the chief's office, he was about to cry out "Report!" when he suddenly hesitated, and stopped himself. He retreated a couple of paces, thinking what if by some chance Liu Shao-ch'iao implicated Third Brother and the Kuomintang organization? What if even he himself were implicated? He muttered to himself:

"How stupid!"

An orderly lifted the chief's door-curtain aside, and the chief came out to see off a caller. He saw Ch'ien Pen-ssu standing there dumbly, and casually asked:

"Do you want something?"

"Nothing," Ch'ien Pen-ssu lied. "Tomorrow I have a little private business, and I wanted to ask a day's leave."

"Fine, I know. Come in, I have something for you."

Ch'ien Pen-ssu went in. There was a pile of red cards on the chief's desk. He selected one and handed it to Ch'ien Pen-ssu, saying:

"The President of the Chamber of Commerce has invited us to dinner tomorrow night; you find time to go."

Ch'ien Pen-ssu agreed.

"Everybody has discussed it, and we think we'll invite some actors down from Peking to give a performance for the general's birthday next month. Everybody can have a good time. The general's been upset lately because of all this shouting down in Kwangtung about some sort of Northern Expedition. It's not convenient for us to suggest it; those on the scene should be seen to be handling it. It was Chief Secretary Chao who let me know. Don't forget, you come too."

Ch'ien Pen-ssu took the card, and withdrew. He struck a match, and burned the report he had just written. He thought:

"How rash! I've got to take care I don't implicate myself."

He returned to his own office, feeling melancholy. He rubbed his lower lip. He hadn't shaved for a week, and the beard pricked his hand. He went out onto the street to get a shave. When he came back, someone was sitting quietly in the reception room, and he didn't know quite how to get rid of her. Suddenly he saw that it was Hung Chin-ling who had come back from outside, and he asked:

"Where did you go?"

"I went to the Post Office to send an express letter."

"To whom?"

"My Mama."

"In Shanghai?"

"Yes."

Ch'ien Pen-ssu was moved, and he smiled and said:

"Sit down and let's talk a bit, all right?"

"All right." Hung Chin-ling said and sat down, very naturally.

Ch'ien Pen-san asked casually about her family situation, and slowly got around to asking:

"Has your brother moved in?"

"He said he was coming over later."

"Do you know Liu Shao-ch'iao?"

"I've seen him a few times."

"Do you know he's in the C. P.?"

"I know, I've heard brother say so."

"Is your brother in it?"

The question put Hung Chin-ling at a loss. She blushed, thought a moment, and then said:

"I don't know. Probably he isn't. He belongs to the Kuomintang; Third Master and Kuo Hsin-ju brought him in."

"There are lots of people who straddle the parties, with their feet in two boats at once."

Ch'ien Shou-yü came in from the back room, heard them, and asked:

"Fourth Uncle, you said straddling the parties, but why do you only see the Communist Party is straddling the Kuomintang? Aren't there any Kuomintang members who straddle the Communist Party?"

"People don't call that straddling!" Ch'ien Pen-ssu said, laughing at himself.

"Isn't that clearly asking for trouble?"

"Who says it isn't?"

"In the future there are bound to be disturbances."

"There's nothing to be done. Wait and see. When the ship reaches the bridge, it naturally straightens out."

"Just so it isn't a case of it being 'too late to fix the leaks when the ship's in the middle of the stream'."

When she heard Ch'ien Shou-yü say this, Hung Chin-ling thought of her brother's attitude toward their mother, and her heart gave a little shiver. She looked at Ch'ien Shou-yü, and she looked at Ch'ien Pen-ssu, and blushing, she hung her head.

Ch'ien Pen-ssu glanced at the mannish leather shoes which Hung Chin-ling wore, and he felt a little inexpressible discomfort. He asked Ch'ien Shou-yü:

"Did Miss Hung bring baggage with her to Hankow?"

Not waiting for Ch'ien Shou-yü to respond, Hung Chin-ling herself spoke first:

"I deceived my mother, and stole away empty-handed."

Ch'ien Pen-ssu heard this and smiled, saying:

"It isn't nice to hear about a young lady stealing away from home."

Hung Chin-ling blushed, laughing, and shifted uneasily. Ch'ien Shou-yü said:

"She did it for the revolution. She almost sacrificed her mother for the revolution."

"You ought to take her to have some clothes made, and buy some shoes and stockings."

When Ch'ien Shou-yü heard this, she pursed her lips, and, smiling sweetly, thrust her open right hand before Ch'ien Pen-ssu's face.

"Money? Haven't you got any money?" Ch'ien Pen-ssu asked.

"My money is rather scarce. I want Fourth Uncle's money."

Ch'ien Pen-ssu looked at Hung Chin-ling, and putting his hand into his gown, he brought out a wallet, and handed it to Ch'ien Shou-yü, saying"

"Use as much as you think you need, and don't say Fourth Uncle is stingy."

Ch'ien Shou-yü opened the wallet and looked. On one side was his official calling card, and the other side contained his unofficial calling cards. There were calling cards and calling cards but not a bit of money inside. Ch'ien Shou-yü threw it back at him, and said:

"Cheater! And you still say you aren't stingy!"

Ch'ien Pen-ssu couldn't keep from laughing. He looked at his watch; it was time to eat lunch. He asked:

"What is there to eat today?"

"For that you'll have to ask the cook," Ch'ien Shou-yü said.

"Never mind, it's greens and bean-curd, nothing good comes whether you ask or don't ask." Ch'ien Pen-ssu turned earnest and said: "Let's go. I'm inviting the two of you out to eat, and after lunch we'll go buy something for Miss Hung, and put it all to my account. All right?"

"As long as you're paying, why not?"

Hung Chin-ling took Ch'ien Shou-yü by the hand and said:

"Sister, how can we let Fourth Master pay? It's embarrassing!"

"Never mind him, just go on. Fourth Uncle is a miserly devil with money. It's rare that he asks anyone out, so don't be ungrateful for his good intentions."

"All right, you little slave, abusing your uncle to his face!"

They all laughed, and Ch'ien Shou-yü and Hung Chin-ling went upstairs.

Ch'ien Pen-ssu, as he watched their backs, and heard the stairs creak, felt a sort of sweet happiness.

That evening Hung T'ung-yeh came with his luggage. There was a small room behind the ground floor reception room, which had already been set in order for him. He asked Ch'ien Pen-ssu to give him something to do. Ch'ien Pen-ssu said:

"Tomorrow morning ask Third Master and he can tell you. He lives in seclusion in the Hotel France and rarely comes out, so he needs someone to be his connection with the outside. Besides, you speak French, so it's convenient for you to come and go in such a place. Perhaps he'll ask you to be his 'communications'."

"Oh." Hung T'ung-yeh didn't say anything else.

Ch'ien Pen-ssu inspected him closely. Except that he was slightly taller, he was almost the image of his little sister Chin-ling. A pair of large, clear eyes, a straight nose that was perhaps slightly too small, and two thin lips. All in all, what came to mind were the two words 'graceful' and 'elegant', and although the impression given was not one of weakness, neither did his various features augur fortune or longevity. Ch'ien Pen-ssu had not been in the Thief-punishing Headquarters for long, but he had already studied physiognomy a little. This was because the entire Headquarters, from Chief Secretary Chang on down, thought a great deal of the art. Most recently, Chief Secretary Chang, not grudging the heavy expense, had invited the famous physiognomist of Shanghai, "Old Muddlehead", to come to Hankow in order to carefully examine the honorable face of General Wu. Not only had he examined his features, but he had also inspected his color before dawn. Old Muddlehead's conclusion was:

"The General has a great future! If the Southern Army doesn't come, there's an end to it, but if it really does come, and meets the General, it will definitely be completely routed, completely defeated."

Chief Secretary Chang and Chairman T'an of the Kwangtung Revolutionary Government had obtained their metropolitan degrees in the same examination, and they were still on good terms with each other. Chief Secretary Chang greatly valued human feelings, and could not bear to see his old friend lost, and the good destroyed with the bad. He especially wrote a letter to Chairman T'an, urging him to draw back while there was yet time, and to think of a way to call off the Northern Expedition, because the mandate of heaven was with Wu, and only Wu could succeed.

Naturally there could be no reply to such a letter. From the standpoint of friendship, he had only done the best he could. But from that time on, an optimistic atmosphere prevailed throughout the Headquarters. Even the sentries all felt that times had changed, and the increase in their morale was obvious. At once, all the subordinate officers competed to pay their respects to Old Muddlehead as their master, and the study of physiognomy became fashionable.

In such an environment, Ch'ien Pen-ssu could not avoid being influenced; he observed, and inadvertently he picked up a bit of it. Now, as he observed Hung T'ung-yeh, he was led to think of Hung Chin-ling, and a feeling of pity welled up strongly. He led the other into the reception room, sat down, and began to talk casually.

"You can relax here, your sister has already arranged things."

"What things?" Hung T'ung-yeh didn't understand.

"Didn't you know? Your sister has already sent word to Shanghai."

"Oh!"

"Besides, today we bought all the things your sister needed."

"Oh."

Ch'ien Pen-ssu, seeing that he seemed indifferent, supposed that he was tired, and said:

"It's late. You rest, we'll talk again tomorrow."

The next morning, Hung T'ung-yeh sent the serving girl up to ask Hung Chin-ling to come downstairs.

"Come on, we'll go out for breakfast."

"They've prepared some here, why go out?"

"It's a good chance to say what I have to say."

"There are many rooms here; isn't there any place to talk here?"

Hung T'ung-yeh saw that she was refusing, and was greatly displeased. His face fell, and he said:

"I really want you to go out!"

Hung Chin-ling saw that he was getting angry, and feared that an argument would be embarrassing, so she said:

"Well, wait while I go upstairs and change clothes, and I'll come."

The two of them walked single file to the street. Hung T'ung-yeh had already noticed that Chin-ling wore new silk stockings and a pair of ochre-colored, semi-high-heeled, sharp-toed leather shoes, decorated with a knot in the shape of a butterfly. He laughed softly, and said:

"What a pretty pair of shoes!"

Hung Chin-ling, hearing him use this tone of voice, turned away and did not answer, but only walked along with him. The day was overcast, but the French plane trees along both sides of the road were already putting forth new leaves. Spring had arrived. They turned toward the river, and a gust of wind blew into their faces. Hung Chin-ling shivered, and quickly pulled up the woolen wrap she had thrown over her left shoulder. Hung T'ung-yeh glanced obliquely at her; her wrap, too, was so brand new that it hurt to look at it.

On the narrow grassy strip along the riverbank, too, the new green was showing itself amid the withered yellow. Hung T'ung-yeh chose a long bench, and the two of them sat down. The river wind carried the spring chill, and Hung Chin-ling grew a little angry.

"Not to enjoy good days, but to prefer looking for trouble—how bitter!"

"From now on, there'll be a lot of trouble," Hung T'ung-yeh said coldly. "I hear you sent money to Shanghai."

"That's right."

"Where did you get it?"

"Ch'ien Shou-yü gave it to me."

"Why should she want to give you money?"

"Wasn't it because she took pity on Mother? She's a good-hearted person."

"You bought shoes and clothes, where'd you get the money?"

"Fourth Master's."

"Why should he want to spend money to buy things for you?"

"I think, it's just that he sympathized with someone who had no resources."

Hung T'ung-yeh looked at her, and said viciously:

"Who would have thought that you'd change so quickly? What good-heartedness? That's just their scheme—don't you understand?"

"I don't understand."

These words infuriated Hung T'ung-yeh. He looked all around, and seeing no one, he pinched Hung Chin-ling cruelly on the leg, pinching her so hard that she couldn't stand it, and cried out "*Ai-ya!*"

"If you dare make a sound, I'll push you into the river!"

Hung Chin-ling was so angry that she turned her head away and just wept.

"Before," she said in a hurt tone, "we used to be one family, and although we were poor, we were close, three people with one heart, with no enmity, and no hatred. How good it was! But since we got to know Liu Shao-ch'iao, you say I've changed, but it's you who've changed! And the first way you've changed is that you don't want Mother!"

"How can you say I don't want Mother? I'm opening a way for the mothers of the whole world!"

"Don't talk nonsense! When you don't care if your own mother lives or dies, how can you be concerned with other men's mothers?" Hung Chin-ling, rushing ahead, had stopped crying. "You see people dying right in front of you and you don't save them, but you say you're going to save people eighteen thousand *li* away, you say you're going to save people three thousand years from now. What kind of a heart do you have? Are you human?"

Hung Chin-ling's courage was multiplied a hundredfold; she stamped her foot and strode away. Hung T'ung-yeh was angry too; he chased after her, saying:

"Be careful, I told you how Liu Shao-ch'iao dealt with me each time!"

"If you're going to beat or kill, I'll follow your example; I'm not a weakling like you!"

She struggled to break away, but Hung T'ung-yeh was unwilling to release her. Placed between Liu Shao-ch'iao and the Ch'iens, Hung Chin-ling as a piece in the game could not be called unimportant; let her show but the slightest fault and it would lead to a complete defeat, in which he too would fall. Hitherto he had only known the ease with which Liu Shao-ch'iao had dealt with Hung T'ung-yeh, and he had never expected that it would be an entirely different affair when Hung T'ung-yeh dealt with Hung Chin-ling. This slave-girl wouldn't be manipulated! He had long ago been disciplined, and he had learned self-restraint; he knew how to steer his boat according to the wind. Seeing that things weren't going well, he became more flexible.

"Sister, just now I was in the wrong. Don't be angry."

Thus, with much sweet talk, he got Hung Chin-ling calmed down. The two of them went back together, and looked for a place to eat breakfast. He begged his sister:

"Don't let the Ch'iens know what happened today. They'd laugh."

Hung Chin-ling smiled and hid her mouth behind a handkerchief, saying;

"Do you think I'm a fool, who doesn't know what it is to lose face?"

As they passed in front of the Hotel France, Hung T'ung-yeh pointed to it and said:

"Third Master Ch'ien lives there."

"The first day in Hankow, I went in there."

Hung T'ung-yeh deliberately took her along the road, and pointed out to her the Liu family's dry goods shop. He said:

"Liu Shao-ch'iao is only waiting until the divorce is arranged, and that woman leaves, and then he can visit the shop. Just look at those people—even though their factory had to close, the disaster wasn't total, and they still have such a big business."

Hung Chin-ling glanced at the doors, and sighed.

"Liu Shao-ch'iao's wife is really to be pitied! With all the men in the world, she had to meet a devil!"

Hung T'ung-yeh glanced at her sidewise, but Hung Chin-ling pretended not to see.

They passed a number of restaurants, but Hung T'ung-yeh did not go into any of them. Hung Chin-ling had walked a long way in her new shoes; she was tired through, and very hungry. The sun had not shown its face, but she saw from clocks hanging in the shops that it was already ten o'clock. She stopped, let out her breath, and said:

"If we're not going to eat, I'm going back."

"Wait a bit more, and we'll eat lunch."

Hung Chin-ling ignored him and turned to leave. But looking about she saw that this area was unfamiliar, and she didn't know the way back to Ch'ien's office. She beckoned to a rickshaw. Hung T'ung-yeh came up behind her, and said anxiously:

"All right, all right, we'll go and eat now."

He told the rickshaw man to carry them to the Two Rivers Cantonese restaurant in front of Ssu-fen-li. As soon as Hung Chin-ling heard Ssu-fen-li, she made a spitting sound and went off. Hung T'ung-yeh, so angry that his teeth itched, chased after her saying:

"Why are you always in such a bad temper? I said you'd changed, and you wouldn't admit it. Were you like this before?"

"Blame yourself!" Hung Chin-ling said as she walked, looking straight ahead. "If you changed and I didn't change, how could I deal with you?"

Hung T'ung-yeh seized her from behind by her pigtail, and said:

"Stand still!"

The two rickshaw men were still trailing after these two prospects, and there were quite a few passersby on the street. Hung Chin-ling blushed, and stamped her foot, saying:

"What kind of way is this to act?"

Hung T'ung-yeh, all smiles, persisted:

"It's just that I'm starved, and I want to eat some Kwangtung fried noodles. Come on with me."

"I'm not going to Ssu-fen-li!"

"Who's asking you to go to Ssu-fen-li? That restaurant is in front of Ssu-fen-li; I'll explain it clearly to the rickshaw man."

"All right, then I'll go with you."

Brother and sister rode in a rickshaw to the Two Rivers. On the way, Hung Chin-ling was secretly concerned for herself: "After we've eaten, I'm going. If he won't let me go, then I can scream, and go anyway. Whatever happens I mustn't go to Liu Shao-ch'iao's place; if I go there, I'll be in for a bad time. At least I'd be beaten, and maybe they'd . . ."

When Hung Chin-ling thought to this point, she almost blushed, and dared not think any further. She turned to regard Hung T'ung-yeh, with a little fear, and a little feeling of hurt. She knew that a wall had already arisen between brother and sister, and there was no way to communicate.

When they arrived at the Two Rivers, Hung T'ung-yeh meant for them to sit in a private room. But Hung Chin-ling was definitely unwilling, and they sat down by the window, near the cashier's desk. She thought, I can avoid a lot of trouble by sitting here.

Hung T'ung-yeh took the thin paper menu, wrote an invitation on it, and sent someone to deliver it.

"It's close by," Hung T'ung-yeh said as he gave it to the waiter. "No. 108 Ssu-fen-li, the last house, upstairs over the tailor shop."

Hung Chin-ling knew she could not prevent this, so she allowed it. She thought, if only I'm determined, and don't set foot in his place, he won't be able to do anything to me on the street.

Liu Shao-ch'iao arrived at once. He seemed to have just come from the barbershop, for his face was clean-shaven, and his head gleamed with oil. The mingled scents of an inferior face-powder and of hair-oil wafted out, and Hung Chin-ling felt that it was irritating; she pressed a handkerchief to her nose. Strangely, she thought that Ch'ien Pen-ssu had also been to the barber the day before, but she hadn't felt that he had any particular smell. Probably he did not use hair-oil, nor powder. She thought and thought about it, but she couldn't remember; at the time she hadn't paid any attention.

As soon as Liu Shao-ch'iao saw Hung Chin-ling, he came forth with a babble of commonplace remarks. He added:

"Why don't we go into one of the upstairs rooms to sit down?"

"My little sister likes it here; it's easy to watch the street," said Hung T'ung-yeh, making an excuse.

"All right, that's fine," Liu Shao-ch'iao nodded helplessly.

With much urging and yielding, they decided on their orders. Liu Shao-ch'iao out of habit ran his fingers through his hair, forgetting it had just been oiled, and so the styling of his hair was ruined. He stuck out an oily hand, gave a loud laugh, and said in self-ridicule:

"Frankly, this is the first time in my life I've had my hair oiled. I'm really not used to it! It's an urban amusement, it's completely—"

What he had meant to say was; "It's completely a pastime of the idle bourgeois wastrels, and fundamentally the opposite of the proletariat's life of blood and sweat—we don't want it!" But he caught himself, feeling that such talk wasn't appropriate in such a public place. Instead, he said:

"It's an urban amusement, it's completely meaningless."

He stood up and went off to wash his hands. Hung Chin-ling said softly to Hung T'ung-yeh:

"Look at your superior, your good friend!"

"He's completely sincere towards you." Hung T'ung-yeh took this opportunity to fearlessly press his attack. "Yesterday, we talked about you almost all day. If you'll only give the nod, he'll get a divorce at once."

Hung Chin-ling shaded her eyes with her left hand, and bowed her head.

"You've seen his shop. I don't see how the two of you aren't suitable. The two of you—'a talented youth and a beauty', 'family backgrounds compatible', 'a match made in Heaven'—there's not a one of these auspicious sayings that doesn't apply."

Having spoken, and seen no response, Hung T'ung-yeh couldn't help asking:

"This won't do. What are you really thinking?"

"I simply haven't thought of such things," Hung Chin-ling said, lifting her head. "I'm only thinking of Mother now. She's old, and she ought to have a bowl of rice to eat. Since you're not concerned about her, then it's my responsibility. I'm telling you honestly: I got confused once in Shanghai, and listened to your wicked talk, and abandoned Mother. Ever since there's been a deep, deep wound in my heart. Every time I think of it, I feel so bad I start to cry. From now on I'm going to make it up to Mother, and I'm going to devote all my heart to that. So you don't need to pay any more attention to me. I can never accept that theory of yours which destroys Mother. If you don't change your ways, then we'll always be people on two different roads."

As Hung Chin-ling spoke her heart was bitter; she rubbed her eyes with the handkerchief, and had she not been in a crowded place, she might have already started to cry. Ever since she had turned her back on her mother, she had lost her girlish mood, and her emotions had turned serious.

"Do you like the Ch'ien family?"

"Never mind that either." Hung Chin-ling shook her head, and laughed bitterly. "Every day I'm figuring how I ought to go back to Shanghai to suffer along with Mother. I can work, and look after her."

"P'eng Wen-hsüeh won't let you get along in peace."

"You're all partners."

"Yes."

"What's the use of exterminating a helpless widow and a lone girl?" Hung Chin-ling's voice was pitched low, but forceful enough to divide steel and cut iron as she said:

"Surely they aren't the bourgeoisie?"

"They represent a certain kind of thought, and a certain system."

Liu Shao-ch'iao came back, and saw by the looks of the two of them that things weren't going so smoothly. He sat down, forcing a happy manner, and pressed them to eat. Because Hung Chin-ling was present, they were drinking Flower-pattern wine. Liu Shao-ch'iao lifted a cup.

"Miss Hung, today I want to offer my respects, please drink a cup."

"Pardon me, Mr. Liu, thank you, but I really can't drink," Hung Chin-ling said coolly, as she barely touched the cup to her pursed lips.

Nonetheless Liu Shao-ch'iao kept on at her, insisting that she drink a cup. He swelled like a goiter, and cried out loudly:

"Miss Hung, you drink one cup, and I'll match you three cups! Five cups!"

This caused all the guests at other tables to look at their table. Hung Chin-ling was shy, and felt very uncomfortable. Her mind was at cross-purposes with itself: if I break with these two, later on it may be very inconvenient for Mother, and for the Ch'iens. So thinking, she raised her eyebrows, and her spirit returned. She said, laughing:

"Well, then, drink your five cups first."

Liu Shao-ch'iao, seeing that she had agreed, reckoned that he had won some face. He poured five cups into a large glass, raised it, and drank it dry. Hung Chin-ling thanked him, and without delay, drank down her little cup. She stood up and refilled Liu Shao-ch'iao's big glass. She said:

"Now I want to return your toast, Mr. Liu."

Liu Shao-ch'iao nodded, and said:

"Good, let me eat a bit first."

Hung Chin-ling held his chopsticks with her hand, and laughed.

"When I was in Shanghai, I heard people say that real drinkers don't eat."

Liu Shao-ch'iao blinked, and then gave in, saying:

"All right, fine."

Again he drained the glass. But he was thinking: "I'll never fall into your hands! Wait a bit, 'til I get you up to my place, then there'll be nowhere for you to run."

Because Hung Chin-ling had been too obvious about it, Hung T'ung-yeh felt that matters weren't quite right, and he said:

"Let's slow down with our drinking, and talk. We don't want to get drunk."

"I'm acting according to Miss Hung's wishes." Liu Shao-ch'iao deliberately filled another glass. "How about it, shall we make it three in a row?"

"All right." Hung Chin-ling raised her little cup.

Thus, one large glass and one small cup were drunk for the third time. Liu Shao-ch'iao's large glass held a good eight ounces. Usually he drank more slowly, and his capacity was forty-eight ounces. Now that he was drinking rapidly, and because of the evil he had in his mind—his calculations were all bent upon Hung Chin-ling's body—he began to waver, as though his head was light and his feet heavy.

"Chin-ling, what are you doing?" Hung T'ung-yeh said in a low voice, meaning to stop her.

"Drinking is fun!" Hung Chin-ling said provocatively.

"All right, enough, we won't drink any more," Hung T'ung-yeh turned to Liu Shao-ch'iao and said: "Let's talk seriously. Chin-ling is young, and it's the first time she's ever been away from home, so she's always thinking of her Mama."

Hung Chin-ling heard, and since she couldn't guess what else he was going to say, she winked, inclined her head, and waited for him to continue. Liu Shao-ch'iao's eyebrows rose, and he ran both hands through his hair, this time without feeling the headful of oil. He squinted at Hung Chin-ling, and asked uncomprehendingly:

"Why is that?"

Thinking of Mother was thinking of Mother, but Hung Chin-ling had not thought why; suddenly she didn't know how to answer. She lowered her head, and drew aimlessly with a chopstick in the wine on the tabletop. Liu Shao-ch'iao's eyes were bleary, but he saw clearly that she had drawn a half-circle and a point; she had drawn a question mark. Then she had added a vertical line and a point; she had drawn an exclamation point. Finally she put the chopstick down heavily, and softly sighed.

Liu Shao-ch'iao cracked his lips, as though to laugh, but he restrained himself. He thought, who'd have thought this little slave would put on such an act? His powers of attention were all at once concentrated upon her face, her complexion, as delicate as that of a baby, pointing up a kind of natural and untouched innocence. Liu Shao-ch'iao unconsciously uttered a sound—"ch"— hesitantly, as though he had just awakened. He thought, she's still a virgin, for sure.

He stuck his right hand into his oiled hair again and scratched, and then thrust the oily hand into his gown to find his wallet. Carefully he took a five dollar note from his wallet, and gave it to Hung T'ung-yeh. Smiling, he said:

"Please go to that pharmacy across the way and buy me some vaseline."

Hung T'ung-yeh took the money and asked:

"What's it for? For your hair?"

Liu Shao-ch'iao nodded.

"I think," Hung T'ung-yeh suggested, "your hair's all right without oil. You're not used to it, and when you oil your hair and then go scratching it wildly, it doesn't look very well."

"No, I'm not going to rub it on that head."

Liu Shao-ch'iao smiled mysteriously. Hung T'ung-yeh then said nothing, but glanced at Hung Chin-ling's face, and saw that she was just getting over her confusion, and obviously did not understand their talk. Hung T'ung-yeh hastily got back to the real topic:

"Shao-ch'iao, just now you didn't understand what I said."

"How didn't I understand?" Liu Shao-ch'iao squinted at him. "Didn't you say that Chin-ling is thinking of her Mama?"

"Yes."

"I don't understand why she thinks of her Mama. I haven't had any Mama since I was little." Liu Shao-ch'iao picked up a half-severed, oily chicken-leg, and began to chew on it, but then stuck out his stomach and leaned his head against the back of his chair.

"As for the feelings between mother and daughter, the two of them have depended on each other for their very lives, and they've been accustomed to this for many years." Hung T'ung-yeh, who was striving to change his sister's mind, could not but take her part.

"Then what's to be done?"

"I think," Hung T'ung-yeh suggested, "it would be best to bring Mother to Hankow, then Chin-ling would have no problem."

"That's fine," Liu Shao-ch'iao said without stopping to think. "Have her come and that's that. The building behind mine is empty, she can live there."

Hung Chin-ling had never thought her brother would make such a suggestion, and she was overjoyed. Hastily she said:

"To have her come is good, only—"

"Only what?" Liu Shao-ch'iao, fearing that a complication had arisen, opened his eyes wide.

"I want to rent another place," Hung Chin-ling said calculatingly. "She and I can live together."

"What's the need for that, I've got a place already."

Hung T'ung-yeh, afraid they would talk themselves out of it, hurried to change the subject.

"Just so she can come, and won't the rest be easy to work out?"

Thus it was decided to send money to P'eng Wen-hsüeh, asking him to send Mother Hung on the boat from Shanghai, and to notify them by telegram of the boat name and time of arrival. At this end, they would go to the wharf to meet her. As for the room, Hung Chin-ling would go and find one. The matter of the room was greatly to the contrary of Liu Shao-ch'iao's inclination.

When they had finished the meal and drunk the tea, Liu Shao-ch'iao began to pick at his teeth with a bamboo toothpick, and he said to Hung T'ung-yeh:

"There's nothing to do now, can you go and buy that vaseline for me?"

"What's the hurry, surely you're not waiting to use it?"

"Naturally I'm waiting to use it. No more delay—today I'm definitely going to do this thing," Liu Shao-ch'iao, staring at Hung Chin-ling, said resolutely.

"No, today certainly won't do. I know the situation, and you must wait until I tell you. You can't be in a hurry; rushing it won't work."

As Hung T'ung-yeh spoke, he couldn't help looking at Hung Chin-ling. Although Hung Chin-ling didn't know what they were talking about, she felt that she was the topic of conversation, and she thought that it couldn't be anything good. So she said to Hung T'ung-yeh:

"Since Mr. Liu is waiting to use it, it's all right if you hurry off and buy a little."

"No, you don't know." Hung T'ung-yeh was a little angry with his sister.

Hung Chin-ling pouted and said:

"Mr. Liu, give me your money, and I'll go buy it for you. It's only a few steps away, and I'll be back in a few minutes."

Liu Shao-ch'iao suddenly felt that this would be amusing, so he told her to go and buy it herself. Giggling, he gave her a bill, and said:

"I want the medical kind. A half-pound jar will do, or a pound jar. Not the scented cosmetic kind."

Liu Shao-ch'iao was afraid he hadn't made himself clear, and that she might buy the wrong kind, which he couldn't use.

"Chin-ling!" Hung T'ung-yeh cried.

"Never you mind. You wait a moment, I'll be back."

So saying, she walked slowly away.

Chapter VIII

They waited and waited, but Hung Chin-ling did not return. Hung T'ung-yeh felt that something was wrong, and that probably she had tricked them. The wine was now making itself felt in Liu Shao-ch'iao; his whole face was flushed, he was exhausted and wanted to sleep, and he couldn't sit still. He said to Hung T'ung-yeh:

"You go and look for her, maybe she's lost the way."

The two of them left the Two Rivers, and Liu Shao-ch'iao said:

"When you find her, bring her to my place. I'm going on back. It's all up to you."

Hung T'ung-yeh watched the other stride away, and then he went slowly searching along the road. He went to two pharmacies, but he did not see Hung Chin-ling. So his suspicions had not been mistaken. Although it was annoying, there was nothing to be done about it, so in a downcast mood he went back to Ssu-fen-li, not knowing what Liu Shao-ch'iao was going to do.

But he also felt rather pleased, because Chin-ling, after all, was clever, and she had made good her escape. Chin-ling couldn't accept Liu Shao-ch'iao's forcible approach, and if it had come to that, there couldn't have been any pleasure in such an encounter, and afterwards things would have been even more difficult to handle. In this matter a gentle approach was definitely called for; rushing it wouldn't do.

Liu Shao-ch'iao, smoking a cigarette, was leaning on the couch, and as soon as he saw Hung T'ung-yeh come in alone, he understood. He snorted, nodded, and then said slowly:

"Sit down."

Hung T'ung-yeh sat down opposite him.

Liu Shao-ch'iao stared at him without saying anything, until he had finished his cigarette. Then he laughed coldly and asked:

"Aren't you turning your back on your own party?"

"No such thing!" Hung T'ung-yeh said in anxious denial. He knew that the question had suddenly become magnified.

"Well, then, why are you wrecking Party work?"

"Are you talking about Chin-ling?" Hung T'ung-yeh was a little unclear.

"Just now in the Two Rivers you were consistently smoothing the way for her, to help her escape."

"It's not important, Shao-ch'iao; let me explain." When he saw Liu Shao-ch'iao getting angry, Hung T'ung-yeh became frightened.

"Speak!"

"I know that Chin-ling has already grown somewhat partial to the Ch'ien family, and you definitely couldn't have managed that business today. So—"

"Why couldn't I have managed it? Couldn't the two of us have gotten her upstairs? And once she was upstairs, we'd have taught her a lesson first, until she was willing to obey, and ready to agree to anything."

"That would be hard to do. Shao-ch'iao, let me finish." Hung T'ung-yeh wished that he could dig out his heart and show it to the other, so that he would understand. "I agreed to Chin-ling's finding another place and living there with Mother, but I didn't mean it. We'll fool her. Get Mother to come, and then she can stay here in your place. Chin-ling will have to come here often to see Mother, and with just a little effort, and my help, there's nothing that can't be managed. She's only a stinking little slave, why do you have to be in such a rush?"

Hung T'ung-yeh, in order to relax this tense situation, deliberately laughed, and added:

"There are plenty of whores here, and you can have a go at one of them."

When Liu Shao-ch'iao heard this, he struck the table angrily, and thrust his flushed and drunken face into Hung T'ung-yeh's. Saliva flew from his lips as he said:

"Do you mean that or are you fooling? Do I lack for women to play with?"

"Softly, Shao-ch'iao, people might hear!" Hung T'ung-yeh was almost begging.

"I'm declaring war on a concept of feminine chastity; I want to destroy that concept of feminine chastity, which belongs to the monopolistic consciousness of the bourgeoisie. For the Party, for the proletariat, she must sacrifice her virginity!"

"I think so too, only when it comes to methods, I'm in favor of going a bit easy," Hung T'ung-yeh said uneasily, holding his breath.

"Many things require the use of force."

"When force has no foundations, it can only be effective once."

"That's because the force is insufficient, and hasn't obtained the absolute superiority that enables it to prevail."

Hung T'ung-yeh hadn't the courage to continue expressing his own view; as usual, the mistake was on his side, and naturally he was forever the one who had to acknowledge himself in the wrong. The more he said, the more he got into trouble. So to make an end of it, he said:

"I was wrong again, Shao-ch'iao, please forgive me. Wait 'til Mother comes, and when the opportunity arrives, we'll do it your way."

"Why do we have to wait until your mother comes? Haven't you any way to get her up here?"

"She's on her guard now, and very alert, we'd better let a few days go by and then see."

"You're useless!"

"All right, let's be serious. Now I'll write to Mother and P'eng Wen-hsüeh, and we've got to send some money." Hung T'ung-yeh sat down at the table and looked for paper and pen.

"Money? I'm nearly starving now. Didn't you say that the Ch'ien girl already sent some money? How is it you still want to send some?"

"All right, I'll tell P'eng Wen-hsüeh," Hung T'ung-yeh agreed.

While Hung T'ung-yeh wrote the letter, Liu Shao-ch'iao lighted a cigarette and smoked. Putting his theory to use, he suddenly had a strange thought. He slapped his right hand down on his thigh, and said:

"Declare war on the old traditions, systems, and concepts!"

Hung T'ung-yeh, becoming aware that the other was very pleased, asked ingratiatingly:

"Shouting slogans all by yourself?"

"It's not a slogan," Liu Shao-ch'iao said excitedly. "Your mother guards her widowhood, and is prepared to stick with it to the end—this too is a kind of inexact concept of chastity. To sacrifice oneself for the monopolistic consciousness of the bourgeoisie—it's not worth it!"

Hung T'ung-yeh's face burned, and he said nothing.

"I'll help your sister, and I'll help your mother too. We have a responsibility to make them both progressive people."

Liu Shao-ch'iao saw that Hung T'ung-yeh's face was immobile and that he was silent. He laughed and said:

"What, aren't you pleased? In order to reach the goal, in order to help them, anyone will do to storm the battlements, it needn't necessarily be Liu Shao-ch'iao. There's someone who's most ideal."

Hung T'ung-yeh blinked, obviously confused.

"That's you!" Liu Shao-ch'iao jabbed his hand against Hung T'ung-yeh's temple. "You ought to do it yourself!"

Hung T'ung-yeh angrily sprang to his feet, and said impatiently:

"That's enough of your crazy talk!"

"Take it easy!" Liu Shao-ch'iao laughed. "Listening in anger, perhaps you didn't take it in. If you take your time and think it over objectively, then you may get it. It's extraordinarily reasonable: it provides the highest degree of struggle, and the highest value of struggle."

Hung T'ung-yeh, like a punctured blister, sank back into his seat. Liu Shao-ch'iao said:

"Write the letter; if you don't write it, I will. Little Brother, you still lack depth; if you can't even swallow a new concept like this, how can you accept even more of them? For the Party, and for the proletariat, sooner or later we're going to sing this opera; you'll be the lead, and I'll be a supporting player."

Hung T'ung-yeh picked up the pen, but he didn't know what to write; he was numb.

Liu Shao-ch'iao, looking at him, smiled, and said no more. He was delighted to have gained, through extension of theory, a new blueprint for action; he had attained his goal without effort. He looked at the photograph on the wall, and softly intoned:

"Shao-ch'iao, see your dappled butterfly Pai Ch'a-hua."

After Hung T'ung-yeh became Ch'ien Pen-san's "communications", he had to run around to several places every day. He himself felt that he wasn't completely suited to this work. For one thing, his speech carried a thick down-river accent, and moreover he had no occupation to serve as his cover. As for his external appearance, he seemed to exude a certain natural elegance, like silk gowns and embroidered slippers, innocent of the slightest trace of dust. Such a personage should have been enjoying himself in the amusement quarter, or among society ladies; he had the manner of the young master of a wealthy family, or of the young boss of a great merchant house, all of whom feel that heaven's disasters may strike others, but never themselves. Now, whenever he had nothing to do, he would be rushing off to the military barracks to hang about with those dusty, coarse soldiers of the Northern Army, or he would appear at a school, with several poverty-stricken teachers. In general, he often appeared in places quite out of keeping with his personal appearance, and unavoidably he attracted attention. Fortunately, the Northern Army's judicial office and constabulary and such organs very seldom took action before matters made themselves plain; they were forever waiting for orders, and had no spirit of independent action. By long-standing custom, they called their positions 'jobs', and performing official duties was called 'muddling through'. They were all the same: "you muddle through, I muddle through, and we muddle through"; thus Hung T'ung-yeh was able, like a victorious general, to be at ease in the face of danger.

Ch'ien Pen-san was responsible for military work: encouraging the Northern Army to mutiny, to collect the secrets of General Wu's headquarters, and to link up with the Revolutionary Party of Kwangtung; this was his responsibility. He saw that, according to Dr. Sun's predetermined schedule, this was the military phase, and he felt that since military matters were important, and he himself was responsible for military work, naturally he was important too. He thought, if we don't clear the way in this military phase, then the phases of political tutelage and constitutional government will never arrive. Therefore, everything ought to serve the military work, and the most indispensable thing is party affairs. So-called "party affairs" was the party attending to one of its revolutionary activities, a kind of mass movement which was the broadening and extension of military activity. So thought Ch'ien Pen-san.

Thus he could not but inquire into party affairs, in order to pair them with military affairs. He had the spirit of bearing responsibility and blame; he thought: for the revolution, how can I dare calculate the slander or flattery of individuals? And he thought, the person who is responsible for local party affairs ought to be in contact with me. And so he began to make such arrangements.

The person responsible for local party affairs was Chu Kuang-chi, the principal of the Wuhan Middle School. Chu Kuang-chi, at the time of the 1911 Revolution, had taken part personally in the fighting, and he had again played an essential role in the Second Revolution against Yüan Shih-k'ai. Now, he had concealed himself in the educational world, but in secret he was still doing party work.

This day he had received a secret letter from Ch'ien Pen-san, delivered by Hung T'ung-yeh, asking him to an interview in the Hotel France. Inwardly, he was quite disturbed. As far as the party was concerned, Chu Kuang-chi belonged to the older generation, and Ch'ien Pen-san ought to have come to him in person, to pay his respects. According to social custom, Ch'ien Pen-san, upon his arrival in Hankow, should certainly have called upon him. He couldn't figure it out, and now here was this urgent letter asking him to call. Chu Kuang-chi couldn't figure it out, and allowed Hung T'ung-yeh to go on standing there. He smoked a cigarette halfway through, glancing several times at Hung T'ung-yeh as though he wished to speak, but did not. Hung T'ung-yeh couldn't help asking:

"Please, Mr. Chu, is there a reply?"

Although he was displeased, Chu Kuang-chi understood the reasoning in the saying "People in the same boat help one another", and he thought, I'll forgive him this time; sometimes these fools are so stupid they don't understand good manners. But he refrained from saying so, and said sourly:

"There's no need to write a letter. You tell Committeeman Ch'ien that Chu Kuang-chi will appear at the time set by Committeeman Ch'ien to hear his instructions. Very well, you go on back."

Hung T'ung-yeh had noticed his manner, and now that he heard him use this tone, knew that he was unhappy. So he said in a roundabout way:

"Mr. Chu is a revolutionary of the older generation, and I want to pay my respects."

"You're paying your respects to me?"

"Yes."

"I'm just a nobody in the ranks," Chu Kuang-chi said with a smile.

"My father was Hung Pai-li. I've heard my mother mention Mr. Chu."

As soon as Chu Kuang-chi heard this he stood up, came forward, and clapped Hung T'ung-yeh on the shoulder. Delightedly, he said:

"Oh, you're Hung Pai-li's boy?"

So he made him sit down, asked if he would smoke, and called a school servant.

"Hurry and pour some tea."

"Pai-li and I were old classmates. When he was at the Japanese school for officials, I was studying medicine. We saw each other often; we were good friends. It's a pity he died early," Chu Kuang-chi said darkly. "Otherwise, since now is the time for military action, he could have shown himself to advantage."

"Did you come to Hankow with Ch'ien Pen-san?" he asked.

"Yes."

Chu Kuang-chi wondered how the other had gotten mixed up with that fool, and he was impatient because he couldn't very well ask. Hung T'ung-yeh saw his suspicious look, and asked:

"Does Mr. Chu know Professor Kuo Hsin-ju?"

"I've seen him, but I don't know him very well. He and I are different: he has standing in the party by reason of his reputation as a scholar, and mine was won the hard way with real swords and real guns, by revolutionary merit. What do you think of him?"

"It was Kuo Hsin-ju who introduced me to Ch'ien Pen-san."

"No wonder! Have you been with Ch'ien Pen-san long?"

"I just got to know him last fall."

"What do you think of him?"

Hung T'ung-yeh did not reply. Chu Kuang-chi looked at him, and asked:

"What's the matter? Our positions are different, so if you have something to say, there's no reason you can't tell me."

"Well, it's nothing," Hung T'ung-yeh smiled bashfully. "I just feel that he's too much like a bureaucrat, and not like a revolutionary. Now that I see your revolutionary style, and compare him with it, I feel even more that my opinion was correct."

"No mistake." Chu Kuang-chi slapped his knee, happy to see that Hung T'ung-yeh had such vision. "Just look at this business today. He sends me this letter telling me to go and see him, when he ought to come and see me! When you said bureaucratic, you were being too polite."

Chu Kuang-chi wore coarse cotton clothing and smoked Golden Rat brand cigarettes, the Nanyang Tobacco Company's cheapest product. Hung T'ung-yeh had discovered, as soon as he entered, that he was a hard-working and frugal, but bigoted, person. Now he added:

"He lives in a foreign hotel, and one day's rent for a single room is sixty dollars."

"There's eight people in my family and we don't use more than sixty dollars a month, and we don't get along so badly. This Ch'ien Pen-san is too extravagant; isn't he spending the revolutionary government's money?"

Inwardly, Chu Kuang-chi was becoming a little angry, but in front of the younger man he had to seem dignified, and so he spoke very evenly.

"Seeing how he behaves cools the revolutionary enthusiasm of us young people."

Hearing Hung T'ung-yeh talk like this, Chu Kuang-chi was slightly shaken, and he hastened to soothe him, saying:

"Don't ever say that! You're not making revolution on his behalf, nor can he represent the party. Be patient for a little while, wait until the Revolutionary Army comes, and then I'll handle this little matter. I'm a native here, and I have the right to speak. Those fools can go back to their own place and fool around there, but not here!"

Chu Kuang-chi looked up at the clock on the wall, and said:

"It's well you came today. From now on, I can advise you on things. Whatever Ch'ien Pen-san's game is, you come and tell me, and never mind him."

Hung T'ung-yeh hastily agreed, and stood up.

"My father is gone, and if Uncle doesn't look on me as a stranger, I'm willing to serve you; I'll do whatever you say."

Chu Kuang-chi was satisfied with Hung T'ung-yeh's attitude, and he added:

"Good, good, I too am pleased to see that Pai-li has posterity."

He thought for a moment, and then continued seriously, in a lowered voice:

"There's one thing you've got to be most careful about, and that's the Communist Party. The Communist Party opposes the Northern Expedition, and it's strengthening its activities in Wuhan. They penetrated educational circles early on. I've got a man among the dock workers who used to get on with them quite well. But most recently the Communist Party sent a Hunanese, Liu Shao-ch'iao, to Hankow to be secretary of the General Labor Union, and it wasn't but a few days until he told the dock workers to beat my man up. You see, they're rather ambitious! With their crafty schemes, from now on there's no telling what they've got in mind. So I want you to pay attention, and be careful of them."

"I know Liu Shao-ch'iao," Hung T'ung-yeh said.

"How could you know such a person?" Chu Kuang-chi hastily asked.

"He and Ch'ien Pen-san have connections."

When Chu Kuang-chi heard this, his heart jumped, and he muttered to himself in deep thought. He felt that matters had grown serious. Telling Hung T'ung-yeh to sit down, he went out for a moment, and then returned, and said lightly:

"I think that you should know how to succeed to your father's enterprise; you come from a true Kuomintang family. I tell you honestly, every morning I hang up Dr. Sun Yat-sen's photograph, and standing before him I reflect upon his last will three times. As Buddhists worship Buddha, and as Christians worship God, so I worship Dr. Sun Yat-sen. I am Dr. Sun Yat-sen's loyal follower. They can take my head, but this faith will never change."

As Chu Kuang-chi spoke, his voice trembled. He was grieved, and two lines of tears flowed down; he wiped them with his sleeve. Calming himself, he continued:

"It may be that Dr. Sun Yat-sen was deeply affected by the October Revolution in Russia, so that he settled on the policy of alignment with Soviet Russia and acceptance of Communists into the party. He was a man of deep learning; one could say that 'from of old he was the only man'. As for the theory and practice of the Communist Party, he certainly must have had his reasons. But these Communists don't understand righteousness and virtue. Their behavior nowadays is completely a case of repaying good with evil, and of ingratitude towards Dr. Sun Yat-sen for his good intentions in raising them up."

Chu Kuang-chi paused a moment, and then said angrily:

"Frankly, I can't stand the wrecking activities of the Communist Party!"

Chu Kuang-chi stood up, clasped his hands, and paced back and forth across the room. He had fallen into a brown study. He had obviously encountered a difficulty, and did not know how best to resolve it. After a moment's irresolution, he relaxed and sat down. He took from his waist a bundle of banknotes and handed them to Hung T'ung-yeh, saying:

"You take these and use them, I'm giving them to you."

Hung T'ung-yeh, stunned, was about to refuse, but Chu Kuang-chi said anxiously:

"If you don't want me to look on you as a stranger, you mustn't refuse. This money is for public as well as private use, so don't be polite. I just want you to do something for me: from now on, you report to me from time to time on how things are with Ch'ien Pen-san and Liu Shao-ch'iao, and that will be enough. I don't think you'll have any problem."

"I'll certainly do it, and definitely won't conceal anything. But this money—"

"If you refuse this, you're refusing me!"

So Hung T'ung-yeh changed his tone, and said:

"Since Uncle says so, I'll just make the most of it, and I won't dare refuse."

"That's what I had in mind, and if you have expenses in the future, just come and get some more from me."

As Chu Kuang-chi spoke, he smiled happily. Now, he had sufficient reason to willingly go to the Hotel France and see Ch'ien Pen-san. He thought, what a bold and reckless fool! So you dare make secret connections with the Communist Party. Perhaps you're thinking of selling out the Kuomintang?

Fortunately the news has come to my ears, so don't think you can get away with anything.

"What's it like in the Hotel France?" he asked Hung T'ung-yeh. "Although I'm an old-timer in Hankow, I've never been in there; I'm like an old bumpkin."

"It's just a hotel."

"Do they all speak French inside? Can Ch'ien Pen-san speak French?"

"The waiters are all Chinese, and Mr. Ch'ien can't speak French."

"Really, why is his room so expensive?"

"Probably the Westerners have a kind of 'respecting what is costly' concept. But this hotel's policy of doubling the price for Chinese is in order to turn away Chinese."

"You see, they turn us away, but there are still those of us who are willing to be taken advantage of!"

Chu Kuang-chi finally got to see Ch'ien Pen-san at the Hotel France. Ch'ien Pen-san, now that Chu Kuang-chi had really taken this polite step, was full of regrets as soon as he saw the other.

"I should have come to pay my respects to you. But, because I'm handling military activities, I've drawn their hatred. If I'm shot to death, it doesn't matter, but it does matter if the work is hindered." Ch'ien Pen-san ostentatiously lowered his voice to say: "I'm constantly reporting Wu P'ei-fu's military dispositions and battle plans to Canton."

"Your contribution is not a small one."

"It's only the matter of a moment," Ch'ien Pen-san drummed his fingers on the tea table and said: "I think that because of my reports Canton understands the enemy situation as clearly as pointing to the palm of one's hand; it won't be any problem to break Wu."

"After Wu is broken, the problem may be bigger still."

Ch'ien Pen-san couldn't understand Chu Kuang-chi's reason for saying this; he paused for a moment, and asked:

"You mean?"

"The Communist Party."

Ch'ien Pen-san heard this and smiled. He said:

"Carry out communism in China? I have a comparison—that's like throwing seed onto a rock."

"Sun Hsing-che has already pulled out his heart and liver to make a swing of them in the Wu-tsang Temple,[6] and you still say it's not serious?" Chu Kuang-chi earnestly and soberly said: "I have some serious words to say on slight acquaintance, so I'm going to say them—don't blame me. Since you're making a contribution to military affairs, just concentrate on military affairs. It's best if you don't go getting in touch with the Communist Party—it's no good to get involved with them."

"I haven't gotten in touch with them"

"What's this business with Liu Shao-ch'iao?"

"We've only met and chatted together a couple of times. How did you know?"

"I'm an old Hankow hand," Chu Kuang-chi laughed, and then added more heavily, "and I'm also a local tiger. Nothing fools me."

"That's why I want to be in touch with you," Ch'ien Pen-san, steering his boat with the current, brought the conversation around to his own goal. "Just now party affairs ought to be coordinated with military affairs. Once Canton shows its offensive strength, Hankow must move: we'll make them suspect spirits and ghosts; their spirits will be upset, and their military morale will be thrown into confusion, they can't help but be defeated."

---

[6] Sun Hsing-che: Sun the Pilgrim, a reference to Sun Wu-k'ung, the magical monkey hero of Wu Ch'eng-en's novel *Hsi-yu-chi* (*Record of a Journey to the West*).

"My plans will of course be reported directly to Canton."

"In order to unify our activities, it would be best if your mass activities followed my military activities. If we each have our own policy, our strength will be dispersed."

"No mistake, our viewpoints are similar, and our principles are the same. But it would be best if your military activities followed my mass activities, because the Party's authority is the highest of all."

The results of this interview and conversation were naturally unhappy. Chu Kuang-chi, before leaving, said, in the manner of one delivering a warning, to Ch'ien Pen-san:

"Everything can still be discussed; there's only one thing I'm uneasy about: you can't cooperate with the Communist Party!"

"You're wrong to use the word 'cooperate'. What qualifications does the Communist Party have to cooperate with us? I'm only using them for a time, that's all," Ch'ien Pen-san said carelessly, in his usual tone.

"If this viewpoint of yours doesn't change, sooner or later you're going to suffer for it. I hope you'll give it deeper thought," Chu Kuang-chi said with complete sincerity and some misgivings.

"All right, I'll certainly do as you say."

These words were obviously meaningless, and Chu Kuang-chi naturally heard them as such. He shook his head, and went out. Ch'ien Pen-san thought of Pen-ssu, and he said to himself:

"Those two are a pair!"

As Chu Kuang-chi left the Hotel France, he unexpectedly ran into his old classmate, Itakura Minoru.

After graduating from the Japanese medical school, Chu Kuang-chi had wanted to take part in the revolution, and so he had never hung out his sign to practice medicine. Originally a native of Kuang-chi in Hupei, he had started out with another school-name, but because he was going to enter medical school he had especially changed his name to Kuang-chi, taking the name of a place and not a person in order to express his desire to save the world through medicine. But after graduation, he saw that the Ch'ing government had lost its way, and he inclined ardently toward the great principle of nationalism. He felt deeply that curing the nation was far more important than curing people, and so he resolutely gave himself to the revolution, and abandoned medicine. After the 1911 Revolution, he commanded a hastily raised section of the People's Army. When Yüan Shih-k'ai tried to make himself emperor, Chu Kuang-chi hurried off to Szechuan to see Ch'en Huan,[7] because he had some personal acquaintance with Ch'en Huan. When he was preparing to enter Szechuan to talk to Ch'en Huan, several people warned him, saying:

"Ch'en Huan isn't like other men; he's Yüan's man to the death. Watch out he doesn't execute you."

Chu Kuang-chi also felt that his head might not be safe on this trip; still he resolutely made his decision and went. Chu Kuang-chi felt a bit like Ch'ing Ko[8] who sang: "*Hsiao-hsiao* soughs the wind, oh—Cold the waters of the Yi", except that his own aim was different.

When he got to see Ch'en Huan, Chu Kuang-chi had a great many principled and stern words to say, urging him to be the public servant of his four hundred million compatriots instead of the slave of a single family. Ch'en Huan listened, and then asked his attendant:

"What day is it by the lunar calendar?"

"The fourteenth," the attendant said respectfully.

---

[7] Ch'en Huan: the military governor of Szechuan Province.

[8] Ch'ing K'o: an assassin who set out to kill the ruler of the state of Ch'in. As he left on his mission, he sang the verse quoted above. The translation here is from *Chan-kuo ts'e*, translated by J. L. Crump (Oxford: Clarendon Press, 1970), p. 559.

"Is it cloudy outside, or bright?"

"Bright."

"Since it's the fourteenth, and bright besides, the moonlight ought to be good," Ch'en Huan said happily and seriously. "Send Mr. Chu to the western reception room, and tonight prepare wine and food so that he can enjoy the moon. When old friends like us see each other, talking about old times is all right, but discussing national affairs isn't called for."

Chu Kuang-chi stayed in the western reception room for two months, obeying the order to drink wine and enjoy the moon, and annoyed because drinking wine and enjoying the moon were two things in which he had no interest. He was interested in leaving the western reception room, but guards would not allow him to. He was also interested in seeing Ch'en Huan again in order to say goodbye, but the guards wouldn't allow that either. He grew very angry, and abused the guards:

"You're worse than I am!"

"It's not that we're worse than you are," the guard said, not giving in. "It's General Ch'en that's worse than you are."

"Tell General Ch'en to come here!"

"If he doesn't come by himself, nobody can tell him to come."

Only when Ch'en Huan had sent off an anti-Yüan telegram did Chu Kuang-chi regain his freedom. Ch'en Huan set out wine to entertain him before he left, and raising the cup, he said:

"Mr. Chu, I've done as you said after all."

Thus, with mutual wishes of long life for the Republic, Ch'en Huan gave him five hundred dollars for travelling expenses, and invited him to return to Hankow.

Yüan had fallen, but Chu Kuang-chi had become a man with no way to go. There was a Japanese who had established the Common Benevolence Society

Hospital in the Japanese Concession of Hankow, and the newly appointed Director was Itakura Minoru, who had been Chu Kuang-chi's colleague and classmate. Itakura Minoru and Dr. Sun Yat-sen's old friend Miyazaki had a certain connection through their wives' relatives; he had studied the writing of ancient Chinese poetry with Miyazaki, and he was reckoned Miyazaki's student. Miyazaki was Japanese, and naturally he loved Japan, but he did not feel that Japan's future had to be founded upon the subjection of China, as was the case with Korea. The proper friendship and cooperation between the two nations of Japan and China could provide Japan with even greater security, and with everlasting glory. While they both loved Japan alike, they had this difference with those military men who advocated plundering by armed force.

How to strengthen the two countries' friendship and cooperation? China's warlord regimes weren't capable of discussing this. When it came to forming a partnership to do business, they wanted to seek a sincere and reliable partner, but the warlord regimes were forever blundering ahead, and couldn't understand a grand strategy. So they turned their eyes toward Dr. Sun Yat-sen's party and the Chinese revolution which he led, and extended their sympathy and hope to this newly risen force.

Miyazaki's view represented that of a segment of enlightened Japanese gentlemen, who naturally could not get along with the Imperial Army's doctrine of subjection. Fortunately, Japan, although under military rule, still had a limited degree of freedom of thought, and of the freedom of discussion necessary to express thought. Kawakami Hajime lectured publicly on Marx's *Das Kapital* at Tokyo Imperial University's School of Economics, and moreover he wrote books and spoke to propagate these ideas, and he was allowed to do so; no one hounded him, nor arbitrarily interfered with him. The Japanese, after all, understood why intellectuals rebel, and did not make such a big thing of it.

Because of this, the point of view represented by Miyazaki could exist, and moreover was able to multiply and extend itself, without interruption, like threads of silk. Itakura Minoru had, since his youth, been influenced by Miyazaki. Moreover, from the practice of dissection, he had obtained sufficiently strong evidence to prove that the physiological organization of 'Chinamen' and men of the Yamato race was not at all different; one could see that 'Chinamen' were people too. Because of this, he gave the Chinese due respect, and did not dismiss them out of hand. His willingness to come to Hankow and assume the Directorship of the Common Benevolence Society Hospital was founded on this view of his. He did not know whether he would have an opportunity to help the Chinese advance towards a more or less brilliant future, but his aim in coming to China had been to find such an opportunity. He hadn't come to pan for gold, and in this he was the opposite of a great many Japanese.

When Chu Kuang-chi was disappointed in politics, Itakura Minoru invited him to be a doctor at the Common Benevolence Society Hospital, and offered him a firm salary of one hundred and twenty dollars in bank notes each month. Chu Kuang-chi accepted, but before he had worked for half a month, he resigned. Because he had lost his medical knowledge while pursuing revolution, and still less did he have any bedside experience, even if he had been bolder yet he would have had no way of dealing with life and death cases, so there was nothing for it but to leave. Itakura Minoru did not press him to stay, but gave him half a month's salary. Twice and three times he refused it, but Itakura Minoru was determined he should take it. After they had been stalemated for some time, Chu Kuang-chi laughed and said:

"Very well, I'll take it. I'll just use this money to buy a little gift for my adopted daughter."

This adopted daughter of his was Itakura Baitai, the only daughter of Itakura Minoru and his wife. Itakura Baitai came from a nursing school, and now she was head nurse at the Common Benevolence Society Hospital. Itakura Minoru hoped that his daughter would have the opportunity to marry a suitable Chinese; he believed that intermarriage between the two countries was a means of eliminating the lack of understanding between the races. Although leisurely action wouldn't help in desperate crises, mankind at last could not but travel the path; the day must come when the mingling of skin colors and the abolition of national boundaries would be realized. This was a grand world view.

Hearing Chu Kuang-chi say that he wanted to buy something for his daughter, Itakura Minoru said:

"That's up to you, but I feel there's no need to. Why do you want to be so polite?"

In the end, Chu Kuang-chi bought a platinum necklace with jade inlay for his adopted daughter, and then he felt that he had fulfilled his wish. Chu Kuang-chi was frugal and cautious by temperament, and even when in an extreme of distress, he would definitely not compromise nor change, but would remain so to the grave.

Later on Chu Kuang-chi entered the world of education.

He worked in secret for the party, economized on what he took in as principal, and contributed all he could to the party. No one pressed him. It was his own wish. Since Canton revealed news of the Northern Expedition, his work had grown more urgent. Various kinds of news of General Wu's army and the northern government, which Itakura Minoru got from the Japanese consulate, he systematically told to Chu Kuang-chi, who then reported it to Canton. Itakura Minoru willingly helped the Revolutionary Army; just as though he were a Chinese he hoped that China might have an enlightened and honest government.

On this day, just as Chu Kuang-chi was coming out of the Hotel France, he happened to see Itakura Minoru coming toward him in a high-wheeled rickshaw. As soon as he saw Chu Kuang-chi, he stopped and dismounted, saying that he had some materials he wanted to give to Chu Kuang-chi, and he asked Chu Kuang-chi to come into his dwelling. He asked Chu Kuang-chi:

"What were you doing in the Hotel France?"

"Seeing a friend."

"A foreigner?"

"No, a Chinese."

"I hear the rents are very expensive."

"Yes."

"It must be an important person with connections."

"From Canton."

Itakura Minoru nodded, and asked:

"Do you want to look for a secure place too?"

"I don't need to just now," Chu Kuang-chi forced a smile. He felt Ch'ien Pen-san was shameful.

"When you need to, you can stay at my place," Itakura Minoru said sincerely. "I know you couldn't stay in that hotel."

"I'll thank you now."

On the fifth day of the fifth lunar month, the Thief-punishing Headquarters put on a birthday party. Everyone, high and low, was busy for several days, and nearly all of the famous Peking opera actors were engaged. Representatives of President Ts'ao in Peking, of Chang the Rain-god of Manchuria, and of Sun the God of Fragrance of Hangchow, and representatives of the military governors of various provinces, as well as important officials and leaders of society, all gathered together in Hankow to celebrate General Wu's birthday. The various regions of the country raised a song of praise, and it was festive indeed.

The prostitutes of Ssu-fen-li were all sought out, so that they could be given to the various representatives at the birthday party to keep them company as they ate, drank, and amused themselves. All of Hankow's hotels and the wine and food trades did a respectable business.

Hung T'ung-yeh and his sister went to two evening sessions of the birthday party with Ch'ien Pen-san. They understood nothing of the Peking opera, but they saw with their own eyes the proud, luxurious, profligate, and idle life of the powerful and honorable, and their false ostentation. Like someone who treads on fire wrapped in paper, they were in the midst of their reckless pleasure.

Hung T'ung-yeh, feeling utterly listless, withdrew and went off alone.

The day after the fifth month festival, when he went to the railroad station to meet a merchandise manager, he saw the southbound soldiers of General Wu's army. They were big fellows, fully equipped, and appeared to be crack troops. He had not seen Canton's Revolutionary Army, and so he could draw no comparisons based on outward appearances. But he hoped that the Revolutionary Army would soon be able to fight its way through. All along he had had the feeling that he was doing something wrong; he didn't approve of Liu Shao-ch'iao's means of devoting full effort to hindering the Northern Expedition army. He felt that if it could advance a step, then it would be well if it did advance a step—why did it necessarily have to be he, himself, who took that step? The revolutionary line staked out by the Kuomintang, "Down with the Warlords!" and "Down with the Imperialists!" corresponded to the interests and demands of the nation and the people. Don't injure it, but give it an opportunity and allow it to do it, and perhaps it would do it well. This was a chance-in-a-thousand turning point for China to move from weakness to strength, and it seemed that everyone had an obligation to lend her a hand.

For the Communist Party to spoil this new run of luck was in the Party's interest, but it was not in the interests of the nation and the people. Hung T'ung-yeh understood this point better than anyone, but because of his change of character and his fallen condition, he was sinking deeper and deeper and could not save himself. He was almost like one of those opium smokers: they knew very well that opium was a bad thing, but they still smoked it, and they could not help but smoke it. That "Buddha's palm" of Liu Shao-ch'iao's was really a minor consideration.

Emotion caused him to abandon reason, and Hung T'ung-yeh followed the Communist Party.

When he came out of the railroad station, he did not take a rickshaw, but walked along, thinking. The weather had already warmed up, and his back, beneath the sun, felt a little as though it were burning. He thought, if I go out tomorrow, I'll certainly have to change clothes. There were pongee trousers and a long gown in his wardrobe.

"Look at those big tall northerners, in the prime of life," Hung T'ung-yeh thought. "Maybe Wu P'ei-fu can make it after all?"

He went directly to the river front, and standing in the shade of the Kiang-Han Customs Station clocktower, he faced into the breeze and drank in the coolness. On the river, spread out like stars and chess pieces, the warships and merchant ships of various foreign countries rode at anchor, with all sorts of flags hanging high on their masts and spreading in the breeze.

As he turned his head, he glimpsed the shadow of a woman on the sidewalk beside the road. She carried a long-handled European parasol, and was just strolling by, waggling her buttocks as she went. Hung T'ung-yeh knew that figure and that gait very well. He fixed his eyes on her, and felt there could be no mistake. "It's definitely her!"

Hung T'ung-yeh had a little repressed dislike, and a little more hatred, for this pile of buxom flesh. So he crossed the road, and followed behind. "I suffered enough of your anger, but I never thought you'd come to Hankow too. Now, if Wu P'ei-fu is defeated, and the Revolutionary Army comes, hah, then it'll be my turn to settle my score with you!"

That pile of flesh, treading with her delicate high-heeled shoes, strode boldly forward with head erect, never imagining that someone was following her. She went straight into the French Concession, and turned down a cross-street. Hung T'ung-yeh, fearing that he would lose sight of her, half-ran to catch up. The woman was standing before a glass door, reaching into her handbag. She took out a key, opened the door, and went in. Hung T'ung-yeh, standing some distance off, saw that a shop-sign with black letters on white hung across the glass door: it was a French person's shop.

"No mistake, it's her!"

Hung T'ung-yeh calmed himself down. He took a watch from his breast pocket. It was just two in the afternoon. Many of the foreign shops opened at just this time in the afternoon. He lighted a cigarette, drew heavily on it a couple of times, and a slight smile of wicked intent appeared at the corners of his mouth. He entered the foreign shop.

A dense row of French plane trees had been planted along the street, and the window was inlaid with colored frosted glass, which made the light in the room unusually dim. The woman, her back to the counter, was bending over, arranging something. Hung T'ung-yeh wore soft cloth shoes and stepped lightly, and she did not know that anyone had come in.

Hung T'ung-yeh looked around. This was a shop selling children's clothing and men and women's lingerie. He thought, when did they change their line of business? Seeing that the woman was still bustling away without stopping, he couldn't resist saying in French:

"Mme. Lefebvre, you're here?"

The woman stood up and turned, and said, as though she were startled:

"Whom did you say?"

Then Hung T'ung-yeh knew he had been mistaken. Although, from the rear, this woman resembled Mme. Lefebvre very closely, her face differed greatly.

Mme. Lefebvre's face was round and clear, and her eyes, which never completely opened, were yellow. This woman had a pair of deeper and darker black eyes, and although her figure was plump, her face was thin, and her lower lip was pointed. And there was another special characteristic: on her upper lip there obviously grew a tiny mustache. This mustache, while not as coarse and thick as a man's, was really a mustache, quite black, and about a tenth of an inch long. Hung T'ung-yeh said hastily:

"Please excuse me, I mistook you for someone else!"

"Where did you know Mme. Lefebvre?"

"In Shanghai."

"How did you know her?"

"I worked in their shop."

"Your French isn't bad."

So he was invited to sit down. The woman continued:

"I've been thinking of looking for someone who can speak French to help out in my shop, only I haven't been able to find anyone. My husband often goes to Peking; he isn't home much, and I really can't handle it myself."

She poured herself a cup of coffee from a thermos and drank it, and took a cigarette from the drawer in the cashier's desk and smoked, but she did not offer anything to Hung T'ung-yeh. Paying no attention to whether he was listening or not, she began to talk about what her husband did: he was a financial and political advisor to the Peking government, an advisor to Ts'ao K'un's Ministry of the Interior, and a military advisor to Wu P'ei-fu; besides that he was Chang Tso-lin's foreign affairs advisor. Because they had such a good advisor, they were making obvious progress on all fronts, and they were all able to manage. As she spoke, she kept asking Hung T'ung-yeh if he understood what she was saying.

She talked for ten minutes straight. As she talked, she kicked off her high-heeled shoes, and pulled off her long silk stockings and circled around the room in her bare feet. Hung T'ung-yeh was her conversational partner, but in her eyes it was as though she had no conversational partner at all, as though there was no one beside her, and she were talking to herself. When her husband was not at home, she had no one to talk to; these past few days she had almost gone mad with melancholy, and her belly was nearly bursting with frustration.

Hung T'ung-yeh listened quietly, and by listening was captivated. He especially appreciated the saucy manner with which she had kicked off her shoes and pulled off her hose, and without moving his eyes, he kept glancing at those feet, so plump and white. Those high-curved arches, which went so well with those rounded and gleaming heels—for a moment Hung T'ung-yeh didn't know what he was thinking of. Suddenly the woman regarded Hung T'ung-yeh and asked:

"What are you looking at?"

Hung T'ung-yeh hastily shifted his eyes, and blushing, he said:

"Nothing. I have to go."

He stood up. At this point the woman introduced herself.

"My husband's name is Raymond, and I'm called Anna. You may call me Mme. Raymond, or Anna, either will do. Tell me your surname and your given name. I hope you'll take the time to come over every day—I love to talk."

Hung T'ung-yeh told her his surname and his given name. Anna reiterated:

"Please come again. There's a lot I haven't asked you. It's wonderful that you can speak French. You can keep me company talking."

Hung T'ung-yeh merely waved and left.

That was an unanticipated encounter.

What that encounter gave to Hung T'ung-yeh were memories and wild hopes. Originally he had been prepared to go straight to the Hotel France to see

Ch'ien Pen-san; there were many matters, large and small, which only he could resolve. Especially there was that economic problem about which Liu Shao-ch'iao had been anxious: "If we don't take in some new funds, we not only won't be able to do any work, we won't even be able to eat," Liu Shao-ch'iao had told him. But, although it was so urgent, Hung T'ung-yeh pushed the matter behind him. He put himself back into an obscure old dream, in which he cherished his scars. He wandered aimlessly, and finally sat down in the six-sided pavilion in the Victoria Park. The gates of this park faced the river. It was the only place in the British Concession where "upper-class Chinese" might enjoy a stroll. Hung T'ung-yeh often passed his afternoons there, sometimes in order to meet with friends, and sometimes in order to rest. Hung T'ung-yeh loved those old trees, which seemed to reach the heavens. They covered the whole pavilion with a deep shade, and lent as well a quiet and refined air. Hung T'ung-yeh spent the whole afternoon there, drinking four bottles of Japanese Sun-brand beer, and smoking British "Zuleika" cigarettes.

The British Concession in Hankow, like the International Settlement in Shanghai, had Indian constables with orders to maintain order on the streets. Frequently, police truncheons in hand, they would chase and beat those rickshawmen, dock workers, and poorly-dressed "low-class" people. Quite different was their treatment of those well-off Chinese gentry and merchants who came into Victoria Park; they were fairly respectful to them, although not nearly as respectful as they were to the British masters.

Hung T'ung-yeh came often to Victoria Park, more or less so that he too could receive this respect.

The image of Liu Shao-ch'iao kept flashing into his memory-dream. He was already without a cent to his name, and had grown stingy in both his official and his private expenditures. Liu the Second held the shop, and the elder and younger brothers had quarrelled countless times over money. Liu Shao-ch'iao thought and thought. He had really exhausted all his sources of money. He said to Hung T'ung-yeh:

"There's only one way, so we might as well try it, and if it doesn't work, no matter. If it should work, then maybe it will open up a way for later on."

"What way? Is it something I can do?"

"Can't do it without you! I think, you can go to Ch'ien Pen-san and see if he can subsidize me by the month. This isn't a loan, because I haven't any way of repaying him; I just want him to subsidize me. I've already spoken with him face to face, and we got along very well. He agreed to cooperate with me. Well, we'll start to cooperate. The Northern Expedition has already set its arrow on the bow, so it's just the time for cooperation."

"Cooperation is between equals," Hung T'ung-yeh said sternly in his role as middle-man. "If he subsidizes you with money, what are you going to subsidize him with?"

"I'll subsidize his ass!" Liu Shao-ch'iao smiled wickedly. "I'll support him, I'll obey him, and I'm willing to do anything he wants me to do for him. Is that enough?"

"What things are you talking about?" The middle-man feared that Liu Shao-ch'iao's side was giving too much, and equity might be lost.

"Yes, even if he tells me to oppose the Communist Party, or to throw myself into the river, or anything whatsoever—I can do it, just let him order it."

"A joke's a joke, but you've got to give him some idea. Then later there'll be fewer misunderstandings, and it'll be easier to get along."

"What are you calling a joke?" Liu Shao-ch'iao poked Hung T'ung-yeh viciously on the buttocks. "I figure to sell it to him, that's all. When the money's in hand, then we'll see."

That afternoon, a melancholy Hung T'ung-yeh sat in Victoria Park until dark. The evening cool of early summer gradually cleared his head. The lined garments, which were too hot in broad daylight, were just right now. He left Victoria Park, stood by the river for a while, and then walked off toward the Hotel France.

Ch'ien Pen-san was sitting on the balcony, smoking. When he saw Hung T'ung-yeh, he told him to sit down opposite. Hung T'ung-yeh asked politely:

"Shall I turn on the light?"

"No."

The two men sat in the darkness on the balcony. The lights in the room and on the street shone distantly, but there was enough light to see by. Hung T'ung-yeh said softly:

"I brought that thing from the railroad station."

"How many men altogether?"

"Not quite twenty, but they were all low-ranking officials and workmen." Hung T'ung-yeh handed over a slender, folded booklet.

"Go and put it in my briefcase, I'll look at it later."

Ch'ien Pen-san hadn't accepted it, but had told Hung T'ung-yeh what to do with it. Hung T'ung-yeh went inside, and then came back and sat down. He said:

"They felt it was best not to let Chu Kuang-chi know, because since he got the organization started, they were afraid he wouldn't be willing for them to develop connections with others."

"That's right," Ch'ien Pen-san nodded. "They should treat Mr. Chu as usual, and whatever they've done before, they should go on doing now, so as not to let him know."

"Can he be depended on, or not?"

This was just what was troubling Ch'ien Pen-san. He well knew that the dependability of these so-called masses was extremely slight, but that if one could just attach oneself to one group, and avail oneself of a single line, one could move in deeper, and establish more advanced leadership connections. When he heard Hung T'ung-yeh's question, he said:

"Don't use those you suspect, and don't suspect those you use. This should be especially true among comrades."

"Yes," Hung T'ung-yeh answered, and continued. "Unfortunately, there were too few people."

"If every one of them is capable, and dependable, then don't be afraid they're too few. If we only counted on numbers, then revolution would be almost impossible. How many people did the revolutionary party have in 1911 in Wuchang? As for now, the Peiyang Army is more than ten times larger than the Revolutionary Army, but does that mean that the Revolutionary Army can never get anywhere? Of course not."

"By his own account, Liu Shao-ch'iao has attracted quite a few people," Hung T'ung-yeh slowly began to make his case.

"That's not necessarily reliable; he may be boasting a little."

"He's also got force. Mr. Chu's workers on the docks were beaten up, and they say it was Liu Shao-ch'iao who ordered it."

"If that's really the case, Liu Shao-ch'iao did wrong. He ought to help Mr. Chu, not hurt him."

"Liu Shao-ch'iao is trying to do something."

"What is he trying to do?"

"He's often poor; he hasn't got any source of operating funds." Hung T'ung-yeh smiled as he spoke. "When he beats someone, it's to knock open a money-fountain. He thinks to beat open a way to get living expenses."

Ch'ien Pen-san shook his head, smiling, and said gently:

"This is truly youth's naive way of thinking. Speak softly, and ask politely—then one can get money. To knock open the money-fountain is the way of ruffians and robbers; it won't do."

"Perhaps, for him, speaking nicely and asking politely won't work, so he's chosen violent activity."

Ch'ien Pen-san lighted his big cigar and inhaled. Wearing his dark glasses in the evening shadows, he was really so well shaded that he couldn't see a thing, so he thought to take them off, and smoothly handed them to Hung T'ung-yeh. Hung T'ung-yeh, who was used to waiting on him, took them into the room. Ch'ien Pen-san said nothing for a moment, and then thought: "Even though it can't be a case of 'ask and you shall receive', still I ought to do something for them, so as to avoid provoking them to violence. This is a method of compromise. Chu Kuang-chi is too obstinate."

In fact, this way of thinking was mistaken. Hung T'ung-yeh's words were in principle only. He hadn't indicated that Liu Shao-ch'iao had already knocked open Chu Kuang-chi's money-fountain.

"Liu Shao-ch'iao has the greatest respect for Mr. Ch'ien. He's often said that you're a far-sighted person, and he's willing to support you, and obey you," Hung T'ung-yeh said.

Ch'ien Pen-san was silent, paying attention only to smoking his big cigar. The puffs of smoke dispersed with the breeze, and a point of red fire moved in the darkness. Because the light was insufficient, Hung T'ung-yeh couldn't see his expression. He knew that the talk could not be concluded from this point, so he waited patiently for the other to reveal himself. As a result, Ch'ien Pen-san spoke again, asking:

"What is he after?"

"He wants to find a source of funds."

"What's he prepared to offer in exchange?"

"I don't know what Mr. Ch'ien wants?"

Ch'ien Pen-san was again silent for a long time, and then he said:

"Do you think he'd be willing to hand over part of the rosters of the Communist Party members in Hankow, and the officers of the Labor Union General Headquarters?"

Hung T'ung-yeh felt that Ch'ien Pen-san wanted too much; this was almost impossible. But still he said:

"That's very hard to say, but I can ask him," Hung T'ung-yeh said, standing up. "I'll go now."

After Hung T'ung-yeh had gone, Ch'ien Pen-san went into the room to study the list of names sent over from the railroad station. Their places of work were dispersed along the right-of-way near each station; their strength could not be concentrated, and that was the great shortcoming. Ch'ien Pen-san pondered deeply on the general and the particular, and got the idea of telling his daughter to take Hung Chin-ling on a tour. No one would pay any attention to two young girls, taking a rail trip on their spring holidays. He thought for a long time, and felt that whether or not things went smoothly for the army of the Northern Expedition, it would certainly be advantageous to sow some seeds along the railroad. Chu Kuang-chi won't necessarily be able to use them, but in a good cause I ought to compete with him, but with discretion.

The next day, Hung T'ung-yeh came to say that Liu Shao-ch'iao was willing to hand over the two rosters, with the explanation that they were not complete, because he himself did not know the complete roster, and in fact there was no "complete roster". Communist Party members, and still more their fellow-travellers, came and went, according to the subjective decisions of several responsible persons. There were a number of people who had already worked a long, long time on behalf of the Communist Party, and who were considered dependable Party members, but he himself didn't know who they were.

So, there was really no roster.

Had there really been a roster to bring, its degree of reliability would have been worthy of suspicion.

But Ch'ien Pen-san, in a sort of commercial transaction, finally took two of this sort of rosters, one of the municipal committee, and one of the Labor Union General Headquarters.

Chapter IX

Hung T'ung-yeh took the time to visit Mme. Raymond's—Anna's—shop
on several occasions. He felt that this woman had quite a few good points. Hung
Chin-ling, before she met Ch'ien Shou-yü, had felt that all people were bad. The
reason was extremely simple: it was that she had not yet run into any genuinely
good people. Hung T'ung-yeh, having been troubled by M. and Mme. Lefebvre
and Dumas in Shanghai, considered that white people, who were not of his race,
all had a kind of racially biassed view, and that none of them regarded the colored
Chinese as human beings. Liu Shao-ch'iao corrected him, saying:

"That's not necessarily so. The Soviet Communist Party members of the
Slavic race look on the Chinese as their brothers. After the October Revolution,
they gave up all their special rights in China. Lenin, before he died, kept thinking
of the Chinese brothers. Didn't Joffe, in Shanghai, join Dr. Sun Yat-sen in issuing
the historically famous joint manifesto?"

Hung T'ung-yeh nodded his agreement, and outwardly accepted this. But
in his heart he greatly disagreed. This was because he felt that political alliances
were based upon mutual interest, and that had hardly anything to do with racial
bias, or with the so-called love of mankind. And as far as the various
manifestations of that "comradely love" spoken of by the Chinese Communist
Party—as in conditions when, for example, a blow with the fist took the place of a
hug and a kiss, when bloodshed took the place of the bestowal of gifts—who

could imagine whether or not the Soviet Communists would ever be able to establish friendly relations between men and men?

When he had been an apprentice in Lefebvre's shop, he had often had to go to a wharf near the T'i-lan bridge to meet an English "Wharf Devil". This Wharf Devil occupied one whole floor of a building, including more than twenty large and small rooms, all by himself. He was already past forty, and still hadn't gotten married. He would frequently hold up his big belly with both hands, and express admiration for the Chinese system of early marriages and marriages arranged by the parents' decision. He was always saying:

"Before you're twenty, without any trouble you've got a wife, and if one's no good, you can get another—what a good thing! We Englishmen have to find our own wives, and that's really not easy. When the girls choose their own husbands, then it's hard to avoid them putting on airs, and finding fault. None of them are any good!"

Perhaps because he had no wife, Wharf Devil would often drink, and when he was drunk he would seize a long, thick piece of rattan and chase people, beating them wildly and cursing them in Chinese: "I'll ___ your mother's ___!" The former verb and the latter noun he had memorized very firmly and clearly.

During the European war, Wharf Devil had been an officer in an engineering unit, commanding a section of Chinese laborers, and responsible for managing road construction. Upon receiving his assignment, Wharf Devil had been rather unwilling, for he felt that he had suffered a slight. But after taking on the assignment, he had been moved by the docility, the industry, and the extremely low material expectations of these young Chinese laborers, and he was satisfied. One of Wharf Devil's relatives of the older generation had held an office in the East India Company, and had gained a fortune, so that he lived like an aristocrat and was respected by everyone. Because of this, Wharf Devil, figuring to follow in his footsteps, had gone to Shanghai after the war. Among those in his unit of Chinese laborers there was a northerner called Little Fish. Originally a beggar who searched for charcoal along the railroad, he had grown up handsome, and with winning ways. Wharf Devil had selected him to be his personal servant; they ate at the same table, slept in the same bed, and got along extraordinarily well. He learned several phrases of northern dialect from Little Fish, especially some curse words—and then considered that he was well-versed in Chinese, and truly understood China. Little Fish had also learned to understand a few words of English, and with the aid of gestures, the two of them got along and despite all, were able to make themselves clear to each other.

After the war, he went to work for Jardine, Matheson and Company, and was assigned to manage the wharf near the T'i-lan bridge. He hired Little Fish to be his household manager and also his cook. Little Fish took this opportunity to cheat and take advantage of his master, and, after a few years of work, he had quite a bit of savings in hand. He got someone to take some of the money back to his home, and his old father then arranged a marriage for him. The bride's family, indeed, were the descendants of a famous official, and the bride the daughter of a learned and refined but poverty-stricken household. Little Fish asked for leave to go home and complete the nuptials, and then he brought the new wife back to Shanghai. Unexpectedly and without any reason, a great many troubles arose from this.

Little Fish's wife had been raised in her country village, and had never been outside the gates of her home. She had never seen a foreigner. When she saw Wharf Devil, she felt that he truly was an evil spirit, and in her heart she was afraid of him. Moreover, she had a pair of bound feet, and Wharf Devil wanted to take a photograph of these bound feet. He meant to send it back to England and show it to his close friends, so that they too could see the world. But a woman's bound feet are mysterious and even sacred; they may be viewed from afar, but may not be lightly trifled with, and how could she allow a foreigner to photograph them? But Wharf Devil insisted on taking a photograph, and there was nothing Little Fish could do about it. He made a hundred arguments to his wife, but she wouldn't give in. Finally, Little Fish got angry, beat his wife half-dead, and then reckoned that he had subdued her. With tears all over her face and a great feeling of having been wronged, she placed her bound feet on Wharf Devil's dining table, and allowed him to take plenty of photographs from the front, the rear, the right, and the left. Wharf Devil wasn't completely satisfied, and wanted her to take off the shoes and remove the bindings so that he could also take some photographs of her bare feet. Naturally the woman was unwilling, and when she was pressed hard, she began to wail loudly.

Wharf Devil took a pound sterling note from his pocket and gave it to Little Fish, saying:

"Tell her not to cry; I'll just take a few more, and I'll give her this."

Little Fish was not impressed by the pound sterling note, but from the pound sterling note he saw that Wharf Devil was determined, and that if the thing couldn't be done, his rice-bowl might be affected. He thought, I know persuasion is no use, so he hardened his heart and once more gave her a cruel beating. This method was indeed effective; the woman became enraged, and not only did she stop crying, she climbed onto the dining table, sat down in the middle of it, and took off her shoes and footbindings, and stuck out her naked feet while she hid her eyes behind her hands.

Wharf Devil took photographs of her feet, and of the woman's whole body. He also measured the footbindings, and even photographed the shoes. Then he ordered Little Fish to take her back to her room. Little Fish knew that she had been wronged, and he felt badly himself, but he didn't know how to comfort her. He put her on the bed, and covered her with a blanket.

The woman slept, and she slept for three days without getting up. Only when Little Fish, exasperated, would have beaten her again, did she put on her clothes and get out of bed. At this time they were still in the middle of their honeymoon.

On account of this affair, Wharf Devil not only admired China's old style marriage system, but he hadn't enough words to praise the virtues of Chinese wives. He said to Little Fish:

"If we Englishmen treated our newly married wives like you treated yours, not only wouldn't the wife stand for it, but social opinion wouldn't allow it. You Chinese are really lucky!"

Wharf Devil had heard that the younger generation of Chinese opposed the old style marriage system, and advocated learning from the West in the freedom of romantic love and marital choice. He couldn't understand this at all. He hoped that the Chinese would preserve their excellent traditions and their excellent customs. He was completely well-intentioned and perfectly sincere. As for the movement for the Chinese to cut off their queues and unbind their feet, he felt that here, too, they were imitating the West, and that there was really no need. A people ought to have their own independent character. The world must have all kinds of skills, and mankind, containing as it did black and white people, masters and slaves, was truly interesting. When all was of a single color or tone, it induced a feeling of melancholy listlessness, and diminished the amusing character of human life; it was an unhealthy path.

The complexity and inequality of social phenomena and human fate manifested God's perfect wisdom; man could not oppose it. So Wharf Devil often thought.

But a new problem arose.

Before Little Fish got married, he had "slept in the same bed" with Wharf Devil. Now that Little Fish had a wife, nature ordained that it should be his wife who shared his bed, and not Wharf Devil. But Wharf Devil would not give up this right, and often, in the middle of the night he would pound loudly on the door, calling Little Fish to come out, and would not let him return. Little Fish's wife, before the marriage, had heard that her parents, because they had gotten some money from someone, were going to give her in marriage to a former beggar and laborer, who was now a foreigner's slave, and she had been most unwilling, secretly blaming her father and mother for their carelessness. But on account of her beliefs that one's parents' orders cannot be disobeyed, and "marry a chicken, follow a chicken; marry a dog, follow a dog", she had a grievance but couldn't speak it out. Since coming to Shanghai she had suffered her husband's oppression over the matter of photographing her bound feet, and she felt deeply that the one she had married was inhuman. She felt that her body was like a floating duckweed, and that she has no one to depend upon. Now, knowing that her husband didn't even have the freedom of sleeping, she really didn't know what to do. She felt it was shameful, but she didn't know where the shame came from. Had her husband brought it upon himself, or had the devil conferred it upon him? She really couldn't think it through. She only felt boundlessly wronged, but she never thought of how she could get redress, or of how she might break out of it. And still less did she know that this behavior of hers was exactly what Wharf Devil admired as the virtue of a Chinese wife.

However there was something still more unfortunate.

One morning, after Little Fish had served Wharf Devil his breakfast, and had seen him go downstairs to the writing-room, he took the vegetable basket and rode off on his bicycle to the vegetable market. Wharf Devil sat on his office table for a while, and smoked a cigarette. Then, with his rattan in hand, he took a turn around the wharf. A number of workmen were busy unloading cargo, with a great "*Ai-yo*" sound. Without knowing why Wharf Devil suddenly felt very impatient and muttered to himself: "I'll ___ your mother's ___!" He tossed the rattan into the river, and went straight upstairs. He went right into the kitchen, but there was no one in the kitchen. He closed the kitchen door heavily and went out into the passageway. This passageway divided the ground floor and the second floor into front and rear sections. The front of the building faced the Whangpoo River, and one could see in the distance the P'u-t'ung plain. The whole front section was reserved for Wharf Devil's use; the rear section contained the kitchen, the store-room, and Little Fish's living quarters.

Little Fish's wife was just then in her room dressing her hair, before going to the bathroom next door to wash her face. When she heard the sound of the kitchen door, she hurried out to look, and came face to face with Wharf Devil. Wharf Devil usually came up and down by the front staircase in the front section, and he had very seldom gone through the passageway between. As soon as Little Fish's wife saw Wharf Devil her heart gave a great jump. She whirled, and was about to retreat into her room, but Wharf Devil hurried forward, pursuing her, and caught her around the waist, trying to kiss her while his hands pawed wildly. Little Fish's wife wasn't strong enough to stop him, and she was frightened and desperate. While she struggled to escape, she cried out wildly "Save me!" By the time Wharf Devil blocked her lips with his hand, the Indian constable who guarded the door of the writing-room downstairs had already heard the noise and come up, and behind him followed quite a few people.

Wharf Devil, in a rage, held Little Fish's wife tightly and withdrew several paces, to the head of the stairs. Then, with sufficient force, he threw her down the staircase. The Indian constable who watched the door saw that Little Fish's wife, after the fall, was moving her hands and feet wildly and was continuously moaning, and he knew that she had been seriously hurt. He was hurrying to go down and help her when Wharf Devil kicked him viciously on the buttocks. The Indian constable couldn't keep his footing, and went tumbling down the stairs. Those people who had followed him, seeing that Wharf Devil was in a rage, hastily retreated through the front.

When Little Fish returned from buying vegetables, his wife had already been taken to the hospital, and Wharf Devil, sitting resolutely at the dining table, was angry. As soon as he saw Little Fish, he started to curse him in a voice to break stone: "I'll ___ your mother's ___!" Little Fish, with no idea why he was being cursed, didn't know what to do, and hastily retreated to the kitchen. It was time to start preparing the noon meal.

Little Chiang-pei was the man-of-all-work in the writing-room downstairs, and Little Fish often joked with him. He came quietly up the rear stairs, and softly pushed open the kitchen door. Little Fish, startled, cursed: "Little Devil, your mother's ___!"

Little Chiang-pei pressed a finger of his right hand to his lips, breathing softly, and nodded and beckoned as he withdrew. Little Fish couldn't make out what mysterious business he was up to, and could only go down with him. In a dark spot across the street, Little Chiang-pei told him in detail what had happened, and only then did he know that his own wife had suffered a great calamity. He longed to rush off immediately to the hospital, but he was afraid he would miss Wharf Devil's lunch and provoke him to a greater rage, so he could only be patient. He begged Little Chiang-pei to telephone the hospital and ask about her injuries.

Wharf Devil insisted upon a big plate of beefsteak for lunch every day. It had to be grilled on odd days, and fried on even days, and he had never permitted any variation. On this day, perhaps because Little Fish's mood was careless, he didn't beat the beef long enough, nor leave it on the fire long enough. When Wharf Devil first cut into it, he saw in the cut a strange, live worm, white and fat, and as lively as a maggot. He called in a great voice for Little Fish, and when Little Fish appeared in response, he flung the whole dish straight at his face. Fortunately, Little Fish was quick-witted, and dodged in time, so that he wasn't struck. Wharf Devil kept shouting furiously at him, and again it was the same "I'll ___ your mother's ___!"

After seeing his master to his post-lunch nap, Little Fish hurried to the hospital to see his wife. Her leg was broken, and she would have to wear a cast, but it would mend. Fortunately there were no other injuries. The brain concussion didn't really count, and wouldn't interfere with anything. Weeping, the wife said:

"If I don't die, when I'm well I want to go home. I don't dare go back to the wharf!"

"Really, how did you make him angry?"

"How did I make him angry? He started it!"

"Did you resist him?"

"What do you mean, resist him? If I had submitted to him, it wouldn't have come to making him break my leg!" his wife said bitterly. "I see you can't even figure it out."

Little Fish said nothing for a while. Finally, he sighed and said:

"You mustn't be too stubborn. I've been with the devil for many years, and I know he's definitely not a bad man. It's not easy to earn money these days. Many people look for an opportunity like this and don't find it."

"Unfortunately you chose the wrong wife; I'm not that kind of person."

Although she spoke thus, when the woman's leg got better she went back, as before, to live upstairs at the wharf. Truly, if you marry a chicken, follow a chicken; marry a dog, follow a dog.

Wharf Devil, after this episode, would often go to a nightclub to drink and dance. Before long, he got to know an Irish girl, and although there was quite a difference in their ages, the girl really seemed to like him. Late one night, Wharf Devil got drunk, and the girl saw him home. They were talking and laughing when suddenly, without knowing why, Wharf Devil got angry and pushed the

Irish girl down from the top of the stairs. She was scratched and bruised about her face and her hands. On this account, he lost that girl.

When Wharf Devil sobered up, he grumbled over his bad behavior when drinking. He had often thought of abstaining from alcohol, feeling that if he didn't give up drinking, circumstances would forever prevent him from taking a wife. Often he would get angry and think of giving it up, but he was always defeated; he couldn't give it up.

A year passed, and Little Fish's wife gave birth to a boy, with yellow hair, white skin, blue eyes, and a prominent nose. Everyone said that they could guess where it came from. Little Chiang-pei would often tease Little Fish by calling the child, "Little Half-breed, you beast!", provoking Little Fish to chase after him, trying to hit him.

M. Lefebvre had business connections with Wharf Devil. He would often have goods to be moved into the warehouse, or loaded onto a ship for export. Hung T'ung-yeh had been dealing with him for a long time, and became quite familiar with such people as Little Fish and Little Chiang-pei. Little Fish had even invited him to sit down in the kitchen and eat some Western dishes, which he had concocted with his own hands, and he gave him some of Wharf Devil's gin to drink. Hung T'ung-yeh felt that Little Fish's skill at the preparation of Western dishes fell far short of Old White-hand Wang's; nonetheless he was full of praise. Little Fish, full of self-satisfaction, said:

"This is really English flavor!"

Hung T'ung-yeh knew about Wharf Devil's many connections with Little Fish's wife, and at that time he had already developed his own ideas on the matter. He felt that the foreigners with whom people like himself, Compradore Chang, Old White-hand Wang, Little Fish, and Little Chiang-pei, came into contact were mostly adventurers and fortune-hunters who were drawn to the colonies and the semi-developed regions. These people belonged to the lower classes, and probably in their own countries too they were a kind of dangerous people. In fairness, we cannot, because we've seen one or two of these people, arbitrarily and generally consider that all Frenchmen, or all Englishmen, or even all white people, are bad. Similarly, there are also some Chinese who misbehave in foreign countries, and so the foreigners often take that minority as the rule, and insist that all Chinese are low-class and worthless. That, too is really lacking in justice, and every upright Chinese must feel pained on this account. The manifestations of human behavior are often many-sided, but among the many sides there is one unifying nature. Take Wharf Devil, who threw Little Fish's wife down the stairs, and kicked the Indian constable down the stairs. If one only looks at it from this angle, he couldn't avoid the suspicion of maltreating colored people. But later on he treated an Irish girl in the same way, so the explanation of racial bias is far off the mark. Thus Hung T'ung-yeh, according to his understanding, came to this conclusion: the wicked behavior manifested by a minority of foreign adventurers in China should be their own individual responsibility, and ought not to damage the image of their country and their people. Still less should it hinder the friendship between their countries and peoples, and our country and people.

This was an extremely simple argument, which a primary school student might have put into an essay, but when Hung T'ung-yeh reached it, he felt that it was his own grand discovery, he felt that he was capable of transcendent conceptions, and was a person of great broad-mindedness. He called his discovery the "Individual Conduct Theory of Race".

This was his intellectual understanding, and his intellectual understanding was clear.

But his emotions were quite different; his emotions did not unconditionally follow his intellect. Emotionally, he still retained a standoffish attitude towards white people; it was one of pride, and also of self-deprecation.

He often had a frivolous thought, feeling that white people did have one worthy thing, and that was their woman-flesh.

This feeling of his was directed not only towards the white women of the imperialist nations, but at the same time towards the socialist Soviet Russians. On this point, he looked upon all with the same benevolence; he wasn't like Liu Shao-ch'iao.

The change in his feelings began with Anna Raymond; unexpectedly he had come upon a living example.

One Sunday morning Hung T'ung-yeh came to see Anna. Inside his shirt he carried a set of pedicure instruments, which his master had given him that year, and for which Mme. Lefebvre had provided a case. This should be the most glorious page in the entire history of Chinese pedicure, and these instruments possessed an unparalleled historical value. In the same manner, the pen with which Marx had written *Das Kapital*, and the smelly socks worn by Lenin, have a glorious place in the history of the proletarian revolution.

As he walked along, Hung T'ung-yeh thought, I'm afraid she'll have gone to church at this hour, and I won't be able to see her. None of the foreign shops did business on Sundays. But as he had expected Anna's shop was open after all, and even the shutters had been taken down. As Hung T'ung-yeh entered, Anna was leaning on the counter reading a paper; in her concentration she was unaware that anyone had come in. Hung T'ung-yeh said softly:

"Good morning, Madame."

Anna looked up, saw that it was Hung T'ung-yeh, wished him good morning, and invited him to sit down.

"I was just wanting to ask you something," Anna said. "This is a Paris newspaper. I just got it, but it's already a month old. Here they've run a telegram from Hong Kong, saying that the Revolutionary Army is already preparing for the Northern Expedition. Doesn't this mean there's going to be more fighting? How is it I didn't know? The people from the Consulate didn't mention it either. Surely it's not that they too don't know?"

"No mistake, I've heard that there is such a thing. If they haven't told you, perhaps it's because they feel it's not worth any attention. China often has civil wars, and rumors of civil war are even more frequent, so there's no need to take alarm."

As Hung T'ung-yeh spoke, he was gazing fixedly at her feet. She wore a pair of white, low, high-heeled shoes, bound front and back with red leather, and her handbag was on the table. He asked:

"Are you going out?"

"Yes."

"To church?"

"No, I've never gone to church, and my husband doesn't either."

Anna took out her cigarettes and gave one to Hung T'ung-yeh. Hung T'ung-yeh quickly stood up to take it, struck a match to light them, and the two of them smoked.

"Are you a believer?"

"Yes. A few days after I was born, I was carried into the church to be baptized, and that was the first time I went to church. The second time was when I got married." Anna raised her eyebrows, laughing at herself.

"You're not like my old employer, Mme. Lefebvre. She was certain to go to church every Sunday, she prayed early and late, and the Bible never left her hand, or her lips."

"Didn't you approve of that?"

"I can't very well criticize her in front of you," Hung T'ung-yeh said with a smile.

"What you mean is you're afraid that if you criticize one Frenchwoman, another Frenchwoman will be displeased. Is that it?"

Anna crossed one leg over the other and swung it gently. Hung T'ung-yeh felt that her legs were really even plumper and more sensual than those of Mme. Lefebvre, and one hand unconsciously stole inside his shirt to finger the case of pedicure instruments he had brought. His lips murmured something, but he didn't say anything.

Anna and Hung T'ung-yeh had seen each other many times, and she realized that he was always consciously or unconsciously looking at her feet. She was a bit surprised. Now she couldn't help studying her own feet in detail. She lifted them, moved them forward and backward, observed them, and really couldn't think of the reason. But she went on to say:

"If that's what you think, then you don't understand me; I'm not so petty. People aren't divided according to nationality or religious beliefs, there are good and bad among all. If I don't go to church, it's on account of my father's teaching. My father didn't go to church either. He would often say that one who truly believes in Jesus will embody the spirit of Jesus' love and sacrifice in his own practical life, and unite theory and practice. My father was most disgusted by those people whose words didn't agree with their actions, like that Mme. Lefebvre you were talking about. As for those who 'eat' religion and look on Jesus as their bread and butter, who force people to enter the church by tempting them with heaven and frightening them with hell, my father thought even less of that sort."

"Your father was really an intelligent man." Hung T'ung-yeh listened to her with fresh interest, and his approval came from the heart.

"He was just a small businessman who kept a general store, and he'd barely graduated from primary school, so never mind his intelligence." Anna spoke very modestly, but she couldn't prevent the very slightest look of pride from showing on her face. "Only on this one point did he refuse to conform to custom and the common practice. He had his own independent point of view, and he maintained his own way of looking at things."

Hung T'ung-yeh kept on expressing his admiration. Anna smiled, and lighted a cigarette, but this time she forgot to offer one to Hung T'ung-yeh. She was proud of her father, and this Hung T'ung-yeh before her eyes counted for little. She continued:

"My mother opposed my father in everything. Only my father's religious opinions met with her sympathy. When she was happy, she'd often tell us in jest, if it wasn't that your father had this worthwhile opinion, he and I would have gotten to the point of divorce. When my father heard my mother talk like this, he'd come back with a big happy laugh. Our whole family always lived very happily."

"Didn't you just say that your mother often opposed your father?"

"That kind of opposition is teasing, it's in fun, it's a different way of expressing love," Anna said happily, dropping her high-heeled shoes and taking off her silk stockings. "For instance, if Father gave Mother a new dress, she might say, you see we're starving to death, and you go spending money wildly. Do I lack for clothes? Wait 'til I put this dress on, and the men pay attention to me, then you'll regret it."

"Your mother was a person who understood humor."

"She wasn't a humorous person. She had two elder brothers. One of them became a pastor, and got married. He raised several milk-goats on the church land, and sold goat milk. The other left home to enter a monastery, and became a priest. The two brothers would attack each other. Elder brother said that younger brother's religion was false, and younger brother said that elder brother's religion cheated people. As long as they didn't see each other, it was all right, but just let them see each other and they'd part without speaking. Whenever my mother mentioned them, she'd get angry, and bitter, so you can see she wasn't a humorous person."

"With two brothers like those, maybe her humor couldn't come out," Hung T'ung-yeh said, and added: "Does your M. Raymond go to church?"

"No," Anna said, shaking her head, "but the reason he doesn't go to church isn't the same as my father's; it's because of his view. He's a capable person, honest and frank, and single-minded about making money. In order to make money, one can do without a conscience; it's drinking people's blood and eating people's flesh. He often says, 'My methods mean turning my back on God and abandoning Him, so I've simply parted company with Him; I've already reserved my ticket to hell!' I think that a person like him, if one took away some of his frankness and added a bit of false benevolence, wouldn't be much different from M. and Mme. Lefebvre you mentioned."

"Your marriage is certainly interesting," Hung T'ung-yeh said lightly, with a little air of disappointment.

"He left school early and studied business in my father's general store. But I didn't love him. When we got married, I was only fifteen. What can a fifteen-year-old girl understand? Even now I haven't thought it through, why I married him then. Perhaps because we were always together, and we got too familiar, so that he took advantage of me. You know, he's ten years older than I."

Anna kept smoking, and since she didn't like the flowing smoke which swirled before her face, she kept waving her hand to disperse it. She coughed twice, got up, and took a handkerchief from her handbag to wipe her eyes. Then she walked barefoot to the door, and leaned against the door-jamb. Probably she needed some fresh air. Hung T'ung-yeh helped her open the back door. At once a cool breeze blew in, and Hung T'ung-yeh felt his spirits rise.

He discovered that there was a lovely rear courtyard, and fairly spacious. In one corner there was a six-sided pavilion with red pillars supporting a rush roof, and a railing worked to represent the character *wan*.[9] Within the pavilion

---

[9] *wan*: ten thousand.

there was a single-legged round stone table and a drum-shaped stone bench. In another corner there was an artificial mountain and a grove of bamboo. A large tree shaded the pavilion and half of the courtyard as well.

Hung T'ung-yeh took a look, and then went on out. Against the wall by the window there was a wooden chicken-coop, where she was raising a few local chickens. A high-ceilinged bird cage hung under the porch roof, and inside was a Mongolian lark, just fluttering its wings and muttering to itself. Colored phoenixes and golden dragons were painted on the white wall, guarding either side of the rear gate. A thin bamboo pole was stretched between the green pillars of the verandah and the red pillars of the pavilion, and on it hung a row of silk stockings and women's underclothing.

Hung T'ung-yeh felt that this was rather common, but he said:

"It's really wonderful that you've got such an elegant courtyard."

"My husband arranged it," Anna said, following him out.

"We both like this kind of Oriental mood. When my husband and I first came to the East, we knocked around in Annam for several years, but the prospects weren't very good. There was a general in Yunnan who engaged my husband as an advisor in order to make connections with the French, and so he took the opportunity to come to China. Who'd have thought it—generals in various provinces competed to get close to him, and he ended up becoming an important foreigner. Because of this, he has some feeling for China, and he loves the Chinese. He often travels in various provinces. For convenience of communications, we moved to Hankow. My husband has no intention of going back to France; he wants to stay in China forever, so he arranged this courtyard."

As Anna spoke, she invited Hung T'ung-yeh to seat himself in the pavilion. Hung T'ung-yeh, laughing, said:

"Let's not sit down; this stone drum's too cold for sitting, and for a woman it's especially unsuitable. Didn't you just say you were going out?"

"I was going out to the tailor shop to have a look. But it's not important, a bit later will do, or tomorrow or the next day."

"Are you going to make some clothes?"

"No, I was going to hurry them up on some goods. These clothes I sell are all bought wholesale from a Chinese tailor shop. They're often not very punctual, and they can never deliver the goods at the agreed-upon time, so I have to go and press them."

"Lack of punctuality is a Chinese trait."

"I didn't say that," Anna laughed as though regretting her words. "I was only speaking of the one shop that makes clothes for me."

She placed particular emphasis on the words "the one shop".

"You needn't explain. I'm not defending the faults of the Chinese. I only know that faults must be corrected."

Hung T'ung-yeh spoke so frankly and naturally that the woman felt there wasn't the slightest unpleasantness, and so they passed safely over this small moment of embarrassment. He went on:

"Shall I go with you? I know the place, and afterwards I can help you with your errands."

"That would be splendid."

The woman cheered up, and sat right down on the stone drum. When Hung T'ung-yeh saw this, he hurried into the house and came out with an embroidered pillow, and gave it to her to sit on. Moreover, he said:

"The stone drum is too cold; it's definitely not for sitting, you'll be uncomfortable."

"I'm not that delicate."

The woman accepted Hung T'ung-yeh's diligent good intentions, and even made another request:

"Could I ask you to bring out the cigarettes and the coffee? Also, my shoes. This cement floor is really unbearably cold on my feet."

Hung T'ung-yeh hurried back into the house, and came out with the tea and the tobacco arranged on a big tray. In one hand he carried her high-heeled shoes. Anna saw this, and said:

"When I'm barefoot, I can't put on my high heels, for fear I might get them dirty inside. If the sweat mixed with the gravel, next time I wouldn't be able to wear them."

"All right, I'll go get your slippers." Hung T'ung-yeh put the tray down on the stone table, and casually asked: "Do you want me to lock the front gate?"

"No," Anna said as she poured tea, "with the back door open, we can be here and still be called. There's often some business on Sunday."

Hung T'ung-yeh came out with a pair of soft rubber-soled slippers of white deerskin, and put them down by her feet. Taking a careful look, he felt that her toenails really needed a trim, besides which the nails were dull, and needed to be rubbed with oil to make them shine. His hand patted the pedicure instruments inside his shirt, but his lips said:

"It would be better if there weren't any business on Sundays. Weren't you just going out?"

He was sitting on the railing near Anna, with his back against a pillar. Anna pushed the tray in his direction, intending for him to help himself to cigarettes and tea. She turned her big, deep-set eyes on him, for a moment, and then laughed and said:

"You don't mind if I criticize the Chinese?"

"As long as it's well-meant, I don't have anything against it." As he spoke, Hung T'ung-yeh stood up and lighted a cigarette.

So Anna straightforwardly revealed her secret. In fact, it couldn't be considered a secret, since she had always been open about it, but this was the first time Hung T'ung-yeh had been told, and she had always avoided giving evidence against herself. She said:

"I use Chinese materials and Chinese labor, in a Chinese location, to tailor all kinds of men's and women's underclothing, for grown-ups and children, according to French fashions, and I add French, English, or American trademarks. This is where my goods come from. Over ninety percent of my customers are Chinese, who glory in the origins of the goods. They like to show off their children in front of their friends and say, 'My precious wears foreign-made clothes; I bought them myself from the hands of a foreign woman in a foreign shop. They're much more expensive than Chinese-made goods, many times more expensive'."

Anna couldn't help laughing as she said this. She looked at Hung T'ung-yeh, and feeling that his face had grown cold, she said:

"You said you wouldn't mind."

"That's right, I don't mind," Hung T'ung-yeh said, and continued: "But I feel that since your husband has ways and means, why do you have to do this business? Your doing this doesn't fit with your own views. You just said that one's practical life should embody the spirit of Jesus' love and sacrifice, but you use the weakness of others, and you use underhanded tricks. Isn't this a contradiction?"

His words made Anna blush. She was ashamed, but she explained:

"My husband wasn't willing for me to open this shop. He wanted me to travel with him to various places. A great many generals' wives, concubines, and daughters would like to make friends with a foreign woman. But I couldn't get used to such a life of constant travelling. I've always felt that such a life couldn't be depended upon; one's always hanging, and the emptiness is frightening. My family has been in trade for a long time, and a shop-front gives me a feeling of security. Besides, I'm a housewife, I want to do all the housework, heavy or light, by myself; I feel comfortable only when I do it myself."

As for selling goods with false trademarks at high prices, Anna had no explanation, and Hung T'ung-yeh did not pursue it. No one could completely integrate emotion and reason, or theory and practice, and make them one, without the slightest difference. Jesus advocated limitless forbearance and limitless forgiveness, but he himself knew anger and grief. And Jesus was considered the son of God! It was difficult enough, and worthy of praise, if one didn't depart too far from His way.

In any case, Hung T'ung-yeh thought that Anna was much superior to Mme. Lefebvre. So, without waiting any longer, he began to work around to the topic, saying:

"Who does your hair every day?"

"I don't have anyone to do my hair." Anna turned her head, so that Hung T'ung-yeh could see her hair. She shook it loose, and pushed it to one side. "I usually just arrange it myself, like this. If it happens to get loose, then I smooth it myself with a curling-iron, and I don't have anyone do it."

Hung T'ung-yeh felt that her hair, which she wore so casually, had a kind of natural beauty. Women in ancient China had had a so-called "falling off a horse" hairdo; he didn't know what it had been like, but according to the meaning of the words, it might have been similar to Anna's hair style. As he thought about it, his eyes had already moved to her hands, and he asked:

"Well, surely you don't do your own nails?"

When Anna heard this she laughed, stretched her hand out flat, and said:

"Can a wife who washes clothes, fixes food, and does odd jobs every day still trim her nails? When they get long, I cut them short myself, that's all."

Hung T'ung-yeh told her how Mme. Lefebvre took care of her hands and feet; she considered the matter even more important than going to church. Anna listened, and said in perplexity:

"I think she must be a fortunate wife."

"As for her being fortunate," Hung T'ung-yeh said with a smile as he blushed, "I learned pedicure. Moreover, I can also use an electric curling-iron to do hair, and I can trim nails."

"What?" Anna felt there was something a bit strange. "Mme. Lefebvre wanted you to give her a pedicure?"

"Yes."

"You said you were their assistant compradore."

"Doing the manager's wife's pedicure was one of the assistant compradore's important jobs."

Anna exhaled with a long-drawn-out "Oh-h!" She puffed on a cigarette, and said lightly:

"So that's how you were."

Two eyes stared fixedly at Hung T'ung-yeh, as though she had some weighty question and was determined to draw the answer from his face.

Hung T'ung-yeh felt a little embarrassed by her gaze, so he went on testing as before.

"If you'd like a pedicure too, I have my knives here, and I'm quite willing to take the trouble for you—I'm willing."

As he spoke, he took the little leather case out of his shirt. When Anna saw it, she reached out and took it. The case, with its red leather and gold clasp, was quite elegant. She opened it, and inside there were ten or so large and small knives. Anna thought this was odd, and she said:

"Do you need so many knives for pedicure?"

"Yes," Hung T'ung-yeh replied. Seeing that she was interested, he went over and explained to her, one by one, the use of each knife: this broad-bladed one was used thus and so, and that one with the sharp, narrow blade was used thus and so.

"I took a master and studied this art with him for three years, and learned the knack."

"Who'd have thought a pair of feet were this much bother!" Incomprehensibly, Anna sounded a little saddened.

"I really hope you'll give my skill a try." Hung T'ung-yeh advanced a step closer, and said plainly: "After I've given you a pedicure, your feet will really be pretty. You have the most beautiful feet."

"No, no," Anna said, shaking her head.

Seeing that she refused, Hung T'ung-yeh felt a little ill at ease, but he continued.

"Try it once, I'm sure you'll like it afterward."

"I don't want to try it." Anna snapped shut the golden clasp, and pushed the case away. "Don't you say anything more about it! There's something else I want to discuss with you."

"What's that?" Hung T'ung-yeh asked listlessly.

"What is it that you do, anyway?"

"I wait on an official; he came from Shanghai to Hankow to take care of something," Hung T'ung-yeh said, combining truth with falsehood. "My superior is a man from General Wu's native district, and he has many friends in the Thief-punishing Headquarters."

"Are you going to be in Hankow for a long time, or a short time?"

"The way things are going, it's not certain."

"I was thinking of asking you to come and help out in my shop, but I don't know if it would work or not."

"Help out with what?"

Anna smiled, and then said:

"I've always done things myself, and in fact, I don't need anyone to help me. I'm asking you to keep me company talking. My husband's not at home, and the few French families in Hankow are all busy with their own affairs. So, there'll often be several days running when I don't get a minute's worth of talk. But I love talking most of all. When my husband's home, I talk day and night without stopping, and talk his head off. He'll often cover his ears, wrinkle his brows, and beg me: 'Dear, can't you give your lips and my ears five minutes' rest?' Five minutes! I get so mad I could slap his face!"

Anna laughed again.

"I can talk about it now and laugh, but at the time I was really annoyed. If you tell me not to eat, it's nothing to me, but what I hate the most is for somebody to get disgusted with me for talking too much. You know I like you very much, because I've realized that you're very patient about listening to me talk, and you're very interested," Anna said happily, and then asked with concern: "But I don't know if you could stand it over a long period?"

"I've been trained to patience," Hung T'ung-yeh said, patting himself on the chest. "Ever since I left school I've been doing things I don't enjoy doing. But I've accepted insults humbly and I've never said an angry word. Patience is a habit that's become natural to me."

"That's good, splendid! I think that my husband's staying away from home so much isn't necessarily because those generals really have so many things they can't do without him; it's because he's avoiding these talkative lips of mine. Well, never mind him, let him go."

With the forefinger of her right hand, Anna patted the tiny mustache on her lip, and lightly stroked it back and forth. Hung T'ung-yeh couldn't help saying to her:

"You're the first woman I've seen who's grown a mustache."

"There aren't many in Europe either. Don't you like it?"

"I like unusual things—it's my nature. When did your mustache start to grow?"

"Probably, when I was thirteen or fourteen? When he asked me to marry him, he'd already told me there were two things about me he loved most: one was that I loved to talk; he was happy to listen to me, he could never hear enough. The other was my mustache; he said my mustache could arouse his sexual feelings. But after we were married I gradually realized that his words weren't entirely reliable, because he's often urged me to pluck it out."

"Don't you have any children?"

"Don't blame me for that, he's the one who got sick. Wherever he goes, he has to play with the prostitutes." As Anna spoke, she kept shaking her head.

"Doesn't it make you angry?"

"Of course it makes me angry! But I love my shop, even more than I love my husband. My shop gives me more of a feeling of security than my husband does."

Although she spoke like this, Anna was obviously disturbed, and thoroughly impatient and hot. She took a cigarette, and Hung T'ung-yeh hastily struck a match and lighted it for her. She inhaled deeply, blew out a long puff of smoke, and then quietly thanked him. Hung T'ung-yeh changed the subject, saying:

"Doesn't your non-stop talking hinder your work?"

"I talk as I work; I'm happy talking, and I can work vigorously too." Anna laughed happily. "If I couldn't talk, if I had to work in silence, then the more I worked the less I'd feel like working, and I'd doze off."

Someone came in from outside. Anna looked, and said:

"A customer. Would you go and attend to her? The prices are clearly marked on everything. Inspect the goods as you please, and collect the fixed price. Thank you."

Hung T'ung-yeh agreed, and went over.

Anna, with a cigarette in her mouth, and wearing her slippers, stood up and stretched. She followed Hung T'ung-yeh, and beside the stairs she turned and went into the washroom.

After a moment, she came out. Hung T'ung-yeh gave her the proceeds of the sale, and he added:

"You're selling these things too high—three to five times what it costs outside."

"There are people who like to buy expensive things. That's what gives me my feeling of security, because my profits are high. But at the same time, it also gives them a feeling of security; they feel that they've certainly bought something good because they paid a lot of money for it. So my business is lovely on both sides."

"Surely they don't lack eyes to tell the good from the bad?"

"Lots of people often cover up their own eyes, especially those who consider themselves clever."

Anna leaned on the sofa, crossed her legs, pulled on her silk stockings again, and mounted her high-heeled shoes. As she did this, she asked Hung T'ung-yeh:

"Just now you didn't answer me—can you come and help out in my shop? If you're willing, I can give you a rather high salary."

"I definitely can't go to work for you full-time. But I can find the time to come and talk with you often; not for a salary, but like friends."

"Fine, I hope you can come every day."

"I've one condition," Hung T'ung-yeh, not letting go of the opportunity, said with a smile.

"What condition?"

"I want to give you a pedicure. Once a week would do."

When Anna heard this, she really couldn't understand the other's psychology.

"Are you addicted to giving pedicures?"

"You could say that."

"I hope you can give up that unwholesome vice. I've heard that it's not a very respectable thing."

"I know that too. But I don't know why, I just like it."

"I think you're like my husband—a little abnormal."

"Possibly, perhaps."

"Would you give me your pedicure set?" Anna patted her bosom.

"What do you want with them?" Hung T'ung-yeh asked, amazed.

"As a keepsake. I like to collect keepsakes. Besides, I can use them to trim my own toenails."

Anna's lips spoke these words, but in her heart she was actually thinking of throwing them away. If he hadn't his instruments, perhaps he'd no longer be interested in that strange idea of pedicures and perhaps he'd break off his weird addiction.

"If you're willing," Anna quickly added, "I've also got a little gift for you. We can make an exchange."

This development was entirely outside of Hung T'ung-yeh's expectations. The pedicure knives had originally been his own keepsakes, and he couldn't help having a feeling of begrudging them. But Anna's request revealed her goodwill and sincerity. Hung T'ung-yeh regretted that he couldn't fully comprehend Anna's feelings. This goodwill and sincerity with which he was unexpectedly confronted aroused another side of his own decent nature, which Liu Shao-ch'iao had almost transformed and gradually destroyed. Excited, without a word he hurried to the pavilion in the rear courtyard, piled the pedicure case with the smoking things and the tea things on the tray, and carried them all back to the front. He gave the leather case of pedicure instruments to Anna, and said:

"I'm giving this to you, and I know I've found the best of all final resting places for it. But I don't want anything in exchange."

Anna happily took it, and immediately put it into a drawer in the counter. She couldn't keep from asking:

"From now on you won't give any more pedicures?"

Then Hung T'ung-yeh understood where her real interest was, and in the midst of his gratitude he felt a little mortified. He said:

"Just as you say, I'll drop it."

"That's my good boy!"

Anna jumped up, caught Hung T'ung-yeh's head between her hands, and kissed him on the forehead. Hung T'ung-yeh felt a light, whirling sensation of giddiness.

Anna fell back on the couch, clasped her hands together upside down, and then pushed them vigorously upwards. She thrust out her feet, and gave a great stretch. Then she said:

"Just now when I mentioned an exchange, I used the wrong expression. What I meant was that I was thinking of giving you a little something."

"What?"

"Let me ask you first," Anna said, staring at Hung T'ung-yeh's face, "do you like to wear Western dress and leather shoes?"

"I like to, and sometimes I wear them."

"Every time you've come here, you've worn a long gown. To tell the truth, what I find hardest to accept in Chinese culture is the men's dress. When I see that long gown, I always think he's a woman, and those thin-soled cloth shoes give me the feeling of going barefoot and not wearing shoes at all. That getup would make even a more martial man appear less impressive, so how much more a Chinese."

Anna felt that she had put it a little too strongly, and she hesitated a moment, thinking what she could say to save the situation. Consequently Hung T'ung-yeh said:

"What do you think are the shortcomings of the Chinese?"

"Please forgive me for speaking too directly." Anna twisted her waist uneasily, and leaned forward. She said with a smile: "I'm speaking from a purely aesthetic point of view, without the slightest racial bias. The shortcomings of the Chinese are that their complexions are too dark, their faces are too flat, and their persons are too small; they're obviously weak and without strength."

"Your criticism is completely accurate," Hung T'ung-yeh spoke very naturally, without showing any resentment. "But God arranged it that way, and what can be done about it?"

"God will have to take the responsibility for His own injustice, so never mind His carelessness. Man ought to understand his own deficiencies, and use his own strength to remedy them."

"Man can't do anything about natural deficiencies."

"If those words of yours represent the general opinion of the majority of Chinese," Anna said seriously, pulling a long face, "then it's just the weak point of the Chinese. For example, those many shortcomings of the Chinese physique, of which I was just speaking. At least they can be remedied by dress. One can improve his appearance at once by changing to Western dress and leather shoes."

Hung T'ung-yeh was just going to say something, but Anna didn't give him the opportunity. She rushed right on, saying:

"What's most to be feared is that, not understanding one's weak point, one simply intensifies it. Women are originally weaker than men, and the way to remedy that should be to improve their physical health. But the Chinese have taken an opposite path: they bind their feet, keep them locked up, and thus use human strength to intensify natural weak points. The first time I saw bound feet, it gave me a feeling of terror. This isn't the beauty of sickliness, it's a cruel punishment!"

"The next generation won't have this business of footbinding."

Hung T'ung-yeh laughed, and added:

"But I saw an Englishman who blamed the Chinese for the movements to get rid of queues and do away with footbinding. He felt that if the Chinese didn't grow queues, and didn't practice footbinding, they'd have none of their 'national characteristics'."

"That was his deliberate perverseness." Anna also laughed. "I think he was probably one of a kind with M. and Mme. Lefebvre, and my husband."

"Your husband?" Hung T'ung-yeh deliberately pretended not to understand, so as to lead her on in this direction.

"Lefebvre, for example: he spent more freely on himself, wasn't a bit stingy, but he would only give you six dollars a month. I understand his psychology all right, because I've already heard my husband say that Chinese don't need money. Their clothes are handed down; if they're hungry they can eat grass roots and tree bark. If money comes into their hands, they simply have no use for it."

At the mention of the Lefebvres, Hung T'ung-yeh really felt a little left-over pain. He didn't know what to say, and despite himself his spirits darkened. Anna regretted that she had spoken too directly, so she changed her tone and said:

"China has such a vast land, and such a large population, and such a long and brilliant history as well; you ought to be able to put things right yourselves, and it wouldn't be hard to become wealthy and strong."

"But too great a land, too many people, and too long a history, have now become a burden for China, weighing down on the Chinese so they can hardly breathe."

Hung T'ung-yeh smiled bitterly and said:

"We need to start over from the beginning."

Anna, who hadn't heard Hung T'ung-yeh's last remark, went on:

"What is this Revolutionary Army from Kwangtung?"

"They want to put China to rights, and make the country wealthy and strong, as you were hoping."

"That's wonderful!" Anna stood up and said excitedly:

"I think they'll succeed sooner or later. The great French Revolution went on for eighty years, and at last we had some foundation of democracy and freedom."

"On the day China becomes wealthy and strong, there'll be no more concessions and special rights for foreigners." Hung T'ung-yeh said this as though he wanted to wake Anna up.

"Let everyone live together in equality, like brothers, like friends—that would be fine."

"When you talk like that, you really sound like a Christian."

"Originally I was a true believer in Jesus," Anna said, looking up.

Both of them laughed, laughed happily.

"Come on," Anna said. She took up her handbag, opened it, and looked at her mirror. "Come with me to the tailor shop. I'll get you a suit of clothes, and at the same time I can press them to send me my goods."

Chapter X

Ch'ien Shou-yü received a letter which her younger brother, Ch'ien Shou-tien, had asked someone to bring from Canton, saying that he was all right. The letter was carried by one of Chu Kuang-chi's comrades, and he delivered it in person. There had been no news of her brother for many days, and she was overjoyed. She thanked the comrade, and hurried to the Hotel France to see her father.

Shou-yü and Shou-tien were Ch'ien Pen-san's only children. There was a saying in their family, which said "a boy, a girl, and a flower". Although most people considered many children a blessing, still it couldn't be denied that many children also meant complications, thus, when at times they saw someone who had few children—for example, one son and one daughter—they would praise them by saying that they were like "a flower", and their feelings of envy would show. Of course, one couldn't simply have none at all, for that would be "cutting off the family". A person who "cut off the family" not only couldn't face heaven and earth, the gods and the spirits, and his ancestors, but he couldn't even hold up his head before his own close relatives and friends.

Accordingly, Ch'ien Pen-san should have been most satisfied, and who knew that this wasn't the case? As for this son and daughter, he loved only the daughter, and didn't love the son. When he was young he had a wife, and he shot his cook dead from behind with a triple-barrelled bird gun, blinding his wife in one eye at the same time. He had to use several thousand taels of silver hidden away by his ancestors, and so he avoided going to court over it. And a large part of that silver, it was clear, had gone to extortionists. Out of this affair he came to deeply understand that a man couldn't get along without influence, and that influence came from being an official. He then resolved to pursue political activities, first as a provincial assemblyman, and then as a member of Parliament.

But he had also come to dislike Shou-tien. He always felt that the child Shou-tien had the greatest resemblance to that dead cook; not only his face and figure, but even his voice and movements were all so similar. He thought back on past events, and calculated the time, and the more evidence he found, the more he felt that he was not mistaken. From then on, he didn't like to see Shou-tien, and even thinking about it made him a bit angry, and still more distressed that he couldn't come out with it. Barely waiting until it was time for him to formally choose the boy's name, he selected the character *tien*,[10] which secretly conveyed his feeling of hopeless dislike. Later on, when he moved away, he took only his daughter along, and concentrated on training her. When they were living in T., he had a household tutor, and made the girl study early and late. But, before two years were out, Ch'ien Pen-san almost killed the household tutor as he had killed the cook before. Had it not been for the painful experience of having had to pay a great deal of grievance money, and suffer a great deal of bitterness when he killed the cook that time, and had it not been that for someone with the prestige and position of a provincial assemblyman to kill a man would mean much harm and little benefit, Ch'ien Pen-san really would have done it again. Now, he forbore, and considered the matter of discharging the tutor. The tutor originally was one of the Ch'ien family's tenants. Because he was a good student, Ch'ien Pen-san had brought him to T., and had helped him take the entrance examination for normal school. It had been Ch'ien Pen-san's idea for him to tutor Ch'ien Shou-yü with her

---

[10] *tien*: a flaw, as in a piece of jade.

lessons; the tutor himself hadn't been too willing, because he was busy with his own schoolwork. Only because he didn't want to give offense, and to avoid that unpleasantness, had he regretfully accepted the job.

After Ch'ien Pen-san discharged the tutor, he also wrote a letter to the president of the normal school, saying that the tutor had misbehaved, and ought to be expelled. Ch'ien Pen-san was a provincial assemblyman, and also managed a newspaper; he was considered a local power. The president didn't dare disobey, but he did not expel the tutor. He gave the student twenty dollars travelling expenses, and told him to voluntarily withdraw from the school and leave.

"You'd better escape quickly; he may be after your life!"

The student lacked little more than a semester of graduating and earning his degree. After withdrawing from school, he had nowhere to go, and no idea of what to do. He drifted to Tsingtao and worked as a redcap at the railroad station. He happened to meet a distant relative, who was passing through Tsingtao on his way to Canton, to enter the military academy. After considering it, he threw away his red cap, and joined his relative and went off with him. The two men entered the military academy at the same time, and in the battle of the Tan-shui during the eastern campaign, they both gave their lives as martyrs at the same time. They did not succeed, but they died for the cause.

This affair left a wound, difficult to efface, in Ch'ien Shou-yü's memory. Originally she had meant to make the best of her mistake and marry that tutor, but her father wouldn't permit it. He flew into a thundering rage, and loudly scolded her:

"The daughter of a land-owning village gentry family marrying the son of a tenant family—have you ever seen or heard of it? You cheap thing!"

An old friend of her father's accompanied her to Peking, and in a Japanese hospital a piece of flesh was taken out of her belly. From then on she was always weighing a question—neither large nor small—in her mind: does my father really love me? And what is the price of his love to me?

After the tutor had died a martyr in the eastern campaign, she would blame her father to his face:

"If you hadn't forced him to leave school then, he could have graduated, and really he could have become a primary school teacher, and not—"

"All right, don't say any more!" Ch'ien Pen-san interrupted her, saying: "He dared to cheat his master and wrong his superior, and this is just his retribution."

"Papa, don't blame me for saying this," Ch'ien Shou-yü was also getting angry. "Your thought is backward!"

This word "backward" was a new provocation indeed to Ch'ien Pen-san. No one had ever criticized him in these terms before, and he knew that it was a fearful thing to be backward. Fortunately, when a sufficient quantity of water is poured onto a newly-lighted flame, the flame will be extinguished at once. Ch'ien Pen-san, in a mood of dejection, coldly carried out a deep self-examination, and moreover he privately asked several intimate friends, "Do you think my thought is backward?"

Although all of his friends' answers were polite: "Brother, you're not backward, you're avant-garde", from then on he was always careful and on his guard, fearing only being backward. He swallowed whole a great many new fads, just to show that he accepted them.

At that time, this mood of fearing only being backward was extremely widespread, and Ch'ien Pen-san was only one example. The Communist Party made use of this mood, using their new face and new manner to attract many promising young people. Ch'ien Pen-san should be reckoned as a confident person, because he still dared to look down on the Communist Party; he still had more or less of his own point of view, and did not simply follow the crowd.

The second occasion on which Ch'ien Shou-yü doubted her father's "paternal love" arose when she had to withdraw from Women's Normal College. She wanted to earn a degree, and her father insisted that she come to Hankow to help operate the organization section. But she wasn't versed in any of the numerous revolutionary enterprises in the organization section, and she really didn't know where to start.

Ch'ien Shou-yü did not deny that her father loved her. But she felt that in the control which he exercised over her, this love had the effect of hurting her. However, a woman, after all, is a woman, and although she was dubious, and even inwardly opposed, still she obeyed.

Her brother's letter also seemed to disapprove of her withdrawal from school. Her brother could only be considered half a soldier, but he too considered that armed force could solve everything. What contribution could a schoolgirl make towards the revolution? The revolution would depend on our rifles!

Ch'ien Shou-tien remained with his mother in their home in the countryside. After he graduated from primary school, he idled about for several years, and was usually to be found in the gambling dens or the brothels. Ch'ien Shou-yü had spoken to her father she didn't know how many times, wanting to bring her brother out to attend middle school, but her father would simply refuse. Later on, some Kuomintang members opened a new style middle school in Tsingtao. Ch'ien Shou-yü stealthily sent some money home and told her brother to go to Tsingtao and enroll in the beginning grade to begin with. At that time, Ch'ien Shou-tien was already nineteen years old. According to his studies, he couldn't enter the beginning grade, but this middle school was a secret organization of the Kuomintang, and its aim was to make revolutionaries, so that studies, or the lack of them, weren't too heavily emphasized. If Ch'ien Pen-san's son wished to enter, could there be any question? Their school wanted Ch'ien Pen-san's help in many things.

Before two semesters of the beginning grade had gone by, the local party leader urged the students to go to Canton and enter the military academy. Ch'ien Shou-tien, under this kind of prompting, resolutely packed his bags and nobly set out. But when he arrived in Canton he couldn't enroll; in both studies and physique he fell short. He felt embarrassed, and didn't write home, but went into the army as a warrant-officer clerk. At the time of Ch'ien Pen-san's last visit to Canton, to attend a meeting, Ch'ien Shou-tien had gone with the army to garrison Tung-chiang, and father and son had been unable to see each other. Later on his unit was ordered back to Canton for some unimportant instruction, then they set out for Shao-kuan to join the vanguard of the troops to be used in Hunan, in preparation for the first act of the fighting of the Northern Expedition.

At this time Ch'ien Shou-tien was a second lieutenant and chief of security in a company.

Reading Ch'ien Shou-tien's letter to his sister, so noble and full of excitement, Ch'ien Pen-san was also gladdened; it seemed the boy had gotten on the right path. Naturally, once the fighting started, there was no avoiding the days on end under artillery fire, and as junior officers were in the front line, their lives were in the greatest danger. But revolution is a kind of sacrifice, and so he didn't worry too much on his son's behalf. The Ch'ien family, since old times, had never produced a military officer; they had considered a military career despicable, and an unlucky thing. As the saying had it, "Good iron isn't beaten into a nail, and a good man doesn't become a soldier." A military career was the end of a man's life, it was the disheartened wanderer's tragic final refuge. But since Kwangtung had established its military academy, the revolutionary concept of fulfilling one's duty to the nation had gradually corrected a great many old, mistaken ideas, and some sons of educated and wealthy families, for a political ideal, were abandoning their books to study war. Although Ch'ien Shou-tien had not come out of the military academy, he had been able to place himself in the ranks of the revolutionary army, and even supposing that he was merely a foot soldier, it was glorious enough.

Ch'ien Pen-san, feeling a certain amount of disquiet, looked at Shou-yü, and said seriously:

"I've had something on my mind for some time which I want to talk over with you. Whether Wu P'ei-fu wins or loses, transportation on the P'ing-Han Line is of life-or-death importance to him."

Ch'ien Pen-san hesitated a moment, removed his dark glasses, and took out a handkerchief to rub his eyes. Ch'ien Shou-yü saw this, and said:

"Papa, your eyes are a little red."

"I know, lately I haven't slept much."

"You can't sleep?"

"That's right."

"Why?"

Ch'ien Pen-san was worried about the strength of General Wu's army. He feared that this time, as in the past, the Northern Expedition's army, after much clamor, would achieve nothing and withdraw. And if, unfortunately, it turned out like that, then all his arrangements and hopes of the past few years would be only bubbles. His loss of sleep actually had a political cause. But it wasn't convenient to say so in front of his daughter. He continued with the previous topic, saying:

"If we can break the southern section of the P'ing-Han Line at the appropriate moment, it's sure to have the greatest effect on military morale."

"I'm just afraid we don't have such talents." Ch'ien Shou-yü expressed her doubts.

"There are a few men, dispersed at various railroad stations near Hankow, but I'm not acquainted with them. I think someone ought to go and take a look at them, and see if we can undertake this job or not."

"Are you going to go yourself?"

"Of course I can't go."

"Well, then, who?"

"I was thinking of sending you and Miss Hung. No one would pay any attention to two girls travelling for fun."

"What could the two of us do? Besides, it would be even easier for people to suspect two young women running about here and there." Ch'ien Shou-yü hesitated a moment, and then added: "It would be proper to look for someone who understands military affairs for a job like this."

"When the time comes to act, of course I'll send military personnel. Now, this is only a first look to see how it is with these men, just an inspection."

"I'm not suitable for that either. You can't tell people's hearts from the outside, and what can you see with a hasty glance?"

Ch'ien Pen-san felt that his daughter's refusal was pardonable, so he did not press her. He thought a bit, and then said:

"Well, you go and ask Fourth Uncle to come over, and I'll discuss it with him."

Ch'ien Shou-yü agreed, and took the opportunity to say:

"There's something I've wanted to tell Papa for a long time. Lately Hung Chin-ling and I have gotten very friendly, and there's nothing we can't talk about. She told me that Hung T'ung-yeh is a member of the Communist Party. He joined the Communist Party even before he joined the Kuomintang, and he and Liu Shao-ch'iao have a special relationship."

"What special relationship?"

Ch'ien Shou-yü blushed and hung her head as she said softly:

"I don't like to say."

Ch'ien Pen-san smiled slightly, and said:

"I've known for a long time that he was a Communist."

"Well, then, why do you still use him? If you keep him beside you, like your heart or belly, aren't you done for?" Ch'ien Shou-yü was utterly amazed.

"This, you don't understand. By using him, I can have a connection with the Communist Party, and also I can show my goodwill to Kuo Hsin-ju; two gains with one effort," Ch'ien Pen-san said with a self-satisfied air, rubbing at his eyes.

"He and Kuo Hsin-ju only saw each other once or twice at Pei-tai-ho, and Kuo Hsin-ju doesn't know the real story about him."

"That's one of my moves." In order to let his daughter clearly understand his mind, Ch'ien Pen-san concealed nothing, and straightforwardly said: "Although the Communist Party has no future, it does represent a certain amount of strength. Besides that, it may contend with the Kuomintang, and that would be Anglo-American style democratic politics, which Kuo Hsin-ju encourages and hopes for. Kuo Hsin-ju often says that Dr. Sun Yat-sen's period of constitutional government ought to be Anglo-American style political democracy, and I think perhaps it might be."

Ch'ien Shou-yü understood her father's motives. His chess piece was placed on a three-cornered square. In the future, it would be all right if the Kuomintang succeeded, or if the Communist Party succeeded, or if Anglo-American style democratic government should actually be realized. His chess piece would be useful in any case. She couldn't help asking:

"Papa, do you really have any political ideals of your own?"

Ch'ien Pen-san was not appreciative of his daughter's question. It was as though he had met an opponent of his own caliber. He laughed, patted his chest, and said:

"Knock down the warlords, and then let me do as I please. Isn't that enough?"

"That's your political wish, it's not a political ideal." Ch'ien Shou-yü was disappointed in her father's shallowness.

"I'm for myself, and for you and Shou-tien; I can't be any other way."

When Ch'ien Pen-san said this, his daughter was even more dissatisfied; she stood up, and said helplessly:

"Very well, I'll go and see Fourth Uncle, and the two of you can talk."

When Ch'ien Pen-ssu learned that the men on the P'ing-Han Line had been stolen out of Chu Kuang-chi's organization, he was shocked, and said angrily:

"Third Brother, I'm not speaking to you as a younger brother, but you're getting more and more mixed up! You acted wildly but now you're really missing the mark!"

"I'll sacrifice everything for the revolution, without taking either slander or flattery into account." Ch'ien Pen-san at once pulled a long face, and pronounced each word with immense weight.

Ch'ien Pen-ssu shook his head and sighed. He no longer had any hope towards Third Brother's stubbornness. Now, he said:

"You're always talking about revolution, you eat the revolution like your regular meals. Now I'm asking you: why are you really making revolution, and how is the revolution going to come about?"

"Talking with you is like talking to those Peiyang warlords and that bureaucratic government—you can't talk sense to them. How can there be any other way, except by overthrowing them?" Ch'ien Pen-san looked at Fourth Brother, and smiled condescendingly.

"But I discovered many years ago that you, too, are a person who can't talk sense. There'll come a day when you, too, will be overthrown by someone!"

As he spoke, Ch'ien Pen-ssu was already heading for the door. He took his straw hat from the hook behind the door, and disappeared. This was because he knew Third Brother's measure very well, and that he would certainly not be able to take these words. When he was exasperated, he was apt to recklessly hit people, for he lost his reason.

"Rotten egg! Worthless thing!"

Sure enough, he heard Third Brother cursing him.

Ch'ien Pen-ssu left the Hotel France, and without hesitation went straight off to see Chu Kuang-chi. They had already spoken together many times, and were reckoned familiar friends. As soon as he saw the other, Ch'ien Pen-ssu said:

"You've been robbed, you've lost something—did you know?"

"I didn't know." Chu Kuang-chi was taken aback. "What is it?"

"Look, you're too careless!" Ch'ien Pen-ssu laughed. "You've lost half a railway, and you're still asleep and dreaming."

"I really don't understand what you're talking about."

Then Ch'ien Pen-ssu told Chu Kuang-chi all about how the roster of party members on the P'ing-Han Line had fallen into Ch'ien Pen-san's hand, and told him the whole story of how Ch'ien Pen-san planned to use them. He said:

"From the party's point of view, I'm against Third Brother doing this."

"His motive is very good." Chu Kuang-chi smoked a cigarette, looked up, and thought a bit, and then said: "The party members aren't my own personal capital. If Third Master can show what he can do on the P'ing-Han Line, and can carry it off, I'll share in the glory."

"Are those men up to it?"

"Now that's hard to say."

"Third Brother is thinking of sending someone to inspect the situation. What do you think of that?"

"I haven't any opinion."

"He feels there's no suitable person to send." Ch'ien Pen-ssu suddenly changed the topic of conversation. "This Hung T'ung-yeh—what's your impression of him?"

"His father and I used to be friends. But I don't know very well what sort of person he is. At first I looked on him as a member of the younger generation and believed in him completely. Later on I began to feel there were some things about him that weren't quite right," Chu Kuang-chi said, and then hastily asked: "Are you clear about him?"

Ch'ien Pen-ssu told Chu Kuang-chi all the news he had gotten from Hung Chin-ling concerning Hung T'ung-yeh. This aroused a great feeling of sadness in Chu Kuang-chi. He smiled bitterly, and said:

"Really, the youth of today aren't simple. I thought I was enough of a crafty old scoundrel, how should I have known I'd be taken in by a kid?"

"This person," Ch'ien Pen-ssu, who was in accord with Chu Kuang-chi, led the conversation on, "is in our little circle, and as you've said, he's a Sun the Pilgrim swinging in the Temple of the Five Viscera.[11] If we don't find a way to get rid of him, sooner or later he'll do us some harm."

"How can we get rid of him?"

"I've got a plan, but I don't know if you'd approve of it?"

"Let's hear it, all right?"

"I'll suggest to Third Brother that he send him to inspect the P'ing-Han Line. After he's gone, we'll send another man to find some out-of-the-way little station and make an end of him. It would be a case without a clue."

As Ch'ien Pen-ssu came forward, speaking so lightly, Chu Kuang-chi's heart jumped, and he said:

"Kill someone?"

"Yes, if we don't kill him, he'll kill us."

---

[11] Sun...Viscera: a reference to Wu Ch'eng-en's classic novel *Hsi-yu-chi*.

"Killing someone is never a way!" Chu Kuang-chi waved his hand, and said: "Especially not Hung T'ung-yeh, he's Pai-li's only son. If we did that, how could I face Pai-li? Fourth Master, it's out of the question."

"Well, then, do we drop him?"

"Actually, we can't drop him either. Wait 'til I call him over; I'll speak frankly with him, and exhort him."

Chu Kuang-chi made Ch'ien Pen-ssu sit down again, and lighted a cigarette for him. He was afraid that Ch'ien Pen-ssu, in his recklessness, would really do it, and so he went ahead, saying:

"The real problem isn't with little people like Hung T'ung-yeh, it's within our own group. In family relationships, you and Third Master are brothers; in unity of purpose, you're far from him and close to me. That's why I can say that Third Master's way of doing things is like picking up a rock only to drop it on one's own foot; if you raise a tiger, sooner or later you're in for a calamity."

When Ch'ien Pen-ssu heard this he got a bit stirred up, and denied it, saying:

"Are you talking about Third Master? How can he be called a tiger? He's no more than a dolt!"

"I didn't say he was a tiger, I said he's the man who raises the tiger."

Ch'ien Pen-ssu took two savage puffs, thought deeply for a moment, and then said:

"You're right. So I suggest getting rid of the tiger. Once the tiger's gone, the man who raised the tiger will have nowhere to stand."

"I can see neither of us is getting to the bottom of it," Chu Kuang-chi smiled. "Just now I wouldn't approve of getting rid of that tiger cub, because I consider that as a skin disease. Now you want to shield the man who raises the tiger, considering that beginning and end could be reversed. Really, each of us has his own shortcomings."

"People can't help having all kinds of selfish motives."

"All right, I recognize what you say. It's just that how are we going to handle it?" Chu Kuang-chi said casually; obviously he had gone from tension to relaxation.

"We'll hold off for a while, 'til the Northern Expedition army comes, before we settle the score."

"That's all we can do; there really isn't any good way."

Chu Kuang-chi agreed.

The city was outwardly calm, with crowds of people coming and going as usual, but inwardly there was trembling and disquiet everywhere. The merchants each made their own calculations, and some tried to sell all of their stocks for ready cash, and to exchange paper money for foreign cash. The Thief-punishing Headquarters, as soon as it was established, had issued a proclamation of martial law. The proclamation of martial law had never been revoked, and now it was reinforced with even greater severity. Patrolling squads of soldiers carrying big placards were given their assignments by the guards unit of the Headquarters. Each squad numbered twenty or thirty men, all of them armed with big swords and pistols. Their footsteps were heard on every street, and not long after one squad had passed, another squad would appear. Disbanded soldiers and roving volunteers, looking for trouble and provoking brawls, spread rumors and disturbed public order. The patrolling squads had the authority to dispense justice. Light punishment was a beating on the street with military cudgels; heavy punishment was to be arrested and locked up to await the court's decision. Every day, along the thoroughfares and main roads, there were notices of executions, and idlers crowded around. Those who could read, read them aloud for those who couldn't read. The general public opinion on the street was that those who had been executed had certainly deserved it, and that the killers had the right.

Scholarly gentlemen knew that General Wu had gotten his Licentiate degree, and that Chief Secretary Chang had been a Hanlin academician, and they respectfully copied these execution orders. Never mind that they themselves could read them, they also taught their sons and grandsons to read them, and they had to read them until they had them memorized. They felt that every one of these proclamations of the Headquarters had been handwritten by a Licentiate or a Hanlin academician, and since the examinations had long been abolished, from now on such good essays would be few. There were some who considered this pitifully dimwitted, but they appreciated their own cleverness, to the point that they were almost intoxicated with it.

Military currency had long been issued, and by law it had the same value as foreign cash. But it had been secretly discounted from the first day of its issue. When soldiers bought things with the military currency, the merchants dared not say they wouldn't accept it, so their method was to raise the price of their goods. For something which should have cost a dime, they would ask one or two dollars, or even three or five dollars, just as they pleased. Thus confusion arose. When the military currency came into the hands of the common people, don't think you could use it to buy anything—it wasn't worth half a cent.

People were shot to death on the street every day for refusing to use military currency.

One day at noon the southbound passenger train stopped at the Ta-chih gate station, and as the crowd of passengers was leaving the platform, suddenly there were sheets of paper flying about, and falling everywhere. Some busybodies examined them, and they were handbills of the revolutionary party. Printed on them were "Down With The Warlords!", "Down With Imperialism!", "Welcome The Northern Expedition of The Revolutionary Army!" and other simple slogans. Instantly all order was lost. Someone cried:

"Catch him, catch him!"

Then many big soldiers were seen binding a boy of fourteen or fifteen, who wore the white cotton jacket and trousers of a student. He had already turned as pale in the face as a sheet of paper, and his whole body was trembling. The martial law unit stationed at the railroad station asked for the issuance of an order. They had the bugler blow the single-note death call. A big soldier pressed his foot down on the boy's back, and there came a string of shots in close succession.

"They've shot a revolutionary party member at the railroad station!" Even before the notice could be posted, word had spread all over Hankow. The next day the morning paper published an editorial about the affair. They were prepared to add their praises when the Thief-punishing Headquarters summarily executed a member of the revolutionary party, the editorial said. But the one executed the day before had only been a minor, and it was extremely likely that he had been used, or hired by someone else. It was rather regrettable that the local authorities had not extracted from this nameless youth the identity of the chief plotter and instigator, so as to make an end of the wicked business.

The newspaper was sealed by the police the same day, and the whole staff, and workers, were jailed.

Chu Kuang-chi went to stay temporarily at Itakura Minoru's home to avoid the danger.

Liu Shao-ch'iao, having been introduced by Hung T'ung-yeh, hid out in Anna's shop, where some bedding had been laid out for him under the stairs. By this time, Anna knew what Hung T'ung-yeh was doing, but she sympathized with them. Impulsively she said:

"Even if General Wu were fiercer than he is, he wouldn't dare come into my house to get anyone. You relax and stay here. I like to see you young people giving your strength for your country; you're really fine. If you go on like this, sooner or later your country will be set to rights. I hope I can see that day."

Hung T'ung-yeh translated this for Liu Shao-ch'iao, and Liu Shao-ch'iao thanked her. Turning away, he said quietly to Hung T'ung-yeh:

"This woman with the little mustache, are you and she . . .?"

"Stop that nonsense!" Hung T'ung-yeh's face went grim, and he said with obvious displeasure: "She's the only person I've ever met in my life who treated me like a human being, and I respect her. Besides, she's helping you without conditions now, so I'm asking you not to insult her. She's not like Lefebvre's wife."

"Look at you and your phony respectability!" Liu Shao-ch'iao stared at him hatefully and said: "I said that you and she were close; surely that's no insult?"

"I return respect for respect. My relationship with her is pure and transcendent. You don't understand."

Hung T'ung-yeh's "You don't understand" was spoken with such complete contempt that Liu Shao-ch'iao couldn't help being a little startled. He put out his hand, meaning to pinch Hung T'ung-yeh's leg, as he had often pinched him until he wept with the pain and could not but submit.

"What are you saying?" Anna asked, as she saw that there was something different about their expressions.

As soon as he heard Anna speak, Liu Shao-ch'iao quickly pulled back his hand. Hung T'ung-yeh smiled, and lied:

"He was asking me, if M. Raymond comes home, would he be against him staying here? I've already told him that it couldn't happen. M. Raymond has the greatest respect for his wife, and regards his wife's words as an eleventh commandment of God, to be kept absolutely. To transgress against his wife's will means going down to the hell of hells."

Anna burst out laughing when she heard this. She said:

"Your answer was very funny, but it's really not like that. My husband neither loves nor hates the Chinese. The Peking government hired him to be an advisor, and gives him a high salary, so he's the Peking government's friend. If one day your southern revolutionary government comes to power, you need only hire him, and he'll be your friend. He calculates only his own interest, and not from any political standpoints of yours."

As Anna spoke, she batted her eyes, and stroked her little mustache with her right forefinger. Then she clapped her hands, and said:

"He's never listened to me! As for me, I'll help you. Little Hung, tell your friend what I've said."

Hung T'ung-yeh translated what she had said for Liu Shao-ch'iao. Liu Shao-ch'iao nodded, and said:

"Who'd have thought this mustached lady of yours would put on such an act?"

"She's really a good person."

"Wait and see," Liu Shao-ch'iao said, nodding at Anna, who nodded back, and then went upstairs. Liu Shao-ch'iao looked after her, and asked Hung T'ung-yeh:

"Have you had a letter from your mother?"

"Yes."

"What did it say?"

"She says she isn't willing to come to Hankow, but she hopes Chin-ling and I will come back to Shanghai."

"Why's that?"

"She's old, and her health isn't good. It's just that it's hard to leave the old home place, that's all."

"What a pity!"

Hung T'ung-yeh said nothing. Liu Shao-ch'iao stared at him, and said:

"You don't speak?"

"There's nothing I can say."

"Why?"

"I really can't accept your plan."

"Your brain can't accept new concepts, is that it?"

"I can accept any new concept, but you can't tell me to test it on the body of my own little sister, and still less on my own mother," Hung T'ung-yeh said painfully. "I can even say that if you wanted me to take a knife and kill them, I could consider doing it. Only what you're hoping for, that I can't do."

"I've already said," Liu Shao-ch'iao said, shaking his head, "anyone can storm the barricades, but you're the most suitable."

"You have a mother too, why haven't you—?"

"She died early. If she were still alive, it would hardly need you to suggest it. I'd have done it long ago."

"You're really a devil!" Hung T'ung-yeh said hatefully.

"No mistake, I oppose God's laws and virtues," Liu Shao-ch'iao said with a grimace. "If only you'd obey the devil, and leave God."

"I don't want the devil, and I don't want God. I just want to be a man with a conscience."

"Your conscience is in a woman's little mustache, is that it?" Liu Shao-ch'iao gestured towards the upstairs.

"You could say that."

"You know I'm taking refuge here, so you won't obey me. All right, just you wait."

So saying, Liu Shao-ch'iao burrowed into his place beneath the stairs and went to sleep. Hung T'ung-yeh relaxed and sat in the leather chair. He felt a boundless sense of having been wronged, and had no idea how to get rid of it. After a long, long time, he heard Liu Shao-ch'iao's light snore. Softly, he shut the gates, and crept stealthily up the stairs. When he was halfway up the stairs, he heard Liu Shao-ch'iao's cold laugh.

"You little hypocrite!"

When Hung T'ung-yeh heard this, he stood still, uncertain whether to advance or retreat. He thought it over, and for fear that the other would go on calling out, he went back down the stairs. He sat down listlessly before the desk. Anna's purse was on the desk, and he opened it to look inside. There was a powder compact, a lipstick, and other such cosmetic items, and there were some folded banknotes. He opened the drawer, which wasn't locked, and there was some loose change. Hung T'ung-yeh at once became suspicious, and regretted that he had brought Liu Shao-ch'iao to stay here. If the other should take it into his head to steal her things, how could he repay her goodwill? When I was at Lefebvre's, and they treated me as they did, I didn't take a single thing of theirs. But this Liu Shao-ch'iao can't be depended upon; he might do it.

Thinking about it, he felt very uneasy, and his face burned. Nor did Liu Shao-ch'iao remain at rest any longer. He got up, and came out barefooted, taking a cigarette from the cigarette-box and smoking as he watched Hung T'ung-yeh. He said:

"I've got two matters which have got to be resolved."

He said this as though he were waiting for Hung T'ung-yeh to ask him, whereupon he would continue. Unexpectedly Hung T'ung-yeh kept his mouth shut, and didn't ask. Liu Shao-ch'iao laughed and asked:

"What, you don't care about my affairs?"

"How could that be? Speak, I'm listening." Hung T'ung-yeh helplessly laughed along with him.

"First, I can't stay in such a place for the sake of my individual safety, and I'm going to leave now. If I hole up here, won't everything come to a halt outside?"

Liu Shao-ch'iao's words struck directly to Hung T'ung-yeh's concern. He was overjoyed, and wished the other *would* go. But he didn't let it show on his face, and said:

"Ch'ien Pen-san never sets foot outside the Hotel France, but doesn't everything get done just the same?"

"He and I aren't the same," Liu Shao-ch'iao said lightly. "He suspends himself in space and does everything by proxy, and the less he goes out, the greater his influence. I'm building a foundation from underground, and I've got to work and sweat in person."

"Well, where are you going to stay?"

"Back at Ssu-fen-li. I figure it'll be safe, unless Old Ch'ien the Fourth betrays me."

Liu Shao-ch'iao spat noisily and heavily onto the carpet. This action aroused Hung T'ung-yeh to anger. He flushed and said:

"That's a carpet, how can you spit on it? If she sees it, how embarrassing!"

"You've been a slave of the foreigners so long you've learned how to fear them."

"This isn't a question of Chinese and foreigners. It's courtesy, and Chinese and foreigners alike ought to have courtesy. Moreover, she was kind enough to take you in, so you're her guest."

Hung T'ung-yeh controlled his anger, and as he spoke, he took a piece of wrapping paper and knelt to wipe the carpet. As he was straightening up, Liu Shao-ch'iao pinched him on the thigh, and Hung T'ung-yeh, in pain, drew away. Liu Shao-ch'iao said:

"What do you think about what I just said?"

"Ch'ien Pen-ssu?"

"Exactly."

"Why would he betray you?"

"Don't you understand that yet?" Liu Shao-ch'iao said, lowering his voice. "He hates the Communist Party, and he loves Chin-ling. If he takes care of me, it'll suit him from both angles."

"That absolutely couldn't happen. Surely he'll have realized you can bite him, and if you really bit him, how could he stand it?"

"What you say is right too. All right, then, I'll relax and go back to Ssu-fen-li. And the second thing is money! If I go back, without money I still can't do anything."

As Liu Shao-ch'iao spoke, he fixed his eyes on Hung T'ung-yeh as though by his stare he could draw money from the other's face. When he saw that Hung T'ung-yeh did not reply, he went on:

"You know that my money comes from only three sources: my family's shop, Ch'ien Pen-san, and there's you. But for a long time now, none of these have treated me with filial respect."

"Your expenditures are too great; nobody can keep you supplied."

"Why are my expenditures great? Is it because I'm living well? Like Ch'ien Pen-san?" Liu Shao-ch'iao looked at Hung T'ung-yeh. "Answer honestly."

"I know that. How do you figure to get money now?"

Liu Shao-ch'iao pointed towards the upstairs, and pressed his hand crosswise on his middle. He said:

"Isn't there ready money right here?"

"How can you get it?"

"Tell her we belong to the Kuomintang. Don't say it's the Communist Party, for fear she'd be frightened. Just ask her directly for a loan."

"She's a foreigner, and a woman besides. I'm afraid it won't do."

"Then say it's my idea, and I asked you to discuss it with her for me. Try it, and if it doesn't work, why, it's no matter."

In his heart, Hung T'ung-yeh was really unwilling to do this, but Liu Shao-ch'iao had suggested it, and he could only obey. He nodded, and said reluctantly:

"All right, then, wait 'til she comes down. I'll be the interpreter, and the two of you can discuss it yourselves."

"Why can't you go upstairs?"

"That's no good, she's a woman."

"Weren't you just sneaking upstairs?"

This one remark stopped Hung T'ung-yeh so that he could no longer open his mouth. Liu Shao-ch'iao said with satisfaction:

"Say something!"

Just as they were quarrelling, Anna came downstairs. She spoke while she was still on the steps, asking:

"What are you talking about?"

Hung T'ung-yeh waited until she had seated herself, and told her that Liu Shao-ch'iao was going to leave.

"Since the situation is still dangerous outside, why not stay a few days longer?" Anna said.

"For the revolution, I can't worry too much about my own safety. I'm going back, I'll brave the danger."

Liu Shao-ch'iao spoke with righteous indignation. This aroused Anna's sympathy; she kept expressing her admiration, and said:

"China's youth have awakened! Very well, then, I won't keep you."

"But there's something else he wants to ask you to help him with."

"That's splendid." As soon as Anna heard this, she stood up excitedly. "I was just regretting that I couldn't do something for you. Since I can be of use to you, speak, and as long as it's something I can do, I'll certainly do it."

"He can't meet his expenses, and he figured on a short-term loan from you."

"How much?" Anna asked, not a bit put off.

Hung T'ung-yeh looked at Liu Shao-ch'iao. Now Liu Shao-ch'iao was in a quandary; he didn't know how large a sum would be suitable. Anna pressed him, saying:

"How much do you want? Say it, don't be polite. I'm very willing to help with this work."

Liu Shao-ch'iao started to discuss it with Hung T'ung-yeh.

"How much do you think I should say?"

"I've no way of knowing. If it were Mme. Lefebvre, I know I could only borrow ten or fifteen dollars. With this one, I don't know how she feels about such things yet—who knows?" Hung T'ung-yeh, guessing, said: "Only, I think it won't do to ask for too much."

"Should I ask for two hundred, or three hundred?"

"I'm afraid that's too much. She might not be willing, and that wouldn't be so good."

"Let's take the chance. Tell her, and we'll see."

So Hung T'ung-yeh told Anna the sum of two hundred dollars. When Anna heard this, she sat down, surprised, and said uncomprehendingly:

"What are you going to do with two hundred dollars?"

"I'm in charge of the General Labor Union. We have several tens of thousands of members, and we have many things to do," Liu Shao-ch'iao said, in suspense, and afraid that he had missed his mark.

"Well, then, is two hundred dollars enough?" Anna asked in wonderment.

At this Liu Shao-ch'iao realized the proper approach, and knew that the sum he had just named was too small. He cursed Hung T'ung-yeh:

"You fool, you spoil so many things for me!"

Then he said:

"In fact, two hundred dollars isn't enough. Since this is the first time I've borrowed from you, I didn't like to ask for more."

Hung T'ung-yeh interpreted this. Anna said joyfully to Liu Shao-ch'iao:

"You really understand courtesy. China's new youth is really fine! I'll give you five hundred dollars now. This isn't a loan, it's a gift, so you don't need to repay me."

So saying, Anna ran happily upstairs, to return a moment later with a roll of banknotes, which she handed to Liu Shao-ch'iao. Liu Shao-ch'iao hastily thanked her. In his heart, he hated Hung T'ung-yeh. If that timid rabbit hadn't guessed short, I could have started with five thousand, or ten thousand, and it wouldn't have been too much. Very well, since there's this opening, I'll see about it next time. He raised his hand to wave goodbye.

"Come again anytime. I'll kill a chicken and invite you for dinner," Anna said to the two Chinese youths, reluctant to let them go. "If the situation isn't right, you can hide here any time. I hope you'll take care."

"Let me go first, by myself," Liu Shao-ch'iao said to Hung T'ung-yeh. "Wait a bit, and then you come along. You can court the mustache-lady some more; your foreign garlic-bud seems to have opened up enough."

"All right, you'd better go. Someone treats you so well, and you talk about them without any respect at all."

"I'm no good; you'll have to instruct me more often."

"I don't dare. I only hope you'll respect her."

Hung T'ung-yeh turned and went to gather up, from under the stairs, the bedding Liu Shao-ch'iao had used. Apologetically, he said to Anna:

"It's all dirty. I'll take it out and wash it for you."

"Never mind, you leave it. Your friend is really fine. It's as though he knows nothing but his work. You see how he doesn't comb his hair, or wash—

such people are truly rare," Anna said with a smile, and asked: "What were you talking about, just now?"

Hung T'ung-yeh, dispirited, sat down and said with a sigh:

"Although you praise him, I regret that I brought him here."

"Why is that?"

"That person is like iron, or stone, he hasn't any feelings at all. You loaned him money, but he only considers that you've fallen into his snare, that you can be cheated; there's no feeling of gratitude in his heart."

"But I didn't want his thanks."

"I'm only afraid that later on he may come often to bother you," Hung T'ung-yeh said painfully, with tears in his eyes. "I regret that I know such a person myself, and it's even worse that I introduced him to you."

Anna, perplexed, looked at Hung T'ung-yeh, and felt that she didn't understand him at all. Since they were friends, they ought to have friendly affection; if there was no friendly affection, why then were they still friends? Were these two people friends after all? Or enemies?

Naturally this was something which Anna could never comprehend.

And even Hung T'ung-yeh himself found it hard to explain.

Chapter XI

Already the season had entered the eighth month of the lunar calendar, and the weather in Hankow was, as usual, extraordinarily hot; the "tiger of autumn" was uncommonly strong. But at first light on the day of the Mid-autumn Festival came a slanting wind and a light rain, and the clouds hung low, giving people a feeling of chill and loneliness. Everyone hoped for a clear evening, so that the festival would not have passed in vain. Unexpectedly, from twilight on, the rain increased, and during the whole of the night the face of the moon could not be seen.

During the past month, there had been frequent stoppages of electrical power in the evenings. Sometimes several adjoining streets would drop into darkness, and the residents would resort to shallow kerosene lamps or foreign candles in order to get through the night. At first the larger shops still did business by kerosene lamps. But in circumstances of such disorder, with inky blackness everywhere, to have only their own lights showing gave people a rather insecure feeling, and gradually they ceased to be used. But only let the electrical current be interrupted, and they would lock the doors and light the lamps. On this account, the city's aspect by night grew ever more lonely.

There was more than one reason for the electrical failures. Some said that the electrical lines were old, and should have been long since replaced with new ones, only the money for replacing them had been taken by the military. So they were not replaced, and there was no avoiding the gradual advance of this chronic ill. But another, and more forceful, rumor said that the revolutionary party was carrying out sabotage aimed at throwing people into confusion.

In the midst of wind and rain, in their lonely situation with neither moonlight nor lamplight, the people of Hankow lost some of their interest in chewing moon-cakes. The common people, who had never concerned themselves with politics, began to put their heads together, furtively inquiring after news of the current situation. It was said that the main force of the forward element of the Revolutionary Army, long forced to remain in southern Hunan, had already seized Hengyang with a single blow, and was moving on Changsha. General Wu had already moved to Yüeh-chou, and of the General Headquarters in Hankow there remained only an empty shell.

The southern section of the P'ing-Han Line, through which the northern army might be reinforced, was unbroken, and it was said that the Szechuan army would come forth to support General Wu. The crack troops of allied General Sun Hsing-yuan held the Nanking-Kiukiang Line, tranquilly observing the changing situation. The Feng-t'ien clique, from Chang the Rain-god,[12] the Jade General Ch'u from Paoting, and the Efficacious General Chang[13] of Tsinan had all rushed to send telegrams full of thief-punishing and anti-Red sentiments; all of them ran to several thousand words. With righteous indignation, they swore to serve as General Wu's rear guard.

The situation was one-sided, and the wrigglings of the Revolutionary Army from Kwangtung were just like trying to smash a rock with an egg. This was the view of all the experienced and knowledgeable men.

---

[12] Chang the Rain-god: General Chang Tso-lin, the warlord of Manchuria.

[13] The Efficacious General Chang: General Chang Ts'ung-chang, also known as the "Dogmeat General".

But the common people did not calculate who won and who lost. They were anxious over the many calamities which could issue from the disorder of battle, when neither life nor property could be protected.

The military currency notes filled the whole sky, while their value sank lower and lower. A man, holding a one-dollar note, went to buy an oily fritter, but he couldn't make the exchange; the other wouldn't sell it at all. The man who wanted to buy the oily fritter got angry, and ran off to report to the martial law patrol. But when the patrol arrived, the man who sold fritters had already disappeared, without a trace. The patrol officer came up empty-handed and didn't like it, so he discharged his anger on the person of the man who wanted to buy the fritter. He blamed him for making a false report. The credit of the military notes had always been good, and there were none, military or civilian, who weren't happy to use them.

"You shouldn't make something out of nothing, spreading rumors and making trouble, and spoiling the army's good name! Looking at you, you ugly fellow, I can see you forgot great principle in your greed for a small advantage, and you're no-good by nature!"

So he was kicked over, and kneeling in the street he suffered fifty strokes of a military cudgel.

The whole patrol, satisfied and even more formidable, counted off, came to attention, wheeled about, and left. News of this incident, in which the military notes had been refused, spread at once, and people no longer turned in reports, but swallowed their sorrows and let it go at that. The officials in charge of managing military currency matters at the Thief-punishing Headquarters quietly investigated public opinion, and felt that the currency's ease of circulation proved that the simple common people knew where their loyalty lay. They submitted a report to General Wu, and the General delightedly issued an order expressing his commendations.

After the patrol left, the man who had been beaten with the military cudgels lay on the ground, groaning and sighing and unable to move. People who lived in the neighborhood came out to take a look at him, but no one recognized him, and when queried he did not answer. The crowd of bystanders kept on growing; they surrounded the scene and would not disperse. It grew so disorderly that several of the nearby merchants couldn't do business. They reported it to the police, but the police refused to intervene, saying that it was the military which had dealt with the man, and it wasn't certain that his case was concluded, so they didn't want to interfere. When inquiry was made of the Martial Law Headquarters, they too said that they hadn't yet received any report, and they knew nothing at all of the matter. With all this pulling and hauling nearly half a day passed.

The neighborhood merchants deliberated, and fearing that he would die, they gave him a little gruel and some morsels to eat. Someone bought him an oily fritter, since a man who had frightened Heaven and shocked Earth going to law over a fritter obviously couldn't have much money. They got together a little money and hired a rickshaw to take him to a hospital, and they sent a man to accompany him, and stay close by his side. This was because they were afraid he might take it into his head to run away, and if the military should by any chance decide that they wanted the man again, and want to know who had let him go, how would that be?

The news had gotten about, and the hospitals did not dare take him in. They went to quite a few hospitals, but they all refused, and say whatever you liked, they definitely wouldn't accept him. Finally the rickshaw man suggested:

"Why don't you try and send him to the Common Benevolence Society hospital? Maybe the Japanese will dare take him in."

The man who had custody saw nothing else to do and could only nod his head, so they set out for the Japanese Concession.

The Japanese marines had recently been added as sentries before the gates of the Common Benevolence Society hospital. The sentries were stationed before the gates of this civil hospital only to demonstrate the Japanese Empire's concern with the tense local situation; it was only the manifestation of an attitude, and they were not examining those who went in and out, nor interfering with business. The man who had custody didn't know this, and watched the Japanese sentries from a distance, not daring to go in. Once again, it was the rickshaw man who said:

"It's all right, come on. I've often done business here; I know."

So he braced himself and went ahead.

It was easier than he could have imagined. Not only did the two sentries let him pass with barely a glance, but as soon as he entered he was able to register his charge as an emergency case, and carry him into the emergency room, and the doctors and nurses appeared at once. After making the examination, the doctor spoke, and a Chinese nurse served as his interpreter.

"His external injuries are very light; they don't matter. But he has heart disease, and should stay in the hospital for examination."

She asked urgently:

"Will he be staying in the hospital?"

The man who had custody of the patient was overjoyed; he had found a place that was willing to take him. Why shouldn't he stay there? He went through the procedure of paying, and carried the patient into a sickroom. The man who had custody got the patient settled, and then sighed, and wiped the sweat from his brow. He calculated the time: from coming in the gates until now had taken, at the most, no more than ten minutes. The man was thinking of making a telephone call and asking them to send someone to take his place watching the patient, so that he could go back. Then he heard someone say:

"The Director's here."

He saw a man with a little beard, wearing a surgeon's gown—probably it was the Director—accompanied by a middle-aged man in a Chinese gown, and they were talking and smiling as they walked slowly along. A slender nurse accompanied them.

He recognized the gentleman in the Chinese gown, and when they approached, he spoke up:

"Principal Chu, are you here?"

"Who are you? You seem very familiar."

"I'm the clerk at the T'ung-feng rice-shop; I've often brought rice to your place."

"Oh, right, right. What are you doing here?"

"The manager told me to bring an injured man here."

So the rice-shop clerk told what had happened. Chu Kuang-chi listened, and kept shaking his head and sighing. While they were talking, Director Itakura Minoru had already seen his patient. When Chu Kuang-chi asked about her condition, Itakura Minoru replied:

"Probably it's not so serious. Wait a bit and we'll ask the doctor in charge, and then we'll know."

Itakura Minoru stopped, and asked his daughter Baitai, who had followed him into the examination room:

"How is that woman patient of mine? Have you seen her?"

"Her sickness is all right, but her state of mind is bad; she's always weeping miserably."

"That's no wonder! Come," Itakura Minoru said to Chu Kuang-chi, "We'll go and see her together."

"I'm afraid that's not convenient, she's always afraid a Chinese man will see her," Itakura Baitai hastily said.

"What does it matter if it's Mr. Chu? Very well, since you say so. Brother Chu, wait a moment for me."

So saying, Itakura Minoru took his daughter into another single-patient sickroom. When he came out, Chu Kuang-chi couldn't keep from asking him:

"What sort of woman patient is it?"

"Wait a bit and I'll tell you in detail."

Itakura Minoru returned to his own office, and after taking off his surgeon's gown and washing his hands, he took Chu Kuang-chi into his home. This dwelling was next door to the hospital, and a small wooden door in the wall between connected it to the interior of the hospital. Itakura Minoru always used this door when coming on and going off duty. The house, in the Japanese style, was surrounded by a broad verandah. The two men removed their shoes, and sat down in rattan chairs on the verandah. A well-scrubbed Chinese maidservant brought tea. Flowering plants flourished on the verandah, and a dense row of tall white poplars circled the wall. As it was the beginning of autumn, the soughing sound produced by the white poplars of north China took on a more urgently moving note. Itakura Minoru enjoyed the sound of the trees; he considered it stirring; like an angry roar of resistance born of the irresistible power of nature, it aroused a man.

Itakura Minoru swallowed a mouthful of tea, and as the leaves of the white poplars swirled by in the wind, he stretched out his hand and caught one. Comparing it, he found it bigger than his hand. Gently he placed it on the tea-tray. With the recent situation so tense, the ruling authorities had been employing larger prisons and casually applied death penalties to stamp out rebellion and guarantee their own rule. Chu Kuang-chi had given himself to the revolution, and had never paid much attention to his own security, but now he too was unwilling to make a useless sacrifice, and he had taken refuge in Itakura Minoru's home. The Japanese cruisers anchored in midstream had removed their gun-covers, as an expression of their resolve to protect their nationals, and their guns were trained on the center of Hankow.

"Relax, and stay here, brother Chu," Itakura Minoru warmly welcomed Chu Kuang-chi. "No matter how stubborn and fierce Wu P'ei-fu may be, he won't dare come into the Japanese concession and seize a person out of a Japanese home, so you can just relax and stay here."

"Thank you," Chu Kuang-chi said with a smile. "I know that if our army men are fierce, it's only toward their own people. As soon as they face a foreigner, they turn as soft as snot. They don't dare touch a single hair of a foreigner's head, or even speak half a word of gossip behind his back. Such subservience is truly shameful, extremely shameful."

"I think," Itakura Minoru said feelingly, "that they have their own reasons. When a people wants to travel the road of wealth and strength, and counts on gaining a place in the sun, the process is a difficult one, and every weakling fears to face such a future. But flattering foreigners and pacifying one's own people is a ready-made sutra—when you bend your legs and kneel on the ground, anything can be accomplished, and you certainly save a lot of trouble."

"That year when we did dissections in physiology, I didn't know the knee had another use, and such an important one." Chu Kuang-chi patted his knee and smiled bitterly.

"This discussion of the knee belongs to political science, not to medicine."

The two men laughed.

Chu Kuang-chi stayed in Itakura Minoru's house, and while security was security, it was inconvenient for outside contacts and work. He was always thinking, I've been at revolution for twenty years, revolutionizing here and there; I haven't made a name for myself, and now I've finally revolutionized myself into the house of a Japanese. There's no getting around it, to secure myself in the face of danger, to beg safety from a foreigner, means that I lose the role of a dignified revolutionary, and chop down the great sign-board of revolution. Under these conditions of complete security, Chu Kuang-chi's mood was worse than when he was risking danger, for when placed amid raging billows and terrifying waves, he felt quite at ease, and even happy.

He kept thinking of going home, of going back to school, and of going on just as he had before, putting life and death, ill fortune or good, out of his calculations. He knew that this was the right thing, and so he made his resolution; it was only that he didn't act on it.

The man who heartlessly attacks a stubborn and unreasonable old system and ancient concepts can abandon himself, and nothing holds him back; he cannot have too much partiality towards himself, because he, too, is the product of that old system and those ancient concepts. It must be so; only then can he be completely independent and do as he wishes without the slightest hesitation.

So Chu Kuang-chi analyzed himself. But it was hard to dissipate the loneliness of seclusion. The chrysanthemums were already full with seeds, and the leaves on the two maples, brought over from Japan, were turning red. Double ninth was approaching, and although it wasn't yet all over the city, it was the beginning of the end of the year, and nature's necessary tragedy had already begun.

Chu Kuang-chi's loneliness grew broader and deeper.

At times he helped Itakura Minoru with one thing or another, and accompanied him to the examining room, or taught Itakura Baitai to speak Chinese. This young girl, never mind her short stature, had unexcelled cleverness and unequalled warmth. Any number of new doctors, finding themselves at someone's bedside and utterly at a loss where to begin, had only to glance at her, and with a few soft-spoken and simple words, she would point out the diagnostic clues and direct them to the source of the illness. She had seen ever so many patients, read ever so many medical histories, and assisted ever so many famous doctors; she had sufficient experience.

But she was always equally quiet and respectful in front of interns, and unless they asked for her help, she never said an unnecessary word. Sometimes she knew very well that they were wrong, but she kept quiet, willing to let the responsibility lie with the doctor who would make another examination.

Such was the nurse's lot. The nurse took the doctor's orders, and the doctor didn't take the nurse's orders. Itakura Minoru would often say:

"Baitai, when we return home, you'd better enter medical school. You could be a good doctor."

"It won't do to have good doctors, if there are no good nurses," Itakura Baitai would turn her sweetly smiling face upon her father, and politely say: "Papa will be a good doctor, and daughter will be a good nurse, then all will be well on both sides."

"Papa can't be a good doctor," Itakura Minoru said with a sigh, with obvious pleasure. "I'm the hospital Director, and there is too much hospital administrative work, so I've gotten out of touch with medicine."

"You ought to give the administrative work to the Assistant Director, and then Papa could concentrate on seeing patients."

"Unless my daughter were the Assistant Director, how could I relax about handing it all over?"

Father and daughter laughed together.

Among all the Japanese at the Common Benevolence Society hospital, Itakura Baitai was one of the best speakers of Chinese, but she still felt it wasn't enough, and she wanted her adopted father, Chu Kuang-chi, to instruct her. Chu Kuang-chi liked teaching, but he said:

"My local accent is too heavy; I'm afraid I'll teach you wrongly."

He did begin to teach her, honestly and frankly. They used a book—*A Course In Chinaman Speech*—commonly used by Japanese, which used Japanese as the main text, and translated it into Chinese. Many Japanese couldn't understand that sort of Chinese, and Chinese couldn't understand it either. But all the Japanese liked to use it.

On this day Itakura Minoru told Chu Kuang-chi the story of his woman patient.

"You'll certainly find it surprising," he said, lowering his voice. "I performed an abortion on her, a child of almost three months."

"Do you do such things too?"

Chu Kuang-chi understood extraordinarily well Itakura Minoru's temperament and character, and knew that for him to have done such a thing, there certainly had to have been an irresistible reason. But, as always when he was shaken, he burst out with this suspicious question.

"This was the first time. For the sake of their individual and family reputations, I couldn't refuse. Although a fetus was destroyed, many people were saved because of it."

Itakura Minoru said this, hesitated a moment, and then went on:

"To prove the kind of person I am, I gave her everything gratis. Not only was the surgery free, but I made her a gift of the room, the bed, the food and drink, and the medication. And in fact she's got money. When they were coming to terms with me, they first mentioned eighteen thousand as though it were nothing."

"You don't need to explain this to me," Chu Kuang-chi hastened to say. "We've known each other a long time."

"One wishes his sentiments to be known," Itakura Minoru said with a smile, "not only by Heaven and Earth, but by you and me, and by others. There are many things on which we want to find out ways to express our own feelings, for our own peace of mind, and also that others can come to peace of mind. This is another way of manifesting the virtue of reciprocity."

"No mistake, what you say is exactly right." Chu Kuang-chi was moved. "If Jesus, having said so many important things, and having left so many moving words, hadn't mounted the cross, and hadn't given his last drop of blood, he wouldn't have achieved anything, and would have been as worthless as grass or wood. I think that's what you meant."

"That's right, action is the best form of expression," Itakura Minoru kept nodding his head.

"Come on, tell me about your woman patient," Chu Kuang-chi urged him.

Since she had been rescued after throwing herself into the river, and since Pai Ch'a-hua had been sent away, Liu Shao-ch'iao's wife Yeh P'in-hsia had hired a new maidservant to live in the house on Chiao-t'ung Road. Like Liu Shao-ch'iao's father, she had all along held to a simple dream, hoping that her husband would one day finally change his mind and that they would be able to establish a regular married life. If it could truly be so, then all the unhappiness she had suffered would change to smoke and dust, and disappear. To be a woman means that, if only one receives one's husband's compassion, then although one doesn't receive offerings from the hand, neither is one trodden underfoot, and one may be reckoned to have attained the ideal of "marry a dog, follow a dog; marry a chicken, follow a chicken". Yeh P'in-hsia's hopes were not extravagant, but because she had experienced a brief and unexpected oppression, she had bowed her head to reality, and had even fallen to her knees.

Before her marriage, when had she ever tasted such experience? In those days, counting on her own beauty and talents, she had naively thought of marital happiness; they would entrust each other with their bodies and minds, and respect each other as though they were guests. In Yeh P'in-hsia's home, just as in many other great Chinese families, they were accustomed to their own tradition of sacrificing to Heaven and praying to the ancestors, and they shut the gates tight, so that not the slightest breath, nor a single hair, of Jesus Christ could get in. But when Yeh P'in-hsia was studying in the school, she had heard the woman English teacher, who was a Christian, happen to mention the great principle that "the husband is the head of the wife". In the beginning, God made man and woman, and it was said that the two alike were of one body, but He did not explain which had how much of the one body, whether it was half and half, or whether one of them had the more and the heavier parts. St. Paul himself did not marry, but he established the position of man, and what he wrote about "the husband is the head of the wife" became one of the tenets of Christianity. Because every action of St. Paul's was in the name of Jesus Christ, this was a serious matter.

Yeh P'in-hsia deeply detested that simple saying. She often thought that that so-called pleasure of the women's chambers was not much more than painting one's eyebrows. Husbands and wives ought to be of equal status, on equal terms, which was to say, the equality of men and women. But who could have known that the ideal and the reality were far apart, and that after marriage, she would try to treat her husband as the head, and be unable to do so?

The method of accepting her position was of course to retreat step by step and to constrict the world of her hopes smaller and yet smaller. By the time she was ready to throw herself into the river, the world of Yeh P'in-hsia's hopes had become so small that there was nothing left of it; she had given up hope.

There's nothing left in the world for me. Living alone, and lonely, in such a big house, Yeh P'in-hsia began to seek another, unknowable world. On the third floor she arranged a small Buddhist shrine. She bought a white porcelain Kuan Yin, two feet high, from an antique shop, and the red sandalwood for the tripodal censer which came with her, as well as the white candles and the fragrant flowers, the oil lamps and the wooden fish. She had also gone cautiously to a Buddhist convent to burn incense, and had tentatively asked those bald-headed women to instruct her in the study of Buddhism. But, for some unknown reason, she couldn't abide their coarse manners, and after one taste of it, she quietly left them.

To be without talent is virtue in a woman—there was something to that old saying after all. Out of the misfortunes she had suffered, Yeh P'in-hsia took herself as an example. On this account, she felt that seeking under someone else's guidance wasn't as good as feeling them out for herself, and that you couldn't say that just reading them blindly wasn't a good way to try. So she began with the simple recitation of Buddha's name, and then gradually learned the Grand Lamentation, until she could recite it smoothly from memory. She would also informally fast, often substituting this for the vegetarian meal she had prepared.

From then on she abandoned her cosmetics, and from head to foot wore only blue cotton. She regretted that her skin was too white, and felt that this would be the only obstacle to her entry into that other, unknowable world. She tried mingling a kind of ashy-yellow chemical liquid into her facial cream, to induce a sick-room darkness on her face.

After closely examining this haggard look in the big mirror, she was pleased, and also hurt, and wept a few tears unawares.

She meant not only to conceal her beauty, but also to block her cleverness and her intelligence.

Several months passed in this manner.

Although Yeh P'in-hsia did not set foot outside the house, she really hadn't gotten to the point of having a heart of wood or stone, as in the saying "no ripples in an ancient well".[14] Sometimes when she was annoyed, she felt that sitting wouldn't do, nor would standing, and she couldn't find a place to settle. Suddenly she thought that Uncle Te-kuang and her father had lived and gained a reputation

---

[14] "no ripples in an ancient well": a saying referring to the absence of sexual desire in an elderly widow.

in the world through poetry and wine; perhaps therein lay another world? She thought a bit, and then made up her mind. Standing at the head of the stairs, she called to her maid to go and buy some wine.

The maid felt there was something a little odd, and she responded:

"Buy which wine, Mistress?"

Yeh P'in-hsia was indeed inexperienced in this matter, and after a moment's silence, she said:

"I don't know what kind to buy."

"There are many kinds of wine." The maid readily named some wines.

"I've seen them drinking kao-liang liquor, but that's too strong. I want something a little lighter," Yeh P'in-hsia said with a little embarrassment. "I just want to amuse myself, and get rid of my melancholy; it's not that I really want to drink wine."

"Well, Mistress certainly knows Shao-hsing wine. And there's red rose, and white rose; they're all slightly sweet, and easy to drink," the maid said, figuring.

Suddenly Yeh P'in-hsia remembered that once a relative, coming from Peking to the south, had given her father several bottles of wine, and said they were a famous product of Tientsin. She remembered that the wine was called Rosy Dew. No mistake, it had come in both red and white varieties. The little girl of those days had liked the wine's name, and had gotten her father to give her a couple of bottles for her to put on her candy-shelf.

All at once a dream, like a floating cloud, swept before her eyes, and Yeh P'in-hsia again possessed the delighted feelings of a little girl. Happily she said:

"Excellent, then buy Rosy Dew. I want both kinds—red and white."

Continuing, she praised the maid.

"You're so familiar with wines, you know so many names."

"My husband had a general store three shopfronts wide, and he drank it all away, and landed in jail for debt, and his wife had to go to work. Mistress, do you think I could fail to be familiar with wines, and not remember the names of a few wines?"

As the maid spoke, she clapped her hands.

"Since you have such a history, how is it I haven't heard you bring it up before?"

"There's nothing so glorious about it, what's the use of me bringing it up?"

"Wine can refine men and their affairs, and it can also ruin families and destroy people."

"As for ruining families, there are many ways to do that. My uncle inherited a fairly large enterprise from his ancestors. He was content with his lot, and originally he was a person who could never have exhausted his fortune. After he turned forty, I don't know what got into him, and he suddenly wanted to be a poet."

Yeh P'in-hsia, because she had been depressed, had never had a heart to heart talk with her maid. The maid, seeing that Yeh P'in-hsia was quiet and taciturn, supposed that she didn't like to talk, and so she had never gossiped with her. Now, as soon as she opened her mouth, she had aroused Yeh P'in-hsia's interest. All this talk of wine and poetry—this maid certainly wasn't a simple person. Feeling rather merry, she pulled the maid in, saying:

"Come, we'll sit and talk."

So the two of them went into the front room, and Yeh P'in-hsia invited the maid to sit down, and treated her politely and sincerely as though she were a close relation or an old friend. The maid didn't stand on ceremony, but sat down opposite her. Yeh P'in-hsia smiled and said:

"What you said is very interesting. Your uncle became a poet, and then?"

"He just wrote poetry, that's all." The maid sighed, tossing her head. "He wrote poetry, and wanted people to read it, and to praise it. But everyone was busy with their own affairs then. Who had the time—who had a full belly and nothing to do but come and read your silly poems, and after reading them go on and praise them?"

Yeh P'in-hsia giggled and nodded, saying:

"No mistake, it is very amusing."

"There was nothing he could do, so he kept some nondescript good-for-nothings in his home, and every day he supplied them with food and drink at a great banquet. He spent a good deal of ill-gotten money with one end in view: to get them to shake their heads as they recited his poetry.[15] After reading it, they would applaud him loudly, and he would be so delighted that his hands danced and his feet tapped."

"That is an intellectual pleasure," Yeh P'in-hsia put in. "Don't blame him, he *did* know how to amuse himself."

"That's nothing. He wanted everybody to have the good fortune of reading his poetry, so he founded a monthly journal, which contained his poems, and essays in praise of his poems. Supposedly it was for sale, but in fact he sent all the copies to people. Thus, before many years had passed, his business was done for. Later on the whole family was so poor they hadn't a mouthful of rice to eat, and of those idlers who had hung around before, not one was to be seen. He still said that, although he was poor, his poems were known everywhere, and he reckoned it was worth it. And he also said that since he was poor, and had no work, his poems would surely get better and better. You see, isn't this just asking for trouble?"

As the maid said this, she shook her head, obviously still resentful. Yeh P'in-hsia couldn't resist asking:

---

[15] In the old-fashioned style of reading aloud, the head is moved back and forth as one reads.

"Who are you, really? To hear you talk, you certainly must have come from a wealthy family. You shouldn't be a maid."

"When things have come to such a pass, it's not up to one any more, so what is this should and shouldn't?" the maid said, growing red around the eyes.

"Tell me, who are you?" Yeh P'in-hsia beseeched.

The maid looked at Yeh P'in-hsia, hesitated a moment, and then said:

"Mistress, do you know a man called Wei Wen-tuan?"

"Doesn't he write fiction?"

"Yes."

"Then I know; aren't his books in the bookcase?"

"He's my little brother." The maid lowered her voice, seemed to want to say something more, and blushed.

"I've heard that formerly he represented the younger generation of some high national official's family. So, it's no mistake. You've been wronged; what an offense!"

Yeh P'in-hsia expressed her heartfelt regret, and asked:

"What of your little brother now? I don't wonder at his stories, but I do wonder at his name. Really, why does he use this *tuan*[16] character for his name?"

The maid laughed when she heard this, and explained:

"He was originally called Wen-tuan,[17] and he changed to that *tuan* to make a pen-name. It's just his sense of inferiority. Mistress, guess my name?"

"How could I guess it? Tell me! From now on we'll call each other sisters. You're older than I, so I'll call you Elder Sister. So don't call me Mistress any more."

---

[16] *tuan* means "short" or "shortcoming". "*wen-tuan*" would suggest "literary deficiency" or "lacking in literary merit". Yeh P'in-hsia's question is natural.

[17] *tuan* means "upright" or "proper". Unlike the same word in footnote 16, which is pronounced in the third tone, this word is pronounced in the first tone.

"I wouldn't dare. Since you didn't think of it, my name is Wen-shu, the *shu* which means 'to shrink'." As she spoke, she couldn't help laughing again. Yeh P'in-hsia said:

"Strange! What does that mean?"

"Originally I was called Wen-shu,[18] but because my little brother changed his name to Wen-tuan, I vented my anger by changing my name to Wen-shu. I told my brother, now that the family is ruined, and your elder sister's husband is a drinker, there's no hope and our branch of the Wei family looks to you. But you won't get ahead; you're neither an artisan nor a merchant, all you want to do is be a worthless writer! Aren't you just making difficulties for yourself? You're called Wen-tuan, and that's no mistake; your life will be a short one."

"You were too hard on him. To be a writer brings fame and profit, and it's considered quite grand. You should have encouraged him; why spoil his hopes?"

"What fame and profit, what grandeur? You see he gets up early and goes to bed late, and sits at a broken-down table racking his brain and sweating until his face turns yellow and his flesh grows thin—how pitiful! When he goes out, it's even worse. As soon as people hear that he's a writer, they know that writers aren't worth bothering with, so they look down on him. And when he goes to see the managers of bookstores, and the newspaper and magazine editors, not only do they act so pompous, they don't even look him in the eye, but he lowers himself, shrugging his shoulders and laughing with them in such an ugly manner that he loses all dignity. I tell him, brother, although we're poor, we ought to protect our honor, and not take ourselves too lightly. Let's not disgrace our ancestors. But he'll still argue with me, and he won't obey me!"

The more the maid spoke the more she raised her voice, and she was growing angry, as though her worthless brother were before her, and the two of

---

[18] *shu* means "clear, pure, virtuous".

them were just starting to quarrel. Yeh P'in-hsia hurried to get the thermos bottle and poured her half a cup of hot water. Smiling, she said:

"Good sister, don't be angry. We won't talk of this any more."

The maid took it and drank a mouthful, and then suddenly realized that this wasn't right; what was her status now, and how had things gotten turned around so that she was drinking the tea poured for her by Mistress? She quickly put down the cup and jumped up, saying:

"Mistress, I beg your pardon, I got mixed up. All right, I'll go and buy wine for you now. Are you still eating vegetarian food?"

"I'm happy today. Let's kill a little chicken, and you can keep me company, drinking a little wine and enjoying myself—all right?"

"I can see that you're happy. I've been here several months, and today this is the first time I've seen you with a smile on your face."

"I have you to thank for that. You brought me my happiness." Yeh P'in-hsia came forward, raised her face, and said sweetly: "You're my good big sister."

"Mistress, I certainly wouldn't dare."

Yeh P'in-hsia seized her and said in a trembling voice:

"You know I'm an unlucky person, and I'm so lonely I wanted to die. Can you really bear to refuse me if I want to be your little sister?"

As she spoke her tears rushed forth like a bubbling spring. Wei Wen-shu's heart was grieved, and she hurried to say:

"Very well, very well, I agree."

That evening the two considered everything very carefully, and both spoke of their innermost grievances. They drank from a little bottle of Rosy Dew for half the night without growing weary. Yeh P'in-hsia took Wei Wen-shu to sleep in her own bed.

Wei Wen-shu originally had no idea of going out to work as a servant. But because she had heard that the daughter of the Yeh family of Changsha and the daughter-in-law of the big cotton merchant Liu lived alone in her own house and courtyard, she decided—for the time being—to give it a try. She had two children, a boy and a girl, at home, with no one to look after them. Yeh P'in-hsia immediately said:

"Tomorrow you go and bring them here to live. They'll add a little liveliness to this big house."

But it was not only the house which became more lively. Even the mistress of the house gradually became more animated. She no longer used ashes to yellow her face, but revealed her own original complexion. As before, she still observed Buddhist rituals in the morning and the evening, but she spent even more of her time playing with the children. The girl was five years old, and the boy was three; they were just at that tender age which people find lovable. Yeh P'in-hsia felt that these two little real lives could give her even more consolation than Buddha and the bodhisattvas. Their father was surnamed Hei. This surname was relatively rare, and Yeh P'in-hsia, who felt that it was quite amusing, called them Ta-hei and Erh-hei. When Wei Wen-shu heard this, she laughed, and said:

"If you call the two names together, then won't it be Hei Ta-hei and Hei Erh-hei? That's quite a bunch of blackness![19] No wonder their Papa fell into the black room!"[20]

"Just so, and I've never asked you," said Yeh P'in-hsia, taking Erh-hei on her lap, and hugging Ta-hei with her other hand, "where is their Papa locked up?"

"The Wuchang prison."

"Don't you go to see him?"

"He and I have nothing more to do with each other."

"How did you come to get married?"

---

[19] *Hei* means "black". Thus, the children's names would read, literally, "Black Big-black" and "Black Second-black".

[20] "fell into the black room" means landed in jail.

"*Ai*, now that you mention it, that's a muddled account!" Wei Wen-shu went over and sat down, saying: "Wen-tuan and I were the children of a concubine, and when our mother died early, they just casually married me off. Their father was originally the son of the Wei family's bookkeeper."

"Good people don't take any notice of lowly origins, so that shouldn't be considered a drawback."

"Was I taking account of his origins? If a person's untalented, then he's useless, no matter how high his origins."

They both sighed. Yeh P'in-hsia asked:

"When will he be released?"

"That's hard to say. He only swindled someone out of a little money, and it should have been a civil case. But since his creditors had influence, they caused it to be handled as a criminal case. Isn't it up to them how long he's locked up? They could just as well shoot him."

Ta-hei and Erh-hei were fighting for a ball, and began to quarrel. Ta-hei struck Erh-hei, and Erh-hei cried. Wei Wen-shu put out her hand to hit Ta-hei, and Ta-hei cried too. Yeh P'in-hsia hastened to soothe them:

"There are lots of balls, why fight over this one? Ta-hei is Big Sister, and ought to give in to Little Brother."

Ta-hei, hearing this, angrily flung the ball she was grasping. Yeh P'in-hsia picked it up and gave it to Erh-hei, and Erh-hei wiped his tears and runny nose, and smiling dashed into his mother's embrace. Yeh P'in-hsia, fearing that Ta-hei would feel wronged, picked her up and went out into the street.

"I'm glad you gave it to your little brother, so I'm taking you out to play."

As she spoke, they walked beside the river. They stood for a while before the Kiang-Han customs building, and she pointed out the river scene to Ta-hei, while Ta-hei asked about this and that. Hearing a commotion on the waterfront, they saw a crowd of men bunching together. Yeh P'in-hsia had never seen any excitement, and now, looking as she did like a nursemaid, she experienced a strange feeling. Without thinking about it, she picked up Ta-hei and went over. Then she heard someone say:

"Isn't it asking to die? A man over sixty, and still trying to lift several hundred *chin*? Crushed to death, and he deserved it!"

"It wasn't that he wanted to," another voice said. "He couldn't help trying it. Unfortunately his boy hadn't learned how yet, the whole family's all girls and little children. If he didn't risk his life to do a little, was he to watch them starve to death?"

"Did they save him?"

"One slip and that was it. A roll of cotton yarn hit him right on the head."

Hearing this, Yeh P'in-hsia no longer had the courage to go forward, and she turned back. Suddenly she thought of her old father-in-law, who was certainly worried enough about his business, and his sons and grandsons. Although he had many sons, only crippled Second Brother was willing to help him. And Shao-ch'iao even opposed him!

Yeh P'in-hsia couldn't help feeling a little sympathy for her father-in-law and hunchbacked Second Brother. She thought, in this family, it's not only I who's lonely and suffering; the two of them are also pitiable enough. She hesitated, and then asked Ta-hei:

"We'll ride in a rickshaw, would you like that?"

"I'd like it."

Yeh P'in-hsia then took a rickshaw to the factory. Old Mr. Liu hadn't imagined she would come so far to amuse herself, and thought that something out of the ordinary must have happened, so at once he asked:

"Has something happened that you've come?"

"Nothing. Ta-hei wanted to ride in a rickshaw and we had no place to go, so we came here."

Old Mr. Liu was delighted to see Yeh P'in-hsia in a happy mood. He hastily said:

"Fine. You really ought to go out often, just for fun."

He also teased Ta-hei, saying:

"The next time you come to play, your mustn't ask your Aunty to take you, you'll wear Aunty out. Today you can eat lunch here and then go back."

"No, Papa, her Mama doesn't know we came over here, so we've got to go back right away."

"What are you worried about? I'll send a car to bring the two of them over here. These past couple of days we've just been thinking about you."

"All right, that's fine, let her Mama come over too and enjoy herself. Just let me go into the kitchen and see what there is good to eat."

This was the first time Old Mr. Liu had seen Yeh P'in-hsia so lively and happy. When he thought of how she had been hurt by the sorrowful and painful life she had had since entering his household, he felt rather sick at heart, as though he had wronged her. Now he hastened to say:

"P'in-hsia, the kitchen here is filthy, don't go in."

"Today let me fix one or two dishes for you to try. I know how to do it."

Afraid of disappointing her, Old Mr. Liu no longer tried to stop her. He laughed and said:

"Well, that's wonderful. Even though I don't have a good son, I've got a good daughter-in-law."

"Second Brother?" Yeh P'in-hsia asked, winking.

Feeling that he had misspoken, Old Mr. Liu gestured toward the interior, saying:

"He's in the office, doing the accounting for the contract workers."

"Second Brother works so hard. Second Brother is your good son."

"Yes, you're quite right."

Yeh P'in-hsia didn't go to the kitchen, but to the office. When she reached the door, she heard them quarrelling inside over some trifling matter of the small change on some transaction. Second Brother Liu wanted to clear the small change on a hundred units, but the other wasn't willing, and said that was no way to do business, and it could only be figured on ten units. When they couldn't agree, Second Brother Liu got angry, and said in a loud voice:

"Well, I haven't any ready cash today!"

"When will you?"

"Ask me again in six months!"

When the other saw that Second Brother wouldn't listen to reason, he too raised his voice. So the words flew back and forth, with tongues serving as rifles and lips as swords, until they began pounding the table and shaking the lamp in their quarrel.

Yeh P'in-hsia, who understood what was going on, pushed the door curtain aside and quietly went in. Casually she asked:

"Second Brother, are you busy?"

When Second Brother saw that it was Third Brother's wife, he was obviously a little embarrassed. Suppressing his anger, he said:

"No, I'm not busy. How are you?"

Yeh P'in-hsia looked at the other merchant, and said with a smile:

"Second Brother, I can't say much about this accounting business. But Second Brother shouldn't get so angry over some small change. It'll spoil your disposition, and that's worth a great deal."

Second Brother Liu, hearing this, seemed to be appeased, and dropped into his chair with a sigh. Yeh P'in-hsia, seeing that her words had taken effect, continued:

"Papa is old, and there's only you to help him. All of us depend on Second Brother. Second Brother must take more care of himself."

Second Brother Liu had long had a kind of inferiority complex, and he had never thought that anyone would depend on him—and this person who depended on him was Third Brother's wife, whom he looked upon as an angel. At once he was at ease, and felt independent, and as though he were a person of some consequence. Without a word, he took up his brush and wrote out a new note, paying in full the sum he had just wanted to discount. Then he took the old note, which he had just written out, in round numbers, and tossed both of them to the merchant, and said carelessly:

"Take them, and from now on don't think of doing any more business with me. I don't want to ruin my disposition."

This unexpected flight of checks put the other merchant at a loss, and he didn't know what to do, because originally he had had no intention of shutting off this avenue of business. "Go, go, go!" Second Brother Liu pressed him, and so, reluctantly, he could only leave.

The success or failure, the prosperity or decline of the Liu family was after all connected with this hunchbacked Second Brother. Except for him, who else did the Liu family have? Yeh P'in-hsia often thought of this, and so she often encouraged him, soothed him, and helped him to have self-confidence instead of slighting himself.

After the failure of the factory, the family moved to Chiao-t'ung Road, and operated a dry goods store. Old Mr. Liu knew well that human life was not forever; one day he was going to die, and although his son was a cripple, all future responsibilities would have to be given over to him to carry on. So he meant to help his son, and allowed him to make all the decisions, while he himself was happy to pay no attention to the business. Yeh P'in-hsia, respecting the wishes of her father-in-law, was especially pleasant to Second Brother, and they became good friends. Second Brother Liu was not ungrateful for their goodwill. As soon as he put his hand to the business, it began to prosper beyond their expectations.

The question of Second Brother Liu's marriage was now Old Mr. Liu's only concern. He knew that although his son had a shortcoming, because of the family's dry goods store and the business, there were those willing to marry him, and to find a wife would be easier than blowing away dust. It was the parents' responsibility to arrange the marriages of their children. But since Liu Shao-ch'iao's marriage had brought on a trouble that could never be resolved, and had caused all kinds of pain, he was afraid of repeating the mistake, and he didn't dare to lightly try it again. The lesson Liu Shao-ch'iao had taught his father had made him understand that the opinions of the two parties involved were most important; their opinions were the final opinions. Because of this, before making a move, he could not but test the principal character's standpoint. So he said:

"Old Second, I ruined the factory, but fortunately you've made a go of the dry goods store. When it comes to doing business, you're better than I, and none of your brothers can compare with you either. You're the 'meritorious statesman' of our family."

As Old Mr. Liu spoke, he smiled broadly. Second Brother only said quietly:

"I can't do anything; it's just that circumstances forced me. You all think for me, but as I see it, except for being good at business, what future do I have, and what hope? I'm not like the rest of you, who follow whatever path you like."

"Although you say we can follow whatever path we like," Yeh P'in-hsia, who was standing by, put in, "there's only one way to success. But the paths are too many, and it's hard to avoid taking the wrong one, and losing one's way. Like—"

Yeh P'in-hsia was about to bring up an example, and say: "Like Shao-ch'iao", to explain her point of view. She did not consider Second Brother Liu inferior to Liu Shao-ch'iao. Although Second Brother Liu was a cripple, he was even more liable than Liu Shao-ch'iao to make such a mistake. But just as the words were on her lips, she suddenly felt that such frankness was not appropriate for one in her position, so she quietly stopped.

Old Mr. Liu, seeing that Yeh P'in-hsia was blushing, and did not continue, then added:

"Anyway, you've been working too hard. And according to your age, you really ought to be married. I've been living alone for many years, and I know that it's very inconvenient for a man with a business of his own not to have a wife."

Seeing that Second Brother Liu hung his head and remained silent and impassive, he continued:

"If you're willing, I'll help you find one. When I've found one, of course I'll want you to see her too, first, and if you're willing, then we can settle on it. This is your own affair, and as a father all I can do is help from the sidelines; I can't act for you."

Second Brother Liu raised his head and looked at Yeh P'in-hsia. His face was like a strip of red cloth. His lips trembled, as though he wanted to speak, but he didn't say anything. After blushing for a moment, he stood up and retreated. Old Mr. Liu then said to Yeh P'in-hsia:

"Surely this is tacit consent."

As he said this he smiled broadly. Yeh P'in-hsia sighed deeply and said:

"That's hard to say; we'll see."

Because neither of the Lius had a wife, and Yeh P'in-hsia paid little attention to such things, Wei Wen-shu became, in fact, the manager of the household. She knew her position, and would withdraw as soon as Second Brother Liu brought home a wife. This cripple was a clever devil, and very loyal to his own family. But to repay the family's goodwill, Wei Wen-shu disregarded these dangers, and assumed the responsibilities of a go-between. Because she was a local person, and came from a good family, fallen on hard times, she was acquainted with many people. She thought, when his wife comes, I'll let her run the house, and then I'll just have to look after myself, and I can relax a bit.

From then on, she frequently brought all sorts of young women to the shop to select yard goods, or to amuse themselves, sitting and chatting. Second Brother Liu usually sat at the cashier's desk, and was used to inspecting every one who came in. This was the disadvantage of a business which dealt with the public; not the slightest carelessness was possible. Naturally, when Wei Wen-shu accompanied the young women, he was still less at ease, and every one of them underwent his rigorous inspection. Although they were plump and lean, tall and short, and had every sort of outward differences, not a one of them but was young, pretty, and healthy. This point attracted Second Brother Liu's attention, and he began to feel more at ease and expansive, and his self-confidence suddenly increased. At first, he had simply felt that the woman he would take as his wife would certainly have some sort of defect, like Pai Ch'a-hua.

Whenever one of them had left, Wei Wen-shu would certainly come over to casually inquire of him:

"What do you think, how about that one?"

Second Brother Liu always shook his head, indicating his refusal. When he had refused many times, Wei Wen-shu grew impatient, and went behind his back to say to Yeh P'in-hsia:

"Isn't he a strange person? You're a hunchback, but someone, seeing your property, is willing to wrong herself and marry you—that's rare enough. But still you can't see anyone—this one won't do, that one won't do. I really don't understand it; what is it that's confusing his intelligence?"

Yeh P'in-hsia's face expressed embarrassment, as though she were troubled. Wei Wen-shu regretted having spoken too frankly. After all they were of one family, and how could she say anything? So thinking, she deliberately slapped herself lightly on the lips, saying:

"What do you think of that? Talking about someone behind his back, what kind of talk is that?"

"No," Yeh P'in-hsia said hastily, "You've already done a good thing, don't you know? You've built up his self-esteem."

She told Wei Wen-shu how the two brothers had fought over Pai Ch'a-hua, and they both laughed. Yeh P'in-hsia said:

"It sounds funny now, but at the time it nearly cost me my life."

"As I see it," Wei Wen-shu said thoughtfully, "he's usually willing to listen to you. Whenever he's acting mulish, as soon as you appear and open your mouth, he's willing to forget it. If you can find an opportunity to advise him on this business of his getting married, perhaps he'll agree."

"Very well, wait until I try." As Yeh P'in-hsia said this, she was gone.

After Liu Shao-ch'iao had come back from Shanghai, quarrelled with them for a few days, and then moved to Ssu-fen-li, the Liu family had settled firmly on one idea: the hunchbacked Second Brother Liu was the Liu family's sole heir, and Liu Shao-ch'iao no longer had any share. Because of this, Old Mr. Liu was especially anxious about Liu Shao-ch'iao's marriage. Yeh P'in-hsia was also aware of the danger of her own position. She thought and thought about it, and felt that only Second Brother's marriage was the road of her salvation.

Wait until I urge him, she thought.

She saw he was not at the cashier's desk, and knew that he must be in the store-room, because aside from these two places, there was no other place for him to go; he had always led such a monotonous life. Recently, he had been busily accumulating tung oil, and was using all the capital he could find for that end. He had already said casually to Yeh P'in-hsia:

"I'm going to make some money with this business. One day I hope to get back the factory Papa lost."

"How can you do that?"

"I have a feeling. Whenever I'm about to make some money, I always get a feeling."

"How does that feeling come?"

"The Kwangtung Revolutionary Army is coming, and with the military disorders right before our eyes, the production of tung oil can't help but decrease."

Second Brother said this, and then hastened to add:

"This is my secret. Don't tell anyone else. You're the only one who knows my secret; even Papa doesn't know, I'm afraid he'd let it out without meaning to."

Yeh P'in-hsia agreed, and in her heart she was moved. A person was not his outward looks, and the hunchbacked Second Brother was really capable.

Now, she quietly entered the store-room. The big door was opened a crack, just enough for one person to enter. Yeh P'in-hsia knew that she had guessed right, and stole inside. The place would soon be full of tung oil. The shade was very dark. Yeh P'in-hsia looked about carefully, and saw no one. She called softly:

"Second Brother, Second Brother."

"Who? I'm here." It was the hunchbacked Second Brother's voice.

Yeh P'in-hsia followed the sound. She heard him ask:

"Is it Third Brother's wife?"

Yeh P'in-hsia didn't answer.

Chapter XII

Amid a life of contradictions—now cold, now hot, now firm, now shaken—Hung T'ung-yeh was the clown in a tragedy. Each person differs in the degree to which he can accept new concepts. Hung Chin-ling had accepted the theory of discarding filial piety in what she considered a moment of confusion, and she had swiftly returned to her original position. That was so-called "obstinacy". Hung T'ung-yeh was relatively "progressive", he accepted the discarding of filial piety, and moreover he held firmly to it; he could ignore his mother's poverty, illness, and death. But when Liu Shao-ch'iao tried to break a long-standing tradition, the firmly rooted concept of feminine chastity, and wanted him to make attempts upon his own mother and sister, he hesitated, and then refused.

Hung T'ung-yeh was well acquainted with the Bible, and he knew when God created man, he originally made only one man and one woman, and all the men on the earth today were their descendants. Human population at that time was very small, nor were there any proper human relationships, so that careless mating and irregular unions between blood relatives were reflected by the authors of the Bible in their great book, nor did they even try to conceal them. Because of this, Hung T'ung-yeh felt that Liu Shao-ch'iao's so-called progressive new concept was in fact a retrogressive restoration of the old. The civilization of mankind was built up, bit by bit, by the accumulation of mankind's own blood, sweat, and mental effort over many years, and Liu Shao-ch'iao wanted to destroy it by violence in one day. Hung T'ung-yeh thought that it was when a person was wearied and discouraged that he enjoyed drinking a little strong wine. From Hsi Shih,[21] who clutched her breast as though in pain, to the women with bound feet who "scattered lilies with every step", to Lin Tai-yu[22] with her lung disease, fashionable gentlemen had considered an air of illness beautiful; this was another way of manifesting the perversions of masochism and sadism. Liu Shao-ch'iao had only attained the remnants of this tradition. He himself considered that he had learned something brand new from the Russian revolution, but in fact he had only brought to light and glorified the fallen tradition of his ancestors, and rendered it even more complete. So Hung T'ung-yeh thought:

"I really cannot follow Liu Shao-ch'iao any longer."

That evening, as usual, he wandered about until it was very late before returning, for he wanted to avoid the ice-cold countenance of Ch'ien Pen-ssu. On many occasions, when he came back at night, Ch'ien Pen-ssu, Ch'ien Shou-yü, and Chin-ling as well, would be talking and laughing together. But as soon as he came in, they would immediately stop talking and laughing, and each of them, with a cold manner, would go her own way. Hung T'ung-yeh often thought:

"Fine, you really look on me as a stranger!"

Sometimes he would mutter disrespectfully:

"I don't believe you'll ever get anywhere with such a narrow factionalism. Can history show any period when there was complete unanimity, without even the slightest differences?"

But this evening he had no such agreeable response. All he had was a discouraged feeling. He saw that Chin-ling was about to go upstairs, and softly

---

[21] Hsi Shih: a legendary beauty.

[22] Lin Tai-yu: the sickly and fragile heroine of Ts'ao Hsüeh-ch'in's classic novel *Hung-lou-meng* (*The Dream of the Red Chamber*).

called to her:

"Sister, I want to talk to you."

Hung Chin-ling couldn't conveniently refuse, so she remained.

Hung T'ung-yeh held his face in both hands, lowered his head, and said nothing. Hung Chin-ling had liked her brother for many years, and her estrangement from him was of recent duration. Seeing him in such a mood, she could not help being moved. And she felt that really he too was a pitiable person. She said:

"What do you want to talk to me about?"

Hung T'ung-yeh raised his head, looked at her, and smiled bitterly as he said:

"Can't you tell what's on my mind?"

"You're too complex, it's hard to make out what's on your mind."

"Our relations are different, and we know each other pretty well; try and guess."

Hung Chin-ling had long wished to have a serious talk with her brother, and grieved that there had been no such opportunity. Most recently Hung T'ung-yeh had treated his sister more or less as an enemy, and had left her no way to make a move. Now that the entreaty had come from Hung T'ung-yeh, she could not abandon it lightly. Getting her own attitude and point of view in order, Hung Chin-ling said earnestly and seriously:

"As I see it, although you seem to be acquainted with many people, in fact you have no real friends. If I were you, I'd certainly feel isolated and lonely, and I'd have no way to carry on."

When he heard these words Hung T'ung-yeh was shaken. He felt that it was his sister, after all, who understood his heart. He felt a little ashamed, and blushed as he said:

"Can you prescribe a remedy for me?"

This question went beyond Hung Chin-ling's expectations, so that for a moment she didn't know how best to reply. Hung T'ung-yeh waited on her for a minute, and then said, laughing:

"I've got a remedy of my own."

"Then why do you need to ask me?"

"I want to discuss it with you."

"All right, let's hear it then."

"I think it's best if the two of us go back to Shanghai and live with Mother. I don't know any important people, and naturally I won't be able to find a good job, but I'm willing to work in a factory, and rely on my own labor to support you and Mother."

This was Hung T'ung-yeh's suggestion. He moved himself, and moved Hung Chin-ling even more. They seemed to have returned to the time of their childhood, when they relied on each other, and had no outside concerns. Hung Chin-ling delightedly asked:

"What made you change all of a sudden?"

"On account of Mother."

"You also realized that discarding filial piety is contrary to human feelings—is that it?"

"It wasn't that."

"When you say that, I don't understand." Hung Chin-ling was obviously anxious.

"Liu Shao-ch'iao demanded me to go a step beyond discarding filial piety; he wanted me to become an animal."

Hung T'ung-yeh knew that Hung Chin-ling still didn't understand, so he went on:

"All right, we won't talk about that anymore. We'll go back to Shanghai right away. Do you approve?"

"It won't do to go back and crowd into Chapei. Since we've come to Hankow, the Northern Expeditionary army has already started its campaign, so why not wait and see? You know, I'm always thinking of going back too. But I think that if the Northern Expeditionary army's campaign goes smoothly, it may create a new situation. We know the Ch'ien family, and that may be a way. If they've something for us to do, it would be better than being a worker. If the Northern Expedition doesn't make it, it won't be too late for us to go back, and we'll know in only two or three months," Hung Chin-ling said, and without waiting for Hung T'ung-yeh to respond, she went on to conclude in a more serious tone:

"I'm for waiting to see how the Northern Expedition goes, and then deciding. Fortunately, Mother still has some money, so her livelihood won't become a problem."

Hung T'ung-yeh was amused to see that Hung Chin-ling, who had been away from home little more than six months, had the seasoned plotter's habit of not yielding her position.

"You've become a genuine opportunist."

"I don't know what you call an opportunist. But I do know that one can succeed by seeing opportunities, grasping opportunities, and making use of opportunities."

"Who taught you to trim your sails to the wind and change according to circumstances?"

"You know I'm always learning."

"From the Ch'ien family?"

"When I compare their behavior to that of Liu Shao-ch'iao, I feel that they're closer to having human feelings. Now that you've had enough of Liu Shao-ch'iao too, you can see that I'm not mistaken." Hung Chin-ling went on to ask with concern: "What are you prepared to do about him? A clean break?"

"No," Hung T'ung-yeh said awkwardly. "I can't leave him just like that, I'd be done for. Right now I have to first separate myself mentally from his bondage, and later on, when I find an opportunity, I can make the change."

"That's right, you'll have to play along with him at first."

"Will you let the Ch'ien family know something of my plan?"

"I think, for the sake of convenience in the future, it's essential to let them understand how your thinking has changed."

This agreement brother and sister had reached not only wiped out that long period of enmity and estrangement, but also had the intimacy of meeting again after a long separation. That emotion was refreshing, and moreover it was poignant. Hung T'ung-yeh happily asked:

"Now you can tell me—when Mother didn't come, was it because you had written her?"

"Sister Ch'ien said I should wait and see if the Northern Expeditionary army advanced or retreated. If they didn't succeed, we couldn't stand, and it would just have been troublesome to have her come here."

"That was a good idea; she's got better sense than we do," Hung T'ung-yeh said, and then he humbly said, "These past two years, I don't know what I've been doing."

"It's not too late to change now," Hung Chin-ling said to encourage him.

But beginning with the next day, Hung T'ung-yeh felt that the Ch'ien family behaved even more coldly toward him. When he was face to face with them, they forced themselves to smile, but otherwise they seemed not to recognize him, almost as though he were a passerby. Hung T'ung-yeh had not eaten at the Ch'ien's for a long time. That morning, when he sat down at the breakfast table, no one said anything during the whole meal, except for the sounds of eating. Hung T'ung-yeh uneasily ate one bowlful, and then, laying his chopsticks across his bowl, he stood up. He cast a glance at Hung Chin-ling, and was about to go off to his own bedroom.

"The way it looks the last couple of days, this side can't hold Changsha," Ch'ien Shou-yü said suddenly, as Hung T'ung-yeh was about to leave. "Fourth Uncle, have you heard anything?"

"This side has already deployed its main force for a decisive battle. Wait until they've fought it, and then we can judge who won and who lost. But the question won't be decided at Changsha," Ch'ien Pen-ssu said. Then Ch'ien Shou-yü asked again:

"Where will the decisive battle be fought?"

"I'm not clear on that yet. Maybe they have more news at Itakura Minoru's. I'm about to go and ask Chu Kuang-chi."

"Has Papa seen Mr. Chu lately?"

"They're both in hiding, one in a French hotel, and the other in the home of a Japanese." Ch'ien Pen-ssu couldn't conceal his melancholy. "Now there's only myself remaining in the tiger's mouth."

"It's really strange the two of them don't cooperate."

It was Hung Chin-ling who said this. When Hung T'ung-yeh heard it, he blamed his sister a little for saying too much, for the words were really not in keeping with her position. But from these words, Hung T'ung-yeh discovered how close the relations between these people had already become, and he sorrowfully restrained his jealous feelings.

"Although they're not cooperating," Ch'ien Pen-ssu said with a cold laugh, "they're waiting for the same thing."

"Waiting for what?" Ch'ien Shou-yü asked.

"Waiting for the Northern Expeditionary army to fight its way through. When that time comes, they'll dare to stick their heads out at once, and display their many ambitions. Just now, they can't do anything."

"You often used to say there was more hope for Mr. Chu."

"That only had to do with his understanding of the Communist Party. Outside of that point, there's no difference between them." Ch'ien Pen-ssu laughed and said: "Fortunately, if the Northern Expedition succeeds, and if the Communist Party is done for, both of them can change direction and go the same way."

Hung T'ung-yeh didn't know why, but when he heard these last words of Ch'ien Pen-ssu, he was pierced to the heart, and his face grew hot. Hung Chin-ling came in quietly, and softly asked:

"You called me?"

"Yes."

"What is it?"

"What we talked about last night," Hung T'ung-yeh said in a low voice. "Did you tell them?"

"Yes."

"How did they react?"

"Naturally they were very glad."

"But their attitude this morning wasn't right."

"Perhaps it's because your relations with Liu Shao-ch'iao are too close. But there's no problem. Gradually you'll prove yourself, and naturally you'll win their trust."

Hung T'ung-yeh felt a slight chill in his heart, and he didn't feel like saying any more. Hung Chin-ling added:

"Fourth Master also said that Mr. Chu had sent letters for you several times, wanting you to come and talk, but that you'd never gone."

"That's because Third Master didn't tell me to get close to Mr. Chu," Hung T'ung-yeh said, shaking his head. "There was something, which I still don't understand. Before, I went several times, behind Third Master's back, to see Mr.

Chu, because I didn't mean to let Third Master know. But—I don't know how—every time I went, Third Master quickly knew about it. It was really scary the way that news was communicated. But I never figured out who it was who passed the reports. Could Third Master have had someone hidden at Mr. Chu's?"

"Where did you see Mr. Chu?"

"At his school."

"There are many people at the school, maybe there's someone there secretly working for Third Master."

When Hung T'ung-yeh heard this, he kept shaking his head. Finally, he sighed and said:

"This is hard."

Ch'ien Pen-san, staying at the Hotel France, was not, as Ch'ien Pen-ssu had said, merely waiting. He was quite willing to do something. Especially something in the military sphere; he was constantly thinking of blocking the army's passage on the southern section of the P'ing-Han Railway, and he deeply regretted Chu Kuang-chi's unwillingness to help in the matter. Chu Kuang-chi said:

"You already have the roster of my people; I hear you paid money to buy it. In fact, you're doing me an injustice. That roster of mine wasn't a secret from my own people, and I wasn't keeping it for myself. If you'd told me frankly that you wanted it, I would have given it to you."

Ch'ien Pen-san felt that these words could not be allowed to wipe out his face, and he immediately disputed them.

"Who says I bought it? Making rumors to stir up trouble is just wrong!"

"All right, we needn't pursue it. You just look at that roster—are there really any there who could cut roads and blow up bridges? To tell the truth, that roster is just a list of names of party members, and there are even a few names I was mistaken about—I thought they would become party members later on, and I wrote down their names first. Do you think such people are going to be willing to risk death and brave danger to sell their strength for us?"

Listening to this, Ch'ien Pen-san felt even worse. He had been staying in Hankow for several months, and all along he had had a very great concern on his mind, to wit: if the Revolutionary Army really did fight its way through, how was he going to account for such a big sum of operating expenses?

Just now, of those leaders he had really contacted, there were only two regimental commanders from Liu Yü-ch'un's command. As to whether these two regimental commanders would accept orders, and act according to them, and to what degree, he had no past experience, so he couldn't know the outcome. None of the other leads were as practical as these two.

If the Northern Expedition were blocked, this stupid account need never be settled. If they came on, then there would have to be something in exchange; that was certain. If he could stir up a bit of disorder on the southern section of the P'ing-Han Railway, then it would be relatively easy to explain things. But the execution of a little boy scattering handbills at the railroad station really wasn't desperate enough.

Still worse was the unconfirmed news out of Kwangtung. The managers there, having analyzed the intelligence reports from Hankow and confirmed them after the events, felt that Ch'ien Pen-san, who spent a great deal of money to buy various kinds of materials, wasn't nearly as good as Chu Kuang-chi, who spent not a dime and relied only on friendship to get more valuable information from Itakura Minoru. And Ch'ien Pen-san was a professional while Chu Kuang-chi did it for nothing, on his own, and his situation was that of an amateur. Comparing them, the difference was certainly striking.

Chu Kuang-chi had made up his mind that wrecking rail connections was the responsibility of the military staff, and his motive was a pure one; he really did not know whether Ch'ien Pen-san's military work was ideal. But since the matter of the roster of party members on the railway line, which had already been revealed by Chu Kuang-chi, Ch'ien Pen-san suspected that he himself had no secrets; every move he made, and even matters which he himself considered absolutely secret, weren't escaping Chu Kuang-chi. He suspected that he was being betrayed by someone close to him. He thought about it; it was most likely Hung T'ung-yeh, so he began to be on his guard with Hung T'ung-yeh, and no longer treated him as a confidante.

Comrades, when facing the enemy, ought to be united in their feelings and share difficulties. Thus Chu Kuang-chi's style of work aroused Ch'ien Pen-san's resentment. When he had covertly bought Chu Kuang-chi's roster of party members on the railway line, that had unavoidably been lacking in righteousness, but Ch'ien Pen-san didn't think of it that way. For the work, even close relatives might be sacrificed for the cause, and why not an ordinary party member? Since Chu Kuang-chi was unwilling to accommodate his party affairs to my military affairs, and since the present is a period of military activity when military affairs are paramount, if I had not dared to take the responsibility, to grasp it, how should I have faced the party, the nation, the revolution, the ideology, and the spirit of the Director in Heaven? So Ch'ien Pen-san thought, and he felt that his thinking was very correct.

When Ch'ien Pen-san heard it said that wrecking the railroad ought to be the responsibility of the military affairs staff, he couldn't help feeling that he was being ridiculed. He felt that Chu Kuang-chi, laughing at him for not having done his military affairs work well, meant to test his strength, and wanted to make him look bad. He thought:

"'In Heaven there's the nine-headed bird, among men there are the men of Hupei'; it's really true."[23]

Thus he remembered that Hung T'ung-yeh had already given him a report:

"Mr. Chu is always saying that you're a fool; he says that Hankow is the Hankow of the Hupei people, and what are fools doing fooling around here? Haven't we people of Hupei and Hunan suffered enough calamities from the northerners? Once that big fool Wu P'ei-fu is down, we'll eat moon-cakes on the fifteenth of August and everybody will kill the northerners!"[24]

At the time, when he heard this, Ch'ien Pen-san had felt a sense of dread; he felt that he was sitting right on top of a stove. No, how could it be only a stove he was on top of? He had placed himself inside a stove, and the flames were all around him. Because Chu Kuang-chi, looking at the province of his birth, considered him in the same category as Wu P'ei-fu, while Wu P'ei-fu's Thief-punishing Headquarters did not recognize the ties of having come from the same district. This was the same sort of thing as when Liu Shao-ch'iao considered him a member of the Kuomintang, while Chu Kuang-chi said that he was too close to the Communist Party. In general, neither side acted human. So he couldn't help grumbling, and there were times when he'd shake his head and say:

"Our revolution means to destroy feudal thinking. It's precisely these localist concepts of Chu Kuang-chi's that are the most extreme expression of feudal thinking. According to this point of view of his, since Sun Yat-sen was a Cantonese, he was a nine-headed bird, or a fool, and there's no need to help him. What kind of talk is that?"

---

[23] *"T'ien-shang chiu-t'ou-niao, Jen-chien Hu-pei-liao"*. *Liao* is a large cat, or a Cantonese term for a boy child. It seems to be a somewhat uncomplimentary term. The nine-headed bird is an ill omen.

[24] Moon-cakes are eaten during the Mid-autumn Festival. Moon-cakes are supposed to have been used to pass messages leading to coordinated massacre of Mongols by the Chinese.

Although this was what he said, Ch'ien Pen-san truly wondered if the course of action he was following in helping the southerners beat down the northerners was, after all, correct. Wasn't this the conduct of an ungrateful traitor? Naturally such thoughts appeared by accident in his mind; it was not to be imagined that he could have made such a change as to help the north oppress the south.

But after Ch'ien Pen-san's grumbling words, after several turns and twists, reached the ears of Chu Kuang-chi, not only was the style changed, but the nature was changed as well. Chu Kuang-chi said to someone:

"I never thought Ch'ien Pen-san's brain was so feudal. He really dared to say that, since Wu P'ei-fu is in power, it's a northerners' world. And when the Revolutionary Army comes, and the southerners are in power, then it's a southerners' world. It matters little if his words are feudal or not, but they can produce a lot of internal dissension. Maybe he's secretly helping Wu P'ei-fu? There's certainly something wrong with the man's head; he can't be depended upon."

The localist concept possessed the thoughts and feelings of both Ch'ien and Chu. Like a devil's shadow dogging their heels, it blocked their eyes, and blocked their intelligence and wisdom as well. Thus they received the Revolutionary Army, which was just then struggling, with the lives and the flesh and blood of several thousand youth, against Wu's army, and was everywhere victorious.

But Ch'ien Pen-san did not forget that he meant to do something on the southern section of the P'ing-Han Railway.

Unfortunately, there was no one with whom he could discuss his great scheme. Fourth Brother, and his own daughter, still weren't willing to obey unconditionally, and there was no need to even mention that little devil Hung T'ung-yeh.

"I used him for the sake of Kuo Hsin-ju. In fact, how should Kuo Hsin-ju have known what kind of a person he was?" It was only because of who his father was, and because he saw him at the beach once or twice, and felt that he was to be pitied If Kuo Hsin-ju comes to Hankow, I'll certainly tell him I don't want the little devil."

So Ch'ien Pen-san thought.

These thoughts led him to think of Liu Shao-ch'iao. He knew that Liu Shao-ch'iao's people were many, for he was a man who had placed himself among the masses, and who carried out mass activities—therefore he had people. He didn't ride on the heads of the masses, nor did he—unlike himself who had not set foot outside the Hotel France—hang suspended in space while hiring the masses to serve him.

Ch'ien Pen-san smiled bitterly in self-ridicule, and kept drawing on his big cigar, so that smoke eddied before his face and did not disperse for a long time.

Since he could no longer trust Hung T'ung-yeh, he ought to have a new "channel" who would undertake to keep him in touch with Liu Shao-ch'iao. To express his candor, and so that both sides should place confidence in each other, it would be best if the person were introduced by Liu Shao-ch'iao. When he used Hung T'ung-yeh for the last time, he would direct him to carry a verbal message to Liu Shao-ch'iao, inviting him to the Hotel France. In his heart, Ch'ien Pen-san thought, if Liu Shao-ch'iao and his Real Strength faction can cooperate with me, and support me, they can make up for my weak points, and extend my reach. In that case, how can that one called Chu stop me?

Liu Shao-ch'iao, living in poverty over the tailor shop on Ssu-fen-li, raised his head every day and gazed to the south, thinking always of his Pai Ch'a-hua. The Northern Expeditionary army, with irresistible force, was attacking Changsha. From the viewpoint of the Communist Party's policy, this was not at all to his liking, because the flames of the Kuomintang's victory in the military sphere would blaze higher, while the Communist Party would be placed in the dark. But for himself, as an individual, this was a rare opportunity; since Hunan and Hupei were linked, he could go back to Changsha and see just what had happened to Pai Ch'a-hua. So far he had no other girlfriends. That was the problem! Liu Shao-ch'iao was not the sort of man to love only one woman for life; if there were a substitute, he was willing to go from one to the other. Originally he had meant for Hung Chin-ling to substitute for Pai Ch'a-hua, but the little slave had put on such airs, and had been such a trickster, that he hated her so badly his teeth itched. It was Hung T'ung-yeh he blamed the most; he hadn't been willing to cooperate.

On that account, he couldn't banish Pai Ch'a-hua's image from his mind. In his entire life, this was the only woman who had ever moved him, she was his first love, and he prized her because her kind was so rare. But he never gave any thought to her origins; if Yeh P'in-hsia hadn't been invited in, how could Pai Ch'a-hua ever have come to his side? That saying about one's love for a house extending even to the crows on its roof had no place at all in Liu Shao-ch'iao's feelings.

The military situation was deteriorating, and the economy was also in dire straits; Liu Shao-ch'iao was already a fish out of water. Unexpectedly, just then Hung T'ung-yeh arrived bearing Ch'ien Pen-san's message.

"Do you know what he wants with me?"

"I don't know."

"You're with him every day, you ought to have some idea."

"No, lately he doesn't trust me," Hung T'ung-yeh said sadly. "He doesn't give me anything to do, he doesn't talk to me, and he doesn't even seem to see me. I never expected such cold treatment."

"No doubt he also doesn't sleep with you, rabbit-boy." Liu Shao-ch'iao smiled contemptuously. "I understand your problem pretty well; you make people hate you and you don't even know it. Mountains are hard to move, and one's nature is hard to change. With you here with me, I guarantee Ch'ien Pen-san can't manage over there."

"I don't understand what you mean, why do I make people hate me?"

"You're always wavering, forward, backward, left, right, it's never certain where you are; isn't that enough? Besides, Little Brother, whatever's on your mind is already displayed on your face so that anyone can see and understand. If you want to play with people, if you want to play with Ch'ien Pen-san and me, you'd better learn to be a bit more cunning—just now you fall too far short."

Liu Shao-ch'iao spoke with a little anger. He threw his cigarette away and came over. Hung T'ung-yeh, frightened, retreated a couple of paces toward the door. He blushed, and asked anxiously:

"When did I want to play with you people? I never have!"

Liu Shao-ch'iao grasped him behind the shoulder, seized the back of his neck, and gave him a long kiss. Then he pushed him away and said cruelly:

"You just rebelled against me, and you thought I wouldn't know."

Hung T'ung-yeh still wanted to say something, but Liu Shao-ch'iao hastily waved his hand and said:

"All right, rabbit-boy, we won't speak of this any more. Let's go and see Ch'ien Pen-san, you go ahead."

Having seen Hung T'ung-yeh out, and locked the door, Liu Shao-ch'iao lighted another cigarette. That packet of ten Golden Rat brand cigarettes had been bought on credit at the tobacco stall at the gate. There was nothing for it; tonight he would have to go back to the family dwelling at the dry goods store for supper, and negotiate with Second Brother for a little money. Truly, it wasn't easy to discuss money with Second Brother. Liu Shao-ch'iao feared neither Heaven nor Earth, but he was afraid of asking Second Brother for money.

Because Liu Shao-ch'iao was utterly careless about his living habits and diet, he had developed a fairly bothersome stomach ailment. Whenever he was a little too hungry, or a little too full, his stomach was liable to hurt, and this gave him a certain amount of trouble. In the past, sometimes when he was very busy he would go a whole day without a grain of rice passing his lips, and though without sleep or rest, he would exert himself as usual, and the busier he was, the greater his energy. When he had money, and leisure, he would sit down at his ease and eat and drink heavily, often exceeding his capacity, so that he would still be full a whole day and night later. Now that would no longer do. The poorer he was, the more he had to take care with his food; one moment's carelessness and his stomach would start to hurt, and then he wouldn't be able to do anything. On this account he couldn't be without a little money in his purse for food, because he really couldn't let himself get hungry.

St. Paul ridiculed those gourmands, saying that "Their belly is their god". And now Liu Shao-ch'iao had to wait upon his stomach as though it were his lord and master. When Hung T'ung-yeh happened to tease him about this, he got a little angry.

"Mother's ___! Didn't I get this ailment from struggling for the proletariat and sacrificing myself for others? Surely St. Paul isn't my son!" He began to curse, somewhat incongruously.

In fact, although Liu Shao-ch'iao's fighting spirit had not lessened on account of this stomach ailment, still the stomach ailment had already begun to hinder his work to some extent, and he was encountering some difficult-to-avoid problems which he had never faced before.

"What does Ch'ien Pen-san want with me?"

He had given serious thought to this question. Ch'ien Pen-san more than once had helped him out with money, but he didn't know for certain just what Ch'ien Pen-san expected to get from him in return. Ch'ien Pen-san, so far, had not made any demands, and that was still more remarkable. When someone did a good turn for another and asked nothing in return, it was possible that he had some unexpectedly heavy demand to make later on. He had already given him two rosters: that of the Municipal Committee, and that of the Labor Union General Headquarters. That list was a complete fabrication, without even a shadow of truth. At the time, he couldn't help feeling somewhat awkward, and had frankly told Ch'ien Pen-san:

"This roster isn't reliable. As for a reliable roster, even I don't know it, because while there's a Municipal Committee and a Labor Union General Headquarters, all right, there simply isn't any roster."

But Ch'ien Pen-san had accepted the two rosters, and he had not seemed to be upset, nor had he pursued the matter. As Hung T'ung-yeh inferred later on, Ch'ien Pen-san wanted the rosters to flesh out his reports. He sent it to Canton, to demonstrate that in addition to his military work he was doing something else as well, and forget about it. But then why hadn't he just made them up himself, why did he want to recklessly spend money to buy them? It was a question of responsibility. If by chance in the future it should be discovered that there were simply no such things, he could explain their origin. Thus with one push he was twice clean; neither mud nor water clung to him, because Liu Shao-ch'iao did really have his men, and if the goods were false, their source was not, and that sounded a lot better.

This gave Liu Shao-ch'iao a certain clue to Ch'ien Pen-san's working style.

But he couldn't guess the reason for today's invitation. Finishing his cigarette, he thought no more of it. When a rogue and a gentleman get into a squabble, it certainly wouldn't be the rogue who suffered. While Ch'ien Pen-san was not necessarily fit to be called a gentleman, it would be strange if I were afraid of him. So Liu Shao-ch'iao thought as he went off to the Hotel France.

This exchange was a fair one, and moreover it represented an attractive source of income.

Ch'ien Pen-san proposed that Liu Shao-ch'iao undertake to cause some disturbance along the southern section of the P'ing-Han Railway, to block the traffic, and he would pay out operating expenses according to the duration of the blockage.

"According to the news in the Hankow papers," Liu Shao-ch'iao said sincerely, grasping at this piece of business, "you can pay me money by the clock. I'm just afraid that if it is blocked for a long time, you won't be able to pay."

"That kind of news certainly won't get into the papers." Ch'ien Pen-san rejoiced inwardly to see Liu Shao-ch'iao's immediate agreement, but outwardly he remained serious. He said, "Changsha has just fallen. If the P'ing-Han line is broken too, do you think they can maintain the morale of the front line troops?"

"Well," Liu Shao-ch'iao thought deeply for a minute and said: "Suppose you send someone you trust to go with my men, and you can pay me according to his reports? This is no small matter; I may have to go myself."

This was a frank and honest proposal, and the method was also a good one. But Ch'ien Pen-san found it difficult, because there was no such person at his disposal. Lately he didn't care for Hung T'ung-yeh, and it was annoying to see him underfoot every day. So he said:

"Suppose I send Hung T'ung-yeh? I trust him, and he's your friend as well."

"If you're sending him, I don't care whether he's my friend or not."

As Liu Shao-ch'iao spoke, he brought his fists together, and said excitedly:

"Sir, just now you said the newspapers won't print the news of the railroad being cut, and your words have just given me an idea. On one hand, we'll make trouble on the P'ing-Han line, and on the other hand, I'll send people to the front line at Yo-yang, and to the Hankow area to spread the news that the P'ing-Han line has been cut; we can throw oil on the fire, talking it up, and ruin their morale. What do you think?"

"If it can be done, it would be excellent!"

"If you can give me extra operating funds, this would be much easier than wrecking the railway."

"How much do you actually need?"

"I can't answer that at once. As an estimate, I'm afraid I'd have to mobilize more than a hundred people. Wait until I go back and calculate it. We'll talk again tomorrow."

"Right. I'll wait for you."

"Sir, it certainly won't be a small sum," Liu Shao-ch'iao warned, studying the other's resolve and economic strength. "Can you really pay?"

"Just so you can do it. I'll have a way."

"I do things honestly; you won't suffer by it. Suppose you give me a deposit, and wait until I've done it. When you're satisfied, then you can pay me?" Liu Shao-ch'iao asked, patting himself on the chest. Such frankness and straightforwardness moved Ch'ien Pen-san deeply, and he felt that Liu Shao-ch'iao was friendly enough, and really was easier to get along with than fidgety weaklings like Chu Kuang-chi and Fourth Brother. Momentarily he felt that he had found someone after his own heart. He seized Liu Shao-ch'iao's hand and kept shaking it, and said in heartfelt tones:

"That would be excellent! We'll work together forever!"

"Of course—we'll cooperate to the end!"

Liu Shao-ch'iao also grasped Ch'ien Pen-san's hand hard and shook it. Ch'ien Pen-san felt that the other's hand seemed to be bigger than the average hand, and hot and strong.

"Sir, the matter should not be delayed. I'll go back and make arrangements."

"All right. I'll tell Hung T'ung-yeh right away to bring you the deposit money."

"Now that you mention it, I have an idea. When Hung T'ung-yeh arrives, suppose you tell him to stay at my place? I'd like to send him to take part as soon as I start my plan. That way, it will be convenient for us to keep in touch, and you can know in detail just what's going on. This is a risky business, and I won't take a single coin in vain."

After repeated mutual assurances, the two parted.

Liu Shao-ch'iao had already seen an underworld leader by the time Hung T'ung-yeh arrived with the deposit money. The man had roots along the southern section of the P'ing-Han Railway, and of his followers nine out of ten were railway workers. At that time, railway workers received average treatment and no more. But for resourceful men it was indeed a golden rice bowl. When the freight agents sold space, they accepted the filial respects of the shippers, and it was really "nothing much", and no one thought anything of it. But the best profits were to be made by shipping narcotics. Narcotics were one of the strange phenomena which had appeared in China since the beginning of the Republic. They spread everywhere at once. It was convenient to sell the paraphernalia, but it was also illegal. But at certain times and at certain places, upon payment of a "special tax", it attained legal status. However, at another time, or in another place, this legal status was no longer recognized. On this account narcotics were smuggled, and not only did this become a flourishing business, but they became "articles of international trade". A number of foreign adventurers and desperate men came to pan for gold in China and suddenly grew wealthy in this flourishing trade.

Narcotics smuggled on the railroads were usually openly smuggled, and as long as the person was someone familiar, the eyes of officialdom were half-open and half-shut. If it were any sort of respectable-looking goods, the officials, although they were not shareholders, had to be given their share of the profits, because after all "we're all one family". But if the division of the profits wasn't equal, then midway through the journey there'd be a transport surcharge, and they'd demand the narcotics. In such circumstances, open smuggling could lead to trouble, and one had to have special means.

There was some "heavenly talent" who discovered that the narcotics could be placed inside a foreign-made metal pipe and tossed into the water-tank of the locomotive. When they reached the destination, and the locomotive went into the roundhouse, it was easy to remove the pipe, and easier still to smuggle it out of the roundhouse, and easiest of all to deceive the inspectors.

The railroads were a state-managed enterprise, but a number of the staff and workers were called "special stockholders". This was because the advantages came to them first, and what was left over was "nationalized". There was a crew chief who smoked heroin in a pipe. He packed the heroin in a two-sided box, as flat as a pancake, within which there was a tiny silver spoon, and some twisted paper spills, all ready for use. He would sit in the engineer's seat beside the big square table, light a spill, open the lid of his box, and use his little silver spoon to drop the heroin into the brass bowl of his pipe. Then, blowing on the spill, he would calmly smoke away. He would cross his legs and begin to waver softly back and forth. The longer he smoked, the faster he wavered. He would hum, in a broken drone like a mosquito buzzing, airs from *erh-huang* or *hsi-p'i*[25] operas.

---

[25] *erh-huang* and *hsi-p'i*: the former is a form of Chinese opera said to come from Huang-pi and Huang-yang districts in Hupei province; the latter is a type of song from Hsi-p'i county in Hupei, used in Peking opera.

Once, happening to see someone smoking heroin in a cigarette, he snorted with laughter, and said boastfully:

"What are you smoking? I reckon I'm throwing away more than you're smoking!"

This crew chief was one of the special stockholders.

The clerk belonged to another rank, and his position was not up to that of the crew chief. He had worked for the railroad for many years, and in the end he didn't even have a place to live, nor even the means to wash up. This was because he always lived in brothels, and every night he hired a double bed. Why was it called a double bed? Because two prostitutes shared it. This was called a "double bath" and "crossing the bridge". This clerk would annoy people by asking them why one got married. He would often say:

"Isn't it convenient, living in a brothel?"

His only close friend was a doctor who specialized in treating venereal diseases. Because he was frequently treated, he struck up a friendship with the doctor, and the two of them went to the Earth God's temple to burn incense and become sworn brothers.

Many Westerners believe in the Christian faith, and daily mumble away, wasting too much time over their prayers. Before and after meals they're muttering their incantations. It's said that if it wasn't for the purpose of begetting offspring, even the affectionate relations of husband and wife would be sinful. Having bored through the cow's horn to this point, it calls to mind the engineer who, before starting the locomotive, was certain to beseech his God to protect the security of his run. Naturally, when the run was completed, he wouldn't fail to offer grateful thanks.

While China's railroad engineers, early in the morning on the first day of the New Year, would at least respectfully prepare the incense table, offer wine and burn incense, set off firecrackers and beat gongs, and kneeling before the locomotive they would pray, begging the "God of the Locomotive" to continue operating steadily, and not to go crashing into any accidents.

An engineer, who was slightly drunk, jumped aboard the train, and when he had fired up sufficient horsepower, he raced for home to eat moon-cakes and pass the Mid-autumn Festival with his wife. He passed through a small station, where he should have stopped and waited to let the other train pass. But he barrelled on through, and after leaving the station he collided head-on with the other train. Afterwards—luckily he had not been killed—he said to someone:

"I didn't think I'd gotten to the station yet, and I just didn't see the station at all, so there was an accident."

Although the station was a small one, all the same it had many lanterns, illuminating the whole station house. The station master on duty held a red lantern and waved it, came out of the station to wave a red flag, and hoisted a red lantern. But the engineer saw nothing at all, and even his assistants' eyes were darkened. This couldn't but be accounted a strange business!

"I think, it was a ghost for sure! A ghost covered up my eyes!"

So the engineer explained it, and so people believed.

When the Western scientists invented the steam engine, little did they think that when it came to China it would be associated with narcotics and with ghosts. The transport and sale of narcotics was certainly inseparable from underworld connections. Liu Shao-ch'iao, having accepted Ch'ien Pen-san's business, first sought out an underworld leader. He calculated that an accidental collision wouldn't spoil the matter, and would be a good beginning.

Hung T'ung-yeh, from being Ch'ien Pen-san's "communications" had become Liu Shao-ch'iao's follower. Outwardly, he was as loyal and obedient as before, but in secret he had already withdrawn his heart. Liu Shao-ch'iao had not given up his desire for Hung Chin-ling, and this was one of the reasons he had borrowed Hung T'ung-yeh from Ch'ien Pen-san. But Hung T'ung-yeh made it plain he wanted to hear no more of it, and Liu Shao-ch'iao was able to guess at his motives.

"Are you using the 'beautiful woman strategy' to get acquainted with the Ch'ien family?"

"Provoke me and tease me all you like—I can't help you with that."

"But I know that you're going to lose your pawn," Liu Shao-ch'iao laughed and said lightly: "I've already discovered, from Ch'ien Pen-san's spirit, that he's turned cold to you. If Old Ch'ien the Third feels like that, you can imagine how Old Ch'ien the Fourth and Old Ch'ien the Third's daughter feel. Perhaps they want your little sister, but they certainly don't want you."

Hung T'ung-yeh was shaken, as though struck upon a painful scar, but as always he said stubbornly:

"I'm not as low as you said."

"I'm telling you frankly—you're thinking of going over to them, but you've no way of resolving the contradictions of the Ch'ien and Chu families, and they'll never believe you. How would you need me to ruin you? Since you've joined the Communist Party, it's like a widow who's slipped—she can never restore her purity. Don't tell me you still don't understand that little point?"

Without waiting for Hung T'ung-yeh to reply, Liu Shao-ch'iao went on:

"Don't be of two minds—follow me in good faith. I can still use you, so I'll never let you rebel against me."

He had spoken with the greatest gentleness, and his manner also was agreeable. In Hung T'ung-yeh's experience, it was rare for Liu Shao-ch'iao to act like that. Generally, it was easy for him to grow violently angry. So he took the opportunity to defend himself, saying:

"I've never meant to go over to the Ch'ien family. But I have thought of going back to Shanghai to get out of this troublesome place, and go and be a worker."

"That's stupid! Haven't I already said I can still use you?"

Liu Shao-ch'iao embraced Hung T'ung-yeh, and would not let him say any more.

The business of the southern section of the P'ing-Han line kept both men busy. Suddenly Liu Shao-ch'iao had a thought, and asked Hung T'ung-yeh:

"Do you go to Anna's often?"

"I haven't been there for some time, because her husband, M. Raymond, came back, and he doesn't like me to come there often."

"Why is that?"

"Half because of the borrowed money; M. Raymond doesn't like helping the revolutionary party."

"All right, that's half the reason. What's the other half?"

"Anna sent me several suits of clothes, and when M. Raymond saw the bills, he asked about it. That's why he doesn't care much for me."

Liu Shao-ch'iao thought for a moment. He felt that the situation was growing more and more tense. It didn't matter if Wu P'ei-fu won a victory, but if he was defeated, he would certainly take out his bellyful of rage on the heads of the common people. If he couldn't beat the Revolutionary Army, he could beat the common people, for he had ample strength to take his rage out on the common people. There might well be a massacre in Hankow on the pretext of suppressing the revolutionaries. As far as readying a bolt-hole for himself, there was no place more ideal than Anna's home. But if M. Raymond was at home, it wouldn't do.

How could M. Raymond be made to leave the house?

"Unfortunately we lack two kinds of things," Liu Shao-ch'iao said, pondering.

"What things?"

"If we had the secret telegraph number that Wu P'ei-fu uses with Shenyang, and the secret telegraph number that Shenyang uses with Raymond, then I could send Raymond away, so that he couldn't come back in a short time."

Experimentally, Liu Shao-ch'iao asked Hung T'ung-yeh:

"Could you manage this?"

"The Ch'ien family has the secret numbers for Shenyang and for Wu."

"Can you get hold of them?"

"Ch'ien Shou-yü's in charge of them. I can ask Chin-ling, but I don't dare say for certain."

"Raymond's will have to be gotten from Anna herself, of course. How about that?"

Hung T'ung-yeh pondered for a moment, and seemed to have some misgivings. Then he said:

"That's not easy! First, with Raymond at home, I've no way of talking with Anna alone. Again, if I did see her, how can I ask her for the secret number? She won't abandon Raymond on our behalf."

"We'll think of a way to steal it," Liu Shao-ch'iao said quickly.

"We'll have to know whether he has the secret number or not, and where he keeps it. How shall we start?"

"Well, first you go and try Ch'ien Shou-yü—I just hope you don't disappoint me."

When Hung T'ung-yeh heard Liu Shao-ch'iao say this, at once his shoulders felt heavily burdened, and he regretted having said so much. If he couldn't manage this, the responsibility would certainly be on his own head, and who could say it wouldn't fall?

When he arrived at the Ch'ien house, he talked alone and in secret with Chin-ling. At first Chin-ling scolded him:

"You already said you'd draw away from him; how is it you're helping him with this? How do you know what he's up to?"

Anxiously Hung T'ung-yeh began to beg his little sister with clasped hands, and beseeched her:

"You know, I didn't say I'd break with him all at once, I said gradually. If you're going to help me, then just do it for him this one time!"

Hung Chin-ling knew that her brother was under another's coercion, and that if he didn't perform, he would have to suffer for it. So she said:

"Sister Ch'ien told me to keep it for her. Wait until I ask her, then I'll know if I can or not."

"As soon as you ask her it can't help but make for all sorts of complications. If she's not willing, how can you avoid hurting me? You get it and let me take a look; it's enough for me to know how it's arranged—it won't take more than two minutes."

Hung T'ung-yeh urged her with all his might to help, and put on a pitiable face to move her. He knew that this slender little sister of his might yield to entreaties where she would never yield to demands.

"It isn't a question of one minute or two minutes," Hung Chin-ling explained her attitude. "Sister Ch'ien believes in me, and she told me to keep it— how could I deceive her?"

"If you ask her, it certainly won't do." Hung T'ung-yeh was obviously greatly disappointed. "You know their attitude toward me. They've always treated me coldly, like a stranger."

"There's nothing to be done about that. If they hadn't asked me to keep it, what would you have done?" Hung Chin-ling was annoyed and a little impatient.

They heard someone on the stairs call: "Miss Hung." It was Ch'ien Shou-yü's voice. Hung Chin-ling responded, and left.

Hung T'ung-yeh was in a rage and wanted to go, but then he thought that he had nothing to give Liu Shao-ch'iao, and he hesitated. All at once he felt anxious and tired. Everywhere he went he ran into a wall, no one took pity on him, and he really didn't know what to do. He felt discouraged and apathetic.

"Maybe I ought to die?"

Just as he was feeling so troubled, he heard a noise on the stairs as Chin-ling came dashing down. She handed a telegraph book to Hung T'ung-yeh and said:

"See—Sister Ch'ien heard everything we said. She told me to give this to you—take a look. Fortunately, I was good. If I'd been like you, it would have made her look down on me."

As soon as Hung T'ung-yeh saw the telegraph book, he no longer paid attention to what Chin-ling was saying, but hurried to write down what he wanted. Afterwards he thanked her again and again. Hung Chin-ling said:

"Stop thanking me! Sister Ch'ien was good to you. You ought to make up your mind not to give people cause to dislike you."

Hung T'ung-yeh paid no more heed to her, and left. Hung Chin-ling, watching his back, shook her head sadly.

A couple of days later, M. Raymond received a telegram, translated as forwarded by the Thief-punishing General Headquarters. Marshal Chang[26] invited him to come to Shenyang, where important public matters awaited discussion. Since M. Raymond had only recently returned home, and moreover did not know what the important public matters were, he did not wish to go. He sent a telegram to inquire, and the return telegram repeated the invitation, so he

---

[26] Chang Tso-lin, the warlord of Manchuria, who at this time was aligned with Generals Wu P'ei-fu and Sun Ch'uan-fang in opposition to the Northern Expedition.

could only respond. He thought that it must be because of the tense situation in Hunan that they wanted to consult with him.

But when he got to Shenyang, he received special treatment: he was followed about, and he could not leave. This was because Marshal Chang's General Headquarters had already received a telegram from the Thief-punishing Headquarters in Hankow, saying that M. Raymond had already taken money from the Revolutionary Army, and given them information; he was no longer the friend of the Peiyang generals.

Fortunately he was a foreigner. Had he been a Chinese, he would long since have been shot to death.

Chapter XIII

Since the fall of Changsha, the Wuhan people were so agitated they couldn't get through the days. At first, amid various disturbances, everyone trusted in General Wu as the Great Wall. Hadn't the Revolutionary Army out of Canton, time and again, made a great fuss about the Northern Expedition? But they had done no more than create disturbances along the borders of Hunan, Kwangtung, and Kueichow, and in the end, unable to catch their breath, they had retreated without having achieved anything, except to weary the army and disturb the people in vain. Who could believe that this time they'd be able to make a name for themselves? Everyone held this superficial view.

As for Wu P'ei-fu, thinking of that year's "From all quarters wind and rain converge on the central region" he made an earnest display of his might. This time, as "East Mountain rose again"[27] to occupy Wuhan and grandly lead the whole nation, he felt that the present day would surpass the past. Relying on this spirited character of his, he paid no attention to the trifling Revolutionary Army from Canton. He had no idea at all that the Revolutionary Army could win; rather, he counted upon taking the opportunity to strike south against the provinces of Kwangtung and Kwangsi, so as to pacify the southern frontiers. Later he would return to the central plain and complete the military unification of

---

[27] *Tung-shan tsai-ch'i*: "East Mountain rises again", a reference to the famous General Hsieh An of the Eastern Chin dynasty, to whom General Wu is pleased to compare himself.

the country, so that the nation might enjoy strength and prosperity for millions of years. To the suggestions from various quarters, to the many battle plans and security preparations brought up by his subordinates, he responded with a cool smile, and after glancing at them, he crammed them into the waste-paper basket. He had his own extremely simple and ideal plan: after one battle in southern Hunan, the Revolutionary Army, beholding his might, would scatter; he would then divide his troops into two columns. One would hasten to Kueilin, and the other would be directed toward Canton. With one or two months of effort, the matter would be settled.

He had long wished to mount a southern expedition, but had feared people would say that he was using his strength to oppress the weak. Having first announced the resort to hostilities, he had deliberately waited patiently and had not yet dispatched his troops. Now the southerners were coming first to attack him, which was exactly what he wanted. From now on, he could go into action without fear that he would be accused of sending the army forth without a righteous cause.

In his capacity as Thief-punishing General, after the grand birthday celebrations in Hankow, he transferred his headquarters to Yüeh-yang. Some people said this was because he was concerned about the military situation in the south, but that was to completely misunderstand him; he could not have taken such a trifling irritation of the skin to heart. In fact, he went to Yüeh-yang to enjoy the glory of Tung-t'ing Lake, to drink wine and compare poems, so as to leave behind a refined spirit. His "baggage" included a hundred jugs of the yellow wine of Shantung, which perhaps expressed the true aim of this journey of his. Amid his poetry, wine, conversation and laughter, he wished to annihilate and destroy the Revolutionary Army, like Chu-ko Liang who pacified the empire while sitting at his ease. Hsieh An, when he received the news of victory, went on playing *wei-ch'i* as before, and Wu P'ei-fu had long inclined toward that kind of casual, carefree manner. Because of this, he meant to make history, so that future historians would write a great book about his effortless destruction of the thieves, and he would not yield to Hsieh An a monopoly on glory.

China has many famous wines, and not a few people who love to drink them, but the yellow wine of Shantung had never before been classified among the great wines. It originated with millet. Millet by nature is glutinous and very sticky, so that after it has been fermented into wine, it is difficult to preserve. It readily turns bad, becomes as bitter as vinegar, and is truly hard to swallow. But Wu P'ei-fu singled it out from among many fine Chinese and foreign vintages for special praise, despite the fact that local opinion found this strange. At the same time, to demonstrate the strength of his conservatism, he would not accept anything that came from abroad—except for real power and false glory.

When Hengyang fell, he was somewhat surprised, and considered that the Revolutionary Army had been lucky. He rearranged the defenses of Changsha slightly, and also made tentative preparations for a counterattack on Hengyang. Unexpectedly, his rearrangements and preparations got nowhere, and Changsha also surrendered.

Then he knew that the bountiful ardent spirit of the Revolutionary Army made up for its inferior equipment, and made one of their soldiers the equal of ten, so that they were like veritable dragons and tigers. His own soldiers would often retreat as soon as they were attacked, without waiting for the battle to be decided. Thus Wu P'ei-fu grew a bit anxious, and did great damage to the calm mood in which he drank wine and compared poems. He thought: to arrange a retreat and bolster up the rear requires time; unless it can be managed within a day and a night, there will be no means of resisting the swift attack of the Revolutionary Army. He had already discovered that the Revolutionary Army moved fast, while he himself was an old procrastinator. And in this instance, he would have to employ some extraordinary stratagem.

The general had his own plan, and didn't have to bother his staff officers and advisors. Flushed with wine, he laughed a chilly laugh. He ordered the unit which had previously retreated from the front line to arrange defenses along the southern border of Hupei, and he added the fresh troops from the north to this line. He used a minority of his units to hold Yüeh-yang.

When General Sun, occupying Hangchow, received the report of the fall of Changsha, he too could not sleep easily. He hurried to Kiukiang, and deployed units to defend western Kiangsi. Wu P'ei-fu sent a coded telegram strongly urging him to proceed along the Chu-p'ing line[28] to attack Hengyang, so as to reap the rewards of a pincer attack. General Sun responded in the affirmative, but he did not move his troops.

Sun Ch'uan-fang's original attitude was one of "sitting on the mountain and watching the tigers fight". He hoped that the Revolutionary Army and the Thief-punishing Army would fight to a draw, and that both sides would waste their strength. Then he could emerge and sweep up the remnants. At that time, he had his fresh crack troops, and with the power of a thunderclap both the Revolutionary Army and the Thief-punishing Armies would have had to submit to him. If this situation did not develop, and the Thief-punishing Army won the victory, he would send a telegram of support to Wu, and preserve the existing situation in the five provinces. If he were unlucky enough to be defeated, Wu would be forced to withdraw, and he, with the strength of five provinces, could gather up Wu's remnant troops, and expand his own area. In retreat he could also protect himself, and later on choose the right moment for a decisive test of strength with the Revolutionary Army. Although the Revolutionary Army had already captured Changsha, in their hearts the allied generals still tended to despise them. Strangely, they never thought that a soldier ought to beware of "slighting the enemy".

---

[28] Chu-p'ing line, the northern section of the railway line linking Canton to Hankow.

His high-ranking subordinates did not know what medicine General Wu was selling in his bottle-gourd. He remained at Yüeh-yang, but sent the bulk of his army north—what kind of battle plan was that? No one dared to ask him too many questions. Only Chief Secretary Chang, when he couldn't stand it any longer, waited for the right moment and then asked:

"General, people are uneasy now. Whatever you plan to do, at least you ought to let your high-ranking commanders and advisers in on it, so they can reassure their subordinates. Just now, you've been drinking quite a bit of wine. Yüeh-yang is an open city—surely you ought to defend it a little."

The general and Chief Secretary Chang were supposed to be friends. As for academic rank, Chief Secretary Chang was a Hanlin academician, and Wu P'ei-fu fell far short of that. So only Chief Secretary Chang could say such words—no one else could have done so.

Wu P'ei-fu smiled when he heard this, twisted his drooping mustache, and shook his head as he said:

"Ch'i-kung, now I'll show you something exciting. Withdrawing troops from Hengyang and Changsha was my plan for deceiving the enemy. Now—"

Wu P'ei-fu stood up as he spoke, and pointed with a rattan pointer at the map on the wall, saying:

"I concentrated my main force here, to avoid tiring them out, so that they can quietly wait for the enemy army. The enemy army, having just won two victories, will be full of pride; for them it's a time of advance, not retreat, and there's no need to fear they won't come. Just let them come, and I'll have them, like catching turtles in a jar."

Chief Secretary Chang's gaze followed his pointer, which indicated the region of southern Hupei. Although Chief Secretary Chang was a literary man, he had read military books, and after considering for a moment, he said:

"If the enemy doesn't attack along the railroad line, but sends out two columns to approach Wuhan, what then?"

"My two defeats and withdrawals have been for this. Now I've nurtured a feeling of pride in the enemy army, and he will surely feel that he need only advance boldly, and needn't have any misgivings. I guarantee he'll take the hook!"

"General, don't blame me for talking too much. If by one chance in ten thousand he doesn't take the hook, then what plan will you use?" asked Chief Secretary Chang, stirring up his courage. The main force had withdrawn, Yüeh-yang was already exposed, and since he himself was in an endangered position, he really felt uneasy. He knew that, out of the Thief-punishing Headquarters, if he did not speak out, no one else had the qualifications to do so, so he could not but speak. But inwardly he was really afraid of giving offense, or of provoking the other's displeasure. The strange thing was, the general didn't get angry at what he heard; on the contrary, he said in a self-satisfied manner:

"If that should really happen, Liu Yü-ch'un would certainly hold Wuchang, and I would return and counterattack, surrounding the enemy army and joining Liu Yü-ch'un in a pincer-movement attack from which he couldn't run away."

Wu P'ei-fu smiled broadly as he said this. Chief Secretary Chang was filled with spontaneous admiration, and said:

"The general's intelligence is marvelous; truly no one can match it!"

"Ch'i-kung," Wu P'ei-fu in return said soberly, "this is something which Heaven knows, Earth knows, you know, and I know. By all means, don't let it leak out."

"Of course not. The general can relax."

Not long thereafter, he secretly departed from Yüeh-yang, personally joined the army in southern Hupei, and secretly transmitted his policy. Feeling that the resistance made at Hengyang and Changsha had been too feeble, he assembled a guard of trusted units, armed them all with light machine guns, and deployed them in a second line behind the combat units. Anyone who retreated in the face of the enemy would be shot to death by the guard unit. The general's idea was to let his combat troops understand that to retreat meant certain death, while to advance offered the hope of life; it was a strategy of placing life beyond the place of death. Thus, if the enemy was unable to destroy them completely, they would necessarily be victorious, or at least they would hold the battle line and stiffen their bearing, and wear out the enemy.

The general's plan was perfect.

But how can such a scheme deceive people? Why had he concentrated all his troops along a single line, if not for a decisive battle? So Chu Kuang-chi and Ch'ien Pen-san were both able to pass on the news to the Northern Expeditionary army.

A "children's rhyme" appeared. Such children's rhymes were printed on tiny strips of paper less than an inch wide, and in the space of a night they appeared everywhere. They were stuck on walls and telegraph poles, and scattered along streets and alleys. They were simple rhymes, and once seen, easily remembered. Thus before long they began to flow—in whispers—from person to person.

> Amid daily losses
> From east to west
> Three times and five times starting a war
> T'ai-shan falls in ruins
> While the virtue of fire rises
> The immortals recognize green youth
> A horse grows horns
> A slave weaves while a slave-girl plows
> Flowers fall and the water flows with blood

At this time the word "disturbed" by itself was inadequate to describe the mood of the people of Wuhan. In fact, they were fearful, and extraordinarily so. Those who had the means to do so had already begun to escape. Just now, the most convenient way was to go into the foreign concessions. Although it was said that the revolution had been provoked by the imperialists, and was aimed at striking down the imperialists, and that the foreign concessions might not offer protection—still, for now, let's go on in. At least they did provide defense against Wu P'ei-fu's Thief-punishing Headquarters. On this account, the British, French, Japanese, and other concessions suddenly declared themselves full up, and the price of a room rose by ten times.

As for means other than those close at hand, one could still take a boat for Shanghai. The Chinese commercial steamboats had all been requisitioned long ago by the military, and there were simply none of them left. All of the foreign steamships were doing business a hundredfold. The Powers, responding to the attacks of the Northern Expeditionary army, had all sent many gunboats, and foreign flags of various colors were as thick on the Wuhan river as the stars in the sky or the pieces on a chessboard.

Another route for those fleeing the disorders was to go to Peking, via the P'ing-Han Railway. But this railway had long before stopped transporting passengers and freight; its traffic was all military. If by chance there were one or two trains symbolically carrying passengers and freight, they wouldn't move more than one or two stations in a day. They had to yield precedence to military cars, and might have to wait for several days without getting a turn. Sometimes the locomotive was taken by the army, and without its locomotive the train couldn't go. Because of such difficulties, relatively few people fled to the north.

Recently there were frequent accidents on the southern section of the P'ing-Han Railway. Scarcely a day passed without burned axles or a derailment. A train's wheels and axles had to be inspected whenever it was in the station, and oil added. If the oil dried out, a fire could start from the friction. A derailment was when the train left the tracks. If one wanted to cause a wreck, the most convenient method was to "burn the axles". If someone stealthily tossed a bit of fine sand in, using sand in place of oil, it would start to burn very soon. While this would not interrupt the traffic, it was enough to cause loss of time.

There was an army train carrying reinforcements south from the Lung-hai railroad, and the highest-ranking officer aboard was a newly promoted regimental commander. He had been ordered southward to do battle, which he felt was a good opportunity for a rising officer. He yearned to bestride Wuhan with a single step, hurl himself into the ranks of battle, and match himself against the Revolutionary Army. Then he could mount rapidly to the rank of brigade commander or division commander, and have some hope of becoming a commander-in-chief or a military governor.

When the train reached Hua-yüan, it stopped as usual to take on coal and water. He couldn't stand to wait, and blamed the train for delaying his military purpose. Somehow he waited until the engine came back, but still it did not start. Then he could endure it no longer, and began to make inquiries. Someone said that they would have to wait for another train.

"I'm not waiting for any other train. Hurry up and start it for me!" he ordered, snorting angrily.

"You've got to wait," the assistant station manager said anxiously. "It's already left the other station."

"Put it in your mother's stinking ass!"

The regimental commander slapped the assistant station manager so that he staggered and nearly fell down, and he ordered a soldier to hold the man aboard the train. Taking a guard with him, he went aboard the engine. He told the engineer:

"Hurry and start it up!"

"We don't have the road pass yet," the engineer said hastily.

"Why don't you have it?"

"We have to wait until the first train passes the station, and then we can have it."

"Your mother's!"

The regimental commander drew his pistol and beat the engineer cruelly about the head with the pistol butt. The engine cab was small, and there was no place to hide. The engineer covered his head with both hands, and kept begging for mercy.

"Don't beat me, don't beat me! I'll start it, I'll start it!"

"Fine, start it and I won't beat you."

There was nothing for it. The engineer sounded the steam whistle, and started the engine. After they left the station, he drove slowly, and kept on blowing the steam whistle. The regimental commander grew impatient again, blamed him for not going faster, and was going to beat him again.

"The first train is halfway here now; we'll run into it!"

"Run into your mother's ___!"

Again a rain of blows from the pistol butt, splitting the flesh on his face.

The engineer, beaten until his head and face were covered with blood, got angry, and at once increased the train's speed. Carefully looking right and left, he chose a flat, sandy stretch, and with a great leap, left the locomotive. While the regimental commander and his guard were still startled, the engineer's assistant also jumped out by the opposite side.

The regimental commander was befuddled and helpless. The oncoming train had already seen their train, and just as it hesitated and prepared to reduce its speed, their train was upon it, and smashed into it head on. With a crashing sound, the two locomotives rose straight up, and then toppled to the ground. The boilers broke, clouds of steam spewed everywhere, and boiling water splashed in all directions. The regimental commander and his guard were buried under glowing coals, and, roasted until half-burnt, gave off a rank odor. The cars of the train had also fallen over. The first train had been carrying wounded soldiers. Of the passengers on the two trains, some died, some were severely injured, and some lightly injured, but not one of them was fortunate enough to escape entirely. The crying and wailing of the wounded suddenly shattered the fields and the woods and startled the mountains and valleys.

At the time of the collision, Liu Shao-ch'iao was staying at a secret location in Wuchang—the small office of the fourth concubine of the favorite retainer of an underworld leader whom he controlled. He had undertaken to manage the work of wrecking the southern section of the P'ing-Han Railway. Hung T'ung-yeh, on his behalf, went to Hankow, and back and forth on the river, maintaining contact with various circles.

Ch'ien Pen-san was not completely satisfied with the reports of trivial incidents of axle-burnings and derailments which came every day to him in the Hotel France. He hoped for some more colorful and violent performance. Liu Shao-ch'iao used Hung T'ung-yeh to communicate with him, which he felt was especially unsatisfactory. He had originally hoped that Liu Shao-ch'iao would keep Hung T'ung-yeh by his side, and he didn't know why Liu Shao-ch'iao was not doing as he wished. He was afraid that his cooperation with Liu Shao-ch'iao was known to Chu Kuang-chi, and that even Pen-ssu and Shou-yü knew. He felt that it was something which ought to be kept secret. With a frozen look, he asked Hung T'ung-yeh:

"I told Liu Shao-ch'iao before to send someone else instead of you to keep in touch—why is it he still hasn't sent someone?"

"I mentioned it, and he said that a new hand wouldn't be experienced."

"For communications, there ought to be frequent changes of face. Too much experience is a defect."

Hung T'ung-yeh felt that this was the time to reveal the words he had long kept shut up inside.

"Third Master," Hung T'ung-yeh said without hesitation, "you shouldn't suspect my loyalty."

Ch'ien Pen-san looked at him, but said nothing, nor did his face reveal anything. Hung T'ung-yeh went on:

"I've had enough of his maltreatment. Really, I want to be on your side!" Hung T'ung-yeh spoke impulsively. His lips trembled, and his voice shook.

"What, are you rebelling against Liu Shao-ch'iao?"

"It's not rebelling against him. From the beginning, the two of us have often quarrelled, but I haven't rebelled. I was speaking of work-styles and lines— I think I belong on your side."

When Ch'ien Pen-san heard this, his heart grew even cooler. Originally, when he hadn't wanted Hung T'ung-yeh to be his channel of communications, it was because he wanted to withdraw a pawn from Chu Kuang-chi; he didn't want Chu Kuang-chi to know too much about him. But he believed in the relationship between Hung and Liu. When he used Hung T'ung-yeh, it was partly to gain the goodwill of Kuo Hsin-ju, but actually to entice Liu Shao-ch'iao. He had always felt that the Chinese Communist Party could never succeed, but still it was a shame to abandon the fraction of strength which the Chinese Communist Party did represent, and one might as well make use of it. Now, if Hung and Liu were apparently in harmony but divided in spirit, Hung T'ung-yeh's usefulness was not nearly so great.

Naturally this could not be explained to Hung T'ung-yeh. So, pretending a different mood, he said:

"I understand what's on your mind. I sent you to Liu Shao-ch'iao—" At first, he was going to continue "because I don't trust him and I wanted you to keep him under surveillance." But then he thought that if these words should come to

Liu Shao-ch'iao's ears, it would certainly have a bad influence upon their cooperation. After a slight hesitation, he changed his tone and said:

"What I really want, is to express my complete sincerity towards Liu Shao-ch'iao. I hope that you'll continue to stay as close to Liu Shao-ch'iao as you are to me, and stop being so changeable."

Such directions were completely out of accord with Hung T'ung-yeh's demands, whether emotional or intellectual. He felt that he could say no more. So he went to the Common Benevolence Society hospital to see Chu Kuang-chi.

Chu Kuang-chi was never one to forget the past. He had not forgotten his old friend Hung Pai-li, and he was more truly concerned than Ch'ien Pen-san for Hung T'ung-yeh. But recently he had had some regrets for this son of an old friend, because he had asked him several times to come and talk, and he had always been turned down. Gradually he had understood: the relationship between himself and Hung T'ung-yeh wasn't deep enough, and the long-dead Hung Pai-li could not serve as a bridge between them. Fathers and sons, in the end, were separate persons. So he thought:

"Forget it; it's no good getting involved with the Communist Party, and I don't want him turning on me, and getting me compromised. Sooner or later it would mean trouble."

Since the fall of Changsha, the situation in Yüeh-chou had grown tense. The martial law troops originally stationed in Hankow had received orders to form an advance guard, and had departed for the front lines. Thus the number of troops left to defend Hankow was suddenly decreased. The martial law headquarters, in order to create a climate of terror, had intensified their oppression, and before the departure of the advance guards, they had arrested many revolutionaries, among whom were quite a few honest citizens wrongfully accused.

Most of the common people feared trouble, and seeing these conditions they became even more suspicious, fearing that they would transgress by mistake.

They stayed at home, seldom going out, and never appeared on the street unless it was absolutely unavoidable.

Itakura Minoru, in order to look after his old friend, urged Chu Kuang-chi not to show his face, and he refused to receive callers unless he knew them very well. He flatly denied that he had any such person there. Such happened to be the conditions under which Hung T'ung-yeh came to see Chu Kuang-chi, and so he had to eat cold door soup.

He was really left with no way to go, like a ghost knocking on a wall. There still were two paths he could take: return to Shanghai, or go and work in Anna's shop, formally accept employment with her, and thus escape from the revolutionary cangue, and regain his personal freedom. But in response to that suspicion of insincerity which he had felt from both Ch'ien and Chu, he felt utterly wronged, and returned to Liu Shao-ch'iao's control. Surely he couldn't have grown a pair of Buddha's hands? Hung T'ung-yeh thought, and he felt it was quite funny.

Because the performance on the southern section of the P'ing-Han Railway wasn't sufficiently striking, not only was Ch'ien Pen-san dissatisfied, but Liu Shao-ch'iao himself felt that it wasn't up to his standards. In order to help Ch'ien Pen-san in this manner, he had first secured the permission of his own higher echelons. His superiors had convened a special meeting on that account, and after some discussion, they had agreed. Because it concerned the policy of "Hindering the Northern Expedition", Liu Shao-ch'iao had no authority to decide for himself. The meeting decided that this small cooperation within the policy of hindering was a reconciling of contradictions, but that in order to obtain certain advantageous conditions from Ch'ien Pen-san's side, such cooperation was necessary.

Thus both sides waited to see Liu Shao-ch'iao's little game. He had to show his superiors his strength, and for Ch'ien Pen-san, he had to provide something in return. But he could not move directly; he had to operate through his underworld friend. This doing a job for someone else's benefit did not entirely suit his own ideals. There were difficulties in blowing up bridges and destroying tracks—to get to the point of it, he just thought he would have to get some more money. Their aim in working for Liu Shao-ch'iao was not the same as Liu Shao-ch'iao's in exerting himself on behalf of Ch'ien Pen-san. This development caused Liu Shao-ch'iao to feel deeply that the revolutionary nature of the lumpenproletariat was dubious; their selfishness exceeded that of the petty bourgeoisie. In fact, they were very unreliable! So he said to himself:

"When the Party develops to a certain stage, it must certainly get rid of the lumpenproletariat, and even wipe them out."

The incident of the train collision was like an unlooked-for lifesaving elixir for him. Now he had some material for his report, and moreover it gave him an inspiration. All news of traffic halted had for a long time been suppressed by the military, and not a word of it had appeared in the newspapers. The newspapers printed endless and wearisome accounts of the victories of the Thief-punishing Army. The Revolutionary Army, since its first appearance, had won a series of victories, from taking Hengyang, and then capturing Changsha, and now it would soon be at Yüeh-chou. As for the truth, every truth was carefully concealed. Thus Liu Shao-ch'iao's report was easy to write. He attributed the collision to his own correct leadership and careful work, and to the bold sacrifices of his subordinates. This collision injured two entire regiments of the enemy's fresh reinforcements, and traffic was interrupted for three days and nights—actual losses which could be counted on one's fingers. And because of this incident, the enemy's military morale was thrown into disorder, and his will to fight was utterly lost; it was hard to calculate how great was the influence of this incident.

As a result, a few days later the Revolutionary Army attacked Yüeh-chou. General Wu withdrew to his line in southern Hupei, deployed heavy concentrations of troops on Ting-ssu-ch'iao, and prepared to make his last stand, to annihilate the southern army and counterattack to victory.

The Revolutionary Army divided its forces, feigned an attack into western Kiangsu so as to engage Sun Ch'uan-fang's army, and then, with a small force of crack troops, launched the central assault against Ting-ssu-ch'iao. A bloody battle developed there. This was the battle which neither side could afford to lose—the decisive battle.

The result of this decisive battle was that the Revolutionary Army, making one man account for ten, with those in the rear taking the places of those in front who fell, defeated the well-equipped and well-fed Thief-punishing Army. When the Thief-punishing Army could not hold, and fell back, they ran into the concentrated machine-gun fire of their own advance guards, which prevented them from retreating. The defeated army, attacked from before and behind, suffered heavy casualties. Finally, the defeated army grew enraged and began to fight against their own advance guard. The advance guard, unable to hold, fell back, and the Thief-punishing troops, dispersing, ceased to be an army.

Wu P'ei-fu retreated to Wuchang, handed the city over to Division Commander Liu Yü-ch'un, and ordered him to defend it and await reinforcements. He himself crossed the river, and sent from Hankow his circular telegram calling for perseverance in chastising the Reds, and asking all provinces to send troops so that with combined strength they might counterattack. Unfortunately no one listens to the remnants of a beaten army, and he never recovered his position.

Liu Yü-ch'un accepted a small part of Wu's defeated soldiers, enrolled them in the city's defense army, and worked with them to hold the city. The greater part, since they had no boats and could not cross to the north of the river, surrendered to the Revolutionary Army. They had thought at first that everyone in the Revolutionary Army had a blue face and long fangs, and ate people alive, like the "long-haired rebels" in grandmothers' tales. But when they saw them, they knew that they were just soldiers like themselves. They differed only in that the northern army wore cloth shoes, and the southern army wore grass sandals over their bare feet.

When the barefoot, grass-sandaled Revolutionary Army made a name for itself, it was said that the soldiers came from Shao-kuan, and that their high-ranking commanders and military advisors all went barefoot in grass sandals, to show that they shared the bitter and the sweet with the common soldiers. Such a spirit of physical vigor readily gained everyone's respect. The atmosphere which the Revolutionary Army brought with it truly left the various Peiyang generals far behind.

Since the organization of the advance guards, there were no longer so many soldiers in Hankow. After Wu P'ei-fu went north, the city froze for a couple of days, and the more cautious shopkeepers stopped doing business and shut their doors until they could see which way the wind blew. As before, there continued to be people who went into the foreign concessions to avoid the wind. Few people frequented the wineshops and teahouses. Every one who understood things wore a cold expression, spoke little, and ate little, since they didn't know just what kind of situation might appear before their eyes.

Gradually they discovered that there were handbills of red and green paper stuck on telephone poles, walls, or shop doors. These said "Welcome the Revolutionary Army", "Support General Commander Chiang", "Down With Local Bullies", "Down With the Warlords", "Down With the Imperialists", etc.

This was a new diversion for the people of Hankow. Under the former Wu P'ei-fu Thief-punishing regime, they had seen only telegrams and newspapers, but these had never been stuck up on walls.

But the Revolutionary Army, wearing its grass sandals, at last entered the city. In general, they were smaller of stature than the northern army men, had bare feet, wore short trousers and puttees, and on their upper bodies rather ill-fitting cotton jackets. An even greater difference was that the northern army had gray uniforms, and the Revolutionary Army's were grass-green. The first time the Hankow people saw them, they felt they were a little extraordinary.

They were singing an army song:

Down with the Powers!
Down with the Powers!
Away with the warlords!
Away with the warlords!
The National Revolution will succeed!
The National Revolution will succeed!
All sing for joy!
All sing for joy!

This army song had several advantages. The tune was simple and easy to learn, and everyone could sing it. The meaning was obvious, and when it was sung loud enough to split steel and divide iron, with no mumbling or muttering, then no one could act pedantic or give a tricky explanation.

Moreover there were the slogans. After the song was sung, then shout some slogans. The slogans and the handbills, in general, did not differ from each other: if written on paper it was a handbill, if cried out on the lips, it was a slogan.

Each handbill, at the bottom, bore the name of the organization which had put it up, and those most often seen were from the Labor Union General Headquarters, the Women's Association, the Peasants' Association, and the political departments of the various armies.

To the Hankow people, this was also something new.

Those who were most rapidly influenced were the children of the streets; within only a day or two they had learned that army song. Their innocent "All sing for joy!" spread to every corner. Their crooked slogans, written in chalk, appeared at the bases of walls and on the corners of buildings. "Down With

Chang the Old Cat! Down With Li the Old Dog!" Shouting and singing, running and jumping, the children were as lively as at New Year's.

There were several newspapers which daily had helped Wu P'ei-fu bait the Revolutionary Army. Now they all changed their tone, did a great turnabout, praised with all their might the Revolutionary army which saved the nation and the people, and abused Wu P'ei-fu as a traitor.

The warships of the various Powers, riding at anchor on the river, all uncovered their guns, cancelled shore leave for officers and men, and prepared to respond to any developments.

But Hankow was peaceful as before.

The five-color flag was no longer to be seen. It was replaced by a somewhat irregularly-made flag with the blue sky, white sun, and red field.

The military assumed responsibility for public order, and the Political Department took over the Hankow municipal government and the police station.

Ch'ien Pen-ssu washed away the strip of paper above his gate which read "Thief-punishing General Headquarters: Military Law Officer Ch'ien" and Ch'ien Pen-san moved out of the Hotel France. He had a long wooden seal cut for himself, which read "National Revolutionary Army Forward Dispatches Military Command", wrote a hasty letter, and sent someone to take over the telegraph office, and began at once to examine incoming and outgoing telegrams. When the Public Order Office came to inquire, he already had everything in order; since he was one of theirs, there was nothing to be said.

The military summoned him to headquarters and asked, with brutal directness:

"What about Wuchang?"

Since Liu Yü-ch'un had been ordered to defend Wuchang, he had closed the gates, and would not come out. The Revolutionary Army, although they had already completely surrounded the city, could not shoot down the walls with their light artillery, and if they used heavy artillery, they were afraid they would crush the people, so they faced a twofold difficulty. Liu Yü-ch'un had sworn to live or die with the city in order to repay the kindness shown him by the Jade General Wu; he preferred to be a broken jade rather than a whole tile. In a word, he did not mean to surrender. When the military inquired of him, Ch'ien Pen-san grew anxious; he blushed, and said honestly:

"There are two regimental commanders under Liu Yü-ch'un who have long had connections with me, but now they're both in the city."

"Why haven't they moved yet?"

"Perhaps they're waiting for the right moment. Since they closed the city gates, I've had no means of communicating with them."

"You should have gotten in touch with them long ago. Of course it's too late now."

"I'll find a way to tell them to move."

The military had no more to say.

Chu Kuang-chi came for an interview. He reported to the military that Ch'ien Pen-san, while in constant collaboration with Liu Shao-ch'iao of the Communist Party, had shown no trust in his own comrades. Speaking as a native of the locality, he did not welcome Ch'ien Pen-san operating in Hankow, or even in Hupei.

A few days later, when the establishment of the local party branch and the government was proclaimed, Chu Kuang-chi was a member of the party committee, and Ch'ien Pen-san was a member of the government committee. This arrangement aroused the greatest resentment in Chu Kuang-chi, and he prepared to strike when the moment offered: "I've got to attack him!"

But from the military point of view, Sun Ch'uan-fang was right before their eyes, and unless this was resolved, the results of the army's victory were completely uncertain. The army's responsibility was to destroy Sun Ch'uan-fang's power. The Eastern Route Army had already attacked Fukien. Sun Ch'uan-fang was in a position where he could not defend both his head and his tail, but his main force was obviously deployed along the southern Hsin River.[29] The army's powers of concentration were likewise directed to this area. Only if there was military victory would party affairs and government have a chance to develop; that was certain.

The revolutionary government, left behind in Canton, decided to transfer itself to Hankow in order to expand its influence.

Within Wuchang, Liu Yü-ch'un's resolve to hold the city was undiminished. But his subordinate military officers saw that circumstances had already passed them by, and they all advocated surrendering. Liu Yü-ch'un held out for more than a month, and when he did not see General Wu making a counterattack, his resolution also weakened. He made an agreement with his subordinates. He would be allowed to go north to serve his old master, Wu the Jade General, and those of his subordinates who wished to could accompany him; the rest could do as they pleased, and he would take no account of it. These conditions, when communicated to the commanders of the besieging army, were immediately agreed to, and soon the national flag borne by the Revolutionary Army flew over Wuchang as well.

The Russian adviser Borodin arrived in Hankow.

Party and government affairs underwent another shakeup. Handbills critical of the military appeared in profusion on the streets, and the newspapers went on the attack.

The common people couldn't understand this. Just a few days before hadn't it been "Welcome" and "Support", and everyone speaking up for the military's "hard work and great merit"?

---

[29] Hsin River: a river near Kiukiang.

There was a man named Ch'en, and through currying favor with no one knew whom, he was suddenly appointed Chief of the Department of Commerce. When the revolutionary martyr Chung was stabbed to death, this Ch'en had been one of the principal instigators. As soon as Madame Chung heard the news she wept with rage. At the time Kuo Hsin-ju was in Hankow. Madame Chung had always respected Kuo Hsin-ju; she considered him a scholar who would certainly stand up for the right. So, weeping, she went to his house, and with many sighs she asked:

"Mr. Chung sacrificed his life for the party and the country. Now, even before his bones are cold, who'd have thought that the murderer who killed him would become a big man in party and national affairs? What kind of a world is this?"

Kuo Hsin-ju smiled but didn't say anything. Madame Chung wiped her runny nose and said:

"Mr. Kuo, you tell me—is *this* politics?"

Kuo Hsin-ju again said nothing and just went on smoking his pipe. Madame Chung grew impatient and pressed him, saying:

"Speak, speak, why don't you say something?"

Kuo Hsin-ju, hard-pressed, then said slowly, word by word:

"Politics is a dark business."

"How can that be an explanation?"

"I don't have any explanation."

Madame Chung, as if she had suddenly understood, seemed to calm down. She dried her tears and said:

"Well, why do we want a revolution?"

"Everyone has his own views on that point." Kuo Hsin-ju put down his pipe, and, as though lecturing in class, said sonorously: "As for myself, I am intoxicated with the Anglo-American style of democratic government. According to my interpretation, I feel that the period of constitutional government decided upon by Mr. Chung-shan should be the Anglo-American style of democratic government. Therefore, I'm willing to bear with the worries of the periods of military rule and political tutelage, in hopes that after the bitter will come the sweet. When that time comes, if it doesn't match my ideals I shan't blame anyone, I'll only blame myself for my mistaken calculations."

"That doesn't explain your remark that 'politics is a dark business'."

"Just now it's the politics of violence, when a murderer can become a Department Chief, and that's a dark business. But that future period of constitutional government as I interpreted it will be bright. If it isn't, then the present revolution is a transition from one darkness into another, and not worth having."

Madame Chung knew that the nomination of Ch'en as Chief of the Department of Commerce was one of the Communist Party's devices: to create disharmony and diminish strength by putting up a questionable person. Madame Chung hated such devices but she could not simply expose the plot, because her beloved boy was in Moscow, and it was a question of a human life. So she deliberately played the fool, and employed the women's precious secret—"first cry, second starve oneself, third hang oneself"—to express her spirit of resistance. She ran about everywhere, she could not be avoided, weeping and talking, and talking and weeping:

"I'm going to starve myself, I'm going to hang myself!"

She proclaimed her resolution.

But as usual no one paid any attention to her.

She knew that unless she became a bit more fiery, nothing would come of it, and Ch'en would be confirmed as Chief of the Department of Commerce. Leading her daughters and younger brothers, she surrounded the office of the Chief of the Department of Commerce, smashed teapots, teacups, and the glass in the doors and windows, and threw a chair at Ch'en's head. Ch'en dodged in a panic and fled through the door.

The next day, early in the morning, various newspapers carried detailed accounts, spiced up and vividly described, which offered their readers a frivolous impression of great party and national affairs treated as a theatrical performance. When this blow to his credibility and violent exposure of his weakness was finished, Ch'en had lost his usefulness, and could only yield the post of Department Chief to another man.

This greatly increased Madame Chung's prestige, and people everywhere praised her. Discovering that she had power after all, she became even more spiteful.

Someone came to feel out Kuo Hsin-ju, hoping that he would serve as Chief of the Department of Propaganda. He was a famous scholar, held in the highest esteem, moreover, because he had been a leader of the May Fourth Movement, he functioned as an idol worshipped by progressive youth. Kuo Hsin-ju coolly asked his caller:

"I don't know what I'd have to propagandize?"

"Just now we must emphasize a part of Mr. Sun Chung-shan's last instructions, such as the policy of alliance with Russia and admitting Communists into the party, the peasants and workers policy, and so forth."

"The Communist Party wants to realize the dictatorship of the proletariat." Kuo Hsin-ju felt that this was very funny. "And Mr. Sun Chung-shan's party has the prospect of a period of constitutional government; do you think they can be a pair of twin brothers?"

The caller extended a rough, hard, muscular right hand and lightly grasped Kuo Hsin-ju's soft, weak hand, and the two men parted.

Since these negotiations had not succeeded, the great responsibility, through Liu Shao-ch'iao's connections, fell upon Ch'ien Pen-san's shoulders.

Ch'ien Pen-san received a meaningless committee appointment. Twice a week he had to cross the river to attend a meeting. At the meeting, on the dais, he listened to the chairman's instructions and to the work reports of various units, and never even had a chance to speak himself. When he happened to put in a word or two, no one paid any attention to him. Although they didn't take him seriously, neither did they slight him; he simply had no role.

He felt that this was not at all to his taste.

It wasn't as much fun as the telegraph office, which was almost like his own son, and now was simply a source of outside income. The inexperienced office chief he had appointed there was eventually recognized by all quarters as having become the real thing. Ch'ien Pen-san did not abandon the responsibility, and every day he hurried to the telegraph office to "manage" it. He personally inspected the texts of incoming and outgoing telegrams, arbitrarily revised them, and then issued them. He paid special attention to all telegrams sent by foreigners to their native countries, no matter whether they were private telegrams or news reports, regarding the situation of the Revolutionary Army. He would not allow the slightest error in reports concerning the Revolutionary Army, for the Revolutionary Army was a nation-saving, people-saving, righteous army. He sought only the momentary propaganda effect, and calculated neither trustworthiness nor consequences. Nor did he care when the fox's tail was revealed, and underhanded plots and tricks were uncovered and reputations lost.

The office chief was a man he had promoted, and even carefully nurtured. He looked upon Ch'ien Pen-san as his sustenance, as his father and mother, and whatever Ch'ien Pen-san wanted would be done. He knew only how to take orders, and hadn't the slightest thought of resistance, or even the slightest doubts. He made me an official, so I'll obey him absolutely: that is a matter of Heavenly principle and Earthly righteousness. Otherwise why should he have made me an official?

The staff under the office chief were all the old staff from before the revolution. They had come through this great change, and not only had their heads and necks remained untroubled, but even their rice-bowls had remained intact. Since they knew of no connections between themselves and the Revolutionary Army, they considered their good fortune Heaven-sent, and if their new office chief wanted to put on airs, naturally they didn't concern themselves with it.

Ch'ien Pen-san came every day to revise the telegrams, and all the telegrams had to pass his scrutiny; without his signature, no telegram could be dispatched. Ch'ien Pen-san considered this the ultimate in power and subtlety. But in the eyes of the old telegraph office workers, whether they were bothered by it or not, it was nothing new. Because for many years back, the head of every occupying army had sent just such a semi-literate old clod to play that game. Such people, it seemed, were always northerners, because the soldiers were always Peiyang men, and for such an important position they wouldn't trust anyone else.

This time it was the southern army, but this person was still a northerner, and moreover he didn't wear a uniform. This point they did find a little strange. A very clever man, who could hear one point and grasp ten, offered his explanation:

"I hear that in the Revolutionary Army there's a Political Department, and a party representative. This person must be the party representative assigned to the telegraph office."

They thought about it, and it did seem rather likely. Ch'ien Pen-san, responding to the tide of the times, took off his gown of brocaded satin and put on a woolen Chung-shan uniform. His Chung-shan uniform was specially tailored. Hung T'ung-yeh introduced him to the Chinese tailor of foreign clothing who normally made clothes for Anna, and the tailor made the outfit for him. According to Ch'ien Pen-san's wishes, the trouser legs were to be twelve inches wide, and the jacket sleeves were to be ten inches wide. At the time, the tailor said:

"It won't look good like that, it won't look like a suit."

"The clothes are for me to wear, not for you to wear." Ch'ien Pen-san was none too pleased.

So they were made to order. Ch'ien Pen-san clutched his black leather official briefcase, wore his dark glasses, and his big cigar, and a woolen cap on top of his head. He was dressed in that big, broad Chung-shan uniform, and shod in low, soft-bottomed Chinese cloth shoes. Over the little pocket on the left he wore a badge as big around as a foreign dollar, and while he didn't know what revolutionary organization it came from, still it gave him a revolutionary air, and was stylish enough.

Although not completely satisfied, he was quite content. Unexpectedly, just at this time Chu Kuang-chi opened fire on him. While delivering a commemorative lecture, he said in public:

"Hupei is the Hupei people's Hupei, and Hankow is the Hankow people's Hankow. These last few years we've put up with enough of the northerners' oppression, and we've been deeply wounded. Who'd have thought that just when we'd knocked down that fool Wu P'ei-fu, there'd come that false revolutionary fool Ch'ien Pen-san? I'm speaking for the Hupei people when I invite that fool to roll on out of here—the fools ought to go back to the fools' own places!"

Fools this and fools that; he delivered a wild tirade. The next day the entire text was printed in the newspapers.

Reporters came to confusedly interview Ch'ien Pen-san, and asked him to express his opinion. In the past Ch'ien Pen-san had made, in confidence, some respectful remarks about nine-headed birds, to quash the epithet "fool". Although "fool" doesn't sound very pleasant, "nine-headed bird" is even harder to listen to, so this was the most convenient response.

But to the reporters Ch'ien Pen-san did not mention nine-headed birds, because to do so would have been the same as declaring war on all the people of Hupei, and he would have become isolated, which was entirely out of the question. Ch'ien Pen-san waved his cigar, smiled slightly, and said in humble tones to the crowd of reporters:

"I haven't any opinion. Ordinarily I hold Mr. Chu in the greatest respect. An elder of the revolution certainly cannot be wrong. I really have no opinion."

"When someone abuses you by name, and tells you to get out, how can you have no opinion?" asked the reporters all together.

Hard-pressed, Ch'ien Pen-san could only say:

"If you agree not to print what I say in the paper, I can say a few words. Because I respect Mr. Chu, I can't very well contradict him and injure his dignity."

"Everyone's concerned about this matter, Committeeman Ch'ien. It would be better to publish your remarks."

"No, I definitely don't want to offend Mr. Chu."

The reporters looked at one another. One of them screwed up his eyes and gave his colleagues a sign. Ch'ien Pen-san pretended not to see. He heard one of them say:

"Very well, very well, Committeeman Ch'ien, we agree not to print what you say, so there."

"Thank you all for your help!" Ch'ien Pen-san said lightly and agreeably. "In fact, I haven't anything to say. Only I feel that Mr. Chu's localist ideas are too deep, and that's an instance of feudal thinking. Our revolution means to change such feudal thinking. The Director often brought up the phrase 'When the Great Way prevails, all the world will be held in common', which means to knock down such feudalistic localist thinking. So a person who holds to such feudalistic localist thinking is in fact counterrevolutionary."

"Are you saying Mr. Chu is counterrevolutionary?"

"No, no, how could that be?"

"That's clearly what you meant."

"No such thing!" Ch'ien Pen-san said with a loud laugh. Clasping his fists together and saying, "So long", he showed the reporters out.

Another newspaper, under the headline "Purge the Feudal-remnant Bastards" printed an editorial which mercilessly flayed Chu Kuang-chi. In conclusion, it said: "The party ought to decisively cleanse itself of those dregs of a backward age who hinder the revolution while preparing to enjoy the fruits of the revolution; the party ought to mercilessly beat down those counterrevolutionary elements who scheme to corrupt the revolution and false revolutionaries who betray the interests of the workers, peasants and the proletariat!"

A big horizontal banner of red cloth, bearing the legend "Down With the Feudal-remnant Bastard Chu Kuang-chi" appeared on the street, and colored handbills bearing similar messages were stuck up on many walls. These handbills appeared first in Hankow, and immediately crossed the river to Wuchang. They were most numerous near the party headquarters and Chu Kuang-chi's middle school.

Chapter XIV

The establishment of the Labor Union General Headquarters' "Workers' Pickets" was proclaimed. They wore civilian clothes and blue armbands bearing white characters around their left arms. Most of them carried wooden clubs resembling Boy Scout batons, while some were unarmed, and others shouldered empty, discarded rifles. Hung T'ung-yeh became the Director of the Workers' Pickets.

To celebrate their founding, they conducted a demonstration. All of the workers in public and private employment in the three townships of Wuhan struck for one day and took part in the march. No one could say for sure how many there were. After the march, a great meeting was held at the race track, and the whole race track was crowded full. The adviser Borodin and all the top personages attended the meeting, and moreover they delivered speeches in succession. Madame Chung, as always, brought up her Mr. Chung, and, as always, wept bitterly, and although very few in the crowd could understand her thick Kwangtung accent, everyone clapped nonetheless.

Borodin said:

"This is the first large-scale demonstration meeting since our arrival in Hankow. Because the proletariat has awakened, the Chinese revolution has already developed to the highest tide."

Ch'ien Pen-san was the last to speak. Before so many important people, he could not imagine that this honor could have fallen to him. But he had long before prepared a speech, in case of some unforeseen necessity, and now he had it ready. At the end of his speech, as he drew his conclusion, the gist of it was: The Chinese revolution was one link in the world revolution. Therefore, we must learn from the Soviet Union, accept their leadership, and press forward in the footsteps of our brothers in the allied Communist Party.

Many important people had spoken before, but Ch'ien Pen-san's speech had the greatest drawing power. The masses, under the control of the Workers' Pickets, had had eight hours of demonstrating and meeting, and this speech increased their spirits a hundredfold, as though they had swallowed a dose of some fiery tonic. Their applause and shouts interrupted Ch'ien Pen-san's speech again and again. Borodin, seeing the excitement, asked those around him about it, and when they interpreted for him the gist of Ch'ien Pen-san's speech, Borodin couldn't help feeling very gratified. The day's great meeting couldn't have had such fine results without Ch'ien Pen-san. Thus, when the speech was over, the cry, "Support Ch'ien Pen-san!" rang out from within the crowd, and did not cease for a long time.

The policy of obstruction was producing no beneficial results. The strength of the army forced the Communist Party to change from obstruction to rebellion, and to raise up some obscure people, who could be directly utilized, to occupy key positions. When General T'ang[30] of the Eighth Army joined his military strength to the Communist Party, the Wuhan regime gained the ability to exist. T'ang understood that there was only one highest seat, and that someone was sitting in it. Unless that man were ousted, he would never have a chance to

---

[30] T'ang Sheng-chih: a warlord in Hunan Province who defected from the side of the Peiyang warlords to support the Northern Expedition, and who supported the Wuhan government until he turned against it.

sit in it. But the Communist Party had agreed to help him knock that man down, and to get that seat for himself. Wonderful!

Borodin's opinion differed from the views of those who represented the army. Beyond Party interests, their strategic views were not the same. Naturally the strategic views were based on Party interest. After the taking of Wuhan, Borodin advocated sending the army north along the P'ing-Han line in a direct attack on Peking—the heart of the Peiyang clique. Once Peking was taken, they could declare war upon, and pacify, the whole country. He considered that Shanghai was the center of the imperialists' power in China. If you collided with it and couldn't struggle against it, then you would have to submit to it. Their strength wasn't great enough to struggle against it, and to submit would be to lose their credibility. It was better to bite at the weak point first by attacking Peking.

The Taiping Rebellion was a painful historical lesson. If the Taiping rebels, after capturing Wuhan, had taken Peking with their main army, then the destruction of the Ch'ing court would have been assured. Unfortunately, that had not been their plan, and they had taken Nanking first, to be defeated in the end by the combined strength of the Ch'ing court and the imperialists in league with each other. How could the National Revolutionary Army disregard this warning?

As for the circumstances, the rise of the Taiping Rebellion had been in response to Heaven and to men; that is to say, it was in keeping with the demands of the times. Because of this, it advanced smoothly from the very beginning. But since those in power were inept in their handling of it and did not know how to control it, they lightly let the great opportunity slip away.

Now, since the National Revolutionary Army was riding the crest of success, its talents would be revealed. Remembering the lessons of history, they would seize the advantageous moments, and the imminent danger would be avoided, and would disappear.

Outwardly this appeared to be his reasoning. In fact, Borodin had another opinion in mind when he advocated moving directly north. He meant to create a *fait accompli* which would make Peking the capital, in order to facilitate the Soviet Union's control of China. Soviet-Chinese unity would suffice to expel Japanese influence from Manchuria and Mongolia. According to Lenin's testament, the shortcut from Moscow to Paris runs through Peking and Jakarta. Military tactics dictate attacking the weak points, and this was precisely one of the weakest points in the world's defenses against Communism.

The governing authorities saw through their villainy, and of course were not taken advantage of. After breaking the defensive line of Sun Ch'uan-fang's army in western Kiangsi, they swept clean the lower reaches of the Yangtze and, when they linked up with the Eastern Route Army, which had attacked and occupied Fukien, one side of the brocade-like rivers and mountains of the southeast was within their grip. Later, in conjunction with several local forces from various provinces in the southwest, they surrounded, resisted, and attacked the Wuhan regime. The governing authorities well understood the international nature of the Chinese Communist Party, and how the Communist Party had abandoned the interest of the nation and the people. Where there was the Communist Party, there was no nation and no people.

Another government was established in Nanking. Besides protecting the already violated "party rule" and "rule of law", it moreover declared the Communist Party illegal, and earnestly set out to eradicate it.

Wuhan published a quarto-sized[31] *Central Daily News*, a surpassingly bold change.

The Guide had already given up on snatching away the role of the *Central Daily News* as the leading theoretical organ. The appearance of a normal-sized

---

[31] quarto-sized: four leaves to the sheet, or approximately 9 by 12 inches.

newspaper in quarto was at the suggestion of a compositor. He had spent many years lying around in the Shanghai bathhouses, having his feet massaged, and reading little newspapers, and he felt that it was unusually pleasurable. He had no use for the majesty of a normal-sized newspaper; that could not arouse his interest at all. When the newspaper was in preparation, he expressed his views through the Labor Union. He felt that the pages of quarto-sized newspaper were easier to turn, especially on board a trolley or bus. Immediately someone contradicted him.

"Hankow hasn't any trolleys or busses."

"In the future this newspaper will doubtless be sold in Shanghai, and in Shanghai they've got trolleys and busses."

"Surely we aren't running this newspaper just for the Shanghai people?"

Another worker brought up a different view:

"Quarto-sized is too small, it's not big enough to wrap things in."

This view was persuasive, and it seemed that the argument for a quarto-sized newspaper would fall. The originator racked his brains, and then said, with a stiff expression:

"The Soviet Union's newspapers are all quarto-sized, and we must follow the example of the Soviet Union."

"How many times have you seen the Soviet Union's newspapers?"

"Borodin said so."

"Who did Borodin say it to, and how do you know?"

"Don't worry, just wait 'til I tell you," the originator said in a satisfied tone. "Borodin has already spoken of this to Madame Chung, and he said that a four-pager isn't as good as a quarto-sized. Madame Chung went home and told someone else, and Old Mother Chien, who cleans the toilets, heard her. Then Old Mother Chien who cleans the toilets went home and told her husband, and her husband told his first cousin. His first cousin is my good friend, and I heard it from his own lips, so how could there be any mistake?"

When everyone heard this and realized the provenance of the business, they no longer made any objection. From the Labor Union the suggestion was forwarded to the Propaganda Conference. When the proposal came up for discussion, the conference chairman raised his eyes and looked at Ch'ien Pen-san, and Ch'ien Pen-san looked at the Secretary of the Department of Propaganda seated next to him. But that one, unnoticed, had gone to sleep with his head resting on the table, so Ch'ien Pen-san did not know what to say, and only stared at the chairman from behind his dark glasses. The chairman made a small sound with his lips, and said helplessly:

"Wait a bit and you can ask him."

Passing over that item, they proceeded to the next. Originally this Secretary had been put forward by the Communist Party. He held membership in both parties, and all major political questions were decided first by him, and Ch'ien Pen-san, as Department Chief, merely gave his assent.

When the meeting concluded the Secretary was still sound asleep. The others left, and Ch'ien Pen-san remained alone, waiting for him. He smoked a cigar, and read that day's newspaper. This was a four-pager, and as Ch'ien Pen-san flipped the pages, and studied it closely, he felt that it really was too big, and inconvenient. It looked as though the suggestion of a quarto-sized newspaper was correct after all. One could see that the Party's peasant and worker policy came not only from the fact that the peasants and workers were the most numerous, and had suffered the most deeply, but also because they surpassed others in wisdom as well. Ch'ien Pen-san nodded, thinking:

"If I should be the one to start this quarto-sized newspaper it would be something to be proud of."

He looked at the Secretary, sleeping on the table, snoring softly, and thought:

"What does the fellow do at night? It's too unseemly to fall asleep at a meeting in front of the chairman."

He glanced at the editorial in the newspaper. It was another attack on the military. The corners of his lips lifted in a cold grin, and he said quietly in his mind, "Dreamers!" and then felt a little uneasy. He knew that the present situation in Hankow would not necessarily last a long time. He understood deeply that the military was the vanguard opening the way for party and government, and was also the shield of party and government. Hankow clutched the empty title of a government, but without military authority its future was difficult to predict.

"This time I've played the fool!"

At this thought he shook his head lightly.

Besides the editorial there was a column. This column appeared every day, and the contributors were all important party and national personages. The contents were monotonous: accusations against the military. Today the writer was Mr. T'an. Ch'ien Pen-san couldn't help thinking:

"Can Mr. T'an be serious?"

Ch'ien Pen-san felt the difficulty of making a move in this confused situation. This present situation—and afterwards? He felt that he ought to place a pawn in concealment, and get word to the other side to let them know that just now he was a hostage. Then, at the next spin of the wheel, he would have a bit of ground to stand on.

The sleeping Secretary suddenly woke up. He yawned, wiped his drooling mouth, and abruptly asked:

"What, the meeting's over?"

"It's been over for a while. I was waiting for you."

"What is it?"

"Look at this."

Ch'ien Pen-san handed him the suggestion for the quarto-sized newspaper. He looked at the Labor Union's introduction first, and then read the resume, and smoothly took up a brush and wrote "pass". He took a seal from the pocket of his Chung-shan uniform, stamped it, and then put the seal back where it had come from. That seal was Ch'ien Pen-san's. Ch'ien Pen-san had given him the seal, along with plenary authority to manage all internal and external affairs.

The Secretary picked up his briefcase and went out, saying:

"I'll see you later. I have to go to Borodin's office on some business."

"All right; I'll see you later," Ch'ien Pen-san said. He picked up the quarto-sized newspaper document and went off toward his own office. But he was still thinking:

"How can I get in touch with the other side?"

When Chu Kuang-chi was attacked, he put on a bold front at first, and affected not to care. But he remained hidden inside his house, and did not dare to go to the school or to the party branch office. His daughter, seventeen-year-old Chu Ling-fen, was a third-year student at the Girls' Middle School. Since the arrival of the Revolutionary Army, the school had held no formal classes, and all the students were taking part in the Women's Association. Every day they held meetings and demonstrations, operated wall-newspapers, stuck up handbills, and were as busy as could be with this movement and that.

Since her father had come under attack, Chu Ling-fen had also come under investigation at the school. A committeewoman from the Women's Association held several mass meetings of students in their school, to get Chu Ling-fen to report to the masses on her father's bad reputation. The first time Chu Ling-fen mounted the stage, she meant to defend her father. Facing so many of her fellow students she blushed, and said hesitantly:

"Father is really a good person. Only . . ."

Scarcely had she said a word when the students got excited, and began to shriek and roar. The Women's Association committeewoman who had called the meeting rolled up her sleeves and jumped onto the stage, shouting:

"Down with the feudal-remnant Chu Kuang-chi!"

The students shouted with her.

"Down with the feudal-remnant Chu Kuang-chi!" She led another chant.

The students again followed along with her.

Chu Ling-fen was so frightened that her face lost all color, and her whole body trembled. The Women's Association committeewoman ordered the meeting to disperse, and took Chu Ling-fen away.

Two days passed, and the Women's Association committeewoman came again to the school, accompanied by Chu Ling-fen. Although it had only been two days, she was quite thin, her eyes were sunken, and her face was a waxy yellow. The Women's Association committeewoman immediately summoned another meeting. The topic was still the same: Chu Ling-fen had to mount the stage and abuse her father.

This time it was different. Chu Ling-fen, with eyes downcast and a face without expression, recited, as though from memory, how before the Republic her father had taken part in the Protect the Emperor Party, how he had slaughtered members of the revolutionary party, and so forth. How, in the early years of the Republic, her father had supported Yuan Shih-k'ai and urged him on, and was the first to submit a memorial and call himself a vassal. How he was greedy and unjust in the school, and perverse at home. It took two hours to say all this, and at last she said:

"Even more hateful was his lustful behavior." Chu Ling-fen said, weeping. "In one year at home, we went through more than ten maidservants, and it was all on account of him, the shameless old—!"

All the students were whispering to each other, and making a great din, with here and there a giggle. The Women's Association committeewoman clapped her hands, saying:

"Speak a little plainer. Go on!"

"Outwardly, he was an old-school Confucian," Chu Ling-fen's face had turned white as paper, her voice wavered, and she gasped as she continued. "But in his heart he was unbearably vile! He had wild thoughts about me, and several times he stealthily tried to do things!"

Upon hearing this several students blushed and looked down. The roaring and the sighing sounds fell and rose. A sharp voice cried out from among the crowd:

"Shameless thing, did you submit to him, or not? If you didn't, you're feudal!"

"Down with the feudal slut!"

Someone took up the shout. The meeting was thrown into disorder, as people surged forward until it looked as though the meeting were out of control.

Everything went black before Chu Ling-fen's eyes, her legs turned weak, and she collapsed to the floor. The Women's Association committeewoman knelt beside her, feeling her brow and checking her breathing, and called:

"Fetch the doctor!"

The students struggled to gain the stage, and crowded around them. One of them answered:

"The infirmary doors are locked; the doctor's not here."

Without waiting for the Women's Association committeewoman to open her mouth, a student put in:

"Quickly, send her to the hospital!"

Ordinarily this student was friendly with Chu Ling-fen, and now she took the opportunity to help her. This was also the Women's Association committeewoman's first experience with such a situation, she was a little at a loss, and she made use of this pretext to get out of the limelight and conclude the performance.

"All right, send her to the hospital," she agreed in a loud voice.

No sooner had she spoken than the students competed to be the ones to run and call a rickshaw.

"The Common Benevolence Society hospital is close," someone suggested.

"The Common Benevolence Society hospital belongs to Japanese imperialism!"

As soon as imperialism was mentioned, the Women's Association committeewoman threw up her right shoulder and shouted a slogan:

"Down with imperialism!"

The students joined in, running about and shouting wildly, and making a confused uproar.

"Committeewoman, Committeewoman, I hear there's going to be a nude march; is it true?" cried some unknown person, with a sound like a broken gong.

"No such thing!" Even the Women's Association committeewoman felt this was a little peculiar. "Who's spreading rumors?"

"If there's really going to be a nude march—"

"That would be too much!"

"Embarrassing!" said a student, covering her face with both hands and looking down.

A rickshaw arrived. The student who was secretly helping Chu Ling-fen asked the Women's Association committeewoman:

"Which hospital shall we send her to?"

The Women's Association committeewoman bent her neck and thought for a moment, frowned, and then said with great indifference:

"It's quite fitting for imperialists and feudalists to get together. All right, send her to the Common Benevolence Society hospital."

Chu Kuang-chi was hiding out at home, hesitant and uncertain. He knew that if all depended upon human feelings and reason, then there could certainly be no problems for him. He was a member of the party committee, and with the reputation of his party he could handle everything that had been published about him. Unfortunately, his party's reputation had been borrowed by others, and was being falsely used; already it had become a wildcat playing the role of the Son of Heaven. Still more fearful, there were people who were glad to be used, who destroyed their own while bowing to outsiders, and saw only what was before their eyes. So many evils were done in the name of party and revolution! Chu Kuang-chi, as he looked around, was naturally aware of his own isolation, and couldn't avoid feeling a little uneasy, so that his heart started and his flesh jumped.

It was the children's situation that he found most frightening. He had trained them for many years to lead regular lives, to go to sleep when they got into bed, and that going to school and returning home, drinking, eating, and doing their homework, each had its definite time. If one kept these rules, needless to say there could be no mistake. Now everything had gone wrong; often they didn't return home for dinner, and even spent the night out. In the past when they came home, they would greet their mother and father, and the whole family had rejoiced that their happiness was complete. Now, they might not come home, and when they did come home their faces were always cold as ice, they hadn't a word to say, and they acted as though they didn't recognize their parents, or even as though they had some grudge against them. Chu Kuang-chi, in his pain, said to himself:

"I always thought that I, named Chu, had foresight. I opposed the Communist Party, and I wasn't a bit wrong in opposing it! Just now is an example—this proves it all. If there are people who still have naive ideas about the Communist Party, and think that they can admit it, align themselves with it, and even use it, that is a fearfully shortsighted view, and no different from bowing a robber inside your house, or leading a wolf inside your house."

For a long time now, a photograph of the late Director-general had hung on display in his home. He used the room originally occupied by a god's shrine, and placed the photograph, more than a foot high, within. A pair of white crackle-glazed flower vases were arranged to either side, and usually contained fresh flowers. Early every morning he would change their water himself. In the middle there was an incense burner, and whenever he happened to think of it, he would light a stick of incense and reverently place it in the burner. With eyes closed he would stand for a while in silence. His friends teased him, saying:

"A real person, with blood and flesh, with happiness and anger, with ideals and calculations, with strong points and shortcomings—that's exactly what's good about Mr. Sun. Once you've deified him, and look on him as a god, he leaves the human race and ascends on high, and has no more to do with us. Since a god has no human nature and doesn't feel human emotions, he's always busy putting creation to rights, and putting on airs; he stiffens his face like a wooden post, and no one's willing to be his friend."

When he heard such criticism, Chu Kuang-chi always responded by smiling a little, and didn't argue. But in his heart he thought:

"I wish Mr. Sun were a venerated deity; it would be better if he had no flaws, or if I never discovered his flaws. I'm not like some people, who have so many unspoken complaints against him, but deliberately lift him up and force him to become a god, and afterwards purposely misinterpret him, and even more wickedly make use of him."

But now, he felt that he had to lie low for a while. The revolution wasn't particular about the means it employed, and the handbills outside had already been written very clearly: Chu Kuang-chi was a counterrevolutionary, and he bore the official titles of school-tyrant, labor-thief, and feudal-remnant as well as many others. Of the thirty-six ways, escape is the best, and there could be no good result if he continued to hang around.

As he looked at that photograph of the Director-general in the god's shrine, he felt a little aggrieved, and a little lonely, as though the melancholy of abandonment had taken him by surprise. He laughed bitterly to himself, thinking:

"When we opposed the Manchus, I risked my life. When we fought Yuan, I risked my life. And now, under the sign of my own party, I'm risking my life again. Surely my life wasn't meant to be like this?"

Thus he hesitated, as though he had just become aware of something: he felt that a man who is dissatisfied with reality, and strives to destroy the existing conditions and improve his environment will always be alone. Only people like Ch'ien Pen-san, who for a moment's advantage would welcome anyone—never mind if it were an enemy or a rival—with a smile, and who would use and be used, would always be surrounded and sought after. His friendly dealings with others, and his haughty airs—there would always be such people. No mistake, he was a lucky fellow, but he was also weak-boned.

"I'll hide out for a while," Chu Kuang-chi decided. "I'd rather seek a quiet place in the midst of the noise, and not have to bow my head."

There was only one place he could go, and that was the Common Benevolence Society hospital. Although it meant putting himself in a foreigner's debt, and wasn't a very respectable thing to do, the situation was urgent, and he would have to adapt himself to it. He calculated that he would wait until it got a little darker, and then try slipping away, for it would be best if no one saw him.

Chu Kuang-chi nodded casually to the Director-general's photograph, as though to a friend, and then went off toward the courtyard. The *Ch'ing-ming* Festival was near, and the branches of the trees which flanked the street, thrusting over the wall, already showed a delicate green. But the weather was dark, and the spring chill was still heavy.

Leaning against one of the mottled and peeling verandah pillars was Shu Tung-mei—the children's mother, wearing her old-person's spectacles as she mended, stitch-by-stitch, a pair of socks. She was scarcely over forty, but already she had the air of an old person. Because he had always been involved in the revolution, and had never made a name for himself, his wife, who had followed by his side for twenty years, had never known a settled life. Under the hardships and difficulties of fear and apprehension on her husband's behalf, and care and labor for her children, she had spent her youth.

When they became acquainted in Japan, they had strolled together under the flowers and beneath the moon. She admired Ch'iu Chin,[32] and had learned by heart every one of Ch'iu Chin's published poems. It was Ch'iu Chin's end that she couldn't accept. She did not deny that such an end was noble and tragic, nor did she feel that, as far as resisting the rule of an alien race, such a death was a meaningless sacrifice. She even felt that such a death was truly worthy of respect. She only knew absolutely that she had no wish to come to such an end. She preferred to live quietly with her head on her shoulders to the end of her life, and did not hope, like Ch'iu Chin, to die a violent death and have her name spread to the four seas.

"At the moment of facing her punishment, perhaps she had some regrets?"

Such anxious thoughts naturally came forth. Shu Tung-mei also frequently reproached herself, and acknowledged that she was a weakling. Naturally she disagreed with her husband's revolutionary occupation. Medicine, and teaching, were honorable professions, but what was the use of revolution? Given the opportunity for free choice, she had finally married Chu Kuang-chi, so of course she had no complaint. In Tokyo, during the cherry blossom festival,

---

[32] Ch'iu Chin: a feminist revolutionary martyr, executed after a failed uprising in 1910.

both infected by the mad joy of the Japanese, they had given themselves over to amusement all day long, and had gotten helplessly drunk. When they awakened, early the next day, they couldn't remember how they had gotten to that hotel the night before. They thought carefully, but not the slightest impression remained. But Shu Tung-mei quickly discovered certain changes in her body, and knew that she could never choose another marriage partner than Chu Kuang-chi. She had never doubted the concept of absolute fidelity.

Shu Tung-mei fully understood Chu Kuang-chi's feelings. He despised officialdom, and thought little of reputation and profit, but he was concerned as to how he could make his nation rich and strong; he schemed to become the citizen of a rich and strong nation, and considered that only in that could he truly take pride. On that account he took part in the revolution, and not out of any private designs. Whenever Shu Tung-mei, in her gentle way, would admonish him, he would always chuckle and say:

"Wait until the revolution is accomplished, then I'll retire, and go back to my old home in Kuang-chi and be a farmer."

Then, with a laugh, he would add, as though in jest:

"If it's a good year and I have a little money, let's go to Japan in the spring to see the cherry blossoms. I haven't eaten *sashimi* in many years, or drunk *sake* in those tiny cups."

Hearing such optimistic and happy phrases, Shu Tung-mei always sighed softly, and absently shook her head. She couldn't say that her husband's way of thinking was wrong: the present authorities, once having gained power, were unwilling to let go, nor would they allow anyone else to interfere, although they themselves were making a muddle of things. Truly, except for using the extraordinary stratagems of revolution, there was no other proper path to pursue. Unless one could sit and watch unmoved as the nation was lost and the race annihilated, one really had to respond to the old saying: the ordinary man bears responsibility for the rise or fall of the empire.

But as far as her feelings were concerned, Shu Tung-mei wished her husband could subside, and even become an average man. It sounded noble and exciting, and even rather amusing, to speak of danger and risk, and of the penalties of maiming and dismemberment, but would it be so interesting to personally experience such things?

But she felt it was not easy to come out with such talk in front of her husband. Withdrawal and indifference might be practiced as regards oneself, but it was not very admirable to pull someone else into the water.

With the Northern Expedition army's succession of victories, Chu Kuang-chi began to express heartfelt joy, since he believed that his dream was going to be realized. Although he still feared the Communist Party, and even remained uneasy over Ch'ien Pen-san, he believed that if only those righteous people, who handled affairs without selfish motives, could stick together, they would stand unshaken, and the Communist Party and the likes of Ch'ien Pen-san would never prevail over them, and would in the course of nature be eliminated. Because of this, his slight misgivings could not conceal his deep joy. Sometimes, stroking his drooping mustache, he would hop onto the stone flower-stand before the stairs, and swing his legs back and forth as he gazed to the south, muttering:

"Come on, come on!"

That simplicity of his always made Shu Tung-mei—she didn't know why—slightly sad. She felt that the old fellow was a little to be pitied. But she didn't say anything.

Once the Revolutionary Army had arrived, and he had made an attempt to strike at Ch'ien Pen-san, Shu Tung-mei felt she could no longer keep quiet, and she seriously admonished him:

"You go your way, and let him go his; well water doesn't mingle with river water, so why offend him? What is there, anyway, that you can't stand about that one named Ch'ien?"

"As individuals, not only is there nothing much, but one could even say we're friends. My opposition to him is on public grounds, not private. He's a member of the Kuomintang, but he eats off his comrades while serving outsiders, and he leans completely to the Communist Party. He thinks he's clever, and that he's using them, but in fact he's stupid, and he's helping them and harming his own people. If such men are not struck down, the revolution will miscarry, and the fruits of the revolution will be snatched away."

Chu Kuang-chi spoke extraordinarily coolly and reasonably, nor was there the slightest trace of emotional irritation in his tone. Even Shu Tung-mei, as she heard him, couldn't help but admire his sincerity and frankness. She looked at him, wanted to speak but stopped, and finally said:

"You're right. But I still think it would be better to forget it. When two tigers fight, one of them is bound to get hurt—and besides, you're such a guileless person."

This criticism of being guileless, coming from his wife's lips, made Chu Kuang-chi feel that he'd been wronged. His face fell, and he said:

"I'm determined to get him!"

Shu Tung-mei had seldom seen him so determined, and she regretted that she had spoken so hastily. She had meant to pacify him, but instead she had provoked him. So she laughed, and said:

"Let's talk about it later. But I wish things were peaceful, and that nothing would happen. The children are still young."

Chu Kuang-chi was moved, and he laughed with her, saying:

"You're changing the subject. As for Ch'ien Pen-san, what can he do to me?"

Shu Tung-mei had no more to say.

But a commemorative week anti-Ch'ien lecture did no harm to Ch'ien, and instead hurt him. Handbills, slogans, attacks in the newspapers, assailed him from all directions, and made Chu Kuang-chi miserable. What made him feel especially apprehensive was that the newspaper which had originally published his lecture had also published an editorial attacking his anti-Ch'ien attitude, and without even giving him a chance to respond.

The prestige of the party committee was not invoked, nor was any notice of a party branch meeting sent out.

Rather, there was a rumor that the Workers' Pickets would take action to arrest and publicly try him.

It was said that such arrests and public trials had been occurring continuously at various places in Hunan, including even the Provincial Assembly in Changsha, but until now none had been seen in Wuhan. Although Chu Kuang-chi was unwilling to give in, he was deeply afraid of being disgraced. He hung around the house for several days, and then felt that it wouldn't do, and that he had better go to Itakura Minoru's place and stay there a couple of days to avoid trouble.

As he left the room, he saw Shu Tung-mei, seated on the roofed verandah, making a pair of stockings, and Chu Kuang-chi looked a little embarrassed. Absently he asked:

"Isn't it cold, sitting there?"

"It's cloudy, and you can't see inside. When I'm done with this pair, I'll go inside."

"Any news outside?"

"No." Shu Tung-mei raised her eyes and looked at him a moment, and then, after a slight pause, she said: "I went out to the vegetable market early this morning, and I saw Ch'eng Tzu-yüan."

This Ch'eng Tzu-yüan was the business manager of the middle school, and recently Chu Kuang-chi had gotten him into the party branch with the title of a member of the propaganda committee, so that every month he drew a little carfare. Ever since the 1911 Revolution, he had been a protegé of Chu Kuang-chi's, and he was considered one of Chu Kuang-chi's intimates, as close to him as his heart and liver. When he heard his wife mention the name, Chu Kuang-chi hastily asked:

"Oh, yes, it's really been a long time since I've seen him. You saw him, how was he?"

"When he was still at a distance he put his head down, and pretended not to see me."

"He couldn't have. Surely he really didn't see you," Chu Kuang-chi immediately corrected her.

"I thought so, too." Shu Tung-mei snorted, and laughed coldly. "So I went after him calling, Mr. Ch'eng, Mr. Ch'eng! He clearly heard me, but he ran off."

"Ah!" Chu Kuang-chi said in surprise. "Why would he do that?"

"That's the way of the world—fickle. You asked for news, and that's the news."

"That's got to be wrong." Chu Kuang-chi stamped his feet, and said: "I was just meaning to discuss something with you—I think I'll go and hide for a while at Itakura's house."

"Hiding is good, but Itakura's place isn't too suitable. They were just accusing you of having connections with the Japanese imperialists. Won't you be proving it yourself?"

So Shu Tung-mei considered. Chu Kuang-chi said:

"I'll have to ignore that, because there's really no place so secure; his place is relatively safe."

"It may not be so safe." Shu Tung-mei couldn't help sighing. "These days there's a rumor they're going to recover the foreign concessions. The newspapers have editorials every day about the wickedness of the foreign concessions."

"Recovery of the foreign concessions is an item in the abolition of the unequal treaties; that's in the Director-general's will. If we can really do it, that's wonderful!"

"And your own safety?"

"If my own safety becomes incompatible with the success of the revolution, then I'm willing to sacrifice myself."

Chu Kuang-chi's face displayed a bitter smile. Shu Tung-mei wordlessly sighed again. She gathered her sewing kit, slowly stood up, and putting a hand behind herself, lightly patted her back. She asked:

"When are you going?"

"I think it would be better to go at night."

Chu Kuang-chi suddenly felt that the household had grown too cold; the atmosphere was too different from that of former days. He looked left and right, and said to himself:

"The children? My children!"

The children had long since ceased to come home at regular hours; Chu Kuang-chi knew this, and obviously he was just asking a rhetorical question. So Shu Tung-mei didn't answer.

Just at that moment someone outside pounded at the door, with a heavy and urgent sound. The husband and wife looked at each other in alarm, and Shu Tung-mei said softly:

"You go into the house, and I'll go and see."

The caller was a handyman from the Common Benevolence Society hospital. Chu Kuang-chi, looking out the window, recognized him. He knew that

Itakura Minoru had sent him, and he came out to meet him. He heard the handyman say:

"The Director told me to tell you that your daughter, the student, has been hurt and is in the hospital."

"Which student?"

"She's called Chu Ling- . . . something!" The handyman couldn't say it clearly.

"Chu Ling-chih, Chu Ling-lan, Chu Ling-fen, or was it Chu Ling-fang?" Chu Kuang-chi prodded the other, and asked: "How was she hurt?"

"The Director said her name, but I forgot," the handyman said with an embarrassed smile.

The husband and wife, with no further hesitation, unlocked the gate and hurried out. The handyman followed them, saying:

"Mr. Chu, I've already quit my job with the Director."

"But weren't you getting on just fine?" Chu Kuang-chi asked absent-mindedly.

"The Labor Union came out with a notice, saying that we were Chinese and mustn't be foreign slaves. All the Chinese at the hospital have to leave. The last couple of days the Labor Union has come forward and is just negotiating with the Director. They want the Director to give us a bunch of money."

"Helping foreigners with their work isn't necessarily being a foreign slave."

"Who knows about all that? I wasn't really willing to quit either, the Director really didn't treat us badly. These days, it's a mixed up situation everywhere. A stevedore on the Japanese dock just said he wouldn't quit, and the Workers' Pickets beat him up, and cut his face."

"What are you going to do after you leave?"

"The Labor Union will give us other work to do."

"What work?"

"That I don't know."

"Can you count on it that they'll really give you some?"

"Who knows, and everybody's worrying about it! Lots of people have families to feed."

So saying, they came to the mouth of the alley, and Chu Kuang-chi hailed a rickshaw to take them to the hospital. At the entrance to the foreign concession there was a pile of sandbags, and the Japanese soldier on guard, drawn back within the sandbags, did not come forward to question those who came and went. Several baggage carts were held up in the street outside the foreign concession, and several Workers' Pickets, wearing armbands, were gesticulating wildly as they spoke. Probably someone wanted to haul baggage into the concession, and the Workers' Pickets wouldn't allow it.

Chu Kuang-chi lowered his head. He was quite uneasy, and afraid of running into someone who knew him. The streets seemed especially noisy; with so many red and green posters, and the rickshaw moving so rapidly, Chu Kuang-chi couldn't go and look at them closely.

They arrived safely at the hospital, and Chu Kuang-chi and his wife first went to see Itakura Minoru. When they learned that it was Chu Ling-fen who was in the hospital, and that she had only fainted because of shock and fear, and had not suffered an injury, nor did she have any severe disease, the couple suddenly relaxed. Itakura Baitai herself accompanied them to the sickroom.

Chu Ling-fen was sitting up in bed reading a newspaper. As soon as she saw Papa and Mama come in, she turned over, burrowed under the blankets, and even covered up her head. This action took the old couple greatly by surprise; they looked at each other and didn't know what to do. Still less did Itakura Baitai understand it. She went over and shook the girl, saying:

"Miss Chu, get up quickly, Papa and Mama have come to see you."

Chu Ling-fen clutched the blanket tightly and paid no attention. This embarrassed Baitai. She made a very deep bow to her adoptive parents, and withdrew, murmuring.

Chu Kuang-chi, mortified, thanked her.

Shu Tung-mei, her eyes full of tears, sat on the edge of the bed. She put out her hand to touch Ling-fen's face, but the girl clutched the blanket which covered her head even more tightly, and twisted away. She hissed angrily, giving full expression to her feelings of disgust and impatience. Shu Tung-mei said pityingly:

"What is it, my child?"

And Chu Kuang-chi added:

"Ling-fen, quickly tell your mother what's the matter."

The couple talked for a long time, but Chu Ling-fen paid no attention. Chu Kuang-chi couldn't help growing irritated, and raising his voice he said:

"What is it, anyway? Don't tell me we've done wrong by you! And if we have done wrong by you, you ought to tell us plainly!"

Shu Tung-mei, seeing that her husband was getting angry, hastily said:

"Don't talk so much. You go and sit in Director Itakura's office, and leave this to me. I'll gradually bring her around."

Unexpectedly, at that moment, Chu Ling-fen, hidden under the blanket, spoke up. They heard her yell:

"Both of you, go, go on! Just pretend you don't know me any more. I hate you!"

"Why, child?"

Shu Tung-mei, hearing the girl speak, felt that she had gotten a thread of hope, and spoke quickly to soothe the girl.

"Go, go! Who is your child?"

Chu Ling-fen, among her sisters, had always been the most agreeable and the quietest one. Today's situation left the old couple absolutely at a loss. Shu Tung-mei, who had been holding back her tears, at last let them come pouring down.

Chu Kuang-chi also felt greatly disheartened. Drawing Shu Tung-mei away, he said helplessly:

"All right, we'll go. Wait 'til she cools off, then we'll come again."

"You don't need to come again. Just pretend I don't exist, just figure I died!" Chu Ling-fen cried.

Shu Tung-mei wanted to ask Itakura and his daughter in detail about the situation, so she stood up, saying:

"Good child, don't be angry. We're going; you rest."

The couple slowly withdrew, and went to Itakura's office. And from then on, Chu Kuang-chi stayed in Itakura's house.

Since Chu Ling-fen had been forced by the Women's Association to attack her own father, and had been humiliated, the strange thing was that she didn't hate those members of the Women's Association who had trampled upon her, but she blamed her father. She felt that if her father hadn't been backward, reactionary, feudal, counterrevolutionary, and laggard, how should she have been persecuted? To be the daughter of a backward, reactionary, feudal, counterrevolutionary, and laggard person, she thought, was such a shameful thing!

We youth are different from that older generation. They're done with, finished, but we still have a long future ahead of us; wait 'til we come forward— no one will be able to take our place! The more Chu Ling-fen thought of the words of the Women's Association committeewoman the more she agreed with them. She knew that since she didn't want her father, she didn't want her mother either, since the two of them were one. In order to get rid of her father, she couldn't help but bear the pain of getting rid of her mother at the same time—although Mother was a great deal nicer than Father. But she couldn't think of just how she was nicer.

After they had gone, she got up, put on her clothes, and when no one was paying attention she stealthily left the hospital. She took a rickshaw to the Women's Association, and fearful of pursuit, she kept urging the rickshaw man:

"Faster, faster!"

Unexpectedly, the more anxiously she urged him, the slower the rickshaw man went. Chu Ling-fen grew desperate.

"What is it? Run a little faster, will you?"

As soon as the rickshaw man heard this, he deliberately stopped, and put down the shafts. With a snort of anger he said:

"You stinking slave, do you take the old man for a cow or a horse? I'll hit you!"

He slapped her, so hard that Chu Ling-fen's eyes were filled with golden stars. She covered her face and wept.

"You're going to the Labor Union with me to settle this!"

"No, I'm not going to the Labor Union, I'm going to the Women's Association!"

"You stinking whore, you don't understand. The Women's Association obeys the Labor Union!"

"I won't, I won't!"

The rickshaw man wouldn't allow her to argue, but took her to the headquarters of the Workers' Pickets of the General Labor Union. Before the gates of the headquarters stood two Workers' Pickets armed with rifles, and before they could register their surprise at seeing a rickshaw bearing a tearful girl student, that rickshaw man burst out:

"This whore oppresses labor!"

When the Workers' Pickets heard this, how could they allow it? As one they said:

"Today labor is sacred; surely you know that?"

Thus, without allowing her to say anything, the two of them conducted Chu Ling-fen into the headquarters. The rickshaw man said:

"She hasn't paid me!"

Chu Ling-fen reached into the pocket under her lapel and brought out her last two brand-new Central Bank notes, meaning to ask for change. A Workers' Picket grabbed them, and handed them at once to the rickshaw man. The rickshaw man took them and went off, hauling his rickshaw and muttering to himself about whores.

Chu Ling-fen was led into a large room inside. The whole floor was covered with straw, and some naked men lay about, sleeping. As soon as they saw the girl student, they immediately began to roar. All talking at once, they cried together:

"A nice little girl!"

"What's she doing here?"

"Has she come to comfort the Workers' Pickets?"

"Let me give her a kiss first!"

"Let me, let me!"

Chu Ling-fen cried, her legs grew weak, and as though paralyzed she fell to the floor.

The Workers' Pickets sentries kept waving their hands, motioning for everyone to quiet down. One of them shouted:

"This whore oppressed sacred labor!"

Thus there was again a great uproar, as they all shouted:

"That won't do! Beat her to death!"

"Beat her to death!"

Then someone came up.

"Don't do anything!" the sentry said, adding: "Wait until the Director comes back."

A worker who had been sitting on the straw mat got up, pinched Chu Ling-fen on the buttock, and said with a chuckle:

"My heart and liver, what a nice tender piece!"

This made everyone burst into loud laughter, and a cacophony of strange cries.

Chapter XV

"The Director has come!"

Chu Ling-fen, hearing the cry, stole a glance and saw someone whom she recognized come in from outside. "Is *he* the Director?"

It seemed that in a hopeless situation a thread of comfort had appeared. Her trembling, weak body straightened at once, and she stood up. Softly she called:

"Mr. Hung, Mr. Hung."

Hung T'ung-yeh recognized Chu Ling-fen, and quickly asked:

"What are you doing here?"

Chu Ling-fen felt so utterly wronged that she didn't know where to start, and could only weep. Hung T'ung-yeh had her brought into his own office, and told someone to bring water for her to wash her face, and to prepare tea for her. He let her rest in the cane chair. When he saw that she was somewhat calmed, Hung T'ung-yeh asked again:

"What are you doing here?"

"They said I oppressed sacred labor."

As soon as Hung T'ung-yeh heard this, he smiled, and said:

"How could that be? You couldn't have."

Thinking that it was certainly inconvenient for her to be there, he added:

"All right, we'll go out."

Chu Ling-fen followed him out. The workers in the large room all called out together:

"Director, so you're going to enjoy yourself!"

"Are you going to keep that little girl all to yourself?"

"Don't we get a share?"

"Let us taste something fresh too!"

The mingled cries and roars blended into a great confusion. Hung T'ung-yeh could not bear to be made a fool of, and he began to grow angry, but when he looked back at all those ill-assorted members of the sacred class, his anger weakened. Lowering his voice, he said to Chu Ling-fen:

"Pay no attention to them. Go a little faster."

Thus the two of them hastily left the headquarters of the Workers' Pickets, and crossed the street. Hung T'ung-yeh hailed a rickshaw and told the man to take them to the Hotel France. Chu Ling-fen stopped, and asked suspiciously:

"Why are we going there?"

"It's quiet; you can rest there, and we can talk."

There was nothing for Chu Ling-fen to do but get into the rickshaw and follow him.

When they had registered at the desk for a room, the two of them went upstairs. A waiter from Shanghai, who knew Hung T'ung-yeh well, met them at the foot of the stairs. He let the girl student pass, then, squinting at Hung T'ung-yeh, he held out his right hand, spread the fingers, and turned it over twice. Hung T'ung-yeh put his right forefinger to his lips, and shook his head, giving the waiter a wink. Going ahead of Chu Ling-fen, he opened the door and allowed her to enter.

"The washroom's on that side."

Hung T'ung-yeh pointed to a closed door, and having made a beginning, he continued:

"What really happened?"

Chu Ling-fen was silent for a moment, and then said with a little sigh:

"It's all Papa's fault. He was backward and couldn't keep up with the times, and even caused us, his children, to have to suffer for it."

She told in detail of everything that had happened.

"But in one respect, Papa was falsely accused. He's an old-fashioned person, and lives very simply. He isn't careless with money, and he's never fooled around with women. But the Women's Association committeewoman insisted that I must attack him on those two points, and I felt it was too unfair!"

"That's the art of attacking someone, and it's a wonderful trick!" Hung T'ung-yeh hastened to explain. "In attacking counterrevolutionaries, you must score quickly, and get your results. Besides, we only care for the end, and not the means. If you can think it over carefully, you'll certainly be able to accept it."

Chu Ling-fen was satisfied with this explanation, which she felt was fresh and lively. Without realizing it she was captivated by Hung T'ung-yeh's intelligence and quick wits. She glanced at him and smiled, blushing.

"What plans do you have now?" Hung T'ung-yeh asked.

"I haven't any plans." Chu Ling-fen, leaning back in the high-backed sofa, twisted a handkerchief in her hands and said vaguely: "I think I'll go to the Women's Association and ask them what I should do."

"These days everyone says," Hung T'ung-yeh said, laughing, "the Women's Association is going to stage a great naked women's march, and just now they're looking for people to take part."

"What?" Chu Ling-fen asked, startled.

"I said, just now the Women's Association is looking for people to take part in their great naked women's march."

"Really?"

"I'm not too clear on it. If there's no wind, the trees don't rustle, so perhaps there is such a thing," Hung T'ung-yeh said lightly.

"What kind of a naked march?" Chu Ling-fen asked, blushing.

"Naked means not wearing one's clothes."

"Nothing at all?"

"Naturally if there's nothing at all, it's called naked."

"How could they stand the embarrassment?"

"It's to break down such unhealthy concepts as that 'embarrassment' of yours that they'd hold a naked march. Only when we've destroyed the false, and returned to nature, can mankind's spiritual life attain true liberation."

Hung T'ung-yeh spoke so earnestly that Chu Ling-fen raised her head, and laughed. She said:

"Embarrassing, embarrassing!"

Hung T'ung-yeh, perched on the arm of the sofa, stroked Chu Ling-fen's beautiful hair, and asked, in a soft, familiar tone:

"Suppose you go too and take part?"

"I couldn't." Chu Ling-fen sat up, moved away from Hung T'ung-yeh's hand, and said, "I'd rather go back to Papa's, and not take part. When I think about it—a bunch of women marching down the street without a stitch on, and huge crowds of bystanders shouting and laughing—I'd really die of shame!"

Hung T'ung-yeh put out his left hand and grasped Chu Ling-fen's shoulder, bringing her head gently to rest against his chest. He bent to kiss her hair. He said:

"When you're used to something, it becomes natural. This so-called 'shame', too, was originally a custom which was nurtured. So the revolution wants to destroy tradition; if the old doesn't go, the new cannot come."

Chu Ling-fen wanted to stand up, but she was held fast by Hung T'ung-yeh's left hand. She felt that his hand was giving off a kind of warmth, which was diffusing over her body. She became weak and without strength. She slowly raised her head to look at Hung T'ung-yeh, and Hung T'ung-yeh took the opportunity to bend forward and lightly kiss her.

They spent the night at the Hotel France. After long consideration, Chu Ling-fen decided to enter the Military-political Academy recently established in Wuchang. Hung T'ung-yeh accompanied her across the river, and as they crossed, the two of them, standing on the deck, leaned against the rail and watched the river scene. There were two warships, flying the British flag, just coming upstream, and as Hung T'ung-yeh saw them, he said:

"We'll see how much longer you can come to China and throw your weight around."

"This slogan, 'Beat Down Imperialism!'—how will it really be carried out?" Chu Ling-fen asked humbly, like a student in the classroom who doesn't understand the lesson, asking the teacher.

"This is a slogan, and people who shout slogans don't know what policies will actually be chosen, and in what order, to realize it." Hung T'ung-yeh smiled casually, and pulled Chu Ling-fen more tightly against him. "But as I see it, these two words 'beat down' aren't entirely appropriate, and it would be better to say, 'drive out'. At least, at present, we can only seek to drive it out."

"Surely you don't mean imperialism will never fall?"

"When revolution breaks out over the entire world, then it will fall, of course."

All the passengers on the boat were looking at Hung T'ung-yeh and Chu Ling-fen. This was not because of their rather loud discussion of revolutionary theory, for not one of the passengers had any interest in such difficult questions. It was their close snuggling which had drawn people's attention. When a young couple could behave so recklessly in public, the way of modesty had been lost, and they were no different from birds and beasts. One bespectacled old gentleman, blinking over his spectacles, and snorting disdainfully, spat heavily, and then softly sighed:

"Revolution, revolution."

A middle-aged woman beside him glanced at him and said angrily:

"What's that to you, that you've got to butt in?"

"Everyone minds everyone's business; how can that be called butting in?"

"Didn't you just hear what happened to Yeh Te-kuang in Changsha?" The middle-aged woman suppressed her anger and lowered her voice.

Then the old gentleman said no more.

But already people were listening to their conversation, for it was obvious that they were quarrelling. Although it took no more than twenty minutes for the boat to cross the river, many passengers found the time too long, and each sought his own way to pass the time. As soon as they saw others arguing, their interest was aroused, and they wanted to investigate. A dense ring of people immediately formed around the middle-aged woman and the bespectacled old man.

An old woman with bound feet, estimating the ages of the couple, couldn't help tugging at the middle-aged woman and asking her:

"What's he to you?"

The middle-aged woman blushed, and did not respond. The bespectacled old gentleman grew a bit irritated. Giving the old woman a look, he said loudly:

"She's my wife."

"Your ages don't match."

"She's my 'little'[33] wife!" The bespectacled old gentleman at once added a word, drawing out and emphasizing "little". The middle-aged woman, furious, began to chatter:

"You old man who won't die! Heaven ought to kill you! You're afraid people won't know I'm your concubine—you don't leave me any face at all!"

---

[33] *Hsiao* means little and here indicates that she is his concubine.

Chu Ling-fen had been among the crowd watching the excitement, and as soon as she heard this, she pushed forward. She forcefully shook the middle-aged woman by the shoulder, and said loudly:

"This is a time of revolution. Taking a concubine is counterrevolutionary. Why don't you go to the Women's Association and accuse him?"

"Fine, I'll do as you say, I'll go and accuse him!" the middle-aged woman said recklessly.

"Now, now, quickly stop this unreasonable talk," the old woman with bound feet hastily tried to interfere. "What is there that can't be settled, that's worth making an accusation about? I'm a concubine myself!"

When Chu Ling-fen heard this, she grabbed the old woman with bound feet as well, and said encouragingly to her:

"Since you're a concubine too, you also ought to go and accuse your old man. All right, the two of you can go together."

"My old man's been dead for many years."

"Then who do you live with now?"

"With my son."

"Then go and accuse your son."

Hung T'ung-yeh, listening to these words of Chu Ling-fen's, felt that what she said was a little unconvincing. He was afraid that a public failure would damage her newly aroused zeal, so he joined the chorus:

"The father's debts are paid by the son, no mistake!"

"Stop making jokes! My son treats me very well. He's filial and obedient, so why should I want to accuse him?" the old woman asked anxiously.

"Not to accuse him won't do; you definitely must accuse him!" Hung T'ung-yeh said, stiffening his face.

"If you don't accuse him—surely you're not willing to go on being a concubine?"

The boat neared the wharf, where the Workers' Pickets had stationed a permanent sentry to keep order, examine the good and the bad, execute the unwritten law of the revolution, and deal with counterrevolutionary elements. They recognized their leader, and Hung T'ung-yeh ordered:

"Take these three people to the Women's Association. The two women are concubines, and in order to struggle for the equality of men and women, they want to make an accusation."

The old woman with bound feet, hearing this, desperately interjected:

"What accusation? I don't want to accuse, I don't want to accuse!"

The middle-aged woman, hanging on to her bespectacled old man, also said:

"I myself was willing to be his concubine. Come on, we'll go home, and the devil can go lay an accusation."

"You are women," Chu Ling-fen said politely. "How can you not want equality of men and women?"

"I don't want it, I don't want it. We're going home."

The middle-aged woman and the bespectacled old man got off the boat, and the Workers' Pickets seized them. They all said:

"Not to make an accusation won't do; you've definitely got to make an accusation. You three people can't get off the boat. You're going back to Hankow on the same boat, to the Women's Association!"

The old woman with bound feet began to cry and beat her hands together.

"What kind of a world is this? How can you force a mother to accuse her own son?"

"You should understand—this is the real world."

So said one of the Workers' Pickets.

Chu Ling-fen and Hung T'ung-yeh got off the boat and took a rickshaw to the Military-political Academy. The broad gates were flanked by two armed guards, and each gatepost bore one line of a couplet in big white characters against a blue background. They read:

Party regulations are like iron
Military orders are like mountains

The walls on either side also bore a couplet:

When the revolution's left wing comes,
Counterrevolutionaries will disappear

When Chu Ling-fen saw this, her heart seemed to shake, and her footsteps slowed, as though she were hesitating. Hung T'ung-yeh, unaware of this, drew her by the shoulder straight on inside. The two sentries made no inspection and allowed them to enter. In the message room, Hung T'ung-yeh asked to see the Chairman of the Political Section of the Military-political Academy, Yün Ta-ying. Yün Ta-ying received them. Hung T'ung-yeh explained why they had come, and Yün Ta-ying looked at Chu Ling-fen, and asked with a smile:

"Can the daughter of Chu Kuang-chi be trusted?"

"She's just left her school and home, to take part in the revolution, in order to oppose her father."

"Don't you know that a great many counterrevolutionary elements pretend to be revolutionary and work their way into the revolutionary camp in order to spoil the revolution? They're more to be feared than external enemies."

"Director Yün," Chu Ling-fen said spiritedly, "I'm not that sort of person! After I enter the school, you just watch me!"

"Watch you what?"

"Watch how I behave! Just now on the ferry boat, I stood up for two concubines, and sent them to the Women's Association to lay accusations."

Yün Ta-ying asked about the matter. Hung T'ung-yeh told him of it in brief, and Yün Ta-ying laughed, and said:

"Since I see you won't leave, you'll get a uniform after all. All right, you'll take part in the Girl Students' Corps."

He pressed the bell on his desk, and in a response to the sound, a little soldier of twelve or thirteen came in. Yün Ta-ying directed him:

"Take her to Commander Yen in the Girl Students' Corps. She's a newly entered student."

Chu Ling-fen hastily stood up, holding in her tears, and said to Hung T'ung-yeh:

"When will you come and see me?"

"I'll come often when I have time. Just relax here, and study well."

"When you cross the river, don't forget to go by the Women's Association. Those two women who were concubines must stand up for themselves, and take part in the revolution, and no longer be content to be some man's plaything!" Chu Ling-fen said in an earnest and excited voice.

"Of course, I'll see to it. Don't you worry about it."

Chu Ling-fen followed the little soldier away.

Commander Yen was a short, plump woman, around thirty years old. Once she had published a book of new poetry, under the title *Spring Heart*. Her poems had this good point: no one could understand them. The self-styled "Military Scholar" Kuo Mo-jo,[34] wrote an essay especially to praise her, and said that her poems were priceless, precisely because no one could understand them. On this account her poetic reputation flourished, and she became an object of worship for the young students. Chu Ling-fen too had long ago been excited by her poetic fame, and now she felt still more deeply the glory of becoming one of the students in her Corps. Seeing that the woman's face was quite round, that she laughed, and acted like someone who was extremely easy to get along with, Chu

---

[34] Kuo Mo-jo was a celebrated poet of the period.

Ling-fen relaxed a little. Commander Yen smoothly took down several blank forms, and said:

"Fill this out first. There's a table over there."

Chu Ling-fen answered, "Yes", bowed slightly, and took the forms. She filled in the spaces one by one, and only with the one headed "Three generations" did she feel any difficulty, because she wasn't clear as to the meaning. So she went over and asked Commander Yen, and Commander Yen said:

"That means the three generations of your father, your grandfather, and your great-grandfather. Fill in their names and occupations and that will do."

Chu Ling-fen thought. She knew the names of her father and her grandfather, but she had never heard her great-grandfather's name. So she frankly told Commander Yen:

"I only know Father's and Grandfather's names."

"Put down those you know first, and later on you can fill in the rest."

"What's the use of having those dead persons' names?" Chu Ling-fen felt that this was certainly strange, and she couldn't help asking.

"The aim is to know the occupations and livelihoods of your ancestors, so that we can understand your class basis, the better to analyze your revolutionary components."

Chu Ling-fen did not completely understand this explanation, but she felt a little ashamed of her own shallowness, and was embarrassed to ask again. She went back to the table and sat down again. But as soon as she thought of her father's name, she couldn't help hesitating, and she felt the greatest disquiet. She gazed at the paper, stunned, for a while, and thought:

"After all, I can't put down something false, so I'll write it and then see. Besides, I just promised Chairman Yün."

Then she no longer hesitated, but stiffened the skin of her head, wrote it down boldly, and then offered it up with both hands. Commander Yen looked at it, and was greatly surprised. She reversed her smiling, laughing countenance, and said coldly:

"Chu Kuang-chi's daughter? How can Chu Kuang-chi's daughter be a revolutionary?"

"Just now Chairman Yün brought up that point," Chu Ling-fen, whose face had turned white, said in a trembling voice. "I'm resolved, Commander. Please just watch my behavior."

"All right, I'll wait."

Commander Yen hummed to herself a moment, and suddenly asked:

"Are you a virgin, or not?"

This question, coming so abruptly, gave Chu Ling-fen a slight convulsion; her heart rose into her throat, and she didn't know how to reply. Commander Yen understood, and she put on a pleasant face and said:

"We're both women, and besides I'm your commander, and you're my student, and there are no strangers here, so go ahead and answer, and don't worry."

Chu Ling-fen still was embarrassed, and could see no way to approach the subject, but Commander Yen was pressing her ever more insistently. Chu Ling-fen saw nothing for it, but to summon up her courage, and hesitantly said:

"I'm not."

"You and who?"

Unbearably mortified, Chu Ling-fen hung her head.

"Don't be afraid, just go on and say," Commander Yen said agreeably and gently, in a soft voice. "To whom did you give your virginity?"

"Hung T'ung-yeh." Chu Ling-fen spat these three words towards the floor.

"The one who's the Director of the General Headquarters' Workers' Pickets?"

"Yes."

When Commander Yen heard this, she was overjoyed. She ran over and squeezed her hands tightly, and said:

"Wonderful, you're really not ashamed of a revolutionary, progressive femininity, because you gave your virginity to the proletariat; your body also belongs to the proletariat. You're really most thorough-going!"

Commander Yen kept on praising her. Chu Ling-fen would have liked very much to know to whom this Commander Yen had given her own virginity, but she felt a certain hesitancy and couldn't ask. Commander Yen also asked:

"Do you know a Ch'ien Shou-yü?"

"I don't know her."

"She's Ch'ien Pen-san's daughter; haven't you two met?"

"We haven't," Chu Ling-fen said, a little embarrassed. "Before the Revolutionary Army came to Hankow, I had nothing to do with the outside world. In those days I was a good student."

These words made Commander Yen burst out laughing, and she said:

"And aren't you a good student now?"

Chu Ling-fen felt that she had made a slip, and not knowing how to explain, she just hung her head, and even her throat flushed. Commander Yen felt that this was amusing, and said:

"Can't even answer such a question? I'll tell you, you could answer like this: 'The times were different then. In those days, you were considered a good student if you never set foot outside the household and the classroom. Now, it is one who resolutely escapes those bounds, and without the slightest hesitation hurls herself into the revolutionary camp, offering herself to the glorious future of the proletariat, who is the good student!' If you give such an answer, then you've got a standpoint."

Chu Ling-fen felt as though the obstacles had suddenly been cleared away, as though a light had flashed in her eyes. Hastily bowing, she said:

"Thank you, Commander, for your instruction. Commander, your intelligence is truly amazing; no wonder that your reputation as a poet is nationwide!"

"My poems were translated into foreign languages many years ago," Commander Yen said, as though a little surprised. "Don't tell me you didn't know that?"

No mistake, Chu Ling-fen really had not known it. But because she was feeling good, and consequently her mind was clear, she added:

"I hadn't finished. I was saying, no wonder that your reputation as a poet is nationwide, and worldwide."

"Good—this time you argued well; you're quick-witted. I'll tell you about Ch'ien Shou-yü. At present she's a unit leader here, but she's very disrespectful, because she studied at the Normal University, and her Papa's a Department Chief. She's always criticizing us, saying that this is wrong and that's no good, that something isn't in accord with educational principles, or that it's destructive of the bodies and minds of the young students. Her mouth's full of these reactionary, backward clichés—really intolerable!"

"I'm not in her unit?" Chu Ling-fen was a little anxious.

"I'm just preparing to enroll you in her unit."

"But that won't do," Chu Ling-fen's heart was chilled. "Her Papa and my Papa are enemies, and if she's such a stubborn thing, how can she not hold it against me?"

"I have a plan; wait 'til I tell you."

Commander Yen rang the desk bell, and a youthful soldier came in. This soldier wore a grown man's military uniform. The upper part covered him to his knees, and the short trousers, though rolled halfway up, still reached to the floor. The cap covered more than half of his face, so he leaned his head back to see where he was going. Chu Ling-fen, seeing him, suddenly laughed. Commander

Yen gave her a look, as though to reprove her for being rude, and quietly said, "What's so funny?" She went on writing on the slip, and gave it to the young soldier, saying:

"Take her to the supply room."

When she received her uniform, Chu Ling-fen gave it a cursory inspection, and felt that it was really too big. She said:

"Please give me a smaller one instead. This one won't fit."

The supply clerk didn't answer. Chu Ling-fen looked at him, and said:

"May I trouble you to give me a smaller one? Thank you."

The supply clerk had already become impatient. He said in a loud voice:

"No exchanges!"

"This is too big; I can't wear it."

"Look at him!" The supply clerk pointed at the young soldier, who had conducted her.

"That looks awful!" Chu Ling-fen was also growing a little angry.

"We're making revolution here, not running a brothel, so what's the use of your looking good?" The supply clerk was enraged, and white spittle flew from his mouth with his harsh cries.

Chu Ling-fen felt grievously wronged. Tears flowed down her face, and she was at a loss. The young soldier, sympathizing with her, hastily bundled up her uniform, and led her away, saying:

"All right, don't cry. Come on, we're going to the unit."

Chu Ling-fen, weeping, went along. When they arrived at the unit, they saw the unit leader, Ch'ien Shou-yü, first. Ch'ien Shou-yü saw that she was crying, and asked:

"What's the matter?"

"Because of the clothes," the young soldier answered for her. "They don't fit, and she wanted to exchange them, but she couldn't, and she got bawled out too."

When Ch'ien Shou-yü heard this, she sighed. She thought for a moment, and said:

"This is a new environment, and perhaps you're not used to it, so you must be patient."

As she spoke, she went over, and dried the girl's tears with her own handkerchief, and lifted her face. Then, stepping back a couple of paces, she regarded the girl's figure, feeling that she was certainly the sort one would take pity on, and love at first sight. All at once, for some obscure reason, she thought of Hung Chin-ling, and felt that the two of them might have been sisters. She drew the girl to a chair, and said:

"It's not so important about the clothes, I'll get a tailor to adjust them for you. Every uniform fits after its been adjusted, mine, and Commander Yen's, too. Lots of the girl students fix theirs themselves. I'll think of what to do about yours."

She pinched Chu Ling-fen's earlobe, and patted her on the shoulder, saying:

"Don't let such a little thing bother you."

As soon as the young soldier heard mention of adjusting uniforms, he tugged at Ch'ien Shou-yü and said:

"Unit Leader, how about fixing mine up too?"

"I'm not running a tailor shop!"

"Take pity on me," the little soldier begged. "There's no one to fix it for me. Do a good deed!"

"No, no, definitely not!" Ch'ien Shou-yü absolutely refused, and moreover she pushed him out. "Go, go!"

Seeing that the young soldier had gone, Ch'ien Shou-yü turned; she sighed, and as much to herself as to Chu Ling-fen she said:

"As for fixing that poor little fellow's clothes, why not? But he works in the Commander's office, and if I fixed his clothes, Commander Yen might not like it. She isn't at all happy with me, and wants to pick a quarrel."

"Why does she want to pick a quarrel with you?" Chu Ling-fen asked at once.

"I think," Ch'ien Shou-yü hesitated a moment, "perhaps it's that there's a difference in our thinking."

"Are you right, or is she right?"

"She thinks she's right, and I think I'm right. It's just like Uncle saying reason's on his side, and Aunty saying it's on hers," Ch'ien Shou-yü said with a smile.

"But who's really right?"

"Perhaps I'm in the wrong, because might makes right, and right now the might isn't on my side."

"Your Papa's a Department Chief, isn't that enough might?"

"He too has to depend on others; he's only a puppet. Besides, I don't rely on my father's influence, and especially not in dealing with such shallow people."

Ch'ien Shou-yü shook her head as she spoke, and asked:

"Your baggage?"

"I haven't any baggage."

"How can you manage without bedding, washcloth, and underwear?"

"I stole away from the hospital empty-handed; where should I have gotten any baggage?" Chu Ling-fen explained.

"Is there anyone who can send you in some things?"

"No one but Hung T'ung-yeh."

"Hung T'ung-yeh?"

"Yes, Hung T'ung-yeh."

"The Director of the Workers' Pickets—you're friends?"

"Yes." Chu Ling-fen blushed.

"Well, you write him a letter now, and ask him to send you some things. For now, I'll see who has some extra they can loan you for a day or two, or you can share a blanket with someone for a couple of days."

When Chu Ling-fen had written the letter, Ch'ien Shou-yü conducted her to the unit dormitory. Originally this place had been a soldiers' barracks, and each dormitory resembled a classroom, or an assembly hall. In Chu Ling-fen's room, there were three rows of bunks, with twenty bunks in each row, and Chu Ling-fen happened to be assigned Number Sixty. Many girls clustered together, chattering and talking. A student was changing her clothes, and had just bared her upper body. Another, standing beside her, looked at her, and said:

"Your breasts are so big, why don't you wear a brassiere?"

"A brassiere?" the half-naked student returned. "Why don't you bind your feet?"

"Binding the feet is harmful to the body; it's not the same."

"Don't tell me wearing a brassiere is good for the body?"

She finished dressing, rolled up her sleeves, and cried in a loud voice:

"Wearing a brassiere is feudal backwardness! Our Corps ought to liberate the breasts. Everybody open up and give us a look, starting with her!"

She pointed at the student who had just asked why she wasn't wearing a brassiere. Everyone roared, and in a moment surrounded that student. In a flurry of confused motion, they stripped her upper body, and tore the tight vest she had used as a brassiere into shreds. The student hid her face and cried.

"Wipe away your tears!" Another student ordered her.

"We revolutionaries shed sweat and blood, but we don't shed tears!"

"Shedding tears is weak!"

"It's like Lin Tai-yü!"[35]

"It's like a concubine!"

"It's like a prostitute!"

"It's counterrevolutionary!"

"Down with counterrevolution!"

Everything was thrown into confusion.

Ch'ien Shou-yü came in, and gradually order was restored. Having inquired into the cause of the uproar, she said:

"It's not good to wear a brassiere."

Before she had finished speaking, the students roared altogether:

"What the leader said is correct; we support the leader!"

Waiting until they were finished, she continued:

"But, we should use peaceful means, and urge those who wear brassieres, so that they will liberate themselves. We shouldn't use force to compel them. Using forcible compulsion against someone's personality and freedom is a kind of violation."

"The leader is not revolutionary!"

One of the students—no telling who—cried out, and everyone took it up.

"The leader is not revolutionary!"

"The leader is counterrevolutionary!"

"Down with what is not revolutionary!"

"Down with what is counterrevolutionary!"

"Down with the leader!"

"Down with Ch'ien Shou-yü!"

"Down with the counterrevolutionary Ch'ien Shou-yü!"

---

[35] Lin Tai-yü: the weak, sickly, and frequently tearful heroine of Ts'ao Hsüeh-ch'in's classic novel *Hung-lou-meng* (*The Dream of the Red Chamber*).

Some of the students were jumping wildly about and shouting, even as they giggled. Ch'ien Shou-yü's face darkened with rage. Chu Ling-fen felt a bit of sympathy for her, but she also knew that 'the anger of the crowd is difficult to oppose', so she stood off to the side and said nothing. A student saw her, seized her and asked:

"What are you doing?"

"I'm a new student."

"Why don't you shout 'Down with counterrevolutionaries!'?"

As she spoke, she gave Chu Ling-fen's cheek a cruel pinch, so hard that it really hurt. Chu Ling-fen could only start to shout "Down with—" along with the rest.

Suddenly someone jumped up onto the windowsill. By the looks of his clothing, he seemed to be one of the Academy's male students. He kept waving his hands, and the girl students, curious, quieted down to see what he wanted. He held up a little book in one hand, showed the cover, and asked:

"Have you read this book?"

The girl students immediately pressed toward the window, and saw the two words *Ling-lung* on the cover. They looked at one another, mystified. Suddenly, a sharp voice cried:

"That's a novel, I read it. It's about an eight-sided romance. One woman has eight lovers at the same time."

"Was it well-written?" the male student asked.

"It was great, it was great, it really moved me!"

"Do you know who was the author of this book?"

"Ssu Ling-luan! Ssu Ling-luan!"

"Do you know who I am?"

Everyone was surprised at this, and no one answered. The male student smiled, and said:

"I'm Ssu Ling-luan, the author of this book!"

"So it's you!" someone said.

"What are you doing here?" another asked.

"I came looking for Ch'ien Shou-yü. Suppose you let me have a few words with her?" the male student said, with a flirtatious laugh.

"You're a friend of hers?"

"Yes."

"All right, Unit Leader, your friend has come looking for you, so go along with him," a student said, indicating that she was pardoned.

"We'll settle that counterrevolutionary score later on."

Ch'ien Shou-yü knew there was nothing more to be said at the moment, so she suppressed her anger and went off to her room. She decided to resign the Unit Leader's position; she could no longer go on with it. Ssu Ling-luan waved his hand in salutation to the girl students, jumped down from the windowsill, and followed Ch'ien Shou-yü into her room. Ch'ien Shou-yü, seeing that it was him, said not a word. Ssu Ling-luan said to soothe her:

"The young students are ardent and excitable, but their motives are good. It's easy to get along with them if only you understand their psychology. You mustn't be angry."

"I'm not angry," Ch'ien Shou-yü said in a low voice. "I only feel that this isn't the right way to educate. Going on this way may spoil their youth."

"Every era has its own political demands, and its own educational methods, and this isn't something that can be exhausted in two or three words, or concluded in an hour and a quarter. I came to ask you—do you have time this afternoon to cross the river?"

Ch'ien Shou-yü had had no plans to cross the river. But now, because she meant to resign the position of Unit Leader, and would need to discuss it with her father and see what he thought about it, she said:

"If I'm going across the river, wait 'til I go and say something to Commander Yen. How about you?'

"I'll go with you."

The two of them left the school. Ssu Ling-luan asked:

"Elder Sister, have you ever seen Yellow Crane Tower?"

"I haven't."

"Let's go and see it, shall we?"

"I don't care much for such famous but broken-down ancient monuments," Ch'ien Shou-yü said with a smile.

"It's just for fun."

Ssu Ling-luan had long admired Ch'ien Shou-yü from a distance. By strict reckoning he probably should have called Ch'ien Shou-yü his first cousin on his mother's side. But because they had been raised far from one another, neither one paid much attention to this family relationship. Ssu Ling-luan was one of Ch'ien Pen-ssu's students, and moreover was one of a small number of his devoted followers; on this account, Ssu Ling-luan was often at the Ch'iens' home. The year before the Northern Expedition, Ssu Ling-luan had graduated from Normal University, and had become a teacher in a primary school. Outside of class, he wrote *Ling-lung*, and experimentally sent a copy to the great writer Chang Chi-p'ing, whom he worshipped, asking him for his criticism. Chang Chi-p'ing had become famous and rich writing multi-angled love stories. When he read Ssu Ling-luan's magnum opus, he expressed his heartfelt admiration. Since Chang Chi-p'ing's love stories sold so well with three or four characters, he had gone on to attain the lofty state of having five or six-cornered romances. He had already come to believe that no more could be added: more, and the protagonist would no longer have time even to eat, and would find it hard to go on living. And now this Ssu Ling-luan, barely out of school, and giving a portent of his future talent, had suddenly brought forth a romance with eight male characters, towards all of whom the female protagonist responded generously and without difficulty. Chang Chi-p'ing spontaneously gave it his great admiration. He then wrote an involved and devious letter to Ssu Ling-luan, the gist of which was "Your magnum opus is excellent; unfortunately the author is an unknown, so people won't necessarily recognize its quality. You had best sell me this manuscript; published under my big name, it will certainly catch on and become a best-seller. If you agree, I've decided to reward you with a high price: ninety-six cents per thousand words," and so forth.

Since Ssu Ling-luan prized fame more than profit, this exchange was not realized. After he had pressed the other with letters and telegrams, he got his manuscript back. He then sent it to a not very famous bookstore on Ssu-ma Road in Shanghai, offering them both manuscript and copyright, and while the bookstore was not very respectful, they did accept it. After the book was published, they sent him two copies, and Ssu Ling-luan felt very well satisfied.

After the Northern Expedition army captured Wuhan, throughout the nation people's hearts were stirred, and Ssu Ling-luan could no longer restrain himself. For many years his grandmother had kept a little savings, perhaps just over two hundred dollars in cash, buried under the bricks beneath the flour jar. He found a way to steal it, and rearranged the bricks and flour just as they had been; neither the spirits nor the devils knew of it. He then went to Shanghai, and bought a steamboat ticket for Hankow. The first person he saw was Ch'ien Pen-san, and to show that he was no stranger to the revolution, he "demonstratively" said:

"I know Sun _____, no mistake, Sun _____!"

Ch'ien Pen-san, hearing him mention Director-general Sun's personal name, was so startled that he turned pale, and his tongue rolled up so that he couldn't speak. Behind his dark glasses, his two eyes stared fixedly at Ssu Ling-luan. He remained numb for perhaps five minutes. Then his color changed from white to red, and then to purple. Finally, with swollen neck, he leaped up from his chair, and cried in an irrepressible rage:

"You muddled egg!"

Ssu Ling-luan couldn't make head nor tail out of this abuse; he left his seat and retreated, saying:

"Third Master, what's the matter?"

"How can you call him Sun _____?"

So that was it. Ssu Ling-luan's spirit relaxed slightly, and he argued:

"He is called Sun _____, and if I don't call him Sun _____, what am I to call him? Everyone knows he is called Sun _____, so why not call him that?"

Ch'ien Pen-san was so angry that he stamped his foot, and said in a loud voice:

"Why not? You ought to call him the Director, or if you don't want to be so formal you should call him Mister!"

Ssu Ling-luan at once grew stubborn, and still wanted to argue, but Ch'ien Pen-san simply pushed him out, and wouldn't listen to him any longer.

"Go, go! What a thing!"

Ssu Ling-luan was angry too, and had it not been for the restraining bonds of many years of accumulated teaching about the difference between seniors and juniors he would really have opposed the other. He thought to himself:

"*Heng*, you called me a muddled egg, but you're really more of a muddled egg than I! You said I'm a thing, but I see that you're really not even a thing."

Ssu Ling-luan had never before been so put to shame, and for several days he was despondent and lonely. He had always respected Ch'ien Pen-ssu far more than Ch'ien Pen-san, and he hoped that he could receive some comfort from Ch'ien Pen-ssu, to make up for the humiliation he had received from Ch'ien Pen-san. But unexpectedly Ch'ien Pen-ssu's face was impassive and he said mechanically:

"He was right to scold you."

"What?" Ssu Ling-luan was terribly shocked. "Fourth Master, do you agree with Third Master?"

"It's true, I've often opposed him. But when he's right, I approve him."

"Do you approve of that feudal practice of avoiding the use of his personal name?"

"That's your crooked argument. Mr. Sun created the Republic; he's the father of his country. When we mention him, we should do so with respect."

"The Americans speak of Washington, and the Soviets speak of Lenin, without meaning any disrespect." Ssu Ling-luan was still arguing.

"That's America, that's the Soviet Union!" Ch'ien Pen-ssu's anger flared up. "We're China, and China has the Chinese tradition; China has China's own moral principles and virtue. You don't want to 'count the records but forget your ancestors'."

Ssu Ling-luan, bearing a bellyful of self-pity, felt even more contrary. On one occasion, when he was with Ch'ien Shou-yü, he couldn't help venting his discontent, and finally he said bitterly:

"Elder Sister, if this is revolution, I'd rather be counterrevolutionary. If this is false revolution, then I want to be even more revolutionary!"

Ch'ien Shou-yü laughed out loud, and shook her head, saying:

"It's really strange to see you so hot for revolution. We're all students of education. Don't tell me you don't believe that only when education is properly handled does the nation have a future? Can revolution take the place of education?"

"Education is important. But education is an empty vessel, and each has his own different content. Formerly, scholars were selected by the examination system; they studied the eight-legged essay, and that was education. The Japanese carried out their scheme to militarize the citizens, with cruel beatings and coercion, and that was education. What is our education at present? 'Distant water doesn't relieve present thirst'! Revolution, let's revolutionize politics, and then we can talk about education."

"At the time of the May Fourth Movement, didn't they advocate science and democracy? In scholarship, the encouragement of free research was very much the fashion—and then society would be able to make progress. Social progress would lead to political progress, and finally to a rich country with a strong people."

Ch'ien Shou-yü spoke with unlimited feeling.

"Wait 'til the situation settles down a bit—the right thing for me is to go back to Peking and finish my studies at Normal University. I've really seen enough of this disorder. I'm not willing to follow after Papa any more—let each look after his own affairs!"

When the Military-political Academy was founded, Ch'ien Pen-san had introduced his daughter to Yün Ta-ying, and Yün Ta-ying had asked her to become a unit leader, and had told her:

"You're a student of education; that's splendid. Our Military-political Academy is educational, of course, but ours is revolutionary education, and not necessarily the same as what you've studied. Our educational goal is to make the students become revolutionaries, who will know how to make revolution."

"Now that we've grasped political power," Ch'ien Shou-yü asked, confused, "whom are we making revolution against?"

This remark was greatly at odds with Yün Ta-ying's thinking. Had not the words just left his mouth, he would have seriously pondered whether or not this person had the qualifications to be a unit leader. At the time, he smiled and let it pass. In secret, he expressed himself to his confidantes, and waited for an opportunity to strike at this unit leader. Thus Ch'ien Shou-yü often received "education" from her colleagues and students, and became the object of their jeers and ridicule.

She well understood that this situation could not go on, and that in due time she would have to withdraw.

She sat with Ssu Ling-luan on Yellow Crane Tower, watching the river, and it did have a calming effect. Ch'ien Shou-yü felt the pleasure of simply breathing. Tea was poured, and they sat in reclining chairs. Originally she had been indifferent when Ssu Ling-luan wanted to come here; now she didn't want to hurry away.

Ssu Ling-luan's eyes were constantly searching her body, as though he were seeking something in what he could not know. He felt that her slender form was really not bad. Wide shoulders, flat chest, but the middle unusually plump. Looking farther down, Ssu Ling-luan stole a glance at her rather large and unbound feet, which were stuck into low-heeled leather shoes, obviously too large. Inadvertently he caught his breath, and quickly averted his eyes.

Suddenly Ch'ien Shou-yü, seemingly without having thought about it, said to him:

"You really shouldn't enter that academy."

"As for me," Ssu Ling-luan said in a self-satisfied tone, "I've decided to study from the beginning and to manage everything thoroughly. I've got to make revolution to the end!"

"So you're going to call attention to shortcomings like a Sun _____?" Ch'ien Shou-yü said to tease him.

"You could say that."

"Can you understand the present situation in Wuhan?"

"Revolution!"

"Can you know who's revolutionary?"

"Outwardly the Kuomintang is making revolution against the Peiyang warlords, and inwardly the Communist Party is making revolution against the Kuomintang; everyone's making revolution back and forth."

"Well, who are you going to make revolution against?"

"Doesn't the couplet on the gate of the Academy say 'The Left Wing of the Revolution is Coming'?" Ssu Ling-luan asked, clenching his fist. "I only want to be Left. I'm Left, I want to be more Left than the Communist Party!"

The sky had quickly turned a dark yellow, and the wind suddenly began to blow hard. The two felt that they could hardly open their eyes. Paying for the tea, they quickly left. When they got down to the shore, the boats which crossed the river had all taken shelter from the wind, and stopped crossing. As twilight passed, the sky grew dark.

Chapter XVI

Looking at the barrier of the river with the fierce wind and furious waves, Ssu Ling-luan suggested:

"Let's look for a place to eat first, and after we've eaten, we'll see."

Ch'ien Shou-yü felt hungry too, so she acquiesced. They went into the city. Because of the high wind there were far fewer people than usual on the street, and it was a little lonely. Ssu Ling-luan was a wizened monkey, and short as well; Ch'ien Shou-yü was about half a head taller than he. He spied a Muslim restaurant, and looked up to ask:

"Let's eat there, all right?"

Ch'ien Shou-yü glanced at it, and said:

"I don't eat beef."

They went slowly on. Ssu Ling-luan asked:

"Why don't you eat beef?"

"It's in remembrance of my mother, a poor, silly old woman; she didn't eat beef."

At the mention of her mother, Ch'ien Shou-yü felt a little distressed, and her voice sank. Ssu Ling-luan, who naturally had no way of understanding her mood, continued:

"If she didn't eat beef, I think there must have been a reason."

"My mother's folks were farmers. Farmers depend on the ox for their living, and they feel that the ox is the farm family's benefactor. It works for you all its life, and for you to still eat its flesh would just be too cruel."

When Ssu Ling-luan heard this, he stopped smiling. He said:

"And to have such false benevolence and false righteousness towards an animal!"

"Their love for the cow really came from the heart. In the dead of winter, on the coldest nights, many, many farmers take their own blankets and cover the ox. And in the spring, when they themselves are half-dead with hunger, they give the bran and sweet potatoes to the ox. I've seen this with my own eyes."

"That's not because they love the ox—it's the price of using the ox's labor power," Ssu Ling-luan said in a rather disappointed tone. "Elder Sister, your thinking!"

"Are you saying my thinking is backward?"

"It deserves some attention," Ssu Ling-luan said suggestively.

"There's nothing that deserves any attention," Ch'ien Shou-yü said coolly. "When the oxen my mother's parents used got old, or sick, they'd look after them, and after they died they'd bury them. Now, old oxen, sick oxen, and even dead oxen can be sold for money. Why was that?"

"False compassion! Reckless waste of natural products!" Ssu Ling-luan said thoughtlessly.

"When did you learn to be so tough?"

Ch'ien Shou-yü was a bit irritated. She snorted in disgust and said no more.

They found a northern style noodle-stall, and had something to eat. Then they went back to the wharves, to find the wind even worse. They could see there would be no possibility of crossing the river that day. Ssu Ling-luan said:

"Elder Sister, what shall we do?"

Naturally, they could have returned to the school, but Ch'ien Shou-yü was really disgusted with that school. No, it was more than disgust, she was a little afraid. That unfeeling contempt shown her by superiors and subordinates alike surrounded her tightly, like insubstantial cords, making it hard for her to breathe. She was no longer willing to enter that circle. She hesitated for a moment, not knowing how to answer Ssu Ling-luan's question.

Ssu Ling-luan saw that she was in difficulty. His heart leaped, and he said:

"If you like, we can find a hotel and spend the night, and tomorrow, when the wind's died down, we can cross the river."

"All right." Ch'ien Shou-yü expressed her agreement at once.

There was a hotel near the waterfront, and each of them took a room. Perhaps because the electric current was weak, or for some other reason, the electric light was extremely dim, not even as bright as a kerosene lamp under a glass cover. The few simple pieces of various kinds of ancient furniture aroused in the beholder a feeling of uncleanness. Ch'ien Shou-yü was extremely tired, but after one dubious look at the canopied wooden bed, she didn't have the courage to lie down on it. She sat down on the wooden chair beside the tea table, feeling quite at a loss. But Ssu Ling-luan stuck as close to her side as possible. He sat down on the edge of the bed opposite Ch'ien Shou-yü, and asked in a loud, animated voice:

"Elder Sister, have you read my book?"

Ch'ien Shou-yü, somewhat annoyed, shook her head.

"You really haven't read it?"

"That's right," Ch'ien Shou-yü said, turning her head away to examine the black and dirty tea things on the tea table, and thinking: How can anyone drink this tea?

"That's really a pity," Ssu Ling-luan lamented. "Elder Sister, you're a student of education, and just now you're taking part in the revolution as a unit leader. If you haven't read my book, how can you guide the students? How would it be if the students knew you hadn't read my book?"

"I've never heard of using fiction to educate students. I only know that truly hard-working good students don't read fiction," Ch'ien Shou-yü said, expressing her view.

"But my fiction is different." Ssu Ling-luan was a little cast down, but he still persisted.

"I don't believe you can write fiction!" Ch'ien Shou-yü felt that in dealing with this self-styled writer, politeness was superfluous and useless, so she prepared to douse him with cold water.

Ssu Ling-luan's face flushed red as fire, and at once he stood up and said anxiously:

"What? My fiction has been critically accepted—by what right do you dare say I can't write?"

Suddenly Ch'ien Shou-yü felt that it was quite amusing. She laughed, and said coolly:

"You needn't get upset. Please sit down, and I'll tell you."

Ssu Ling-luan came a step closer to her, arms akimbo, and said, snorting with anger:

"Tell me, tell me!"

"Sit down!"

"All right, I'll sit down."

Ssu Ling-luan poured himself a cup of tea from the tea table, using this action to calm his anger somewhat, and sat down again on the edge of the bed.

"Let me explain first," Ch'ien Shou-yü said, drawing a deep breath and collecting herself, "that I'm a complete novice as far as fiction is concerned. But I think that a person who writes fiction at least ought to understand human feelings and the ways of the world, and comprehend the psychology of all sorts of people—then he can pick up his pen. Fiction is born out of men in society; it isn't trumped up out of nothing."

"What you say is exactly right," Ssu Ling-luan said excitedly, noisily swallowing a mouthful of tea. "I truly do understand human feelings and the ways of the world, and I really do comprehend human psychology. My fiction is created precisely out of man in society."

Ch'ien Shou-yü stared at him for a moment, and then shook her head, saying:

"I don't see that at all."

"Why not?" Ssu Ling-luan stood up again.

"Let's take something right before our eyes for an example. A woman has her own private life; she has her own affairs. You've already been with me for a long time, we've come to this hotel, and you ought to leave me alone to rest for a little while. If you wanted to come into my room, you should have asked my consent first. Besides, in a city as big as Wuchang, surely there must be a clean, proper hotel? But you wanted to come here. Look, how can a person stay here?"

Ch'ien Shou-yü spoke slowly, and Ssu Ling-luan smiled broadly as he listened.

"Elder Sister," he said, as though he didn't take her seriously, "I said before that your thinking deserved some attention, and I wasn't mistaken. You demand to have your own private life, you want to stay in a pretty hotel—these are all the individualistic pleasures of the bourgeoisie! Frankly, such demands are counterrevolutionary."

"Stop, stop, don't say any more, I've heard enough of this! Ch'ien Shou-yü waved her hand. "All right, go. I'm going to sleep."

Ssu Ling-luan came over, put down his tea cup on the tea tray, and patted Ch'ien Shou-yü's shoulder, saying earnestly and softly:

"Elder Sister, let me sleep with you, all right? My Elder Sister."

Ch'ien Shou-yü, shocked, jumped up and shoved violently with both hands against Ssu Ling-luan's chest. Ssu Ling-luan fell helplessly over, to land before the bed. Ch'ien Shou-yü was so angry that she was trembling all over. Her legs felt weak, and she dropped back into the chair she had been sitting in.

Ssu Ling-luan got up, blushing, and said:

"A man and a woman ought to sleep together, why do you refuse me?"

"You're talking nonsense!"

"But really, why can't we?" Ssu Ling-luan persisted in failing to understand.

"Your mother's a woman too, why don't you sleep with her?"

Ch'ien Shou-yü was so very angry that this coarse phrase burst from her lips. But at once she felt that she had said the wrong thing, and had lowered herself; she was upset, and began to cry. No longer able to remain dignified, she wiped her face with a handkerchief and hiccoughed.

"Didn't you recognize my good intentions? It's because I love you that I want to sleep with you. Won't you accept my love?" Ssu Ling-luan was still unwilling to give up.

Ch'ien Shou-yü felt that this person before her was truly unreasonable, and truly hateful, to an extreme. Her anger rose again, and she stopped crying. With a cold smile she said:

"That's why I say you aren't qualified to write. You simply don't understand love. Love comes gradually. To want to jump into bed with someone as soon as you set eyes on her, without having gone through the stage of beseeching her love, is the conduct of an animal."

Ssu Ling-luan smiled when he heard this, and said, as though now he understood.

"Oh, so that's what you want! According to this theory of yours, you've got an old-fashioned brain—fundamentally bad. But that doesn't matter. Perhaps there still are people who like sad, sentimental poetry, who want to first exchange keepsakes in the rear flower garden, and send messages through Hung-niang,[36] and make private vows of lifelong fidelity before they'll get into their refined beds. Such persons are certainly phonies who love to make a great show, and they're not in keeping with today's trend. I don't care for all that stuff. But, Elder Sister, if that's how you want me to act, I can do it; I'm willing to sacrifice myself for you."

As he spoke, he took a filthy handkerchief from the pocket of his uniform trousers, lifted it by a corner, and shook it so violently that it snapped.

"Elder Sister, you've probably read *The Dream of the Red Chamber*. Once, because Chia Pao-yü had played at taking part in a theatrical performance, his old man beat him 'until his skin was broken and his flesh split', until 'death went and life came'. Lin Tai-yü came to see him, with her eyes running tears like a rotten peach. Later on Tai-yü left, and Chia Pao-yü sent a slave girl to give Lin Tai-yü a handkerchief he had used. The slave girl didn't understand, and feared that the gift would irritate Lin Tai-yü, but Pao-yü guaranteed that it wouldn't. Sure enough, Lin Tai-yü accepted the gift, and not only was she not annoyed, she was grateful for being understood. She dried her tears, and wrote a poem in her own hand, which went something like this: 'A foot of silk, given from your suffering—how should it not make one suffer?'. Elder Sister, if you like sentimental poems, isn't that sentimental enough for you? Now, supposing I'm Chia Pao-yü, and you're Lin Tai-yü, I'll give you this keepsake, completing the first step of the process, and then we can go on to the second stage."

Ssu Ling-luan, with a disgusting leer, and paying no attention to the other's response, handed the filthy handkerchief to Ch'ien Shou-yü. Ch'ien Shou-yü leaped to her feet, and slapped him across the mouth. Because she was at the peak

---

[36] Hung-niang: the heroine's maidservant, in the play *The Romance of the Western Chamber*. She serves as a go-between, facilitating the love affair between the scholar and the beauty.

of her rage, she struck as hard as she could.   Ssu Ling-luan saw golden stars dance before his eyes, and nearly fell down.

"You shameless thing!"

Ch'ien Shou-yü, cursing him, rushed out of the door and hastily left the little hotel.

Ssu Ling-luan rubbed his stinging face, and remained stunned for a moment, like a defeated rooster.   Then he drooped wearily onto the bed, and muttered to himself:

"She didn't like the direct approach, and she didn't like sentimental poetry—what a strange woman!"

Tossing and turning, groaning and sighing, he passed half the night, and it was nearly dawn before he got to sleep.

It was close to noon the next day when he got up.   He left the hotel.   The weather was bright, and the wind had dropped.   He hurried to get on the ferry-boat, crossed to Hankow, and went first to the Ch'iens' house.   For several days he had been quite poor, and he was prepared to borrow a little walking-around money from Ch'ien Pen-ssu.   It was quiet downstairs, and there was no one about. Ssu Ling-luan sat on the sofa.   He saw a copy of that day's *Central Daily News*, which carried a special article entitled "Put-on Appearances and Manufactured Atmosphere".   The writer was Kuo Hsin-ju.   This man had been one of the leaders of the May Fourth Movement, and since then Ssu Ling-luan had always considered him rather important.   He had heard that Kuo Hsin-ju was in Wuhan, but had not seen him take part in any activities.   On this day, he had delivered a speech.   He said there are only two things which the present government authorities in Wuhan are interested in.   One is putting on appearances; they make big talk, but in fact there's nothing inside; they strive to create a revolutionary atmosphere of terror, so as to stiffen their own courage.   In fact, neither of these two things is urgent, and they are quite unnecessary.   Kuo Hsin-ju's prescription was to bring up Mr. Democracy and Mr. Science, of whom he had spoken during the May Fourth period, and to hope that material and political construction might be attended to in that spirit. With a firm footing, one could proceed cautiously. Revolution and nation-building were different from sleight-of-hand, and magic charms were of no use.

Ssu Ling-luan felt that this essay put it very well. But it was like the old scholar's oft-repeated phrases, and he opened the paper. Turning to another page, he saw a local correspondent's dispatch. It reported that Yeh Te-kuang of Changsha had been struggled against, and had died. The gist of it was that in the household of one of Yeh Te-kuang's nephews, there was a servant girl called Pai Ch'a-hua. Her master had maltreated her, and had moreover deprived her of her freedom of movement, so that for many years she had led the life of a prisoner and a slave. After the revolution, when the Wuhan labor leader Liu Shao-ch'iao learned of this, he suggested to the Changsha Women's Association and the Workers' Pickets that an investigation be made. After the Women's Association and the Workers' Pickets had rescued Pai Ch'a-hua from this fiery pit, they arrested her master and his whole household. During the investigation, it was discovered that this local villain of a rich family, who maltreated his servant girl, had mutual connections with the Peiyang warlords, and had a plan to counterattack against the Revolutionary Army, in order to carry out the duties given them by the imperialists. The leader of the counterrevolutionary clique in Changsha, as the investigation had shown, was the widely known and famous gentleman Yeh Te-kuang. So Yeh Te-kuang was arrested. This counterrevolutionary clique, which included Yeh Te-kuang's whole household, and that of his nephew as well, altogether some thirty-odd people, men and women, old and young—among whom were two infants still at the breast—were all alike sentenced to the death penalty by a specially-summoned mass meeting. The sentences were carried out on the spot, by Pai Ch'a-hua herself, who used a soldier's rifle and shot them to death one by one. Pai Ch'a-hua, who had received the highest praise from the Women's Association, had already set out for Hankow to assume her duties as a Women's Association committeewoman.

Ssu Ling-luan read this straight through, sighed deeply, and brandished his fist, saying:

"She sure did it! Good for Pai Ch'a-hua and her glorious revolutionary femininity!"

This led him to think that Pai Ch'a-hua must certainly be very different from Ch'ien Shou-yü. Such femininity surely would not want a stage of beseeching love, or any such meaningless procedures as private vows of lifetime fidelity. He thought spontaneously:

"Such a woman is really too lovable, too lovable!"

Suddenly he was seized by an intense desire, impossible to satisfy: how he wished he could snatch her at once to his side.

"I must think of a way to see her, to get to know her!" he thought.

Suddenly there was a commotion outside. Ssu Ling-luan put down the paper and went out. He saw a man on a stretcher carried in, with Ch'ien Pen-ssu and Ch'ien Shou-yü following close behind. The stretcher was set down in the courtyard, and the man slowly sat up. Ssu Ling-luan recognized him, and called out in startled delight:

"Little Brother Shou-tien?"

"Oh, is it Elder Brother Ling-luan?"

Thus, with everyone helping, they supported Ch'ien Shou-tien inside, and helped him into the little room originally occupied by Hung T'ung-yeh.

The battle of Ting-ssu-ch'iao had been fiercely fought, and each soldier of the Revolutionary Army fought like ten men. Ch'ien Shou-tien commanded a security detachment, and had taken part in the fighting, carrying a rifle in the front lines. As a result, a bullet had passed through the fleshy part of his left leg. It was not a serious injury, and had damaged neither tendon nor bone, so that it was a light wound which could probably be healed within ten days or a couple of weeks. From the front lines he had been withdrawn to Yüeh-yang, where he convalesced for three months. Because the medical facilities were insufficient, not only did his wound fail to heal, but it grew worse day by day, until half of his leg was swollen as big as a water-bucket.

Placed in circumstances where he absolutely couldn't help it, with extraordinary regret he wrote a letter to his Department Chief father, reporting on the condition of his wound and his illness. Ch'ien Pen-san sent Ch'ien Pen-ssu to Yüeh-yang to bring him back to Hankow.

Seeing that he was settled, Ssu Ling-luan went over and shook his hand, and said with warm concern:

"You've suffered!"

"It's nothing," Ch'ien Shou-tien said, gritting his teeth. "We revolutionaries must sacrifice ourselves."

"I really have to admire your spirit."

"We must press forward in the bloody footsteps of the revolutionary martyrs, we must make the flower of revolution bloom!" Ch'ien Shou-tien glared with wide eyes.

"You're really something!"

"We revolutionary party members must beat down the warlords!"

Ch'ien Shou-yü saw that he was gritting his teeth and glaring, and she felt for him. She couldn't help asking:

"Does your wound hurt?"

"No!" Ch'ien Shou-tien said, shaking his head. "We men of the Revolutionary Army don't fear the pain of wounds."

She hadn't seen her little brother in several years, and her little brother had changed. He was still leaner, and still yellower, than before, and the whiskers on his cheeks were thicker. Of those naughty smiles of his childhood, which had always remained part of Ch'ien Shou-yü's impressions of him, not the slightest trace remained. Now, he was somber, but within this somberness it could clearly be seen that he was numb; there was something of the spirit of one who is completely unaware of his individual existence.

"Are you uncomfortable with a fever?"

Ch'ien Shou-yü, her two eyes full of tears, went over to feel his forehead, and she felt that she had nearly scalded her hand. She looked at Ch'ien Pen-ssu and said:

"Fourth Uncle, what shall we do?"

"Let's send him to a hospital."

"Which one is good? Should we discuss it with them first?"

"Japanese hospitals are good."

"Do you mean the Common Benevolence Society hospital?"

"Yes." Ch'ien Pen-ssu considered for a moment. "But there's only one difficulty. I hear that Chu Kuang-chi has taken refuge there, and that he and Itakura Minoru are good friends. Would they do anything to hurt our patient?"

"Doctors have their code of ethics; that couldn't happen! Besides, Shou-tien hasn't done anything to offend the Chus." Although Ch'ien Shou-yü said this, in her heart she wasn't certain, and she kept looking at Fourth Uncle, waiting for him to make up his mind.

Ch'ien Pen-ssu couldn't endorse it all at once, so he said:

"We'd better call your Papa and ask him."

They called for some time but couldn't locate him anywhere. When Ch'ien Shou-tien heard that he was to enter a Japanese hospital, he said:

"We members of the revolutionary party must beat down the Japanese imperialists!"

"Look, I'll go ahead and see how things are," Ch'ien Pen-ssu said, and went off. Ssu Ling-luan followed him, and kept calling: "Fourth Uncle!" from behind him.

Ch'ien Pen-ssu pretended not to hear him, and walked faster.

"What is this? Fourth Uncle!"

Ssu Ling-luan hurried around to get in front of Ch'ien Pen-ssu, and turned to block his way. Then Ch'ien Pen-ssu halted, and asked:

"What do you want with me?"

"Are you angry with me?"

"No mistake—I guess you understand."

"It was only because of love, Fourth Uncle, surely you'll forgive me."

"I won't talk about such nonsense. What do you want?"

"I want to borrow a little loose change."

"How much?"

"Thirty or fifty would do."

Ch'ien Pen-ssu took a ten-dollar Central Bank note from his wallet and pressed it into Ssu Ling-luan's hand. Then he hailed a rickshaw and left. He called out:

"From now on, don't come looking for me any more."

Ssu Ling-luan flushed, caught up with him, and forced the banknote back upon Ch'ien Pen-ssu. Without a word, he left, in a rage.

"Just turns his face and doesn't recognize a person—what a thing!"

Thinking of it, his footsteps fell ever faster and heavier.

A rickshaw came towards him, and he saw to his surprise that it carried Ch'ien Pen-san. Just as he was thinking of avoiding the other, Ch'ien Pen-san's rickshaw stopped, and he called loudly:

"Ssu Ling-luan, come here!"

Ssu Ling-luan could only stand still, and without waiting to say anything, Ch'ien Pen-san dealt him two slaps across the mouth.

"You rotten egg, you've gone too far in cheating people! Didn't you think of who I am?" he scolded.

Passersby, seeing the quarrel, at once stopped to watch the excitement. Ch'ien Pen-san, becoming aware of this, hastily got into the rickshaw and left. Ssu Ling-luan, watching his back, spat heavily.

Nursing a bellyful of hatred, Ssu Ling-luan returned to Wuchang. On the street, there was a handbill, just pasted up; the paste was not yet dry. "Down with Kuo Hsin-ju!" Ssu Ling-luan was puzzled: What was the matter with Kuo Hsin-ju?

The school was just then conducting small group meetings, and they were mercilessly attacking Kuo Hsin-ju's essay, "Put-on Appearances and Manufactured Atmosphere". They recognized it as the aggressive thought of imperialism, and as an attack upon the present policy of alignment with the Soviet Union and alignment with the Communists and the peasants and workers. Their conclusion: Kuo Hsin-ju's thought was counterrevolutionary, Kuo Hsin-ju was a counterrevolutionary!

Ssu Ling-luan seized this opportunity to boldly and provocatively advance a step further and point out that Kuo Hsin-ju represented a counterrevolutionary clique, of which the brothers Ch'ien Pen-ssu and Ch'ien Pen-san were the essential members. As soon as Ch'ien Pen-san was mentioned, Yün Ta-ying, Director of the Political Section, asked eagerly:

"What evidence do you have for what you've said?"

"The Ch'ien brothers are my uncles on my mother's side, and Ch'ien Pen-ssu is my teacher as well. This morning in Hankow Ch'ien Pen-ssu told me to take a letter to establish connections with Kuo Hsin-ju!" Ssu Ling-luan said smoothly. Yün Ta-ying asked:

"Do you know Kuo Hsin-ju's address?"

Ssu Ling-luan hesitated a moment, and then hastily said:

"I don't know it. It was agreed that the letter would be given to someone on Pier No. 1."

"What sort of person?"

Ssu Ling-luan was unprepared for Yün Ta-ying's close questioning, but he could not change his story, so he could only toughen the skin of his head and plunge ahead as if it were true.

"A middle-aged woman, plump, like anyone's wife."

"What was her name?"

"Ch'ien Pen-san told me not to ask her name, and not to speak to her."

"Obviously there's an organization," Yün Ta-ying said judiciously.

"Ch'ien Pen-san's daughter is a unit leader in the Girl Students' Corps of this school," Ssu Ling-luan said casually.

Alerted by the very mention of the name, Yün Ta-ying shouted:

"Send for unit leader Ch'ien!"

Having looked everywhere without finding her, Commander Yen of the Girl Students' Corps said:

"Probably she heard something and slipped away."

"Exactly so; they've got an organization."

Such was Yün Ta-ying's conclusion. Because Ch'ien Pen-san was a lofty Department Chief, and moreover appeared to be properly Red, Yün Ta-ying could not act on his own authority. He decided to cross the river to Hankow to seek instructions.

That night Ch'ien Pen-ssu was arrested by the Workers' Pickets.

The instructions received by Yün Ta-ying were: to conduct an all-out propaganda attack on Kuo Hsin-ju, so that he would be sensible of his difficulty and withdraw, and speak as he pleased no more. This action was to be carried out under Ch'ien Pen-san's direction to see how he performed. The political requirements of the present demanded that Ch'ien Pen-san be protected, because he possessed the value of continuing usefulness. No better could be found, because while he did not belong to the Communist Party, he was willing to speak and act for the Communist Party.

For the sake of his face, his daughter Ch'ien Shou-yü had to be protected as well.

In order to make him still more attentive, obedient, guileless, and loyal, they selected the stratagem of "killing a chicken to frighten the rooster" and picked up Ch'ien Pen-ssu. Being picked up is being picked up, but he would be well-fed, well-housed, and well-treated. As a hostage, he could never be released.

Ch'ien Shou-yü, having gotten her father's agreement, wrote a letter resigning her position as a unit leader. She stayed at the Common Benevolence Society hospital, looking after Shou-tien. Itakura Minoru considered Ch'ien Shou-tien, because he had been wounded for the revolution, a promising youth, and moreover told his daughter Baitai to attend to the patient's room and person. Not only did the Itakuras, father and daughter, treat him well, but even Chu Kuang-chi, who was staying in the Itakura home, often came to see him, and loved to make sure that all was in proper order. Chu Kuang-chi often said to Itakura Minoru:

"You see how fortunate Ch'ien Pen-san is, that he has such a revolutionary son."

Sometimes, half in jest, he would say:

"Don't you want to marry your Baitai to a Chinese husband? I think this one is very suitable—do you want me to be the go-between?"

"You know I'm against marriages by the parents' decision and the matchmaker's words," Itakura Minoru said happily.

"Well then, let them have 'free love and enlightened marriage'."

The two old friends laughed loudly.

Ch'ien Shou-yü stayed by Shou-tien's bed, and carefully arranged his diet. Ch'ien Shou-tien had strange tastes: he liked to eat steamed things, and disliked anything prepared with oil or salt. Steamed green vegetables and beancurd, steamed chicken, duck, and fish—things other people considered insipid and tasteless—he enjoyed and never tired of them. Ch'ien Shou-yü felt that this might be a symptom of some illness, and asked Itakura Minoru. Itakura Minoru carefully examined him, but could see nothing wrong. Half-joking, he said:

"Probably it's just a habit, or it may be a psychological abnormality. The ancients had low tastes, and liked to smell women's smelly, bound feet. Master Shou-tien's enjoyment of insipid foods is much higher, much higher—extremely noble."

In the midst of this praise, Itakura Baitai, with her snow-white complexion ornamented by a face powdered faintly pink and two large black eyes which flashed like stars, came floating in, and those in the room (including Itakura Minoru) were all emotionally shaken. She carried in one hand a squarish carved plaster flower-vase of I-hsing ware, within which were distributed several purple butterfly orchids and several long, green leaves. She placed these on the tea table at the head of Ch'ien Shou-tien's bed, and said:

"Look, aren't these pretty? They're for Mr. Ch'ien."

Everyone admired them. Itakura Minoru said:

"Did you cut the orchids in the tub?"

"Yes."

"It's a pity to cut the orchids. You should have brought the tub in."

"The tub's too coarse; the leaves are many and the flowers are few. This way is much more cheery and bright, and nice to look at." She turned to Ch'ien Shou-tien. "Mr. Ch'ien, what do you say?"

Ch'ien Shou-tien turned half around, frowned, and muttered to himself:

"Our revolution must beat down Japanese imperialism!"

Everyone in the room halted for a moment. Ch'ien Shou-yü's face turned yellow as beeswax, and she anxiously asked:

"Shou-tien, what's the matter? Are you feverish again?"

She went over and felt his brow, and he did have a slight fever. Itakura Baitai rang for a thermometer, and Itakura Minoru went to listen with his stethoscope, and then hastily stood up. Everyone forgot about the purple orchids.

Half a month later, the excessive swelling of Ch'ien Shou-tien's wounded leg had completely disappeared, and the intermittent fever had also cleared up. Itakura Baitai brought a pair of canes, and wanted him to get out of bed for some exercise. At first Ch'ien Shou-tien tried walking a few steps in front of the bed, with Itakura Baitai and Ch'ien Shou-yü, one on each side, supporting him. They led him outside the sickroom, onto the porch, where there were several rattan chairs, and helped him sit down. It was midsummer weather, and although the sun had not yet risen, there was already more than a little of that extreme heat. Itakura Baitai took a tiny folding fan, gilt with red tracery, from the pocket of her uniform, and gently fanned herself. The sandalwood ribs of the fan spread a subtle, pure scent. Ch'ien Shou-yü couldn't help glancing at her, and felt she was rather like a sylph.

"It's quite a hot day; let me send someone for an electric fan," Itakura Baitai said.

"No, Miss Itakura, you're busy enough. Sit down and rest," Ch'ien Shou-tien said politely, pointing to a rattan chair next in line to his own.

Ch'ien Shou-yü was pleased to hear her little brother say something human, and felt that it reflected well upon herself. She drew Itakura Baitai to the seat.

"Miss Ch'ien," Itakura Baitai said, "is your old home near Tientsin?"

"Yes, only two or three hours by train. But from our home to the railroad station, you have to ride the whole day in a mule-cart."

"It would be convenient if the railroad also came to your home," Itakura Baitai said.

"Our revolution will build railroads," Ch'ien Shou-tien put in. What he meant was that after the revolution had succeeded, they would repair the railroads, and then before long there would be a railroad to his old home. What he wanted to make clear was that a revolutionary's ambition was also a beautiful prospect. Facing a foreign girl, he was willing to plot how to gain the advantage. The past was the past, and now, empty-handed, he was sacrificing to the "future".

Ch'ien Shou-yü blushed, and gave him a look.

"In a few more days," Itakura Baitai said, "Papa is going to take us to Tsingtao, to avoid the heat. Tsingtao is really nice, especially in the summer."

Ch'ien Shou-yü nodded, smiling, to express her agreement.

"Mr. Ch'ien," Itakura Baitai went on, "when you're well, you ought to go to Tsingtao to rest for a while."

"That's the territory of the Peiyang warlords; I can't go there. Our revolutionaries will beat down the Peiyang warlords. Our revolution doesn't try to avoid the heat."

Ch'ien Shou-tien spoke with a thick rural accent, and he was always talking of revolution. Itakura Baitai blamed herself because she couldn't understand him very well. But from his expression one could more or less tell that he was not going to Tsingtao, so she smiled and let it go.

Ch'ien Shou-yü blushed even to her throat. She almost slapped him, as she would have done ten years before. She thought, who can blame Papa for not liking you, you're really not worth the effort!

Since Ch'ien Shou-tien's arrival in Hankow, Ch'ien Pen-san had never been to see him, nor had he ever asked about him. He gave Ch'ien Shou-yü a little money for him, and that was all. Ch'ien Shou-yü would say:

"Little Brother is a revolutionary, and he has the air of a revolutionary. He's no longer the worthless Little Brother he used to be. Papa ought to take another look at him, and encourage him to get on in the world."

Ch'ien Pen-san would shake his head wordlessly.

While the condition of his wound grew better day by day, Ch'ien Shou-tien's anxiety increased day by day as well. The Military Academy Graduates' Association had somehow turned into two organizations: one of them undertook secret activities, and protected the Commandant; the other publicly opposed the Commandant. Ch'ien Shou-tien was not a product of the Military Academy. He had been a warrant-officer clerk, and a second lieutenant commanding a security detachment, but strictly speaking he was not a real soldier. Since he had left school when he was young, and his natural gifts were modest, most probably he could never have become a regular Revolutionary Army soldier. But since he had been wounded at Ting-ssu-ch'iao, he felt that he had achieved something for the revolution. He swallowed a few handbill slogans whole and hung them on his lips, sternly considered himself a Revolutionary Army soldier, and gave special thought to military matters. Pressed between the two graduates' associations, whose origins had nothing to do with him, he had a mysterious feeling that trouble might lie on both sides.

One day, he happened to get hold of a printed "Letter to the Military Academy Graduates", which exhorted the graduates of the Military Academy to be firm in their faith, to clearly recognize friend and foe, and to guard against being taken advantage of by the Communist Party. Although it was an ordinary pamphlet, it was written with great beauty and feeling. He read it, and felt very moved; he read it again, and spontaneously wept; the third time he read it, tears and mucus poured down his face, and he could not control himself.

As luck would have it, Ch'ien Pen-san, suffering from bleeding piles, rushed to the Common Benevolence Society hospital to see the doctor. Afterwards, he remembered that Shou-tien had been staying at the hospital for some time, and father and son had not yet seen each other, so he took the opportunity to go and see him. When he saw him, Shou-tien was lying on the bed crying, and didn't even know his father had come in. Ch'ien Shou-yü hastily pushed him, and said:

"Papa has come, Papa has come."

He paid no attention.

Ch'ien Pen-san, standing there, shook his head, and asked:

"What's the matter with him?"

Ch'ien Shou-yü sighed helplessly, picked up the pamphlet from beside the pillow, and handed it to her father.

Ch'ien Pen-san took it, glanced at it, then tossed it down and left, shaking his head. Ch'ien Shou-yü understood him, and knew that the gap between father and son had grown a little deeper.

After Ch'ien Shou-tien, his wound healed, left the hospital, he quietly boarded an eastbound steamboat, and went to Nanking. Ch'ien Shou-yü returned to her father's office, and served as her father's household manager. Every day, she found time to review her studies, preparing to return to Peking and finish at Women's Normal University. She deeply regretted having delayed her studies to come to Hankow, and she felt that her father had taken advantage of her, but she couldn't very well say this.

Ch'ien Pen-san was busier and busier: meeting guests, holding meetings, delivering speeches, assemblies; his Chinese-linen Chung-shan uniform was always damp with sweat. Ch'ien Shou-yü had never seen him take a moment's quiet thought, or ponder and question deeply: he was just busy, busy, busy. Whenever anything came before him, he always said: "Ask Secretary Feng to come in," or "Ask Secretary Feng to go."

When the conditions of the time had settled down, and he had accepted the position of Chief of the Propaganda Department, Liu Shao-ch'iao had given him two secretaries. One of them, whose name was Ching, worked in the Department office. He held Ch'ien Pen-san's private seal, and opened letters and acted in his name. The other one was this Feng, who was his travelling secretary and followed him like shadow following substance; he also had one of Ch'ien Pen-san's private seals.

The first time they met, Ch'ien Pen-san ran into difficulties with the one called Ching. Because this name, the character *ching*, was clearly the one used in "respect", "salutations", and "respecting the spirits but keeping one's distance from them". As soon as he saw the name-card, Ch'ien Pen-san shook the man's hand, saying:

"Ah, Comrade Ching!"

"Mr. Ch'ien, you're wrong, how is it you don't recognize the character? This character is read *kou*. My name is Kou."

"Oh, excuse me, Comrade Kou."

Ch'ien Pen-san blamed himself for not having studied the characters used as surnames, and when he turned to the second one, Feng, he was very cautious, hesitating for perhaps five or six seconds, pondering whether or not this character *feng* ought to be read as *ma*. He even removed his dark glasses, to see clearly, and then extended his hand, and said with a chuckle:

"Comrade Feng!"

Feng did not find any fault, and stuck out his own hand in a friendly manner, but he said:

"Comrade Ch'ien!"

This form of address gave Ch'ien Pen-san the greatest displeasure. Ch'ien Pen-san had always considered the appellation "Comrade" to be common, and when used to a superior, Comrade was lacking in respect. It would do for Ching, and for Feng, but when addressing their highest superior they ought to call him Department Chief, or Committee member, which wouldn't be so far off the mark. Just now Ching had called him "Mr. Ch'ien", but Ch'ien Pen-san was already uncomfortable with that, he felt that it wasn't quite to his taste. And now this "Comrade" comes up! Blushing in spite of himself, he said:

"I like that, I like it."

What he meant was, "I like your calling me Comrade". He was taking this opportunity to show that he could keep up with the times, and had not fallen behind. But in his own heart, he simply couldn't overcome his lingering regrets. Unfortunately, those opposite him couldn't understand this tortuous thinking; they thought that what he "liked" was that the two of them had come to work for him as secretaries.

Ch'ien Pen-san was a Department Chief, but in the eyes of his daughter, he had fallen. She could not help recognizing that he was only a genuine puppet, and that it was those two secretaries who had the real power to act. None of the essays, speeches, or even the letters, which bore Ch'ien Pen-san's name contained Ch'ien Pen-san's own ideas, and Ch'ien Pen-san, seeing his own name in the paper every day, felt that it was a spiritual victory. But Ch'ien Shou-yü suffered for him, and felt that he was pitiable.

Still harder to bear were the rebukes which poured in, by letters and telephone calls, from various quarters. At that time the two most active organizations were the Women's Association and the General Labor Union Headquarters. Their activities were frequently directed against tradition, and shocked many people; thus they were the most frequently criticized. When the newspapers reported such stories as that the women would hold a naked march, or that they had already done so, or that a factory owner had held the chamberpot for his workers, or that a house-boy had raped his Western mistress, it was hard to avoid reading their criticism between the lines. This was a question of editorial technique, but they brought all these accounts and laid them against Ch'ien Pen-san, as though his leadership were at fault. Among those who frequently called to scold him over the phone were Hung T'ung-yeh, the leader of the Workers' Pickets, and the Women's Association Propaganda Bureau Chief Pai Ch'a-hua.

Ever since the arrival of the Revolutionary Army in Hankow and the grasping of "real authority" by Liu Shao-ch'iao and Hung T'ung-yeh, Hung Chin-ling's freedom had been more than half lost. At first, Hung T'ung-yeh came to the Ch'ien home, to say that he had already found work for her, and wanted her to move at once. She was to be the Assistant Bureau Chief of the Women Laborers' Bureau of the General Labor Union Headquarters, and concurrently a member of the Worker and Peasant Women Committee of the Women's Association. Not only did Hung Chin-ling ungratefully fail to accept her older brother's well-meant promotion, but she immediately refused it. She had another plan of her own. She and Ch'ien Shou-yü had already developed deep feelings for each other, and were as close as if they had been natural sisters; indeed, their friendship was such that there was nothing they couldn't discuss. Ch'ien Shou-yü had known for a long time that Ch'ien Pen-ssu was especially interested in Hung Chin-ling, and Hung Chin-ling seemed to be interested. She was quite willing to forward a good thing. One day, when she and Hung Chin-ling were upstairs passing the time of day, and talking of their individual futures and ambitions, Hung Chin-ling asked:

"Someone said that a woman's best vocation is to marry a husband. Elder Sister, what do you think?"

"That's one point of view, and a very natural one."

"Are you getting ready to do that?"

After a few moments of silence, Ch'ien Shou-yü said quietly:

"I haven't sufficient qualifications."

"Oh, Elder Sister, you're too polite," Hung Chin-ling said, upset. "If you don't have sufficient qualifications, who does?"

"If you want to just casually marry somebody, then it doesn't matter if you're not perfect. But if we're speaking of seeking an ideal partner, a perfect husband, then I know my own shortcomings."

"What shortcomings do you have?"

Ch'ien Shou-yü was obviously displeased that Hung Chin-ling pursued the question. She looked at Hung Chin-ling, and said with some emotion:

"When you ask me that, are you being serious, or just prying?"

"Of course I'm serious," Hung Chin-ling hastily replied. "You're my good Elder Sister, how could I be prying?"

Ch'ien Shou-yü sighed, and said dejectedly:

"Surely you've seen my feet?"

Hung Chin-ling's glance fell at once on Ch'ien Shou-yü's two little gleaming ochre-yellow leather shoes, which were stuffed with cotton-wadding. Hung Chin-ling at once felt pained, and so overcome with pity that she did not know what to say. Ch'ien Shou-yü smiled, and said lightly:

"In times past, people had to suffer too much!"

"Why *did* women bind their feet in the old days?"

"I suppose that the men's perverted maltreatment was one reason. But in my opinion, it was really a manifestation of our surplus population. A thousand years ago, to cripple the women—who make up half the population—in a country with a shortage of human labor, would have been unthinkable. By the same reasoning, the mechanization of industry cannot develop rapidly in China at present because of the surplus of human labor-power. Last year, I wrote an essay for the Women's Normal University quarterly, and brought up this shortcoming of mine. In history, whenever there was a change of dynasty, people were cut down like grass. One side killed to protect their power, and the other side killed in the struggle for power; both sides competed, and whoever killed the most gained the victory. What is in short supply is dear, and the reverse of that, naturally, is that what is plentiful is of no account. Surplus population is the sole cause of disorder. The present revolution, unveiled, also has as its goal the reduction of population, or to put it more honestly, to kill people—that's all!"

As Ch'ien Shou-yü said this, she sighed deeply with emotion. She paused, and went on:

"Someone took issue with me at the time, and said that in ancient times the population was very small, and the land was wilderness, so why were there wars even then?"

"Yes, and how did you answer him?" Hung Chin-ling asked at once.

"I didn't answer him. If man is a war-making creature, he must seek his progress through war. Then, to be human and to suffer comes with being born, and there's no way to improve the situation, nor to avoid it. Isn't that even more frightening, and even more tragic?"

Ch'ien Shou-yü shook her head. She stood up, drew a long breath, and smiled.

"Let's not pursue the subject so long we beat it to death. Let's be serious. Little Sister, I ask you, are you willing or not for me to call you by a different title?"

Hung Chin-ling felt that the other meant something by this. After a moment's hesitation, she said:

"I don't know what you mean to change it to?"

"If you'll come up by a generation, I'll call you Fourth Uncle's wife. How would you like that?"

Hung Chin-ling immediately blushed, gulped, and said:

"You're making fun of me—is that nice?"

"Such a day generally comes to young women. I've considered everything. Fourth Uncle's shortcoming is that, compared to you, he's too old. Outwardly, he may seem a little rustic. But he's also got quite a few good points, enough to make up for his shortcomings. He's honest, he's got firm views, and he would never be fickle or opportunistic; he's not like Papa. Besides, he's thrifty, and knows how to manage money. He's a very dependable person."

Hung Chin-ling said nothing.

Both of them considered the matter in silence. It only remained for the problem of Ch'ien Pen-ssu's work to be resolved, and the marriage could be arranged. Ch'ien Pen-ssu had in mind finding a suitable position in judicial circles, and hoped that then he could pass his days in a settled fashion. The documents proving his academic qualifications and record all having undergone Ch'ien Pen-san's consideration, he asked someone to bring them over to him. From Ch'ien Pen-san's office there came oral agreement, only nothing was issued.

Because of this, when Hung T'ung-yeh wanted Hung Chin-ling to go to work for the General Labor Union Headquarters and the Women's Association, he ran into a wall.

Chapter XVII

One day Ch'ien Pen-ssu happened to be walking on the street with Hung Chin-ling. At the exit gate of the British Concession, there were Workers' Pickets on one side, and on the other side British soldiers and Indian constables. Although wire barriers had not yet been raised, both sides were on their guard. In addition, a noisy crowd of idlers had gathered at a distance, and the situation was obviously somewhat tense. Ch'ien Pen-ssu and Hung Chin-ling stopped and reflected for a moment, and felt that it would be safest not to leave the Concession. But Ch'ien Pen-ssu, because of the question of his taking office, had to go out. So, concealing their unease, they went tentatively ahead.

The guards on both sides scrutinized the couple, but neither questioned nor halted them, and they passed peaceably into, and out of, the Concession gate. Ch'ien Pen-ssu sighed with relief, looked down at Hung Chin-ling, and forced a smile. Hung Chin-ling drew a little closer to him, and at once felt a feeling of security never before experienced.

There was a sudden commotion of footsteps behind them. The two involuntarily turned. There were some ten-odd Workers' Pickets in blue uniforms, carrying wooden cudgels, running after them. In their surprise, they couldn't understand what was happening, as the Workers' Pickets caught up with them, swept up Hung Chin-ling, and went their way. Hung Chin-ling, anxious and frightened, yelled:

"What are you doing, what are you doing? What are you doing?"

"We're doing this!" one of the Workers' Pickets said, giggling and grinning as he jabbed Hung Chin-ling in the small of the back. At this, aching and hurting from the jab, Hung Chin-ling burst into tears.

Ch'ien Pen-ssu, seeing that it was the Workers' Pickets, was at first a little frightened, but he toughened the skin of his head and went after them. He said with a smile:

"What ever it is, it will be better if you'll explain it clearly. This dragging people off on the street looks very bad."

A Workers' Picket bringing up the rear turned and aimed a cudgel blow at his head. Ch'ien Pen-ssu saw him raise his cudgel, instinctively raised both hands to protect his head, and quickly turned around to run. The cudgel blow fell on his right elbow. The pain ran right into Ch'ien Pen-ssu's chest, his whole body turned weak, and he knelt down.

The Workers' Pickets paid no more attention to him, and carried Hung Chin-ling off.

After ten or so minutes had passed, Ch'ien Pen-ssu had more or less overcome the pain, and he looked at his right arm. Although there was no external wound, still, as though a joint had been dislocated, his whole arm would not respond. Ch'ien Pen-ssu knew that the injury was to the bone and muscle. He pushed his way slowly through the dense crowd which had surrounded him to watch the excitement, walked back to the Concession gate, and hired a rickshaw to take himself home. His shoulder had indeed been dislocated, and the bone of the elbow broken, but after a couple of months of treatment, it slowly mended.

Not long afterwards, he too was arrested.

Hung Chin-ling was hustled into a building at the rear of the General Labor Union Headquarters and taken upstairs, and locked up in a vast, and pleasantly cool, room. Several tall and robust middle-aged women took turns watching her. There was good tea and good food, attentively served, and outwardly they were completely courteous. By this time, Hung Chin-ling knew that force would be of no use, and she could only be patient and wait. When she had the chance, she tried to test their attitude, but it was "three don't-knows to every question", and they let nothing slip.

But Hung Chin-ling knew that this testing was, in fact, unnecessary. If the arranging of this affair wasn't Liu Shao-ch'iao's and Hung T'ung-yeh's deviltry, then whose was it?

And indeed, after three days had passed, late one night Hung T'ung-yeh arrived. He came in and said:

"I knew you'd come. I was busy, so I've only come to see you now."

By now Hung Chin-ling deeply understood the ways of the world. She knew that the elder brother of today was not the same as he had been in the past. The feelings of brother and sister in their childhood days, that natural and innocent affection, did not necessarily exist any longer. This caused her manner to become cold and even more courteous. She said:

"What's the idea of your having me brought here?"

Hung T'ung-yeh sat down opposite her, lighted a cigarette, and said with a sigh:

"We two were born of the same mother, and we've relied on each other since we were little. I don't want you to part company with me in the high tide of this revolution. I want you to come back to my side, and that we can cooperate all the way."

"We've both grown up and maybe our views are no longer the same; we each have our own way of looking at things. I don't think you could force me to suffer; you can forgive me," Hung Chin-ling said, frankly and politely.

"My experience ought to be of some benefit to you. I tell you honestly, I spent a long time walking back and forth in a narrow place—now left, now right, without being able to make up my mind. But finally I came back. Because you shouldn't forget that we do come from a worker's household; we belong to the working class."

"Papa was an old People's Party man . . ."

"We're alive, let's talk about living people's business!" Hung T'ung-yeh, not wanting Hung Chin-ling to go on, waved his hand. "Papa is dead, the dead don't bother with living people's business, so what's the use of bringing him up?"

"I was only going to say, we're not from a worker's household." Hung Chin-ling felt a bit uneasy as she said this.

"Have you forgotten when Mama needed that appendicitis operation? The foreign boss and the Bureau Chief weren't willing to loan us the money. Who finally gave us the money for the doctor and the medicine? Wasn't it P'eng Wen-hsüeh of the Chapei Labor Union?" Hung T'ung-yeh said angrily, raising his voice. "Now you're 'counting the records but forgetting the ancestors'; you've surrendered to the enemy and forgotten your own origins."

Hung Chin-ling didn't know what else to say, so, with an injured air, she fell silent.

Hung T'ung-yeh, too, paid attention only to his smoking, as though sunk in deep thought. Finally, he stood up, tossed his cigarette butt out the window, and said with a forced smile:

"Anyway, we two shouldn't part company. I've already decided to send someone to Shanghai to bring Mama. Perhaps after she comes, she can help the two of us be close again, like we were before."

"You want to bring Mama here?"

"Yes."

"I hear that river traffic stopped long ago."

"No, British and Japanese river steamboats were never interrupted."

Hung T'ung-yeh looked at his watch, and said:

"It's late; one o'clock. Are you hungry? I'll go get us something to eat."

So saying, he went downstairs. In a moment, he came back up, carrying a bamboo tray with peanuts, melon seeds, biscuits, and a bottle of *kao-liang*, and set it on the table.

"You drink *kao-liang*?"

"Yes."

"You didn't use to drink."

"Nowadays I need the stimulus, so I drink hard liquor."

As he spoke, he poured a teacup full, took a great gulp, and handed it to Hung Chin-ling, saying:

"You drink a little too, we'll use the same cup."

"I don't drink wine."

"When you were with those fools, didn't you learn to drink *kao-liang*? The fools drink *kao-liang*," Hung T'ung-yeh said seriously.

"None of the Ch'iens drink wine."

"Well, you must have learned to eat scallions and garlic," Hung T'ung-yeh said in jest.

"No mistake, I can eat scallions and garlic," Hung Chin-ling said deliberately.

"Later on you'll have to drop that, and change to hot peppers."

"Why?"

Hung Chin-ling understood what he meant, but asked on purpose.

"Do you really not understand, or are you pretending not to understand?" Hung T'ung-yeh smiled.

"Really."

"That's because of Liu Shao-ch'iao; Hunan 'mules' grow up eating hot peppers."

When Hung Chin-ling heard this, she was at first going to say something like "I'll never—" but then she considered her situation, and held back the words, saying nothing. Hung T'ung-yeh took another drink of wine and asked:

"What? You're not saying anything."

"I don't know what to say."

"Talk about anything you like. I'll tell you, the day before yesterday, I killed someone with my own hands!"

When the wine's power rose in him, Hung T'ung-yeh's waxy-yellow face turned as red as a great swatch of red cloth, and his eyes filled with blood and became as red as his face.

"What's that? Really?" Hung Chin-ling, frightened, asked.

"Since I said so, of course it's true." At first Hung T'ung-yeh manifested a casual attitude towards his little sister's question. Then he went on: "It was a Kuomintang party member, who went to Nanking, and after he came back he kept saying that the Workers' Pickets organization was illegal. And he also said that they had already deployed their units so as to surround Wuhan, in order to wipe out the Wuhan regime. When we heard these rumors, we secretly arrested him."

Hung T'ung-yeh drank another swallow of wine, ate a few more salted seeds, and smiled with deliberate calm. He continued:

"Shao-ch'iao just wanted me to put him in mourning clothes and throw him into the river around midnight. But I thought that was letting him off too cheaply. I remembered that in the *Shui-hu-chuan*[37] there was a good fellow who stopped people on the river, and he had a way of giving people 'chopped noodles' to eat. I ordered my people to prepare a small boat and we went downstream by moonlight, and I took care of him myself with a slaughtering knife."

"You killed him yourself?"

---

[37] *Shui-hu-chuan*: a classic novel about the adventures of 108 Sung Dynasty bandits, containing many incidents of violence, murder, and cruelty.

Hung Chin-ling had grown more anxious the more she heard, and when she saw Hung T'ung-yeh's face change again from red to yellow, and saw his hand on the winecup trembling, she couldn't help asking in fright.

"Unh," he mumbled, nodding. Hung T'ung-yeh poured another full cup of wine, and drank it down. He put the cup down heavily on the table, slumped in his chair, shook his head, and said to himself:

"Drunk, I got drunk all by myself. That's really funny!"

He fixed his eyes on Hung Chin-ling, and Hung Chin-ling was a little frightened by his gaze.

"Bring me cigarettes!"

Hung Chin-ling hastily got up and handed him the cigarettes and matches he had left on the table. Hung T'ung-yeh took advantage of this to seize the hand which gave him the cigarettes. He pulled, and Hung Chin-ling fell into his lap. Hung T'ung-yeh embraced her, and kept kissing her, saying:

"My good little sister!"

Hung Chin-ling, so frightened that her face turned the color of earth, struggled free. Gasping, she said:

"What are you doing, what are you doing?"

"Why can't I? At least it's better than giving it to the Ch'iens on the cheap."

As he spoke, Hung T'ung-yeh picked up the cigarettes and matches, which had fallen under the chair in which he reclined, and lighted a cigarette. Then, deliberately calming himself, he went out. He turned, on the stairs, to say:

"Shao-ch'iao will be along soon; you'd better behave yourself, otherwise somebody may ask you to eat 'chopped noodles'. It's no fooling now, like it used to be."

As soon as Hung T'ung-yeh went downstairs, two of the serving women came upstairs. Hung Chin-ling, looking at them, was a little afraid. The one who was in her thirties went to clear the table, and the one in her forties sat down opposite Hung Chin-ling and asked:

"Just now the Director said that Committeeman Liu is coming to see you."

"I don't know what he wants," Hung Chin-ling said dully.

"He loves you; don't tell me you didn't know?"

"That can't be!" Hung Chin-ling blushed.

"It can; why can't it?" the woman in her thirties said, turning around.

"Never mind, Third Sister, let me encourage her," the one in her forties said. "Comrade Hung, since I've been here watching you, I've been reminded of my daughter; she's only two years younger than you. When she was fourteen she ran off with a fellow who sang the martial role in the opera, and I haven't had a word from her. I'll soon be fifty, this year; I've been married three times, and I've raised eight children. Now I haven't even half a husband, and not one child is left. Just think, is there anything I don't understand? You listen to me, I won't hurt you."

As she listened to this mystifying talk, Hung Chin-ling grew more and more anxious. Suppressing her anger, she said:

"Mother, you didn't know it, but I already have someone, and we're to be married soon."

"What does that matter?" The woman's lips cracked in a grin. "You know that Committeeman Liu is wonderful! At my age, and he still promoted me. And if you obey him—need I say more?"

"Mother, I beg of you, just as if you were my own mother!" Hung Chin-ling could no longer restrain herself, and her tears flowed down.

The woman saw that she was to be pitied, but she only sighed, and kept shaking her head.

"In this place what Committeeman Liu says is 'jade words from a golden mouth'," the one in her thirties said. "Who can save you? Besides, this isn't doing some terrible thing, so don't be ungrateful. This Corps has leather whips, and branding irons, all ready. Pretty soon you'd be a cripple, and you'd have brought it on yourself. 'Chopped noodles'? It wouldn't be so easy!"

"Is there really 'chopped noodles'? Are you telling the truth?"

"I don't know you and we're not related, so why would I deceive you?"

"All right, enough of this!" The one in her forties went over to sit down beside Hung Chin-ling, took her hand, and said gently:

"It's late, you'd better sleep a bit first. He'll soon be coming."

. . . . . .

The fiery hot days of summer came.

Mrs. Hung arrived in Hankow on a Butterfield and Swire steamboat. The young man who had been ordered to go to Shanghai and fetch her was surnamed Miao and called Feng; his nickname was Little Miao. Originally from Ma-chiang, he had been apprenticed to an older man from the same district in a hardware store in Hankow. Hung T'ung-yeh could speak a few words of Ma-chiang dialect, and on the strength of that the proprietor of the hardware store considered him another Ma-chiang man, so he called there frequently. Later on the Revolutionary Army came, and Little Miao joined the Labor Union. Hung T'ung-yeh provoked a struggle between Little Miao and the proprietor. First it was a wage increase, and then it was division of shares, with equal sharing of the proceeds of cash sales. What was "equal sharing of the proceeds of cash sales"? It was that the cash proceeds of each day's business, after they had been gathered up and accounted for each night, should be divided equally between the proprietor and the employee.

Naturally, business conducted in such a fashion soon failed. Since neither the courts nor the police would concern themselves with the affairs of the Labor Union, the Peasants' Association, or the Women's Association, there was nowhere for a grievance to be redressed or a complaint lodged. The proprietor could only withdraw, giving his business unconditionally to his employee. But after the employee took over, he couldn't stock his shelves because he had no capital, so it was "Congratulations—going out of business."

Thus Little Miao's hardware store came to an end. After the proprietor and his family went down to Shanghai, Little Miao inherited the management of the large building housing the hardware store. There was a residence behind the store, private property which the proprietor had bought long ago. The back wall of this dwelling was right up against the store-room of the textile shop operated by Liu Shao-ch'iao's family. The two buildings were back to back, although their stores faced two different streets. There had never been any connection between them; they were like two different worlds.

Although Little Miao had suddenly come into possession of this building, business had fallen off, and he had no means of livelihood. At first he thought to sell the building, but since the deed was incomplete and unsigned he couldn't find a buyer. Moreover, since the times were so uncertain, and market conditions were chaotic, he couldn't even sell the furnishings. Little Miao was thus somewhat agitated.

Fortunately the Workers' Pickets were established, and Hung T'ung-yeh became their Director. He summoned Little Miao and appointed him Manager of the "Director's Office", so the problem of his livelihood was temporarily resolved.

All the way back from Shanghai, Little Miao carefully served Mrs. Hung and tried hard to ingratiate himself with her. Mrs. Hung asked:

"What are the Workers' Pickets? What do they investigate?"

"The workers are the masters of the country now, and everything is decided by the workers. They investigate everything. All the Party, government, and military organs, and the popular organizations, have to obey the Workers' Pickets," Little Miao gushed, glibly and mindlessly.

"Can T'ung-yeh handle such a big job?" Mrs. Hung was delighted, but deliberately let on that she couldn't believe it.

"The Director? Of course! Everybody wants to get along with the Workers' Pickets, and the Workers' Pickets want to get along with the Director. You can just imagine how lofty his position is now."

Mrs. Hung was nearly fifty years old, and having just struggled her way out of distress, was there anything she didn't understand? She greatly discounted Little Miao's report, and felt that, although there was only one chance in a hundred of its being true, since he had sent someone to fetch his old mother, his circumstances must be acceptable; that she could believe. For many years she had hoped that her son and daughter would find themselves in "acceptable circumstances" and that would be enough.

Because of this, her mood had been happy ever since she had seen Little Miao in Shanghai.

When she disembarked at Hankow, Hung T'ung-yeh met her on the pier. Mrs. Hung did not see her daughter, and quickly asked:

"Chin-ling? Why didn't she come?"

"She's working at the Women's Association now. She was sent to Changsha a couple of days ago; she'll be back soon," Hung T'ung-yeh lied.

"You knew I was coming, so you shouldn't have sent her," Mrs. Hung said, disappointed.

"She's working for them, so she has to do what they tell her. How could it be so convenient?"

Mrs. Hung sighed, and said helplessly:

"Well, you write a letter right away and tell her to come back."

Hung T'ung-yeh agreed. After a moment's thought, Mrs. Hung added:

"Tell her to finish up matters there and then come back. I won't quibble over a day or two."

Hung T'ung-yeh agreed again.

Mrs. Hung was settled in Little Miao's hardware store. After getting out of the rickshaw, she entered a large store, the doors and windows of which were shuttered. Mrs. Hung paused for a moment. The shelves were all empty, and a thick layer of dust had fallen on the counter. A disorderly heap of miscellaneous objects lay on the cashier's table, beside which stood a bed, and several wooden chairs with missing legs and broken backs. Having gone through the store, she saw several rooms to each side of a central footpath paved with bricks. Along both sides of the footpath were rows of plants in tubs, but some of the plants were withered, and some of the tubs were broken. Wild grass, fruit peels, and scraps of paper littered the narrow footpath so that Mrs. Hung felt there was no place to put her foot down.

"What are these rooms on each side used for?" she asked, stopping.

"Originally they were store-rooms, now they're empty," Little Miao answered.

"This looks like it was once a prosperous business," Mrs. Hung said in surprise. "Why did it fail?"

Neither Little Miao nor Hung T'ung-yeh responded.

At the end of the footpath there was a spacious courtyard, paved with square tiles. Within were three upstairs rooms, with flying eaves and painted roof-beams, and a latticework verandah railing patterned to suggest the character *wan*.[38] But it was quite clean, and entirely unlike the rooms in front.

A maid in her thirties, in a short jacket and long trousers, with her hair done up in a tall, shiny black hairdo, and wearing a pair of Cantonese style yellow leather slippers, came running out of the house to meet them, and asked, giggling:

"Is this the Old Mistress?"

---

[38] *Wan*: ten thousand.

"Yes, my mother," Hung T'ung-yeh answered, and turning to Mrs. Hung, he said: "This is Second Sister Sung. I asked her to come and serve you."

"Thank you, Second Sister," Mrs. Hung said with a smile, looking Second Sister Sung over. Since her husband's death, more than ten years before, she had had no servants. Now that the boy seemed to have ambition and a will to fight, although she could not return all at once to the status of a vice-minister's wife, still she would never again have to go to work as a temporary laborer in a factory. As Mrs. Hung thought, her heart grew distressed, but she did not know if it was from happiness or from pain.

Stepping over the threshold, which was more than a foot high, she saw that the whole room was full of redwood furniture, inlaid with marble. Directly opposite her, there hung a wide scroll of Ma-ku[39] making a longevity offering Ma-ku was painted nearly as big as a living person. On the stand behind the eight-place dining table, in a glass box, stood a white porcelain Kuan-yin, two feet tall. To either side were displayed large flower vases, over two feet tall. The five-branched glass hanging lamp was suspended from a painted beam. Mrs. Hung looked at everything with pleasure, and then, with her hand on the chair beside her, sat down. The marble was cold, and she quickly got up again. Second Sister Sung lifted the white satin door-curtain, embroidered in the Hunan style, to the chief suite of rooms on the right, and said:

"Old Mistress should come in here and rest; this is your bedroom."

Mrs. Hung went in. A brass bedstead and a dressing table stood under the rear window, and a sofa, with a low, squarish table, faced the door. Everyone sat down, and Second Sister Sung brought out towels for them to wipe their faces.

Mrs. Hung drank some tea. On the wall behind the door hung a large photograph of an elderly couple seated side by side, as though husband and wife. Mrs. Hung immediately asked:

---

[39] Ma-ku: an ancient fairy, featured in a legend of the Eastern Han (23-220 AD) Dynasty legend.

"Whose photograph is this?"

"It's the original owner of this hardware store."

"If he left you such a big photograph as this when he went away, he must have been pretty good to you," Mrs. Hung said. "Such good-hearted people are rare nowadays."

"It wasn't that he was good-hearted," Little Miao said, grinning. "When we workers took charge, there wasn't anything he could do about it."

"How long were you in business with him?"

"Mother, I'll tell you the truth. I was an abandoned child. He brought me in off the street in the middle of the night, and they said that I wasn't more than a few days old at the time. He raised me, and he treated me pretty well," Little Miao said frankly.

"No wonder that I took the two of you for flesh and blood," Mrs. Hung said, nodding.

That evening, Liu Shao-ch'iao held a welcoming dinner in the hardware store for Mrs. Hung. Hung T'ung-yeh, Little Miao, and Second Sister Sung attended. When the talk turned to conditions in Shanghai, Mrs. Hung said:

"It's not too peaceful there. I've heard that many people have gone astray in the party purification movement, and P'eng Wen-hsüeh's whereabouts are unknown. Uncle who's a Bureau Chief went to Nanking, and Nanking has a new government too."

"Don't mention him again!" Hung T'ung-yeh, as he thought of the past, was still angry.

"Old White-hand Wang came by once," Mrs. Hung said.

"How was he?" Hung T'ung-yeh asked anxiously.

"He came to say goodbye to me, he was going to Nanking too. He was wearing a brand new Western style suit, and the way he stuck out his belly and wore his glasses made me think of a Doctor of Philosophy. Really, he was just like that," Mrs. Hung said, smiling, as she lifted her cup and drank some wine.

"I didn't know Mrs. Hung paid so much attention to outward appearances," Liu Shao-ch'iao, whose face was streaked with saliva, said. "Mother, what do you make of my face?"

"The working class is in charge here, and you're the head of the Labor Union, and that's the best, so what use is physiognomy?"

"This isn't physiognomy, this is a discussion of outward appearances."

"As for outward appearances, you're tall and slender, with long hair and a little mustache, and you don't pay much attention to your appearance, just like a famous gentleman who drinks wine and composes poetry."

"Thanks for the compliments! You don't feel I'm like a murdering, burning, devil?"

"No. Except for the cruel light in your eyes, you're entirely like a literary man," said Mrs. Hung, offering him a further word of praise.

"When will you bring Pai Ch'a-hua to meet Mama?" Hung T'ung-yeh asked.

"She ought to come to see Mrs. Hung," Liu Shao-ch'iao said happily, raising his eyebrows. "But lately she's been really busy."

"The Women's Association has been ever so much better managed since she came. You appreciated her, and she's really quite a hand."

"That goes without saying," Liu Shao-ch'iao said, with a deliberate smile. "Who doesn't know that Liu Shao-ch'iao has special insight?"

"What are you talking about?" Mrs. Hung asked.

"Pai Ch'a-hua, my family's former servant."

"She killed more than thirty people of the Yeh household, young and old, by her own hand," Little Miao said, sticking out his hand with the thumb up. "I guess that satisfied her anger!"

Mrs. Hung didn't understand, so they explained the situation to her in detail. When Mrs. Hung heard this, she felt extremely uncomfortable. She thought: don't bring such a person to see me, it would scare me dreadfully.

Mrs. Hung had her old complaint of sleeplessness. She had dragged along for more than ten years in the Chapei district of Shanghai, in that narrow half-attic where you could scarcely draw breath. Now, transported all at once to this almost extravagantly comfortable new environment, she couldn't help feeling emotionally stimulated, and since she had also had several cups of wine that evening, she felt quite excited. The clock on the wall outside had already struck twelve, and her eyes were still wide open as she tossed and turned on the bed. Stretching out her hand from the pillow to turn on the electric lamp, Mrs. Hung saw, in the mirror set horizontally into the bedstead, the sleeping image of herself, wrapped in a silk coverlet as yellow as a gosling and embroidered with dragons and phoenixes. She had done up her hair before going to bed, but perhaps because of her tossing and turning, it was already disheveled, and one long strand of hair, bound near the root, had fallen beneath the soft double pillow. Mrs. Hung sat up, and did up her hair. She wore a closely-buttoned, snow-white, form-fitting, sleeveless vest, which served as a brassiere. This had long served Mrs. Hung as underclothing, for she had been lean and wiry for many years, and her chest was flat. Indeed, she really didn't need a brassiere.

Mrs. Hung took another glance at her face in the mirror. The wrinkles at the corners of her eyes were already multiplying, and when she raised her eyes a little, there were obviously some horizontal wrinkles concealed upon her forehead. Mrs. Hung had long known that she was old, but never before had she found in her aging anything to grieve about. The difficulty of life, and the lack of hope, had made her feel there was nothing so serious about old age, or even death.

Now, as though she had fallen among the clouds, she couldn't help thinking of the days of her youth.

Although her husband, Hung Pai-li, had studied military affairs, and had taken part in the revolution, still he had been a man of great charm. She remembered that, on their wedding night, their bedroom had contained a big bed with an inset mirror, much like this one. She had secretly told the servant girl to cover it with a piece of red silk. According to tradition, the lamp is not extinguished on the wedding night. Hung Pai-li had been drinking, and was slightly drunk; he glanced at the red silk covering the mirror, and whisked it away.

That had happened back in the twenty-sixth year of the Kuang-hsü emperor.[40] In that *keng-tzu*[41] year, the Eight-nation Allied Army entered Peking, so Mrs. Hung had always remembered it clearly. At that time customs had not yet become enlightened, marriages were still decided upon by parents, and frequently the bride and groom first set eyes on each other on the day of the wedding. Mrs. Hung, however, had been Hung Pai-li's cousin on his mother's side, and because they lived in the same city, and the two families often went out with their children, they had become well-acquainted early on, in their days of "green plums and bamboo horses". The two families, seeing how well they got on, got the idea of arranging a marriage.

Because of this, after Hung Pai-li had whisked away the red silk, his bride, seated with head bowed, said softly:

"Oh, cover it up again."

"Why?"

"It's so embarrassing!"

---

[40] The twenty-sixth year of the Kuang-hsü emperor's reign was 1900.

[41] *Keng-tzu* year: one of the sixty-year cyclical year names. 1840, 1900, 1960, etc, are *keng-tzu* years.

The bridegroom came over and put his lips on his bride's ear, and said softly:

"The mirror is just what's good about this bed."

The new bride was just thinking that he smelled strongly of wine, and that she would move away a little, so she was not on guard when one hand planted itself against her back, and the other hand seized her ankles, and she was gently picked up. He released her onto the bed, and the two of them twisted about together. The bridegroom was determined that the bride should look in the mirror, and the bride, twisting her head and shutting her eyes, was determined not to look. The bridegroom put out his hand to tickle her, and the bride was afraid of being tickled, so she began to laugh.

When Mrs. Hung remembered her first night, it seemed that some of her ticklish hesitancy still remained, and she spontaneously laughed.

Now, she was already forty-six, but if Pai-li were still present, and the time was right, the bedroom wouldn't be so lonely. When such thoughts came to Mrs. Hung, she would sigh, and say to herself:

"A pity he died so early."

Mrs. Hung could not sit still, so she threw on some clothes and got out of bed. Facing the dressing table, Mrs. Hung turned on the electric lamp over the mirror, with its thin pink gauze shade, and studied her face. She applied some powder, and lightly rubbed it in. Finally, she rubbed her face all over with a dry handkerchief.

"More than ten years," she sighed.

She happened to look up and see the photograph of the old couple which hung on the wall, and she felt lonely and discontented, and quite at loose ends. Idly, she pulled open the dressing table's drawer, and saw that many things were tossed carelessly inside. Turning them over, she discovered a thick stack of large and small photographs. No sooner had she set eyes upon the first one than Mrs.

Hung quickly dropped it, and at once pushed the drawer shut. Her heart was jumping, jumping so hard she felt a little dizzy.

She shut her eyes, and held her head in both hands, and calmed herself, until slowly she settled down. Then she couldn't help opening the drawer again, and holding her breath, she looked at the photographs one by one. Now and again she turned to look at the door and the window. When she twisted her waist, her two legs seemed to convulse. Finally Mrs. Hung recognized the man: it was Liu Shao-ch'iao, no matter that he was always seen from behind, or from the side. There was more than one woman! There was one in this pile of photographs, and another in that pile; all in all, there were four or five. What excess! How could such photographs have been taken? Who could have taken them? This was some low racket of the Shanghai trash!

As she thought, and thought, Mrs. Hung's whole body turned weak. Putting the photographs down, she shut the drawer, and forced herself to stand up. Leaning on the wall, she went to the sofa and sat down. Since her husband's death, Mrs. Hung would occasionally—when no one was around—smoke a water-pipe just for fun; she considered it a kind of compensation. Later on, when she was troubled with an illness which made her cough at night, she stopped smoking. Now, ready-made cigarettes were there on the table before her, and Mrs. Hung couldn't help but pick one up, light it, and smoke it. She was afraid of coughing, so she didn't dare inhale, but just blew it out of her mouth. But even this was a stimulus, and Mrs. Hung's eyes grew wider and wider.

The sound of laughter, and of desultory chatter, came to Mrs. Hung's ears. She listened, but couldn't make out the direction. Curious, Mrs. Hung stood up, and quietly opened the door; then she discovered the sound was coming from the opposite room.

Second Sister Sung lived in the opposite room, and who was she talking to, this late at night? Mrs. Hung inclined her ear and listened carefully. It was a man's voice. In the darkness, she could see that the rear door was open. Mrs. Hung quietly went out, and from the rear window, whose glass pane opened inward, she could see clearly that two people lay on the bed. The man was Little Miao. Mrs. Hung's heart leaped, and a painful wave of heat rose from her throat to her eyes. She thought:

"Isn't Second Sister Sung more than ten years older than Little Miao? And the two of them have been—"

Just as she was going to go with her thought, she heard Little Miao's voice saying:

"Don't consider Mrs. Hung old, she's quite cultured, and not a bit inferior to young people. The woman is bound to be really something; it's no wonder her husband died young!"

"You men—it's just like inviting a beggar to eat dead crabs—every one is good!"

Second Sister Sung started to tickle Little Miao, causing Little Miao to laugh until the whole bed shook. Second Sister Sung said meaningfully:

"Do you still dare?"

"I don't dare."

When he had calmed down, Little Miao went on:

"You're mistaken, I hadn't any intention. Liu Shao-ch'iao has praised her; he says she's better than her daughter."

"Can the old one be better than the young one? I can't understand that."

"You didn't know it, but Liu Shao-ch'iao has a little quirk."

"What quirk?"

"His quirk is abnormal: he takes the stinking for the fragrant, and the ugly for the beautiful."

"Is there such a thing? It's new to me."

"Haven't you seen Liu Shao-ch'iao infatuated over Pai Ch'a-hua? Pai Ch'a-hua is a cripple," said Little Miao. He tugged on Second Sister Sung's underclothes, and she pretended to guard them. Little Miao asked:

"The Women's Association is just pushing their campaign against wearing brassieres and panties, so how is it you're still wearing such things?"

"They have too many campaigns. I really can't understand it. How can women do without wearing panties? I'm not used to it."

"Soon they'll be making inspections on the street. Whoever is found wearing a brassiere or panties will have to take part in the naked march as their punishment."

"There may be some reason not to allow brassieres. But not to allow panties—what's the point of that?" Second Sister Sung asked, annoyed.

"Because none of the women in the countryside wear panties. Wearing panties is a wasteful pleasure of the urban bourgeoisie, so down with it!"

"Every day it's down with this, down with that—really, it's too much 'down with!'."

"Revolution means beating down."

"Why does the Women's Association have so many movements?"

"Since Chinese women have suffered the most oppression and restrictions, so their problems are the most numerous."

"After I've taken off my panties, I don't know what more can happen next," Second Sister Sung sighed, as though slightly exasperated.

"There are many other things. Soon they're going to make widows get married."

As soon as Mrs. Hung heard this, her heart jumped, and her whole body gave a convulsive start. Hastily catching herself, she composed herself and listened once more.

"Why is that?"

"You see, there are all these poor men who have no wives, and yet there are all these widows who want to preserve their widowhood. It isn't fair, and it's a reckless misuse of Heaven's gifts. The Women's Association is just now making an investigation, and before long single men and widows will draw lots and pair off; we must make sure that each one of them gets somebody."

"Draw lots? Suppose they draw someone who isn't suitable?" Second Sister Sung laughed. "If a pretty young bachelor drew a seventy or eighty-year-old widow, what then?"

"Nothing to be done about it. If we let everyone choose for themselves, everybody would want to choose the good ones, and who would want those left-over second-best ones? Wouldn't that be unfair?"

"To match up by drawing lots—that's really a joke." Second Sister Sung sighed softly. "How long can they go on so recklessly?"

"What? To hear you talk, you don't support it? If you don't support it, you're a counterrevolutionary, and counterrevolutionaries are to be killed," Little Miao said, raising his voice a little.

"I was just joking. How could I not support it? If I'm doing all right today, who was it helped me out? I'm no fool!"

Second Sister Sung turned over, hugged Little Miao, and began kissing him, saying:

"You're always finding fault with me!"

"No mistake, I'm always finding fault with you."

Mrs. Hung drew away, and quietly withdrew to her own room, as though moving in a dream. "Marrying off widows by drawing lots." Surely that couldn't be true? If there were such a thing, then why did they bring me here? Surely they don't want me to draw a lot too?

Tomorrow I'll definitely ask about this. I'll go back to Shanghai!

Her whole body seemed to be burning up, and again she fell onto the bed. She thought, I've suffered hardships and preserved my widowhood for more than ten years, and for nothing else than the sake of the two children. Now that the children are grown up, and can manage on their own, can't I think of my own affairs?

The image of her late husband appeared clearly before her. The slender figure, when seen from the back—wasn't it just like that of the present Liu Shao-ch'iao? Mrs. Hung snorted, and rebuked herself for thinking such things; why was she thinking of that animal's body? That animal!

Too shameless! To take such pictures with women!

And to say that I'm more beautiful than my daughter! Nonsense!

She tossed and turned until the window grew light, and then Mrs. Hung, in the early dawn, fell asleep.

When she woke up, it was already noon.

Mrs. Hung, with black circles around her eyes, got dressed. Hung T'ung-yeh had been sitting there for some time, abstractedly reading a newspaper. Mrs. Hung thought, you came at just the right time, I want to ask you something.

"Ma, it's so late and you're just getting up?"

"I couldn't sleep all night," Mrs. Hung said, blushing.

"Is that insomnia of yours still with you? I'll bring you a sleeping medicine tonight."

"I've had this trouble ever since your father died. After so many years, how could it ever get better?"

Mrs. Hung caught up her disheveled hair behind her head, and sat down opposite Hung T'ung-yeh. She went on:

"You've just been reading the paper—is there any news?"

"Nothing. It says that several more British warships have arrived, and the people of Wuhan are excited and angry, and afraid there may be trouble," Hung T'ung-yeh said carelessly.

"I hear that the Women's Association makes the most news. What are they up to, anyway?"

Hearing Mrs. Hung get up, Second Sister Sung poured water, and brought in tea. She smoothly asked Hung T'ung-yeh:

"It will soon be twelve o'clock. Would Old Mistress like some breakfast, or will she have some lunch? We've got both."

"Naturally, I want to eat lunch now."

"Director, will you be eating here as well?"

"All right, I'll keep Ma company."

Mrs. Hung hastily washed up, and when she came out, she drank a cup of tea, and then asked again:

"What news is there about the Women's Association?"

"Just now they're going to force widows to get married."

"Did you know about this when you sent Miao Feng to Shanghai to fetch me?"

"Yes," Hung T'ung-yeh said candidly.

"Then why did you bring me here?" Mrs. Hung was a little angry.

"They hoped I would personally set an example. Because I'm a leader of the Labor Union now, I must be a leader in everything." Hung T'ung-yeh spoke with great confidence, glancing at his mother's face.

"Do you want me to get married? You should be ashamed!" Mrs. Hung put her teacup down heavily.

"Marriage is a good thing," Hung T'ung-yeh said calmly and slowly, drawing on his cigarette. "These ten-odd years, you've sacrificed yourself for Little Sister and me. Now that we're grown up, you've no ties and no dependents, and it's quite right for you to marry again, and enjoy a little of the pleasures of being alive. As I see it, you're too lonely and solitary, and you ought to have a mate."

"How filial of you!" Mrs. Hung expressed her firm refusal. "I'm going back to Shanghai right away; I won't stay here and make a fool of myself."

"It will be the same in Shanghai. There's a high tide of revolution now, and no force can hold it back. Soon this tide will engulf all China, and of course Shanghai will be included, so no matter where you run, you can't avoid it. Supposing you fled to a foreign country, sooner or later the foreign countries will also be engulfed by this high tide."

"You're dreaming, I don't believe it can be as bad as you say."

"Later on the facts will prove it. But I won't wrangle about it with you now, and you needn't get angry." Hung T'ung-yeh smiled, puffing casually on his cigarette.

"It's not that I'm angry." Mrs. Hung calmed down at once. "How old do you think I am this year?"

"Even old widows of seventy or eighty still have to draw lots and pick mates; by comparison, you can't consider yourself old."

"What did you say? Draw lots?" Mrs. Hung pretended ignorance.

"Yes, draw lots."

"How are they to be drawn?"

"The men will be given numbers and the women will draw, or the women will be given numbers, and the men will draw, and whoever you draw, that's it. With everyone depending on luck, there can't be any fault-finding. It will be so fair that no one will have anything to say against it."

"And are you going to let me go and draw a lot?" Mrs. Hung quickly asked, as though her heart were suspended in space.

"Naturally you don't have to draw a lot. You can choose a mate according to your own wishes. Your affair will be arranged beforehand, and moreover your mate will certainly have to be someone famous, so that they can make a great deal of propaganda out of it. The two of you will serve as a model to break the man-eating custom of the widow preserving her chastity and establish a trend of widows getting married. Then later on it will be much easier for the Women's Association to conduct their campaign to get the widows married."

As Hung T'ung-yeh spoke, it was obvious that his plan had been determined well in advance.

"Wait until your Little Sister comes back, and see what she thinks of this," said Mrs. Hung, again trying to change the subject.

"Little Sister cannot oppose it," Hung T'ung-yeh said with great confidence.

Second Sister Sung raised the door-curtain to say:

"Director, the meal is served."

Hung T'ung-yeh immediately stood up and allowed his mother to precede him out of the room.

Although only the two of them were eating, the table was covered with big dishes and small bowls of both meat and vegetables. Mrs. Hung said:

"For dining at home there needn't be so many dishes. Wouldn't one or two have been enough?"

"They're here to eat now, so eat them," Hung T'ung-yeh said.

"I only wish I could have them more often."

"Now that the revolution has been accomplished, at least there will never again be a problem about eating a little better."

The weather was hot. Hung T'ung-yeh said:

"Strange that that fellow didn't have an electric fan put in. This afternoon I'll send someone to have one put in."

"There used to be several electric fans," Second Sister Sung put in, picking up a palm-leaf fan and standing to one side to fan them. "Little Miao said that after his boss left, there was a time when he didn't have anything to eat, so he took them out and sold them for what he could get."

"Good, I always thought he was a likely lad," said Hung T'ung-yeh, making both Mrs. Hung and Second Sister Sung laugh.

Chapter XVIII

After the noon meal, Hung T'ung-yeh wanted to take his mother out for a walk. But because she was tired, Mrs. Hung told her son to go out, and she went back to bed to sleep. But again she couldn't sleep, and she tossed and turned. As soon as she closed her eyes, her late husband's image would appear clearly, just like a ghost. Alarmed, Mrs. Hung said in her mind:

"Don't tell me you're unwilling for me to marry?"

Thinking of the grief of the past, Mrs. Hung then said:

"For more than ten years I've suffered, and you never came to help me. Now that I've raised the children and I want to look for whatever else Heaven and Earth may have arranged for my remaining years, you appear to hinder me. Is the love between husband and wife really so selfish?"

Mrs. Hung glared at him, and said:

"Don't tell me you've forgotten that you're already dead?"

Mrs. Hung snorted, and her husband's image disappeared. Another image, obviously that of Liu Shao-ch'iao, appeared. Mrs. Hung thought:

"Animal, off with you! How many years older than T'ung-yeh can you be? Shameless!"

But Liu Shao-ch'iao was not as obedient as her late husband, and order him or scold him as you please, he just hung about without leaving, like a vagabond. Mrs. Hung grew a little irritated, and suddenly sat up. She calmed herself, and thought again of Little Miao the night before. Looking in the mirror she arranged her hair, and went toward the opposite room, but there was no one there. Hearing a noise in the rear courtyard, she turned and went to the rear door. The rear courtyard was spacious, with the kitchen and the servants' quarters on one side, and the bathhouse and toilet on the other. There was a tall water-tower. Directly opposite there was a large building, two stories high, but completely without doors and windows.

Second Sister Sung was just tidying up the kitchen, and Mrs. Hung asked her:

"What's that building facing us? It's so big."

"It's the dry goods shop of Liu Shao-ch'iao—Committeeman Liu's—family. It fronts on the street behind this one, and on this side it's back to back with ours. The big building is their store-room."

Liu Shao-ch'iao again! Mrs. Hung felt a little disappointed, so she changed the subject, and said:

"Is Little Miao around?"

"He works at the Labor Union; he's not around in the daytime."

"Where does he sleep at night?" Mrs. Hung blushed.

"He sleeps in the front room, facing the street," Second Sister Sung said casually, with a crafty smile.

"Have you known him long?"

"No. Before Little Miao set out for Shanghai, the Director sent me here to take care of the place and to wait on you. I got acquainted with Little Miao only after I got here."

"How did the Director get to know you?" Mrs. Hung was truly puzzled as to these connections of theirs.

"I used to live in Wuchang. I won't fool you—I was somebody's number four concubine," Second Sister Sung said with a laugh.

"I asked how you got to know the Director."

"When General Wu was in power, the present Committeeman Liu and the Director stayed in my house, so we got to know each other. At the time, the two of them, and my dead devil, and my dead devil's old man, would discuss every day how to wreck the railway. They agreed that once the Revolutionary Army arrived, they'd make my dead devil and my dead devil's old man both officials. Who knew my dead devil and my dead devil's old man didn't have such luck? Not long after the Revolutionary Army came, not only did they not get to be officials, but somebody quietly killed them; they were shot to death!" Second Sister Sung said, and laughed again.

"What was it, that they got themselves killed?"

"There's no telling, and they never caught the killer." Second Sister Sung smiled again.

"What? Your husband died, and you're happy about it?" Mrs. Hung saw her smile, and felt that it was strange.

"Yes. Old Mistress, you didn't know I hated him to death!"

"Why?"

"That dead devil of mine was a gang leader, with I don't know how many followers. I didn't have any father when I was little, and Mama and I had a little business in a shed at the Hsüs' place at the railroad station. When I turned thirteen dead devil had his eye on me. He tossed my Mama twenty foreign dollars and carried me off to be his concubine. My Mama wouldn't go along, and discussed it with him, and his men beat her to death, and dragged her off and buried her."

"Didn't anything come of it, beating someone to death?"

"He was in with the officials, and we were poor people, so it didn't matter a fart!" Second Sister Sung said, as though she still felt some leftover pain.

Mrs. Hung looked at her, and sighed in sympathy. She asked:

"Have you finished tidying up? Let's go in my room and sit down. It must trouble you, me asking about this and asking about that."

"No, Old Mistress, I like to talk about these things; talking makes me happy. I was with him twenty years, and I was unhappy all the time, so unhappy I could have died."

Speaking, she entered Mrs. Hung's room. Mrs. Hung urged her repeatedly to sit down, and said:

"Just sit down and we'll chat, like friends. Don't consider me a stranger. From now on you needn't call me Old Mistress, just call me Mrs. Hung and that will be sufficient. Most of them call me Mrs. Hung, haven't you heard Liu Shao-ch'iao?"

Unconsciously she had brought up Liu Shao-ch'iao again. Mrs. Hung silently snorted at herself, and felt that her face had grown hot.

"This morning, before he went out, Little Miao told me that this evening several Committee members from the Labor Union will be having a banquet in your honor here. Committeeman Liu, the Director, and Little Miao will all keep the guests company."

Second Sister Sung, patting her lips with a handkerchief, kept smiling.

"What are you smiling about?" Mrs. Hung saw that the other's smiles were out of the ordinary.

"He also said that I should also keep the guests company."

"That's good; you ought to eat with us. Didn't I say so last night, and again at noon today?" Mrs. Hung asked politely.

"Mrs. Hung, you're really a good person." Second Sister Sung saw that Mrs. Hung was looking at her, and suddenly she felt happy. "Your son is good too. When the Director was staying in my house, he was good to me, he was always calling me Second Sister, Second Sister this, Second Sister that . . ."

"Why did he call you Second Sister?"

"My name is Erh-hsi. Dead devil and his followers all just called me Erh-hsi. Only the Director, from the first time he set eyes on me, called me Second Sister. So I like him—he's got such a sweet lip."

"Since he calls you Second Sister, you ought to call him Little Brother. You're always calling him Director, and it sounds so strange to my ears."

"That's what he says too, but I'd be embarrassed." Second Sister Sung smiled, pursing her lips.

"You really needn't be formal."

"I can't be formal now." Second Sister got up and came over to Mrs. Hung's side. She put her lips to Mrs. Hung's ear and said in a low voice: "Mrs. Hung, I can't tell you, but who do you think killed that dead devil of mine and his old man?"

"How could I guess that? Who?"

"It was Little Miao!"

Mrs. Hung's heart jumped, and she asked anxiously:

"Why?"

"The Director ordered him to do it."

Mrs. Hung felt even more amazed. She asked:

"What was it really about?"

"He was avenging me!" Second Sister Sung said loudly, standing up. "Your son is really good, really good, he's wonderful!"

Mrs. Hung couldn't say what she felt. Her son had grown up, and become independent; that was good. But he had also changed too quickly: to have killed two people, and to urge his own mother to remarry—these were truly not ordinary things! Surely the world hadn't really changed to his ways?

"I don't understand, I really don't understand," Mrs. Hung said to herself, shaking her head.

"Don't you understand yet? Mrs. Hung, he avenged me because he loves me!" Second Sister Sung explained still further.

"I know." Mrs. Hung made a smiling face, and nodded.

That evening, Hung T'ung-yeh first came by alone. Mrs. Hung, evading Second Sister Sung, steathily asked him:

"Did you order Little Miao to kill Second Sister Sung's husband and his father? Is that story true? Never mind whether it's true or not, such wild talk is no good!"

"It's true," Hung T'ung-yeh said unconcernedly and casually. "Liu Shao-ch'iao ordered me to, and I ordered Little Miao to go and do it."

"How is it that again it's Liu Shao-ch'iao's idea? Now, I really don't understand."

"It wasn't Liu Shao-ch'iao's idea either." Hung T'ung-yeh hesitated a moment, and then said gravely: "Ma, it's best if you don't ask about such things; if you don't understand, then you don't understand."

"When I see you so relaxed about taking two people's lives, how can I help but be anxious for you?" Mrs. Hung asked in a trembling voice.

"You don't need to grieve over dead men," Hung T'ung-yeh said, smiling. "I've killed a lot of men; how should I have stopped with those two?"

"To kill people is to give up your own life. Are you crazy?"

"I'm not crazy, don't you worry."

"Really, why do you want to kill people?"

"Revolution! If I don't kill people, people will kill me! Revolution isn't playing games," Hung T'ung-yeh said sternly and excitedly.

"In your father's time there was also a revolution, but he didn't talk of killing people."

"That revolution and this present revolution aren't the same."

Holding back her tears, Mrs. Hung stared at her son for a long time, and then said:

"You've changed."

"No mistake, I have changed. The times are changing, and of course I have to change too. If I didn't change, I'd fall behind." Hung T'ung-yeh paused a moment, and then went on: "Ma, don't you feel that you're changing too? I hope you'll change."

Mrs. Hung sighed, and after a time she said:

"Now that I think of it, ever since you got to know Liu Shao-ch'iao, you've gone wrong step by step. I really don't understand this person Liu Shao-ch'iao."

"If I hadn't known Liu Shao-ch'iao, then I might have known someone else like Liu Shao-ch'iao, and taken the same path I am on today. Or if Little Miao hadn't met this Hung T'ung-yeh, then certainly he would have met another Hung T'ung-yeh. Today's Little Miao is still today's Little Miao; there can't be two different ones."

Hung T'ung-yeh seemed to be instructing his mother. His conclusion was:

"This is the tide, and the tide is pressing on; no one can change its direction."

"I don't understand, I really don't understand." Mrs. Hung only felt that her head hurt.

"It's best we don't talk about this." Hung T'ung-yeh changed the subject, and asked in a happy, casual tone: "Ma, have you thought about your husband? What kind of a person do you hope for?"

"I told you already, wait and ask your little sister."

"Since it's for your good, Little Sister will certainly approve; you should go ahead and think about it," said Hung T'ung-yeh.

Mrs. Hung said nothing.

That evening, the Labor Union leaders all toasted Mrs. Hung. Mrs. Hung could not refuse their kind intentions, and she drank a little more than her capacity.

After the banquet, she seemed to hear someone ask Liu Shao-ch'iao:

"Nanking has set up a government, and the British keep sending warships to Hankow; clearly this is intimidation. Aren't we going to do anything at all?"

"Of course we must do something," said Liu Shao-ch'iao. "The reactionary armies are just now surrounding Wuhan tighter and tighter. We must do something that startles Heaven and shakes Earth. If we're going to finish, then we must really finish, and leave a little trouble behind for them!"

Mrs. Hung, in her befuddlement, put in:

"Right, if you're going to play, then play to your heart's content!"[42]

The images of last night's Little Miao and Second Sister Sung came dodging in from the corners of her eyes. She felt a little disgusted, and a little irritated as well. She stood up and said:

"You people talk, I'm going to sleep. Thank you."

Hung T'ung-yeh saw that she was a little unsteady, and quickly helped her into her room.

"I hear that Wang Ching-wei and Ch'en Tu-hsiu were both wanting to talk to you."[43]

"Yes," Liu Shao-ch'iao said, nodding. "They urged me to be careful. They both feel that the Labor Union and the Women's Association are going too far."

---

[42] Liu Shao-ch'iao used the verb *wan* (to finish). Mrs. Hung misunderstood and thought he meant *wan* (to play, to amuse oneself).

[43] Wang Ching-wei was the Chairman of the Wuhan government. Ch'en Tu-hsiu was the General Secretary of the Chinese Communist Party.

"Wang belongs to the Kuomintang and can be forgiven for saying such things. But what a thing that Ch'en Tu-hsiu is! Surely he hasn't forgotten who he is?" someone burst out.

"Both of them consider themselves leaders," Liu Shao-ch'iao said with a cold smile. "Do you still remember that Wang-Ch'en joint statement they issued in Shanghai? It seems that after they said it, they forgot about it."

"Never mind them, we'll act on our own."

"That's just what I think," Liu Shao-ch'iao poured the last of the wine from the table and took a drink. "And what's even funnier is that Wang doesn't approve of attacking Kuo Hsin-ju. He says the man is some sort of a scholar and that he has prestige just now, and drawing power. When we try to draw such people to us and they won't come, how can we kick them out?"

"Perhaps he thought you'd come from London or Washington?" Hung T'ung-yeh said, drawing a laugh from everyone.

"Ch'ien Pen-san can be counted on to exert himself in attacking Kuo Hsin-ju."

"He's a rather intelligent person," Liu Shao-ch'iao said. "He knows that if he doesn't attack Kuo, he won't be able to protect himself."

"But for propaganda purposes, his defect is that he doesn't have enough of a reputation."

"Kuo Hsin-ju has enough of a reputation, but will he obey you? But reputation is something that can be built up." Liu Shao-ch'iao inclined his head to the side as he thought for a moment, and said: "Wait until there's an opportunity, and we'll make him look good."

"So as to make him even more obedient?"

"Yes, needless to say."

Everyone laughed. Amid the laughter, they dispersed. Some still asked: "How is it we don't see Mrs. Hung?"

"She got drunk and went to bed."

"All right, then we'll be going, don't bother her."

It grew so quiet that no longer could any sound be heard. Mrs. Hung, still agitated, took off her long gown and trousers. Mrs. Hung's liberated and enlightened[44] feet depended upon a pair of silk stockings for "concealment". Except for bathing and changing, and when she was sleeping at night, she always wore them. But now she took off these silk stockings as well, and lightly tossed them aside.

She turned over once or twice, and still feeling depressed, she removed her "riding jacket" vest as well. With eyes confused by drink, Mrs. Hung gazed at her own body in the bed's mirror—that frightfully thin, bony body. She turned the light off at once. She remembered that when her husband was alive, scarcely a night passed when he did not comment approvingly on her moderate plumpness. Ten-odd years of widowhood had not only done away with her dreams, they had also consumed her body as well.

Mrs. Hung heaved a long sigh. She was sick at heart, and she began to feel aggrieved. She felt deeply that human life was not forever. Now that her son and daughter had grown up, and she had fulfilled her responsibilities toward them, she really didn't know where the meaning lay in going on suffering so.

Here and now, not only was it no longer shameful behavior for a widow to remarry, but it was being held up as a kind of feminine virtue. Sons and daughters could take pride in the remarriage of their widowed mother; it had become a model, the praiseworthy action of the avant-garde. Strange, too strange, Mrs. Hung thought, the world had really become too strange!

Weren't the children always saying so? Everyone, man or woman, young or old, must keep up with the times and respond to the tide, otherwise you would

---

[44] enlightened feet: natural, or unbound, feet.

fall behind. Surely the remarriage of widows couldn't be the tide of the times, Mrs. Hung thought.

Would Chin-ling really be certain to approve, she wondered.

Turning the light back on, she glanced at her body in the bed's mirror. At once Mrs. Hung shut her eyes, feeling a little disappointed, and also—as might have been foreseen—a little defeated.

Mrs. Hung, feeling hot, got out of bed, went over to the dressing table, and without the slightest hesitation opened the drawer and carefully enjoyed the photographs, those unbearable-to-look-at things which she had already seen the night before.

From the room across the hall came once more that hateful, provocative laughter. Mrs. Hung snorted, put the photographs down, and without shutting the open drawer, went quietly out. She felt her way along the wall, turned toward the rear window of the room across the hall, and looked in through the glass window-panes.

After some time, she felt her way back again. As she was just lifting the door-curtain, someone seized her and lifted her up.

"Who?" Mrs. Hung was so startled that her whole body broke out in a cold sweat.

"Who do you think?" The person kept kissing Mrs. Hung all over the face, kissing and sniffing. The odors of wine and tobacco were so strong that Mrs. Hung couldn't breathe. She thought, I must get free, but she was held too tightly, and she hadn't even the strength to cry out.

Mrs. Hung hid her face with both hands, just like an ostrich which, trying to avoid trouble, buries its head in the sand.

. . . . . .

It was nearly noon the next day, and Mrs. Hung hadn't gotten out of bed yet. Her eyes were a little reddened; obviously she had been crying. She felt a certain satisfaction, a satisfaction which made good her long isolation and loneliness, but of which she herself had never been clearly aware, for it was hidden behind a still heavier and greater shade. All that she felt then was a deep grievance; that she had been violated, and injured.

If you want to play, then play to your heart's content. No mistake, play was play, and heart's content was heart's content. But she had never, never dreamed that this was a trap, a shameful plot. Mad sensual pleasure, the long-contained bursting forth of animal nature, left one, once the storm had passed, with a kind of indefinable melancholy. But what Mrs. Hung had encountered was an absolutely unexpected and unusual shock, so unusual as to render her mind incapable of accepting it; she simply couldn't follow this turn of events.

"What will I do when Chin-ling comes? Shall I put my head in my arms and cry a while with her, or shall I just quietly accept it, and lift my hands while I crouch in submission?" Truly she couldn't think what to do.

"How humiliating—how can I see her?" she thought. "Otherwise, I might deceive her for a while. I don't know if that rotten egg will tell her—could I deceive her?"

"Ma," Hung T'ung-yeh appeared before the bed, "so late, and you haven't gotten up yet?"

"I'm not getting up!" As soon as she saw him, Mrs. Hung felt inexplicably angry.

"Why act like this? I know all about it."

"What do you know?" Mrs. Hung couldn't help feeling afraid.

"Last night, you and—"

"Did you take part in the plot?" Mrs. Hung asked, without waiting for Hung T'ung-yeh to finish.

Hung T'ung-yeh, wordlessly and with a slight smile, nodded.

"Animal!"

Mrs. Hung suddenly turned toward the wall, and shut her eyes tightly.

"Ma, I did everything for your own good," Hung T'ung-yeh said gently, sitting down on the bed. "Unless the rotten concept of chastity is broken down first, you'll never enjoy good fortune. You've already suffered for many years, and I'm not willing for you to go on suffering."

"Well, did you ask him to do it?"

"No, not at all; I only knew about it beforehand."

"Animal, animal!" Mrs. Hung cried furiously, and began to weep.

"However, you can trust me, Ch'ien Pen-san has many good points too. If you marry him, you'll be satisfied. On that point, Liu Shao-ch'iao's not deceiving you."

"Since you've decided I must get married, I'll get married. Why did you have to add this on too, letting that rotten egg violate me?" Mrs. Hung said angrily, as she turned over and sat up. As she spoke, she feared that her voice was too loud, and that someone would hear. In shame and anger she covered her face with her hands and wept again.

"It was necessary, in order to change your attitude," Hung T'ung-yeh said, shaking his head. "Your weeping and carrying on like this makes me very disappointed."

He wrung out a cold hand-towel and passed it to his mother.

"All right, wipe your face, and get out of bed and sit up. We're going to eat soon."

Mrs. Hung took it, and wiped her face, and got dressed. She rinsed her mouth, and sat down on the sofa to smoke a cigarette. She felt utterly exhausted; her head ached and her eyes were blurred, and it was hard to stay upright. She thought of that rotten egg last night—to molest a woman twenty years older.

What a shameless fellow! Mrs. Hung snorted silently, in disgust, and—she couldn't help it—almost laughed.

Hung T'ung-yeh saw Mama's face relaxing and expressing pleasure, and he said:

"Have you thought it through? You know I love you, I couldn't hurt you."

"Shameless!" Mrs. Hung regained control of herself, and turned away.

"Little Sister Chin-ling thought it through early, and she didn't cry and carry on like you. So we can see that young people can accept new thoughts and new concepts more easily."

"Why hasn't she come yet?" Mrs. Hung asked with concern.

"Liu Shao-ch'iao will soon be bringing her, and we'll all eat lunch here."

At the very mention of Liu Shao-ch'iao's name, Mrs. Hung frowned, and said no more. Silently she attended to smoking her cigarette. After some time had passed in silence, she said in a low, sorrowful voice:

"This is another world of yours here, and it's different from the former world that I was used to. In this world of yours, people who are high up can fall, and low-class people can ride on the heads of others. This world of yours is abnormal!"

Mrs. Hung sighed, and held back her tears. She went on:

"If I had known it was like this, I wouldn't have come. Really, it would have been well if I hadn't come! I think I'll go back to Shanghai."

"That can't be done. Didn't Chin-ling and I try time and again to leave, but time and again we didn't make it? Ma, you'll have to give up that idea."

"I used to think, now that you two were grown up, that I ought to enjoy a little happiness, to make up for all the difficulties and suffering I've put up with these ten-odd years. Now I know that thought harmed me. If I hadn't been thinking that way at the time, nothing would have happened."

As she spoke, Hung Chin-ling came in with Liu Shao-ch'iao. As soon as Mrs. Hung saw her, she felt that her daughter had grown a little taller, and thinner, and that her spirit seemed a little withered. Hung Chin-ling hugged her mother, but without even saying the word "Ma", and her tears poured down. The two of them held one another without speaking for some time. Liu Shao-ch'iao looked at Hung T'ung-yeh, and said impatiently:

"Shall we eat after they've cried their fill?"

"What's there to cry about?" Hung T'ung-yeh drew his sister away, and pointing to the dressing-table he said: "Hurry and wash your face so we can eat."

Mrs. Hung followed her.

After lunch Liu Shao-ch'iao and Hung T'ung-yeh went away. Mrs. Hung made her daughter lie down flat on the bed to rest. Chin-ling said to her mother:

"For the present we must obey them in everything. They really are killers, and they pay no mind to family relations. Truly they're a pair of devils!"

"When T'ung-yeh was little he was so dutiful and so good-hearted. Who would have thought that today he'd be so changed?" Mrs. Hung thought of Hung T'ung-yeh as he had been when he worked at the foreign shop, and couldn't overcome her feelings as she compared past with present.

"If your brother's no good, it's M. and Mme. Lefebvre and your Bureau Chief uncle and his wife who must bear the full responsibility. If they had had the slightest human nature, your brother wouldn't have been driven to this point."

"You can't blame them entirely. If I hadn't gotten sick, he wouldn't have run into P'eng Wen-hsüeh and Liu Shao-ch'iao, and perhaps he wouldn't have changed so quickly."

"Pushed from one side, and enticed by the other—the two forces combined to ruin him," Hung Chin-ling said pityingly.

"Do you have any ideas?" Mrs. Hung asked.

"I have a friend; he's Ch'ien Pen-san's fourth brother. They were suspicious of him, and they've locked him up."

"Your friend?" Mrs. Hung asked nervously.

"I only had an oral agreement with him to be engaged. I've been calling his niece Elder Sister; we haven't done anything else," Hung Chin-ling said with a smile.

"Then I certainly can't marry Ch'ien Pen-san. How could a mother and daughter ever be sisters-in-law?"

"When they've decided the matter, can you turn away from it?"

"I'd rather die!"

"That wouldn't be worthwhile, either." Hung Chin-ling put her lips to her mother's ear and said quietly, "I don't know why, but I've felt for a long time that this situation before our eyes can't last very long. They've got half of Hupei Province, and half of Hunan Province, and they're surrounded by other people's armies. Shutting the outer gates and carrying on recklessly, what kind of an atmosphere do you think they can create? I don't know how brother is going to end up."

"If that's what you say, then there's still less reason for me to marry into the Ch'ien family."

"Let's see what they're going to do. The matter isn't up to us."

"On the contrary, you've both grown up already. And the worst thing that can happen is death, so what am I afraid of?" In front of her daughter, Mrs. Hung's attitude stiffened.

The circle which the outside armies had formed around the Wuhan government grew ever tighter. The Szechuan army in western Hupei had already formally broken with the Wuhan government, and even the students of the Military-political Academy in Wuchang had taken part in the fighting.

This was no good news, for the students of the Military-political Academy were the Wuhan government's favorite soldiers, and they were also its trump card. Forced to play their trump card before there had even been a regular battle, the regime's emptiness could be imagined. Because of this, although they beat back the Szechuan army, not only did they fail to obtain a decisive victory, but they thoroughly exposed their own weak point.

The foreboding feeling that "good prospects don't last forever" grew ever sharper, and Ch'ien Pen-san felt that unless he quickly sought an escape route, he would really die without even a spot to be buried in. He thought of Shou-tien, and said to himself: "Don't think the boy was so stupid; at least he was clever enough to see ahead. If I can't get out of this after all, there's him, so it won't be the end of me."

The image of that dead devil's kitchen reappeared in his memory, and Ch'ien Pen-san snorted.

Chairman Wang's office telephoned, to say that the Chairman summoned his presence at once. Ch'ien Pen-san was shaken; he felt that while all along he had been serving as a publicity agent for the Communist Party, he had not established any special ties with Chairman Wang, and that he had certainly made a mistake. So he thought:

"This is a lucky chance after all!"

It was even luckier that Secretary Feng was not with him, and he was able to go alone to Wang's office. He sat for a bit in the reception room, and Madame Wang came out.

Of all the important personages in Wuhan, Ch'ien Pen-san most feared two women: the widow Chung and this Madame Wang. Behind their backs he had always said they were a pair of shrews.

Madame Wang, stern-faced and looking straight ahead, sat down heavily opposite Ch'ien Pen-san, and threw the newspaper she clutched in his direction.

Ch'ien Pen-san, who had already stood up to welcome her, dropped his hands and made a formal bow, and the newspaper fell to the floor. He hastily bent to look for it, still not understanding what this was about.

"You see," Madame Wang snorted angrily, "you're more and more ridiculous!"

"What? Madame!"

"Look for yourself."

Ch'ien Pen-san riffled through the newspaper but still did not understand where the trouble was. He flushed and said:

"Madame, what is it, really? Explain it, so I can understand."

"Department Chief Ch'ien," Madame Wang said with a cold smile, "I ask you, when did you enter the party?"

"At the time of the Anti-Yüan expedition," Ch'ien Pen-san, acting deliberately obtuse, suppressed his anger.

"I think it must have been that when Yüan Shih-k'ai dispersed the Parliament, you found yourself at a loss, so you took this path. Didn't you?"

"Mr. Chung-shan sent me a letter inviting me to join the party," Ch'ien Pen-san said quite clearly. "And when Chu Chüeh-sheng organized the Anti-Yüan Army in eastern Shantung, he also invited me to help out."

"And so on the strength of that little bit of an achievement you look down on the martyr Chung's widow. Don't you?" Madame Wang laughed coldly.

At this, Ch'ien Pen-san realized his offense. An essay appearing over his name in the paper, pointed out that the women's movement was practical work which penetrated deeply among the masses. Through practical work they were proving theory and gaining experience; later on theory and experience would direct the next stage of their work. They needed no lofty, impractical leaders.

Madame Chung was the Department Chief of the Women's Department, and this was obviously a veiled barb at her. It was a manifestation of the struggle for leadership between the Women's Association and the Women's Department. Ch'ien Pen-san, as though suddenly waking up, thought:

"It's certainly the widow Chung who's accused me!"

He acted as though it didn't matter. Putting the paper down, and suppressing a bellyful of mortification and anger, he said, with a gloomy, pained expression:

"As for that, perhaps you won't believe me. Nowadays, all of the essays that are printed under my name in the newspapers, and the speeches and remarks as well—they're all written by someone else, and I know nothing of them beforehand. Now, as for today's essay, I simply wouldn't have known about it if you hadn't alerted me. It's the Women's Association—in my heart I've always been opposed to them, but it's not convenient for me to say anything."

Pausing a moment, and sighing, Ch'ien Pen-san went on sadly:

"Everybody knows I'm a puppet Department Chief. For a long time now, I really haven't been able to stand being a puppet Department Chief."

Seeing that Madame Wang said nothing, as though she were listening attentively to his pleading, he lowered his voice and went on:

"Unfortunately, no one understands my position. My position is that of the Kuomintang. No, my position is really that of Mr. Wang. Mr. Wang is our leader; we obey Mr. Wang. If we didn't obey Mr. Wang, who would we obey?"

Madame Wang shifted on the soft chair, as though quite gratified by Ch'ien Pen-san's words. Ch'ien Pen-san then continued:

"I'd really like to have a good talk with you. This present situation is truly extremely dangerous. Mr. Wang's party—since the Director died, I always call it that, because only Mr. Wang can succeed the Director, and be the Party's leader; it's undoubtedly Mr. Wang's party. This party is just now being robbed from us; it's being transformed from within!"

Madame Wang put her forefinger to her lips and sighed softly. Ch'ien Pen-san stopped talking. She looked deliberately right and left, and then said quietly:

"Very well, this business today is finished; you can go back. I'll meet with you another day. If you have something to say, you can talk to Mr. Wang alone."

Ch'ien Pen-san stood up, bowed, and with a "Thank you, Madame" he took his leave and went away.

He felt that he had "drawn advantage from misfortune"; he was good at grasping opportunities. Not at all careless, he discussed it with his daughter, and the two of them stealthily hurried off to an Englishman's jewelry shop and bought several kinds of valuable jewelry.

From then on, he visited Wang's office frequently, and no longer had to go through the process of sending in his card and waiting to be seen; he appeared in his dignity like someone who belonged to Wang's office.

The other thing on Ch'ien Pen-san's mind was Kuo Hsin-ju.

Although he often said that he had joined the Kuomintang upon receiving a letter of invitation from Director Sun's own brush, the true circumstances were that he had been introduced by Kuo Hsin-ju. And after he had entered the party, Kuo Hsin-ju, deliberately or otherwise, had often helped him along. Whatever "utility value" Ch'ien Pen-san had now was owing, more or less indirectly, to Kuo Hsin-ju, and in his heart Ch'ien Pen-san understood this. On this account he had always cherished a special respect for Kuo Hsin-ju.

After the publication of the essay "Put-on Appearances and Manufactured Atmosphere" the Communist Party decided to attack Kuo Hsin-ju. The first essay was written by Secretary Ching, and published under Ch'ien Pen-san's name. Because it was a "major affair", Secretary Ching showed the draft to Ch'ien Pen-san before it was published. Ch'ien Pen-san knew that he didn't have the power to stop the essay, so he said nothing. This was because he had already experienced this kind of thing many times.

He had visited the Soviet Union, and Secretary Ching brought that up in almost every essay he wrote for Ch'ien Pen-san. The Soviet Union was just fine, just fine; how could I be wrong about what I saw with my own eyes? But that's enough. Once he presumed to write:

> Two years ago, on my world tour, I passed through England, France, and other countries, and having met people from all walks of life, I know that all of them inclined towards the Communist Soviet system. It won't be long before the whole of Europe turns Red. This is an historical tide which no one can turn aside. Without doubt the Chinese Revolution must follow the great Soviet Union motherland, and advance like a fly on a horse's tail. The Chinese Revolution is part of the world revolution; it cannot go it alone.

Even a bolder person than Ch'ien Pen-san could not have helped having some misgivings. Because he had simply never toured the world, and except for his visit to Moscow, neither had he ever set foot in any part of Europe. Even in lying one shouldn't stray too far from the truth.

He suggested this point to Secretary Ching, but before he had finished speaking, Secretary Ching flushed and grew very displeased.

"To do propaganda you must understand mass psychology," Secretary Ching said, as though delivering instruction. "The Chinese people have an attitude of worshipping what is foreign. Communism comes from the West, so of course it's good. If even the people of England, France, Germany, and Italy believe in it, who are the Chinese to doubt it? Besides, these are things you've seen with your own eyes, which is all the more reason they can't help believe it. This is a kind of marvelous skill I have with propaganda. It's an art. How can you say it's telling lies? Committeeman Ch'ien, you've been in politics for many years; really, I'd never have thought you didn't know this little trick."

Secretary Ching laughed expansively. Ch'ien Pen-san, blushing, said nothing more.

In addition to such incidents, one thing had made him sick at heart and extremely uncomfortable. This was when, at the beginning of the attacks on a certain official, he "received an order" to publish a most provocative essay, abusing that high official so as to leave him not an inch of whole skin. He had always held that certain official in the highest esteem, and that certain official had treated him very courteously. In general their relations, on both sides, had been quite good. He resisted with the greatest strength the publication of that essay under his name, but in the next day's paper, there it was, as usual.

The business had upset him, and he had remained depressed for some days.

Ch'ien Pen-san cared nothing about such epithets as "ingrate". It might be said there was no difference between "great ideals override kinship" and "ingrate"; both were only lawyers' phrases. It was the question of how, after this episode was finished, the two of them could meet face to face again that concerned Ch'ien Pen-san. His foreboding that "when the play is over, the guests disperse" made him suffer much self-restraint, and prevented him from getting right to work.

Ch'ien Pen-san still remembered Kuo Hsin-ju's phone number, so he put through a call. He planned to tell Kuo Hsin-ju:

"There's an essay attacking you in tomorrow morning's newspaper, and although it appears under my name, you know that it's not my essay, and still less is it my idea. There aren't the slightest problems between the two of us."

But the person on the other end of the line said that Kuo Hsin-ju and his wife had already left.

"Where did they go?"

"I don't know."

There was no one to whom Ch'ien Pen-san's explanation could be delivered. He consumed half his cigar at one puff, paced a hundred circuits around his room, and wrinkled his brows into a knot, but in the end he couldn't think of a good way.

Much later, he learned that Kuo Hsin-ju and his wife were staying at the Wangs' office. "Waiting at the door is like the ocean", and he couldn't get close. When he telephoned, the person at the other end would not acknowledge that such a guest was at the office.

Now that he was a frequent guest at the Wangs' office, he found an opportunity to say to Madame Wang:

"I hear that the Communist Party is going to attack Mr. Kuo again."

"Didn't they attack him last time?" Madame Wang asked, confused. "Why do they want to attack him again?"

"It's because when they attacked him before, he didn't show his face, nor did he respond. This time they want to force him to surrender."

"How can Mr. Kuo surrender to them? They don't understand at all the kind of person Mr. Kuo is!" Madame Wang sighed.

"That's why I respect Mr. Kuo so," Ch'ien Pen-san said, falling in with Madame Wang's attitude. "A person like me who's a puppet for others, a speaking-tube—what use am I?"

"It's not just you nowadays. There are many men, in positions higher than yours, whose circumstances are just like yours; they're all using someone else's people as confidential secretaries. Commander T'ang has military authority, and he's under their coercion as well," said Madame Wang with deep emotion.

"If this is how it is, the Kuomintang exists in name, but in fact is lost. Mr. Wang must think of a way!"

"Let's look at the circumstances and then say. Just now they want to introduce a secretary to Mr. Wang."

"If they've such great ambitions, matters can't wait!" Ch'ien Pen-san wrung his hands anxiously.

"No need to be so anxious," Madame Wang nodded gently, and said seriously and gravely. "Only let all the comrades unite in support of Mr. Wang, and allow Mr. Wang to pursue his own path. The Communist Party will never overthrow him."

"To support Mr. Wang is ordained by Heaven and decreed by Earth!" Ch'ien Pen-san slapped his thigh forcefully. "I'll attack anyone who dares say a word against it!"

"How fine that you have such a resolve; certainly it's a good one. Just wait until I tell Mr. Wang; he'll surely want to take especial care of you," Madame Wang at once encouraged him.

"Thank you, Madame."

Ch'ien Pen-san jumped up from the easy chair to bow. He sat down again, and asked:

"May I ask Madame, do you know where Mr. Kuo is staying?"

Madame Wang stared at him, remained silent for a moment, and then said:

"He's staying here, upstairs. Whatever you do, don't tell anyone else."

"Yes," Ch'ien Pen-san was overjoyed. "I'll certainly keep my mouth shut like a bottle. But I was hoping to see Mr. Kuo. Could I trouble you, Madame, just to ask on my behalf?"

"Wait until I ask him and then I'll tell you." Madame Wang yawned, and said, as though she were tired, "All right, you'd better go."

Ch'ien Pen-san hurriedly withdrew.

When, after many days, Madame Wang hadn't brought up the matter, Ch'ien Pen-san couldn't stand it. He sought an opportunity, and tentatively asked:

"About that matter of my seeing Mr. Kuo—has Madame asked on my behalf?"

"I asked, and he won't see you."

"Why?"

"He didn't say why."

"I know, he certainly despises me!" Ch'ien Pen-san flushed.

"Since you know, why did you have to ask me?" Madame Wang asked, wooden-faced.

Chapter XIX

Ch'ien Pen-san hurried back from Wang's office.

His daughter Shou-yü was sitting in the sitting room, under the big ceiling fan, reading a thick book. In front of her was a big cup of red tea. Ch'ien Pen-san was in no good humor, and since it was in the full heat of the summer, he thought that the big cup of red tea must be iced. Putting down his briefcase and straw hat, he picked it up and took a great mouthful. With a "*tung-lung*" sound, the porcelain cup dropped to the floor and shattered. Ch'ien Pen-san's anger blazed up thirty thousand feet high, and he leaned across the table to hit Shou-yü, but Shou-yü ran off.

The cup of red tea set before Ch'ien Shou-yü had been boiling hot. Ch'ien Shou-yü had a quirk: she liked to drink hot red tea in hot weather; the hotter it was, the better, and she would add a great deal of brown sugar. It had to be that way, she said, in order to relieve thirst. Ch'ien Pen-san, through having failed to check, drank it in a hurry and blistered his lips.

After perhaps ten minutes, Ch'ien Shou-yü came downstairs. She knew her father's temper: by this time the rain should have passed and the skies cleared. She quietly poured a big cup of fresh iced lemonade, and placed it on the table, and then hesitantly and very timidly she said:

"Papa, please help yourself."

Ch'ien Pen-san took off his dark glasses, glared fiercely at his daughter, turned his head away, and then his tears came gushing down. Ch'ien Shou-yü had never seen her father cry like this, and she had no idea why. She hastily wrung out a cold towel and gave it to him. Ch'ien Pen-san took it, and wiped his face with the towel, and began to sob in an ostentatiously grief-stricken manner.

"Papa, it was my fault," Ch'ien Shou-yü tried to comfort him.

"I don't blame you!"

"Then why do you feel so badly?"

Ch'ien Pen-san rubbed his face, drank some lemonade, and stopped crying.

"I've decided to resign as Chief of the Propaganda Department; I can't go on with it."

"Why?"

"It isn't something for a person to do," Ch'ien Pen-san said with a long sigh.

He went on to tell his daughter about the business of Kuo Hsin-ju refusing to see him.

"According to Hsin-ju's lofty reputation and clear principles, if you compare him with me, am I even a human being? If I go on, then I not only can't face myself, I can't face my father and mother and my ancestors," Ch'ien Pen-san said with deep pain.

"If you can quit, of course that's best; what do you have to do with the Communist Party anyway?" Ch'ien Shou-yü had rarely seen her father so changed and resolved, and she hastened to encourage him.

But when he submitted his letter of resignation, it was not accepted. The reason was that it was a "fiery pit" and none of the important members of the Kuomintang were at that time willing to jump into the fiery pit. As for the Communist Party, it was trying to avoid using its own comrades to "head the assault"; they were looking for real benefits and did not seek position.

Wang himself summoned him to an interview, and after he had been soothed by the other in person, Ch'ien Pen-san could only withdraw his resignation. At the same time, Kuo Hsin-ju's wife agreed to see Ch'ien Shou-yü. At one time Mrs. Kuo had lectured on educational psychology at Women's Normal University, and Ch'ien Shou-yü had been one of her students. Because of the friendly relations between Kuo Hsin-ju and Ch'ien Pen-san, they had been especially close as teacher and student, and had always gotten on well together. Mrs. Kuo told Ch'ien Shou-yü:

"Isn't politics something? Wait until the situation calms down a bit; then we'll go back to Peking. I'll teach, and you'll study—that's proper."

These words touched exactly on Ch'ien Shou-yü's concern. She seized Mrs. Kuo's hand, and said:

"That's just what I think. I've always regretted leaving school to come to Hankow; it was all Papa's idea. And now look what he's doing!"

Kuo Hsin-ju was leaning on the writing-desk writing something, and when he heard Ch'ien Shou-yü's words, he put down his brush and said with a laugh:

"Tell your Papa, when in Rome, do as the Romans do, but the performance needn't be excessive. Does he understand now whether or not the Communist Party is his friend?"

"I think he's already eaten plenty of bitterness, but he hasn't necessarily truly awakened."

Ch'ien Shou-yü's words caused Kuo Hsin-ju and his wife to laugh.

When Ch'ien Shou-yü left Wang's office, she felt frustrated, and walked slowly instead of taking a rickshaw, and observed the street scene. Conditions on the streets were disordered. It was still early, but already there were shopkeepers putting up their doors. Troop after troop of Workers' Pickets set out in various directions. Everyone's faces wore chilly expressions, which couldn't cover up their alarm.

While Ch'ien Shou-yü stood puzzled, she chanced to come face to face with Hung T'ung-yeh.

"Mr. Hung," she quickly asked. "What's going on?"

"The British marines struck one of our Workers' Pickets, and arrested one of our Women's Association committeewomen. The Foreign Ministry is already with their important negotiators. If the negotiations don't work out, our Workers' Pickets will occupy the Concession. We absolutely won't submit to the imperialists. Elder Sister, you'd better hurry home."

Hung T'ung-yeh spoke rapidly, and went away, but before going more than a few steps, he stopped, and called out to Ch'ien Shou-yü:

"Originally Liu Shao-ch'iao was going to call on Third Master at home tonight, to discuss some little matter. With this business of the British Concession, perhaps he won't come."

"What did he want to discuss?"

"He wanted to discuss a suitable marriage with your father," Hung T'ung-yeh smiled craftily. "Elder Sister, let me beg of you first: whatever you do, don't refuse."

"Who and who?" Ch'ien Shou-yü felt this was odd.

"I can't let that out just now, but I want to ask you to help," Hung T'ung-yeh said, and left.

Ch'ien Shou-yü suddenly thought of her own body, and couldn't help blushing. She muttered quietly: have you gone crazy and gotten some idea of picking on me? Then you people don't understand me! Don't think that I—"

Ch'ien Shou-yü bent her head and looked at her feet—

A crowd of people like you have never meant anything to me.

As she thought, she grew a little angry. She wanted to hire a rickshaw and go home. As luck would have it, an empty rickshaw was just then passing, and Ch'ien Shou-yü hailed it. The rickshaw man said:

"Excuse me, but I'm not hauling anyone. We are putting our rickshaws down in the Labor Union, to go and attack the British Concession."

And he was gone.

Ch'ien Shou-yü was amazed, and hurried home. She was very uneasy, because she lived in the British Concession, and now she had heard that they were going to attack it. She telephoned to find her father, but couldn't locate him anywhere. Nor could she learn any news. She carelessly ate a few mouthfuls of dinner, then sat in the courtyard to enjoy the cool, and fanned herself with a big banana-leaf fan. Aunty Li, the old woman who cooked and washed, went out to dump the trash, and came back saying excitedly:

"Missy, everyone in the street is saying that the English are all moving down to their ships, and the Workers' Pickets have recovered the Concession. On the street ahead of us there's an English family who've been held up by the Workers' Pickets because they haven't paid their servants their wages, and they won't let them go, so they're still sitting there."

Aunty Li clapped both hands, and went on:

"Look, isn't this something to marvel at? Before there were only Chinese who were afraid of the foreigners, and now the foreigners are afraid of the Chinese. Everybody on the streets is discussing it. Missy, you watch the door, I'm going back out to see the excitement. They say the Workers' Pickets are going to recover the Concession; how is it I haven't seen them? I never thought they could really do it!"

So saying, she slipped away like a puff of smoke.

Ch'ien Shou-yü, watching her retreating back, smiled to see her in such high spirits, although there was something a little dull-witted about it, like the Boxer psychology of the past. But the psychology was quite subtle. Those especially noble white people, who felt that they had received Heaven's favor, who held the superficial concept of despising the colored races—no matter whether they were swindlers, missionaries, businessmen, adventurers, or escaped criminals—as soon as they arrived in the so-called backward territories, not a one of them but thought himself God's representative, and a lord, and thus, inevitably, they aroused psychological and physical resistance like that of the Boxers. Could one blame only those backward colored races?

Ch'ien Shou-yü was a little uneasy, but at the thought that the Workers' Pickets had already recovered the British Concession, she felt, without knowing quite why, a kind of mysterious satisfaction. And so again she thought: the present clamorous shouting of the slogan "Down With Imperialism!" was an extension of the Boxers' thinking, because the revolutionary party itself, and this action which it supported, did not have sufficient strength to beat down imperialism. Their shouting was meant to incite and arouse that long-repressed anti-foreign psychology. Having stirred up the strength of the masses with this anti-foreign psychology, they would also make use of it, and then they could obtain political power. "Down with you; I'm coming!"

As for after "I'm coming", would they really want to beat down imperialism? One thing could be foreseen: at that time, they would have to carefully calculate the opponent's strength against their own, and if they should discover that the disparity was too great, they would certainly have to furl their flags and muffle their drums, and make other calculations.

Having thought thus far, Ch'ien Shou-yü inadvertently felt her heart jump, as though invaded by a faint chill.

"I wish I could go back to Peking. What Kuo Hsin-ju said was right. This is what politics is," she thought.

Having turned off all the inside and outside electric lights, Ch'ien Shou-yü went back to the courtyard and leaned back in a rattan chair, looking up at the cloudless sky. She was quite ignorant of the stars, but as a child she had often sought the cool breezes on summer nights—summer nights whose rural atmosphere was completely different from the mood of the day—and had learned from her mother's lips about the River of Stars, the Weaving Damsel, and the Herdboy; she knew the Dipper, and the Southern Dipper, and the simple stories about these stars. Her mother had no gift of speech, and even stammered, but those not particularly appealing nor reasonable stories she told were deeply imprinted upon Ch'ien Shou-yü's mind, enduring and ever-new.

Ch'ien Shou-yü first saw that overflowing River of Stars, and then found the Weaving Damsel and the Herd Boy. Ch'ien Shou-yü felt a deep aversion to this story. The couple, in love with one another, were separated by a river and could look but could not meet. Only on the seventh night of the seventh month out of the year could they meet on the Magpie Bridge, and since antiquity they had been so parted. Was there anything crueller than this among the dwellers in the heavens?

On account of the strike news which the newspapers printed every day, Ch'ien Shou-yü was led to think: if the magpies were unhappy and went on strike, then on the seventh night there would be no bridge, and wouldn't the pair of lovers then have no chance to be together?

Then what would they do?

Ch'ien Shou-yü grew quite anxious, and thought no more of it. She remembered her mother, far away at home in the countryside. What was she doing now? Was her mother, like herself, looking up at the heavens and grieving over unrelated and mysterious matters?

"If I go back to Peking, I ought to think of a way to bring Mother to Peking to live with me. No matter what she's like, she is my mother, and I can't let her suffer too much."

For some reason she thought of Hung T'ung-yeh. Ch'ien Shou-yü snorted:

"You think too much of yourself, and you've made a mistake about me! Even if Papa agrees, I won't do it!"

So she thought, and felt extraordinarily resolute.

There was a commotion outside, and the sounds were familiar.

Ch'ien Shou-yü turned on the electric light. Her father came in with Liu Shao-ch'iao and a pale, plump and lame young woman. The three of them were flushed, and had obviously been drinking.

"Elder Sister, come on over," Liu Shao-ch'iao said loudly. "Let me introduce you, this is Comrade Pai Ch'a-hua."

"Committeewoman Pai," Ch'ien Shou-yü hurried over to shake hands with her, "I've heard so much about you, 'like thunder in my ears'. I'm Ch'ien Shou-yü."

"Miss, you certainly can make jokes," Pai Ch'a-hua looked up, to inspect Ch'ien Shou-yü.

So they sat down, and iced tea was poured. Ch'ien Shou-yü, while seeming to behave casually, was thinking: in this great city of Wuhan there are no more powerful organizations than the Labor Union and the Women's Association, and in the Labor Union and the Women's Association there are no more powerful people than Liu Shao-ch'iao and Pai Ch'a-hua. Surely these two powerful people didn't come here this evening just to talk. "Even if you put forth even more formidable power, I won't consent, and there's nothing you can do!"

"Elder Sister, you must know already that today, without a single rifle or bullet, we recovered the British Concession!" Liu Shao-ch'iao said happily.

"I heard a little about it, but I don't know the details." Despite herself Ch'ien Shou-yü was anxious to ask: "How did it really happen?"

"For public consumption, we have another explanation," Liu Shao-ch'iao said, gesturing with his cigarette and shaking his head. "But I don't mind telling you the true circumstances."

That afternoon an Englishwoman had gone to the Kiang-Han Customs Office to pick up something, and after finishing her business, she had walked

alone along the sidewalk beside the river. As she passed the wharf, a group of
workers were idling and chatting by the iron railing along the road, and others
were leaning against it. As the Englishwoman passed before them, she covered
her nose with a handkerchief, and quickened her pace, intending to cross the road
to the opposite side. By that time, all the workers were concentrating their
attention upon her person, and one of them, swallowing his saliva, said:

"A nice piece of fat meat, so white and tender!"

This brought a laugh from everyone, and some confused yelling. When it
quieted down, someone else said:

"It's nice all right; very nice. Too bad you like her, but she doesn't like
you! See, she's holding her nose while she runs away."

"That won't do! Now is not like it was before; the world belongs to us
workers! What kind of thing is she?"

"But I do love that big ass," said the one who had originally approved of
the woman, as he went after her.

He stuck out his hand and pinched her. The woman gave a piercing cry
and stood still in the middle of the street. On her dress there remained the black
and oily print of a dirty hand. The woman, angry, began to chatter; certainly she
was scolding him.

Another worker grimaced and asked the one who had just stuck out his
hand:

"How was it? What did it feel like?"

"Great!" The one who had stuck out his hand raised his thumb. "Soft—I
felt like I'd gotten an electric shock."

As he spoke, he raised his dirty hand to his nose and began to sniff at it.

"Good, I'll try that foreign meat too."

"Everybody come!"

Thus in a moment there were seven or eight of them, some pinching her buttocks, some feeling her breasts, and some squeezing her cheeks, and laughing and cursing in a disorderly crowd. Chinese seeing foreigners were like rats seeing the cat, and this tendency had given rise to the foreigners' opinionated and contemptuous attitude. The Englishwoman had lived in China for many years, and to these yellow-faced sons and grandsons of the dragon she was like a representative of the gods on high, as proud as the Emperor, and as beautiful as the Empress. What had just happened—that these yellow devils would finally dare rebel—was something she had never thought of, even in a dream. She was mortified and angry, and raising her parasol she struck about wildly. A workman snatched away the parasol, snapped the handle, and tossed it down.

"A foreigner striking a Chinese—don't let her go!"

At this ridicule turned to anger. The workers hustled the woman over to the ladder leading to the receiving lighter, and someone proposed stripping her naked, so that they could really appreciate this morsel of meat. Someone else opposed it, saying that they shouldn't go too far and make the incident even more serious. Then the one who had spoken out in opposition was immediately surrounded and beaten half-dead with fists and feet.

"Traitor!"

"Foreign slave!"

"Counterrevolutionary!"

"Running dog of imperialism!"

And many other "official titles" were applied.

Amid the confusion, the Concession police cars arrived. The British marines, who were always in a state of readiness, the British police, the Indian constables, and even a few Chinese policemen, arrived in succession. Besides pistols, rifles, and bayonets, there were light and heavy machine guns as well. The British warships on the river had long since removed the covers from their guns, and now they were loaded with live ammunition and aimed. Because of the British action, the warships of the Japanese, the French, and the Italians had also made ready for combat.

The Englishwoman was first gotten out of danger, and then the British police arrested several workers and carried them off towards the police station. The British immediately piled up sandbags at the entrance of the Concession near the Kiang-Han Customs Office, set up machine guns, and allowed no one to enter or to leave.

Outside the sandbags, and in front of the machine guns, a crowd of idlers collected at once to watch the excitement. They tugged their lower lips, stared straight ahead, and occasionally whispered to each other. But these idlers were suddenly dispersed, because a large detachment of armed Workers' Pickets had arrived and formed into a group opposite the British sandbags.

Gradually the sky grew dark.

The public and private addresses of every Englishman went without electricity, without water, and without telephone service that night. All of their hired Chinese staff and workers stayed close and did not leave, but they stopped working. They prepared the Englishmen's dinners, and ate themselves, but wouldn't allow the Englishmen to eat. They wouldn't permit the Englishmen to leave by so much as one pace.

By twos and threes the workers infiltrated the Concession, until it was calculated that at least one hundred thousand were inside, until every street and alley was packed full.

The British and the Foreign Ministry of the Wuhan government engaged in non-stop negotiations. The Foreign Ministry kept urging the British to withdraw, otherwise the lives and property of both sides must suffer incalculable damages.

The "Chinese government" did not underestimate the power of the British warships; they had sufficient might to render the three townships of Wuhan a levelled wasteland. But the "Chinese government" had already decided that while it might be rendered a levelled wasteland, it absolutely could not contemplate submitting to the imperialists.

This was the message to the British which brought fame to the Minister of Foreign Affairs, Ch'en Yu-jen, who spoke plenty of English but understood not a word of Chinese. This communication differed little in spirit from the rascally spirit of the Boxers of some twenty-odd years before, but happily he was able to utilize the might of the masses, and manifest the popular awakening, and so, luckily, he gained the victory.

The British told him that the British Army and British subjects would quickly withdraw, and they requested the "Chinese government" to send people to recover the Concession and keep order.

Ch'en responded that the "Chinese government" would accept the British suggestion, but that it would be necessary for the British side to issue a formal, written request.

When the British added such a communication, the matter was considered settled. Ch'en sent his vice-minister to take over the administration of the Concession, and the Chinese police entered the concession. The British Army and the civilians had cleared out that night, withdrawn to their ships, and departed for Shanghai.

Liu Shao-ch'iao recounted all of these events to Ch'ien Shou-yü, and then Pai Ch'a-hua spoke up, saying:

"It was that Englishwoman's fault. When they patted her behind, it was just because they liked her, it was an expression of friendship. She should have accepted it gratefully. If they hadn't really loved her, who would care for that frowzy, smelly, big behind?"

This made everyone laugh.

Without her knowing why, Ch'ien Shou-yü's mysterious feeling of satisfaction on the "recovery of the Concession" expanded, and she felt that her body was as light as a cloud, that it almost floated. Ch'ien Shou-yü's face flushed, and she despised herself for this shallow attitude of revenge which took pleasure in the difficulties of others. But she had no means of eradicating the feeling. The feeling eroded her intelligence, and even made her disbelieve that one and one equalled two.

Madness—she understood why a person could slip down into madness.

And she understood also how the feelings of an individual, or of a crowd, cunningly utilized, as though by some devilish art, could produce whatever sort of mad behavior.

A very black shadow flashed before her eyes, and Ch'ien Shou-yü felt a little frightened. Her face turned from red to white; she stood up, and uneasily drank a cup of tea. In her heart she felt a chill.

Ch'ien Pen-san lighted a cigar, drew on it twice, and said as he looked uncertainly at Liu Shao-ch'iao:

"You people talk; I'm going inside to wash. I've been up since five and haven't stopped until just now."

"That's fine, you take a rest," Liu Shao-ch'iao responded.

Since matters were being handled so casually, Ch'ien Shou-yü relaxed slightly. But since she was already psychologically prepared, she didn't care. On the contrary, she coolly sat down, and watched to see how they would begin.

"Miss," Liu Shao-ch'iao said agreeably, all smiles, "there's a matter we've already discussed with Third Master, and he's willing. But Third Master feels that it needs your agreement as well."

"That depends on what it is." Ch'ien Shou-yü's tone already carried three parts of resistance.

"You'll never have guessed; it's a marriage." Liu Shao-ch'iao was deliberately mysterious.

Ch'ien Shou-yü said nothing, but took a banana-leaf fan from beneath the tea table and began to lightly fan herself.

"It's that we feel that Third Master is too busy at his work every day, and his life is too sedate; taking his age into account, he ought to have a little compensation. That's why we want to be a matchmaker for Third Master."

"A matchmaker for Papa?"

Ch'ien Shou-yü had all along felt that they wanted to be her matchmakers, and she had her response in mind; she was prepared to refuse at once. She had never imagined that their intentions were directed at Papa. She felt deeply shaken, and suddenly sat up straight, afraid that she hadn't heard right.

"Yes," Liu Shao-ch'iao and Pai Ch'a-hua answered together.

"But I have a Mama, she's back at our old home. How can Papa get married again?" Ch'ien Shou-yü couldn't help feeling a little angry. "Don't tell me this means taking a concubine?"

"This is a serious matter, don't you make jokes!" Pai Ch'a-hua snapped. "The Women's Association has forbidden taking concubines. As for those who've already become concubines, we're forcing them to leave one by one, and to marry someone else. How could we allow someone else to take a concubine?"

"Then, how?" Ch'ien Shou-yü truly didn't understand. "Would they both be treated as equals?"

"The Women's Association doesn't permit multiple wives; the one husband one wife rule must be strictly carried out." Pai Ch'a-hua, feeling that Ch'ien Shou-yü was lacking in candor, and was being deliberately obtuse, unconsciously raised her voice.

Liu Shao-ch'iao knew that Ch'ien Shou-yü would not necessarily be able to think it through, so he hastily said:

"Our plan is to ask Third Master and his original wife to get a divorce first, and then he can take a new one. Naturally afterwards his first wife must also remarry."

Ch'ien Shou-yü was convulsed, and a chill penetrated her four limbs. Calming herself, she said:

"Mr. Liu, I can't agree to his divorcing Mama. Papa doesn't like her, and he left her at home many years ago; she's suffered enough already. What's wrong with her that Papa has agreed to divorce her?"

"Third Master doesn't like her, the two of them have no feelings for each other, they can't live together, and they're vainly bearing an empty name; isn't that sufficient grounds for divorce?" Pai Ch'a-hua asked.

"That's where Papa has wronged her. She isn't the kind of low-class woman who can get a divorce and remarry!" Ch'ien Shou-yü felt greatly upset on her Mama's behalf.

"What?" Pai Ch'a-hua had truly stood all she could stand. "What kind of brain do you have, saying that a woman who divorces and remarries is low-class? Your thought is reactionary; you'd better be careful!"

"I certainly don't approve of his divorcing Mama!" Ch'ien Shou-yü would not retreat.

Liu Shao-ch'iao seized Pai Ch'a-hua and kissed her on the cheek, and then as he drew back his hand, he slapped her on the shoulder, and said in a familiar tone:

"Take it easy, darling, and wait 'til I explain it to her."

Ch'ien Shou-yü, seeing their performance, was even more mortified and angry. She stood up and would have gone, but Liu Shao-ch'iao seized her by the arm, and she heard him say:

"Miss, this should be a happy occasion, it's no good your being angry."

Ch'ien Shou-yü felt that his grip was quite strong, and knew she couldn't leave. She could only suppress her anger, and she perched on the rattan chair and turned her head away. She heard him continue:

"The matter's already been decided, and it's no use for you to oppose it. We came to tell you out of respect for Third Master's opinion. As for this so-called seeking your agreement, that's only a polite phrase. If you don't appreciate it, then forget it. I'll tell you again, so you'll understand: the announcement of the divorce has already been sent to the newspaper office, and it will be printed tomorrow morning."

"I'll go and withdraw it; I'll oppose it even if it kills me!" Ch'ien Shou-yü's words were even more determined.

"I'm telling you, you can't withdraw it, and I don't believe you'll try. I sent that announcement in the name of the Women's Association!" Pai Ch'a-hua said with a cold smile.

Alone and with nowhere to turn under this absolute and wicked power, Ch'ien Shou-yü, nursing a bellyful of injured feelings, gave herself to tears. She accepted defeat; for the first time she tasted a savage force, added to that pain in the head of the weak person who has no defenses whatsoever, and she comprehended the real reasons which gave rise to revolutions. What was strange was that the revolutionaries, after making revolutions against others, took the pains which they themselves had once suffered and laid them on another weak person's back, and scarcely realized they were sowing the seeds that would allow others to make revolution against them. Revolutions never ceased, and tragedies continued without pause; this was the genuine pain of human life.

Ch'ien Shou-yü wiped away her tears, and sighed a long sigh of utter helplessness.

Liu Shao-ch'iao and Pai Ch'a-hua looked at her coldly for some time, and then asked:

"Now do you understand?"

"No, I don't understand!" Ch'ien Shou-yü said recklessly. "Your insistence on breaking up their marriage is truly meaningless!"

"How is it meaningless? This is a declaration of war against an ancient system!" Liu Shao-ch'iao cried loudly in great excitement. "When the ancient system is beaten down, a new concept can arise, and then it can be spread about and accepted. That's what revolution is for!"

"But you don't necessarily have to start the operation in our family."

"Because Third Master is relatively progressive, he's most able to accept new concepts. Otherwise, why should we support him?"

"You're really doing it because he has weak points, and he can be taken advantage of! I know that in your hearts you despise him most of all." Ch'ien Shou-yü spoke plainly and without the slightest hesitation.

"There you've got it just wrong; we have the greatest respect for Third Master," Liu Shao-ch'iao patted his chest, and stuck up his thumb.

"What a mess this is," Ch'ien Shou-yü sighed sadly. "Certainly we want to beat down old systems and old concepts. But what harm have these old systems and old concepts really done you? They've been operating for several thousand years and I haven't heard anybody say a word against them."

Pai Ch'a-hua, without waiting for Ch'ien Shou-yü to finish, grew thoroughly impatient. She rolled up her sleeves, spat heavily upon the just-waxed wooden floor, knit her brows, and was just about to deliver a tirade. Liu Shao-ch'iao, realizing this, nudged her with his elbow and said:

"You sit down, and listen to me."

He turned to Ch'ien Shou-yü and said in a calm, even voice:

"Miss, you've brought up a fundamental question. Yes, it is necessary to ask: what are you people really after? That you could have such a question shows that you're not an ordinary person, and it wasn't in vain that you drank ink at the university."

"Thanks for your compliments, and it won't hurt for you to give me an explanation," Ch'ien Shou-yü said politely. "I'm glad to see that you can study questions coolly and objectively, and use intelligence to move people's hearts, but I'm still afraid that in your strength and power, you'll only know how to use violent means to force others to submit, or that you'll compel those of a different pattern to fit your pattern by 'cutting off what is too long to fill up what is too short', by 'cutting the foot to fit the shoe'."

"Miss," Pai Ch'a-hua burst out laughing, "this talk of yours is so pedantic that it's sour!"

"I forgot myself," Ch'ien Shou-yü said, also laughing, "because Mr. Liu complimented me on not having drunk the university's ink in vain."

"It just happens that I'm not afraid of sour things," Liu Shao-ch'iao said with a chuckle, "and I have my own way of dealing with these 'sourpusses'."

"What's a sourpuss?" Pai Ch'a-hua asked.

"A sourpuss, to use the new phrase that's going around, is an intellectual."

"Don't you want intellectuals?" Ch'ien Shou-yü asked.

"If they're willing to accept our new concepts, we want them."

"What are your new concepts?"

"We should take that up from what we were just talking about. First, you must understand why old systems have to be beaten down." Liu Shao-ch'iao drank a great gulp of iced tea, and frowned somberly as he said: "No mistake, this system has operated for several thousand years. But the results of its operation are before our eyes, and the reality which everyone can see is: a tiny minority of privileged people have grasped the capital and the land, and they cheat the great majority of poor people of their labor; they sit enjoying their wealth, and indulging their desires to the utmost. The poor people they've cheated spend their sweat and blood and never get to eat a full meal. And there isn't a one of those privileged people who got his capital and land by his own labor. They stripped it from others, they got it by underhanded tricks. This system protects that minority privileged class who specialize in robbing others; this system is a vampire, a death-warrant, to the broad majority of poor people. Besides, this system forces ever so many unhappy couples to maintain their status as husband and wife and to suffer for the rest of their lives and allows them no escape. This system also restricts countless young men and women who are in love, and forcibly separates them, leaving their hearts separated and forever suffering the pain of thinking of one another . . ."

"Perhaps what you say is right," Ch'ien Shou-yü said, interrupting Liu Shao-ch'iao. "But you use the methods of fighting force with force; change is change, but the question hasn't been resolved. For example, my Papa and Mama: how are they themselves willing to divorce? In forcing them, aren't you on the contrary causing them pain?"

"Their unwillingness is the result of many years of conforming to tradition, and the rights and wrongs of it are unclear. They are situated in a mood of confusion; it's most pitiable. Our first responsibility is to awaken them."

After washing, Ch'ien Pen-san had put on grass sandals, and when he came in from behind he made no sound. He stood outside the rear door of the sitting room for some time, listening, and blamed his daughter for arguing with Liu Shao-ch'iao. Because, argue back and forth as you might, they were always right, and finally if you didn't acknowledge that you were wrong, then there was some question about your thought; without doubt you must be a reactionary, who deserved to be locked up, or even to "disappear".

Ch'ien Pen-san had given no outward sign of it, but inwardly he had been tied up in knots on account of Old Fourth losing his freedom. He felt that although he was a Department Chief, he possessed no dignity, nor any face. In that case, what did the Department Chief's daughter count for? Wasn't it just asking for trouble to speak so recklessly? At least this once, let her put up with it!

Ch'ien Pen-san, after all, had experienced much and seen many things, and he understood the danger. He put on white cotton trousers and a Chinese-linen jacket, and came out, all smiles.

"What, haven't you come to an agreement yet?" he asked.

"We're just discussing a fundamental question," Liu Shao-ch'iao said.

"What fundamental questions does Shou-yü understand?" Ch'ien Pen-san sat down. "If you're talking about revolutionary theory, she doesn't know the first thing about that. Don't waste your efforts on her."

"No, she understands quite a bit."

"That's absolutely impossible, absolutely impossible!" Ch'ien Pen-san hastily changed the subject. "Have you come to an agreement on that matter yet?"

Ch'ien Shou-yü understood something of what her father meant, and regretted having openly argued with them in her anger, because she too knew that it was dangerous and without profit. So she said:

"I still don't know what kind of a partner they're seeking for Papa. I'm going to have to call that person Mama. If we can get together on the matter, then it's done."

"That hardly needs saying," Liu Shao-ch'iao, seeing Ch'ien Shou-yü's change of attitude, was delighted. "If they weren't a match we wouldn't introduce them. The person is Hung T'ung-yeh's Mama, one year younger than Third Master—"

"Forty-one this year?"

"Yes."

"That's not right. Chin-ling told me her mother is forty-six this year."

"She made a mistake, or you heard it wrong." Liu Shao-ch'iao seemed a little anxious. "She told me this herself, so it's absolutely reliable."

"A woman's age is secret; it's a riddle," Ch'ien Pen-san said loudly, with a smile. "We needn't pursue it."

"Listen to that!" Pai Ch'a-hua said, clapping her hands. "It's Third Master who sees things clearly—aren't forty-one and forty-six the same thing?"

"You can't just say that forty-one is the same as forty-six." Ch'ien Shou-yü truly couldn't stand this and started to scold the other.

Ch'ien Pen-san glared at her and said angrily:

"Forty-one is the same as forty-six; what do you understand?"

"All right, Miss," Liu Shao-ch'iao said, "you see that Third Master is a thousand and ten thousand times willing, so you too will surely approve."

"It's no use for me to oppose it," Ch'ien Shou-yü said with a bitter smile and a feeling of having been wronged.

Thus it was settled, and on the following day, at noon, Liu Shao-ch'iao would invite Ch'ien Pen-san and Mrs. Hung to their first meeting.

After they had seen off Liu Shao-ch'iao and Pai Ch'a-hua, father and daughter returned to the sitting room and sat down. Ch'ien Pen-san asked gently:

"Who's at home?"

"They've all gone out to see the excitement, and haven't come back."

"Go and shut the front gate."

"And when they come back?"

"When they come back, then open it again," Ch'ien Pen-san said with great impatience. "Such a little thing and you don't even understand it!"

Ch'ien Shou-yü hastily went and closed the gate, and then came back and sat down again. Ch'ien Pen-san reached out and shut off the electric fan, and then said seriously, in a quiet, calm voice, to his daughter:

"This is all just a farce, so you needn't oppose it. Divorce?" He gave a cold laugh. "What do I want with a divorce? If I wanted to, who could stop me from taking three wives and four concubines? Why do I need a divorce?

Remember your Mama is my wife, and there'll never be any mistake about that. Whether I like her or not is another matter, which is no one else's business. In order to deal with this situation, let them print whatever announcements they please—what do I care? As for that Hung woman, I'll be happy to marry her just for fun."

"Chin-ling and Fourth Uncle are engaged," Ch'ien Shou-yü said, pondering that point. "In the future, what shall we call each other? What kind of proprieties shall we have?"

"In the future?" Ch'ien Pen-san laughed coldly. "In the future—we'll see! In the present situation nobody can guarantee tomorrow. In the future maybe I'll get rid of her; in the future maybe your Fourth Uncle won't make it. We can't be certain of things in the future, so let's watch out as we go along."

"Suppose we take this opportunity to get Fourth Uncle out? How long do they mean to keep him locked up?"

"That's my idea exactly." Ch'ien Pen-san nodded cunningly. "Wait until she comes, and I'll have a way to get her to get Fourth Uncle out on her own, without our needing to ask for it."

"Don't you take her too lightly; maybe she's coming to keep an eye on you."

"Don't they have plenty of people to keep an eye on me? What's the use of keeping an eye on me?" Ch'ien Pen-san puffed incessantly on his cigar, and said: "Shou-yü, we two, father and daughter, can only rely on each other. If you'll obey me, and understand my meaning, then we can certainly get over this difficulty. I've always believed that I've got the strength to deal with the Communist Party. Just now I'm taking advantage of their strength to climb up, and to make my own position into something important. Wait 'til the right time comes, and I'll smash them down!"

"I only hope things can be peaceful. In man's life on this earth, too much doing makes for anxiety, and thinking doesn't mean anything." Ch'ien Shou-yü, without knowing why, felt sad. "I've studied education, and I believe in proceeding in an orderly manner, and in getting one's feet firmly on the ground: a measure of effort, a measure of gain. I don't know why but I've never cared much for 'good profit from desperate deeds' or 'taking a chance despite the danger'."

Seeing that his daughter was holding back her tears, Ch'ien Pen-san felt that he couldn't bear it. In the quiet of the night, as they faced each other by the light of the single lamp, he thought of his half a lifetime of sorrow. He had only one wife and one son, neither of whom pleased him; he had only this daughter, who was barely satisfactory, who occasionally said a few understanding words, which he supposed was a comfort. Ch'ien Pen-san felt that he was alone; he was placed in a boundless loneliness, and all at once he had lost his brother. Several minutes of silence passed, and then Ch'ien Pen-san said, as though talking to himself:

"We'll certainly get Fourth Uncle out. At first, I wasn't willing. Because—you know that temper of his—as soon as he gets out, he's sure to run off to Nanking. And if he goes, that's no good for me." He sighed deeply. "But now I don't care about all that; get him out first and then we'll see. Out of five brothers, there are only the two of us left. If I don't look out for him, who will?"

Ch'ien Shou-yü experienced a comfort and satisfaction she had never known before. It was the first time, within memory, that such emotion-laden words had come from her father's mouth. The tears she had been holding back flowed down at last, reflecting the glow of the lamp and sparkling like two strands of pearls.

Hearing someone knocking at the door, she stood up.

"When you see her tomorrow," Ch'ien Pen-san said anxiously, clutching his daughter's hand across the table, "act happy, and just be sure to call her Mama in a loud voice; be just as familiar as though you were really mother and daughter, and don't show any aloofness."

Ch'ien Shou-yü nodded, and started to weep again.

The meeting was quite lively after all. But Ch'ien Pen-san and Mrs. Hung each had other things on their minds. Neither temperament nor habits could be discerned from their outward appearances; one could only investigate by putting oneself in their place, and slowly groping forward. What remained, then, was only the outer form. Ch'ien Pen-san's original mate was a country woman, withered, dark, and lean, who sat forever on the low bench beside the fireplace, with her pipe in her mouth, gossiping about people. She would never see the larger world, nor would she appear before the public. On this account, Ch'ien Pen-san had always preferred ladies who were relatively tall, plump, light-skinned, and well-bred. Formerly, in Peking, Ch'ien Pen-san had been a frequent guest of the Eight Famous Lakes sing-song girl house. Nearly all the people of the house knew Third Master's temperament, and generally would introduce him to ladies of the "Yang Kuei-fei type".[45] He was never determined to amuse himself with a particular woman, for he liked to change partners frequently. His reasoning was that since a woman never made up her mind to receive only a single guest, why should a free-spending gentleman, who was only looking for a good time, settle for only one woman? Surely one wasn't really going to speak of love in a brothel?

Later on, when he was taking part in the revolution, he stopped going to the brothels. But his eye for beauty didn't change. He divided women, in general, into three major categories: small, clever, and beautiful; plump, white, and tall; and talented, learned, and ideal. He himself preferred the second category: plump, white, and tall.

---

[45] Yang Kuei-fei: the favorite concubine of the T'ang Dynasty emperor Ming Huang. Said to have been full-figured.

Officials in the Peiyang government paid great attention to acquiring their concubines. Actresses, drum-singers, prostitutes—as long as they suited one's taste, they'd be bought for great sums of money, brought in, and registered according to number (she was ninth concubine, thirteenth concubine, there was even a twenty-seventh concubine), and taken as one's possession. Although the saying was "taken as one's possession", except for being used now and then, she had her freedom. She could call on her girlfriends, play mahjongg, go to the theater, and amuse herself with actors, rickshaw men, military guards, junior officers, and even with the sons of her patron by his original wife whom he had left behind in the countryside. As long as they were able to deceive their masters, they could do as they pleased. Their patrons entertained outside, and when they called for girls to come to the banquet, they behaved quite differently, and they didn't bring their concubines along.

Upon arriving in Canton, Ch'ien Pen-san discovered the new manners of the Revolutionary Government. There they weren't interested in taking concubines, and women's rights were held in high esteem. When important men appeared in public, it was the fashion for them to be accompanied by their wives.

Ch'ien Pen-san had never thought of divorce, for that would have brought on many nameless difficulties. Preserving that empty name allowed her to go on living in the countryside. If only the other party were willing, when he had a chance he would marry her again. Surely a man like me was unlikely to be accused of the crime of bigamy? First of all, who would accuse me?

He kept calculating thusly: if there should really ever be such a day, surely she must be plump, white, and tall. Since he had extended his experience in Canton, and learned the direction of the tide, it was still such women that he wanted to take out and bring back. He went through a period of careful pondering, and then added to "plump, white, and tall" a new condition "talented, learned, and ideal".

As for this Mrs. Hung now, she was no more than one hundred and eight thousand *li* from Ch'ien Pen-san's ideal. There was simply no need to mention "plump, white, and tall". As for the "ideal", that was an ideal of beauty, and in a woman who was close to fifty, she was nothing more than middle-aged, and her refinement still remained, which perhaps should be prized because it was so difficult to find—but how could one speak of an ideal of beauty?

On this account, Ch'ien Pen-san was no longer concerned as to whether or not she was talented or educated; on the contrary that was that.

Since the May Fourth Movement the youth had been struggling for self-determination in love and marriage, and the movement had gradually been accepted by society; they had largely achieved their aims. Unexpectedly, at the age of forty-odd years, he himself, Ch'ien Pen-san thought, was now confronting the strange situation of being forced to divorce and forced to marry. And this was called a new concept, which must be unconditionally accepted. This was the progress of the times, and the results of the revolution.

Out of a kind of feeling of forced humor, Ch'ien Pen-san couldn't help laughing, a natural and genuine laugh.

"I toast Mrs. Hung."

He stood up, and raised the long-stemmed, translucent goblet. The clear yellow Shao-hsing wine seemed to flash with golden stars, as though winking with tempting, mysterious eyes. Mrs. Hung also stood up, raised her glass in the same fashion, and thanked him. She took a swallow, and sat down. The business of the second marriage was settled, and the partners in the second marriage were also settled, but Mrs. Hung was not at all used to the person across from her—this coarse fellow with half of his face shaved blue! Looking at Liu Shao-ch'iao's elegant features, Mrs. Hung felt aggrieved. She fixed her gaze upon Hung T'ung-yeh. It was as though she were rebuking him: you've offended your Mama!

After the gathering dispersed, Ch'ien Shou-yü found an opportunity to quietly exchange a few words with Hung Chin-ling in the bathroom.

"You see, what kind of carrying on is this?"

"Let it be, accept it," Hung Chin-ling said in a terrified voice. "They really do kill people; we can't offend them!"

"What about your and Fourth Uncle's engagement after this?"

"Afterwards, we'll see." Hung Chin-ling seized Ch'ien Shou-yü's arm. "Perhaps I can't marry Fourth Master!"

"Because of your mother?"

"Not entirely. I've really done something for which I must beg Fourth Master's pardon. Elder Sister, he asked me, several times, and I refused him."

"What was it?"

Hung Chin-ling looked at her, and then continued:

"What I mean is that I originally thought to wait until our wedding night. I meant well."

When she heard this, Ch'ien Shou-yü understood, and at once she almost blushed.

"But now I've already run into their wicked trick," Hung Chin-ling said bitterly. "If I had known before, I'd have been willing to give it to him. Now how can I have the face to see him?"

"There's nothing to be done about it. I know you were raped."

"Does being raped deserve to be forgiven?"

Hung Chin-ling smiled coldly, and then, hearing a sound outside, she raised a finger to her lips, and hurried out.

Ch'ien Shou-yü deliberately remained within for a while, and then came slowly out.

Chapter XX

On the day on which the announcement of Ch'ien Pen-san's divorce appeared in the newspapers, quite a few reporters came to interview him. Ch'ien Pen-san patiently saw them one by one. He expressed his opposition to the old-fashioned arranged marriage, and he advocated self-determination in love, and civilized marriage. Secretary Feng, who sat by his side to assist him with the interview, added:

"It's not civilized marriage; what the Department Chief means is free marriage."

"What's the difference?" one of the reporters asked.

"The opposite of civilized is barbaric." Secretary Feng looked up, and rapped lightly with his right hand on the table. "The old-fashioned arranged marriages were a kind of forced behavior, which is naturally barbaric. But the word civilized very easily makes a person think of the style of the wedding ceremony. For example, the old way was to have the bridegroom wear red flowers in his hair, and for the bride to wear the phoenix cap and cloud collar; the elders would lead them to worship the ancestors and bow to Heaven and Earth. Now, in keeping with the fashion, the bridegroom wears a swallow-tail coat, the bride wears silk, and they bow three times to each other. We often get a wrong impression, and consider that the civilized style is the civilization. Anyone with a mouth full of jargon and a bellyful of curses need only put on black formal dress and he's taken for a civilized person. This is a great mistake, a special mistake! The word freedom in its associations, generally carries the meaning of lack of form, of casualness, and even of absence of responsibility. Naturally, that is not the real meaning of freedom. But what Department Chief Ch'ien really meant to say was free marriage, and definitely not civilized marriage."

"Lack of form, relatively casual; that'll do." There was a reporter who still didn't understand, and who pursued: "No responsibility, did you say that in a free marriage the couple haven't any responsibility towards their marriage?"

"I said that it needn't be for a lifetime, as it was in the past. Since you can freely marry, you ought to be able to freely divorce as well."

Secretary Feng rubbed his lower lip, as though he couldn't fathom the question.

"Suppose we say it's free civilized marriage? If it's free, and also civilized, then both form and content are taken care of," Ch'ien Pen-san inquired of Secretary Feng.

"No, free is enough, there's no need for civilized," Secretary Feng said, wooden-faced.

"I really don't understand," another reporter, deeply anxious, said to this pedant of the propagandists.

"Such a little thing, and you still don't understand." Secretary Feng's whole face expressed his displeasure. "That's because there's a problem with your thought."

"I understand, I understand." The reporter hastily changed his tune. "Department Chief Ch'ien is getting this divorce to set an example, to advocate free divorce. Once free divorce becomes popular, then it will be easy to promote free marriage."

"No mistake, that's exactly it." Secretary Feng held up his thumb. "So we can say, Department Chief Ch'ien is not only a revolutionary theorist, he is also a thorough-going revolutionary activist, a great revolutionary theoretical activist!"

"Come, come," Ch'ien Pen-san said modestly, standing and bowing.

The reporters, with a great din, departed.

The next day the newspapers announced Ch'ien Pen-san's divorce with appropriate applause. It was praised as a heroic and grand revolutionary act without precedent in history, an act which destroyed the several thousand-year-old tradition of arranged and forced marriages contrary to human nature, an act which established the unalterable and eternal foundation for the new society's new marriage system of free marriages and free divorces. Because he proved the grand revolutionary theory in his own individual practice, and did not leave it in the realm of fancy, Department Chief Ch'ien Pen-san is a forerunner of our era!

Each paper alike went on in this vein. Although each paper had sent a reporter, for certain matters considered important the Propaganda Department sent out mimeographed sheets. Once these mimeographed drafts had been issued by the Propaganda Department, there was no longer any need for the reporters to move their pens. The editorial staffs in the same way were also saved effort, for they too had no need to move their pens; they could go ahead and issue the finished product, because both the major and minor headings had been provided. You couldn't add a word, nor could you take away a word. Every compositor was controlled by the Labor Union, and the Labor Union and the Propaganda Department were as one, cooperating perfectly. If you wanted to run a paper according to your own ideas, that was too bad!

Because it was given excessive prominence by the newspapers, the announcement of Ch'ien Pen-san's divorce gave rise to talk in the streets and discussion in the alleys. For the conservative element of social psychology, this was like hurling a bomb.

In fact, they still didn't know that the female party to this "divorce by mutual consent" was still in her home in the countryside, several thousand *li* away. Every day she crouched by the fireplace, working the bellows, and her eyes were reddened by the smoke. She gnawed sweet potatoes to get through the days, and she simply did not know that such an announcement of her divorce had appeared in the Hankow newspapers.

Barely had this earth-shaking affair quieted down, when it followed directly that Ch'ien Pen-san would marry the famous Miss Liang Yün-feng. Although the wedding was not much publicized, well-wishing guests filled the gates, and nearly every large and small personage in Wuhan attended the wedding. The various newspapers used entire sections to report the news. Since Ch'ien Pen-san was already a news personality with whom the masses were familiar, the reports concentrated upon the person of Miss Liang Yün-feng, and pointed out that she was the widow of the former revolutionary figure Hung Pai-li, that she was the granddaughter of the first-ranked metropolitan graduate from Nanking, Liang Shou-kuo, and that now she was the mother of Hung T'ung-yeh, an important figure in the Labor Union. This great revolutionary woman was carrying forward her heroic declaration of war on the cannibalistic old ethical system: she was remarrying!

The long-winded remarks of every committeeperson of the Women's Association were printed, and they unanimously expressed their praise for the remarriage of Miss Liang Yün-feng. They went on to develop this point, summoning all widows to imitate her and advance in her footsteps. The world was truly changing, and widows must all remarry.

Whether or not the revolution succeeds depends on whether or not widows are all willing to remarry!

Among the wedding guests was one rather special personage, and that was Mme. Anna Raymond. But as a Frenchwoman, she did not understand what was so startling about a widow's remarriage. Hung T'ung-yeh seized her hand and said:

"I'm happy for my mother."

"Yes," said Anna, without a clue, "you ought to be."

The bride's floor-length white wedding dress hid her rather large enlightened feet. The former wife's daughter, Ch'ien Shou-yü, kept stealing glances, and she felt that the relatively old-fashioned floor-length wedding dress was ever so gallant and attractive. Had the skirt been shorter, half of her leg would have been revealed, and it would certainly have looked rather cheap. Ch'ien Shou-yü, abashed, glanced at her own feet. Mme. Raymond, wearing a pair of white leather high-heeled shoes, was turning ahead of her, and Ch'ien Shou-yü, from behind, glanced at her.

Dressed up, Mrs. Hung seemed to have become at least ten years younger. No, from now on she was no longer Mrs. Hung, she was already of the Ch'ien family, she was Department Chief Ch'ien's wife, she was Mrs. Ch'ien. Ch'ien Pen-san felt that it was all a little strange. A year before, he'd had no idea he was to have such good fortune; usually when such strange things befell him, they caused his eyes to blur and gave him a headache.

But the feeling which this wedding brought him was wholly one of happiness. This new person, compared to his country wife, was certainly much better in both features and figure. Suddenly Ch'ien Pen-san remembered that when he was in Peking as a member of the Parliament, the former Foreign Minister Han Chia-t'an had a girl from a sing-song house who knew physiognomy, and once as a gift he had been given a reading. She said that after forty he would take a concubine. Who'd have thought that now it would be fulfilled after all? Just a girl from the brothel, and able to read physiognomy—if only he could thank her.

Ch'ien Pen-san laughed easily, a satisfied, natural laugh. Ch'ien Shou-yü, seeing this, pursed her lips and turned her head away.

Liu Shao-ch'iao, who had drunk until his face was red, came lurching over.

"Miss, this is an auspicious day, so just go over and drink a cup to your Papa and your new Mama."

He took hold of her arm. Ch'ien Shou-yü broke away, and said, all smiles: "I've already toasted enough."

"Won't do, I haven't seen you, so it doesn't count."

"I really have toasted them. If you don't believe it, go and ask them."

"Well, toast them once more."

"That's right, toast them once more," Secretary Feng added. "When Papa takes a new Mama, it's an occasion for great rejoicing."

Ch'ien Shou-yü, feeling a bit irritated, made no further reply, but raised her winecup to her father.

"Third Master," Liu Shao-ch'iao called out in a deliberately loud voice. "Your daughter is offering a toast to you, and to your wife."

Secretary Feng hastily fetched Hung T'ung-yeh and Hung Chin-ling.

"Go on, go on, go on and toast your Mama and your new Papa."

The guests' attention was now concentrated on the scene.

Ch'ien Shou-yü raised her cup before her father. Ch'ien Pen-san looked embarrassed. He said nothing, and took a drink of wine. He was thinking:

"The girl's too old; it's really inconvenient. Although they say there's nothing wrong with taking a concubine, still this business today is really inviting ridicule."

When it was Hung T'ung-yeh's turn, Ch'ien Pen-san hastily stood up and lifted his cup, saying:

"It's I who should drink to you; please forgive me."

"No, Third Master, I'm toasting you," Hung T'ung-yeh said.

"You can't call him Third Master any more, he's your new Papa," Secretary Feng said loudly.

"No, no, that's too much!" Ch'ien Pen-san said, and fearing that it would get even more complicated, he quickly stretched his neck and drank down the wine. Afterwards, in a low voice, he told Hung T'ung-yeh:

"Can I trouble you to call the Hotel France for me, and reserve a room for me?"

"Why?"

"Tonight we're staying out, and we're not going back, so as to avoid quarrels," Ch'ien Pen-san said with a smile. "Don't tell anyone else."

Hung T'ung-yeh understood; he nodded, and went off.

At the urging of the crowd, Hung Chin-ling also drank a toast. Her mother, the bride, seeing her daughter's eyes full of tears, felt a little aggrieved in her own heart. She touched her lips to the cup and then put it down. Then she took her daughter's hand, but she did not know what to say.

The dignitaries sat for a time for form's sake, and then they left. Those who remained belonged to the glorious ranks of the Labor Union and the Women's Association. The wine tables were set up on the verandah outside the reception hall, and in the open air of the courtyard, and the singing and shouting combined to make a great din. Everyone fought to drink toasts to the newlyweds. Pai Ch'a-hua cried in a loud voice:

"Let the bridegroom drink a skin-cup toast to the bride!"

"What's a skin-cup?" asked someone who didn't understand.

"That's passing it from mouth to mouth," Pai Ch'a-hua explained.

"Oh-ho, how could I do that?" Ch'ien Pen-san said with a nervous laugh. "Committeewoman Pai, you'll have to excuse me."

"You're a Department Chief, and you can't even do such a little thing?" Pai Ch'a-hua said, disregarding him. "Wait 'til I teach you—look, it's like this."

Pai Ch'a-hua smoothly put out her hand and seized a familiar worker who was standing beside her. The worker was taller than she by a couple of heads, his cheeks were covered with whiskers, and his whole face was greasy. Pai Ch'a-hua ordered him:

"Sit down here!"

The worker, mystified, sat down on the designated chair. Pai Ch'a-hua took a great mouthful of wine, seated herself on the worker's legs, turned about, and placing both hands on the sides of his face, she pressed his head back so that he was looking at the sky. Pai Ch'a-hua leaned forward, put her lips to the worker's lips, and with a snorted sound—"*heng, heng*"—ordered him to open his mouth. Then she poured forth her mouthful of wine. The worker, taken by surprise, nearly coughed.

Everyone exclaimed in amazement, and there were sharp cries. One worker, excessively excited, leaped onto the round table, breaking the table-top with a loud sound, and smashing all the cups and dishes on the table. He too fell head over heels and hit his forehead, drawing blood.

A woman worker saw this and quickly helped him sit up, as she gave him a skin-cup of wine mouth to mouth and stroked his cheeks, saying:

"It doesn't hurt, it doesn't hurt, my good boy, don't cry."

This also drew a burst of laughter.

"Committeewoman Pai, Committeewoman Pai!" A worker who would not be repressed pushed forward to call out: "Give me a skin-cup too!"

"Roll on out of here!"

Pai Ch'a-hua pushed him forcefully, and he stepped back, and happened to bump into Hung Chin-ling. His vision blurred by drink, he seized Hung Chin-ling and began to kiss her wildly. Her mother, the bride, seeing her daughter in such distress, came over and pulled at the worker. The worker then released the daughter and grabbed the mother about the waist.

"Get him off her!" Pai Ch'a-hua yelled.

Then people came up and pulled the worker away, and dragged him outside. Confused cries diminished. Pai Ch'a-hua thrust a cup of wine into Ch'ien Pen-san's face, and squinting until her eyes were mere wrinkles, she said with a giggle:

"You've learned from me, now drink a skin-cup toast to your new wife!"

"Pardon me," said Ch'ien Pen-san with a laugh, standing up. "I couldn't learn that, that's a game for you young people."

"A revolutionary is forever young; you can't plead your age."

Pai Ch'a-hua came over and raised the cup of wine to Ch'ien Pen-san's lips. Ch'ien Pen-san looked in embarrassment at his bride, at his daughter Shou-yü, at Hung Chin-ling, and then involuntarily retreated two steps backward. Wringing his hands, he said:

"Committeewoman Pai, let me trouble you to represent me in toasting her."

"You can't delegate this business!"

"You can't delegate it, you can't delegate it!" The crowd of men and women guests who were watching the excitement cried.

"Department Chief," Secretary Feng said, "loosen up a bit."

"If you won't do it, I will!" The speaker was Liu Shao-ch'iao. He took a mouthful of wine, took the bride's head in both hands, and put his face to hers. The bride struggled to escape, and shut her lips tightly, unwilling to open them. Liu Shao-ch'iao could not back down, and at once growing angry, he spat the mouthful of wine into her face and shoved her away. The bride fell backwards, and those near her hastily helped her get up. Unable to bear it any longer, the bride covered her face and wept. The wine spat by Liu Shao-ch'iao mingled with the tears flowing down her face.

Hung Chin-ling, seeing her Mama so mistreated, began to sob hysterically.

The guests immediately broke into a confused discussion, criticizing this and carping about that, and everyone blamed the newlyweds for not being sufficiently revolutionary. Secretary Feng, shaking his head, said:

"It simply won't do; it's really not easy to reform a petty bourgeois!"

Amid sighs of disappointment, the guests dispersed. Hung T'ung-yeh had just returned and didn't know that the wedding banquet had already broken up. He drew near to Ch'ien Pen-san and quietly said a few words, and Ch'ien Pen-san nodded, and thanked him. He helped the bride outside, saying:

"Don't cry, it's no use crying, come along with me."

Hung Chin-ling was about to follow them. Hung T'ung-yeh called to her:

"Chin-ling, don't you go! It's their wedding night, what are you going to do?"

Hung Chin-ling halted, not knowing what to do. Her Mama, the bride, said:

"You come with me, it doesn't matter."

"It's no matter, brother T'ung-yeh, let her come with us," Ch'ien Pen-san added.

Hearing such words from her new husband, the remarried bride felt an unequalled warmth, and received an unexpected comfort. She looked up at his coarse face, took her daughter's hand, and went on out.

"Elder Sister? How is it I don't see Elder Sister?" Hung Chin-ling said, stopping and looking back.

"Come on, hurry up," Ch'ien Pen-san said. "I know about her."

They had already reserved a car. Hung Chin-ling meant to sit beside the driver, but her Mama, the bride, pulled her into the back seat, and told her to sit in the middle. Hung Chin-ling, squeezed in between the newlyweds, felt that she was a little waxen-faced. With the greatest uneasiness, she kept saying apologetically:

"Excuse me, excuse me!"

This made the newlyweds smile. The bride reached over, and pinched her cheek, and said intimately:

"Are you joking?"

"Third Master," Hung Chin-ling said, turning her head, "I've enjoyed the warmth of your household, and I've depended on Mama, I only hope I can always have such freedom."

Ch'ien Pen-san pouted his lips forward, and made a sign with his eyes to Hung Chin-ling, for the driver was a member of the Labor Union, and he wanted Hung Chin-ling to be careful what she said. At the same time, he said:

"Relax, there's no problem with me. I won't mind if you and your Mama are close."

So everyone smiled, and even the driver smiled with them.

In the room at the Hotel France, Ch'ien Pen-san took off his upper garments, and facing the window which opened toward the river, he drew a long sigh, thinking: "Miss Hung said it right: if only I could always enjoy such freedom."

"Chin-ling," he said, turning, "call the house, and see if Elder Sister is there or not. Just now when they were bothering me about the wine, I saw her get angry and leave. She had nowhere else to go. If she's at home, tell her to hurry and come over here; I'll rent another room for the two of you, and we'll all stay here tonight."

Hung Chin-ling agreed. Ch'ien Pen-san, having seen her go out, sat down before his new wife, and said with a sigh:

"I feel I must really beg your pardon for what happened. Liu Shao-ch'iao has such a hot temper. When he insulted you, it was the same as insulting me."

The new wife blushed, and forced a smile. She watched him take out a cigar, and bite off the sharp end. She struck a match and lighted it for him.

Ch'ien Pen-san inhaled, said "Thank you," and casually pinched his new wife on the thigh. Although it was not a completely sensual gesture, still Ch'ien Pen-san, who had been as though single for a long time, felt a kind of light giddiness.

"Are you friendly with Liu Shao-ch'iao?" the new wife asked in the lowest of voices.

"We have business dealings," Ch'ien Pen-san said, very carefully and hesitantly. "I've had business dealings with him all along."

"Then you're not friends?"

"Enh, enh . . . ."

"Since you and he aren't friends, it would be well if you could keep your distance from him a little," the new wife said in an abashed tone. "These last two years he's injured everyone in my family."

"But," Ch'ien Pen-san hemmed and hawed for a moment, and then said seriously but gently: "T'ung-yeh and he get along well; their friendship is out of the ordinary."

"T'ung-yeh drank his bewitching soup early on, I know. Now Chin-ling and I are the enemies they've destroyed."

Feeling that conversation represented an opportunity, Ch'ien Pen-san moved his chair a little closer, and while his left hand held his cigar, his right hand clutched tightly his new wife's skinny hand. The new wife felt that this coarse hand of her new husband's was strong, and hot, and her other hand came to rest on the back of his hand. Finally, her tears glittered brilliantly as she earnestly said:

"I know that Elder Sister Shou-yü and Chin-ling get on well, and that Chin-ling and Fourth Master have an oral agreement to be engaged. If you don't find the two of us, mother and daughter, too tiresome, and you could look after us, that would be well."

"That goes without saying!" Ch'ien Pen-san was delighted to hear this, and spontaneously exclaimed in a loud voice: "Could there be anybody in the world closer than husband and wife?"

Chin-ling had gone to make the phone call, and soon Ch'ien Shou-yü arrived. The four of them discussed Ch'ien Pen-ssu. Ch'ien Pen-san said:

"So far no one knows where they've got him locked up, but he's certainly there. Because on several occasions I've received short notes reporting his well-being, written in his own hand, and no mistake."

"If T'ung-yeh is willing to listen to his Mama's words," Ch'ien Shou-yü said, looking at her new Mama, "perhaps you can ask them to let him go."

"I'll try," the new Mama said, obviously troubled. She glanced at Chin-ling. "Liu Shao-ch'iao considers Fourth Master a personal enemy, it's got nothing to do with T'ung-yeh."

"You estimate the situation, and do what you can," Ch'ien Pen-san said. He yawned, and added: "This day has really been tiring enough!"

Liu Shao-ch'iao's divorce announcement also appeared in the papers.

Pai Ch'a-hua, in her capacity as Committeewoman of the Women's Association, took several corpswomen of the Labor Corps with her to the Liu family textile shop. Old Mr. Liu and Old Second just happened to be sitting at the cashier's table. They were stunned to see Pai Ch'a-hua appear. They had long understood the powerful position occupied by Pai Ch'a-hua, and they often recalled her bold deed in slaughtering the Yeh family of Changsha. Now, as though by unspoken agreement, they respectfully got to their feet, nurturing a helpless fear and awe.

Old Mr. Liu was after all the more experienced, and hastily saluting her with folded hands, he said:

"Committeewoman Pai, how nice that you've come. Welcome, welcome."

"We're looking for Yeh P'in-hsia."

"All right," Old Mr. Liu said to Old Second. "Quickly, go and tell your elder brother's wife to come."

Old Second hurried off to the rear of the house. Pai Ch'a-hua surveyed the condition of the shop, and saw that most of the shelves were empty. She laughed coldly, and said:

"What, your goods have all been taken up?"

As she spoke, she was off, close behind Old Second towards the rear of the house.

Yeh P'in-hsia was in the kitchen, washing bowls. Her hair was dishevelled and loose, and she was wearing blue cotton trousers and a white cotton dress. She had leather slippers on her bare feet.

"P'in-hsia," Old Second said coldly. "Someone's looking for you."

Yeh P'in-hsia wiped her dirty hands on a rag, and was just going to ask, when she saw that it was Pai Ch'a-hua. "Oh!" she exclaimed, and didn't know what to say.

Pai Ch'a-hua came up and took her hand, and smiling all over her face, said:

"P'in-hsia, are you well? When I see you in this get-up, doing this kind of work, I know that you've made great progress. Excellent—people must work! I always said you had a future, and that there was hope for you."

"Thank you, Sister Pai." Yeh P'in-hsia forced a smile.

"No, P'in-hsia, don't call me sister, I'd like you to still call me Pai Ch'a-hua. Outside, everyone calls me Committeewoman Pai, or Bureau Chief Pai, but you needn't."

"Oh, Committeewoman Pai!"

"All right, never mind that. Come, we'll sit outside. I've something else to tell you."

As she spoke, she led Yeh P'in-hsia into a small sitting room behind the shop front. Old Second followed, turned on the electric light, and then went to fetch tea. Ever since they'd joined the Labor Union, the clerks and apprentices had stopped pouring tea and serving at the table, so Old Second and Yeh P'in-hsia had had to assume that job. Wei Wen-shu, since her husband had already been released, and she could see that the Liu's business was going downhill, had long since quit. At first they still had a cook, who prepared tea, rice, wine, and dishes, and who looked after everything very well. Later on the cook joined the Labor Union, and came back to the house to let fly a great blast of temper, scolding them and saying:

"We're all human beings, so why do I fix your food? Why do you want me to fix the food you eat? This world is too hateful!"

So he issued an order: Yeh P'in-hsia should be the cook, and bear on her shoulders the burden of life in the kitchen. He then had nothing to do. Food came to his mouth and tea to his lips, and every day he sat in front of the shop, watching women pass by and humming a little tune.

Next came equal sharing of the cash proceeds, and he got his share of that. With a little money in his wallet, he was even more satisfied, and often praised the way the Labor Union managed things, raising the leaders of the Labor Union as high as the heavens.

"There isn't one good thing in this whole den! Who'd have thought the old dog would produce a tiger cub and finally bring forth a Liu Shao-ch'iao?"

Sitting in front of the shop, he would laugh aloud.

"Liu Shao-ch'iao is an outstanding fellow! A real hero!"

Old Mr. Liu and Old Second, hearing this remark, looked at one another, at a loss. They could only bow their heads and go, furious, but unable to do anything about it.

Liu the Second's tung oil was sold in the spring, and as a result he earned a great profit. Unfortunately, by that time his business had already come under the labor-capital joint management system, and equal sharing of cash proceeds also was in effect. Half of the money went to the workers, and the workers took it and spent it as they pleased. But on his part it was neither so convenient, nor so free. The Labor Union ordered him to use the money as capital to buy more stock, and to share the proceeds once again.

At that time, the shelves in the Liu family textile shop were not yet entirely empty, and proved after all more reliable than Liu the Second's tung oil. The foundation was thick, and slow to be exhausted, and so it was; indeed, there was no other supernatural explanation.

After Pai Ch'a-hua had drawn Yeh P'in-hsia into the little sitting room to sit down, she called in Old Mr. Liu and Old Second as well. Then she opened the newspaper and showed them the announcement of Liu Shao-ch'iao's divorce.

The three of them remained coldly silent.

"Those two haven't the right to speak," Pai Ch'a-hua said to Yeh P'in-hsia, waving her hand at Old Mr. Liu and Old Second. "You should read it clearly."

"I've already read it," Yeh P'in-hsia said casually.

"What do you think of it?" Pai Ch'a-hua asked at once.

"I don't have any opinion."

"That won't do." Pai Ch'a-hua immediately seemed to grow a little impatient. "You certainly must have an opinion!"

"I agree to the divorce," Yeh P'in-hsia said with a smile.

"Splendid." Pai Ch'a-hua pounded the table and said in a loud voice: "You're really a progressive element, you've got the revolutionary spirit! P'in-hsia, you've really changed for the better; I admire you!"

"Not at all, not at all. I only recognize the situation. If I didn't agree to it now, what do you think would happen to me?"

"That's also valuable, that's understanding the present conditions." Pai Ch'a-hua rolled her sleeves up high, and then changed the direction of the conversation. "But, P'in-hsia, according to the ways of the Women's Association now, divorced wives are the same as widows, they both have to marry. If you don't marry on your own, we'll choose someone for you by lot."

"I can marry on my own." Yeh P'in-hsia, frightened by the prospect of drawing lots, hastily said: "Committeewoman Pai, I can certainly marry on my own."

"You're limited to three days. If you haven't gotten married within three days, you must go to the Women's Association to draw lots."

Yeh P'in-hsia didn't know what to say. In the midst of her anxiety, she heard Liu the Second interject:

"Committeewoman Pai, we don't need three days, we can settle it right now. P'in-hsia and I will get married, is that all right with you?"

Pai Ch'a-hua had never imagined that Liu the Second would make such a move. She said:

"P'in-hsia, what do you think of this?"

"I'm willing," Yeh P'in-hsia said without the slightest embarrassment. "Second Brother and I will get married, so let's hurry up and announce it in the papers, and tomorrow we'll have the ceremony. Committeewoman Pai, please be our witness, and invite Shao-ch'iao to come to the house to drink some wedding wine."

"You can't go on like this!" Old Mr. Liu could stand it no longer, and stood up, saying: "P'in-hsia, Old Second, what are you doing? How can you do this?"

"Why can't they do it?" Pai Ch'a-hua fixed her eyes on him and said fiercely: "Are you opposing it? If you're opposing it, then we'll give you P'in-hsia for your wife! You've lived alone for many years, you ought to take part in drawing lots too!"

"No, no!" Old Mr. Liu was so frightened that his face turned the color of earth, and he hastily said: "I don't oppose it, I don't oppose it, it's best if the two of them do get married."

The clerks had gathered around the door to watch the excitement, and came crowding in to congratulate Yeh P'in-hsia and Old Second, and discuss how to manage the next day's wedding. The cook who didn't prepare food said:

"Committeewoman Pai, you're always playing the Old Man in the Moon,[46] why aren't you married yourself?"

"I'm an advocate of polyandry," Pai Ch'a-hua smiled lightly. "I've got several tens of husbands; which one do you want me to marry?"

These words made everyone laugh. A happy and lively atmosphere filled the Liu family shop.

But Old Mr. Liu felt that he couldn't support himself. He dragged his weakened body to the wall and leaned against it, and went to one of the side rooms in the back to lie down and rest. He could not believe his eyes, and he could not believe his ears: surely what he had seen and heard could not be real? Madness and license mingle together—am I dreaming or not?

Could even such a person as Yeh P'in-hsia have changed? The more he thought, the more confused he became.

No mistake, Yeh P'in-hsia's ready acceptance had been unanticipated even by Pai Ch'a-hua. The credit, as Pai Ch'a-hua analyzed it on the way back, ought to be given that blazing demonstration when the whole Yeh family died at her hands. That demonstration firmly established her authority; she caused people to look at her and hold her in awe, so that her mere reputation intimidated people. Pai Ch'a-

---

[46] Yüeh Lao, the Old Man in the Moon, is the matchmaker in traditional Chinese fairy tales. He ties together the life-strings of couples destined to wed.

hua realized, in a vague way, the reason why, in a time of revolutionary disorder, many things cruel beyond people's imagination could yet happen.

That had its repressive function.

At the end of the street, leaning against a telephone pole, was the naked corpse of a woman. Both breasts had been cut away, and the lower part was stuffed with clumps of rice-straw, which had already been set afire. Not far away there was another, this one with a wooden stake instead of rice-straw.

—Such scenes as this Pai Ch'a-hua had already witnessed. Thinking back on it, she still felt a little remaining fear.

"That's how men vent their abnormalities," Pai Ch'a-hua thought. "In times of disorder it's generally the women who suffer, and I'm a woman. I'm not content to be weak; I want to vent my feelings on men!"

Nursing this feeling of having won victory in a struggle, Pai Ch'a-hua told Liu Shao-ch'iao of the results of her meeting. Pai Ch'a-hua still thought that Liu Shao-ch'iao did not know to express his delighted acceptance, and would never have imagined that as soon as he heard it, he would get angry.

"How can it be? You're too muddled!"

"Was I wrong?" Pai Ch'a-hua asked, startled.

"Of course you were wrong!"

"Why?"

"How can she marry Old Second?"

"Since you've divorced her, she can marry whomever she wants to marry; what's it to you?" Pai Ch'a-hua felt that it was very funny.

"She can marry anyone at all, but she can't marry Old Second, I hate Old Second."

"Oh, so it's harming public interests for the sake of private!" Pai Ch'a-hua said with a cold laugh. "This isn't the attitude that you as a leader of the Labor Union ought to have. Yeh P'in-hsia marrying Old Second is a case of the younger brother's wife marrying husband's elder brother; it's the best kind of a blow against the old ethics, and the kind of propaganda material that's hard to find nowadays—but you don't approve of it!"

"I don't approve of it!" Liu Shao-ch'iao wouldn't discuss it with her.

Pai Ch'a-hua looked at him, and for some time said nothing. She thought a bit, and then suddenly burst out laughing.

"What's so funny?" Liu Shao-ch'iao was even more impatient.

"I was thinking," Pai Ch'a-hua said mildly, "her marriage to Old Second, from our point of view, really isn't too ideal."

"Ah, so you recognize it too."

"There's someone who would be even more ideal."

"Who?"

"Your Papa. If the daughter-in-law was given in marriage to her father-in-law, then her original husband would have to call his divorced wife Mama—that would be even more provocative!" Pai Ch'a-hua said as excitedly and happily as though she had discovered a new continent.

"I'm willing for her to marry Papa but I don't approve of her marrying Old Second."

"But just now I gave them permission, and I must maintain my authority," Pai Ch'a-hua said, wooden-faced. "This is the business of the Women's Association. The Labor Union needn't bother with it."

"The Women's Association is also under the authority of the Labor Union!" Liu Shao-ch'iao said loudly, coming forward, as droplets of his spittle sprayed Pai Ch'a-hua's face.

Pai Ch'a-hua suddenly stood up and fled outside, saying:

"I'm going back to call a meeting, and I'll ask the Party Committee to examine your case. You mustn't harm the public interest with your private interests; you're counterrevolutionary!"

"Let the Party Committee show its face!" Liu Shao-ch'iao was still not giving in. "I still oppose her marrying Old Second!"

Although that was what he said, the Women's Association exerted pressure, and Pai Ch'a-hua obtained the full support of the Party Committee in the dispute, while Liu Shao-ch'iao got a "reprimand". Thus, on the evening of the following day, the wedding took place as scheduled at the Liu family textile shop. Since the tung oil had been sold, the big store-room in the rear was empty, and now it served as a wedding hall. Wedding guests, chief among them committee members of the Women's Association, and the Labor Union, filled the entire store-room.

Liu Shao-ch'iao, under Party compulsion, also attended the wedding, called Yeh P'in-hsia "Aunty", and drank a toast.

Old Mr. Liu, ill as he was, also came out. He was considered the person in charge of the wedding, and was expected to thank the guests. In his heart he was completely opposed to the marriage, but he dared not show this. But afterwards he relented a little, and felt that it was well for Old Second and Yeh P'in-hsia to be joined. They were the two people he loved most, and with Old Second's ability, and with such a good helpmate as P'in-hsia, perhaps in their hands the Liu family reputation might be revived and past prosperity restored.

"How odd that P'in-hsia was willing to marry Old Second," Old Mr. Liu thought. He felt somewhat uneasy on P'in-hsia's behalf, but he couldn't help feeling that Old Second had been very lucky, and between these contradictions he obtained some comfort.

Pai Ch'a-hua's affair had been handled so smoothly, with even Liu Shao-ch'iao having gotten the worst of it at her hands, that her gall grew bigger and bigger, and she no longer had any doubts. Even as the drama of Yeh P'in-hsia's divorce and remarriage was being portrayed and boasted of in the propaganda, the affair of Commander Ko's residence arose.

Commander Ko's residence was right next door to Pai Ch'a-hua's on a certain lane. Commander Ko was responsible for protecting the section of the railroad from Hankow to Hua-yüan, and he controlled three divisions, but in fact he was afraid that in men and rifles he had no more than three regiments. The Commander's headquarters were at Hua-yüan, and the Commander usually stayed there.

The Commander's widowed mother lived in his Hankow residence. She was over sixty, and although her bound feet made walking inconvenient, she was sharp of ear and keen of eye, and her body was still very vigorous. Besides the mother, there was also the Commander's wife, and his son and daughter. In addition the Commander had a concubine, who had formerly been one of Old Mistress' maids. Old Mistress liked her, and was unwilling to marry her off, so she gave her to her son as a concubine. According to the custom in their native place, many of the farming families would take concubines in order to supplement their labor power. Such a concubine's greatest use was in working; she was a tool of production, and entirely different in nature from the concubine of a powerful and wealthy family. The former was a slave in different guise; the latter was a plaything: one side by means of wealth and influence, and the other by means of beauty, mutually used each other; animal lust and greed were exchanged to mutual satisfaction. The Commander's concubine belonged to the former category. Because of the Commander's connections, everyone addressed her respectfully as the concubine, but in fact she was a kitchen maid, and the Commander didn't like her.

Old Mistress was fond of playing mahjongg, and sat at the mahjongg table every day.

The Commander's wife was a virtuous woman, wholeheartedly devoted to raising her son and daughter.

Because of this, the concubine was in fact the manager of the household. Early each morning she would take up the basket and go out to buy vegetables.

Pai Ch'a-hua had long known that a military commander's family lived on the other side of the wall, and she had also encountered the woman who was on the street daily. At first, Pai Ch'a-hua had considered her one of their servants. One day, she had deliberately hailed her, and in the course of some pleasant conversation on the street, learned the truth about her.

The concubine had heard of the Women's Association, and had been in awe of Pai Ch'a-hua's reputation. She was good-natured, and not inclined toward the revolution, nor did she greatly marvel at the deeds of the Women's Association. But in order to attract attention, she said that she was the Commander's concubine. Her motive was to glorify herself, and to raise her own status, so that this famous Pai Ch'a-hua wouldn't look down upon her.

Who could have known that this was a mistake?

Pai Ch'a-hua took several workers and visited Commander Ko's residence.

When Old Mistress heard that it was Committeewoman Pai of the Women's Association, she was puzzled. She quickly rose from the mahjongg table. The Commander's wife came out also, and the concubine as well, and everyone expressed their welcome.

"Commander Ko, the revolutionary army man!" Pai Ch'a-hua said. "Wonderful! Who doesn't respect him?"

"Committeewoman Pai is truly polite," Old Mistress said uneasily.

"But whoever is a revolutionary army man ought to set an example. So I've come especially today to notify Old Mistress and the concubine to hurry and get married on your own—there's a three-day time limit. After three days, you'll have to come to the Women's Association to choose a mate by drawing lots."

"What did you say?" Old Mistress was confused, and afraid she hadn't heard it clearly.

"Every widow and concubine must get married, no matter who they are," Pai Ch'a-hua said clearly, in a loud voice.

"My son is a Commander . . ." Old Mistress was so angry she couldn't speak.

"I was willing to be the Commander's concubine," the concubine tried urgently to explain.

"If the Commander doesn't set an example himself, he's a counterrevolutionary!" Pai Ch'a-hua made plain her resolution.

"Counterrevolutionaries must be beaten down!" The several women members of the Labor Corps who had accompanied Pai Ch'a-hua said at once, striking their breasts.

It was the Commander's wife who had the sense to see that nothing would come of such an argument. With a pleasant expression, she said:

"Committeewoman Pai needn't be anxious; aren't we all for the revolution? Didn't you say the limit was three days? Let Committeewoman Pai go back, and within three days we'll certainly have found a way. Please don't worry about it."

"Very well, that's the kind of talk. You encourage them, and don't let them be obstinate."

Pai Ch'a-hua stood up to leave, and the Commander's wife saw her out, with some more polite talk.

The Commander's wife was afraid that neither letters, telegrams, nor messengers could be relied upon, for a single slip would ruin everything. She calmed Old Mistress and the concubine, and she rode the train to Hua-yüan in person.

The next day Commander Ko, accompanied by his wife, returned to Hankow. Old Mistress, in her rage, was already sick in bed. She wouldn't eat or drink. Commander Ko comforted his mother, and went immediately to see Commander-in-chief T'ang. When T'ang received the report, he was furious.

"What kind of talk if this? This is pushing people too far!"

At once he took Commander Ko to see Wang. Wang was also enraged, and ordered the dissolution of the Women's Association. But T'ang said:

"The problem isn't with the Women's Association. This is the problem of the Communist Party, and also the problem of our whole work-style. This problem also involves the basic problem of 'cooperation between the Kuomintang and the Communist Party'."

Wang said nothing.

That day T'ang sent his personal bodyguard corps to escort Commander Ko's whole household to Hua-yüan.

At the same time he warned that if the families of military officers were bothered again, he would not hesitate to take action.

Not long thereafter, the so-called "*Ma-jih* Incident" took place in Hunan. Hsü K'o-hsiang, with one regiment, dispersed the Peasants' Association, dispersed the Labor Union, dispersed the Women's Association, and with a puff of air dispersed the supposedly 700,000 man strong Peasants' Self-defense Army like a drifting cloud.

Wuhan blustered and cursed Hsü K'o-hsiang "until his dog's blood squirted from his head".

But such cursing could only vent a moment's anger, it could not solve the problem. Wuhan, at that time, was completely surrounded, and as the circle grew smaller and smaller, Wuhan found it more and more difficult to breathe.

Thus, unless they could break out, it was plain that they were done for.

One way was the "Eastern Campaign" with Nanking as the target. One way was the "Northern Expedition" with Peking as the target. The third route was to return their forces to Kwangtung and Kwangsi, restore the old base, and wait for a chance to move.

But every way depended on military strength. And with matters as they were, there were no military units willing to risk danger with no confidence of success, or become nameless sacrifices for this storm-buffeted regime. Everyone looked on, and everyone husbanded his strength.

The military units controlled by the Communist Party were too few, and still immature.

Wang and the Communist Party had originally been able to use each other. But as the Communist Party's arrogance became excessively blatant, Wang's utility was correspondingly diminished.

Wang felt the disadvantages of his position.

So he sought reconciliation with Nanking, hoping to break out of this disintegrating situation.

He dispatched secret envoys.

Nanking's response was favorable.

He then decided to "break with the Communists".

Chapter XXI

Ch'ien Shou-yü and Hung Chin-ling slept in the same bed that night. Although they had only been separated for a few months, because of the strange changes in the world situation and human affairs both of them felt a little as though "separate worlds had met". Hung Chin-ling, on account of her sorrow which could never be fully told, and the limitless wrong she had suffered under violent oppression, couldn't stop crying. She said:

"I'll absolutely do everything I can to save Fourth Master. But I know I'm no longer fit to talk about marrying Fourth Master."

These words stirred Ch'ien Shou-yü's feelings about her own experiences, and she thought of that family tutor. She couldn't help thinking:

"Where does it say that chastity has to be so important to a girl? When the blessings of a lifetime marriage are determined by a few drops of a virgin's blood, then it's no wonder some people are willing to be 'rebels against Confucianism'."

She wiped Hung Chin-ling's tears, and said with a sigh:

"Of course, I too know that Fourth Master is not a modern-minded man. But your situation deserves a person's sympathy. Your engagement was only an oral agreement, and it's such a disordered time just now."

"It's just the disordered times that are a true test for a woman. If the times were peaceful, and there were no external pressures and temptations, then what would be so special about preserving one's honor?"

Ch'ien Shou-yü was utterly startled to encounter such depth in a girl like Hung Chin-ling. She seized the tip of her pigtail and kissed it lightly, and said:

"We can't demand that every woman consider preserving her chastity more important than saving her life. If there are such women now and then, they are certainly exceptions, and don't deserve to be examples!"

Because "people who suffer from the same ailment commiserate with each other", and in order to comfort the weak girl whose mind and body alike were filled with pain, Ch'ien Shou-yü spoke of her own family affairs and personal experience, of why her father didn't like her mother, and of why her family tutor had gone to Kwangtung to join the army and finally to lose his life. At last she said:

"So, you should see now why you mustn't go on being anxious and melancholy. We could almost say that every one, and every household, has his 'secret'. The rituals can only exist so long as they're camouflaged; once uncovered, they're not worth a dime. What's even more laughable is that whoever uncovers them becomes a rebel."

Ch'ien Shou-yü sighed, and continued:

"Who knows how many years we've been cheating one another with this ancient tradition of ours?"

Hung Chin-ling was moved by Ch'ien Shou-yü's complete candor. She had always respected Ch'ien Shou-yü, considering her somewhere between teacher and friend. Now she felt strongly that here was someone who truly understood her, and that it was not merely a case of "those who suffer from the same ailment commiserating with each other".

"Elder Sister, you're several years older than I, you've read many more books, and you have the deepest understanding of women's sorrows. In your opinion, what does the future hold for women?"

Without waiting for Ch'ien Shou-yü to respond, she quickly continued:

"Liu Shao-ch'iao and Pai Ch'a-hua also say that they want to liberate women, and struggle for the equality of men and women. Do you think their methods are correct?"

"I've always felt that the meaning of equality of men and women doesn't lie in equal pay for equal work. Suppose a man is a soldier, should a woman be a soldier too? But through division of labor and cooperation, each fulfills his own responsibilities. The concept of lifelong chastity must change. But absolute sexual liberation becomes license, and it's still the woman who gets hurt, because she has one more problem than the man—pregnancy. I'm a middle-of-the-roader; I believe that concepts are formed gradually, and must also change gradually. Therefore, I oppose the methods of Liu Shao-ch'iao and his friends."

"Their methods have already led to the sacrifice of many people, including my mother and me. Elder Sister, do you think that my mother and Third Master can last very long together?"

"Since they've already gotten married, I hope they can. If they can make the best of it, and manage to get along somehow, then it may be their good fortune."

"Without Liu Shao-ch'iao, they certainly wouldn't have gotten married. If this is cause and effect, then Liu Shao-ch'iao is truly the Old Man in the Moon who drew their threads together, and it would be proper for all of us to thank him."

As Ch'ien Shou-yü said this, they both laughed.

One night had passed, and the attitude of Hung Chin-ling's Mama—Liang Yün-feng—toward her new husband had changed greatly for the better. Ch'ien Pen-san, having lived alone for a long time, did have needs, and although this twice-married bride came from a "fallen household", when compared to his country wife she was certainly much cleaner and better looking. A woman's beauty or ugliness is always derived from comparison. Ch'ien Pen-san, in "winding the ties of marriage" exerted himself to the utmost to win over his new wife, and made pleasant small talk to earn her goodwill. This did a great deal to gloss over his coarse nature and vulgar ways, and it gave the new wife a feeling of security.

The four of them got up around noon, ate lunch at the Hotel France, and then went home together. The new wife had already talked things over with her daughter, and agreed that somehow or other, Ch'ien Pen-ssu should be saved. The steps they had decided to take were that while her mother asked Hung T'ung-yeh, Hung Chin-ling would go and look for Liu Shao-ch'iao, and thus, pursuing two lines at once, they would separately advance.

Hung Chin-ling went first to the Labor Union. She wanted to see Liu Shao-ch'iao, and at the same time she had a letter to give to her brother, asking him to come and see his mother. Originally Hung Chin-ling had been able to come and go freely through the outer gates of the Labor Union Headquarters, since the Workers' Pickets on guard all recognized her as the Director's little sister. But on this occasion she was halted, and told that she must go to the message room and register, and wait to report. Out of past experience, Hung Chin-ling knew that in such a situation, reasonable speech was not only useless, but could get one in trouble. So she restrained her anger and went obediently to the message center, where she filled out a visitor's form and then sat down on a bench to wait. After some time, seeing that they hadn't even carried the visitors' forms in, Hung Chin-ling couldn't help asking:

"Why don't you send the visitors' forms in?"

"What are you in a hurry about?"

"It's not that I'm in a hurry, but I've already been waiting quite a while."

"If you don't want to wait, you can go, nobody's keeping you!"

"I have some important business with Committeeman Liu and Director Hung," Hung Chin-ling said with a smile, and all the courtesy she could muster. "It's putting you out; thank you."

"There are many visitors here, I can't go running for each one; I'd run myself to death that way. Just sit down, and wait 'til there are three or five of them, and then I'll take them in."

"Fine!" Hung Chin-ling forced herself to respond.

A great many people went in through the outer gates, but not once during the afternoon did any of them come to the message center to register. Then Hung Chin-ling understood. She asked:

"Did they already say that they wouldn't see me?"

"You should know your own business. What's the use asking me?"

"Well, I'll go." Hung Chin-ling walked away.

"You shouldn't have come."

Hearing this behind her back, Hung Chin-ling almost started to cry.

Back at the Ch'ien house, she told them of the situation and no one could guess what it meant. Hadn't they all been friendly enough at last night's wedding banquet? Why had they changed so quickly? Ch'ien Pen-san thought, and said to Hung Chin-ling:

"Give them another telephone call now, and see."

The call went through, but as soon as the other end heard that it came from the Ch'ien house, they hung up. Everyone was still more in doubt. Suddenly Ch'ien Pen-san realized that some great change might have transpired during the night. He said:

"I'm going around to Wang's. Last night Mr. Wang sent someone with his best wishes, and he also sent a gift. I should go in person to thank him."

So saying, he hurried off alone.

There was a thin shadow concealed in the new wife's heart; she felt a certain unhappiness. She considered that this was a new era, and that in this new era, when her Department Chief husband went out to pay a courtesy call, he certainly ought to be accompanied by his wife; that was more in keeping with the customs of the new era. But now he took no account of this, so one could see that—"He's a coarse fellow after all!"

The new wife muttered this quietly to herself, and nothing showed on her face. Her new husband was an unfathomably changeable politician, so she would overlook this little matter. Since she had never before had such an experience, it was no wonder.

Towards evening there was a telephone call from Ch'ien Pen-san, saying that he would probably be returning late, and asking them to go ahead and eat supper without waiting for him. Ch'ien Shou-yü took the call, and she told her new Mama and Hung Chin-ling what her father had said.

At the mention of dinner, Hung Chin-ling thought at once of the Two Rivers Cantonese restaurant. She knew that Liu Shao-ch'iao and her brother T'ung-yeh always ate there. So she thought:

"Why don't I go to the Two Rivers now, and maybe I'll run into them. For Fourth Master's sake . . ."

So she said to her mother and Ch'ien Shou-yü:

"You eat; I'm going out for a little, and then I'll come back."

The two of them were still trying to ask why, but she had already hurried off, half-running.

The street was full, as usual, with people coming and going, and it was noisy, and chaotic. But Hung Chin-ling had a vague premonition, as though something unforeseen was going to happen. When she arrived at the Two Rivers, she didn't see a sign of them upstairs or downstairs, so she sat at a table near the entrance. She told the waiter that she was waiting for friends. The waiter brought tea, and she carefully drank a mouthful. She casually glanced at the menu while paying attention to the diners who came and went.

After having waited for more than an hour without seeing them, Hung Chin-ling had to order for herself. But she didn't give up, and remained sitting there after she had finished. Finally, past nine o'clock, when the restaurant was almost ready to close, Pai Ch'a-hua rushed in, with Liu Shao-ch'iao and Hung T'ung-yeh behind her. Hung Chin-ling at once stood up and greeted them. Hung T'ung-yeh, somewhat surprised, said:

"What, you here alone?"

"I've been waiting for you."

"What is it?"

"I went to the Labor Union this afternoon to see you, but they wouldn't let me in, and they wouldn't send a message for me."

"We were holding an important meeting today, and no visitors were admitted," Hung T'ung-yeh immediately explained.

"I called . . ."

"No telephone calls were accepted either."

"Why so tense?" Hung Chin-ling asked.

"That takes a while to tell. Let's go upstairs and sit down," Liu Shao-ch'iao said, pulling Pai Ch'a-hua toward the stairs.

"Let's go upstairs and talk," Hung T'ung-yeh said.

Hung Chin-ling followed them upstairs.

When they were seated, Hung T'ung-yeh asked:

"What is it you want?"

"Mama wants to see you about something, she wants you to come over."

Hung T'ung-yeh hesitated a moment, looked at Liu Shao-ch'iao, and then said:

"She's already gotten married to someone else, she's no longer my Mama. I won't go."

Hung Chin-ling had never expected such an answer, and it startled her so fiercely that she almost lost control of herself. Calming herself, she said:

"I don't understand what you're saying. How should Mama herself have wanted to marry? Wasn't it you people who made her do it?"

"I can't say it's wrong for her to marry. I'm only saying she and I are no longer mother and son!" Hung T'ung-yeh's face flushed, and it was obvious that he spoke with extreme pain.

Hung Chin-ling paid no attention to him. She thought for a moment, and then said to Liu Shao-ch'iao:

"I want to talk to you alone, all right?"

Without waiting for Liu Shao-ch'iao to speak, Pai Ch'a-hua broke in:

"You can't talk to him alone. Tomorrow at noon, he and I are getting married in the assembly hall at the Women's Association. He doesn't belong to you."

Liu Shao-ch'iao said:

"I've already gotten what I wanted from you. You look for your Fourth Master Ch'ien; I don't need you any more."

He pulled Pai Ch'a-hua close and gave her a kiss.

Hung Chin-ling kept her temper with great effort, and said calmly:

"That's just why I came to find you. Since you don't need me, how about letting Fourth Master Ch'ien go?"

"Let him go to you?" Pai Ch'a-hua asked contemptuously.

"I'm not fit for that any more."

"That's just your polite talk," Liu Shao-ch'iao said. "I tell you honestly, even I don't know where Fourth Master is right now. Wait until I find out, and then I'll tell you."

"When will I get your reply?"

"I'll call you, or write."

"Well, thank you. I'll go now."

"Why not drink a couple of cups with us here?"

"I've just eaten," Hung Chin-ling said, and she was gone.

"Come to the Women's Association tomorrow for our wedding!" Pai Ch'a-hua called.

Hung Chin-ling didn't answer her.

It was already close to ten o'clock when she returned to the Ch'ien house. Her mother and Ch'ien Shou-yü were seated in the downstairs sitting room, talking. Ch'ien Pen-san still hadn't returned. Hung Chin-ling told them in detail about her meeting at the Two Rivers Cantonese restaurant.

His mother was especially surprised, and enraged, to hear of Hung T'ung-yeh's attitude. In front of her new husband's daughter, she felt even more embarrassed. He was really too worthless! Holding back her tears, she said helplessly:

"It goes without saying this is certainly more of Liu Shao-ch'iao's doing. But T'ung-yeh himself is too confused: he's over twenty, but he hasn't any convictions of his own, and he lets that person manipulate him in everything."

"Under the pressure of the environment," Ch'ien Shou-yü said quickly, "sometimes one can't act freely. We can't blame T'ung-yeh alone. Ma, I'm afraid you're tired. You go on up to bed; Chin-ling and I will wait for Papa to return."

"No, I'll wait a while longer." Her mother queried Chin-ling again. "Do you think Liu Shao-ch'iao can be trusted when he said he would help find Fourth Master?"

"That's hard to say," Hung Chin-ling said. "He can't catch me again, that's for sure."

"This is good news," Ch'ien Shou-yü said, laying her hand on Hung Chin-ling's back. "Just now we'll take each one as it comes, and try our luck."

Seeing the maid who cooked and cleaned returning home, Ch'ien Shou-yü hastily stopped talking, got up, and asked:

"Aunty Li, have you had supper?"

"I beg your pardon, Miss, I've already eaten. And you?"

"We ate earlier, too, and there's some for you in the kitchen."

Aunty Li casually seated herself, gave Hung Chin-ling's mother a careful inspection, and smacked her lips as she said:

"This is Third Master's new wife, right?"

"That's right, my new Mama," Ch'ien Shou-yü replied.

"Quite a beauty!" Aunty Li clapped her hands. "No wonder Committeeman Liu has been praising her everywhere. Third Master Ch'ien is really lucky."

The new wife flushed, and with her mind in confusion she experienced the greatest distress. She didn't know what Liu Shao-ch'iao had been saying about her outside; such men weren't likely to guard a woman's intimate secrets. At the same time, she was afraid, because she didn't know what else that Aunty Li was going to say. If she were disgraced before her new husband's daughter, how would she be able to maintain her position as mother in the future? Today was only the second day of her marriage! She didn't know that the secrets between mother and daughter had already been secretly exchanged by her daughter and Ch'ien Shou-yü. She stared at Hung Chin-ling, and asked Ch'ien Shou-yü:

"This Aunty Li is—?"

"She helps our family with the cooking and washing."

"I'm the maid here." Aunty Li delightedly introduced herself. "But I spend a lot of time at the Labor Union. Now labor is sacred, and women are number one, so maids are sacred number one. Mrs. Ch'ien the Third, if I didn't say this you probably wouldn't know: I'm the sacred number one maid."

As soon as Mrs. Ch'ien the Third heard this, she quickly said:

"I know, that's splendid!"

She asked Chin-ling:

"Are those iced candied lotus seeds that we boiled this afternoon frozen through by now? Bring them out so that we can eat a few with Aunty Li."

"Mrs. Ch'ien the Third is too polite," Aunty Li said firmly, seating herself.

In a moment, Hung Chin-ling and Ch'ien Shou-yü brought in a tray with four small bowls of lotus seeds. In each bowl was a little silver spoon. Mrs. Ch'ien the Third said:

"Did you save some for your father?"

"I did, there's plenty," Ch'ien Shou-yü replied.

"Mrs. Ch'ien the Third, you're really kind and good," Aunty Li extolled her as she ate.

After they had eaten, Hung Chin-ling cleared up the bowls, while Ch'ien Shou-yü gave napkins to her new Mama and Aunty Li. Her new Mama thanked her, and said:

"Elder Miss, from now on you needn't wait on me. Let me do it myself."

"I like to serve Mama."

"But I don't deserve it."

Aunty Li saw and heard this, and couldn't leave off complimenting them.

"Look how polite the two of you are, mother and daughter. Mrs. Ch'ien the Third is really fine!"

"Now, now, I'm just an easygoing person."

As Mrs. Ch'ien the Third said this, she was quite surprised, and didn't know what the other meant by her repeated compliments. She heard Ch'ien Shou-yü ask:

"Aunty Li, you're so late coming back was something going on?"

"Look at that—I'm so fond of sitting and talking I forgot the important business," Aunty Li said, clapping her hands. "Tomorrow at noon, Committeeman Liu and Committeewoman Pai are getting married in the assembly hall at the Women's Association. There'll be an announcement in the papers tomorrow, but they're not sending cards. I came back to tell Third Master Ch'ien how to prepare the gifts. I myself want an advance on my wages; we have to send gifts too. The two of them, one a labor leader and the other a women's leader, are the great benefactors of us laborers and women. We've got to really celebrate tomorrow!"

"That's certainly proper. We'll definitely come to congratulate them," Ch'ien Shou-yü said. She asked Aunty Li how much of an advance she wanted, and gave her the sum she asked for. In addition, having stuffed a red envelope with a thick wad of banknotes, she handed it to her, saying:

"This is for you, from my new Mama, to thank you for coming with your good wishes."

Aunty Li took it, and said with a giggle:

"Miss, you certainly know how to act! Your new Mama sure must be pleased with you."

Turning her head, she asked:

"Mrs. Ch'ien the Third, isn't that so? Speak up!"

"Of course, Miss is very good to me."

"Well, Mrs. Ch'ien the Third, I still have something else to ask of you," Aunty Li said respectfully.

"What is it, just tell me."

"I see that's a very pretty ring you're wearing. You don't care about such trifles, so suppose you give it to me? I've never had a proper ring on my hand."

"This is my wedding ring," Mrs. Ch'ien the Third said hastily. "Third Master just gave it to me yesterday."

"It doesn't matter that it's a wedding ring, give it to me so I can enjoy it too."

"You can't give away your wedding ring!" Mrs. Ch'ien the Third grew slightly desperate.

"As long as you're willing, it doesn't matter." Aunty Li still hadn't given up.

Ch'ien Shou-yü hurried to break the impasse, and said in a pacifying tone:

"Aunty Li, wedding rings really can't be given to anyone. I originally bought that ring, and I know where to get another one. Look here—you come by tomorrow morning, and I'll take you there, and buy you one just like it. All right?"

"That's fine," Aunty Li said, pulling a long face. "This Mrs. Ch'ien the Third is a petty sort after all, and they say she came from Shanghai. To have come from Shanghai and still be so unfamiliar with the world!"

As she went out, she was lamenting to herself:

"I'd really never have thought it, really never have thought it, that I could be so wrong about someone."

Ch'ien Shou-yü saw her out, and told her:

"I'll wait for you tomorrow morning, and when you come we'll go together to buy the ring."

"Miss, I see you're still the generous one," Aunty Li stopped and said in a loud voice, and then she left.

Mrs. Ch'ien the Third, mouth agape and tongue-tied, was speechless.

"Ma, don't be angry," Hung Chin-ling went over to pat her mother on the back. "Nowadays everything's all different."

"We'll see how long they can carry on like this," Ch'ien Shou-yü sighed and shook her head.

"It's so late, how is it your father still isn't back?" Mrs. Ch'ien the Third looked at the clock hanging on the wall. Obviously she was a little uneasy.

"Wait 'til I call and see."

As she spoke Ch'ien Shou-yü picked up the phone. Ch'ien Pen-san was still at Wang's home, and over the telephone he told his daughter:

"Wait until the meeting breaks up, and then I'll be home. You go on to sleep. Whatever you do, don't call up again."

Ch'ien Shou-yü put down the telephone, and told her new Mama. She heard the doorbell ring, and went to open the door. Unexpectedly, it was Hung T'ung-yeh, alone. First he thanked Ch'ien Shou-yü, and helped her close the gate, and then he came in.

"Ma, did you want to see me for something?"

"Are you speaking to me?" Mrs. Ch'ien the Third asked angrily. "Didn't you say that I wasn't your Mama any longer?"

"I'm sorry," Hung T'ung-yeh said with great remorse. "In front of Liu Shao-ch'iao and Pai Ch'a-hua I couldn't help it—they told me to act that way."

"Are you a three-year-old child, without any views of your own?"

"Now, in this environment, no one's allowed to have his own views." Hung T'ung-yeh sat down, clasped his head in his hands, and said painfully: "I don't know why, but they've always paid special attention to me, and beaten so many ideas into my body. I don't think I have to explain it, you'll all understand: if I don't obey them, I'll soon cease to exist. I confess that I'm greedy for life and afraid of death. You'll have to forgive me."

Seeing how pitiably he spoke, she could no longer bear to scold him. Mrs. Ch'ien the Third, needless to say, had a kind of passionate love for her only son. She said sorrowfully:

"I know that I can't entirely blame you. If it weren't for the times, there couldn't be a Liu Shao-ch'iao and a Pai Ch'a-hua. Without such people, you wouldn't have fallen to such a point. Now that I think of it, you're the victim of your Bureau Chief uncle and of the Lefebvres. If they had treated you a little better, you wouldn't have gone to such an extreme."

"It's the times, and it's the tide." Hung T'ung-yeh was grieved to hear his mother speak of past matters, and he held back his tears. "I've sacrificed myself for the times and the tides."

"There's no need to talk about that any more, and it's no use either," said Hung Chin-ling, now trying to comfort him. She asked: "We have lotus seeds; do you want some?"

Hung T'ung-yeh then felt a kind of long-lost warmth, as though he tasted once more that very bitter, and yet very sweet, family life of Chapei days. He hesitated a moment, and then said:

"Thank you, Little Sister, but I won't have any. I've been drinking, and right now I don't feel very well."

When Ch'ien Shou-yü heard this, she quickly went and got a cold hand-towel and invited him to wipe his face. Hung T'ung-yeh stood up to take it. He felt both grateful, and ashamed. People like his little sister and Ch'ien Shou-yü, he felt, were truly rich in the spirit of forgiveness. And such a spirit was simply indispensable in human relations. Its value was far above that of hatred and struggle. Hung T'ung-yeh knew that it would be improper to vainly say "Thank you" at this time, but at last he did say:

"Thank you, Elder Sister."

His voice trembled a little, and was very low and weak.

Ch'ien Shou-yü was immediately aware that this sheeplike Hung T'ung-yeh before her eyes was not the powerful and arrogant Labor Union leader. She muttered to herself in surprise: "What's the matter with him? This certainly bears looking into."

Having taken the cold hand-towel, Hung T'ung-yeh sat down. Suddenly he looked left and right, and asked softly and uneasily:

"Is there anyone else in the house?"

"No one."

"Third Master?"

"He's not here either."

"Isn't he at a meeting at Wang's house?"

"I don't know," Ch'ien Shou-yü, alert, fired back. "We're just waiting for him to come back."

"He must be at the meeting at Wang's home," Hung T'ung-yeh said positively. "It may be he'll be very late coming back."

"How do you know?" Ch'ien Shou-yü pressed him.

Hung T'ung-yeh didn't answer, but said, as though to himself:

"I came earlier, but I didn't come in because I could hear that Aunty Li was here. I hid in the shadow of the trees across the street, and when I saw that she had gone, I came in. That Aunty Li is Liu Shao-ch'iao and Pai Ch'a-hua's agent; she's responsible for telling them what goes on in Third Master's household. She can make trouble where there's none; her tongue is two feet long."

"That can't be," Ch'ien Shou-yü said hastily. "Although Liu Shao-ch'iao introduced Aunty Li, she was very seldom in here, so you can see she didn't come to keep watch on us. Liu Shao-ch'iao is Papa's good friend, so how could it be?"

"You've forgotten when Aunty Li had just come. Wasn't she in here a lot then?"

As he spoke, Hung T'ung-yeh suddenly seemed to come awake, and he stopped talking. Then he changed the subject, saying:

"No, no, I came today looking for Third Master. We won't talk about that other. Elder Sister, it's no wonder you don't believe me. You suspect there may be some other motive behind my words, and you're right."

Seeing him so confused, as though his mind were a little out of its usual order, the three of them didn't know how to answer him. Then he added:

"No wonder, no wonder, nobody will understand me until I kill myself!"

"Stop this nonsense!" Mrs. Ch'ien the Third said anxiously. "What is wrong with you?"

"The news today is bad, don't tell me you haven't heard?"

"What news?"

Hung T'ung-yeh's face grew cold. He seemed to want to speak but stopped, and only gazed fixedly at them.

"What *is* it?" He was making Ch'ien Shou-yü anxious in spite of herself. "There are no strangers here, so if you have something to say, say it. What are you afraid of?"

Hung T'ung-yeh hesitated a moment longer, and then leaned forward, and said soberly, in a low voice:

"The Kuomintang has decided to break with the Communist Party."

"Why?"

"Because the Communist Party's methods have caused the Kuomintang to suffer abuse. But the most important factor is that the military situation is disadvantageous. Wuhan has been surrounded on all sides for a long time, and they can't fight their way out. Now the encirclement is growing tighter and tighter, and since the Wuhan military themselves know that they can't beat them, they're thinking of getting in bed with them."

"They needn't break with the Communist Party on that account," Ch'ien Shou-yü interjected deliberately.

"The Nanking Central Government insists on purging the Communists. If they don't purge the Communists, then they absolutely can't go to bed together. Already the Communist Party is the only obstacle in the way of their unification."

Hung T'ung-yeh looked at Ch'ien Shou-yü as he spoke, and added:

"Besides, food is becoming a problem on the Wuhan side. Our food is insufficient, but the outside forces have us locked up, and nothing's coming in. Most recently even the army's rations haven't been distributed. If the army hasn't anything to eat, won't there be trouble? And then there's the inflation. Ever since we carried out the 'Concentration of Cash Reserves', the Central Bank notes have been pouring forth like the military scrip of the warlord period, and when you get them you can't buy anything with them. In order to stir up divisions between labor and capital, industry and commerce were bankrupted early on. In such a situation nobody has the means to support himself. So circumstances are forcing them to break with the Communist Party and seek a reconciliation."

Ch'ien Shou-yü was utterly delighted to hear this news; it was as though the light of dawn had shone in the midst of darkness. But she did not change her expression, and said nothing. She heard her new Mama ask Hung T'ung-yeh:

"This 'breaking with the Communist Party'—is it like the Party Purification movement in Shanghai?"

"I don't know. I've heard that Wang has in mind only for the Communists to withdraw from the Kuomintang, and after they've withdrawn the government will drop it," Hung T'ung-yeh said vaguely.

"What do the Communists think about all this?" Ch'ien Shou-yü couldn't help asking.

"The Kuomintang's army is already deployed, and the Communists will naturally accept reality. The Labor Union and the Women's Association both held meetings today, and I took part."

"What did you decide?"

"I've been ordered to withdraw to Kiangsi with Liu Shao-ch'iao."

"Why go to Kiangsi?"

"That's the Party's decision," Hung T'ung-yeh said gloomily. "When we get there, we'll get our orders."

"Are you really going to go?" Mrs. Ch'ien the Third hastily asked.

Hung T'ung-yeh paused a moment, and then said with great hesitation:

"I don't want to go. Besides, they don't trust me, and if I go, I don't know what they'd want me to do. I'm a little afraid."

"It's best you take this opportunity to leave them," Hung Chin-ling couldn't let such a chance pass. "Whatever you do, don't add one mistake on another."

"That's why I came to see Third Master. I wanted to ask Third Master to help me. I'm willing to leave the Communist Party." Summoning up his courage, Hung T'ung-yeh burst out with what was on his mind. His lips and hands trembled.

"If there's really going to be a break with the Communists, then I don't know how Papa himself is going to come off."

Ch'ien Shou-yü thought of all the deeds through which her father and the Communist Party had used each other. These would not necessarily be forgiven by the comrades of the Kuomintang, and might give rise to deep suspicions.

"There's no question about that," Hung T'ung-yeh said positively. "Third Master belongs to the Kuomintang, and the Kuomintang is always the Kuomintang. Besides, he's drawn very close to Wang lately, and Wang can certainly protect him."

"Wait 'til he comes back, and we can all discuss it." Mrs. Ch'ien the Third said.

The clock on the wall had already struck two when Hung T'ung-yeh stood up, saying:

582

"I'm going back, I can't stay any longer, I'm afraid they'd suspect me. You tell Third Master what I have in mind. I'll come back when I have time."

Hung Chin-ling at that moment felt that Hung T'ung-yeh was truly in a dangerous position. She said:

"Since you've already decided to leave them, just don't go back. Find a place and hide out. It's a tiger's mouth—why go back?"

"No," Hung T'ung-yeh said decisively. "Breaking with the Communists is still inside news. It's not certain it will be made public; that will depend on circumstances. It wouldn't be in my interest to leave too soon. Right now I'm still playing their game. Tomorrow Liu Shao-ch'iao and Pai Ch'a-hua are getting married. I'm in charge of the preparations and I'm also the intermediary; it wouldn't look right if I weren't there."

"You'd better take care." Mrs. Ch'ien the Third felt extremely uneasy. "Don't be too stubborn. They're not as trusting as you are."

"I know, Ma, don't worry."

As Hung T'ung-yeh spoke, he walked away. Suddenly he stopped, turned, and said:

"I just thought of something—my uncle the Bureau Chief was right. When you're a compradore in a foreign firm, you can eat a bowl of rice in peace without being in constant fear."

These words made everyone feel distressed, and his own eyes were moist. Calming himself, he said to Ch'ien Shou-yü:

"Elder Sister, there's something else I'll ask you to tell Third Master. I'll definitely do all I can to protect the safety of Fourth Master. I know I'm no good, and I haven't the face to ask Third Master in person. I hope I can send Fourth Master back safe, so as to express a little of how I really feel."

"Thank you," Ch'ien Shou-yü said quickly. "Fourth Uncle is totally dependent on you."

"How *is* it with Fourth Master?" Hung Chin-ling asked anxiously.

"He's been kept in Hankow," Hung T'ung-yeh said honestly. "Liu Shao-ch'iao decided at today's meeting to send him across the river, by night. He has a secret place near the station at the Hsü family shed; I've been there."

"Will they harm him?" Hung Chin-ling pressed him.

"Not right away. Liu Shao-ch'iao means to use Fourth Master as human collateral to discuss terms with Third Master so as to guarantee his and Pai Ch'a-hua's safety."

"Don't they want to go to Kiangsi?" Ch'ien Shou-yü asked.

"He said that he wanted to wait until several important matters in Hankow had been taken care of, and then he would go to Kiangsi."

"What important matters?"

"That I don't know. When I asked him, he just smiled and shook his head."

Mrs. Ch'ien the Third was endlessly worried about her son. She repeated, again and again, that he must take care, and then she let him go.

The three of them, mother and two daughters, stimulated by the news, forgot their fatigue and sat in the reception room waiting for Ch'ien Pen-san. It was past two-thirty when he returned.

"It's so late, how is it you're not sleeping?" Ch'ien Pen-san felt it was a bit strange.

"We were waiting for Papa, and also waiting for news," Ch'ien Shou-yü said as she gave him a cold hand-towel.

Hung Chin-ling spread lotus seeds on an imitation silver tray.

Ch'ien Pen-san took off his dark glasses and rubbed his eyes, as he smiled and nodded at Hung Chin-ling and thanked her. Then he asked his daughter:

"What news were you waiting for?"

"We hear that the Kuomintang has decided to break with the Communist Party."

"What did you say?" Ch'ien Pen-san, greatly startled, suddenly leaped to his feet.

"We hear that you're going to break with the Communist Party," Ch'ien Shou-yü repeated timidly, retreating a couple of steps.

"Where did you get that news?" Ch'ien Pen-san relaxed back into his chair, and pushed the tray of lotus seeds which had been set before him towards the center of the table.

"Younger brother of the Hung family just came and told us. The Labor Union and the Women's Association held meetings all day today to discuss their response, and moreover the Communist Party has already given them its orders."

Ch'ien Shou-yü spoke gently, afraid of the embarrassment of angering her father in front of her new Mama.

Ch'ien Pen-san said nothing. He picked up the lotus seeds and lowered his head to eat them, all by himself. When he was finished, he put down the bowl, and then, recollecting himself, he said:

"How is it I'm eating alone?"

"We've all eaten already," the new wife said with a slight smile.

"Thank you."

It made them all laugh to see Ch'ien Pen-san being so polite. Hung Chin-ling said:

"It wasn't very courteous of us to go ahead and eat, and yet Third Master is thanking us."

"This is just because no one can blame me for being too polite." Ch'ien Pen-san also smiled.

"You're in your own home, who would blame you?" asked his new wife happily.

"I thank my wife for her good wishes." Ch'ien Pen-san clasped his hands and gestured to his new wife.

Everyone laughed. The new wife pursued the question.

"This news about breaking with the Communists—is it the truth or not?"

Ch'ien Pen-san composed his features, nodded soberly, and said:

"It's true. Just recently Wang saw a document from a Russian adviser. That document was a genuine order from the Third International to the Chinese Communist Party. If those orders were all carried out, the Chinese Kuomintang would be totally annihilated, and China would become a Communist world. Because of this, Mr. Wang and several of the people close to him have discussed breaking with the Communists, and moreover to get in touch with Nanking, so as to coordinate internal and external responses."

Having spoken to this point, Ch'ien Pen-san stopped for a moment, and then, obviously with great distress, continued:

"But these things are extremely secret. I just happened to come upon the meeting today, and Mr. Wang told me to take part, so I got to know the inside situation. How did the Communist Party find out so soon? And the Labor Union and the Women's Association have completed their preparations—how strange!"

"Certainly one of the trusted people close to Mr. Wang must have leaked it to them." So Ch'ien Shou-yü conjectured.

Ch'ien Pen-san thought a moment, and said:

"It must have been the Widow Chung! That old woman has a son who joined the Communist Party in Moscow, and she herself was close to Borodin. If there's a traitor close to Mr. Wang, I think it's certainly her."

"Since that's the case," Ch'ien Shou-yü put in, "Mr. Wang should be told, so that he can be on guard against her."

"Her relations with Mr. Wang are ten thousand times deeper than mine! How should Mr. Wang not know about her affairs? Just as long as she doesn't carry tales about me to Mr. Wang, I'll be satisfied. I haven't the qualifications to say anything bad about her."

Ch'ien Pen-san laughed loudly in self-ridicule as he said this.

His new wife, seeing him in such good humor, brought up the matter of Hung T'ung-yeh. Ch'ien Pen-san listened attentively, and impulsively said:

"There's absolutely no question. Isn't your child my child? If I have the power, I will certainly protect him. Even if a person has taken the wrong path, so long as he repents and changes to the good, he's considered a good fellow."

"He used to be a decent and honest boy, but he fell in with bad companions and was captured by the devil. If you're willing to bring him back, so that later on he can struggle upwards, then not only will I be grateful, but even his dead father—if there is consciousness in the Nine Springs—will surely be grateful to you."

As she spoke, her painful feelings were aroused, and her eyes filled with tears.

"You needn't feel so bad." Ch'ien Pen-san removed his dark glasses, put them on the table, and gazed lingeringly and sincerely at his new wife. "I shall certainly do this thing, you can relax."

This act on Ch'ien Pen-san's part moved his new wife. Liu Shao-ch'iao's image flashed through her mind, arousing the ugly dark side of her own nature, and she felt endlessly ashamed before her late husband, and her new husband as well. She glanced at Hung Chin-ling, and her tears fell like linked pearls.

A person's purity, once defiled, may be ever so cleverly concealed, but by no means can one ever wash it clean, or restore its original state. The scars on her spirit could never be healed, unless by omnipotent God.

One false step makes for a thousand regrets. That, Mrs. Ch'ien the Third thought, was really a truthful saying. But the environment surrounded one's entire life in such a special atmosphere as to often determine the shape of an individual's future and his choice of the light or the darkness. Mrs. Ch'ien the Third had clearly examined "herself" when she was at Little Miao's place, and "herself" as she was today as a new wife in the house of Ch'ien Pen-san. Her psychology was in these two instances fundamentally different; there was a great distance separating the two.

What power had created this separation?

Suddenly Mrs. Ch'ien the Third came to herself.

"We must take advantage of this moment when he wants to repent," she said, wiping her eyes. "We must quickly think of a way to make him leave them. Their group is like an enchanted place—unless you escape you can't awaken from it."

Mrs. Ch'ien the Third had really only understood one-half of the problem; she didn't comprehend why, after all, her boy suddenly wanted to repent. A "magic weapon" had just penetrated that "enchanted place", and news of the break with the Communists was that "magic weapon".

But her new husband and her two daughters all agreed with her suggestion. and felt that he should be made to leave before any action had been taken, so as to avoid future oppression and feel completely safe. Hung Chin-ling added:

"Just now I felt that I should keep him back, and not let him go. But he himself was unwilling. I'm afraid he's too changeable, and not resolute enough."

"Keep him?" her mother said, looking at her daughter. "People come and go here; we couldn't hide him."

"We can think of a way around that," Hung Chin-ling said.

"Yes, there's a way," Ch'ien Pen-san concluded. "Tell him to stay at the Hotel France, I'll take care of the bill for him."

"Sixty dollars a day?" the new wife said dubiously.

588

"Yes," Ch'ien Pen-san said proudly and loudly. "What does the money matter? Just so the child is safe."

This caused his new wife to incline her heart towards him, and to trust him even more. She had had no idea, before, that her new husband was so reliable. A grateful and sincere gaze sought her new husband, and did not leave him for an instant.

Ch'ien Shou-yü said:

"Papa, speak a little more quietly."

"What's to be afraid of so late?"

"You can never be certain where they're concerned; they *might* be eavesdropping outside, especially now when such a great change is coming," Ch'ien Shou-yü said lightly.

"No mistake." Ch'ien Pen-san looked at the clock. "It's really late. Let's all get some rest."

He supported his wife up the stairs.

The two girls watched them up the stairs, until they reached the top and could no longer be seen. They looked at one another, and pursed their lips, smiling. Hung Chin-ling said:

"I hope they get along well."

"And for a long time, too!" Ch'ien Shou-yü added.

At noon the next day, as though there were nothing on his mind, Ch'ien Pen-san attended the wedding of Liu Shao-ch'iao and Pai Ch'a-hua. He took care to look at every one of them, those usually active left-wing elements and Communist Party elements, of whom nearly all were present. They were in high spirits, as usual, and gave no sign of being aware that any sudden change was going to take place.

Ch'ien Pen-san couldn't help feeling a little surprised; he didn't know if these fellows were deep, or just numbed.

Liu Shao-ch'iao saw Ch'ien Pen-san arrive, and came over especially to thank him. He drew him off to the side to talk.

"Third Master, our cooperation is soon going to end."

Ch'ien Pen-san was profoundly surprised by this frankness, which seemed to hold back nothing; he couldn't help being slightly shaken. Fortunately he was quick-witted, and at once he seized Liu Shao-ch'iao's hand, squeezed it, and said in a pitying voice:

"It's really unfortunate news!"

"There's nothing unfortunate about it!" Liu Shao-ch'iao shook his head lightly, and then said listlessly: "But for myself, I'm not too pleased. Never mind those outside the Party, what do they understand? Within the Party, I've been criticized. They say that the Labor Union and the Women's Association behaved too 'excessively'! And it was actually I, Liu Shao-ch'iao, who directed the Labor Union, as Pai Ch'a-hua directed the Women's Association. It seems that everything's going to be smeared on the two of us."

As he spoke, he sat down on the grass beside the stone-paved sidewalk. Ch'ien Pen-san was most unaccustomed to this style of sitting, but he could only sit down with him, linking his hands together around his knees. He said:

"How can that be, how can that be?"

Liu Shao-ch'iao paid no attention to him, and went on:

"Formerly they wanted to destroy the Kuomintang. Now that the Kuomintang is preparing to break with the Communists, they are no longer willing, and hope to go on cooperating. Their rebuking the Labor Union and the Women's Association is for no other reason than because they want to push the responsibility off on myself and Pai Ch'a-hua, to sacrifice Pai Ch'a-hua and me in order to show the Kuomintang their goodwill. They consider it a trade-off, which will sweep away all obstacles to cooperation between the two parties. It's a case of voluntary stupidity—the matter isn't that simple at all."

Ch'ien Pen-san and Liu Shao-ch'iao conversed for some time. Never before had he known Liu Shao-ch'iao to speak of any of the Communist Party's business, let alone criticize them. Now, just listen to this resentful talk, which even seemed to carry a hint of opposition. With a sudden inspiration, he asked:

"You and Pai Ch'a-hua's performance today—it was to spite them!"

"No mistake, it was for that, a little." Liu Shao-ch'iao looked at him, and smiled.

Ch'ien Pen-san, unwilling to let the opportunity pass, sought an opening. He hastily continued:

"Brother Shao-ch'iao, Mr. Wang has often mentioned your talents, and with extraordinary appreciation. Many people have heard him, and not just I alone."

Liu Shao-ch'iao heard this and couldn't keep from grinning. He asked:

"Third Master, do you mean that I should revolt against the Communist Party and surrender to Wang?"

"It is the talented man who understands the affairs of the day," Ch'ien Pen-san said with complete sincerity. "The man of character decides on the spot."

"If that's what you think, you're mistaken." Liu Shao-ch'iao's smile disappeared, and he sounded a little hurt as he said: "The Communist Party is the Communist Party after all. I may struggle inside the Party, and clash with them, and if I lose, then I deserved to. I could never take advantage of my comrades to curry favor with outsiders, or turn on my own!"

Hearing Liu Shao-ch'iao speak like this, Ch'ien Pen-san looked embarrassed, and for a moment he couldn't wipe it away. In a tone of disapproval, and even more of shame, he said:

"All right—if such a day should really come, we can go our separate ways. Only, Brother Shao-ch'iao, if we should meet again, no matter when or under what circumstances, I hope we'll still be friends."

"We can never meet again."

Liu Shao-ch'iao jumped up from the grass.

"Let's go into the hall—quite a few people have come."

"It's time now."

As Ch'ien Pen-san got up, he dug out his watch and looked at it.

The hall was full of people, yelling and calling, and all jostling together. The day was fiercely hot, without a breath of wind, and the reek of sweat struck Ch'ien Pen-san, almost making him dizzy. On this account, no sooner had he pushed inside, than he pushed out again, to stand by himself in the shade of a tree in the courtyard, completely at a loss. But in his mind he was still thinking of his own affairs.

Will this shouting, crowding scene still be here tomorrow?

A moment's celebration—what it represents is not that moment, but the whole of a person's life. The dream of Huang-liang wasted only a dream; after awakening from the dream, I am still myself, and whether I advance or retreat, I must leave myself a little space on which to turn around.

The blood spilled in revolution wasn't so cheap! How many lives had been lost on that account? How many families separated? How many cultural records and historical traditions had been cut off on that account? It was nothing to play with!

"I've always been lucky myself," Ch'ien Pen-san thought. "From 'Kuomintang-Communist Cooperation' to 'Kuomintang-Communist Contradictions' I've gotten my political position. I've been used, but I've also been elevated. When the final accounts are settled, it'll be they who were used, and not I! Now I've received Mr. Wang's order to go to Kuling and talk with the representatives from Nanking, while you are about to withdraw in defeat, but there's no place for you to retreat!"

"What a laughable bunch," Ch'ien Pen-san thought. "A bunch of trash!"

Ch'ien Pen-san caught sight of Hung T'ung-yeh, and taking advantage of a moment when no one was looking, he drew near and said:

"They've already told me about your business. It's fine, I guarantee there'll be no problem. Don't worry."

"Someone is looking for you to talk over something," Hung T'ung-yeh said hastily in a quiet voice. "What place and what time is good?"

"Secret?"

"Yes."

"Who?"

"Raymond."

"He's come back?"

"Yes."

"What does he want with me?"

"When you've talked with him in person, you'll know."

Ch'ien Pen-san hesitated a moment, and then said:

"You go to the Hotel France and take a room."

"When? Today or tomorrow?"

"Tomorrow definitely won't do, you can only do it tonight."

Chapter XXII

That evening, when Ch'ien Pen-san and M. Raymond met at the Hotel France, Hung T'ung-yeh served as their interpreter.

After M. Raymond had been tricked into going to Shenyang by two forged telegrams, he had received, ever since getting off the train, especially courteous treatment, and an interpreter had followed him everywhere. This interpreter was named Kao, and his personal name was Tsui-ming. But he himself had chosen the nickname of Wei-ming; as the characters were arranged, this meant nothing else than humility and self-restraint. Nominally, his position was that of an official sent by the local office of the Provincial Commissioner of Foreign Affairs to escort visitors; in reality he was a counterespionage agent from Marshal Chang Tso-lin's General Headquarters. M. Raymond from the outset was amazed by his linguistic skills. Needless to say, he was fluent in French. M. Raymond was fond of visiting brothels, and what elicited his startled respect was that when they entered a Japanese house, the other spoke Japanese, and when they went to a White Russian house, he spoke Russian.

The two of them roistered their way up to Harbin, and in a White Russian house they met a pretty Spanish girl. The interpreter, speaking in Spanish, tried to ingratiate himself with her. At this M. Raymond could not but look upon him in a new light. He had always looked down on the yellow-faced sons of the dragon, and considered those precious fellows no more than God's remnants, constructed of coarse leftovers, and not quite right. Now, as though he had picked up a precious stone from a rubbish-heap, his feeling changed, and he asked in amazement:

"Mr. Kao, how old are you?"

"Twenty-eight."

"Ah—who would have thought that a person of twenty-eight could speak so many languages, and moreover speak them so well."

"M. Raymond, you flatter me too much," Kao Wei-ming said humbly.

"How did you learn these languages?"

"You'll laugh when I tell you." Kao Wei-ming smiled ingratiatingly, and blushed.

"How could I?" M. Raymond said sincerely. "I have the greatest respect for you."

"I had to drop out of school," Kao Wei-ming said. "Since I was little, I worked as an attendant on the South Manchurian Railway, and because of the requirements of the job I learned a few words of Japanese, and Russian. Once, on the train, I met a Spaniard who had taken Japanese citizenship, and he took me to work in his business. His business was established in Shenyang, and in fact it was a gambling house. Every day he had customers from various countries, so I learned the languages of quite a few countries."

"That's really not an easy thing! And you speak them so well, too."

"I can speak them, but I can't read them so well, or write them."

"That's not easy, either."

The two of them amused themselves in Harbin until their joints were tired and their strength exhausted, and suddenly M. Raymond came to himself. He said:

"Damn, damn! Why did I come to Manchuria? Mr. Kao, we must go back to Shenyang at once, I have to see the Marshal."

"The Marshal is not in Shenyang; he went to Peking some time ago, surely you knew that?" Kao Wei-ming felt that the other was really laughably confused.

"All right, then we'll go to Peking." M. Raymond blamed his own carelessness. "Ah, look at me, concerned only with pleasure and completely slighting my proper business. Mr. Kao, if I may trouble you, hurry and reserve a berth for me in a sleeping car."

Kao Wei-ming, not at all anxious, slowly smoked a cigarette, and asked in a cold voice:

"What's this urgent matter you have to see the Marshal about?"

"He sent a telegram telling me to come. He wants to discuss something with me, possibly because the Kwangtung army wants to mount a Northern Expedition," M. Raymond said with a little hesitation.

"Well, don't you know the Marshal is in Peking?"

"I know," M. Raymond put his hand to his mouth to cover a yawn. "But no matter where the Marshal is, his secretaries can handle things in his name; all the generals do things that way."

"But this time things are different," Kao Wei-ming said with a laugh. "This time he has gone to Peking to manage the Central Government, and it's from Peking that he should give out orders."

"Then I don't understand it." M. Raymond stretched, and said indifferently: "But once I see him, then I'll understand everything."

"All right, then I'll accompany you to Shenyang. When we get to Shenyang, you can discuss the matter of going to Peking with them yourself, and I won't be concerned with it." Kao Wei-ming gave a cunning smile. "How about that?"

M. Raymond nodded, signifying his agreement. Suddenly he thought that while he had been many years in China, going often to various provinces as an advisor and coming and going among generals and marshals, he had never before encountered a situation in which some Provincial Foreign Affairs Office sent an interpreter to escort him, following him about and never leaving him by so much as a single pace, and even settling his bills in the brothels.

"What am I doing, that deserves such impressive treatment?"

The more M. Raymond thought about it, the odder it seemed, until he came directly and straightforwardly out with his thoughts. He asked tensely:

"We've been with each other these past few days, and we seem to have the same temperament. Mr. Kao, if you consider me a friend, please tell me the true situation."

"Since you're asking, you'll have to promise me something first." Kao Wei-ming was straightforward too.

"Say it, and I'll certainly promise."

"You've got to keep the secret, you can't tell others that I told you anything."

"Of course."

"Well, it's nothing much," said Kao Wei-ming and then repeated: "but if you leak it, I'll become someone who bites the hand that feeds him, and I won't be able to mingle with the officials."

M. Raymond took Kao Wei-ming's hand, shook it firmly, and said with sincerity:

"Relax, why should I do you any harm?"

So Kao Wei-ming told how the Marshal's headquarters in Shenyang had received a telegram from General Wu in Hankow, saying that M. Raymond had already switched his loyalty to Kwangtung, and requesting the Marshal's headquarters in Shenyang to "give this visiting official a special welcome when he arrives". Then he added:

"Thanks to you, I've had a wonderful time these past few days."

The two men clapped their hands and laughed aloud. M. Raymond said:

"If this is surveillance, I'll willingly give up my freedom."

Then he asked:

"How did they happen to pick you? We'd never seen each other before."

"The Marshal's headquarters asked the Provincial Commissioner of Foreign Affairs to lend them someone who could speak the language and knew how to have a good time, and the Commissioner's Office didn't have any such person, so they borrowed one from the gambling house."

The two men laughed again, and decided to go to Shenyang.

The train stopped for a long while in Changchun. In the passageway connecting two railroad cars, Kao Wei-ming encountered a fashionable young woman as they brushed past one another. The young woman gave Kao Wei-ming a captivating smile, and dropped the handbag clutched under her arm to the ground under the coach.

Kao Wei-ming, begging her pardon, opened the door and got out of the coach. He jumped down onto the tracks, and picked up the handbag. By that time the young woman was standing on the station platform. She took the handbag, and thanked him again and again. Kao Wei-ming said deliberately:

"It seems as though I've seen you before; your face is very familiar."

"What is your honorable surname?" The young woman asked with a smile.

Kao Wei-ming told her, and also gave her his card. On one side of the card was a great deal of closely printed Western writing, and on the other side Chinese characters.

"So you're Mr. Kao," the young lady said, putting the card into her handbag, and taking the opportunity to inspect her face in the little mirror in the handbag.

"I haven't asked yet, Miss; your name is?"

"Governor Yin Ch'ang-jen is my Papa."

"Miss Yin, forgive me, forgive me!"

Kao Wei-ming shook her hand. M. Raymond also got off the coach, and the three of them strolled on the station platform. When they learned that Miss Yin was alone, and going to Shenyang, they invited her to the dining car. Inwardly, Kao Wei-ming was amazed. The Provincial Governor's daughter travelling alone like this?

As they travelled the two of them got on very well, and talked of gambling, of singing, of dancing, and of all sorts of dining, drinking, and amusements and the young lady seemed acquainted with them all. Moreover, she was quite easygoing and seemed extraordinarily experienced, without the slightest trace of the restraint and timidity of a sheltered young lady.

Kao Wei-ming became a little more suspicious.

After the evening meal, they returned to their sleeping cars. M. Raymond asked:

"Mr. Kao, are you married?"

"No."

"Chinese marry early, and you are a very resourceful person; why haven't you gotten married yet?"

"Early marriages are often at the parents' orders. I've been an orphan since childhood; I was entrusted to the nuns to raise, and when I was twelve-years-old, they sent me to the South Manchurian Railway." Kao Wei-ming laughed at himself. "I hadn't the good luck to get married early!"

"But now you certainly ought to get married."

"There's no suitable mate."

"What about the one you met today?"

"That's impossible." Kao Wei-ming shook his head with a smile. "Her family status is too high, beyond my reach. Besides, there are a lot of things about her that make a person suspicious."

"After we get to Shenyang, you can go around with her for a while, and then see how it goes." M. Raymond's interest was aroused, and he said impulsively: "As for family status, that will be no problem. I can ask the Marshal to show his face, and make the proposal on your behalf, and then your family status will be even higher than hers. I've visited various provinces and I've never paid any attention to such Provincial Governors. In front of the generals, they don't even have a place to sit down—they're really pitiable."

As M. Raymond spoke, he laughed loudly, fully revealing his feelings of contempt.

In the middle of the night, M. Raymond suddenly awakened to find that Kao Wei-ming's berth was empty. M. Raymond threw on his clothes and went into the lavatory. As he came out, he happened to see Kao Wei-ming coming out of a compartment at the opposite end of the car. But as soon as he had shown himself, he dashed back inside. His movements were extremely quick, as though he were hiding. But M. Raymond was sharp-eyed, and had already seen him. In M. Raymond's mind a layer of suspicion formed.

The next day, M. Raymond noticed that the compartment was occupied by a white-haired old Western lady and a younger woman with red hair. M. Raymond knew a little of the white-haired old lady: she was a German widow and she operated a grocery store in Shenyang, supplying local European residents with various commonplace foodstuffs. However, in reality she was an agent for Soviet military intelligence in Shenyang. On one occasion M. Raymond, through the introduction of an Austrian businessman, had brought in a shipment of German arms. The Austrian businessman had taken him along to the white-haired old lady's grocery store to buy something, and after they came out the Austrian businessman asked him:

"Are you interested in making a few rubles?"

"I've never had anything to do with the Russians."

"In fact, it's just a way to make some money, so why shouldn't you? If you're interested, I can introduce you. That white-haired old lady you just saw in the grocery store—she can pay you the money directly, in pounds sterling or American dollars, whichever you like."

The Austrian businessman added in a serious tone:

"You two would deal directly; I wouldn't want a commission."

"Well, why are you doing it?"

M. Raymond didn't understand why the other was so eager to help.

"Isn't that easy to understand?" The Austrian businessman smiled. "I'm depending on you to find an outlet for my arms."

Although they had discussed it, M. Raymond had never earned any money from that quarter. His hands were spattered with blood, but he did not like the Soviet Union's Communist system. He had no ideology, it was just the way he felt, and he couldn't make a sudden change.

It had been two years, but M. Raymond remembered the whole affair clearly, and the white-haired old lady's features remained as though before his eyes. Now, having discovered her aboard the train, M. Raymond would follow the "adventurers' code" and protect her secret. He had never mentioned the affair to anyone before, and still less, of course, would he give any sign now.

What was Kao Wei-ming doing, going to their compartment in the dark of night? And why, having shown his head, did he then dart back inside? Had he already seen me? He certainly must have, because at that hour there was no one else in the passageway.

M. Raymond returned to his bed and lay down. He lighted a cigarette and smoked, thinking that such people as Kao Wei-ming would naturally have extremely complex social relationships. His background, and his occupation, would cause him to have numerous unexpected encounters, which he would have no means of refusing, and from which he could not extricate himself. That my thoughts had never run in this direction since meeting him must be due to my own naiveté. So thinking, M. Raymond felt that it was rather amusing.

But at the same time, he was deeply concerned with his own good fortune, because his activities from beginning to end, were within the scope of commerce. Although he assumed the title of advisor to various quarters, this was only to facilitate his business, and was absolutely apolitical in nature.

M. Raymond suddenly felt his own nobility. In this old Eastern country, he had done honor to his own name, and he had also done honor to his country, and to himself as a Frenchman. M. Raymond had never had such a feeling before.

No mistake, it was good to deal fairly. M. Raymond was a businessman, and it was proper for him to have such feelings. What he glossed over was the nature of his trade goods: the munitions which killed directly and the narcotic drugs which killed indirectly.

It is just oneself whom everyone considers may be forgiven.

The international relations of the northeast, squeezed between the two great powers, Japan and the Soviet Union, were complex. What M. Raymond couldn't understand was: why did the Chinese want to do anything for the Soviet Union with its Communist dictatorship? Surely they were not really that helpless and desperate?

Extinguishing his cigarette, M. Raymond smiled disdainfully.

Kao Wei-ming returned. He turned on the lamp, and glanced at M. Raymond's berth, saying:

"You haven't slept?"

"That's right."

"What is it? Are you thinking of your wife?"

"We were in the brothels every day; you know I don't think of her."

"Well, she must certainly be thinking of you."

"She doesn't think of me either; she loves her shop more than she loves her husband."

"In that case, the two of you are very well-matched."

"I often think so." M. Raymond thought for a moment, and added: "What is it really like in that foreign company where you work?"

"Didn't I tell you? It's a gambling house."

"What I mean is, what is it like in that gambling house?"

"It's like a hotel. There are rooms, there's a restaurant, and there's a bar."

"You only neglected to say if there are girls."

"Naturally there are girls, what kind of a good-time place would it be without girls?"

"Can someone like myself, who doesn't gamble or drink, stay there?"

"You would be welcomed."

"What about your Spanish boss?"

"I can guarantee the two of you will become good friends."

"Since that's how it is, I've decided to stay at your place," M. Raymond said happily. "I'll take this opportunity, and not go back to Hankow; I'll give my ears a little peace and quiet. My wife talks too much; I'm really afraid of her."

"You're not going to Peking, then?"

"I think I'd best send a telegram to the Marshal, and see whether or not he wants me to come," M. Raymond said, yawning. "I haven't anything on just now, and I'd be glad to show him my devoted loyalty, and express my obedience. I really can't think why he wanted to put me under surveillance. Sending me on a false errand—surely he doesn't want to arrest me?"

"They didn't say to keep you under surveillance," Kao Wei-ming said with a laugh. "They're giving you special treatment."

"I thought he understood. That business of his is only useful in dealing with the common people of his own country, it's of no use at all in dealing with foreigners. In the future there will come a day when even the common people of his own country won't stand for it."

"Not necessarily in the future, but even now the common people are no longer willing to say yes when they mean no, nor afraid to show their anger."

"Once things change, he can't fix them up."

"How long do you think he can last?"

"That I can't say for sure. Hasn't Kwangtung already mounted their Northern Expedition?"

"Do you think they can succeed?"

"That's very hard to say. But that is a newly risen force, and a newly risen force can often win. Otherwise, the empire would always have been ruled by the same family, and never have changed hands."

"If they do succeed, what are you going to do?"

"Think of a way to adapt to them. I work for the Chinese, and not for any particular Chinese. Only . . ."

Then M. Raymond hesitated for a moment, and said nothing.

"Only—only what?" Kao Wei-ming pursued.

"Only, I've heard that the Communist Party is on that side, and I don't approve of the Communist Party."

"Why?"

"I'm satisfied with the present situation; this present world is fine. Our colonies are several tens of times larger than our own country, and we have many places to go," Mr. Raymond said frankly. "I don't approve of any plans to change the world."

"From the standpoint of the colonial peoples, they certainly wouldn't listen to these words of yours."

"Yes, I know."

M. Raymond grunted his assent, and yawned again. He was exhausted.

"If there were no Communist Party on the Kwangtung side, I would certainly think of a way to adapt to them, and to help them—if they were able."

As he said this, he was already falling asleep.

The next morning they got off the train in Shenyang. On the station platform, Kao Wei-ming asked Miss Yin's address.

"I live at the Aoyama Villa."

This answer further aroused Kao Wei-ming's incomprehension. For a Provincial Governor in the northeast not to have an office in Shenyang, and for his daughter to stay in a hotel, and moreover in a hotel run by a Japanese? Kao Wei-ming was really a bit puzzled. Miss Yin went on:

"Mr. Nomura of the Aoyama Villa is my adoptive father."

This was obviously a significant explanation.

Kao Wei-ming, hearing this, nodded and said:

"Good, then we'll see you there."

The three of them hired a car, and went first to the Aoyama Villa. As they clasped hands before parting, Miss Yin asked:

"Mr. Kao, can I come to your foreign establishment to see you?"

"If you want to, we would especially welcome you," Kao Wei-ming said happily, and added a word of explanation: "It's a splendid mixing place."

"I've heard Mr. Nomura speak of your Spanish employer, and say that he's a very good and charming gentleman. I hope this time I'll have a chance to meet him."

After they parted, Kao Wei-ming kept smiling at the thought of it all the way back.

"Can those who run gambling houses be good gentlemen? Can good gentlemen run gambling houses?"

But once they arrived at the gambling house, M. Raymond had the pleasurable feeling of a "guest treated as though returning home". First of all, he and the Spanish master of the house, as soon as they set eyes on one another, were like old friends, and got on very well. Several Japanese military police lived in a row of the "foreign" establishment's rooms facing the street. One entered by a small and unimpressive gate, to find oneself in a marvelous Japanese style courtyard, with an artificial mountain and winding paths, dense trees and clear ponds, all extremely subtle and refined. M. Raymond thought of his arranged courtyard in Hankow, and felt immensely mortified: "Look at this! It's so well-done! This truly deserves to be called 'Oriental mood'!"

He stood on the small, curved bridge of blue stone, gazing appreciatively in all directions, and gave the Spanish owner, who stood beside him, a hearty clap on the shoulder. He said admiringly:

"You certainly know how to arrange things!"

"No, this was all my wife's plan."

"For your wife to be such a hand at it—it's wonderful!"

As M. Raymond expressed his heartfelt pleasure, the image of his own Anna flashed through his mind, and he seemed to hear a chattering beside his ear.

"My wife is Japanese."

"Is that why you became a Japanese citizen?" M. Raymond, with a little amazement, gazed at the Spanish owner.

"Yes." The Spanish owner nodded happily. "My wife's family name is Kiyosui, and I changed my own name to Kiyosui. I would like you to call me Mr. Kiyosui."

"Fine, Mr. Kiyosui. Your wife must certainly be an extraordinary person, to have such magical power."

"Wait a bit and I'll introduce you."

Passing through the courtyard, they came to an old-fashioned two-story Western house, with a broad covered verandah. The gambling hall was downstairs, with single rooms to both sides. The hotel was upstairs.

After they had seen the rooms, Mr. Kiyosui led M. Raymond around to the upstairs rear verandah. Here again was a broad courtyard, which contained a tennis court, encircled on four sides by green pine trees. Mr. Kiyosui pointed and said:

"See, over there is a Japanese style house."

"Yes."

"That's where my wife and I live. We can enter from the small gate beside the tennis court," Mr. Kiyosui said, pointing it out.

"Your business isn't a small one, Mr. Kiyosui; this building alone must be worth quite a bit. Is this property your own?"

"Yes."

"When I see your style here, I know there's no hope for me," M. Raymond spoke candidly. "To have lived so many years in the Orient, in vain!"

"I've relied on the help of the Japanese Kuantung Army."

Mr. Kiyosui led M. Raymond to sit down in one of the reclining chairs on the verandah. A plump, middle-aged white woman came over and said a few words to Mr. Kiyosui. Mr. Kiyosui answered her, and she went away. Pointing in her direction, Mr. Kiyosui said:

"That woman is the manager of this upstairs hotel; she's a White Russian widow, all alone. She can speak a few words of French, so if you want something, you can ask her. Her husband used to be a count, but he couldn't stand the hardships of being a refugee, and he died. She likes people to address her as Countess. She knows Japanese too, and she's accustomed to using Japanese with my wife and me."

A yellow-faced servant boy brought coffee. He wore a dark red, dapple-patterned long Chinese gown, and over that a yellow riding jacket with "horse-hoof" sleeves, an official's hat with red hatband and red button, and high-legged court boots. M. Raymond, who had never before seen such a get-up, looked him over and asked:

"What nationality is he? What kind of clothes is he wearing?"

"He's a Chinese boy," Mr. Kiyosui said, drinking some coffee, and smiling. "He's wearing the court dress of an aristocrat of the Ch'ing Dynasty period."

"You certainly know lots of ways to amuse yourself."

"In the evenings in the gambling hall, I have a maid with bound feet. Out of ten million, I picked the smallest of small feet."

"No wonder you've gotten rich—you're really something!"

The two men laughed. M. Raymond looked again at that Japanese style house of Mr. Kiyosui's, and couldn't help asking:

"How did you happen to marry a Japanese woman?"

"I fell ill while I was visiting Japan, and entered a private hospital. The daughter of Dr. Kiyosui, the hospital director, looked after me herself, and now she is my wife."

Seeing that he was half-bald, plump, and short, and truly failing to understand how he could have gained his wife's affection, M. Raymond once again doubted that his wife could be a beauty.

"You're truly fortunate."

"But I paid a great price. I returned to my country, got a divorce, and broke off relations with father, mother, son and daughter, and with many relatives, abandoned my country, and abandoned my religion as well, because according to religious teachings it is not permitted to divorce and remarry."

"I think that when you add it all up, you certainly don't regret it."

"Of course I don't regret it. I live very well now, and every day my wife and I burn incense and worship Buddha," said Mr. Kiyosui with a satisfied smile. He took out his pocket-watch, looked at it, and said:

"She'll be coming out to eat soon. Today, she and I are inviting you to eat lunch with us, to welcome you."

"Thank you."

"Good; we'll go down to the restaurant and wait for her."

The two of them went downstairs together.

Mrs. Kiyosui's personal name was Ho-tzu. Ho-tzu was far more lovely than M. Raymond could have imagined. She had a tall and slender body, and a subtle, natural smile was forever on her features; she was moreover very quiet and taciturn. In her refined Japanese kimono, she seemed to float above the ground, making M. Raymond think of those fairies and Oriental princesses in the children's stories.

By M. Raymond's calculation, the Spaniard had to be twenty years her senior. Even if he wore high heels, he would hardly match her height. So M. Raymond didn't understand how she could love him. In private, he asked the Spaniard:

"Mr. Kiyosui, by what means did you win the affection of this beauty?"

"I don't understand it myself," said the Spaniard with a shrug. "Perhaps it's because I'm a white man. Although Japan is a great power, the colored races still feel a little inferior before the white race. This feeling of inferiority causes them to have two opposite reactions toward the white race: one is blind worship, and the other is blind opposition."

"I'm a white person, too, but I've never run into such good luck as yours." M. Raymond smiled bitterly, and inexplicably felt a little jealous.

He returned to his room, shut the door, and carefully examined himself from head to toe in the dressing mirror. Then he made an extremely objective comparative study of the man in the mirror and Mr. Kiyosui as to age, features, figure, and manner. He felt positively that truly there was no point on which the man in the mirror did not surpass Mr. Kiyosui several times over. He thought:

"As for nationality, France too far outshines Spain. Bullfighting is so barbaric, and we have Paris, the city of flowers!"

After that he calmed down, and thought no more of leaving. He said to Kao Wei-ming:

"I'll help you out. As long as I don't slip away, you've got something to offer the Marshal's headquarters, which is your 'meritorious service'. You can report to them a little extra 'special welcoming expenses' and the two of us will go equal shares in the business."

"That goes without saying, and I guarantee you'll have a good time," Kao Wei-ming answered. "Whatever kind of woman you want to play with, here it can be arranged."

"No, Mr. Kao, I've already sworn off lechery."

"Why?" Kao Wei-ming felt this was a bit strange.

"No reason, only that I fooled around too much, and I'm tired of it."

"All right, rest a few days, and you'll be all right. You certainly can't swear off it."

"Kao, you watch me!"

As M. Raymond said, so he did; he no longer amused himself with women. He even gave up cigarettes. He didn't gamble, he didn't drink, he went to bed early, and rose early, and he lived as simply as a Puritan. He importuned Kiyosui Ho-tzu to teach him to worship Buddha, and to teach him how to study the sutras and pronounce charms. Aside from this, he seemed to have no other interests.

After a few days, Kao Wei-ming began to understand his intentions. When they were alone he said:

"M. Raymond, would you like to have a Japanese girlfriend?"

"I told you, I've sworn off lechery."

"I don't mean a prostitute, I'm talking about a girlfriend."

"No, I haven't any such thing in mind."

"Japanese women are fine. M. Raymond, I advise you to get a Japanese girlfriend. You see how nice Madame Ho-tzu is. Mr. Kiyosui loves Madame Ho-tzu to an extreme."

"Yes, I know."

"I dare say," said Kao Wei-ming seriously, making a gesture with his hand to catch M. Raymond's attention, "that if anyone had improper intentions, or actions, toward Madame Ho-tzu, that Mr. Kiyosui would kill that person with his pistol, because Mr. Kiyosui loves Madame Ho-tzu to an extreme, and he often practices with his pistol, shooting at targets. His skill with the pistol is magical; nine hits out of ten."

"I didn't know Mr. Kiyosui had such a skill; sometime I'll have to study it with him," M. Raymond said carelessly.

Two days later, he had a string of Buddhist beads in hand. Madame Ho-tzu had already begun to teach him the Buddhist law.

Suddenly one evening Miss Yin came to the foreign establishment, alone, especially to call on Kao Wei-ming. Kao Wei-ming was in the bar to welcome her with a cup of tea, and later he conducted her to the main room in the rear to see the sights. He introduced her to his Spanish employer, Mr. Kiyosui, and when Mr. Kiyosui learned she was the daughter of a famous Provincial Governor, he called Ho-tzu to come out especially to keep her company. Although Ho-tzu was the woman manager of the gambling hall, she seldom came out to the front of the building except to dine. Recently she had gotten quite involved with M. Raymond, but she would often come out to the front to get some exercise. Originally she had enjoyed playing tennis, and Mr. Kiyosui had built the tennis court in the rear courtyard especially for her. But although there was a tennis court, usually there was no one to play with. M. Raymond had played as a young man, but since coming to the Orient he had left off. Now, seeing a rare opportunity, he took up the racquet again. Often, in order to exhibit the temperament of a loser, he would give up a game to Ho-tzu.

But in the evening Ho-tzu was still unwilling to come to the front. On this occasion, in order to keep the Provincial Governor's daughter company, she broke her rule.

"Would the Provincial Governor's daughter like to gamble?"

The roulette wheel had already started to spin, and an assorted crowd of men and women, old and young, of various nations were crowding around the gaming table.

"No, I came to see Mr. Kao."

"Well, then, let's go into this little room and sit down."

Ho-tzu in her heart blamed her husband; since the girl was Mr. Kao's girlfriend, Mr. Kao ought to keep her company; what was the use of calling me out without any reason? But she sat down, and said:

"Provincial Governor's Miss, you speak Japanese very well."

"Thank you, Madame, but please don't call me Provincial Governor's daughter."

When Ho-tzu heard this, she pursed her lips, and smiled. Looking at Kao Wei-ming, she asked:

"How should I call her?"

"I call her Miss Yin."

Miss Yin heard, and said quickly:

"My name is Wen-tzu, please call me Wen-tzu."

"Oh, Miss Wen-tzu," Ho-tzu said. "Your name is a little like that of a Japanese girl."

"It was my adopted father Mr. Nomura who chose the name for me."

"So that's how it is, you're no stranger after all," Ho-tzu said, looking at Kao Wei-ming. "You keep Miss Wen-tzu company; I'll go and ask them to bring tea."

"I don't drink tea, Madame, thank you."

While Yin Wen-tzu was being polite, Ho-tzu had already bowed and withdrawn. She went into her Spanish husband's office and told him:

"She's Kao Wei-ming's friend; it's not very convenient for me to be sitting there."

"It was only to show off a bit for her, and also to get you to come out." In order to show his guilty feelings, her Spanish husband hurried over and kissed her lightly on the cheek.

"I'm not very used to coming out to the front at night," Ho-tzu said gently, nestling close to him. "I'll go on back."

"All right, you go ahead," her husband agreed.

When she came to the tennis court, Ho-tzu paused, to look at the many stars in the heavens. It was the time of the Mid-autumn Festival, and the weather was already chilly. Ho-tzu clutched her wrap a bit closer, and half-ran toward the house.

Suddenly someone jumped out from the shadows of the trees. Ho-tzu halted, stepped back, and asked;

"Who?"

"It is I, Madame Ho-tzu."

"M. Raymond?"

"Yes."

"What are you doing here?"

"May I come into your house and see you?"

"You can't, we have never received friends in our home."

"Well, then, let's just walk about out here."

M. Raymond came closer and caught Ho-tzu by the arm. Ho-tzu was a little frightened, and speedily freed herself, saying:

"No, M. Raymond, it's late, and it's cold."

"I'll give you my overcoat to wrap up in," M. Raymond said, taking off his coat.

Ho-tzu, seeing that he would not relent, turned and began to walk rapidly ahead. Raising her voice, she called:

"Countess, Countess!"

M. Raymond didn't understand why she was so terrified. He hurried up behind her, asking:

"What is it, what are you doing? Madame Ho-tzu!"

The Countess appeared from under the upstairs hotel verandah and urgently asked:

"What's going on? Mistress!"

Ho-tzu calmed herself, blushing as she smiled, and took the Countess' hand. She said:

"I don't know why, but I became frightened when I saw the shadows of those big trees."

The Countess, catching sight of M. Raymond coming along after her, already understood a little. Laughing, she said:

"What were you afraid the tree's shadow was going to do? Come on, I'll see you home."

They spoke in Japanese, and M. Raymond did not understand. Seeing them go off hand in hand, he wandered off listlessly by himself toward the gambling hall in the front.

He made a circuit of the hall, disliking the clamor of the already numerous drinkers and gamblers. He was about to withdraw when he glimpsed two people coming out of one of the side rooms: it was Kao Wei-ming with Miss Yin. He went over and greeted them:

"How are you passing the time, Miss Yin? Drinking or gambling?"

"I didn't come for either. I only came to see the excitement."

"Good, it's the same with me. Miss Yin, when you've seen enough of the excitement, I'll invite you upstairs, to the hotel verandah for some of the Countess' coffee. It's quiet up there; quite a different atmosphere."

"We were going there anyway for some quiet conversation," Yin Wen-tzu said with a captivating smile, leaning closer to Kao Wei-ming.

No sooner had she spoken than the big glass double doors were suddenly thrust open, and two Japanese military policemen took their positions, one to each side. A Japanese Army officer proudly entered, and the two military policemen hailed him and raised their hands in salute.

Mr. Kiyosui, who had been sitting in the office, heard their hail, took a careful look, and then came rushing out to welcome the officer, saying:

"Commissioner, welcome, welcome! You seldom come here."

The Commissioner took off his cap, pistol, and sword and handed them to Mr. Kiyosui. Kao Wei-ming came over to stand behind Mr. Kiyosui, and Mr. Kiyosui, having reverently accepted the articles with both hands, turned and handed them to Kao Wei-ming. Kao Wei-ming bowed to the Commissioner, and then took the articles off to the cloakroom.

Mr. Kiyosui stood to one side, yielding the way to the other, and said:

"Won't the Commissioner please come into my office and rest a bit?"

The two military policemen withdrew, shutting the big glass doors.

Following along behind the Commissioner, Mr. Kiyosui continued:

"What is the Commissioner's pleasure tonight?"

Catching sight of M. Raymond, he beckoned him over, saying:

"Come along, I'll introduce you to Commissioner Kuriyagawa, an excellent friend."

M. Raymond went in with them, and when Commissioner Kuriyagawa, speaking in French, had made small talk with him for a little, and knew that he lived in Hankow, the Commissioner said:

"The Kwangtung Revolutionary Army has already occupied Hankow; didn't you know?"

"I haven't read the papers for many days, and I haven't gone out. And no one brings up such important matters in here," M. Raymond said frankly, and asked: "Are things quiet in the Concessions there?"

"Of course. I don't believe anyone would dare invade the Concessions."

"I'd never have thought Marshal Wu would be so badly beaten."

Commissioner Kuriyagawa looked fixedly at M. Raymond for a minute, and abruptly asked:

"M. Raymond, which side do you work for?"

"I'm for the generals of the various northern provinces."

"Why did Marshal Wu send a telegram saying that you had given your allegiance to the Revolutionary Army?"

"That's a joke!" M. Raymond said boldly. "I still can't understand it. I've been staying here at Mr. Kiyosui's, and I've cut off my connections with the outside world; I haven't even written my wife—all in order to make my intentions clear."

"I can see that you're very clever. There was a need for further clarification." Commissioner Kuriyagawa professed himself satisfied, but he went on to ask: "You work for the northerners, I know. How about foreign countries? What country do you belong to?"

This question caused M. Raymond a good deal of unease. He knew that he had probably run into trouble. The Commissioner's visit this evening seemed to be meant to trouble him, because his talk had already exceeded the limits of social intercourse; it was absolutely not the sort of talk appropriate for new-found friends. M. Raymond understood his situation. If his responses were unsatisfactory, he might be laying future trouble for himself. Summoning his wits, he said carefully:

"I'm a broker, pure and simple. I belong to the merchants of various countries."

"Is it really that simple?"

"It's really that simple," Mr. Raymond said courteously and gravely. "I have nothing to do with politics, but I'm not one who doesn't understand politics. China is the Japanese Empire's China, especially the coast, the north, Manchuria, and Mongolia. Since I make my living in China, I certainly have to get along with the Japanese."

Commissioner Kuriyagawa stood up, grasping M. Raymond with one hand, and said a little excitedly:

"Splendid, your understanding is extremely correct. If all Westerners were like you, there simply wouldn't be any 'China problem'. Come on, drink up!"

He hauled M. Raymond off toward the bar, and Mr. Kiyosui followed.

"Commissioner, let me substitute water," M. Raymond said in a courteously beseeching tone. "I don't drink."

"Stop that foolish talk at once," the Commissioner laughed. "Is there a Frenchman in all the world who doesn't drink wine?"

"Commissioner, I'm that one."

Kuriyagawa's face went stiff, as though he were a little displeased.

"M. Raymond," he said slowly, "it looks as though your words just now were false. So you weren't sincere at all!"

"No, Commissioner, I really don't drink," M. Raymond hastily broke out of the encirclement and turned the direction of the conversation. "But, since the Commissioner orders it, to prove my loyalty I'll break my rule."

"Champagne, champagne!" he cried.

So the two of them drank a toast, and Mr. Kiyosui joined them. Commissioner Kuriyagawa said lightly:

"I hope that in the future you can do a little work for the Kuantung Army. If you're willing, we'll drink another toast."

M. Raymond, hearing this, knew that refusal was useless, and preferred to be straightforward. He said:

"Commissioner, you're my friend, and I'll do whatever you want me to. What do you think—isn't that all right? I haven't the patience to have to do with other people."

"It's the same thing, I represent the Kuantung Army," Commissioner Kuriyagawa said with a loud laugh. The two men then drank another toast. Kuriyagawa pointed to Mr. Kiyosui and said:

"All right, we've settled it with a word, and Mr. Kiyosui will be our go-between. We're going to wait a bit longer, and see how this battle of Sun the Fragrant General's goes. If Sun can beat the Revolutionary Army, then there's no problem. If Sun is beaten again, then the Revolutionary Army has matured."

Kuriyagawa paused at this point, thought for a moment, and then continued:

"If that time really does come, then I will probably ask you to go back to Hankow. The Kuantung Army cannot just sit looking on!"

"Commissioner, I'll stay here, awaiting your orders," Mr. Raymond said in an extraordinarily obedient tone.

Kuriyagawa was satisfied, and the two men drank three more toasts. Kuriyagawa directed Kiyosui:

"From now on put all of M. Raymond's bill on my account."

"There's no need, Commissioner, Marshal Chang's headquarters has already reimbursed me for everything."

"Why is that?"

Once he understood that M. Raymond was receiving "special treatment" Kuriyagawa laughed loudly. He said:

"That's fine. You take his money for doing my work."

So saying, he went off alone towards the crowd at the gaming tables.

M. Raymond withdrew. He stood for a moment on the little bridge in the courtyard, shook his head, and smiled a cold smile, and then went upstairs to the hotel. He stopped before the door of the Manager's office, and asked the Countess:

"Have you seen Mr. Kao?"

"He's in that room over there, with a young lady."

"Miss Yin?"

"Yes." The Countess opened the registration book on the counter and looked. "Miss Yin Wen-tzu."

"What room number?"

"Number Nine."

Seeing that the door to Room Number Nine was closed, M. Raymond returned to his own room. He remained alert for any movement in Room Number Nine, until it grew very late, and he was truly so tired that he couldn't go on with it. Then he got ready and went to bed. He looked at his watch and saw that it was already three o'clock.

The next day Mr. Kiyosui invited Yin Wen-tzu to lunch, and he was asked to accompany her. But neither Kao Wei-ming nor Ho-tzu were to be present at the meal, and M. Raymond, feeling that it was a little odd, secretly hesitated.

He simply didn't understand why Ho-tzu had been so alarmed at him the night before.

Later on, Sun Ch'uan-fang was defeated, and the government was established at Nanking. Commissioner Kuriyagawa arranged to see M. Raymond again, and the two men exchanged views. They considered that the "Nanking-Hankow Split", with the two governments at odds, like two tigers fighting, must result in injury.

"Wait 'til they start fighting amongst themselves," Kuriyagawa said. "We still have time, we can look on a bit yet."

When the British returned the Hankow Concession, M. Raymond feared the French Concession would not be protected either; he began to be concerned for Anna, and wanted to go back to Hankow, but Kuriyagawa wouldn't let him. Kuriyagawa said:

"I'm still waiting for something."

"What are you waiting for?" M. Raymond asked urgently.

"I don't believe the British would have given back their Concession willingly. Perhaps the Revolutionary Army will have trouble with the Western powers. If they start to quarrel, the Great Japanese Empire will adopt a policy of neutrality, and happily 'sit on the hill watching the tigers fight'."

Kuriyagawa was laughing loudly as he said this.

There was nothing for M. Raymond to do but be patient and stay on. Several times he thought of going to the French Consulate and asking for a safe-conduct pass out of the country, but he didn't actually do it. At least in "Manchuria" that would not have been the cleverest thing to do. M. Raymond lived off of China; he had in mind his destiny, and was not seeking a momentary advantage.

Chapter XXIII

Upstairs in Room Number Nine at the hotel.

Early in the morning, the sun that filled the window awakened Kao Wei-ming from his dreams. He threw on his clothes and got up, and went to draw the curtain. At the same time he silently reproached himself for his carelessness the night before—how could he have forgotten to draw the curtain before going to bed? Fortunately, beyond the window was the courtyard, and the tall trees, so he wasn't anxious that the beauties of spring might have been seen. Otherwise, it might have given rise to jests.

Drawing the curtain tightly, he returned. Looking down at Yin Wen-tzu's cheeks, as delicately red as apples, Kao Wei-ming felt a certain itch. He lay down, and lightly kissed her. First with a sweet, subtle smile, and then opening her eyes, she awakened. She hugged Kao Wei-ming with both hands, and asked in an intimate voice:

"Don't you like me?"

"Nonsense!"

"Then why don't you make love to me again?"

"The sun dazzled me, and I got up to draw the curtains."

Yin Wen-tzu nibbled Kao Wei-ming's lower lip with her two lips, and wouldn't let him say any more. Turned over so that he was looking up, Kao Wei-ming's feet had already left the ground, and he felt slightly suffocated because she was holding him so tightly.

After a time, Kao Wei-ming leaned back against the head of the bed, smoking a cigarette. Yin Wen-tzu's head was buried on his chest, and with one hand he was stroking her glossy hair. Divided to the sides to be coiled on top, her hair, which was now loose, would be gathered in the morning into a coil. Kao Wei-ming gently removed those clasps and hairpins, one by one, and made a pile of them on the lampstand at the head of the bed.

As he thought, Kao Wei-ming couldn't help smiling.

"What are you smiling about?" Yin Wen-tzu asked, looking up.

"I'm asking you," Kao Wei-ming said in an intimate voice. "Are you satisfied?"

"I don't know, I won't answer you. Is that really what you're smiling about?"

"No. I've drawn a question mark in my mind. If I say it, I'm afraid you'd take offense."

"I'd prefer that if there's something on your mind, you'd come out with it, then you wouldn't be treating me like a stranger."

"I feel," Kao Wei-ming said, taking her hand and kissing it, "that you aren't a young girl."

"You're very experienced with women."

"The chess piece has met its match." Kao Wei-ming put down his cigarette, laid flat, took her face between his hands, and said in banter: "I've met a woman who's had experience with quite a few men."

"Do you like it, or don't you?"

"Of course I like it; this is called 'households are suitable and families are a match'."

"I deployed my forces so obviously, first of all, in order to help you, because I was afraid you didn't understand," Yin Wen-tzu said very naturally, with a slight smile.

"Well then, you ought to tell me the truth. Who are you?"

"In fact I'm Provincial Governor Yin's third concubine."

"Did you use to sing in the Peking dialect, to the drum?"

"No mistake."

"No wonder I felt that your face was familiar, I remembered seeing your photograph."

"Now you're talking nonsense. I've never been photographed, I avoid photographs."

"Why?"

"I know that you've never been photographed either, why is that?" Yin Wen-tzu asked with a smile, deliberately batting her eyes at him.

Kao Wei-ming's heart gave a start. Yes, he too had avoided being photographed, and that was because of a reason he couldn't tell anyone. For Yin Wen-tzu to ask about it like this—surely she didn't know the reason? How strange!

Kao Wei-ming hesitated for a moment.

"You still can't answer it?" Yin Wen-tzu said, smiling. "Can't make it out, you're not quick-witted enough."

"It's because I can't figure you out, so I hesitated a bit," Kao Wei-ming also smiled.

"What's on my mind is all plain to see now. I'm speaking honestly: I love you very much." Yin Wen-tzu sighed. "You're in a dangerous position, and you don't even know it."

"I don't understand you."

"You're pretending to be stupid! You consider yourself clever, but in fact you're a fool!" Yin Wen-tzu was angry and spoke impatiently. "I'm pointing it out to you, and still you don't get going. I ask you now: what were you doing going to the old German lady's compartment on the train, in the middle of the night?"

Kao Wei-ming was startled. He had fallen head over heels into the hands of a woman, and he was very embarrassed. He remembered that, when he was about to leave the old German lady's compartment, he had caught a glimpse of someone, and that had been M. Raymond. Outside of that, there couldn't have been a second person. He couldn't help thinking:

"Could she have some connection with M. Raymond, and have gotten the information from Raymond?"

But in any event he knew that he had met his match, and that it was an intelligent opponent. And so without further evasion, he said frankly:

"Do you belong to the Kuantung Army?"

"Yes, the same as you."

"You know me, but I don't know you; your position must certainly be higher than mine." Kao Wei-ming was deliberately deferential.

"Not necessarily; on the contrary, you don't come under my direction," Yin Wen-tzu said in a low voice. "You didn't get the Kuantung Army's permission before you went to work for the old German lady; you didn't think about whether the Kuantung Army would agree. Russians are the great enemies of the Japanese in Manchuria and Mongolia. The Kuantung Army has been paying special attention lately to the old German lady, they want to know just what it is she's up to."

"The two countries have contradictions over the profits of Manchuria and Mongolia—this situation I understand."

"Well, then," Yin Wen-tzu said with a sigh, "aren't you 'feeling around for advantage between two pairs of bloody jaws'? Don't you feel that it's dangerous?"

Kao Wei-ming kept kissing her neck and shoulders, and murmured:

"Tell me, what should I do? From now on, I'm yours. I'm willing to accept your orders, and I'll do whatever you tell me."

"That's not what I meant. I only hope that you and I can sincerely love each other. I'm so alone and so lonely I could die, and I need a lover to comfort me."

As Yin Wen-tzu said this, she felt terribly distressed, and her eyes filled with tears.

"We're truly two sufferers from the same illness, sympathetic with each other," Kao Wei-ming, also moved, said. "My background isn't very different from yours. If you don't despise me, I could marry you."

"Marriage?" Yin Wen-tzu said sadly. "A special agent of the Kuantung Army, a Provincial Governor's concubine, and formerly a famous drum-singer to boot—do you think that such a woman can get married?"

"I was speaking of later on, when you've gotten free of these relations, when you've recovered your freedom; I wasn't speaking of now."

"Then wait until later on to speak."

"Well then, what shall we do now?"

"For now we'll just meet in secret." Yin Wen-tzu smiled. "Tell me, how did your connection with the old German lady begin? I have a way to save you. I've been ordered to keep her under surveillance. I've been at it for several months now, and she's never discovered me."

"It started in the gambling hall." Kao Wei-ming sighed. "I was threatened by one of the gamblers. If I didn't give him the things he wanted, then I couldn't protect my life."

"Did Mr. Kiyosui know?"

Kao Wei-ming hesitated a moment, and then said:

"I don't think he knew."

"Why didn't you tell the Kuantung Army? The Kuantung Army could have done away with him, and removed the threat to you."

"He also had plenty of pounds sterling."

"Did he use pounds sterling?"

"No, it was I who asked him for the pounds sterling."

"Why?"

"I was establishing some property in Hong Kong, preparing another retreat for myself. I wasn't ready to go on doing what you see for the rest of my life, and when the opportunity came I was going to wash my hands of it. Just now, when I said I was willing to marry you, it was with that in mind."

Kao Wei-ming spoke with utter sincerity.

"The plan was a good one, but you forgot that the Kuantung Army can take your life."

"I hope you won't report me."

"I definitely won't report. But this secret of yours can't be kept for very long; if I don't report it, there are others who will; the ears and eyes are many."

"Well, what do you think I should do?"

"You should report voluntarily to the Kuantung Army, and say that you took the opportunity to penetrate in order to learn the old German lady's secrets."

"They won't be that easy to fool."

"If you can give them some relatively valuable materials, they'll be busy sorting them out, and then you'll have time to lie, and change the whole situation."

"All right, I'll rely on you. What a blessing that you're saving my life!" Kao Wei-ming, moved, kissed her again and again.

They rested a little longer, and then got up and dressed. Yin Wen-tzu, seated at the dressing table, looked at Kao Wei-ming in the mirror and smiled.

"Kao, I may have committed a great crime."

"What do you mean?"

"In our line of work, emotional involvement is most to be shunned. I've gotten emotionally involved with you. Now, I'm in your hands."

Kao Wei-ming leaned down and hugged her from behind. He kissed her, and said:

"If you're in my hands, you're safe."

After combing their hair and washing, they went downstairs, and it happened to be lunchtime. M. Raymond was already seated and he politely called them to share his table. Kao Wei-ming said:

"Miss Yin, you sit with M. Raymond a minute, I'm going to see Mr. Kiyosui."

"We can't talk to each other, and it would be embarrassing sitting together."

"Just for a moment; I'll hurry back," Kao Wei-ming said, and went off.

Yin Wen-tzu found nothing for it but to smile and nod at M. Raymond, and quietly sit down. M. Raymond especially called a Chinese waitress who could speak English to interpret, and he became unbearably attentive, asking Yin Wen-tzu about this and about that.

Mr. Kiyosui had not yet come out, so Kao Wei-ming placed a telephone call from the Manager's office to his residence, and said that he wanted to speak to him alone, and asking the other to meet him on the tennis court. He put down the phone, returned to the table, and told Yin Wen-tzu:

"Mr. Kiyosui wants me to come to the rear, but I'll hurry back."

"Where in the rear?"

"In his house."

"Isn't he coming out to the front?"

"He'll come. I can tell him that you're here."

M. Raymond, blinking, asked the Chinese waitress:

"What are they saying?"

The waitress told him, and he said to Kao Wei-ming:

"Would it be convenient for you to invite Madame Ho-tzu to come out and eat with us?"

"I can give her your message."

On the tennis court in the rear, Kao Wei-ming in a low voice told Mr. Kiyosui:

"Yin Wen-tzu has already discovered the secret of the old German lady and me."

Kiyosui asked about the details, thought it over for a bit, and was greatly disturbed.

"She's doing this to uncover the truth about you, you shouldn't have spoken so frankly with her."

"I didn't at first, and later on I felt that she was completely sincere, so then—"

"Never mind that," Kiyosui broke in, saying: "How can we make the best of it now? If she reports to the Kuantung Army, you'll be for it, and it will be hard for me to avoid being involved, because everyone knows of our connections."

"Miss Yin loves me, she absolutely won't."

"If that's what you think, then matters are messed up for sure. That kind of woman can't have genuine feelings."

Kiyosui rubbed his hands together, and smiled bitterly. He looked in all directions, and then said:

"That fresh lemon that we used last time can be used once more."

"No, Mr. Kiyosui!" Kao Wei-ming, terribly frightened, grabbed the other by the shoulder and said anxiously: "Don't ever do that! If it ever got out, it would be even worse!"

"Relax, it absolutely can't get out. Fatal paralysis of the heart, and no one can determine the cause." Kiyosui shrugged and smiled an easy smile.

"No, I'm saying that you can't use it on Miss Yin, she really does love me, I can tell."

"You don't understand how serious it is; you haven't enough experience . . .!" Kiyosui said, and went off toward the front.

"Mr. Kiyosui, stop, I'm talking to you." Kao Wei-ming held him. "This is what I've decided now: if Miss Yin does as you suppose, and really does go to report the secret, then I'll confess to it myself, and even to the death I won't implicate you. How about that?"

"The matter isn't that simple. I've already decided." Kiyosui glanced at him impatiently. "You're always making trouble for yourself, and I have to make it right."

"If you're really going to do it, Mr. Kiyosui, then I'm going to tell Miss Yin, and get the Japanese military police to protect her safe departure!" Kao Wei-ming cried loudly, as though breaking off with the other.

Kiyosui said no more, but turned, and taking advantage of the other's inattention, struck him with all his strength in the chest and knocked him down. He quickly jumped onto the other and kept striking him hard about the head, until he lost consciousness.

Kiyosui laughed coldly, called one of his people, and told him to carry Kao Wei-ming down to the underground room. He ordered:

"After you've woken him up, lock him in there."

Kiyosui smoothed down his clothes and headed for the dining room. With his face all smiles, he told Yin Wen-tzu:

"Kao is back there helping Ho-tzu with something. I've come to dine with you in his place—all right, Miss Yin?"

"But it's putting you to too much trouble." Miss Yin, bowing, thanked him.

Kiyosui stood up, patted M. Raymond's shoulder, and said:

"I've invited Miss Yin to lunch, and you're invited too."

M. Raymond nodded his thanks. He asked:

"Why is it Madame Ho-tzu hasn't come out?"

Kiyosui didn't answer him. He said:

"You two sit. I'll go to the kitchen and see about the dishes."

Kiyosui returned at once. After the soup, the fried fish arrived with a slice of fresh lemon beside it. Kiyosui said, by way of introduction:

"This dish is my chef's specialty. Taste it and see: it's crisp and tender. He can prepare the same kind of fried fish with a different flavor. This way, squeeze some fresh lemon-juice on the fish first, and then cut it and eat it. Miss Yin, try some; it's good, it's extremely good. M. Raymond, what do you say—isn't it?"

As he himself set to, while praising the dish and urging on his guests, a slice of the fried fish soon went down. Then he wiped his lips and said:

"Miss Yin, how do you feel? Was I mistaken?"

"Even if it hadn't been good, it would have become good after all your praising." Yin Wen-tzu, finding Kiyosui slightly comical, spoke half in jest. "But in fact, I forced myself to eat some out of regard for your face."

"Why, wasn't the flavor good?"

"It wasn't that the flavor wasn't good, it's just that I don't like to eat flesh-food."

"Why?" Kiyosui asked with a smile. "Are you afraid of getting fat?"

"Not entirely that."

"Women are willing to undergo any sort of hardship in order to keep a good figure." Kiyosui communicated this to M. Raymond in French. "How about your wife?"

"She doesn't pay any attention to that. She has a thick waist and fat thighs—a country woman."

"You're being polite, M. Raymond."

After the meal, they dispersed to rest. Yin Wen-tzu wanted very much to see Kao Wei-ming again and to say a few words to him, but though she waited and waited again, he never came, and she herself was beginning to feel very tired. She excused herself to Kiyosui, and he did not try to keep her, but saw her out. Yin Wen-tzu told him:

"Tell Kao I'll come and see him again. Tomorrow."

Kiyosui agreed, and saw her into the taxi.

The next morning, the members of Nomura's household discovered that, at some unknown time, Yin Wen-tzu had died in bed, and the corpse had already grown stiff. Nomura wired the Kuantung Army, and a military doctor came to examine the body. The examination produced nothing; Yin Wen-tzu had "died without any illness".

After that, the Kuantung Army also investigated Kiyosui and Kao Wei-ming, and the investigation produced nothing. Provincial Governor Yin sent someone to Shenyang to manage the funeral of his third concubine. Kao Wei-ming did not attend the burial, but hid in his own room and wept.

"How lucky that I didn't tell Kiyosui that M. Raymond had also discovered that business of mine; otherwise it would have cost another life! How fearful to kill people like that!"

So Kao Wei-ming thought.

After several months of stalemate, with the greatest attacks having been made with the spoken and written word, and each side having made their military arrangements, the "Nanking-Hankow Split" situation remained as before. What was strange was that they had not actually begun to fight. And the British, after having returned their Concession, seemed to have washed their hands of the matter, and were no longer looking for trouble. The Kuantung Army now recognized that the situation was grave, and that it could no longer just observe.

Moreover, the convergence of Nanking and Hankow, in which both sides sought ways of destroying obstacles, was still more urgent. A newly risen force surely gives people hope, and hope often causes men to act, without any misgivings.

No mistake, China was the Japanese Emperor's China, but in the eyes of the Kuantung Army, China ought to be the Kuantung Army's China, because the Kuantung Army represented the actual strength of the military based in China, and the life of the Japanese Empire was entrusted to the actual strength of the military.

The special affairs agents of the government of the Japanese Empire had already spread throughout China, but that was the affair of the government of the Japanese Empire; the Kuantung Army had many reasons for believing its own direct emissaries could be of still greater use. The "Nanking-Hankow Split" could be advantageous to Japan; the "Nanking-Hankow Convergence" would absolutely mean the rejection of the Japanese. That was certain.

So Commissioner Kuriyagawa came to Kiyosui's establishment to see M. Raymond. As Commissioner of the Japanese Imperial Army holding full power over special affairs, his position was higher than that of a cabinet minister in a democratic country, or even that of a cabinet premier. He used no titles, and behaved humbly, "ever aware of his humble origins", but not a single Japanese failed to recognize his honor. M. Raymond, however, took no great account of him; not only did he fail to consider him honorable, but on the contrary, he was humiliated as an Oriental military officer, for M. Raymond considered Japanese and Chinese of equal consequence.

"I think that it is just the time now for you to go back to Hankow," Kuriyagawa suggested.

Calling it a suggestion was a way for dealing with M. Raymond. Commissioner Kuriyagawa considered it an order. His tone was just a little subtler and more gentle with a Frenchman. Kuriyagawa considered this an instance of his international courtesy.

"How shall I travel? Neither the P'ing-Han nor the Chin-P'u is clear."

"Go to Dairen. A Japanese warship will take you directly to Hankow, via Shanghai."

"Won't that expose me, and let everyone know I've got connections with the Japanese military?" M. Raymond asked, surprised.

"It cannot; we can convey you to your home, to your wife's shop, under conditions of such secrecy that neither gods nor devils will know of it."

M. Raymond suddenly had a thought, and he thought deeply for a moment, muttering to himself.

"I'm going now, and who knows if I'll ever be able to come here again. If I did come back, who knows whether the situation would still be what it is now?"

Commissioner Kuriyagawa, hearing this, thought about it, and said with a slight smile:

"I hope that one day I'll be able to welcome you in Peking, in Hankow, or even in Shanghai or Canton."

M. Raymond made no reply, and after a moment said:

"After three days, I'll go."

"Why not today, or tomorrow?"

"I have my personal reason."

"What personal reason?"

"I won't tell you."

"Kiyosui isn't a good one to annoy; you'd better take care." Kuriyagawa gave him a well-meant warning.

"I don't know what you're talking about!" M. Raymond said in a startled voice.

"We know that he killed Yin Wen-tzu, but we cannot find any proof." Kuriyagawa laughed coldly. "If he were a Japanese, or a Chinaman, wouldn't we have dealt with him already?"

"Hasn't he already taken out Japanese citizenship? Don't Japanese laws control Westerners who've taken out Japanese citizenship?"

"The laws are for everyone, only the methods are different."

Commissioner Kuriyagawa seemed to receive a kind of limited indication of M. Raymond's problem. After pondering for a moment, he looked to see that no one was about, and said softly:

"What is it that makes you so suspicious?"

"When I board the boat at Dairen, I hope you'll see me off."

M. Raymond, in a joyous mood, raised his glass.

"This is Japanese whiskey, so it's not much good, but I drink to you."

"I can't accept it, if you say that whiskey's no good." Commissioner Kuriyagawa was a little displeased.

"All right, I drink to you with the best, the very best Japanese whiskey!"

Kuriyagawa smiled, and the two men clinked glasses and drank.

That evening, as the casino had just opened, M. Raymond, seeing that Kiyosui was busy welcoming guests, went off alone toward the rear. His calculations were of long-standing, and his deliberations had matured; he had not the slightest hesitation as he crossed the tennis court toward Kiyosui's dwelling.

He hopped onto the low, four-foot-high wall and looked about. The lights in the house shone brightly, and there wasn't the slightest sound. Just as he was about to jump down, he suddenly thought that there might be a dog, so he stopped himself, and looked again in all directions. The weather was that of the late spring, and the new moon was just a crescent; the darkness was thick amid the dense trees. M. Raymond cautiously got down from the wall, picked up a clod of earth, and boldly threw it ahead of him. Still he saw no movement, and he determined there was no dog. Then he did not fear to go over the wall and in. Moving with great care, he made a circuit of the house, and saw no one. M. Raymond's suspicion intensified. He rallied his courage, removed his shoes and placed them on the stone porch step, and went quietly inside. The lights were on in every room, but no one was there, and he went round and round, as though he had entered a labyrinth. Suddenly M. Raymond discovered a narrow stairway. He looked up, and a fresh scent struck his nostrils. All at once M. Raymond felt that he was young again, as though he had returned to his boyhood days; he had placed himself in an Oriental emperor's palace out of the *Arabian Nights*. With no more doubts or apprehensions, he went quietly up the stairs.

It was a narrow little room. There was a gilded Buddha image nearly ten feet tall, standing solemnly erect. Crosswise before it stood a low table, and on the table were two mottled green, long-legged incense burners, each of which stood more than two feet high. The incense smoke was just curling upwards. A woman, whose body was swathed in white silk and capped with her long hair, was prostrated in worship before the Buddha image, and for a long time she did not move.

M. Raymond, watching, grew anxious, and couldn't keep from softly calling:

"Madame Ho-tzu!"

The woman, startled, immediately sprang up, and cried out in an uncontrollable rage:

"Go, go, get out!"

"Ho-tzu, don't be angry, I've come to worship Buddha," M. Raymond said gently, as he came to the top of the stairs.

Ho-tzu moved quickly to the side, as though she wanted to dash away. But M. Raymond was unwilling to let her go; he reached out and drew her against his chest.

Ho-tzu no longer struggled; on the contrary, she said smoothly and warmly in a low voice:

"Carry me downstairs to the bedroom. The Buddha's here; I don't dare to do anything."

M. Raymond, delighted, pressed her face to his as she descended the stairs.

"That way, that way," Ho-tzu said, pointing.

There was a pale yellow night-light in the bedroom. Ho-tzu said:

"Put me down, and go over there and spread out the bedding. I'll turn on the lamp."

Beneath the dragon-headed floor lamp there was an alarm bell, directly connected to the offices of the Countess and Mr. Kiyosui. Ho-tzu turned on the lamp, casually pressed the button, and then went to help M. Raymond spread the bedding.

M. Raymond, overjoyed, began to reproach himself that he hadn't "braved the danger" earlier, and had thus wasted more than half a year of precious time. There was the sound of hurrying footsteps, and the Countess charged into the room.

"Madame Ho-tzu, have you been frightened?"

"No, Countess, it's M. Raymond, come to worship the Buddha," Ho-tzu said easily.

M. Raymond, whose hand still clutched a corner of the mattress, was so stunned he didn't know how to respond, as Mr. Kiyosui also came rushing in. Taking one look at the situation, he said hotly:

"M. Raymond, I'm very sorry that I was out when you called. Since you're gracing my humble abode with your presence, why didn't you let me know in advance, so I could have made proper preparations?"

"I just came to study Buddhist worship with Madame Ho-tzu," M. Raymond said in great embarrassment, with a wink at Ho-tzu.

"Excellent—*A-mi-t'o-fo!*" Mr. Kiyosui laughed aloud, and told the Countess: "Tell them to bring wine, and I'll drink a cup with M. Raymond."

"I don't drink, Mr. Kiyosui, and I'm really too tired, so please forgive me," M. Raymond said, heading for the door. "It's late, I'm going to go to bed."

So everyone followed him out.

M. Raymond himself felt dispirited; he tossed around all night and couldn't get to sleep. But just as dawn was breaking, he got to sleep.

When he awakened, it was already nearly noon. The Countess came to say:

"It's noon, and Mr. Kiyosui invites you to dine with him."

"Thank you."

As M. Raymond spoke, he suddenly thought of Yin Wen-tzu, so he changed his tune, and said:

"Yesterday Commissioner Kuriyagawa made an appointment to have lunch with me today. I'm to go to the Commissioner's office. Mr. Kao?"

"He's been ill these past two days, he's lying down in his room."

"Wait until I go and see him, and ask him to go to the Commissioner's with me."

But Kao Wei-ming made it clear that he would have to get Mr. Kiyosui's permission before he could accompany him. M. Raymond did not know the

Commissioner's address, and Kao Wei-ming said that he didn't know it either. There was nothing for it but to ask Mr. Kiyosui.

Mr. Kiyosui called the Commissioner on the telephone. The Commissioner said there was no appointment. Kiyosui was displeased.

"M. Raymond, I took you for a friend. What is the meaning of this?"

"To tell the truth, my stomach is upset today, and I meant to decline your invitation," M. Raymond said evasively.

Kiyosui felt that something strange was going on, and he was troubled.

M. Raymond went hungry for two days. He didn't even drink anything, and at night he locked the door, and slept. Early on the third day, Commissioner Kuriyagawa arrived. M. Raymond had his baggage all packed, and went away with him. The Commissioner personally accompanied him on the train to Dairen. Aboard the Shanghai-bound warship, M. Raymond told the Commissioner certain things. Concerning the death of Yin Wen-tzu, he suspected that there must have been some powerful poison, capable of fatally paralyzing the heart, in that fried fish and the fresh lemon juice. On that account, after having burst into Kiyosui's residence, he had refused Kiyosui's invitation, and had rejected food and drink, in order to guard against the unexpected. In addition, there was the connection between Kao Wei-ming and the white-haired old German lady.

Commissioner Kuriyagawa listened, and shook his hand joyfully, saying:

"Splendid, M. Raymond, at our first collaboration you're giving me so much precious information!"

Kuriyagawa arranged the method of correspondence with him, and when the transport weighed anchor, bade him goodbye. Before parting, Kuriyagawa repeatedly charged him:

"M. Raymond, I hope that from now on you will have even more worthwhile information."

"I will certainly do my best," M. Raymond replied.

M. Raymond returned to Hankow. On the face of it, he felt, it had not greatly changed since he had left. But while passing through Shanghai, he had gone to the French Consulate General, and had also called upon several friends of his own nationality. He knew that the Central Government established in Nanking, flourishing in the vigor of youth, had obtained the support of the Chinese people; it was a genuine government of the Chinese people. And he also knew that Wuhan had a government which falsely bore the name of the Kuomintang, but in reality was controlled by the Communist Party.

M. Raymond had no intention of exerting himself on behalf of the Kuantung Army, but he could not but do something for them. Seeing that the Peiyang party was already on the way down, if he wanted to continue getting along in China, he couldn't do without some channel into the Nanking government.

As for the Wuhan regime, it had no way to go—neither military, political, nor economic. Its situation was extraordinarily clear: it could not maintain itself for long.

The meeting of husband and wife after long separation, upon his arrival in Hankow, held a certain special excitement. He didn't find it difficult to listen attentively to every word Anna said, and indeed he took pleasure in it. He kissed her little mustache again and again, and carried her upstairs.

"Have you put on a little weight?" M. Raymond asked, panting as he put Anna down.

"Do I look it?"

"You feel a lot heavier than you used to."

"Can't you carry me?"

"It took a little effort!"

"Perhaps you wasted yourself too much, and ruined your body." Anna seized him by the shoulders with both hands. "Tell me, did you go with a lot of prostitutes?"

"I'm telling you the truth," M. Raymond kissed his wife's throat. "I absolutely didn't. You'll be able to tell in a little while."

In their casual talk M. Raymond brought up Hung T'ung-yeh. He said:

"I'm in sympathy with the revolution now. I think you were right when you helped him before. You think of a way to ask him over. I want to talk to him."

"He often comes here, and we talk about everything. He's always very troubled in mind."

"Why?"

"He's squeezed between two parties. He worked for them both, and neither will forgive him."

"That's no wonder, because the two parties' positions are different."

M. Raymond thought deeply for a moment, and then said as though to himself:

"He must certainly be quite familiar with conditions on both sides."

"Yes, he knows a lot of inside stuff."

"Well, then, perhaps I can find a third way out for him, and rescue him from his tight crack."

Anna was happy that her husband was concerned for Hung T'ung-yeh, but she could not pursue the reason. Her brain was domestic, but not political.

Because he had been gone for a long time on this occasion, M. Raymond made a point of going to the French Consulate. He considered this reporting in, and a courtesy call as well. A middle-ranking officer in the Consulate warned him:

"The situation in Wuhan is complex. The Communist Party is biting people at random, like a mad dog. You must take care; it's no longer the Peiyang era."

"I know. I want to just observe, quietly and simply, for a time."

So M. Raymond indicated. He added:

"Wang has often lived in France, and quite a few of the people around him have studied in France; he can't have become a problem for France?"

"At present he's all for the Communist Party, all for Russia!" the consular official repeated earnestly. "Whatever you do, don't have any thoughts about good luck. The British couldn't protect their Concession, and France isn't any tougher than Britain."

"Relax, I won't go rushing into trouble."

After meeting with Hung T'ung-yeh on several occasions, he discovered that indeed the youth was not an ideal target, and could serve only as a contact through which to seek his target. Liu Shao-ch'iao had a definite superior, but they did not speak of that. After Hung T'ung-yeh's mother married Ch'ien Pen-san, he felt that, by way of the feudal relations among the Chinese, through Hung T'ung-yeh he could gain access to Ch'ien Pen-san.

By chance, he unexpectedly discovered Kao Wei-ming in the dining room of the Western Chamber of Commerce. In amazement as they shook hands, he asked:

"Mr. Kao, how is it you came to Hankow too?"

"I escaped from Mr. Kiyosui."

"Why?"

"No reason." Kao Wei-ming smiled bitterly. "I've been upset since Miss Yin died. That's why I wanted to change my surroundings."

"Why didn't you come to see me first, when you arrived in Hankow?"

"I wanted to, but I've been so busy that I put it off," Kao Wei-ming said regretfully.

"What are you busy with?"

"Friends introduced me, and I saw Mr. Wang, and Mr. Wang sent me to the Ministry of Foreign Affairs."

"You're an official in the Ministry of Foreign Affairs? Congratulations, congratulations!" M. Raymond happily shook hands with him again. "What duties have you taken on?"

"I'm a secretary. When my official work at the Ministry is done, I also do some private work for Mr. Wang. I stay at his establishment."

"Right—no wonder you're busy."

M. Raymond calculated that Kao Wei-ming, in his position, would certainly know many secrets. He thought of the old white-haired German lady of Shenyang, and he thought of Kao Wei-ming's tangled connections with Marshal Chang Tso-lin's General Headquarters, with the Kuantung Army, and with Mr. Kiyosui—so tangled that it couldn't be told at once just which side he was really working for now. Mysteriously, he broke into a cold sweat for Wang. He asked:

"Are Mr. Kiyosui and Ho-tzu all right?"

"They've gone back to Japan."

"What for?"

"The Kuantung Army took over his business and forced him to go back to Japan. He's restricted to staying in Tokyo, under the Army's supervision," Kao Wei-ming said lightly, as though mentally somewhat numbed.

"What's the reason for such severity?" M. Raymond asked uneasily.

"Mr. Kiyosui suspected it was something you said to Commissioner Kuriyagawa," Kao Wei-ming said, fixing him with a cold stare.

M. Raymond was obviously startled. His lips trembled slightly as he asked urgently:

"How can he say that? His relations with Kuriyagawa were much deeper than mine. Kao, do you believe I have such great power?"

"An accidental opportunity, an unconcerned person, a casual word, can all develop a very great influence, and the magnitude of such power is unimaginable."

Kao Wei-ming spoke casually, and smiled mildly.

"What do you want me to say, to make you believe me?" M. Raymond was a little anxious.

"I don't want you to say anything." Kao Wei-ming responded with a question of his own. "Do you know how I got out of Manchuria?"

"I don't know." M. Raymond, inwardly, felt a little bored on that point.

"Someone sent me a secret message. I hid in that nuns' convent where I had sheltered when I was little. I wasn't like Kiyosui and his wife. They could go back to Tokyo and be under surveillance, but I couldn't. I'm Chinese, so I wouldn't have gotten off so easily. They wanted only one thing from me, and that was my life. So I shaved my head, made myself up as a nun, and escaped to Harbin, and from Vladivostok I took a Russian ship to the mouth of the Huang-p'u. Then I stole across to Shanghai."

Kao Wei-ming spoke slowly, and rubbed his bald head.

"You see, my hair hasn't grown out yet."

"You've really been through great dangers."

"I think so."

"The person who sent you that secret message, and the person who introduced you to Mr. Wang, are certainly your great benefactors." M. Raymond made a tentative move ahead.

"I think so."

Kao Wei-ming seemed deep in thought for a moment, and suddenly said, seriously and quietly:

"M. Raymond, there's something which you'll understand even if I didn't say it. I've only one life, and I'll die only once. Beginning today, we'll be friends all over again, and we won't speak of what's past. From now on, you look after your affairs, and I'll look after mine, and we won't cross each other. Otherwise, it won't do either one of us any good."

"Very well, Mr. Kao." M. Raymond welcomed Kao Wei-ming's suggestion. "That's how I had figured it too. If Mr. Kiyosui hadn't been so obstinate about inviting me to dinner that day, I wouldn't have concerned myself with other people's affairs."

"Asking someone to dinner isn't a bad thing."

"But after one meal with him, Miss Yin went away and didn't come back." M. Raymond sighed.

Kao Wei-ming was pained, and tears welled up in his eyes. He nodded, and said:

"That was Mr. Kiyosui's big mistake. His luck had been good these last few years, and everything had been going smoothly. He'd done it several times and nothing had happened, so his gall got bigger and bigger."

"Unfortunately, I think Miss Yin was wrongly accused."

Because Kao Wei-ming was in a poor mood, the two men drank several melancholy glasses of wine and then parted. M. Raymond repeatedly invited Kao Wei-ming to his shop, and reiterated:

"But don't say anything of consequence in front of my wife."

"Does she have a long tongue?" Kao Wei-ming smiled.

"If you know, it should be easy to manage."

Despite having sworn their good faith, and both of their lives being in danger, M. Raymond, when he saw Ch'ien Pen-san for the first time at the Hotel France, could not restrain himself from bringing up Kao Wei-ming. The reason was that he opposed the Communist Party, bitterly hated anyone who worked for Communist Russia, and especially Chinese who worked for Communist Russia. In this M. Raymond was both naive and righteous.

"Splendid—you're splitting with the Communist Party! But since you're going to split, you must split clearly, and split thoroughly. You can't allow them to hide within your ranks, to wreck you from inside. That way, you can't guard against them."

"Yes, we will pay attention to that."

"As I happen to know, there are some unreliable people in Mr. Wang's entourage."

So he spoke of Kao Wei-ming. His intention was to ask Ch'ien Pen-san to send a note to Wang. But he didn't understand Ch'ien Pen-san. Ch'ien Pen-san never discussed the good and bad points of others in front of Wang, firstly because he knew that his relations with Wang were not that close, and secondly because he deeply understood that if one discussed others, one would also be discussed by others; if he spoke of others, others might also speak of him. His not speaking of others was precisely so that others would not speak of him, for he knew that he was not invulnerable. Besides, although at present there was to be a split with the Communists, he still had no wish to offend the Communist Party. In man's life on earth, it's never certain at what time one may meet one's enemy on a narrow road, so rather than cutting them off utterly, he would leave them ground for retreat.

He did not feel that the Communist Party would definitely be unable to recover from its mistake.

This is what was in his mind. But he had something else to say:

"Thank you, M. Raymond, I will certainly tell Mr. Wang, and he'll quickly find a pretext for dismissing that person. How should we want such people? And especially among those close to Wang!"

After M. Raymond had left, Ch'ien Pen-san told Hung T'ung-yeh:

"For safety's sake, your mother and your sister hope that you won't go back there. Now, if you're willing, you can stay here, without showing your face again, and wait until things quiet down."

"Thank you for your good intentions, Third Master." Hung T'ung-yeh was moved, and ashamed. "There's a piece of unfinished business, and now I don't want to hide any longer. Besides, this place couldn't protect me against Liu Shao-ch'iao."

"What's your unfinished business?"

"Fourth Master," Hung T'ung-yeh said sincerely. "I'm prepared to watch for the right time to think of a way to rescue Fourth Master. I know where he's being held now. When the split with the Communists actually happens, there will be great confusion, and in the confusion it may be that Fourth Master will be unguarded."

"How rare it is that you have such a good heart. I'll thank you now," Ch'ien Pen-san said, nodding.

"I hope that I can redeem myself in this way. Third Master, I beg you to forgive all the bad things I did in the past; I didn't know what I was doing."

Hung T'ung-yeh was troubled at heart and shed tears unaware.

"I don't blame you for that. In such a time and environment, sometimes one can't help oneself. And it's not as though I never made any mistakes!" Ch'ien Pen-san was also moved. "From now on, we'll start fresh; we'll make a new start."

"I hope I'll have such a chance."

After Hung T'ung-yeh had gone, Ch'ien Pen-an sat for a while. His interview with M. Raymond, he felt, had been extraordinary, and even stimulating. A person's encounters, whether lucky or unlucky, were often contrary to what one had imagined. Strange illusions were rare, and life still held much color and beauty.

Ch'ien Pen-san felt a little as though he had been placed amid floating clouds.

He returned home, and packed several articles of clean clothing in his suitcase, and then he set out for Wang's residence. He told his family:

"I may not be home for a few days. Don't you worry. If anyone comes to look for me, say you don't know where I went."

"What's going on, really?" Ch'ien Shou-yü asked anxiously.

The new wife also had such a question, and the words were almost to her lips when she saw Ch'ien Shou-yü had already spoken. So she didn't open her mouth, but stood to one side and listened.

"Wait 'til I come back and then I'll tell you," Ch'ien Pen-san said, and was gone as he spoke.

The new wife looked at the clock on the wall; it was past one. Suddenly she felt very suspicious, and muttered in surprise:

"Where's he going, so late?"

Chapter XXIV

After a few days, Ch'ien Pen-san accompanied a group of Wang's representatives on their return from Kuling. They had concluded their negotiations with a group of representatives from Nanking. Wuhan would split with the Communists.

The formal announcement of this news came not as a clap of thunder on a clear day, but as rain finally falling on a thickly clouded and long overcast day. Circumstances brought it about, and what had to happen at last happened.

Every soldier and civilian cheerfully sighed, as though while suffocating in the darkness they had seen the light of dawn, and had returned to the world to breathe again the fresh air of freedom.

The newspapers published Wang's remarks: he demanded that the Communist Party members leave off their membership in the Kuomintang and the positions they occupied in various organs of party, government, and army. Those Communist Party elements had already, during the period when the split with the Communists was brewing, made their planned withdrawal. Now, stilling their voices and hiding their tracks, the others scattered in disorder like birds and beasts.

Ch'ien Pen-san was one of those who had been instrumental in realizing the plan of splitting with the Communists. The realization of this plan depended entirely upon military force. Had it not been for the suppressive function, how should the Communist Party have so readily obeyed?

From then on, Ch'ien Pen-san had ample opportunities and military connections. Before long, he established excellent relations with the military men, and gained their trust, just as during the previous years he had established relations with the Communist Party and gained their trust.

Chu Kuang-chi, staying at Itakura's home and keeping quiet, neither sticking out his head nor showing his face, had long been forgotten. This was to his advantage, because through being forgotten he gained security.

On the night when the Workers' Pickets created the incident at the British Concession, the Japanese at the Common Benevolence Society hospital all received notices from the Consulate, directing them to temporarily board a naval warship, for safety's sake. Many of the Japanese went.

Chu Kuang-chi, at the sincere invitation of Itakura and his daughter, also put on Japanese clothing and followed them on board the warship. By this time he understood that while the Communist Party held power in Wuhan it wasn't worth it to sacrifice himself. If the warship went downstream, he meant to disembark in Nanking. He knew, from the Japanese newspapers, of conditions there, and he responded enthusiastically to the announcement of the "party purification". He felt that the Kuomintang was already under the guidance of correct principles.

He had no use for Wang. Once he said sadly to Itakura Minoru:

"That year when he was in jail in Peking, with his poem—

> Proudly singing in the city of Yen,
> happy to be a prisoner from Ch'u.
> Let the knife flash quickly,
> then I'll no longer carry this young head!

—if he had really been killed then, it would have been well for him. Then he wouldn't have disgraced himself as he has today by making underhanded deals with the Communist Party."

"This is called 'things play with man'." Itakura Minoru also clutched his wrist and sighed, unable to overcome his grief. "Between birth and death a man's success and failure are decided—such examples are plentiful in both Chinese and Japanese history."

The situation in Wuhan became much more settled after the reclamation of the British Concession. The Workers' Pickets did not extend their activities to the concessions of other nations. Because of this, after staying aboard the warship for several days, Itakura and his daughter returned to the Common Benevolence Society hospital. This hospital was their business, and it was also their hearts' blood; neither father nor daughter could bear to abandon it. Itakura Minoru said to Chu Kuang-chi:

"If you've decided to go to Nanking, just remain aboard ship. They'll be leaving for Shanghai before long, and they can take you. I've already worked it out with them."

"No," Chu Kuang-chi said, laughing. "Since you're going back to the hospital, I've changed my plans; I'm not going to Nanking."

"That isn't necessary."

"Didn't the hospital's Chinese staff and workers all leave? You'll be short-handed; I'll help you out."

"You're too good to your friends; it makes me very uncomfortable," Itakura Minoru said with emotion. Both of them were deeply loyal men, so they dispensed with further polite speech. Itakura Minoru looked at his daughter and said:

"I really owe Baitai an apology. I told her I'd take her to Tsingtao to avoid the summer heat, but because of the local disorders in Hankow, I couldn't feel easy about going."

Baitai heard this, and bowing deeply to him, she said a little mischievously:

"When Papa's so polite to his daughter, daughter really can't face it. Thank you, thank you."

This made Itakura Minoru and Chu Kuang-chi both smile. Itakura Minoru said:

"Next year, I hope that next year is peaceful, and we'll go to Tsingtao for the summer."

Baitai once more thanked them repeatedly.

Chu Kuang-chi knew nothing at all beforehand of the development of the split with the Communists. He had only felt, like other informed people, that this was not a situation that could go on for long. Itakura Minoru could obtain various kinds of inside news from the Japanese Consulate, but since the "mass movement" had taken an anti-foreign direction, even to the point where foreigners had been treated rudely on the streets, he had tried to avoid going out. Besides, in his mind he felt that since there wasn't any good news, he was reluctant to go and inquire after it.

On this account, only when the evening paper formally published Wang's remarks breaking with the Communists did Chu Kuang-chi know that the Communist Party was done for, and that with hope for a reconciliation between Nanking and Hankow, his party might proceed from division to unity.

After conferring with Itakura Minoru, he decided to return to his home. His wife, Shu Tung-mei, came to the hospital. Shu Tung-mei told him happily that the Workers' Pickets had already been disbanded, and that the Labor Union General Headquarters and the Women's Association had ceased their activities and were awaiting reorganization. The headquarters of General T'ang, who had pressed Wang to split with the Communists, had long been reorganized, and had already taken stern precautions, so that public order was very good.

Chu Kuang-chi was delighted. He thanked Itakura Minoru again and again, and then left the hospital. Because all at once none of the numerous rickshaws were to be seen on the streets, the husband and wife walked slowly back to their home. In the clear weather of mid-autumn, Hankow, as usual, was extremely hot. Chu Kuang-chi said excitedly:

"After all, evil can't prevail over good, and I'll see prosperity and peace after all!"

"Don't be too happy," Shu Tung-mei said in a warm, quiet voice. "It's hard to predict changes in the situation. What I mean is, I hope you can escape this quarrelsome place, so that I won't always have to be afraid."

Chu Kuang-chi was moved, and he said sadly:

"This time I'll certainly do as you say. I won't be a principal any more, either, I'll just look for a school where I can teach, and raise the children."

"That's a good idea. I hope you won't just make a momentary show of doing as I said."

"I'm serious. Tung-mei, I must beg your forgiveness for these past few years."

"Unfortunately we no longer have any children now," Shu Tung-mei sighed.

"What, there's no news of them?"

"That's right. We can only see whether they come home after this split with the Communists. But early this morning there was news of Ling-fen."

"Where is she?"

"The Wuchang Military-political Academy."

"How did you get this news?"

"Ch'eng Tzu-yüan came to see you this morning. The news of Ling-fen came from him." Shu Tung-mei smiled bitterly. "Don't you think that Ch'eng Tzu-yüan is very odd? He's never been to our door for the past six months, and when I'd meet him face to face on the street he'd pretend he didn't recognize me; he feared me as though I were an evil spirit. Now the newspapers have barely published the split with the Communists and here he comes offering his attentions. What kind of person is he after all?"

"There are lots of people in this world who haven't enough character; you mustn't judge others by too high a standard. Tung-mei, forgive him."

"Oh, you!" Shu Tung-mei said sadly. "Your heart is too good, I'm only afraid that in the future you'll have to suffer endlessly."

"If I suffer, then I suffer, but I cannot wrangle with small people."

They stayed quietly at home for several days, and not one of their children did they see coming back. Ch'eng Tzu-yüan came several times, and he was always saying:

"Now we've split with the Communists, and you're an old party member, and a local man besides—why don't you go and see Wang? He would certainly put you in an important position. With your qualifications, even if you didn't become chairman, you could still become a department head. It would be such a pity to miss the opportunity!"

"I've no such ambition," Chu Kuang-chi said calmly. "Next semester, I expect to look for a teaching job."

Seeing Chu Kuang-chi so aloof, Ch'eng Tzu-yüan thought about it some more, and felt that since—wishing to avoid suspicion and fearing involvement— he hadn't come to call during the past half a year, perhaps he had provoked the other into treating him like a stranger. In his heart, he blamed Chu Kuang-chi for being a small-minded person, who couldn't understand the difficulties of others.

Thus something arose out of nothing, and whenever he met anyone on the street, he would say that Chu Kuang-chi wanted to be Chairman of Hupei Province.

"It's true—Chairman Wang already asked him, face to face, to agree, and it's going to be published."

The news reached Ch'ien Pen-san's ears, and he went to report to Wang. As soon as Wang heard it, he was greatly displeased.

"I've been in Hankow for a good six months, and I've never seen Chu Kuang-chi coming to call on me. What makes him think he can be a Chairman?"

Ch'ien Pen-san saw the sense in this, and said no more.

Because none of the children came back, Chu Kuang-chi found that the hardest thing to bear was the loneliness of his home. He thought and thought, and decided that he would go across the river to Wuchang to look for Ling-fen.

"I'll go with you," Shu Tung-mei said.

"No, you wait at home. Maybe one of the children will come home. If the door was locked, I'm afraid they might misunderstand, and think that their family was no more."

Shu Tung-mei thought that this was very correct, so she nodded and agreed, and let him go alone.

He had not been across the river for a long time, and the scenery, as he crossed on the steam ferry, gave Chu Kuang-chi the greatest happiness. He thought innocently:

"The warlords have been struck down, and the Communist Party has been purged. My party will make China rich and strong; it's already settled. From now on, I'll get out of the revolution and be a simple ordinary person, and I'll be content."

He recalled the garden in his native village, he recalled the cherry blossom season in Japan, and he even remembered the western flower garden in the General's residence in Szechuan, and how, at Ch'en Huan's order, he drank wine and enjoyed the moonlight there. By now General Ch'en had already slipped into old age, and would no longer return to people's minds. While he, Chu Kuang-chi, had finally obtained a place among the people of a great era.

As he thought, he felt a happiness he had never known before.

The Wuchang streets were full of sentries, and no rickshaws were to be seen. Chu Kuang-chi was familiar with the location of the Military-political Academy, and he walked slowly towards it. He remembered the year 1911, when they hastily founded the People's Army. There were still some people wearing queues, and some who wore long gowns. He and several other youths who were making revolution together, with big scissors in hand, organized themselves to cut queues, and to cut long gowns. They would shout:

"Attention!"

When the People's Army got organized, the backs of people's heads immediately turned bald, and their lower halves were now clad in trousers. Queues, and the lower halves of long gowns, were heaped up, forming a small mountain. They threw away their scissors, and clapped and laughed loudly. Then—one, two, three—they reported for duty, and set out empty-handed for the river-front.

As he thought back on the past, on the hot-blooded, restless emotions of that "inexperienced youth", the corners of Chu Kuang-chi's mouth drew up in a slight smile. In those days, he thought, if my father and mother had come to urge me, or order me, to leave the battle front, I certainly wouldn't have accepted it, and moreover, wouldn't I have considered them too timid?

Yes, I certainly would have, Chu Kuang-chi answered himself.

His steps slowed, and finally he stopped.

He thought of why he was going to Wuchang that day.

Will my Ling-fen, here and now, feel as I did then? If I do see her, what shall I say?

If I urge her to return home, to content herself with her lot, to prepare to be a good wife and a loving mother, can she agree? Chu Kuang-chi felt, as though it were still before him, that estranged alienation manifested in her annoyance with her parents in the sickroom at the Common Benevolence Society hospital. On this account, his answer was uncertain. Ling-fen—she certainly wouldn't listen to him.

Chu Kuang-chi felt like turning around and going back.

But a different feeling prevented him. Today's conditions and those of 1911 weren't the same, there was 108,000 *li* of difference between them. The youth of that day stood up for the righteous principle of "Revolution to Oust the Manchus". But now, they've swallowed poisoned cakes, and lost themselves in a labyrinth.

Parents had an inescapable responsibility to save their children from poison, and to rescue them from the labyrinth. Chu Kuang-chi struck himself on the brow, and said, as though jeering at himself:

"Have you gone slow-witted?"

And he kept on straight ahead.

The Military-political Academy's signs had already been taken down, and the slogans on the gates had been rubbed away. Chu Kuang-chi went straight in, and saw no one at all. Every room was missing its doors and windows, and contained only broken tables and smashed benches, and scraps of cloth and paper littered the floors. There were two poor trash-scavengers searching for something usable, and they couldn't help being a bit startled to see someone enter. But they relaxed when they saw it was Chu Kuang-chi, with his old country fellow's manner, and paid no more attention to him.

Chu Kuang-chi wandered through the buildings, and knew that they had already gone; he had come too late. At the thought of Ling-fen, he knew boundless grief, and he felt that in such a disordered world, it was really endlessly shameful when a man couldn't even protect his wife and children.

"Ling-fen, it's Papa who begs your pardon!" he thought in his heart.

He stopped, and looked all around, and saw some blue smoke issuing from a corner. Nursing a thread of hope in his heart, Chu Kuang-chi went slowly over there. A skinny, sallow-faced boy, wearing an army uniform, perhaps twelve or thirteen years old, was pressing weeds into a tiny stove to make a fire, and he kept wiping his face with his hand, as though he were crying.

Chu Kuang-chi approached quietly, and the boy remained unaware. He coughed softly, startling the boy, so that his head whirled around and his eyes went wide with fear. At first Chu Kuang-chi found nothing to say, and just looked at him with suspicion and pity. Finally it was the boy who spoke:

"What are you doing?"

"I'm looking for someone."

"Who?"

"Chu Ling-fen."

"Why are you looking for her?"

"I'm her father."

"Oh," the boy said softly, frightened. "So you're that counterrevolutionary Chu Kuang-chi?"

Chu Kuang-chi was startled. He calmed himself, and then said with a smile:

"How is it you know me?"

"One time the school held a meeting to examine your case, and Chu Ling-fen reported on a whole lot of your crimes, and said that you were a one-hundred-percent diehard counterrevolutionary."

As the boy was slowly talking, Chu Kuang-chi found himself quietly sobbing. When he had calmed himself somewhat, he asked:

"Do you know where Chu Ling-fen has gone?"

"She's gone to Kiangsi with them."

"Why have they gone to Kiangsi?" Chu Kuang-chi spoke as though to himself, as he turned and started to walk away. But he had only gone a few paces when he turned and asked the boy:

"Then how is it you're here alone? What are you doing?"

"I used to belong to the school's labor corps. But when they were leaving, I happened to get these sores on my leg, and I couldn't walk, so I didn't go with them."

As he spoke, he pulled up his trouser-leg so that Chu Kuang-chi could see. His left leg was swollen like a small water-bucket, and looked as if it were ready to burst at every point. Chu Kuang-chi felt the boy's forehead; he had a fever. He became a little anxious for him, and hastily said:

"You can't go on like this, you've got to get into a hospital."

"Hospitals are for the bourgeoisie to stay in. I belong to the proletariat, so I can't stay in a hospital," the boy said coldly, shaking his head.

Chu Kuang-chi couldn't help smiling at this.

"Not only is your leg poisoned, but your mind's been poisoned too. I tell you, you'd better not listen to their nonsense. Hospitals aren't only to serve the bourgeoisie, but poor people too. If you don't believe me, I can take you to a hospital right now, it won't cost you a cent, and they'll fix your leg."

"You make it sound so good—what are you really plotting?"

When Chu Kuang-chi heard this, it made him laugh, and at the same time it made him sigh.

"I won't answer that question. Please, you tell me: you're a child, and your leg's so bad that I'm taking you to a hospital. What kind of plot do you think I have?"

The boy seemed about to say something, but Chu Kuang-chi knew it was hard to make it clear, so he quickly added:

"All right, all right! I haven't time to talk about it with you now. Right now just say whether or not you're willing to go to the hospital. If you're willing, I'll take you there. If you're not willing, I'm going."

The boy thought a moment, and then said:

"All right, I'll go with you. I'm not afraid of the shabby plots of the counterrevolutionary bourgeoisie!"

Chu Kuang-chi paid no attention to him. Realizing that there were no cars on the street, and unable to carry him on his back, he discussed it with several of the trash-pickers, gave them a little money, and they took turns carrying the boy on their backs to the ferry landing. Chu Kuang-chi asked the boy:

"What is your name?"

"I'm called Ta-tzu."

"You're called what?" Chu Kuang-chi didn't understand.

"It's the *ta* and *tzu* of 'Beat down the bourgeoisie!'"[47]

"How is it you've got such a name?"

"Originally my name was Ta-chih, but at the school Commander Yen changed it for me. Commander Yen is really revolutionary!"

"What's your family name?"

"I used to be called Li, but Commander Yen changed it to Lieh for me."

"What did he change it to?"

"The character *Lieh* of *Lieh-ning*. I've got the same family name as Lenin now; Lenin and I belong to the same family."

So the boy replied. He was perfectly serious, and utterly certain.

Chu Kuang-chi deeply understood that the boy's attitude couldn't be changed by a few words, so he said no more. But his heart felt as though a great

---

[47] *ta-tao tzu-ch'an chieh-chi* (beat down the bourgeoisie) is a Communist political slogan.

stone had been placed upon it, and the more he thought about it, the more uncomfortable and painful he felt.

When they got off the ferry in Hankow, Chu Kuang-chi carried the boy on his own back onto the receiving lighter. Then he hired someone to carry the boy to the Common Benevolence Society hospital. As they went along the road, the boy became aware that he was going to a Japanese hospital, and he kept lamenting:

"The counterrevolutionary bourgeoisie are forever in league with the imperialists. But I'm not afraid of them!"

The boy was taken to the emergency room, and Chu Kuang-chi went to look for Itakura. When he faced his old friend, he smiled painfully and said:

"I've brought you trouble."

Then he told him, in general, about the boy's illness. Itakura said:

"According to what you've told me of the situation, it's curable. You needn't feel badly about it."

"I don't feel badly about his leg, but about his mental illness. He's been hypnotized by the Communist Party, and the poison has gone very deep."

After hearing the whole story from Chu Kuang-chi, Itakura Minoru also sighed. He said helplessly:

"Very well, first we'll treat his leg, and then we'll find a way to treat his mind. But treating the mind isn't so easy as treating the leg."

After the boy had been settled in a room, and everything had been arranged, and after having taken supper in Itakura's home, Chu Kuang-chi left the Common Benevolence Society hospital. Because of "Lieh Ta-tzu" Chu Kuang-chi thought of his own children. None of them had come home again after the split with the Communists; naturally this was all the worse, and their fate would certainly be the same as that of "Lieh Ta-tzu".

He thought of his efforts of half a lifetime, of his hopes for his son and daughter, which were simply that they might become respectable Chinese within the Chinese tradition, satisfied, like himself, with poverty, and taking pleasure in things of the spirit. Such hopes could not have been considered extravagant, and his dream was a simple one. Yet even such a weak and vague thing he had also lost.

He felt an emptiness he had never known before.

He didn't go directly home, but walked slowly along the river bank, and sat down on a stone bench by the shore, watching the river in the night. He didn't know if he felt embittered or aggrieved.

"Perhaps Tung-mei is right. It's quite difficult enough for a person to just maintain his own integrity. But I wanted to save people from calamities, and as a result I missed my goal, and I almost lost this old life of mine."

So Chu Kuang-chi reflected. He thought painfully of his sons and daughters, but his sons and daughters had already been caught up in the flood, and it would be difficult to see them again.

On the eastern side a large moon had just risen.

"Tomorrow is the Mid-autumn Festival. And my family can no longer be whole."

Chu Kuang-chi thought that with it so late, Tung-mei would certainly be waiting, and would certainly be uneasy. A wind blew over the river, and he felt very cold. He stood up, intending to go home.

Just at that moment, two men came up quietly behind him. One grabbed his head tightly from behind, and stopped his mouth with a handkerchief, while the other seized his legs. Both men were very fierce and strong, while Chu Kuang-chi was a wizened, undernourished old man whose hands lacked the strength to tie up a chicken.

He couldn't cry out, and he couldn't struggle. Chu Kuang-chi was thrown into the river.

The next morning his corpse was discovered. It had become entangled in the steel cables of the receiving lighter, and hadn't been able to drift far.

Chu Kuang-chi had been a well-known man locally, and all the newspapers carried notices of his death. As for the cause of death, it was unanimously assumed to be suicide. Itakura Minoru, with tears all over his face, said to Shu Tung-mei:

"Suicide—yes, I think so. Yesterday evening, when he was eating dinner at my home, he was feeling very badly. His children were nowhere to be seen, and Ling-fen had followed the others to Kiangsi. And the spiritual condition of that 'Lieh Ta-tzu' made him especially pessimistic. I know he was never pessimistic! I tried to comfort him, before we parted, but I never imagined he could take his own life."

Shu Tung-mei believed Itakura Minoru's words.

To resolve the problem of the survivor's livelihood, Itakura Minoru asked Shu Tung-mei to take up the light duties of a file clerk in his hospital, since she was able to speak Chinese and Japanese as well.

Most of those Communist Party elements commonly seen in public had quietly departed while the split with the Communists was in the making. But only when the news was proclaimed, and the split with the Communists was already being carried out, did Liu Shao-ch'iao slowly leave Ssu-fen-li. He moved to the Hsü family shed near the station, a place to which people seldom paid any attention. With him went Pai Ch'a-hua and Hung T'ung-yeh. For a long time they had had at their disposal a small ferry boat.

Liu Shao-ch'iao and Hung T'ung-yeh changed into long gowns and broad-brimmed woolen hats.

What was impossible to disguise was Pai Ch'a-hua's gait. So she made a point of not changing, and went ahead of them by herself. She knew that in this period in which the work was being wrecked, it was the Women's Association that had attracted the most hatred, and she, as the principal leader of the Women's Association, was the object of everyone's attention. But she said:

"If they execute me, I've a clear conscience. I came out way ahead!"

Yes, she had killed quite a few, and she only had one life.

The Hsü family shed was one of Liu Shao-ch'iao's several refuges. Formerly, when he was "cooperating" with Ch'ien Pen-san, and directing the wrecking of transport on the southern section of the P'ing-Han Railway, he had lived here. Originally it had been the residence of the fourth concubine of the favorite follower of an underworld personage whom he controlled, and later on it had been the dwelling of Second Sister Sung, who had waited on Mrs. Hung at Little Miao's hardware store. Although Second Sister Sung's man had a wife and four concubines, he only liked Second Sister Sung, and so he had bought this house for her in her name. Second Sister Sung's man kept a lodge and accepted followers; he attracted workers from the southern section of the P'ing-Han Railway, and from the northern section of the E-Han Railway.[48] His wife, and his three other concubines, lived together near the Ta-chih gate Station in Hankow; like four horses at the same manger they quarrelled constantly and had no peaceful days. He got angry, set up Second Sister Sung on her own in Wuchang, and from then on seldom went to Hankow.

Liu Shao-ch'iao, on account of the wrecking work on the southern section of the P'ing-Han Railway, paid the man a personal call, and came across the river to stay in his house, from which one can see the depth of his dependence on the other.

---

[48] E-Han Railway: the Canton-Hankow Railway.

Later on, not long after the arrival of the Revolutionary Army, Second Sister Sung's man and his principal lieutenant were assassinated. Liu Shao-ch'iao then generally sent Hung T'ung-yeh to keep in touch with Second Sister Sung, and the house became one of his secret refuges; many things which never saw the light of day were done there.

Second Sister Sung and Little Miao had long since moved there from the hardware store in Hankow. Their assignment was to look after Ch'ien Pen-ssu.

When Liu Shao-ch'iao had had Ch'ien Pen-ssu arrested, it had been in order to coerce Ch'ien Pen-san, and to ruin Hung Chin-ling. But with the split with the Communists in the works, the captive's value suddenly changed. Liu Shao-ch'iao's thinking was: as long as I hold Ch'ien Pen-ssu, Ch'ien Pen-san must protect my security, and this life of mine will be safe.

It was already very late when Liu Shao-ch'iao and the others came to Second Sister Sung's place. It was raining, and pitch-black everywhere, and very few people were on the streets. As soon as Liu Shao-ch'iao was inside, he asked:

"Is there any wine?"

"There's a bottle of hard liquor," Second Sister Sung replied.

"Bring it out, let's have a little."

"There's also a little tea, left over from dinner."

"Never mind if it's left over, bring it," Liu Shao-ch'iao said.

"We're imposing on you, Second Sister. Shall I come and help you?"

As he said this, Hung T'ung-yeh followed after her.

Hung T'ung-yeh had been meaning to rescue Ch'ien Pen-ssu, so as to make up for his own offenses, and thus to leave the Communist Party. But he had waited for several days without finding a suitable opportunity. He knew well how alert and cruel Liu Shao-ch'iao was, and he was especially careful not to mention Ch'ien Pen-ssu. He knew that Second Sister Sung liked him, and he followed her back to the kitchen and then softly asked:

666

"How's that one?"

"He's locked up in the bathhouse in the rear."

"Is he behaving himself?"

"He's very quiet. The poor fellow."

"He's suffered a few times," Hung T'ung-yeh said casually, with a smile. "He knows it won't do not to be quiet, so he's being really quiet."

"Keeping him locked up all this time—what's really going to be done with him?" Second Sister Sung felt a little uneasy.

"That will be up to Shao-ch'iao. He'll certainly have a way."

Hung T'ung-yeh kissed Second Sister Sung lightly on the cheek, and asked:

"Who took the key to the bathhouse?"

"Isn't it hanging on the door of the dish-cabinet?"

Hung T'ung-yeh's gaze followed the direction pointed out by Second Sister Sung, and he nodded.

The two of them carried the wine and the food into the dining room in the front, and they seated themselves around the square table. Liu Shao-ch'iao lifted the wine bottle, and drank from a little porcelain cup. Then he said:

"These last couple of days my stomach hasn't felt well."

"Then you shouldn't drink wine," Second Sister Sung, the only one of them who was sitting in an easy chair, said. "I'll go and fix you some vermicelli."

"No," Liu Shao-ch'iao said, laughing. "I'll try and treat my stomach ailment with big noodles, and see if it works or not. It's just one life, after all."

"You'd better take care of yourself, especially at this critical point," said Hung T'ung-yeh. He felt that Liu Shao-ch'iao seemed—outwardly—almost negative, and his emotions were extraordinarily low. Within his memory, the man had seldom been so.

"Thanks for your concern." Liu Shao-ch'iao glanced lazily at him.

"Besides, Shao-ch'iao," Hung T'ung-yeh said warmly and tentatively, "almost everyone's gone now. Wuhan today is a tiger's mouth—why do you still want to stay here? Since we have this boat, as I see it we ought to go too, in a hurry."

"I'm not so easily dealt with as you are; I'm not satisfied." Liu Shao-ch'iao set his cup down heavily, and laughed coldly.

"What aren't you satisfied with?" Second Sister Sung asked, perplexed.

"I'm not satisfied to leave just like that."

"Then what are you going to do?" Little Miao asked hesitantly.

Liu Shao-ch'iao didn't say anything and just looked at Pai Ch'a-hua. Pai Ch'a-hua spoke for him, rolling up her sleeves and speaking in a loud voice:

"We'll leave them something to remember us by when we go! We can't let them off too easily."

"What do you really have in mind? How about telling us so we'll all know?" Hung T'ung-yeh said softly, drinking a little wine. He too was anxious.

"As for that, you needn't ask. When the time comes, you'll know, of course."

Liu Shao-ch'iao laughed, looked at Hung T'ung-yeh, and said:

"I want to ask you now—what do you think we should do about that fellow in back?"

Hung T'ung-yeh was startled and didn't know how to reply at once. He calmed himself and then said:

"I haven't any suggestions. That's your business. It will be however you say; I haven't any opinion."

"You certainly can push off the blame! Unfortunately, I'm not a three-year-old child and I can't be tricked so easily."

"What kind of talk is this? Who's tricking you?" Hung T'ung-yeh disputed sharply.

"Then why did you just ask in the kitchen where the bathhouse key was?"

"It was just casual talk."

"I don't think so."

Liu Shao-ch'iao turned, lifted from under the table the little blue cloth bag he had just brought with him from Hankow, and took out a revolver, which he gripped in his hand. Then he said in a serious but quiet tone:

"Since you 'haven't any suggestions' and say that it will be however I say, well and good. We'll take advantage of the rain and dig a hole in the back courtyard, and bury him there. We'll do it now."

As he spoke, he suddenly stood up, and waved his revolver to hurry them to the rear of the house. They all looked at one another, not knowing what to do.

"Go on, go on, this isn't a game," Pai Ch'a-hua kept urging them.

Second Sister Sung had knocked around in the underworld for more than ten years and was rather experienced. As soon as she saw the situation, she fell on her knees before Liu Shao-ch'iao, knocking her head on the floor and beseeching him.

"Committeeman Liu, didn't you agree long ago that I could stay? This is my house, I want to live here the rest of my life. If you bury a dead man in the back courtyard, how could I dare live here? I don't care if you kill him or not. I'm only begging you—not in my courtyard!"

As she spoke, she wept profusely, and knocked her head on the floor before Pai Ch'a-hua.

"Committeewoman Pai, here's the boat all ready. Wouldn't 'chopped noodles' be good enough? Committeewoman Pai, you're the leader of our Women's Association. Say a few words for what's fair!"

This performance, however, made Pai Ch'a-hua laugh.

"Look at that pitiful face of yours!"

"I'm a pitiful person, Committeewoman Pai! Neither Little Hung nor Little Miao is willing to marry me, or ask me to be his wife. I'm a widow too, how come you don't pick a husband for me?"

"All right, Shao-ch'iao, get that piece of wire of yours and we'll look for another place to take care of him." Pai Ch'a-hua laughed so that the skin around her eyes crinkled. "Look how pitiful Second Sister Sung is! Let's solve her marriage problem first."

"No good." Liu Shao-ch'iao was still a little angry. "We'll take care of the one in back first."

Pai Ch'a-hua, still giggling, went over to him, took his revolver away, put her hands on each side of his neck, and sweetly said:

"Have some regard for my face, and don't be angry. Let me exercise my authority as Committeewoman of the Women's Association this one last time, and 'marry a widow' for Second Sister Sung."

She pushed Liu Shao-ch'iao down onto a chair, and the others all sat down around them. Pai Ch'a-hua first questioned Hung and Miao:

"Why do you both refuse, and don't want to marry Second Sister?"

Hung T'ung-yeh hurried to answer first.

"I was being polite, I was afraid Little Miao wanted her."

"I was being polite, too," Little Miao said hastily. "I was afraid the Director wanted her."

"From now on, you can't call me Director anymore."

"That won't be a problem; let's not talk of it now." Pai Ch'a-hua waved her hand, forbidding them to evade the topic. "According to what you say, you're both willing to marry her, are you?"

Neither one of them said anything.

"Since you're both willing," Pai Ch'a-hua said, "you'll draw for it."

Hung T'ung-yeh suddenly had a thought, and he asked Little Miao:

"How do you feel about it? Let's not draw lots. You let me have her, all right?"

As soon as Liu Shao-ch'iao heard this, he understood the other's motive. At once he said:

"I approve of Little Hung's suggestion. Let Second Sister Sung go to Little Hung without drawing lots."

"That wouldn't be fair." Pai Ch'a-hua didn't agree. "I'm definitely going to draw lots. This is a Women's Association matter, so don't concern yourself with it."

The result of the argument was a decision to draw lots. To save trouble, both men twined their fingers: the thumb pressing on the index finger, the index finger pressing on the middle finger, the middle finger pressing on the ring finger, the ring finger pressing on the little finger, and the little finger pressing on the thumb. The one pressing down would get the woman.

When they were ready, Hung and Miao put their right hands on the table. Pai Ch'a-hua gave the order, and at the first pass Little Miao's thumb was pressed down by Hung T'ung-yeh's little finger. So Second Sister Sung went to Hung T'ung-yeh.

Pai Ch'a-hua told Little Miao to act as the go-between, while Liu Shao-ch'iao served as a witness and she herself, as the marriage broker, ordered the bridegroom and the bride to embrace and kiss; thus the wedding was immediately completed. There was wine, and the five of them each drank a glass and then sent the newlywed husband and wife off to the nuptial chamber. That was the bedroom in which Second Sister used to live with her husband, the Dead Devil, and it contained a shiny brass bed hung with snow-white curtains.

"Save some energy so you can get up early tomorrow and see Ch'ien Penssu off to eat 'chopped noodles' in the river," Liu Shao-ch'iao said to the bridegroom, Hung T'ung-yeh.

"About what time are we going?" Hung T'ung-yeh asked.

"They lift the curfew at five o'clock. We'll get up a little after four, and get ready, and leave at five. It just gets light at six, so there'll be quite enough time."

"If I'm sleeping, come and call me," Hung T'ung-yeh said.

"Fine, you just relax and sleep," Pai Ch'a-hua said, going over to pull at Little Miao.

"Little Brother, don't feel bad. Come on with Shao-ch'iao and me, the three of us can all sleep in the same bed."

Second Sister Sung had always liked Hung T'ung-yeh, and he had known it for a long time. It had only been because in those days he really had too many "social obligations", and besides he knew that she was already living with Little Miao, that despite Second Sister Sung's constant attempts to arouse his interest and express her concern, Hung T'ung-yeh had never been able to respond to her. Now that he had thought to avail himself of Second Sister Sung's help in order to rescue Ch'ien Pen-ssu, he had taken the chance to draw lots. Heaven, after all, follows the wishes of man, and since he had drawn the lot, he was inwardly pleased.

As for Little Miao, that was only a diversion on his part. He liked Second Sister Sung too, but he wasn't very interested in getting married. Second Sister Sung was big and tall, and older than he by ten years; Little Miao did not consider that an ideal mate, nor a perfect match. So, when Pai Ch'a-hua ordered him to draw lots, he had still hesitated. But without knowing why, when she had been drawn by Hung T'ung-yeh, he felt mysteriously aggrieved, as though he had been wronged.

Although he slept in the same bed with Liu Shao-ch'iao and Pai Ch'a-hua, he was still extremely uncomfortable. He tossed and turned all night and sighed constantly.

Second Sister Sung, having suddenly and unexpectedly gotten as her husband a man with whom she had long been infatuated, was extremely happy. She embraced Hung T'ung-yeh and kissed him greedily again and again. All sorts of tender feelings and secret thoughts came spilling forth.

"Are you going to Kiangsi with them?"

"Not now. After they've gone and things calm down, I want to formally marry you while my mother's still alive. I hope you'll have sons and daughters for me, and we can settle down. I'm an only son, and my mother has hoped for years for grandsons and granddaughters."

Hung T'ung-yeh spoke softly, with his lips against her ear. His hand roved over her body.

These words made Second Sister Sung feel as light as a fairy, and a wave of warmth, starting at her ear, at once permeated her whole body; she felt paralyzed and without strength. Heaving a long sigh, Second Sister Sung composed herself, thought for a moment, and then said:

"It would have been much better if you'd said these things a bit earlier."

"It's not too late now."

"If you'd said these things when we were wrecking the railroad, I'd never have let Little Miao take advantage of me." Second Sister Sung sighed.

Hung T'ung-yeh couldn't help laughing.

"What are you laughing about?" Second Sister Sung asked.

"You still had a husband then, so how could I have spoken of these things?"

"Oh, I remember," Second Sister Sung said regretfully, as though she had just understood. "Afterwards you came here and told me to go to Hankow and stay at Little Miao's hardware shop and look after your mother, and you were interested in me then. Is that right?"

"Exactly, you're just right," Hung T'ung-yeh murmured, as he passionately embraced her.

"If you hadn't been interested in me then, surely in a city as big as Hankow you could have found someone else to wait on your mother, and you needn't have come all the way over here to look for me?"

"Yes, yes."

"Besides, I'm not a maidservant. You wanted me to go, so your mother could see her daughter-in-law first. Am I right?"

"Right, right, that's what I had in mind."

"Well, it's really a pity. Why didn't you explain it to me?"

"You know, I not only love you, I respect you too," Hung T'ung-yeh said in a trembling voice, as though he were deeply moved. "I was just afraid I wasn't fit for you, so I didn't like to say anything."

"I really can't see it, your being so narrow-minded! Do you know what I thought? I was always afraid you looked down on me."

Second Sister Sung sighed deeply and said:

"After all it's a good thing, but what a pity there's this little problem. Now that I think of it, it's Little Miao that's to blame."

"No, don't blame anyone. All right, let's not talk about what's past. Let's make plans for the future."

Hung T'ung-yeh soothed her, and said warmly:

"I've studied it and studied it, and there's a difficult business now."

"What difficult business?"

"Early tomorrow morning we're going to execute that one in back. Once they're gone, it's over with for them. But if the two of us stay behind, we can't avoid trouble. If the authorities should find out—killing someone is a capital offense."

"Who'd know about a case of 'chopped noodles'?"

"There are no walls under Heaven through which the wind doesn't pass."

"But haven't you killed quite a few people recently? Aren't you afraid about that?"

"When we had power, what did a few lives mean? But it's a different situation now. If it goes to court, the two of us will never get to grow old together."

Hung T'ung-yeh spoke as though in great distress, and his tears fell on Second Sister Sung's face.

"Little Brother, don't feel so bad! Let's think it over, and see if there isn't a way."

"There is one way."

"Well, tell me!"

"I think," Hung T'ung-yeh said, lying on Second Sister Sung and nibbling her ear, "we'd better take advantage of this rainy night to steal away with that one called Ch'ien, and find a place to hide for a couple of days. Wait 'til they've gone, and then we can come back."

"I couldn't feel easy, abandoning my house."

"You get along all right with your neighbors, and either of them can look after it for you for a couple of days. What are you afraid of?"

"Where would we hide?"

"I have a place. We'll wait there 'til daylight, and catch the first boat across the river."

After further discussion, they dressed, and with cautious movements they softly opened the door and went out. Feeling her way into the kitchen, Second Sister Sung reached toward the dish-cabinet for the key, but the key was no longer in its original place. She said softly:

"Turn on your flashlight."

But the key wasn't there. Hung T'ung-yeh pulled Second Sister Sung and the two of them went to the bathhouse. The bathhouse door was locked as usual.

Just as he was feeling baffled, he heard a voice behind him say:

"Little Hung!"

Startled, Hung T'ung-yeh turned, and shone his flashlight. It was Liu Shao-ch'iao.

"What is it, Shao-ch'iao?"

"I'm asking you, what are you up to?"

"I couldn't sleep, so I got up to have a look."

"I'm standing watch, so you two go back to sleep."

"Well, sorry to have troubled you." Hung T'ung-yeh, squeezing Second Sister Sung's hand, went back to their room. Having locked the door, he said quietly but with great anxiety:

"No good! What'll we do?"

"Wait a little and then try again."

"It's no use trying again. Liu Shao-ch'iao is already on guard against us, and besides we haven't the key."

The two of them lay down in their clothes, and tossed back and forth, fretting and worrying. Second Sister Sung made nothing of it, but Hung T'ung-yeh understood the danger, and had a bellyful of fear of Liu Shao-ch'iao. He thought much of stealing away alone, but he hadn't the resolve; he only thought about it. He didn't actually flee.

Sometime after four o'clock everyone got up. All the preparations were made. Liu Shao-ch'iao himself went to the bathhouse and brought out Ch'ien Pen-ssu.

"Fourth Master, we've imposed on you these few days," Liu Shao-ch'iao said regretfully. "Today I'm going to see you across to Hankow. Third Master and Elder Miss are still staying in the old place, and Chin-ling is there too."

"Thank you."

Ch'ien Pen-ssu clasped his clenched hands together. His body wasn't in such bad shape, and his hair had recently been cut. At times he had thought of fleeing, and of taking care of them, but his hurt leg still wasn't right, and it wasn't easy for him to walk.

He had known for a long time of the marriage between Third Brother and Hung T'ung-yeh's mother, and seeing Hung T'ung-yeh there, he felt somewhat more at ease.

At five, leaving Second Sister Sung and Pai Ch'a-hua to watch the house, Liu Shao-ch'iao, Hung T'ung-yeh, and Little Miao accompanied Ch'ien Pen-ssu to the river's edge. The "comrades" on the boat had everything ready in advance. As soon as they were aboard the boat the lines were cast off, and they left the bank and rowed out toward the channel. It wasn't yet light, the stars were points of light, and there was a half-sickle of waning moon.

Ch'ien Pen-ssu looked about uneasily, and muttered to himself:

"Why not wait 'til daylight and take the ferry?"

"Don't worry," Liu Shao-ch'iao said with a laugh. "We all want to avoid being seen just now. The Communist Party has always done a few things which don't bear the light of day."

"You've got your own ideals," Ch'ien Pen-ssu said casually.

Liu Shao-ch'iao suddenly raised his voice and asked:

"Old Eighth?"

"I'm here." In the rear of the boat the upper half of a man's body came into view.

"Come on, you can do it now!"

In the midst of Ch'ien Pen-ssu's alarm, "Old Eighth" struck him a heavy blow on the temple, and he dropped. They put him into a hemp sack, and tied the mouth of the sack shut. A piece of granite, more than two feet long, was bound tightly to the sack with wire. Several of them, moving together, lifted the sack and threw it into the river.

Liu Shao-ch'iao turned, seized Hung T'ung-yeh, and kissed him on the mouth.

"Rabbit-boy, it's your turn now!"

Before he had finished speaking, Hung T'ung-yeh too was knocked senseless, and went the way Ch'ien Pen-ssu had gone.

Liu Shao-ch'iao returned and told Second Sister Sung:

"Little Hung saw Fourth Master Ch'ien across the river, and he was going to visit his mother and his little sister."

"Will he be back soon?"

"I didn't ask him."

Then Second Sister Sung was a little uneasy.

Liu Shao-ch'iao and Little Miao idled with Pai Ch'a-hua, passing several days in bed in nervous slumber. Since Hung T'ung-yeh still hadn't returned, Second Sister Sung grew even more anxious. She said to Liu Shao-ch'iao:

"Could he have changed his mind? I'm going across the river to look for him."

Liu Shao-ch'iao was just reading that day's newspaper, in which was printed the news of Chu Kuang-chi's suicide. He couldn't help being surprised: Chu Kuang-chi was a leading anti-Communist, and had suffered not a few blows in the recent episode; why, after the split with the Communists, should he have taken his own life? Extraordinary, truly an extraordinary business!

"I can't go on with this stupid waiting any longer; it's better to go a little earlier."

So he decided. Then he answered Second Sister Sung:

"All right, tonight we'll cross the river together. Maybe we can help you."

"That's not necessary," Second Sister Sung said reluctantly, in her confusion. "When it's daylight, I'll go myself. He's my husband, and it's best if outsiders don't interfere in matters between husband and wife. Committeeman Liu, just give me the Ch'ien family's address."

"No mistake, you're right," Liu Shao-ch'iao said with a leer. "But except for myself and Pai Ch'a-hua, other people may not recognize your marital connection. Especially the Ch'iens. We'll go there with you, to be your witnesses, so the Ch'iens can't refuse to recognize it."

Pai Ch'a-hua and Little Miao joined in to agree with this, and so pressed Second Sister Sung that she could no longer maintain her own opinion, and could only agree.

They waited until it was dark. It was mid-autumn, and there was plenty of moonlight. After locking the gate, the four of them crossed to Hankow in their own boat. Liu Shao-ch'iao said:

"You all come with me to my family's dry goods store. I'm going far away, and I want to say goodbye to my father. After this parting, it's hard to say if we'll ever see each other again."

"Committeeman Liu, how filial of you!" Little Miao felt that this was something new.

"Naturally. I can become the twenty-fifth filial son, just wait and see."[49]

So the four of them crept furtively into the dry goods store.

Little Miao's old employer, the hardware store proprietor and his wife, stayed for a time in Shanghai. Hearing that Hankow had split with the Communists, and that order had been restored to industry and commerce, they returned to Hankow by steamer. The gates of their hardware store were locked.

---

[49] A reference to *Erh-shih-ssu hsiao* (*Twenty-four Examples of Filial Piety*) by Kuo Chu-ching of the Yuan Dynasty.

The proprietor didn't have a key, so he got a coppersmith to come and break open the lock. He pushed the door open and went in, to find a corpse lying athwart the door, and already stinking in all directions. The proprietor and his wife, and even the coppersmith, were greatly frightened, and turned and fled.

Before long a large group of police officers arrived, and bringing with them a coroner. The corpse was that of a woman, and her skull had been broken by the blows of a heavy iron bar. The neighbors recognized her; it was Second Sister Sung.

They went inside, and in the rear courtyard they found a strange thing. A hole had been broken through the rear wall, into the Liu family's storehouse. Going through this hole, they found another body in the storehouse. When identified, it was that of Little Miao. His body showed no wounds, but blood ran from all seven orifices.

When they opened the front doors of the storehouse, the smell in the Liu family dry goods store was even stronger. There, upstairs and down, in the front room and in the back courtyard, there were altogether seven corpses: Old Mr. Liu, Second Brother Liu, Yeh P'in-hsia, the cook, the clerks, and an apprentice.

The front gate of the dry goods store was barred from the inside. In the little reception room behind the gate wine cups were scattered about, and a few dregs of wine remained.

Later on, when it was chemically analyzed, it was found that the wine contained poison.

This was the most earth-shaking "Strange Case of Nine Murders" since the split with the Communists.

According to one analysis: during the period in which the Labor Union and the Women's Association were troubling society, two of the most active characters had been Liu Shao-ch'iao and Pai Ch'a-hua, and both were of the Liu family. They had harmed quite a few people. Most probably, this was a revenge killing. Because the two of them had fled, their enemies had satisfied their anger by plotting the murder of their families.

Double Ninth passed, and Hankow, often referred to as a steaming-basket, gradually cooled off.

Wang finally dissolved his government. He took a steamer to Shanghai. Among his entourage, in addition to his numerous confidantes, were Mr. and Mrs. Ch'ien Pen-san and their two daughters. Kao Wei-ming was also in the company.

The steamer stopped briefly at Kiukiang, and then continued on.

Not far behind the steamer, a cargo boat was also proceeding downstream, and stopped at Kiukiang. Two people disembarked there; a short, plump woman leaned close to a tall, thin man as they walked, and seen from a distance they much resembled the English letter "d".

This letter "d" kept moving ahead, and before long disappeared into the twilight vastness.

CHINESE STUDIES

1. Eve Alsion Nyren (trans.), **The Bonds of Matrimony/Hsing-shih Yin-yüan chaun (vol. One), a Seventeenth-Century Chinese Novel**

2. Jean M. James, **A Guide to the Tomb and Shrine Art of the Han Dynasty 206 B.C.-A.D. 220**

3. Shiao-Ling S. Yu (edited & translated with introduction), **Chinese Drama After the Cultural Revolution, 1979-1989: An Anthology**

4. Kylie Hsu, **A Discourse Analysis of Temporal Markers in Written and Spoken Mandarin Chinese: The Interaction of Semantics, Syntax, and Pragmatics**

5. TBA

6. William J.F. Lew, **Understanding the Chinese Personality: Parenting, Schooling, Values, Morality, Relations, and Personality**

7. Richard A. Harnett, **The Saga of Chinese Higher Education From the Tongzhi Restoration to Tiananmen Square: Revolution and Reform**

8. **A Translation of the Chinese Novel *Chung-yang (Rival Suns)* by Chiang Kuei (1908-1980),** translated from the Chinese by Timothy A. Ross